OVERCAPTAIN

TOR BOOKS BY L. E. MODESITT, JR.

L. E. MODESITT, JR.

OVERCAPTAIN

TOR PUBLISHING GROUP

NEW YORK

OVERCAPTAIN

A Tor Book
Published by Tom Doherty Associates / Tor Publishing Group
120 Broadway
New York, NY 10271

www.torpublishinggroup.com

Tor® is a registered trademark of Macmillan Publishing Group, LLC.

The Library of Congress Cataloging-in-Publication Data is available upon request.

ISBN 978-1-250-90290-0 (hardcover)
ISBN 978-1-250-90293-1 (ebook)

Our books may be purchased in bulk for promotional, educational, or business use. Please contact your local bookseller or the Macmillan Corporate and Premium Sales Department at 1-800-221-7945, extension 5442, or by email at MacmillanSpecialMarkets@macmillan.com.

First Edition: 2024

Printed in the United States of America

0 9 8 7 6 5 4 3 2 1

ALYIAKAL'ALT,

OVERCAPTAIN

Oldroad Post, Guarstyad

I

In late midafternoon on threeday of the second eightday of Summer, as Overcaptain Alyiakal sits behind the modest writing table in the post commander's small study, a Mirror Lancer ranker appears in the open doorway.

"Overcaptain, ser . . ."

Alyiakal looks up from the maps before him, closes the atlas, and says wryly, "Nomads wanting water or traders coming up from Stonepier?"

Not that Stonepier is much of a port. It sits some seventeen kays east of Oldroad Post with a small Kyphran stone building and is nothing more than a barracks for a squad of Kyphran troopers, with a stable for possibly a half score of horses and a single wagon. Then again, two years earlier, right after the border-readjustment conflict, all that had been left was the stone pier—and the ashes of hundreds of Kyphran troopers.

When the Kyphran post was built at the pier, Alyiakal had wondered why the Duke of Kyphros exempted the small port from levying tariffs, then realized no traders would land there if they had to pay tariffs at the port and again at Oldroad Post. Instead, the troopers collect a small landing fee. *And the Duke hopes in time to see a small town that will raise more golds.* The Duke's actions also require Cyador to spend golds to maintain Oldroad Post.

The Mirror Lancer scout clears his throat, politely trying to get Alyiakal's wandering attention. "Two wagons, ser. With guards. They've crossed the border and should be here in another glass. Second Company's third squad is escorting them."

"Wagons and guards mean wealthy traders." Alyiakal wonders why wealthy traders would take three or four days on the road when they could afford to sail into Guarstyad directly, even skipping the need for wagons. He stands. "Very interesting. Wealthy or not, they'll be too late to take the road tonight and will have the waystation to themselves. You can return to duties." Alyiakal heads for the door. "I'll let the gate guards know."

As he walks from his study toward the gate at the east end of the old road, he can't help but think how his discovery of the forgotten road and how it had been blocked led to so many changes over the past two years. One of the first changes after the annihilation of the Kyphran troopers had been the destruction of their rough fort and the removal of the half-destroyed building created by the dissidents a century earlier, followed by the construction of Oldroad Post and the repair of the old road.

Traders deciding to enter Guarstyad through Oldroad Post essentially forced Alyiakal and the lancers of the two companies to build a waystation to the south and east of the post, including diverting water to a rough fountain and drains, a matter requiring Alyiakal to employ more than a few concealed uses of order/chaos magery. The waystation rules are simple. No one can enter Cyador and use the old road to Guarstyad without the Mirror Lancers approving the condition in which they leave the waystation. Nor can they set up camps within Cyadoran territory, which extends ten kays east of Oldroad Post.

The Kyphran troopers at Stonepier are somewhat laxer about travelers or others setting up camps on Kyphran territory, but not much. The Duke of Kyphros made it clear that camping didn't bring in silvers the way an inn would, and discouraging camping might cause an inn to be built sooner.

As Alyiakal leaves the post building, he smiles ironically. The Duke might even regain a few silvers out of his ill-considered attack on the Mirror Lancers. Then Alyiakal glances at the wall that encloses the Mirror Lancer post, except for the rear of the post, cut into the stone that looms a good fifteen yards high behind the post. He walks alongside the wall to the gatehouse guarding both the post and the entrance to the old road to Guarstyad.

"Ser?" says the lead duty guard.

"There are some traders heading in. They'll get here too late to use the road safely and will complain about it. Just tell them the road is closed until sunrise tomorrow. Don't argue with them. Send for me."

"Yes, ser."

Alyiakal turns and goes to find Torkaal, who is working on blade skills with the recent recruits from Guarstyad. Although blade skills are usually a last resort, if they're needed, they're needed desperately. The other aspect of blade skills is, as Alyiakal knows well, that they're extremely useful for teaching a certain amount of caution and wariness, often the only way with some recruits . . . and even officers.

Alyiakal stops in a shaded courtyard archway and watches Torkaal spar under the hot Summer sun with one of the recruits. Half a quint later, when Torkaal finishes with that recruit, Alyiakal steps forward.

"You've got a half quint to catch your breath," the undercaptain says to the recruits before walking to meet Alyiakal. "Ser?"

"You got the report about the traders?"

Torkaal nods.

"What do you think?"

"Wealthy traders in good wagons? Something's up."

"That was my first thought," agrees Alyiakal, "but then I recalled something. Remember the hamlet near where we thought the road from Guarstyad ended?"

"The one where that mage attacked you?"

"Exactly. They have two kinds of goods that those with wealth would be interested in—the musk ox wool and that mushroom that grows on holly oak roots."

"The last thing they'd want the tariff enumerators in Guarstyad to know is their interest in those," replies Torkaal.

"They might also be using that for a cover. Or they're wary of the Imperial tariff enumerators in Guarstyad for another reason."

"Ser, how could we possibly imagine anyone being wary of those upright officials?" Torkaal's every word drips sarcasm.

"I would never imagine anything of the sort," returns Alyiakal with a cynical smile, "but it might occur to an outland trader."

"It hasn't happened yet," rejoins Torkaal, "but I've wondered when it might."

"I'm not holding my breath." Alyiakal laughs softly, then asks, "How are the recruits coming along?"

"They're all green and soft as Spring growth. Good thing is that they haven't had a chance to learn bad habits." Torkaal smiles happily. "In a season, they'll be better than anyone coming out of Kynstaar. Be a while before any of them'll need to spar with you."

"There's always someone," replies Alyiakal.

"Not near as many here. Won't be long before some of the more experienced rankers we've trained will be getting orders."

"Most likely to the northern borders."

"Everyone serves there, sooner or later."

"And usually often," rejoins Alyiakal. "I'll see you later." He starts back toward his study, then stops for a moment as his order/chaos senses alert him to riders from the north. After a moment, he nods and continues. *Vaekyn and first squad returning from patrol.*

Two quints later, Vaekyn knocks on the open door to Alyiakal's study.

Alyiakal motions for the senior squad leader to enter and take one of the two straight-backed chairs in front of the small writing desk. "How did it go?"

"Caught sight of some nomads, but they stayed on the Kyphran side of the border. No signs that anyone's been using the east pass road. Not since we took care of that bunch in late Spring."

"I still can't see the point of smuggling spices overland and then over the east pass. Not when they'd have to take the west pass road and travel more than a hundred kays to Luuval, and as many more to Fyrad. The tariffs aren't that high on spices. Well, except for tri-spice and vanilla. If they'd been trying to get iron blades into Cyador or gems . . ." Alyiakal shakes his head.

"Have you heard anything about the silvers we get from the sale of the spices we confiscated?" asks Vaekyn.

"You and the men will get them. I got the acknowledgment from head-quarters last eightday. When they'll arrive is another question."

"Do you think the nomads here will turn to raiding, like along the north-ern borders?"

"Not any time soon. There's not enough to support them year-round, and nothing to raid. Even if they avoid our patrols and get over the east pass, there are only a handful of steads north of Guarstyad post, and it would take at least a well-armed squad, if not two, to mount an attack on the mine. Before they could take it, the subcommander would have them cornered. It's not like the Duke of Kyphros, who wanted the silver mine and all Guarstyad so that he could have a sheltered harbor and another port."

Left unsaid is the fact that the Oldroad Post primarily exists to protect access to Guarstyad, and the lancers' greatest enemies are not smugglers or Kyphran troopers, but weather and boredom. He'd kept them occupied ex-ploring and mapping the entire border area, building and rebuilding the dan-gerous trail down to the tiny cove pier twice, so that the ride down and back is merely arduous, rather than potentially deadly.

After Vaekyn leaves, Alyiakal picks up the tariff manual. *You might as well refresh your knowledge before the traders arrive.*

A glass passes before a ranker from the road gate arrives.

"Overcaptain, ser?"

"The traders have arrived and want to know why the gate is closed?"

"Yes, ser."

Alyiakal stands, dons his visor cap, and follows the ranker back to the road gate, where two well-kept, if dusty, wagons wait short of the iron-bound gate. He enters the gatehouse from the post side and then steps out to meet a heavyset and red-bearded trader standing beside the first wagon. On the wagon seat is a teamster, holding the leads for the wagon's single horse.

Facing the trader is the duty gate guard.

"You the officer in charge here?" demands the trader.

"I am," replies Alyiakal. "What seems to be the trouble?"

"This gate is, officer."

"Overcaptain," corrects Alyiakal politely.

"Well . . . Overcaptain . . . can you get this gate open so that we can be on our way?"

"The gate will open at sunrise tomorrow."

"That's absurd. Why can't you open the gate now?"

"Because being on the next ten-fifteen kays of the road in the dark gets people killed," replies Alyiakal. "We used to let people do it, until too many fell two hundred yards onto the rocks into the ocean." *Including several Mirror Lancer messengers.* "It's perfectly safe when you can see where you're going. It's not when you can't, and parts of the road are in heavy shadow even in full sunlight."

The other reason is to bar the road to unwelcome persons, such as brigands posing as small traders and, of course, armed nomads or Kyphran troopers, not that either would attempt to use the road after the border-readjustment conflict. "Since you're merchants or traders, your wagons will need to be inspected for goods subject to tariffs. That will take a little while."

"And for an additional fee . . ." snorts the trader.

"We go by the Imperial tariff manual," says Alyiakal coldly. "I'll be happy to have you look at it if you have any goods that are subject to tariffs."

Alyiakal can sense the trader's surprise.

For a moment, the red-bearded man says nothing. Then he asks, quietly, "You said sunrise tomorrow?"

"I'll be happy to go over your goods tomorrow at sunrise. After determining and paying the tariffs on your goods, you'll be free to go—if it's not raining. We don't expect rain, but the first ten kays are smooth rock that's slick when wet."

Those words elicit some little surprise.

"You'll need to use the waystation. The fountain water is clean. There's a refuse barrel and a jakes house. Use them. If you don't, you'll have to clean up the waystation before we open the gate." Alyiakal projects a slight feeling of unyielding law.

"Yes, ser. We'll be back at sunrise."

"I'll be here." Alyiakal nods, then turns and enters the gatehouse, where he watches as the traders turn the wagons and head back to the waystation.

II

Early on fourday morning, Alyiakal makes his way to the duty squad leader's desk, where Saavacol has just taken over.

"Good morning, ser."

"We'll have some traders showing up shortly."

"The ones at the waystation? I've already sent some of the duty squad down to check the waystation. If there's a problem, I'll let you know."

"Let's hope there's not. I did caution the lead trader late yesterday."

"If you cautioned him, there won't be."

"Hopefully."

From there, Alyiakal walks to the enumerator's three-room building on the south side of the still-closed iron-bound gate. While he waits for the traders' wagons, he goes over the procedures and makes sure all the forms are ready.

Slightly after sunrise, the first wagon nears the enumerator's building, and Alyiakal steps out before it comes to a stop. He carries a polished wooden hand desk holding the necessary forms.

The red-bearded trader climbs down from the wagon.

"I have the shipping manifest for you to look at and compare, Overcaptain."

"Thank you." Alyiakal smiles politely, then adds, "Before you say anything more, trader, you should know several things. First, we follow the Imperial tariff code, as close to the letter as possible. Second, copies of all tariff bills and import fees are sent to the Senior Imperial Tariff Enumerator in Cyad. And, third, in addition to being a Mirror Lancer overcaptain, I'm also a Magi'i-trained field healer." Before the trader's puzzled expression can fade, Alyiakal continues. "While I do not have enough order skills to be a magus or a Mirror Engineer, I do have enough to be a better than usual field healer and can discern when someone is not telling the truth or the whole truth."

The trader swallows slightly, "I appreciate your directness, Overcaptain."

Alyiakal reads through the manifest listing the goods. Nothing on it appears different from goods most outland traders might carry, items of comparatively high value for their weight and size. Among the herbs and spices are brinn, burnet, cumin, cinnamon, peppercorns, and others he's never heard of before he'd had to act as a tariff enumerator. There are also dyes and aromatics, and ten amphorae of olive oil. One listing catches his eye—"20 s/s scarves, each 4/5 yard."

"Shimmersilk scarves?" he asks.

"Yes, ser. From Hamor."

"In all colors?"

"Not all," admits the trader.

Alyiakal doesn't pursue the matter, although he wonders if there are any scarves in Merchanter blue that might suit Saelora. Even if there were, he cannot ask or offer to buy anything the trader might have. Besides which, the scarves would cost more than a gold, close to what Alyiakal makes in an eightday.

After reading through the manifest, Alyiakal says, "Let's take a look. What is your name, or the name you usually trade under and where are you from?"

"Byjaan, out of Brysta."

"Brysta?" asks Alyiakal, sensing a possible evasion.

"That's where I'm from."

Alyiakal understands. Byjaan is the name he's known by, and he was probably born in Brysta, but that's not his trading base. Since that's not relevant to levying tariffs, Alyiakal just nods and asks, "Do you wish to declare a trading name, in addition to your true name? That's not required, but some traders prefer it that way on the documentation kept on file."

"No, ser."

After that, as he goes through the goods in the two wagons, Alyiakal asks various questions:

"Peppercorns in these kegs?"

"Ehrenflower? Is that a perfume?"

"Why shimmersilk scarves, rather than a bolt or half bolt?"

To that question, the trader replies, "Hamorians won't sell shimmersilk cloth to traders not from Hamor, only finished goods."

When Alyiakal completes the inspection, he turns and asks, "Is there anything else you should have listed? Have you misstated any of the values?"

"No. After what you said earlier, I would have told you. The values are based on what I paid for them. They may sell for more . . . hopefully not less."

Alyiakal can sense the honesty. "Why don't you join me in the study while I figure the tariff and import fee? That way you can check my mathematics."

Alyiakal's words surprise the trader, who pauses, then says, "Thank you. I will."

The two walk to the study. There, Alyiakal methodically tallies up what is due. Some of the goods are only subject to the one-part-in-twenty import fee, while others have additional tariffs of one part in ten.

In the end, the fees and tariffs total forty-seven golds, by far the greatest amount that Alyiakal has ever collected. Not surprisingly, since only a handful of traders have come through Stonepier over the past two years.

The trader looks over the forms and signs them, and then counts out forty-seven golds. "I won't say it's a pleasure, Overcaptain, but it's been quicker and far less burdensome."

"I take it you'll travel by the winding road from Guarstyad to Luuval, or what's left of it, and then to Fyrad and Geliendra?"

"What else? It takes longer, but no one else is doing it, and we can sell goods along the way. Not as much as in years past."

"You have quite an array of goods for Luuval."

"For now, but before the better half of the town was destroyed, the families of many wealthy Merchanters spent the colder seasons there."

Alyiakal didn't know that, and while he can sense that the trader's telling the truth, he has the feeling that the man isn't telling everything.

"I wish you well."

"Thank you."

Even after the gate to the old road is open, and both wagons have passed through, Alyiakal is still considering what he doesn't know. Are the enumerators in Guarstyad or Fyrad so incompetent or corrupt that it's worth adding four days' traveling time? Especially since it's improbable that Trader Byjaan could possibly sell all the goods in his wagon in Guarstyad or Luuval . . . or any of the villages or hamlets along the way from there to Fyrad. Whatever those reasons, Alyiakal is certain Byjaan didn't choose to offload his goods and wagons at Stonepier just to travel the old road to Guarstyad.

He shakes his head and begins to write up the trader's visit for his eightday report. After finishing, he returns to the post commander's study, where he locks away the tariff fees. With this amount, he'll have to dispatch a squad to convey the forms and the golds to the Imperial enumerators in Guarstyad, and they'll have to leave at first light. The enumerators don't like being forced to accept the golds in the evening, but they'll certainly take them. The squad won't mind it because they'll get a day's rest in Guarstyad, and a chance to visit one of the alehouses in the town before returning.

III

Alyiakal reins up some thirty cubits from the slant-roofed dwelling, aiming his lance at the planked wall, giving it the quickest touch of chaos. The firebolt strikes the rough wood, immediately creating a charred and ashen circle a cubit across with small flames at the edges that begin to spread.

He's about to turn the bay gelding toward the next barbarian dwelling to flame when a slender, girlish figure steps around the corner of the dwelling, with bow in hand and arrow nocked.

Whhsssst! The firelance bolt flares into the figure, consuming the archer, bow, and arrow just as the shaft would have been released.

Alyiakal bolts upright in his pallet bed, sweat running down his face.

That same dream . . .

Except it's not exactly a dream, and he hadn't realized the archer was a mere girl until after he'd flamed her. *And she was trying to kill you.*

But no matter how often he tells himself that, every so often, the dream comes back.

He stands and walks to the basin, splashing his face with lukewarm water, and begins his preparations for the day.

Because it's sixday, after breakfast and muster, Alyiakal leads First Company out of the post heading north to the old trading road from Felsa, seldom used after the Mirror Lancers and Mirror Engineers blocked the east pass to wagons or carts.

Since the grasslands nomads tend to avoid the borderlands reclaimed by Cyador, on most patrols, the lancers only catch sight of endless grass and vulcrows sweeping out of the Westhorns looking for carrion or careless coneys. This patrol begins no differently, although Alyiakal continues to sharpen and extend his order/chaos senses, and especially his shields.

By midmorning, First Company reaches the trading road and follows it east to the border, without seeing a single bootprint or hoofprint. From there, the company turns back south along a border trail various patrols have created over the past several years.

Just before noon, Alyiakal reins up his chestnut gelding at the border between Cyador and Kyphros—a point ten kays east of Oldroad Post where the terrain shifts and the ground begins the long gradual slope down to Stonepier. He surveys the road, then turns to Vaekyn, and says, "Looks like two groups of wagons headed our way. We haven't gotten two traders in the same eightday, let alone on the same day since we opened the old road."

"We didn't see a single trader all Summer that first year," recalls Vaekyn.

Alyiakal nods. "Only Mirror Engineers and Magi'i until sometime in Harvest."

"Magi'i left as soon as they could."

Once they discovered there wasn't any real difference between the old order/chaos stonecutter we found and what they use now. "They weren't all that interested in helping to repair and remove the breaks in the old road."

"Begging your pardon, ser," says Vaekyn, "but it seems like the Mirror Lancers and the Mirror Engineers are the only ones really interested in what's right for Cyador. Or am I missing something?"

"I've known some Merchanters, and a few Magi'i who are. I don't know enough of either to make an accurate judgment." *But I haven't been that impressed by most Magi'i, except Healer Vayidra.* "Offering judgment of either, especially anywhere in public, is unwise for lancer officers and squad leaders."

"I've heard—"

"Too much obvious interest in Merchanter affairs, I've been told, does not benefit one's duty . . . or future." Alyiakal smiles wryly, and adds, "Even when it's on a very personal basis."

"Ser?"

"I've known distinguished and accomplished officers who were not promoted above a certain rank because they consorted a woman of Merchanter background. I've known of others who waited to consort until they were stipended out, just to avoid that difficulty. Headquarters can be . . . rather particular." *And if the Majer-Commander ever found out that I'd once been involved with Adayal, a woman of the Great Forest with mage's skills . . .*

Vaekyn grins. "Even if I'd be fortunate enough to get a field commission, like Undercaptain Torkaal, that wouldn't much bother me." He pauses. "Did you know that, ser? I mean before you became an officer?"

"I suspected but didn't learn it until later." *As with so many things.* Alyiakal takes a last look eastward. "Time to head back to the post."

First Company returns by early midafternoon. By the time Alyiakal unsaddles and grooms the chestnut and returns to his study, Chavaar, one of the border scouts, is waiting.

"How many trader wagons?" asks Alyiakal as he stops outside the study doorway.

"Three, ser. Two different traders; one has two wagons. They should be here in less than three glasses. Graanish is escorting them in."

"Did they mention any other traders?"

"No, ser. They were the only ones who disembarked at Stonepier."

"Did they say anything about the ship?"

"No, ser. Were we supposed to ask about the ship?"

Alyiakal smiles wryly. "No. I can ask when I'm acting as enumerator, but not as a lancer officer." At the look of confusion on Chavaar's face, Alyiakal adds, "As I've been occasionally reminded, our duty is to make the borders and roads safe for Merchanters, not to inquire into their business. That doesn't mean we can't listen."

Chavaar grins. "Yes, ser."

"Is there anything else?"

"They've each got a pair of mounted guards."

"Good to know. Thank you."

After Chavaar leaves, Alyiakal enters the study and looks at his inbox. There's nothing in it, not that he expects otherwise. He only receives communications from a Cyadoran cutter or fireship delivered to the cove pier, or from Guarstyad Post. The lookouts haven't sighted any ships, and any messenger from Guarstyad won't arrive until close to sunset.

Then he sits down, thinking.

IV

With two traders at the waystation wanting to get on the old road to Guarstyad as soon as possible, on sevenday Alyiakal rises before dawn. The white sun is barely above the grasslands to the east, and the sky more gray than green-blue, when two high-sided wagons halt before the enumerator's building. Alyiakal steps out carrying the wooden hand desk and the necessary forms.

Two mounted guards flank the lead wagon. Their sabres look roughly similar to lancer blades, but Alyiakal senses both are iron. The guards' bearing suggests both are former outland troopers, but nothing reveals their origin. The trader is a well-muscled brown-haired man, a head shorter than Alyiakal.

"You're the Mirror Lancer officer acting as Imperial Enumerator?"

"I am."

"Then we might as well get on with it," says the trader.

Alyiakal takes out the worksheet and asks, "Your name?"

"Saantyr, out of Sagana."

Alyiakal detects the unease and untruth and replies, "That's not your real name. Is that the name you trade under in all lands?"

"It's the name I'm giving to you, Captain."

"Overcaptain," replies Alyiakal politely. "And if you want to enter Cyador, you will give me your real name or the name you most often trade under. That's your choice."

"How can you tell me that Saantyr isn't my real name?"

"Because it's not . . ." Alyiakal explains as politely as he can, in the same way he had with the trader Byjaan.

After a long moment, the trader says, "Tyrsaan."

Sensing the truth of the declaration, Alyiakal writes down that name on the form, yet there's a certain unease. "And you're out of Sagana?"

"I am."

"Are you carrying forbidden items, such as cammabark?"

"That would be madness and stupidity. I'm neither mad nor stupid."

When Alyiakal asks about declaring a trading name, Tyrsaan shakes his head.

"Do you have a manifest listing your goods, or do you wish me to list each as you present them?"

"I have a list for you. It's not a manifest."

"Are all the goods you intend to bring into Cyador on that list?"

"They are, Overcaptain."

Again, Tyrsaan's words ring with absolute truth.

"Then let's look at them and verify the quantities."

The trader opens the rear doors to the lead wagon, and points out the cases holding spices, then those holding modest jewelry that consorts of smallholders might be able to afford, followed by an array of tools, and then an assortment of other goods. Alyiakal has to admire Tyrsaan's organization. He can see that more of Tyrsaan's goods might be sold in Guarstyad and Luuval and various hamlets than those of Byjaan. While Tyrsaan carries some shimmersilk scarves, they are smaller than Byjaan's goods, and there are none in green, white, or Merchanter blue.

In the end, the tariffs and fees total thirty-nine golds and two silvers, despite the fact that the trader has two wagons and far more in total goods than Byjaan. Once Tyrsaan pays the tariffs and fees, and receives his receipts and clearance papers, Alyiakal signals for the guards to open the old road gate. The trader inclines his head.

"My compliments, Overcaptain. Would that all enumerators were so precise and efficient. I do appreciate it."

"I appreciate your organization, trader. It made the enumeration far easier and swifter."

Once Tyrsaan's wagons have passed through the gate, Alyiakal turns his attention to the trader standing beside the next wagon—a graying and slender figure, accompanied by two mounted guards.

"Greetings, Overcaptain, I'm Saarkyn, from Surien, in Nordla."

"Is that your true name or the one you trade under?"

"One and the same," returns Saarkyn with an amused smile. "I have a terrible memory. Telling the truth means I don't have to remember when I lied and when I didn't."

Alyiakal senses no deception, but all that means is that Saarkyn is a very good trader. He writes down the names. "That's a long voyage."

"All voyages are long."

"I wouldn't think that Stonepier Port and Oldroad Post would see two traders at the same time," says Alyiakal cordially. "What brings you here?"

"Trade. What else?" replies the trader.

"To a Mirror Lancer post in the middle of nowhere, serving a middling town a hundred kays from the next middling town?"

"Sometimes, the best profits are to be had by going where others don't wish to travel. I learned that a long time ago."

"There's something to be said for that," agrees Alyiakal, although he has a feeling that the trader's words, honest as they feel, have a meaning he'll decipher later. "Do you have a manifest or a listing of goods?"

"I do." Saarkyn hands over a comparatively short list.

Alyiakal scans the list, which contains several items he has never seen, then says, "We might as well begin."

Saarkyn nods.

The spices are similar to those Tyrsaan carried, but there are several that

Alyiakal has heard of but never encountered, especially achiote and memnyt, as well as a wide range of dyestuffs, and kegs of various aromatics.

"Next are the half amphorae of lavendula oil."

"I can't say I've ever heard of it, and it's not on the tariff schedules."

"It's a fragrant oil that discourages insect pests and is good for skin rashes and some lesions."

"It still falls under import fees," Alyiakal points out, wondering at the same time whether the oil has healing properties.

"I'm aware of that. It's fragrant, but not a fragrance. Unknown liquids, four coppers per amphora, or two coppers for each half amphora."

"You're certain it isn't a fragrance?"

"It was not listed the last time I came to Cyador, and I'm not aware of anything that would change that."

Alyiakal can sense the certainty and writes down, "Lavendula, fragrant oil, 8 half amphorae." Then he sees two wooden crates filled with what look to be identical small glass bottles. Those in one crate are slightly smaller than the liqueur bottles that Saelora uses, while those in the second crate are half the size of those in the first crate—and all are empty. "Are you selling those?"

"Not exactly. I sell the lavendula oil and put it in those, then cork and seal the bottle with wax. I discovered that no one would buy the oil without smelling exactly what they were buying, and I ended up having to open every bottle and then reseal it. That's why I carry the oil in the amphorae and fill the bottles as I need to."

Alyiakal knows he must apply a fee to the bottles as well, but he has no idea how exactly to do so. "Empty bottles?"

"There's nothing in your schedule for that, Overcaptain."

"Fifteen coppers?"

"Fair enough."

Since the trader is neither surprised nor outraged, Alyiakal knows his valuation is low, but not excessively so. To be careful, he only writes down, "Empty glass bottles."

When Alyiakal finishes the inspection, the total of tariffs and fees comes to sixteen golds and eight silvers, yet he has the feeling that Saarkyn will have a far wider margin of profit than will Tyrsaan.

Before he signs and seals the papers for Saarkyn, he asks, "Do you know a trader named Byjaan?"

"I can't say that I know him. I've only encountered him twice before."

Again, the statement is without deceit, but Alyiakal senses more left unsaid.

After Saarkyn, his guards, and his wagon are through the gate and on the old road to Guarstyad, Alyiakal finishes his paperwork and takes it, with all the fees and tariffs, to his study—and the hidden lockbox. He'll be relieved when he dispatches the papers and golds to the enumerators in Guarstyad, even if it will be early on eightday morning.

It would have been helpful to have had Saelora here . . . very helpful. Yet he cannot afford to write her about his doubts and possible misvaluations, not when every letter might be read before she receives it.

From three traders and four wagons, the tariffs and fees exceeded a hundred golds. All three of the traders had a listing of goods ready for Alyiakal. Not a one was concealing anything. All paid readily and without complaint.

Yet, from what Saelora has said, all traders complain about tariffs and fees. In that, he trusts her judgment more than his own. He continues to worry over Saarkyn's statement that the best profits come from going ways that others don't wish to travel, a worry compounded by the fact that the trader said so without deceit or any unease.

He frowns, then shakes his head.

V

Over the next eightdays, the weather at Oldroad Post remains similar to the previous eightdays, and to the previous two Summers. There are more traders than before—a half score outland traders with more modest trading goods than Byjaan or Tyrsaan. By comparison, Alyiakal had seen less than a handful over the two years since establishing the post. That may be because outlanders hadn't yet learned about the post, but Alyiakal doubts that's the only reason for the increase.

On twoday of the fifth eightday of Summer, in the late afternoon, Alyiakal returns with First Company from a patrol well north of the closed east pass. While he and the scouts have discovered hoofprints of a single mount on a trail bordering the east side of the Westhorns, those tracks do not reach the east pass road before turning back north.

The rider might have been a hunter, but Alyiakal doubts this, primarily because the tracks, only glasses old, suggest the rider saw the dust of First Company and decided to withdraw. *So we'll have to carry out more patrols to the north for at least several eightdays.*

After Alyiakal takes care of the chestnut gelding, he heads to his study. As he approaches the doorway, the duty messenger hands two envelopes to him. "Ser, dispatches from Subcommander Laartol."

"Thank you." Alyiakal takes the envelopes and enters the study, lays them on the writing desk, and sets his visor cap on one of the wall pegs before slitting both envelopes open with his belt knife. Extracting the single sheet from the smaller envelope, he begins to read.

> *Alyiakal—*
>
> *I just wanted you to be among the first to know I've been promoted to commander, in large part, for reasons I suspect you know all too well. Effective immediately, I'll be posted to Mirror Lancer headquarters for duties yet to be assigned. I thought it would be a suitable occasion to open a special bottle of brandy someone was kind enough to send me. It was most excellent, and Majer Jaavor agreed. He was detached and sent to head the border post at Inividra . . .*

Alyiakal smiles at the reference to Saelora's greenberry-pearapple brandy. He hopes Commander Laartol will mention the brandy in Cyad. Whether he does or not, the brandy has been well-received in Geliendra and in Fyrad. Hyrsaal's consort-to-be Catriana has something to do with the sales in Fyrad and to outland traders porting there. Catriana has been working part-time for Loraan House while she waits for Hyrsaal's home leave when the two can be consorted. Unlike most factors and Merchanters, Saelora did not name her factorage after herself, but chose the name Loraan House after she purchased it from Vassyl—who holds a one-fifth interest, at Saelora's insistence.

> *. . . By the way, Majer Jaavor's replacement is Majer Bekkan, previously in charge of firewagon security at Ilypsya.*

Alyiakal couldn't help but think Bekkan might be like Jaavor.

> *You will be up for assignment this coming Autumn, if not sooner, but it's too early to speculate on your new post, and that decision may depend upon events yet to transpire.*

*I thought you'd like to know that the long-awaited enumerator for Oldroad
Post . . .*

"Long-awaited"? Alyiakal shook his head. *That must be what's in the
other envelope.*

> *. . . comes from a distinguished Merchanter heritage; his grandfather was
> the head of the Dyljani Clan before his death last year. Given that you don't
> have a background as a Merchanter, high altage, or elthage, nor are you
> from Cyad, I'll just mention that the Dyljani are one of the five clans that
> dominate trade in Cyad and throughout Cyador . . .*

*The other envelope likely deals with the appointment of an enumerator for Old-
road Post. But why is a potential Merchanter heir even deigning to be an Imperial
enumerator, let alone accepting a position as far as possible from Cyad?*

Abruptly, all the pieces click into place. More outland traders choosing
to come through Stonepier and Oldroad Post. All of the traders landing
at Stonepier coming from ports in Nordla. Jaavor, who always follows procedures scrupulously, whether they make sense or not, has been posted to
Inividra, where he's likely to be proved incompetent or killed . . . and where
Alyiakal's father died mysteriously. Laartol has been promoted to Mirror
Lancer headquarters, where he's in reach of powerful Merchanter clans.

And not in a position to support you.

While Alyiakal cannot prove it, he would wager that Imperial enumerators
add significant extra "fees" to tariffs or extort golds from outland traders. *And the
Nordlan traders have realized that by coming through Oldroad Post and taking extra
time they can get their goods into Cyador more cheaply with fewer "complications."*

All that, and Laartol's words about Alyiakal's next post depending on
events yet to occur, suggests that it will greatly depend on how he deals with
the situation . . . and the new enumerator.

The remainder of Laartol's short letter contains pleasantries and vague
appreciations for all that Alyiakal has done, both while at Guarstyad Post and
as officer in charge of Oldroad Post.

After rereading Laartol's letter, Alyiakal extracts the sheets from the larger
envelope. It contains exactly what he suspects—a letter from the Emperor's
Merchanter Advisor announcing the appointment of Donaajr'mer of Cyad,
and of the Clan Dyljani, as the enumerator for goods and trade entering
Cyador through Oldroad Post. The envelope also holds a copy of the dispatch

announcing that the enumeration duties of the officer in charge of Oldroad Post will cease upon the arrival of the new enumerator, and that all documentation and collected fees not already remitted to the Senior Enumerator in Guarstyad shall be turned over to Enumerator Donaajr, who will arrive in Guarstyad in the seventh eightday of Summer.

About two eightdays from now.

Alyiakal replaces both sheets in the larger envelope and takes a deep breath. He knows exactly what he'll be doing evenings for the next few days. *Making copies of every tariff-related form you've signed.* He'd thought about that earlier, but with Laartol's veiled warning, there's no choice.

He slips the two envelopes into his small personal file chest, stands, and heads for the compact mess room to find Torkaal.

The undercaptain is there, seated at the small table.

Alyiakal takes a seat across from him. "We're getting an enumerator." Then, he explains.

Torkaal nods when Alyiakal finishes. "Sounds like the Merchanters in Cyad aren't happy with outland traders getting honest tariffs."

"The official reason will be that it's time to appoint a real enumerator because of increased trade."

"Do you think this Enumerator Donaajr will come by boat or by the road?"

"He'll come by the old road because he has to meet with the Senior Enumerator in Guarstyad first." *Not just to be briefed, but to deliver a message from the Emperor's Merchanter Advisor.*

"At least you won't have to deal with him for too long." Torkaal smiles wryly.

Alyiakal understands the smile because, when Torkaal accepted the field commission as undercaptain, he agreed to extend his tour at Oldpost Road for an additional year.

"I don't like it," Torkaal continues. "Not if you're posted out, not with an enumerator being sent from Cyad. There's nothing I could do to stop any abuses. You're an overcaptain. Your words would have some weight."

"How long before you could draw a stipend?"

"Another four years."

Alyiakal winces.

"You see?"

Alyiakal definitely does. "We'll just have to see. Maybe we're worrying too much."

Torkaal raises his eyebrows.

"We can hope."

After a quiet dinner in the officers' mess, Alyiakal returns to his study, where he writes a letter to Saelora, then rereads it.

> Saelora—
>
> The Summer here has been even hotter than in previous years. That might be why we've seen no nomads or travelers from Kyphros. Quite recently, though, we've had more traders coming to Stonepier and entering Cyador through Oldroad Post, many of them from Nordla, and I have to wonder why. That won't be my problem, though, after the coming seventh eightday of Summer, when the official enumerator will arrive. His name is Donaajr'mer, and he has relatives in the Dyljani Clan. I'm guessing that he's taking a post as an enumerator to gain some experience before he returns to trading, but that's only a guess . . .
>
> Subcommander Laartol has been promoted to commander and will be posted at Mirror Lancer headquarters next, while Majer Jaavor has already been posted to Inividra to take command. I'll receive a new posting later this year, but I've heard nothing yet. Unless matters are unusual, I should have at least several eightdays of home leave. I do hope that your schedule will allow me to have a more leisurely visit than the last time . . .

The remainder of the letter makes a few mentions of trade, especially the lavendula trader who couldn't bottle the oil until customers could smell it, and where Saelora's brother Hyrsaal might be posted next, as well as the timing for Hyrsaal and Catriana's consorting ceremony and whether Alyiakal will be able to attend.

After he finishes the letter, he seals it so that it will be ready to go with the next dispatches to Guarstyad.

Not for the first time, he wishes he could send letters to Healer Vayidra to thank her for all she taught him and to Adayal, just to find out how she is faring, but he has no addresses for either and hasn't for years.

Then he takes out paper and the older tariff records, knowing he cannot delay copying them.

VI

Over the next several days, Alyiakal turns the patrols over to Torkaal while he checks for any discrepancies in any of the tariff and post records. Only one trader returning to Luuval appears. He has but a cart and a pony, and very limited goods, on which he pays seven silvers and three coppers.

When Alyiakal asks why the trader doesn't disembark at Luuval or Guarstyad, the answer is short and direct.

"Port hasn't been rebuilt at Luuval. Never liked the enumerators at Guarstyad. Good day, Overcaptain."

Alyiakal can't say he's surprised, but a Cyadoran trader willing to pay a one-silver landing fee to Kyphros and add days of travel in order to avoid Guarstyad or Fyrad indicates problems with the Imperial enumerators.

Just before sunset on fiveday, the lancers guarding the old road report a lancer squad less than two kays away.

"The escort for our new enumerator," Alyiakal tells Torkaal, who has joined him in his study. "Laartol, or whoever is in command of Guarstyad Post, had to send an officer. Who do you think it might be?"

"An undercaptain or a junior captain would be seen as an insult. The two most senior captains left there are Craavyl and Baentyl. Baentyl would be my guess."

Alyiakal nods. Baentyl would be the most likely, given his probable ties to Mirror Lancer headquarters, probably to Captain-Commander Mheryt, or a very senior commander. In addition, since Craavyl wasn't promoted after the border conflict, Laartol wouldn't put Craavyl in an awkward position of reporting to Alyiakal, not in front of an enumerator. *But if Laartol already left for Cyad . . . then Majer Bekkan might not know or care.*

"Are you going out to greet the enumerator?"

"He'll get here sooner or later." Alyiakal grins. "Besides, I have all the keys to the enumerator's building."

"Best keep spares, ser."

"I intend to."

A quint passes before duty squad leader Chaartes appears. "Ser, Enumerator Donaajr and Captain Baentyl are here to see you."

"Have them come in." Alyiakal stands, as does Torkaal.

The fair-haired Baentyl leads the way, followed by a figure in white-trimmed Merchanter blues. Donaajr is slender, but not wiry, half a head shorter than Alyiakal. Under slicked-back black hair, his muddy brown eyes seem to meet Alyiakal's without doing so.

"Enumerator Donaajr," says Baentyl politely, "Overcaptain Alyiakal."

"It's good to see you here, Enumerator," says Alyiakal pleasantly. "We've all wondered when the Emperor's Merchanter Advisor would send an enumerator."

"So did quite a few Merchanters, I heard," replies Donaajr politely.

"I imagine you'd like to see your quarters," says Alyiakal. "You have your own building, within the post, of course, which contains both your personal quarters and space for your official duties. It's adjacent to the gate to the old road."

"The head Enumerator in Cyad will be pleased that traders will not be able to evade paying their lawful tariffs."

"That has certainly been the case so far," replies Alyiakal, "between the effective closure of east pass and Mirror Lancer patrols." He pauses, then adds, "I'll take you to your building. After you have a chance to freshen up, the four of us will have dinner in the mess here."

Before he can say more, Baentyl steps forward and extends two envelopes. "Majer Bekkan sent these. He suggests you open the one from headquarters first."

From Mirror Lancer headquarters? Alyiakal doesn't care for the sound of that, but merely says, "Thank you. I appreciate your making sure they got to me." He sets the envelopes on his desk. "I'll get to them as soon as I take Enumerator Donaajr to his study and quarters."

Then he leads Donaajr from the study and out of the building past the closed gate to the old road. "As you can see, Enumerator, any trader has to pass through two gates."

"Who controls the gates?"

"The senior Mirror Lancer officer," replies Alyiakal, "after any traders or travelers have paid any entry fees and tariffs. How could it be otherwise?"

"How indeed?" says Donaajr blandly.

Although Alyiakal senses the arrogance behind the words, he says nothing and continues to the enumerator's building, unlocking the door and handing the key to Donaajr, then steps inside. "This is the study."

"The furnishings are . . . rather spare."

"For all of us," replies Alyiakal. "That's true of most border posts, and

Oldroad is definitely a border post. I'm sure you'll be able to change things more to your liking. Given the difficulty of transporting goods here, it didn't make much sense to furnish beyond the basics until we had an enumerator, especially since we had no idea what you might need."

Donaajr inspects the private quarters, then says, grudgingly, "These are more spacious than what junior enumerators have in Guarstyad. The bed appears adequate."

Alyiakal understands. "As soon as I get back to my study, I'll have someone on the duty roster deliver clean linens and blankets . . . and towels."

"I'd appreciate that."

As he turns to leave the enumerator's building, Alyiakal hands Donaajr a smaller key. "For the lockbox."

"I brought a special lockbox with me. It wasn't clear whether there was one here."

"Then you'll have two," replies Alyiakal.

When Alyiakal returns to the Mirror Lancer building, after arranging for the linens and blankets, he enters his study. Both Baentyl and Torkaal have gone, doubtless dealing with settling Baentyl's squad and mounts.

Alyiakal looks at the envelopes, deciding to open the one from Mirror Lancer headquarters. He immediately realizes it contains the orders he has not expected for at least another season, orders signed, as is usually the case, by the deputy commander, Captain-Commander Mheryt. The key provisions are more than clear, in both direction and implication.

> *Alyiakal'alt, Overcaptain*
> *Officer in Charge*
> *Oldroad Post, Guarstyad*
>   *You are hereby ordered to Luuval Post, for temporary duty as acting post commander. You are to report to Guarstyad Post no later than oneday of the eighth eightday of Summer 101 A.F. for expedited travel to Luuval . . .*
>
> *. . . You are to complete the Luuval Post closure no later than the end of the eighth eightday of Harvest, 101 A.F., and within an eightday of closure to transport all lancers, horses, wagons, and valuable gear and equipment, as physically possible, to the Mirror Lancer post in Fyrad . . .*
>
> *Following the satisfactory closure of Coastal Post Three, in accordance with applicable Mirror Lancer procedures, and your satisfactory arrival at*

Fyrad, you are entitled to up to six eightdays of home leave. Following home leave, you are to proceed to Lhaarat Post as deputy post commander with emphasis on directing and conducting longer-range field patrols . . .

Directing longer-range field patrols? Is something going on with Gallos or Cerlyn, or in the northwest of Kyphros? Once again, there's far too much he doesn't know, including why they need an overcaptain in Luuval temporarily, especially since the "better" part of the town was destroyed.

The envelope also contains the form to accept or reject the orders, as well as other requirements and instructions for indicating how much home leave he intends to take, although he doesn't have to declare that until mid-Harvest.

Still wondering about his orders and all the implications, Alyiakal opens the envelope from Majer Bekkan and begins to read.

> *Overcaptain Alyiakal—*
> *I've been notified of your temporary duty and your further assignment as deputy post commander at Lhaarat, and I'd like to offer my congratulations.*
>
> *To accommodate the requirements set forth by headquarters, Captain Craavyl will be promoted shortly to overcaptain to replace you. First Company of Oldroad Post will be rotated back to Guarstyad, while Fourth Company will accompany Captain Craavyl to Oldroad Post and become the post's First Company. Second Company will be getting a new undercaptain, and Undercaptain Torkaal will be receiving orders, possibly to Kynstaar. Please feel free to share that information with him . . .*
>
> *The Senior Enumerator in Guarstyad asked me to convey his appreciation for your precise recordkeeping and your timely remittance of tariffs and other fees. He trusts that the lancers at Oldroad Post will continue to afford the same secure transmission of funds and records from Enumerator Donaajr and that there will be a smooth transition in the handling of tariffs. . . .*

The lancers at Oldroad Post? And a smooth transition? Alyiakal can tell there was much more behind those words.

> *. . . since the Imperial tariff enumerators rely on long-established procedures not always codified.*

Meaning that they overtariff and pocket the difference? Or take bribes and look the other way for the traders of certain clans?

The remainder of Bekkan's letter contains vague generalities.

Alyiakal shakes his head slowly. In effect, nearly every experienced and good officer will be gone from Guarstyad and Oldroad Post within another season. Alyiakal is still thinking over what he has learned when Torkaal returns.

"They're all settled for now, ser."

"Close the door and sit down," says Alyiakal quietly.

"What is it, ser?"

"First . . . Majer Bekkan says you'll be getting orders to Kynstaar." Alyiakal relates those details, followed by the orders he has just received. "And that means I'll have to leave at first light on sevenday with Baentyl and his squad."

"They're not giving you much notice. Sounds like they've got trouble in Luuval. Maybe in Lhaarat as well."

"What do you know about Luuval?"

"Not much. Word has it that men who weren't that good got posted there. Usually a command for a loyal but tired majer or sub-majer about to get his stipend, before half of the town fell into the ocean. After that, I haven't heard anything."

"You were posted to Lhaarat, weren't you?" Alyiakal laughs wryly. "That's a dumb question. You've been posted to every border post that requires fighting."

"Except Syadtar."

"That's the one with the fewest raiders and brigands. At least, you won't have that problem at Kynstaar. That's probably why you're being posted there—so no one can say that it's different somewhere else."

Torkaal offers a cynical smile. "You might be right there."

"One of the best instructors I had there was an Undercaptain Faaryn. Came up through the ranks like you."

"Never met him, but I heard about him. Good man, everyone said."

"What can you tell me about Lhaarat?"

"It was run-down when I was there. Doubt that's changed. It's there to keep mountain brigands from attacking the fertile holdings northeast of the Accursed Forest. It's about a hundred kays north-northeast of Northpoint."

"Many brigands?"

"Some years. Never could tell."

"A friend of mine serves there now. He wrote that there were more brigands, and there's talk of problems with Kyphros and Gallos. I don't get that, given that's the widest stretch of the Westhorns."

"I haven't heard anything about that, ser."

Before either officer can say more, there's a knock on the door.

Alyiakal senses Baentyl's order/chaos pattern. "Come in." Then both he and Torkaal stand.

As Baentyl opens the door, Alyiakal adds, "We were about to head to the officers' mess, such as it is. We'll wait there for Enumerator Donaajr."

The three make their way to the mess, where the small table is set for four.

"The smallest officers' mess you'll ever see," Alyiakal says to Baentyl. "If we had a bigger table, we could seat eight or ten—tightly, but with the Mirror Engineers here we usually had four, sometimes five with a visiting magus."

"Weren't there two Magi'i here for a time?" asks Baentyl.

"They left before the building was finished—after they'd done what was needed of them and after they discovered that the devices weren't much different from what they currently use."

"Typical elthage snobbery," says Baentyl.

Alyiakal decides not to say more when he senses Donaajr approaching.

When the enumerator enters, Alyiakal gestures to the table, and the four seat themselves. After the mess ranker pours the wine, Alyiakal lifts his glass. "To the first official enumerator of Oldroad Post." After he sips the wine, a passable red, he adds, "And one of my last toasts here."

While Alyiakal senses surprise from Baentyl, he senses none from Donaajr. Hardly unexpected, not with what Alyiakal suspects about the ties between Merchanters, Mirror Lancer headquarters, and possibly even the Palace of Light.

"One of your last?" asks Baentyl.

"One of those envelopes contained my orders. I'll be returning to Guarstyad with you for expedited transportation, whatever that means. I'm being posted to temporary duty to oversee the closure of Luuval Post. Then, after home leave, I'll be going to Lhaarat as the deputy post commander."

"Congratulations!"

Baentyl's words are genuinely meant, Alyiakal can tell, and that is a surprise. "Thank you."

At that moment, the mess ranker serves their meal.

Donaajr looks askance at the fare.

"Roasted coney, cheesed potatoes, and roasted quilla," replies Alyiakal cheerfully. "You're fortunate. In the Winter it could be salt pork and spring beans." He's exaggerating a bit, because he hasn't seen spring beans since Pemedra, thankfully, but he already doesn't care much for Donaajr.

"Oldroad Post is a border post," adds Torkaal pleasantly. "The coney is quite tasty, and a change from the usual fare."

After taking a small bite of the coney, Donaajr looks to Alyiakal. "You're rather young for an overcaptain, aren't you?"

"I'm on the youngish side, but there are others. We tend to have extensive experience fighting on the borders in common."

"There hasn't been much need for fighting here recently, I've been told," observes Donaajr.

"That might be because the overcaptain and his company destroyed a thousand Kyphrans in the conflict," interjects Torkaal. "The Kyphrans still call him the Lance of Fire."

"Much of that was due to my senior squad leader and now undercaptain of Second Company," adds Alyiakal before Donaajr can reply. "He was promoted as a result."

"Ah . . . very strategic of the Mirror Lancers. A most effective deterrent, to have the most effective . . . warriors remaining to guard the border."

"It should make your work easier," says Baentyl pleasantly.

The more Alyiakal thinks about it, the more he feels he's misjudged the situation. Putting any true enumerator at Oldroad Post will eventually stop most of the outland traders. The only reason most have come through Oldroad Post is to avoid the enumerators in Guarstyad and possibly Luuval or Fyrad. That suggests Donaajr was chosen to stop traders while getting him away from Cyad, possibly because the Dyljani Clan doesn't know what else to do with him.

"How did you come to be an enumerator?" asks Alyiakal.

Donaajr shrugs. "When you grow up in a Merchanter family, you either become a Merchanter or an enumerator."

"I've seen both Imperial enumerators and Merchanter enumerators," says Alyiakal.

"They're different," explains Donaajr. "Imperial enumerators are like . . . Mirror Lancers or healers. They spend their life at it. Senior Enumerators control trade entry at the largest ports and make sure the revenues go to the Palace of Light so that there are golds to pay for all those who work for the Emperor, the Magi'i, or the Mirror Lancers. Some advise the Emperor's Merchanter Advisor. A Merchanter enumerator is one of the lower positions in trading concerns. Some Merchanter enumerators may spend their lives working for such concerns. The best sometimes become Merchanters and traders."

Alyiakal replies, "So, as an Imperial enumerator, you could go on to be a Senior Enumerator at Guarstyad or another port of entry, and be promoted and posted in different places? Like Mirror Lancers?"

"It's similar. Enumerators don't get moved from port to port as much as lancer officers do."

While Alyiakal doesn't particularly care for Donaajr, he feels slightly sorry for the young man.

The remainder of the dinner conversation covers the weather, the traders who have come through, and how the post came to be built.

After dinner, Alyiakal returns to his study, where he writes a letter to Saelora, explaining his orders—and the fact that he will definitely get home leave after his temporary duty at Luuval. He worries about problems he will encounter in Luuval, but he's not about to put that in a letter.

VII

Alyiakal rises early on sixday morning since he has a great deal to accomplish in the single day before he leaves Oldroad Post. After a quick breakfast in the mess, where Donaajr and Baentyl appear just before Alyiakal and Torkaal excuse themselves, Alyiakal spends the next several glasses with Torkaal going over matters, since it will be some time before Craavyl arrives.

When Alyiakal has covered all he can think of and Torkaal has no more questions, the undercaptain asks, "What do you think of the tariff enumerator?"

"I'm not impressed, and I feel a little sorry for him. As soon as word gets out that he's here, there won't be many traders coming through, and he'll be doing nothing—"

"Instead of *almost* nothing," interjects Torkaal. "Wouldn't it be more effective to clean up the way tariff enumerators work?"

"Effective for whom? And who would do it?" *And manage to stay alive after the attempt.*

"I see your point."

"You, or Craavyl and your successor, will be chasing smugglers by around Harvest, while Donaajr will suffer, or turn to some pastime, if not both, unless he only imposes the rightful amount of tariffs . . . and keeps his personal take low, in which case some traders will continue to come here. If he takes much at all, none will come. If he takes none, he'll face other problems." Alyiakal laughs sardonically. "He'll need to be very careful."

"You never even considered a personal take."

"Neither would you. We're Mirror Lancer officers." Alyiakal doesn't have to mention that it also would have been stupid and shortsighted. He stands. "I need to check my gear and figure out what to take, then pack."

"As if you have much to pack."

Alyiakal shrugs, then smiles. "It'll be your turn before long. No more fighting raiders, troopers, or brigands."

"Just infighting. That's almost as bad," Torkaal replies.

"There's always something."

"Are you going to see that Merchanter lady who writes?"

"After my temporary duty."

"Until you told me about her, I'd never heard of a woman who wasn't from a Merchanter family who became a full Merchanter on her own."

"She started out as an apprentice scrivener."

"There aren't many woman scriveners, either. I can see why you think she's special." Torkaal then says carefully, "I've never heard you talk about her to anyone but me."

"You asked. I can trust you."

"You serious about her . . . really . . . Isn't there something . . ." Torkaal stops, then says, "It's not my place—"

"It's not spoken of, except quietly, but very few officers who consort women from Merchanter backgrounds get promoted beyond overcaptain, and none, I've been led to believe, beyond majer. We've never discussed consorting. We've been writing each other for over eight years, but we've only spent a few days together, and that was around her family. We'll see what happens on my leave."

"What does her brother think?"

"He was the one who suggested she write me." Alyiakal offers an amused chuckle. "He's the officer who's at Lhaarat now. Since he's due for reposting this Autumn, we won't cross paths at Lhaarat. I hope to see him on leave because he's getting consorted around then." Alyiakal stretches. "I'll see you in the mess for dinner." He offers a wry smile, turns, and heads for his quarters.

He finishes his tasks well before the evening meal and takes time to write a letter to Hyrsaal and a shorter one to Liathyr, who commands a port company in Chaelt, a modest coastal town roughly two hundred kays southwest of Kynstaar.

Baentyl is waiting when Alyiakal enters the mess, and he turns. "Not a bad post, all things considered. How are the Winters?"

"A trace warmer than Pemedra, or the other posts in the Grass Hills. The air's damper and bites more here, but we don't get near as much snow as at Guarstyad."

"For that alone, it might be worth being posted here."

"Until you have to chase smugglers," says Torkaal as he enters. "The Grass Hills are flat compared to the Westhorns."

"Are there that many smugglers?" asks Donaajr, who has followed Torkaal into the mess.

"No, not many," replies Alyiakal, gesturing to the table, then waiting for a moment before seating himself. "But there'd be a lot more if we weren't here."

Once the four are seated, their wineglasses filled, and their platters full, Alyiakal lifts his glass. "The best to us all in an uncertain world." He sips from his glass, sets it down, and surveys the meal, which consists of slices of pork in gravy-like white sauce, with roasted potatoes, and, again, roasted quilla.

It could be worse. And it definitely has been in the past at times.

Alyiakal takes bite of the tender pork, followed by some of the potatoes.

While the two other officers begin to eat, Donaajr looks warily at his platter before taking a tentative small mouthful of roast potato.

"How soon can we leave tomorrow?" asks Baentyl.

"A quint after first light. We don't let traders start until sunrise."

"Why do you make them wait?" asks Donaajr, with a hint of challenge.

Alyiakal gives him the same explanation he's given traders. Even before he finishes, he senses the enumerator's irritation, but he waits to see what Donaajr will say.

"Merchanters have more at stake than lancers. Why do you think they'll be any less careful?"

"First, none of them have traveled the old road. Second, most of them have wagons, and there's not much room to spare with a wagon, as you must have seen on the ride here. Third, because they *do* have more at stake, it's even more important to the Mirror Lancers that they travel the old road safely. Even if they're outland traders, I'm certain neither the Emperor nor the Majer-Commander would like the rulers of other lands believing that we carelessly let their traders kill themselves." Alyiakal takes a sip of his wine, a drinkable but indifferent red. *And you're not paying for it.*

"You kill hundreds, and you worry about outland traders?"

"We follow orders," replies Alyiakal. "We had orders to hold this area against the Kyphran attack, land that actually belonged to Cyador. They tried to take devices developed by the First . . . and they attacked us first. Our current orders are to protect the border, to ensure only those authorized can use the road, and that they use it in safety. Until you arrived, my orders were to follow the schedules and requirements for tariffing traders and others entering Cyador. Now, those orders apply to you."

"Do you come from a Merchanter family, Overcaptain?"

"No. I'm from an altage background, and a third-generation lancer officer, Enumerator."

"I've gone through the records you left. They're certainly adequate and competently done."

Meaning that you can't find anything obviously wrong with them. "My father was a lancer majer. He always emphasized the need for complete and accurate records."

"Ah . . . yes. Before he left Guarstyad, Commander Laartol mentioned you were known for your detailed and thorough reports."

"He left while you were there?"

"He departed on the fireship on which I arrived. The *Kiedral,* as I recall," says Donaajr off-handedly. "I spent several days with the enumerators at Guarstyad."

"I'm sure those days were useful," comments Torkaal blandly.

"I doubt I'll encounter many of the situations on which they briefed me, but one never knows."

"Did the enumerators mention whether any tariff enumerators plan to remain at Luuval?" asks Alyiakal.

"Luuval was never mentioned, but I imagine there must be some provision for one so long as the port is open."

Baentyl clears his throat. "I talked to Overcaptain Shenklyn last fall before he took his stipend. They offered him the command of the Mirror Lancer post there. He said there was no point in taking it because there wasn't anything left of the harbor—that it had all turned into a swamp."

"That might explain why I'm being sent there," says Alyiakal. *They need an officer who can be effective finishing an unpleasant job.* He can't help wondering what all the problems are, because he has no doubt that's why he's being posted there.

"If Overcaptain Shenklyn chose getting out . . ." offers Torkaal.

"There are problems," finishes Baentyl. "He said he didn't know what they were and that he had no intention of finding out."

"So they give you temporary duty before you become a deputy post commander," says Torkaal. "Makes it hard to reject those orders."

If you ever want to be more than an overcaptain. "It does," agrees Alyiakal, even as he senses Donaajr's surprise.

After a long moment, Baentyl says, "It looks like the ride to Guarstyad will be pleasant, at least as pleasant as a long, Summer day's ride can ever be."

The rest of the dinner conversation revolves around the weather at various border posts, and Alyiakal excuses himself early, claiming that he needs to finish packing, which is true except for the fact that what he has left might take two quints, at the longest.

VIII

Alyiakal is up before first light on sevenday, but the mess ranker still has ham slices and fried eggs for him and Baentyl, which he presents with a smile, and says, "You'll need a good breakfast. It's a long day's ride."

"Thank you, Haanst," replies Alyiakal. "We appreciate it."

"My pleasure, ser. Been a good two years." Then the mess ranker turns and makes his way back to the kitchen.

Alyiakal eats quickly, but as he finishes, Torkaal arrives, a wry smile on his lips. "Might have known you'd be up early. Just wanted to see you off. Won't be the same without you here."

"You'll handle everything just fine." Alyiakal grins. "Especially given how much I learned from you." He lowers his voice. "Let the enumerator find his own way."

"Yes, ser." Torkaal pauses. "Still won't be the same."

"You'll let me know where you'll be posted?"

Torkaal nods.

"Until later, then."

After his farewell to Torkaal, Alyiakal leaves the mess, picks up his two duffels, and makes his way to the stable, where he saddles the chestnut gelding, straps his gear in place, leads the chestnut from the stable, mounts, and then joins Baentyl while the captain musters his squad.

As the sky lightens in the east, the two lead Baentyl's first squad to the old road gate and then through it.

Alyiakal gives a last look at the neat stone enclave—*that shows no sign of all the blood shed to make it possible*—then turns to the smooth-cut stone road before him.

"Best of fortune, Overcaptain!" one of the gate guards calls after Alyiakal and Baentyl ride past. The road carves a topless half tunnel through the rock. The echoes of hoofs on stone and a few low words between lancers are the only sounds.

For the first two kays, the road gradually climbs, then levels out for the next kay or so, gently descending over another two kays, until it reaches the eastern edge of the inlet. Sheer cliffs, more than two hundred yards above the ocean, surround it on three sides. At the cliff edge, the road turns north along cut stone. After running nearly a kay, the next section of the road appears to end in a rugged, rocky mass rising several hundred yards above the road—except another section of the road heads west above the end of the inlet for little more than a kay.

"I can't believe that this was lost for almost a century," says Baentyl as he turns his mount north, "until you rediscovered it."

"I just followed orders," replies Alyiakal. "Commander Laartol told me to find the end of the road. I didn't really find the end of the road—only where it went before part of it was destroyed."

Baentyl gestures to his left and at the water below. "The First must not have had any fear of heights. They built a road some three yards wide with a two-hundred-yard fall if they took a misstep."

"Given that they came from the Rational Stars, is it that surprising?"

"Not surprising, but I'll be happier when we're around the inlet."

Alyiakal nods, admitting, if only to himself, that he'd had similar feelings, especially when he'd had to ride partway around the inlet to be able to give a detailed report.

When they near the corner where the road resumes its westward heading above the end of the inlet, Alyiakal notes, again, how deeply the builders cut into the stone to allow wagons to turn safely.

When they reach the open road beyond the inlet at the top of the southern cliffs, the white sun has risen well above the inlet's rocky east point. Alyiakal says nothing when he hears Baentyl take a deep breath and senses the captain's relief.

After a short break, the squad and the two officers resume their journey, and the next eight kays on the bare and open stone cleared by the Mirror Engineers are easy riding, a far easier ride than Alyiakal's first experience.

Then, it had seemed little more than a narrow path hemmed in by gnarled evergreens creeping out of the tangle of rocks to the north and encroaching on the then-hidden road.

Except that it was pleasantly cool then, and now it's midday in full Summer and there's hardly a hint of a breeze.

As Alyiakal, Baentyl, and the squad near the side road leading to the only village between the Oldroad and Guarstyad posts, Baentyl looks to Alyiakal. "Time for a break, don't you think?"

"That's an excellent idea. Are you planning on stopping at the village up ahead?"

"I am. They have a fountain. Commander Laartol arranged it. We pay a silver each time we stop, regardless of the number of mounts."

Before long, the squad turns north on the narrow road—now stone paved—leading through the trees to the open heavy-timbered gate. The neat gray stone fountain stands on the east side of the main street, just north of the gate.

"They must have built the fountain for us, or for traders," Alyiakal says to Baentyl. "I don't recall it when I was here."

The few villagers out in the village move away from the fountain basin as the lancers ride in and dismount, but the locals don't seem disturbed in the slightest.

Alyiakal lets the chestnut drink, and then leads him away from the fountain, where he takes out his water bottle and has some of the remaining ale.

Baentyl joins him. "Seems peaceful enough, but you had some trouble here, didn't you?"

"A little. We kept it from being more."

Alyiakal sees a gray-haired woman walking toward them. From her appearance and the unseen rough order/chaos shield she carries, he senses she is the one he encountered more than two years ago.

Baentyl steps forward and hands her a coin. "Your silver, Headwoman."

"Our silver," she replies with a faint but pleasant smile. Then she turns to Alyiakal.

He inclines his head. "I'm glad to see that you're well."

She studies him without speaking.

Alyiakal waits.

"You are even more powerful now," she says. "You are leaving?"

"I'm being posted elsewhere."

She nods. "That is best for all, especially for you."

Alyiakal raises his eyebrows.

The woman smiles, sadly. "Great power needs to be used or it destroys those who possess it. Use it well." Then she turns and walks away from the fountain.

"What was that about?" asks Baentyl.

"The trouble was her brother. He was a bit of a mage and tried to attack us. I had to kill him. I imagine she saw that I'd been promoted." Alyiakal hopes that statement will suffice to allay Baentyl's curiosity.

"She recognized you, though."

"That's because I had her escort us through the village to make sure that this road didn't lead anywhere else. It doesn't. It ends downhill beyond the holly oaks."

"Holly oaks?"

"A little-known variety of oak trees. Maybe their acorns are useful for something. I wouldn't know."

Baentyl shakes his head. "We need to get moving. We've still got a ways to go."

Once mounted, the squad leaves the hamlet and continues west on the cliff road, now a mixture of rock and clay, a composition that remains largely the same until close to Guarstyad.

More than a glass passes before Alyiakal sights the rounded point where the cliffs running east-southeast join those running north-south, bordering the small gulf that leads into the Guarstyad harbor.

From the point, the ride gradually descends over ten kays to the port town, which they reach in late afternoon. Alyiakal notes small sailing craft are the only vessels at the two harbor piers, and he wonders how "expedited" his travel to Luuval might be, since riding there, if even possible, would take five to six days.

After riding east through the town and heading north along the only real road outside of Guarstyad, they cover another five kays before reaching the stone causeway to the walled post.

By the time Alyiakal takes care of the chestnut, gathers his gear, and carries it to the officers' quarters, which are in the same building as the mess, it's close to sunset. He pauses in the entry, wondering about his quarters, when a tall majer with thinning sandy-red hair appears.

"You must be Overcaptain Alyiakal. I'm Majer Bekkan. It's good to meet you."

"It's good to meet you, ser."

"Take the visiting officers' chamber," says the majer. "Some of the empty officers' quarters aren't fully furnished."

"The furnishings were sent to Oldroad Post for the companies there. I doubt headquarters felt any immediate necessity to replace them."

"Not with golds as tight as they are," replies Bekkan dryly. "Just leave your gear in quarters for now. The evening meal will be in a quint. We'll talk about your travel and a few other matters tomorrow after morning mess."

"Thank you, ser. I'll join you as quickly as I can."

While Alyiakal has misgivings about "other matters," there's not much else he can say, but he's happy to be assigned the visiting officers' quarters. They're closer than his former quarters. He washes up quickly, brushes and straightens his uniform, and then makes his way to the mess, where he sees Craavyl, Baentyl, and an undercaptain.

Before Alyiakal can say a word, Majer Bekkan appears and gestures to the table. As acting post commander, Bekkan seats himself at its head, with Alyiakal, as the next senior officer, to his right.

"As you can see, Alyiakal," says the majer, "we're a bit understaffed. I believe you know Captain Craavyl and Captain Baentyl. This is Undercaptain, soon to be Captain, Nuultyn. Nuultyn, this is Overcaptain Alyiakal, who's been the officer in charge at Oldroad Post."

Nuultyn nods politely.

Once the mess orderly has poured the wine, Bekkan lifts his glass. "In the hope of good news and good times to come."

"In the hope of good news," Alyiakal repeats with the others before taking a small swallow of wine and puzzling over the majer's words.

After Bekkan sets his wineglass down, he clears his throat. "Some of you may wonder about my toast. We've received word that the Emperor Taezyl is quite ill. What you may not know is that his sole heir is . . . shall we say, far less well-regarded in Cyad than is his sire, and there is considerable concern about who should succeed the Emperor . . . and who will."

Considering that the Emperor Taezyl is generally regarded as adequate, if that, Alyiakal gets the feeling that the heir is considered far less than that.

"Is the heir old enough to rule in his own right?" asks Craavyl. "I had heard that the Empress might be considered as regent."

"The heir turned twenty in early Spring," replies Bekkan.

Barely old enough to rule. Alyiakal does not voice this, but asks, "Does the Emperor have any daughters?"

"He's not known to have any other children by the Empress," replies Bekkan dryly.

"Which son by what other woman is considered more fit to hold the Malachite Throne?" asks Craavyl.

"Kaartyn'alt is a promising magus. He's around thirty, and the result of a brief liaison between Taezyl and a young Magi'i healer well before his uncle died in that fire aboard the Imperial yacht . . ."

A fire that not only claimed the Emperor Kieffal, but his wife and both his male heirs before they had heirs.

". . . The fire thrust Taezyl onto the Malachite Throne, without a consort, and he quickly consorted Elynia, another Magi'i healer—"

"Then the rumor that he's always been sickly is true?" asks Baentyl.

"Most likely," admits the majer, "but saying that publicly has never been wise, especially around or near seniors in the Triad or in Cyad."

"So Kaartyn is Magi'i, of Imperial blood, and considered competent by some in power," asks Alyiakal, "or the issue wouldn't be troubling . . . so the conflict is between precedent and perceived competence?"

"Precisely. We will need to stand together, behind the Majer-Commander and whatever decision he makes. Our duty is to support Cyador against outside enemies and forces and not to be involved in affairs of the Palace of Light."

Not to be involved in affairs of the Palace of Light . . . an interesting way to put it, suggesting the Majer-Commander cares more about competence than "affairs." Alyiakal's private observation will definitely be staying private.

"Now that you know," the majer continues, "I suggest that we enjoy dinner."

While giving attention to Bekkan, Alyiakal has scarcely looked at what the orderly has served: veal cutlets in brown sauce, with lace potatoes, and young asparagus, a vegetable Alyiakal considers the same as quilla—necessary and edible, but little more.

The five officers eat in silence before Craavyl looks to Alyiakal. "Do you know what you'll be doing in Luuval?"

"Only that I'm supposed to close down the post and all operations before the end of Harvest," replies Alyiakal dryly.

"Don't know why it's taking this long," says Baentyl, "the subsidence or whatever it was happened over three years ago. If they were going to close it, why not before now?"

"Closing any Mirror Lancer post has a great many ramifications and repercussions, *and* certain requirements," replies the majer. "Overcaptain Alyiakal will have to complete dealing with them. Headquarters may have decided on him, precisely because he's an outsider . . ."

That very well may have been a decision by Mirror Lancer headquarters, but Alyiakal knows his position will be near impossible. If he succeeds, the accomplishment will be considered competent, at best. *After all, how hard can it be to close down a coastal post in a town that's lost its harbor to a natural disaster?* He smiles politely and makes pleasant comments for the rest of the meal.

IX

After morning mess on eightday, as Majer Bekkan stands to leave, he addresses Alyiakal. "I'll see you in a quint."

Alyiakal inclines his head. "Yes, ser." He takes his time getting up, while Nuultyn and Baentyl hurry from the mess.

Craavyl, who has waited, as if he wishes to speak privately with Alyiakal, looks at him questioningly. "Could I have a moment? I was hoping you could tell me more about events at Oldroad Post. I don't know if you've heard—"

"Majer Bekkan informed me that you'll be promoted and take over as officer in charge. Congratulations."

"It's only a one-year posting, but somehow Commander Laartol managed it."

"That was good of him." *Especially since the tour of duty is short, while the promotion is permanent.* Craavyl will still be making overcaptain earlier than normal, even if it's not as fast as Alyiakal's promotion. "I'll be happy to tell you what I know." *And even some of what I suspect.* "Since I have to meet with the majer before long, perhaps I could meet you in the officers' study afterward?"

"I'd appreciate it. Thank you."

Alyiakal manages a warm smile, then makes his way out of the building to the post headquarters.

The door to Bekkan's study, the one for the deputy commander, is open. "Come on in. Please close the door."

Alyiakal does and takes the center chair facing the desk.

"First, your transportation. You won't be traveling by fireship. Instead, you'll take a fast naval sloop to Luuval. It's expected to port here late today or early tomorrow. Either way, you'll depart tomorrow. The sloop has a shallow draft, but they still may have to ferry you ashore by boat, since there's no harbor or port left at Luuval." Bekkan pauses. "That's not quite true. When the headland collapsed, it filled the entire harbor and turned it into a bog. Initially there had been hope that the engineers could open a channel, but even with chaos-cutters the Mirror Engineers couldn't do it."

"How many lancers are still at the post?"

"Roughly three squads and a captain."

"Closing the post presumably means removing equipment, horses, and lancers," says Alyiakal. "If there's no port and no easy access to the ocean . . ."

"Exactly . . . you'll have to load the most valuable equipment onto wagons and take the road from Luuval to the Lower Ford across the Great East River. From there, it's about five kays to the Great Canal . . . and two days beyond there by wagon to Fyrad." The majer hands a thick envelope to Alyiakal. "All the requirements are detailed here."

"It seems like the post is rather isolated, more so than Guarstyad or Oldroad Post," Alyiakal observes. "How does the post receive orders and directives from headquarters? How are the lancers there paid?"

For the first time, Alyiakal senses irritation from the majer.

"Those details are in the information I just handed you."

"Thank you, ser. I'm glad to know that."

"That's all I can add. I'll have someone let you know when the sloop arrives." The majer pauses, "If you wouldn't mind briefing Captain Craavyl . . ."

"I'm meeting him after we finish here, ser."

"Excellent . . . excellent. I'll see you later." The majer stands.

Alyiakal does the same, inclines his head, and leaves the study, thinking.

Did you get the temporary duty assignment partly because you've been in charge of an isolated post?

Carrying the thick envelope, he leaves the post headquarters building and walks back to the officers' study in the mess and quarters building.

The only officer there is Craavyl. Alyiakal takes a chair from the desk that used to be his, brings it to Craavyl's desk, and sits down. "You've been to Oldroad Post a few times and know the basics. What else would you like to know?"

"Anything you'd care to tell me, especially about the traders, the Kyphrans, smugglers, and the nomads."

"There's not much new about the any of those, but an enumerator just arrived, and the situation with the traders could be interesting . . ." Alyiakal explains his suspicions about the recent number of traders arriving at Oldroad Post and the fact that Donaajr is related to the former head of the Dyljani Clan.

When Alyiakal finishes, Craavyl nods, then says, "Thank you. That will be very helpful."

"It'll be a long year," replies Alyiakal.

"It's been two for you," points out Craavyl, "and I won't have to build and organize the post."

"No, but you'll be dealing with a dissatisfied enumerator connected to a powerful Merchanter clan."

"The majer didn't mention that."

"I imagine he has a great deal on his mind." Alyiakal manages not to frown, wondering why neither Majer Bekkan nor Commander Laartol had told Craavyl. Then again, Bekkan hadn't mentioned it to Alyiakal. Had it slipped Laartol's mind? "You said that Commander Laartol managed to get you the posting and promotion. Was that before he left?"

Craavyl looks slightly embarrassed. "It doesn't matter now, but when he left, he said that he'd try to get me named as your successor and not to say anything about it. I don't see that it could have happened any other way."

"I don't either." But that means Bekkan either doesn't know about Donaajr or had reason not to tell Craavyl about the Dyljani connections. *Of course! Bekkan told you to brief Craavyl . . . if Craavyl doesn't know, both you and Craavyl could end up in trouble . . . and that's not the sort of information Bekkan could be faulted for not passing along.* "Just be very precise in any reports you make."

"I'd thought about that, and I appreciate the caution."

After talking with Craavyl for another quint, Alyiakal leaves and makes his way back to his temporary quarters, where he opens the thick envelope and begins to read.

Some of the material is so poorly written that he has to read it twice, and he suspects it was written by a ranker pressed into service. If Alyiakal understands what he has labored through, some of the town was lost, not by the collapse of the headland, but afterward. The only effective rapid communications use a small pier east of the now-ruined harbor—a pier unusable in bad weather. One payroll delivery vessel lost their boat rowing the payroll courier to the pier, along with the courier and payroll. The interim post commander, a sub-majer, died of a suspected flux, and the next officer selected refused the orders. *That had to be Shenklyn.* Currently, the acting post commander is a Captain Aaltyn.

For a moment, Alyiakal wonders why Aaltyn can't just close the post, but he recalls Bekkan's comment about "certain requirements." With a sigh, he gets out the small manual he'd received as officer in charge at Oldroad Post and searches through the pages. He finally finds what he remembered reading:

> Mirror Lancer Posts must be commanded, except for short transitory periods, by a senior field-grade officer or by a command-grade officer. Any act significantly affecting the status of that post must be carried out by a fully qualified commanding officer . . .

So they need at least an overcaptain to even close the post.

That does explain a few matters, but it raises other questions. Is Alyiakal being ordered to temporary duty at Luuval so that more favored officers aren't inconvenienced, or because he has to travel in that direction to get from Guarstyad to any posting?

He continues reading.

When he finishes, Alyiakal shakes his head. He replaces the material in the envelope, then completes his letter to Saelora, only adding a few lines, one of which reads "the harbor at Luuval is reported to resemble the bog behind the distillery, except it is far larger." That will give her some idea of what he faces without raising the suspicions of whoever reads his letters. He then seals it, and takes it, with the letters to Hyrsaal and Liathyr, to the duty squad leader for dispatch with the next fireship.

From there he strolls to the stable, where he spends some time with the chestnut gelding who has served him for nearly three years.

X

The fast sloop promised for Alyiakal's "expedited" transportation doesn't sail into the pier in Guarstyad Harbor until midmorning on oneday, and a ranker informs Alyiakal that he's expected on the pier as soon as possible. Alyiakal carries his gear to the stable and straps it onto the chestnut he'd saddled earlier, suspecting he might require a precipitous departure, and rides down to the pier, accompanied by a junior squad leader he doesn't know and two rankers.

He's no sooner reined up on the pier just short of the gangway than one of the sailors standing there hurries over.

"You the overcaptain, ser?"

"I'm Overcaptain Alyiakal."

"The captain would like you on board quick, ser."

Alyiakal dismounts and hands the reins of the chestnut to the nearest Mirror Lancer ranker. "Be kind to him. He's a good mount."

Then he unstraps both duffels and says to the sailor, "If you'd show me the way?"

"Yes, ser."

As Alyiakal nears the gangway, he sees that the nameplate on the bow reads ZAENTH. He doesn't recognize the name but supposes it was someone once noteworthy. Extending his order/chaos senses, he detects nothing of the confined chaos permeating Imperial fireships. Nor is the *Zaenth*'s hull iron, which makes sense, given that there's no chaos to contain.

When he reaches the gangway, he asks, "Permission to come aboard?"

"Permission granted, Overcaptain," replies the weathered figure with the insignia of a squad leader on the collars of his light gray uniform. He belatedly recalls that the navy calls them petty officers. "Dhapres will take your gear to your cabin. If you'll come with me, Captain Haeryn asked to see you as soon as you came aboard."

Alyiakal follows the petty officer aft to where an even more weathered officer with the insignia of a naval lieutenant stands.

"Overcaptain Alyiakal, ser," says the petty officer.

"Thank you, Jaarvyt." Captain Haeryn studies Alyiakal for a moment, then says, "Welcome aboard, Overcaptain. Have you been on a cutter before?"

"No. I've only been on a fireship, just once."

Haeryn nods. "We've been ordered to get you to Luuval, or as close as we can, as quickly as safely possible. Would you care to tell me why?"

"No one has told me, Captain—"

"Haeryn, please. You outrank me."

"Only on a rank chart," replies Alyiakal, "and certainly not on board your ship."

Haeryn smiles wryly. "Any ideas, then?"

"The Mirror Engineers are trying to close the post. The previous commanding officer was reported as dying of a flux. My last tour was cut short, and I've been detailed to Luuval on temporary duty before taking my next posting. I'm guessing that everything's disorganized, at best, and a complete disaster at worst."

"You had any experience in command of a post?"

"Officer in charge of a small border post for the past two years."

"Makes as much sense as anything. Anything more you'd care to pass along?"

"That's what I know. Anything else would be speculation." Alyiakal adds dryly, "Speculations often miss the mark, usually by being too optimistic."

Haeryn barks a brief laugh.

In the background, Alyiakal hears, "Gangway aboard! Stand by to cast off all lines!" He waits for a moment, then says, "In short, don't risk the ship or the crew to get me there. It's not that critical. There wasn't a fireship available, and besides, headquarters wouldn't divert one for me, but traveling by road right now could take an eightday or more."

"There are always brigands between Guarstyad and Luuval."

"They wouldn't be the problem. What passes for a road could be."

"The way you say that . . . you wouldn't be the one who massacred that Kyphran army, would you?"

From the way Haeryn phrases the question, Alyiakal senses that the captain already knows the answer.

"It wasn't an army. Maybe the equivalent of twenty or twenty-five companies. We had five companies and lost two."

Haeryn nods. "Make sure your gear is secure. It's a bit rough in the outer harbor and worse than that farther out. Take the hatch in front of the helm. Your cabin is the one on the port forward of the captain's cabin. We don't have staterooms, like they do on fireships." He pauses, then grins. "The *Zaenth*'s a cutter, not a mere ship, or a chaos-powered barge like the fireships."

"I won't forget that, Captain." Alyiakal smiles back. "I'll get out of your way." He turns and makes his way down the ladder. On reaching the bottom of the ladder, he discovers that he has to stoop to keep from hitting the overhead.

His cabin is even smaller than the one on the fireship, and his two duffels take up all the space on the lower bunk. After studying the two bunks, Alyiakal stuffs the duffels under the lower bunk, then heads back topside.

ALYIAKAL'ALT,

Overcaptain

Luuval

XI

As Captain Haeryn predicted, the voyage from Guarstyad to Luuval is rough, until late midafternoon on twoday, when the *Zaenth* sails past the headland to the northeast of Luuval, where the waters become merely choppy.

Alyiakal stands to the rear and on the port side of the helm, while Haeryn directs the helmsman, and occasionally calls out orders to the small crew.

The captain points and addresses Alyiakal. "To the west and just a touch north, inshore of that low hill . . . there used to be a headland close to a hundred fifty yards high. It all just slid over the south end of the town. Flattened everything, especially the seasonal mansions of some wealthy Merchanter families . . ."

Alyiakal gets the feeling that Haeryn isn't terribly sympathetic to those Merchanter families.

". . . can see what's left of the town to the right, and that flat lumpy area in front of it . . . that's where the harbor was. Ahead, to starboard, about two kays," adds Haeryn, "there's a point, and a small wooden pier. We'll ease in. Right now, it looks like we might be able to tie up long enough that we won't have to use the cutter's boat."

Alyiakal would prefer that, since the boat is less than three yards long and he's not a great swimmer. *Your swimming is more like staying afloat . . . badly.*

Alyiakal doesn't breathe easily until the cutter is moored to the shaky-looking wooden pier; two rankers and three horses wait for him. He turns to Haeryn. "I appreciate the transportation, Captain. You saved me a long ride and a great deal of time."

"Our duty, Overcaptain." Haeryn glances at the rankers and back to Alyiakal. "We wish the best to you. If you don't mind, we'd like to get you ashore. Currents and wind here change quickly."

Alyiakal senses Haeryn's concerns without strain. "I'm on my way. Again, my thanks."

The gangway hasn't been used, and there's a gap of more than a cubit between the wharf and the cutter. One of the crew already has Alyiakal's duffels on the weathered planks of the small wharf before Alyiakal jumps from the cutter onto the wharf, which moves ominously under the impact. He grabs the duffels and strides off the wharf before turning back to see the *Zaenth* already opening the distance between the cutter and the shore.

"You the new undercaptain?" asks the older of the rankers standing on the dirt road a few yards from the foot of the pier.

Alyiakal offers a pleasant smile, his voice hard, as he projects a feeling of absolute authority. "Did you mean to ask, 'Are you the new overcaptain, ser'?"

Both rankers freeze where they stand.

"I'm Overcaptain Alyiakal, and Mirror Lancer headquarters sent me to take command. Who else would arrive on a naval cutter?" *Except possibly your payroll, but we're not getting into that right now.* His senses range over the two rankers—one older and overweight, who had sneered as Alyiakal approached, and one who looks too young to be even the freshest of recruits. Then he senses the horses, who don't seem to be in much better shape than the two rankers.

He looks to the older ranker. "Your name, lancer?"

"Ollscaat . . . ser."

"And you?" Alyiakal asks the younger.

"Kaytynn, ser."

"Excellent." Alyiakal's senses go to the mounts. While he doesn't sense any injuries, he does sense a lower level of order and chaos. "Ollscaat, how do these mounts compare to the rest of those at Luuval?"

"Ah . . . they're about the same, ser."

If that's the case, they haven't been exercised enough. Alyiakal takes the mount intended for him, a gray mare, strapping the duffels behind the saddle, and patting the mare's shoulder, reassuring her with a touch of order and comfort before mounting. "Lead the way, Kaytynn. Ollscaat can fill me in on a few matters."

"Yes, ser," replies the younger ranker.

"Ser . . . you're on temporary duty, aren't you?" asks Ollscaat cautiously.

"Why all the gear? I'm permanent until the post is closed. But I have orders to Lhaarat as deputy post commander afterwards. Now . . . Captain Aaltyn is still acting post commander?"

"Yes, ser."

"About how many mounts are left?"

"I wouldn't know exactly, ser. Maybe two score, and the draft horses."

"Are you from Luuval?"

"No, ser. Topcrass. It's a hamlet on the road to the Great Canal. Fifteen kays west, ser."

"What are your duties?"

"Whatever Squad Leader Dettlas orders, ser."

"What's your squad?"

"Third, ser."

"And all the squads are understrength?"

"Ah . . . yes, ser."

"Now . . . tell me what you know about what we're riding past. Start with the wharf."

"East of the old wharf, the water gets deep. North of it, it gets shallow real quick . . ."

As Ollscaat talks, Alyiakal studies the area. The narrow dirt road from the rickety wharf curves north, following the ocean for half a kay, then cuts across another point that barely rises above the ocean. Beyond the point, on the left side of the road, are boggy shallows, into which protrude neglected docks, while run-down and bedraggled cots line the right side of the road. These give way to modest wooden dwellings, run-down or abandoned. The ground around the dwellings appears to be a combination of rock and dirt with no sign of sand, nor much in the way of grass or bushes, only scattered low evergreens behind the houses.

Absently, with the back of his hand, Alyiakal blots away the sweat oozing from under his visor cap. While on the cutter, he'd forgotten that it's Summer.

"Where is the road from Guarstyad to the Great Canal?" asks Alyiakal when Ollscaat pauses.

"It's to the north of the post. Sort of follows the line of the harbor, but on higher ground. After a little less than a kay, it turns west."

"Does Luuval see many traders since the harbor filled up?"

"Don't see many outsiders at all, ser. When the headland collapsed, the better part of town went with it. Most of the folks who had golds, too."

"What buildings were south of the post? Are they still there?"

"There aren't any left beyond the cleared space."

"Did it happen at night?"

"No, ser. Just after dawn."

While that seems strange to Alyiakal, he hasn't sensed any unusual flows or concentrations of order or chaos. Less than a hundred yards ahead, the dirt road ends, and a yellow, brick-paved street begins, one flanked on the right by slightly more imposing dwellings that give way to two small brick buildings. A hundred yards beyond them are the faded, yellow-brick walls of the Mirror Lancer post.

When Alyiakal first catches sight of the post, all four brick walls appear to be intact. There's no indication of structures to the post's immediate south, just a flat area with occasional rushes and water weeds. The post gate divides the east wall, and a brick-paved causeway extends from the gate to a wooden pier slanting down into the muddy bog of the former harbor. The brick-paved way on which Alyiakal rides crosses the causeway and ends where the swampy area begins, slightly past a point parallel with the southern wall of the post.

When he nears the two neat brick buildings just back from the foot of the sunken pier, he notes both seem to have a slight imbalance in order and chaos, and he points. "The brick buildings there?"

"They're for the Imperial tariff enumerator. The front one is for their work, the rear for quarters."

Alyiakal quirks his lips into a wry smile. *Enumerators and chaos imbalances— that fits.* "The enumerators are still here?"

"There's one, I think. You'd have to ask Captain Aaltyn for sure."

As Kaytynn turns onto the causeway heading to the post gate, Alyiakal studies the post walls, noting how the south wall leans and sags in places.

Then he concentrates on the swamp, but he still senses no apparent concentrations of order or chaos. He has the feeling there's something odd. He just can't pinpoint what, and he turns his attention to the post as he nears the open, sagging gate where he sees no lancers on guard duty.

Kaytynn reins up outside the small brick building fifteen yards directly back from the open gate.

Alyiakal reins up beside him and asks, "Is this the headquarters building?"

"Yes, ser."

Alyiakal dismounts, and leads the gray mare to the short hitching rail, where he ties her securely. "You two can return to your squad leader."

"Yes, ser."

Alyiakal extracts his orders from one of the duffels and enters the building. Inside, at the back of the entry area sits a duty desk, empty. From the dust on the desk, no one has been posted there recently.

Is anyone in the post on duty?

He senses someone hurrying toward him, and the faint echo of boots on the stone floor of the hallway behind the vacant duty desk.

The captain appearing out of the dim corridor wears a worn but clean cream lancer jacket as wrinkled as Alyiakal's own travel-stressed uniform.

His face is angular, with dark circles under his deep-set eyes. Aaltyn has to be a good ten years older than Alyiakal, too young to have come up through the ranks and old enough that he should have made overcaptain by now.

"Overcaptain, ser . . . we didn't expect you so soon."

Then why were two rankers waiting for me? Alyiakal isn't about to get into that, one way or another. "I was granted expedited travel on a naval cutter from Guarstyad."

"Your last posting?" asks Aaltyn.

"No. My last posting was as officer in charge at Oldroad Post, on the Kyphran border. Guarstyad was the closest port." Even before Alyiakal finishes speaking, he can sense the captain's growing concern.

"That's quite a journey. I'm sure you'd like some time to recover."

"That won't be necessary. We can go through the post. After that, I can stable my mount and drop my gear in my quarters." Alyiakal would rather deal with the mount and gear first, but he has the feeling both will have to wait.

"Ah . . . I don't know that your quarters are ready, ser."

"I'm sure that you'll find a way to have them ready during the time I'm inspecting the post," Alyiakal says firmly but without raising his voice. "You can take me to the post commander's study, and we'll go from there."

Aaltyn simply nods, in quiet resignation.

"Lead the way," says Alyiakal. *Exactly what did you expect of a senior officer encountering this situation?* "By the way, why isn't there a lancer at the duty desk? It doesn't appear that anyone's been posted there in days."

"We're rather shorthanded, ser." Aaltyn heads back down the corridor.

Alyiakal follows, asking, "How many men did you lose when the headland collapsed?"

"Just four. The sub-majer died later."

"How did he die?"

"The duty squad leader found him dead in his bed. I reported it as from a flux. Several rankers had fluxes, possibly from the flies and snap-bugs that infest the bog."

"Reported?"

"He didn't look like he'd had the flux, but there were no marks on him, no insect bites, no signs of poison, and his door and shutters were bolted from inside. I had to report something."

"That's odd."

"I thought so, but what else could I report? There was no indication of anything else, and the sub-majer was rather . . . hefty."

Alyiakal has the feeling that, while Aaltyn is telling the truth, there's something he's not saying. He wonders how many more discrepancies, for lack of a better word, he'll discover over the next few days. "Then . . . was the post understrength before the collapse?"

"It has been for some time." The captain stops at the first door on the right. "Here, ser."

The study holds a desk with a chair behind it and two in front, a single, half-filled bookcase, and four wooden file chests set on a long narrow table against the wall to the left. Overall, the study appears comparatively neat.

"The file chests hold the lancer records by squad?"

"Yes, ser."

"Where are the post records?"

"In the fourth chest, the one on the right end."

"What about the post payroll? Where is that kept?"

"There's a strongroom in the rear of the armory."

Alyiakal nods. "Let's see the rest of the post, starting with the stables."

Aaltyn leads Alyiakal down the corridor, out the back entrance into the rear courtyard. "The barracks are to the left. The kitchen and mess hall are on the right end. The building ahead has the officers' quarters and mess, studies, and a meeting room. The stables are the two buildings against the north wall. The armory is at the west end of the stables."

Alyiakal surveys the western courtyard, where he sees a half squad of lancers returning to the stables through the area north of the headquarters building. He presumes they've concluded either exercises or a patrol. Then he turns to Aaltyn. "We'll start with the barracks."

"The upper level is closed, ser. It has been ever since reducing the complement to one company."

"Then we'll start with the lower level." Alyiakal finds himself checking his shields, realizing that too many words that Aaltyn says raise some flags.

For all his concerns, Alyiakal finds the condition of the barracks passable, although the cleaning has been hasty and haphazard. *But then, who really wants to spend too much time on a building that's going to be abandoned in a season?*

The same is true for the kitchen and mess hall, and Alyiakal barely glances at the building holding the officers' quarters, while Aaltyn instructs the orderly to make the changes to the commander's quarters. The stable is dusty, with more of a hint of manure than Alyiakal would like, as if it had been recently cleaned, but not exceptionally well.

As they near the locked door of the armory at the west end of the stable, Aaltyn produces a key, unlocks and opens the door, then gestures for Alyiakal to enter.

"After you, Captain," says Alyiakal dryly.

Inside the armory, Alyiakal senses that none of the firelances racked against the wall are fully charged. As he inspects them, a quick count comes up with fifty-three, half of which contain so little chaos as to be effectively useless. *Against whom would they use them?* "Why only fifty-three?"

"I couldn't tell you, ser. The firelances haven't been used much since I ended up in command. I was ordered not to use them except where absolutely necessary because of the difficulty in replenishing them."

"What are the necessary uses?"

"A few with each road patrol, and three with the occasional dispatch run to Fyrad. If we send less than three riders with firelances, there's a good chance they'll be attacked by swamp brigands from the south. That's why we limit dispatch runs."

Strangely enough, Aaltyn's words ring totally true. "Before that, what were they used for?"

"Patrols against smugglers, ser. They'd try to use the old east wharf at night or bring goods in on the far side of the headland . . . well, when there was a headland. There was a little cove beyond the south seawall, too shallow for fishing craft, but ships' boats could land, when the water was calm. All that's vanished."

"What about brigands around Luuval?"

"There weren't many before. Now . . . what would they steal? The better part of Luuval is gone. The only brigands to worry about come out of the delta swamps. They like to attack traders, especially those without guards. Once in a while, we kill or catch them, but they usually stay west of our road patrols. If we patrol five kays farther west, they move another five kays. We don't have enough lancers to patrol all the way to the Great Canal, and there aren't that many brigands."

"If you catch them, what then?"

"If the post commander or acting commander finds them guilty of brigandage, they're executed. Very few are captured. They know what will happen."

Alyiakal can see that anything less will just encourage more brigandage. He doesn't like the need for such stringent penalties, but he knows that barbarians and brigands only regard mercy and forbearance as weakness.

He turns his eyes to another wall rack, holding cupridium sabres, roughly a score, with a separate rack for scabbards. There is a single mirror shield hung on the wall, and Alyiakal wonders how long it has been there. "The strongroom?"

Aaltyn walks to what appears to be a closet door and unlocks it. Behind the first locked door is an iron-banded second door with an iron lock.

"That will do." *For the moment.* "I'd like to inspect the walls, especially on the south side of the post. We'll go around the headquarters building on the south side."

Alyiakal takes his time walking through the southern part of the court-yard. He can't sense any chaos or lack of order in the walls, but still has the feeling that the southern wall is leaning toward the encroaching bog.

From the east gate, the two officers walk outside along the walls facing the swampy area of the former harbor, walls that are perhaps two and a half yards tall. When they reach the corner, Alyiakal looks up, but there's no sentry post there. Then he realizes that Luuval is not and never has been a border town. Studying the south wall, he notes it leans slightly to the south. The ground looks solid for five to ten yards out, where the marshy area begins, although the boundary between solid ground and marsh is hardly regular.

The rushes and weeds are two yards into the marsh from the apparent shore . . . and it's late Summer. That alone tells Alyiakal that the boggy area has recently edged at least two yards toward the walls, possibly over the last few eightdays, given how fast weeds can grow—and that's worrisome.

He extends his senses to the boggy area south of where he stands and is struck by the much lower level of order. *Much lower, and the chaos is stronger and deeper.* He frowns for a moment and walks west along the wall, scanning for cracks in the bricks and the mortar while monitoring the levels of order and chaos in the ground. When he reaches the southwest corner, he stops and studies the terrain behind the post and farther to the southwest. For fifty yards west of the post's rear wall, the ground slopes gently upward, generally bare, except for patches of grass and stringy weeds. Beyond the empty ground stand more of the neglected-looking houses, only a few appearing inhabited.

Alyiakal clears his throat, then says, "Most of the houses look abandoned. What's left of the harbor is useless. The one usable wharf is in poor condition and located in a dangerous position. I haven't seen signs of fishing boats. I don't see any factorages or mills remaining. How long has Luuval been like this?"

"Since before I was posted here two years ago." Aaltyn adds, "There are still a few fishing boats."

Alyiakal won't ask why Aaltyn was posted to Luuval, not until he looks at the captain's records, but it appears that the captain did something, failed to do something, or angered someone higher up, if not all three . . . and that there's some reason why he couldn't be released from duties. *Or someone doesn't want him released from duties.* "Why has there been such a delay in closing the post?"

"I don't *know*, ser."

"But you have an idea."

"There's still an Imperial tariff enumerator here, ser. Along with his assistant and a few guards."

Alyiakal shakes his head, although he can sense that there's a great deal that Aaltyn hasn't said, but he isn't ready to press the captain yet. "Let's head back to the headquarters building. Have you drawn up the papers for the transfer of command?" Alyiakal turns and heads back toward the east gate.

"They're mostly compiled," replies Aaltyn. "Except I didn't know who was assigned, and I didn't see any point in a final version yet."

"We'll take care of that in the morning, after I've had a chance to go through all the files and records."

"Ser?"

"Once I take command, I'm responsible for everything. I'm not about to sign any acceptance of command without knowing what's here and what's not." Alyiakal smiles politely. "You won't be blamed for anything. Whatever's not here was obviously destroyed when the headland collapsed and in the confusion that followed. We are going to do a thorough inventory of everything and list its condition. That will allow us to determine what to transport to Fyrad and what to leave behind, and account for everything one way or the other."

Alyiakal senses some relief from Aaltyn, but a great deal of apprehension remains, and that suggests more problems. *You just hope you can find them all before it's too late.*

XII

In the two glasses after leaving Aaltyn, Alyiakal stables and grooms the mare, lugs his gear to Aaltyn's hurriedly vacated and cleaned quarters, unpacks his uniforms, and returns to the post commander's study.

Once there, he reads through the most recent reports to Mirror Lancer headquarters. If the reports are accurate, the Mirror Lancers' current duties involve road patrols and apprehending the very occasional smugglers attempting to land along the coast northeast of Luuval. There are only trails, if that, south or west of the town, and those end short of the extensive delta of the Great East River, the only area outside the Great Forest to harbor stun lizards, night leopards, and the chaos panthers, but not the tawny cougars.

Perhaps because the delta is too swampy?

He turns to the individual ranker files, looking through them, then counting them—forty-nine in three squads, little more than the full complement of two squads spread across three. *And patrolling with only a few firelances?* Alyiakal wonders about the patrols' effectiveness.

While he's nowhere close to going through everything, he turns to Captain Aaltyn's file to learn more about the captain before they have dinner. He begins to read, discovering that Aaltyn was commissioned at Kynstaar in Autumn of 88 A.F. after successfully completing a year of officer training. The only other information prior to Aaltyn's commissioning is that he was born in Cyad in 68 A.F. No family references. *He has to come from a privileged family or clan but can't be recognized by his parents.*

Aaltyn's first duty post was Syadtar, and after two years as an undercaptain in command of Syadtar's Second Company, he made captain. Two seasons later, he was "wounded and suffered severe injuries . . ."

Wounded and severe injuries? That's a wording Alyiakal hasn't ever seen.

. . . during recovery, temporary administrative duties at Syadtar for a year, then posted to Klehl as port company commander for three years, extended one year, and posted to Summerdock as senior port company commander for two years before being posted to Luuval . . .

But not promoted to overcaptain . . . and not given any combat postings after Syadtar.

A single bell chimes from the rear courtyard, and Alyiakal closes the file, stands, and stretches. Then he walks from the post commander's study to the next study, where Aaltyn is writing something.

Aaltyn looks up. "Ser?"

"We should get something to eat."

"Of course." Aaltyn sets aside his pen and stands, leaving the document on the desk as he joins Alyiakal.

Alyiakal extends his senses, trying to discern the injuries that the captain had incurred, but cannot sense anything definite, although he has the feeling Aaltyn's order levels are lower than they should be for a man of his age, especially since Aaltyn is trim, although the circles under his eyes are suggestive of fatigue, worry . . . or possibly some health condition that Alyiakal cannot discern.

"The officers here usually eat what the rankers eat," offers Aaltyn as the two leave the building and walk across the rear courtyard.

"It was that way at Oldroad Post," replies Alyiakal.

"How many officers?"

"Two, mostly, after the post was completed and the Mirror Engineers and Magi'i left, but sometimes three."

"Magi'i?"

"They were there to help rebuild the two sections of the old road, between the post and Guarstyad, that had been destroyed a century ago. They left quickly. The two engineers remained for a season."

Aaltyn nods, and opens the door to the building containing the officers' quarters and leads the way to the small mess, containing a short oblong table that might seat six, but has only two place settings.

As soon as the two seat themselves, the mess orderly appears, pours wine into their glasses, then leaves the carafe on the table, along with a small basket of warm bread. The orderly returns in moments with two platters, each containing pork cutlets with boiled sliced potatoes, both covered with the gravy, and some limp green beans—then departs.

Aaltyn raises his glass. "Since I'm technically still in command . . . to your safe arrival, ser."

Alyiakal lifts his glass in return. "With my appreciation, Captain." Then he cuts a morsel of pork and eats it. "It's quite tender."

"We have a great deal of pork here."

"Partly wild from damaged and abandoned holdings?"

"Exactly. Mostly from the hill holdings west of the area that collapsed."

"You don't have difficulty getting provisions?"

Aaltyn shakes his head. "The post has silvers. More than anyone else who's left."

"What do you think will happen once we close the post?"

"Luuval will turn into another impoverished hamlet at the mercy of smugglers."

Alyiakal nods, although he has his doubts, but because those doubts are based on quick impressions, he prefers to say nothing.

After several moments of silence while the two eat, Aaltyn says, "You're either older than you look, ser, or you've been promoted more quickly than usual."

He offers a pleasant smile. "A bit of each. I entered the full officer candidate training young. I did well and was posted to Pemedra. I had the fortune, or misfortune, to be involved in the action against the Jeranyi-supported barbarians in the West Branch valley of the Jeryna River. Later, I led a successful patrol force into the grasslands separating Cyador and Cerlyn. That led to my being posted to Guarstyad, which, in turn resulted in my being assigned to develop and hold Oldroad Post." Alyiakal smiles wryly. "Once I was assigned there, Mirror Lancer regulations required the promotion."

Aaltyn's eyes widen, just slightly. "You commanded the company that destroyed most of the Kyphrans, then, didn't you?"

"We didn't have much choice, not if we wanted to survive." At the same time, Alyiakal wonders how Aaltyn knows that, since he didn't know that Alyiakal was the new commander at Luuval.

"Why are you here? Do you know?"

"I don't *know*. I suspect because the overcaptain originally assigned to close the post refused the orders and took an early stipend . . . and I was due for orders in Harvest anyway. So they sent me here. After we close the post, I'll get home leave, before becoming deputy post commander at Lhaarat."

Aaltyn nods slowly. "Lhaarat's getting more and more dangerous. Sending someone like you makes sense."

Before Aaltyn can ask more, Alyiakal says, "Let's talk about you. You're from Cyad, aren't you?"

"I don't believe that's in my file, ser."

"It isn't, but you only spent a year at Kynstaar before commissioning. That doesn't happen unless you've had a great deal of education and background in Cyad." *And a well-connected family.* "You weren't even the slightest interested in hearing about the Magi'i who were at Oldroad Post. Then, too, you speak exceedingly well." Alyiakal senses a certain surprise from the captain but says nothing more and waits.

Abruptly, Aaltyn laughs softly. "You're right. I am from Cyad. From a checkered background, as you obviously deduced. I'd appreciate it if we left that background alone. I did well at Syadtar, until a certain subcommander ordered a single company to destroy a village along the West Branch, and not to come back until that was accomplished."

"And they had polished mirror shields from the Jeranyi, archers, and spear-throwers and three times your forces?"

"Something like that. We never had a chance to find out. I wasn't supposed to live. But there was an incredible Magi'i healer at Syadtar." Aaltyn pauses. "There's always a place for good administrative officers." His smile is both amused and brittle.

"That had to be before Subcommander Munnyr."

"It was."

Alyiakal doesn't press. Sooner or later, if necessary, he can find out. After a moment, he asks, "Do you want to remain in the Mirror Lancers?"

"I do. My other options . . . are even less desirable."

"Once we close the post, we'll be moving what we can to Fyrad."

"Closing the post might not be quite what you envision, ser."

"Oh?" Alyiakal has a very good idea why, but he wants to hear what Aaltyn has to say.

"The Imperial tariff enumerator may have other ideas."

"Against the commands of the Majer-Commander?"

"His assistant is a magus."

With that, Alyiakal recalls his sensing the order/chaos imbalance around the Imperial Tariff Enumerators' building. *Would the Merchanters really go that far? Especially after effectively abandoning the town. Or is headquarters using you to deal with something that, if it goes wrong, all the blame will fall on you? That way, whether you succeed or not, the Mirror Lancers can claim that they didn't have anything to do with it, and that you only had orders to close the post. Are the ties between Merchanters and the Imperial Tariff Enumerators that strong? Does a sabre cut? Does the Great Forest contain stun lizards?*

After the briefest hesitation, Alyiakal asks, "Has the enumerator or the assistant ever said anything about the post closing?"

"I've only talked to the enumerator a few times. The last time, when I informed him the post would have a new temporary commander to effect the post closure, he told me closing the post was unwise because, without a Mirror Lancer presence, Luuval would become a haven for smugglers and all sorts of ruffians."

"What did you say to that?"

"I told him that was unlikely—that no one here has the silvers to buy smuggled goods, and that offloading wagons to carry such goods elsewhere was dangerous. His assistant insisted smuggling was far too profitable to be deterred." Aaltyn clears his throat. "The assistant then said it was in my interest to persuade the new commander to keep the post open or everyone in the company would suffer."

"Did you pass that on?"

"That was on oneday. There's been no opportunity to do so. Both would deny their words, and I'd be disciplined for lying about what an esteemed tariff enumerator said."

Alyiakal senses Aaltyn believes every word he has uttered. He also has no doubt the enumerator made such a threat, and he has a good idea how the sub-majer died. "I can believe that . . . unfortunately. I'll have to have a talk with the enumerator before long." He pauses. "Are you sure that the assistant is a magus? Wearing white doesn't make a man a mage."

"He created a small fireball in midair when he spoke."

"Interesting. He might be a renegade magus." *But if he's not . . .*

"No offense, ser, but . . ."

"There's more chaos in a fully replenished firelance than most Magi'i can raise at one time. That's something I learned a long time ago. But it might be a good idea to bring one with me when I visit the enumerator." Alyiakal smiles.

"Are you certain, ser?"

"A mage once attacked me. My firelance held enough chaos to deal with him. You can't hesitate if one starts to throw chaos at you. Enough of that. I'll deal with the enumerator and his assistant in due time." Alyiakal pauses. "By the way, did the sub-majer meet with the enumerator the day before he died?"

"I wondered about that, but I was on a road patrol with first squad during the day. He didn't mention it at dinner, and none of the lancers knew anything about any meeting, but I suppose it could have happened. There's just no indication that he did."

Alyiakal manages not to take a deep breath. "We may have to look into that. For now, have you a current inventory of what's valuable that can be transported by the wagons we have?"

"There's an inventory, but it needs to be updated."

"Then you should start on that tomorrow. We'll need a listing of equipment and goods in order of value. Then we'll decide what goes and what remains."

"You'll just abandon the post?"

"I don't think the post will survive that long anyway. The swampy land is creeping northward. Isn't it closer to the southern walls than it was in the Spring?"

"A few yards, perhaps."

"Even if the post buildings do survive, we have orders to close the post," Alyiakal points out. "If we don't follow orders . . ." He leaves the words hanging.

"We don't have any future in the Mirror Lancers," Aaltyn finishes.

"So . . . I'll finish inspecting records and a few other things, and you can work on the inventory. After that, you can draw up the assumption-of-command papers, and I'll sign them."

Having finished dinner, Alyiakal returns to the study and works his way through the remaining records and papers. When he finishes, well into the evening, he's puzzled; all the records are satisfactory, even more than satisfactory. In fact, the files, records, and other paperwork are all in pristine condition. The stables and barracks are all functional, and that's more than Alyiakal expected.

What he hasn't expected is an Imperial tariff enumerator with a magus as an assistant trying to keep the post from closing. While Aaltyn has that impression, Alyiakal will have to meet with the enumerator to determine whether the captain is in error, and, if not, what to do without angering the Merchanters and the enumerators.

If that's even possible.

XIII

Alyiakal wakes in the gray light before dawn. After dressing, he makes his way from his quarters out the east gate, past a single gate guard who stares and manages, "Good morning, ser."

"Good morning to you." Alyiakal walks south along the east wall. He doesn't see or sense anyone along the brick-paved road that now borders a swampy morass. When he reaches the southeast corner of the post walls, he stops and extends his order/chaos senses toward the area that had once held various structures and houses. If the headland had been all that collapsed, there'd be a mass of rock and dirt covering that part of the town. Since there's a swampy bog, the ground under the town had to have given way, either first or immediately afterward, under the weight of the headland.

He studies the bog, realizing that there are no insects, no flies, no mites or midges. *Because of the lower amounts of order and chaos?*

He compares order and chaos levels. There's a minimal amount of order in the morass to the south, far less than beneath Alyiakal's boots. He takes several steps south and studies the ground again. The concentration of the order and chaos below is less. He takes another few steps and halts, feeling a softness beneath his boots in addition to an even lower concentration, especially of order.

Before that long, this will collapse as well. He steps back and makes his way back to the gate.

Halfway there, he stops. Standing in the light of the white sun just after dawn, Alyiakal creates the same invisible order funnel he'd used before the battle with the Kyphrans. Using it, he collects the tiny diffuse pieces of chaos streaming from the sun, knowing that he'll need to collect as much as he can over the next few eightdays so that he can surreptitiously begin replenishing the chaos in a few of the firelances in the armory.

He has no doubt they'll encounter brigands on the long ride from Luuval to Fyrad, or possibly stun lizards or great black panthers from the delta. He stands before the wall for perhaps half a quint before he collapses the funnel and links the small amount of chaos he's gathered to his outer shield, something he normally wouldn't do, but the only possible mage around is the assistant to the enumerator, and Alyiakal will be using the chaos before he meets with either the enumerator or his assistant.

He walks swiftly past the gate guard and to the officers' mess. He waits only a fraction of a quint before Aaltyn arrives.

"You were up early this morning, ser," says the captain.

"More things to look into," replies Alyiakal.

The mess orderly serves the two fried ham strips, an egg casserole, and a basket of warm bread, accompanied by ale.

Alyiakal takes a sip of the ale, better than at Pemedra, and similar to what he'd had at Guarstyad and Oldroad Post. After several bites of the casserole, heavier on cheese than he would have preferred, he says, "When we finish the inventory and take care of the assumption-of-command papers, I'll need keys to the armory and strongroom. Then you'll muster the lancers, and I'll inspect each one personally. That way, I'll get to know each face, and they'll see who I am. Following muster, I'll conduct a blade-skills evaluation of the company by squads—"

"Ser?"

"You're wondering what that has to do with closing a post? Where do you think most of these rankers will be posted next? I'd wager most of them need some retraining if they want to survive their next posting. We'll also be making a long journey to Fyrad along a road that's not the safest in Cyador." Alyiakal cuts the chewy ham strips into small pieces, then slowly eats them, interspersed with mouthfuls of bread. "After breakfast, we'll go through the old inventory and update it as we go. That will help determine what to take and what to leave. We have less than a season, and that includes transporting what we can to Fyrad."

Aaltyn nods.

Alyiakal can sense the captain is discomfited, if not stunned, by Alyiakal's plans. "I took another look at the morass to the south. It's definitely creeping toward the post walls. I worry because something has to be happening deeper underground. If the headland had just collapsed, there would be a large hill that covered the town, not a flat marsh. What's under the post can't be all that solid."

"The sub-majer mentioned that, ser."

"Right before his death?"

"A few days, as I recall."

"What did you do after that?"

"I passed on his concerns to Mirror Lancer headquarters, and was told that the matter would be handled by the new post commander."

"I didn't see that correspondence."

"I kept it out of the files, ser . . . just in case. I can show you after breakfast."

Why would headquarters ignore such a report? Alyiakal decides not to speculate until he reads the correspondence. "I'd definitely like to see it."

"Yes, ser."

Alyiakal concentrates on finishing his breakfast.

A quint later, he follows Aaltyn to the captain's study, where Aaltyn opens a strongbox and retrieves several sheets, which he hands to Alyiakal.

The copy of the first letter, since the original went to headquarters, mirrors closely what Aaltyn told Alyiakal. The reply is more interesting. The first paragraph essentially restates what Aaltyn reported. Alyiakal has to reread the second paragraph just to make sure that he has read it correctly.

> . . . *while the Majer-Commander appreciates the concerns expressed in your report, Mirror Lancer regulations require that any post closure, or any steps taken to effect such a closure, can only be authorized and effected under the direct orders of a senior field-grade officer or a command-grade officer authorized to command and close such a post. In response to your concerns, the Majer-Commander will be appointing and dispatching such a qualified officer as soon as practicable . . .*

Then Alyiakal checks the dates. Aaltyn's report and request to proceed with closure operations is dated sevenday of the sixth eightday of Winter, and the response, signed by the Captain-Commander of the Mirror Lancers, is dated threeday of the second eightday of Spring.

Half a season to reply, and more than a season after that before you got orders to Luuval.

Alyiakal wills himself to composure, and asks, "The dates on these and the contents are accurate?"

"To my knowledge, yes, ser."

The captain's response is truthful. "I can see why you wanted these locked away." Alyiakal hands the papers back to Aaltyn. "Keep them safe." Alyiakal doesn't need the papers, but Aaltyn well might, especially if matters do not work out well. *And if we don't close this post quickly, matters aren't going to go well.* Unfortunately, if he doesn't close the post according to regulations, they also won't go well.

Aaltyn looks surprised as Alyiakal returns the correspondence, but merely says, "Yes, ser."

"Now . . . if you'll get that inventory . . ."

"Of course."

Going through the inventory takes three glasses, and there are a number of items that Alyiakal doesn't look at closely, simply because they aren't about to be moved—such as the large ceramic stoves in the mess kitchen. Each one would fill a wagon, and there aren't that many wagons. But in the process of inspecting the firelances, he does use the chaos he gathered earlier to increase the amount held by one of the weapons.

Another glass passes before they finish with the assumption-of-command paperwork, again necessary, because without it Alyiakal doesn't have the authority to close the post, and it's clear from the response Aaltyn received, the Captain-Commander—or one of the commanders advising him—is a stickler for following procedures. In the end, it's a glass past midday when the company musters in the post's rear courtyard.

Going through the ranks, inspecting and talking to each ranker, if only briefly, takes another glass. Alyiakal's overall impression is a certain slackness and lack of precision, but his next task will give him a better idea.

It takes a quint for Maert, the first squad leader, to come up with practice sabre wands, a delay that doesn't set well with Alyiakal. He doesn't show it, but merely smiles pleasantly as he turns to the squad leader once he returns with the wands.

"Who's the best in the squad with blades?"

For a moment, Maert is silent, then says, "Naelkyn or possibly Zaalt."

"Excellent. Both of you step forward." Alyiakal studies the two, then looks at the taller and more muscular lancer and says, "Naelkyn, take one of the wands. We'll see how much you recall."

"I'm sparring against you, ser?"

"When else will you have a legitimate way to try to strike an officer? Don't worry. That's why we're using wands." Alyiakal senses the wands still held by the squad leader, picks one, then steps back and lets the ranker pick from the remaining three.

Once Naelkyn chooses a wand, Alyiakal moves slightly, to an open space where all the rankers can see, then lifts his wand. "You choose when we start."

After several moments, Naelkyn lunges, but even as he moves forward, Alyiakal moves forward to his right, past the tip of Naelkyn's wand, bringing his own wand down on Naelkyn's just below where the ranker grips it. Alyiakal drops back, saying, "In a real fight, my blade would have come up and across your throat."

Naelkyn pivots and goes for Alyiakal's forward leg, but Alyiakal has already anticipated that and slams his wand into Naelkyn's arm just above the elbow. Naelkyn drops the wand.

"Anyone else care to try?" asks Alyiakal as the ranker massages his temporarily numb arm.

No one volunteers.

"I suspect that all of you need some work on your blade skills. Over the next few eightdays, we're going to remedy that. You won't like it now, but you'll be glad later."

The expressions on the faces of the rankers range from puzzled to skeptical.

"There shouldn't be any secret why I'm here. This post is being closed. Where do you think most of you will be posted next? Some border post. It won't be Guarstyad or Oldroad Post. They are reducing the number of companies now that the Kyphrans have decided not to lose any more troopers there. Instead, you'll be going to places like Lhaarat, Pemedra, Inividra, or Isahl . . . and you'll be fighting barbarians or brigands, if not both. Real fighting, sometimes in rain, occasionally in snow. What many of you may have forgotten is that firelances don't work well in rain . . . or if a long patrol has left little chaos in your firelance. That's why, starting tomorrow, all of you will be working on blade and riding skills . . ."

After he finishes with first squad, Alyiakal repeats the performance with second squad . . . and later with third squad.

By the time he finishes, he's sweating heavily, not because of the heat, but because the air is damp and still.

After he dismisses the third squad rankers to their usual duties, Alyiakal makes his way to the armory, where he takes a firelance with a third of its full chaos and brings it with him to the stable, where he saddles the gray mare. He leads her out and ties her behind the headquarters building to wait while he finds Aaltyn, working on drafting an updated equipment and supply inventory.

The captain looks up as Alyiakal appears in the doorway to his study. "Ser?"

"Aaltyn, I'm going to ride around what's left of the town to get a better feel for things. After that, I may stop by the enumerator's building."

"You don't want an escort?"

"Have there been any brigands in town lately?"

"Ah . . . no, ser."

"Good. Then I'll see you in while." Alyiakal makes his way back to the mare. He mounts, then creates the unseen order funnel, making it as wide as possible. The ride will serve several purposes, giving him a better sense of how and where the bog is expanding and how many houses are occupied, as well as allowing him to replenish the chaos in the firelance.

After riding out the east gate, Alyiakal expands his sensing to discern possible concentrations of order or chaos. He finds none, but gets the same impression from the harbor morass as he had from the area south of the post.

He rides down the stone causeway to the foot of the pier that slants into the swampy mess, then turns the mare north-northeast along the narrow road bordering the edge of the harbor. Alyiakal passes the brick buildings for the Imperial enumerator, his putative assistant, and staff or guards assigned there. The harbor edge road ends less than a kay farther at the short dirt road leading to the rickety wharf. He reins in the mare and studies the area for a while before heading back, but this time he takes a side road that heads gently uphill and due west. Less than half a kay later, it joins what has to be the road to Fyrad. While there are scrub trees on the left side of the road, Alyiakal can make out the post below. On the right side, smallholdings hug the ground that slopes upward into scattered woods and pastures. Most of the holdings appear to be inhabited.

Alyiakal rides another kay, but encounters no one and sees little difference along the road—except for the semicircular depression that once marked the major part of the town, now filled with muddy water and floating swamp weeds. Something about the muddy water bothers him, but he can't quite pinpoint it. After riding a bit farther, he turns the mare back.

Abruptly, he realizes what he missed. The headland collapsed three years earlier. Mud settles out of still water fairly soon, and seawater doesn't have mud. *So a goodly amount of water and mud are coming from somewhere else, and that's why the morass is creeping toward the post.*

He shakes his head, knowing he should have caught that earlier. *Except you haven't been here even a day and you've had a few other matters on your mind.*

As he turns the mare off the road to Fyrad and heads down toward the post, he debates stopping at the enumerator's main building, then decides postponing the visit will only make matters worse. When he reaches the yellow brick building, he compresses all the free chaos he has collected on his ride and pushes it into the reservoir of the firelance, making sure no free chaos lingers about him. Then he dismounts and ties the mare to the hitching post, leaving the firelance in its holder, but putting a small order block inside it before he walks toward the door, beside which stands a guard in pale blue, with a sheathed sabre on one side of his belt and a truncheon on the other. A puzzled expression crosses his weathered face, then vanishes.

After making sure that his outer shield reveals a modest surplus of order, consistent with a field healer, Alyiakal stops short of the guard and says, "Overcaptain Alyiakal to see the tariff enumerator."

"Just a moment, ser." The guard opens the door and announces, "Overcaptain to see the enumerator." Then he steps back.

"Thank you," says Alyiakal, before opening the door wider and stepping inside.

The small entry chamber holds a table desk with a chair behind it, and a side table against the wall on which rests a single file chest. Alyiakal also senses a residue of free chaos.

Behind the desk sits a gray-haired man in gray who looks up as Alyiakal enters. Since the man is in gray and manifests no excess of chaos, he's a clerk of some sort.

"Ser?"

"I'm here to see the enumerator."

"Just a moment, ser." The clerk rises from the desk and moves to the door behind and to one side of the table desk, which he opens and steps through, closing it behind himself.

Alyiakal waits several moments before the door again opens, and a smooth-faced man attired in the white garb of a magus appears.

His eyes widen slightly as he takes in Alyiakal, and he inclines his head in a fashion just slightly more than perfunctory. "Overcaptain, are you perhaps the new Mirror Lancer post commander?"

"I am. Alyiakal'alt, temporary post commander."

"Khyental'elth, assistant to Enumerator Chysrah. How might I help you?"

"A Magi'i assistant to an enumerator. That's a bit unusual, isn't it?"

"Luuval is a rather isolated port."

That doesn't answer Alyiakal's question. A tariff enumerator with a lancer post some hundred yards away wouldn't seem to need the protection of a mage, especially with a guard outside the building. "No more isolated than many."

"How might I help you, Overcaptain?"

"I came to pay my respects to the enumerator. If you would inform him?"

Khyental frowns slightly. "You have the air of a healer. That, too, is most unusual."

"You're very perceptive. I received training in field healing in addition to the other skills required of a combat officer. The Mirror Lancers don't like to waste talents." *Of junior officers, at least.*

"That is most unusual."

"No more than a mage assistant to an enumerator." Alyiakal offers a coolly pleasant smile. "And now, if you'd inform Enumerator Chysrah that I'm here to pay my respects."

"Of course, Overcaptain."

Khyental turns and leaves the entry area, closing the door.

Within moments, he returns. "At the moment, the enumerator is not available. Perhaps you could come another time."

Alyiakal can sense the duplicity, but merely says, "I'm very sorry to hear that." His smile is icy. "You both know where to find me. He'll be welcome any time he chooses to visit." He does not nod even to acknowledge what the other has said, but turns and leaves the tariff building, closing the front door quietly.

He nods to the guard and says, "Thank you," once more.

As he unties the mare and mounts, he reflects on the brief meeting. Since he had been able to sense the order/chaos pattern of two others in the second room and since Khyental had been lying about the enumerator not being available, Chysrah either does not wish to meet with Alyiakal or he's attempting to assert his superiority. Alyiakal would wager on the second possibility.

Either way, Alyiakal has offered a courtesy since there's no requirement for him to meet with the enumerator. He will make an entry in the post log that, even though present in the tariff building, Enumerator Chysrah declined to meet with the incoming post commander.

Once he returns to the post and stables and grooms the gray, he returns the partly replenished firelance to the armory and then makes his way to Aaltyn's study.

"I see you're back, ser."

"I am. I have a better sense of what's left of the town, and that will help. I stopped to pay my respects to the enumerator, but he declined to see me."

Aaltyn nods. "The sub-majer tried several times before he met with the enumerator."

"I'm not that patient with arrogance. I told his assistant that the enumerator would be welcome here whenever he chooses to visit."

"Ah . . ."

"You're wondering if that's wise? I have no idea. I do know it's unwise for a post commander to be at the beck and call of a tariff enumerator. That sets a bad example." Alyiakal pauses, then asks, "Have you finished with the updated inventory?"

"I should be finished within a glass, ser."

"Excellent. Have someone else copy it. Over the next few days, we'll go over the copy and begin to determine what are the most valuable and useful items to take to Fyrad."

"What about the other items? And the fort itself?"

"Unless I'm greatly mistaken, before long the fort will sink into the expanding morass. Our job is to close the post and transport to Fyrad those items most useful or most valuable to the Mirror Lancers." Alyiakal knows full well that most of the lancers will try to find items that they can sell in Fyrad. One of his and Aaltyn's tasks is to make sure none of them pocket items that can be used or sold more effectively by the Mirror Lancers and that they don't weigh themselves down or sneak items into the wagons to the extent that they overload them.

XIV

Alyiakal makes sure the next four days follow the pattern he has laid out on threeday. By eightday, he can see definite improvement in formation riding and blade skills. Over those days, he has added chaos to another ten firelances, bringing them up to half full. More than that would be suspicious, because everyone knows the chaos levels are low, but not how low.

Under Alyiakal's supervision, Aaltyn has completed a priority listing of the equipment, tools, and devices from the post that can theoretically be carried by wagon. The post only has four wagons, and it will take almost an eightday for a fully loaded wagon to reach Fyrad and, with a day for rest and repairs, another eightday for the return. The wagons can only make four round trips before the closure date specified by Mirror Lancer headquarters. That limits what can be transported to sixteen wagonloads, assuming none of the wagons break down, that the Mirror Lancer post at Fyrad cannot provide any additional wagons, and that the road remains passable for all of Harvest.

In addition, the crumbling and disintegrating ground has moved a yard closer to the south wall, and Alyiakal has the feeling that the wall will collapse well before he can close the post. Unsurprisingly, Enumerator Chysrah has yet to make a visit.

When Alyiakal wakes on eightday morning, he feels tired, possibly because he has been dreaming about loading wagons, but he forces himself awake. Even before breakfast, he inspects the ground next to the southern wall. While the visible crumbling doesn't seem to have advanced much, he can sense that the concentration of order beneath the soil continues to decrease.

He makes his way to the mess, then sits down at the table, where Aaltyn joins him.

"How are your riding skills these days?" asks Alyiakal.

"I've taken some of the road patrols," replies Aaltyn, his tone wary. "Why?"

"Because you're going to be in charge of all but the last set of wagons ferrying equipment to Fyrad." Alyiakal explains the logistics, then takes a small swallow of ale, and a mouthful of the cheesed eggs containing small chunks of leftover ham.

"That could be difficult with so few effective firelances, ser."

"I've been checking them. There are enough that appear half full to supply a squad, and you can take extras that have no chaos left. You should be able to get replacements for all the firelances you take at Fyrad. That's where they replenish them. Then, if you don't encounter too many brigands on the way back, the next squad can take some more of the firelances that are exhausted."

"You don't have any orders about conserving the firelances, ser?" Aaltyn sips some ale, then looks dubiously at the eggs on his platter.

"Not yet. If you run into difficulty in Fyrad, just tell them that you're carrying out orders. If some higher officer complains, tell them your overcaptain insisted because he didn't want to incur casualties and have equipment damaged or lost because someone was concerned about saving chaos in firelances." Alyiakal offers an amused smile. "I doubt anyone will ask you. They might ask me when I arrive with the last wagonloads of equipment and supplies, although I think it unlikely."

"You still haven't heard anything from the enumerator or his assistant?"

"They may be waiting for me to prostrate myself before them." *Which isn't going to happen.*

"Seems strange to me that the Senior Tariff Enumerators want to keep an enumerator here when there's no usable harbor."

"It's only a guess on my part," replies Alyiakal, "but the Merchanter clans may worry that if there's no tariff enumerator here outland traders will bring in goods to avoid paying tariffs." He takes another mouthful of the eggs, followed by some bread.

"It's a long journey to anyplace else they could sell those goods . . . and time can cost more than the silvers saved."

"Not always. Some of the tariffs are hefty. I had to act as an enumerator, and some traders ended up paying twenty golds or more in tariffs. Several as much as admitted they were coming through Oldroad Post because it cost less."

"Because you were going by the posted Imperial rates?"

"That was my guess, but I don't have any hard proof." Alyiakal pauses, then asks, "Do you know when Chysrah got his assistant?"

"Not exactly. Probably less than a year before I was posted here."

"After the headland collapsed, then, and after headquarters began considering closing the post."

"You think they arranged for a Magi'i assistant to protect the enumerator?" asks Aaltyn.

"I don't see how it could be otherwise." *The real questions are why any magus would agree to accept such a post and whether, besides protecting Chysrah, he's here to keep Chysrah moderately honest, or to keep the levied tariffs high.* Alyiakal almost shakes his head. All the Merchanters care about is keeping the price of goods imported by outlanders high.

Aaltyn nods.

"How are you coming on the list of what we'll send to Fyrad next sixday?"

"I'll have it to you by the end of the day." Aaltyn sighs softly and begins to eat the eggs, each mouthful of egg followed by one of freshly baked bread.

"Good. We can go over it then and have first squad start loading out on threeday."

"That early?"

"I haven't done this before, and neither have you. In fact, I don't know of another post closure. The weights and balances have to be right, and we have to balance lighter and heaver goods and equipment, and space out the heavier equipment. If it takes longer, we might only be able to send the wagons three times, and that won't be good for either of us." *And there will be problems we can't foresee. There always are.*

After a moment, Alyiakal adds, "I've decided to accompany second squad on today's road patrol. We'll be going a fair distance toward Fyrad. According to all three squad leaders, the stretch of road west from Luuval for the next thirty kays is the roughest and the worst. I want to see exactly what the road is like, and how it might affect the wagon loading. I'll be taking a firelance as well." He offers a wintry smile. "Just in case."

Less than two quints later Alyiakal has saddled the gray mare, obtained three firelances from the armory, and reined up beside second squad leader Khenn.

"Ser . . . any special orders?" asks the squad leader, looking questioningly at the firelance Alyiakal extends.

"Take the firelance."

Khenn does and places the weapon in his empty holder.

Alyiakal extends the second firelance. "Give this one to whatever ranker is a good marksman, *and* coolheaded, and have him ride rearguard. We're going to head farther west on this patrol. I need to see the road conditions."

"It's passable, ser. Not much more." Khenn frowns. "We usually ride east first, then come back to Luuval and head west. Sometimes, west first and then east."

"Since we have to send wagons filled with equipment west, we'll just head west today."

"Yes, ser. The firelances have chaos?"

"These do. They're not full, but there should be enough to deal with the usual brigands—if we encounter any." What Alyiakal isn't saying is that none of the three is more than a third full, but that he intends to change that during the patrol, because, even as he waits for the squad to form up, Alyiakal uses his unseen funnel to gather the tiny chaos bits that stream from the white sun.

One scout precedes the squad while Alyiakal and Khenn lead the squad proper. After heading northeast past the enumerator's buildings, the squad turns northwest on the side road.

Half a kay later, the squad rides west on the road that eventually leads to the Great Canal and Fyrad. Although Alyiakal doesn't expect great cats or brigands, he still extends his senses and studies the terrain, knowing he can't afford to let those skills get rusty, not when he'll be headed to Lhaarat.

After a time, Alyiakal clears his throat and asks the squad leader, "Besides occasional brigands, have you encountered any stun lizards, night leopards, or great panthers?"

"Only a few brigands, ser, but we usually don't go as far as where swamp brigands have attacked traders. I've never seen a stun lizard. Panthers and night leopards, once in a while. They avoid the squads. A few times every year, we see signs that they've killed someone, close to the delta swamps. Once we found a grower's cart and what was left of his horse, pretty much just bones, hoofs, and hide. No one in town knew who it was, but the cart was gone in a few days."

"Is there anything else that could cause problems for loaded wagons?"

"Some dips in the road that fill up with water if it rains a lot. Doesn't rain that much in Summer. Not like late Harvest and especially Autumn, when there's more rain."

Another reason to start shipping gear and equipment to Fyrad as soon as possible. "How long have you been posted here, Khenn?"

"Four years at the end of Harvest."

"And before that?"

"Klehl."

Alyiakal struggles to recall its location, then nods. "Another small port few have heard of. Smuggler patrols or something else?"

The squad leader shakes his head. "A little bit of everything. There are hidden reefs and strong currents just offshore. More wrecks there than almost anywhere . . . and sea-reivers. Merchanters hate them, especially since the clans have a salvage post there. Between the reivers, the smugglers, and the hill brigands, it could be busy at times. Still as death at other times, like here right now."

"Don't all Mirror Lancer posts have down times when nothing happens . . . until everything happens all at once?"

A faint smile crosses the squad leader's face.

"Are there other roads off this one? That go to more than hamlets?"

"Only one. Five kays west, there's a winding back road that ends up in Geliendra. I wouldn't want to take it, but the sub-majer told me smugglers used it years back. That's one reason why they built the post in Luuval."

"The other reason?"

"All the Merchanter families who had holiday houses here felt better with a Mirror Lancer post. That was what the sub-majer said." After a brief hesitation, Khenn adds, "The men liked it better then, too."

"I can see that," replies Alyiakal. "Are there many rankers in second squad from Luuval or nearby?"

"Yharan and Dellor from second squad, Kaytynn from third squad, and Ollscaat's from some nearby hamlet. I don't know of any others."

Alyiakal nods, turning his full attention to the road, which has traces of gravel packed into the dirt and clay, suggesting that it might once have been metaled and more heavily traveled. Scattered smallholdings separate the stretches of scruffy and barely tended woods.

Were the holdings always like this . . . or did everything get run-down after the town's destruction and the golds of the Merchanter families vanished?

Alyiakal pushes the thought away and concentrates on the road ahead.

Within kays, the few holdings to the left of the road give away to bushes and trees, with some intervals of high grass. Grasslands stretch away to the right, and farther north, Alyiakal sees a flock of sheep.

In time, they come to the road to Geliendra. Despite what Khenn has said, the north road looks in good repair, with signs of recent use in the dirt.

Over the next glass, the grasslands to the north sport more bushes, as if not as many sheep or cattle graze there, while the trees on the left grow taller, although not nearly as tall as the trees of the Great Forest. Alyiakal notices the road has become more uneven, although the dips in the surface aren't deep.

But heavy rain could create mud that's difficult for wagons, especially if they're heavily loaded. Maybe they should carry some planks in case of rain.

Given the warm day and the damp air, Alyiakal almost wishes for rain, except that, as soon as the rain ended, the air would be damper but not any cooler. *You never thought you'd prefer the heat and dryness of Oldroad Post.* He shakes his head.

Close to another glass passes before Khenn says, "This is about as far as we usually go. It's about fifteen kays from the post."

"We'll go a bit farther. I'd like to see what lies ahead."

"Yes, ser."

After another two quints or so, Alyiakal gets a vague sense of chaos/order patterns to the west. Then, after another quint, he senses the chaos patterns of a horse-drawn wagon ahead, surrounded by several riders. The lack of movement suggests brigands. If not, a quiet approach and a charge will provide some practice for the squad.

"Squad Leader, call in the scout, or get him to halt quietly."

"Ser?" asks Khenn.

"I have the feeling something's amiss, but we'll see in a bit." Alyiakal eases the firelance from its holder.

Khenn whistles, then gestures, and the scout halts.

"Silent riding. The scout and I will lead. Stay ten yards back and keep the squad to the right."

"To stay out of sight as long as possible?"

"Until we know."

The squad moves to the right and approaches the beginning of the curve in the road.

Alyiakal senses five or six horses around the wagon, but only two carry mounts, suggesting that some brigands are looting the wagon. He wants to get within a half kay before the brigands notice him, but the riders and the wagon are at least three hundred yards from the end of the curve and will be able to see him before he can use a firelance.

But if you and the scout keep riding quietly and they only see two riders at first, that might give you enough time.

When Alyiakal and the scout near the end of the curve, he says, "We'll keep riding silently at the same pace until they notice us. Then we'll charge."

"Yes, ser."

Once Alyiakal and the scout come out on the straight section of the road, he sees the wagon tilts slightly and the wheels on the right side have gone off the shoulder into the drainage ditch.

Chased or scared off the road?

Then Alyiakal senses a black mist of death, likely from the teamster. He forces himself to keep riding quietly. He and the scout cover a hundred yards more before one of the still-mounted brigands looks up, freezing for a moment as he sees the two riders, and then those behind Alyiakal.

The brigand yells something and turns his mount to flee.

Alyiakal extends the range of the firelance and drops the two already-mounted brigands before they move more than a few yards. Another brigand mounts and turns his horse. Alyiakal's third bolt takes him down, as well as his mount. Alyiakal winces at the death mist of the horse but continues riding.

One of the remaining brigands ducks behind a horse tied to the tilted wagon, then sprints toward the south side of the road. Alyiakal looses another firelance bolt that he guides to the fleeing brigand, who vanishes in a gout of flame.

The last brigand struggles to untie his mount, then climbs into the saddle. Alyiakal takes his time and guides the last firebolt into the brigand's back, careful to avoid hurting the horse. Then he urges the mare into a fast trot toward the wagon. At the same time, he scans the trees on the south side of the road for brigands, but he doesn't find any.

When he reins up short of the wagon, he sees one man slumped over the teamster's bench seat, with at least two arrows in his body, and a second figure sprawled on the road, with an arrow through his chest and a slash across his neck.

Alyiakal looks in the open wagon and finds little there—a half score of kegs, most likely of spices, and four large slabs of what looks to be stone. *Stone?* After a moment, he recognizes the slabs as salt from the mines in the foothills east of Geliendra. Then he studies the wagon, which shows little sign of wear, and seems nearly new.

He shakes his head. *Salt and spice traders, with the only real value in the spices and salt . . . and the wagon.*

While the salt slabs would bring a few golds in Fyrad, as would the spices, they're of limited value to brigands—anyone would know they were stolen— and it would be difficult to sell them in any market square without raising questions.

At that moment, Khenn rides up and reins in his mount beside Alyiakal. He looks at his overcaptain.

Alyiakal slips the firelance back into its holder. "That took pretty much all the chaos. They were spice and salt traders. I doubt we'll find many silvers in any of the brigands' purses. The salt's worth a lot, and so are the spices. We'll have to take the wagon, the mule, and the dead men back to Luuval. Round up the brigands' horses, those you can find easily. If there are any coins among the brigands, they're spoils. Anything held by the traders isn't."

"Yes, ser," replies Khenn.

As Alyiakal recalls, if recovered property isn't claimed within a season, the nearest enumerator must put it up for sale at a reasonable price. The sale proceeds, as well as any coppers, silvers, or golds, go to Mirror Lancer headquarters.

But you can't get a reasonable price in Luuval. That means you'll have to send them to Fyrad, with a letter of explanation.

A quint later, with the wagon back on the road, the squad rides back toward Luuval.

Khenn eases his mount closer to Alyiakal. "I've never seen anyone that accurate with a firelance, especially at that distance."

"I've had a lot of practice . . . and those five blasts took most of what I had." The first sentence is true; the second is not.

"Yes, ser."

Alyiakal can sense that Khenn isn't satisfied but won't press. He has no doubts that what the squad leader saw will pass to the entire company. That should prove useful, but what should happen doesn't always, Alyiakal knows.

XV

Early on sixday, Alyiakal and Aaltyn sit across the mess table from each other, finishing a quick breakfast.

"I've said this before," says Alyiakal, "but make sure you get a written acknowledgment from either Subcommander Quellyt or the supply officer that the post has received the contents of the wagons, as well as the recovered wagon. If he proves difficult or unwilling to provide such an acknowledgment, you know what to do."

"Send a copy of the inventory and the recovered-property report to Mirror Lancer headquarters with an explanation of why the Captain-Commander is receiving it," says Aaltyn dryly.

"I doubt that will be required. It doesn't matter to him what we send, as long as we send what's in the manifest." Alyiakal pauses. "Of course, if you weren't prepared to send a manifest to headquarters, then you'd have to."

"You've dealt with headquarters before, ser?"

"Only by observation at distance, but it was . . . instructive."

"Then you see more than most officers."

"It helps that my father was a majer without illusions." Alyiakal stands. "We need to get you and the wagons off."

Aaltyn gets to his feet quickly. "Yes, ser."

The two walk out to the rear courtyard, where first squad and the teamsters of the four wagons prepare to depart. The seventeen rankers all carry fire-lances, but none of the firelances hold more than half the chaos they should. That's the best Alyiakal could do surreptitiously over the past five days.

But that should suffice against brigands and any stray beasts. With that thought, Alyiakal says to Aaltyn, "Don't push it. Those wagons have to make three more trips after you bring them back." He pauses, then adds, "Make sure the supply officer issues you decent rations and fodder for the return trip."

"If he doesn't, I'll tell him you'll be coming later." Aaltyn grins.

"Given some supply officers, that won't go far." Alyiakal steps back and lets Aaltyn take charge. He still wonders about the captain's order and chaos levels, which remain slightly lower than those of most officers Aaltyn's age, but those levels haven't changed since Alyiakal arrived.

Once the wagons have rumbled away, Alyiakal walks from the gate to the outside of the southern wall, where he checks the slow but inexorable expansion of the bog, whose leading edge is a yard closer to the brick wall than when he arrived. Despite the heat, the water foliage remains sparse and the insects few, which bothers him, little as he cares for flies and midges.

He walks back into the post, and through the front door to the head-quarters building, nodding to the duty ranker. Once in his study, Alyiakal has time to review the completed inventory and wagon-loading plans now that the first loads have left. There's no point in writing Saelora, because Aaltyn and first squad carry letters from the post for dispatch in Fyrad, including a letter to Saelora, as well as Alyiakal's report to headquarters on the closing progress, including the brigands' attack on the salt and spice trader.

Alyiakal takes out his much-amended atlas of Candar to see how detailed the map of the Lhaarat area is, particularly the border between Cyador and Kyphros. As he suspected, there's little detail, because the most accurate maps in the atlas deal with the coastal areas. His own personally made maps of the grass hills around Pemedra and of Guarstyad and southwestern Kyphros are much more detailed. Then there is the detailed map of Biehl that Alyiakal copied from the one made by Saelora's father.

He turns the pages of the atlas to the map including Luuval. The detailed coastline largely matches what Alyiakal has observed, with the exception of the missing part of the town. The map shows the road from Luuval to Ge-liendra, suggesting it was known and used at the time.

Alyiakal takes out the pen he uses for making additions to the atlas and painstakingly begins to add details to the coastal section of the Luuval map.

A glass passes before the duty ranker knocks on the side of Alyiakal's half-open study door. Alyiakal looks up. "Yes?"

"Overcaptain, the Imperial tariff enumerator and his assistant are here to see you."

"Escort them in, if you would, Daarenz," says Alyiakal cheerfully, checking his outer shield to make sure he shows no mage-like traces.

The smooth-faced, black-haired Khyental is the first into the study, followed by a slighter man only a few years older than Alyiakal, wearing green-trimmed Merchanter blues. Chysrah's short curly hair is brown, and his eyes are a watery gray. His mouth and eyes present a cheerful smile, but Alyiakal has no difficulty sensing the chill beneath the superficial warmth.

While Alyiakal momentarily considers remaining seated, he stands, offering a warm smile. "Welcome to the post, Enumerator Chysrah, Magus Khyental." He gestures to the chairs. "I'm sorry you were indisposed when I came to pay my respects."

"These things happen," replies Chysrah, taking the chair directly across the table desk from Alyiakal.

As Khyental seats himself, Alyiakal does the same and observes that the magus has a single moderately strong shield and shifts his chair quietly so that he can more easily see both men without obviously changing his focus.

When Chysrah shows no sign of speaking, Alyiakal asks, "Have you been the enumerator here long?"

"Senior Enumerator Lyang unfortunately perished when the headland engulfed most of Luuval. He was visiting friends at their dwelling. I was sent as his replacement."

Since the tariff building has a separate structure for quarters and since the headland collapsed sometime after midnight, Alyiakal suspects the late Senior Enumerator was more than merely visiting, but he only remarks, "The disaster was most unexpected, but then most are." He pauses. "It was only at my last posting that I ever met an Imperial tariff enumerator—Donaajr'mer. I believe he was sent from Cyad. Did you know him?"

"I do not remember an enumerator of that name, but most enumerators come from Cyad," replies Chysrah. "Occasionally from Fyrad, and even fewer from Summerdock."

"Then you're from Cyad."

"How could it be otherwise?" Chysrah offers an enigmatic smile. "I did notice wagons leaving the post earlier this morning. There was also a trader's wagon."

"We're under explicit orders to close the post and to transport the best of the usable gear and equipment to the Mirror Lancer post at Fyrad. The trader's wagon we recovered when a road patrol caught brigands just after they'd killed the trader and his assistant. Since we were sending wagons to Fyrad anyway, we sent the trader's wagon, its cargo, and the clothing and personal effects to the Mirror Lancer post in Fyrad, under the provisions for recovered property."

"Shouldn't you have turned them over to the nearest tariff enumerator?" asks Khyental, unctuously.

"The provisions state that efforts need to be made to return the property to the heirs, and, if not, to obtain a reasonable price. While the cargo and papers did not provide the name of the teamster or the owner, they suggested that the trader was trading between a place east of Geliendra and Fyrad. It seemed reasonable that we should send the wagon and contents to Fyrad."

"That would seem rather unnecessary," declares Chysrah. "I could have provided the service far more easily."

Alyiakal ignores the enumerator's displeasure and says politely, "I was following Mirror Lancer requirements to maximize the chance for the owner or heirs to recover their property, or if not, for the Mirror Lancers to obtain the best price for the wagon and goods."

"Then you are proceeding with plans to close the post?"

"We are."

"That would seem . . . unwise."

"The harbor is unusable, and the morass still expanding. The remaining wharf is unusable at times. Outland traders would more likely port at Stonepier or Guarstyad and come by road."

"Outland traders are not the problem, Overcaptain," declares Chysrah. "Smugglers have always been the problem here, and that problem will increase if the Mirror Lancer post is closed."

Alyiakal can sense that Chysrah feels strongly, but not necessarily that he believes what he says, except for the problem increasing. "I can understand your concerns, Enumerator Chysrah, but I am under orders to close the post."

"Those are most unwise orders, Overcaptain. I would suggest that you make an effort to keep the post open as long as possible . . . until someone more senior comes to their senses."

As Chysrah speaks, Alyiakal senses the faintest chaos probe from Khyental, exploring Alyiakal's outer shield . . . and trying to pry order away from it. "I appreciate your recommendations, Enumerator, and I will consider them in the light in which they were offered, especially given your experience."

"I hope so, Overcaptain." Chysrah pauses. "I could not help but notice that you are carrying a sabre, even in your study."

"It's a matter of habit and custom. I've been posted mostly where there was a possibility of going into action on short notice, and it would be an unnecessary delay to find and belt on a sabre." Then Alyiakal stands and smiles politely. "I do appreciate your taking the time to offer that advice, and I will certainly inform you if someone more senior than I should change the order to close the post." As he finishes speaking, he can definitely sense consternation from Khyental.

Chysrah rises easily. "Matters will certainly go more easily if you receive such orders, but I understand the difficult position in which you have been placed."

"And I appreciate your concerns, Enumerator Chysrah, but, as a lancer officer, I'm bound to the interests of the Emperor of Light, as expressed in my orders from the Majer-Commander."

Although Chysrah maintains a pleasant smile, Alyiakal notes that something in his words has disconcerted both the enumerator and the magus.

"Then let us both hope that matters will be quickly resolved." Chysrah offers the slightest of nods. "A good day to you, Overcaptain."

"And to you, Enumerator Chysrah . . . and to you, Magus Khyental."

Alyiakal remains standing after the two leave. While he would have liked to follow the two under a concealment, that would reveal far more to Khyental than Alyiakal would like, without gaining much information. He does follow the two with his senses until they walk down the causeway.

Then he considers what he has learned from the meeting. First, from Khyental's attempt to deplete Alyiakal's order levels, that's how the sub-majer was killed. While Alyiakal cannot prove that, even raising the fact that Khyental made the attempt would reveal Alyiakal as a mage of sorts. Second, by coming to see Alyiakal, Chysrah is either in a difficult position and desperate to stop the post closure or he's totally contemptuous of Alyiakal. *Possibly both.*

That leaves the apparent consternation caused by Alyiakal's parting words. *Was it the reference to the Majer-Commander, with the implication that you have orders directly from him, contrary to what the Captain-Commander has promised the Merchanters? Is that why they sent an overcaptain, the lowest rank with the authority to command or close a post?*

At that possibility, Alyiakal almost shivers, but he takes out the post log, and notes that Enumerator Chysrah and his assistant, the magus Khyental, returned the post commander's visit, eleven days later. He also notes Chysrah's concerns about closing the post and his lack of interest in proper handling of the recovered property.

XVI

Over the next eightday, Alyiakal increases his efforts in extending his senses and strengthening his shields. He spars daily with Khenn and Dettlas, usually left-handed, and with the better rankers. He leads the majority of road patrols, drilling whichever squad he leads in Mirror Lancer tactics and maneuvers. While he hopes that will keep him sharp for Lhaarat, those efforts are also improving the rankers' skills.

From the increased diffuse chaos around the post, he knows that Khyental has been observing the fort and his activities but has only approached closely when Alyiakal has been elsewhere. As long as the magus only observes, there's little Alyiakal can . . . or should do.

At night, he works on his map of Luuval. He believes his growing collection of more accurate maps will be useful, based on his observations that most maps used by the Mirror Lancers leave much to be desired. He also practices moving under a concealment, which sharpens the details he can gather with his order/chaos senses.

On fiveday morning before breakfast, he sets out to make his daily inspection of the collapsing ground near the south wall. As he walks out the gate, past the lancer guard, he senses more free chaos directly before the gate.

He turns to the ranker. "Have you seen anyone near the post this morning?"

"No, ser. Not even down by the pier or near the enumerator's place."

"That's good to know." *If not for the reasons anyone might think.* Alyiakal walks south toward the corner of the fort, immediately sensing someone—who has to be Khyental—near the midpoint of the southern wall.

When he stops short of the corner, he sees the ground crumbling as close as four yards from the base of the wall. Alyiakal shakes his head. *Parts of the southern wall, if not most of it, could come down even before we can close the post, possibly before half the gear and equipment is sent to Fyrad.*

That problem will have to wait, because the concealed magus around the corner is a more pressing concern. Alyiakal considers, then nods. *Concealments can work both ways.*

He gathers a bit more free chaos, compresses and concentrates it, and strengthens both shields before he steps around the corner and walks toward the middle of the wall as if he has no idea that Khyental waits, seemingly hidden under a concealment. Then he stops several yards short of Khyental and asks conversationally, "Do you take your orders from the Merchanters or the Magi'i?"

Receiving no response, Alyiakal focuses the compressed chaos into a thin blade, even thinner than the one he had used against the Kyphran mage, and forces it against Khyental's shields. For an instant, the mage's shields hold, before they give and a flash of light and chaos surrounds Alyiakal, whose shields are more than adequate.

Little remains of Khyental, except a few metal objects and a strand of charred weeds and vines. Given the amount of chaos that surrounded Khyental, that doesn't surprise Alyiakal.

After several moments, Alyiakal retrieves the objects and tosses them out into the boggy morass. One or two remain slightly visible, and he extends an order probe and presses them beneath the surface. Then he scuffs the ground with his boots to grind the few charred bits into powder that he mixes with the dirt.

As he walks back to the gate, he reflects that, even if anyone had been watching from a distance, all they could have seen was a flash of light and Alyiakal apparently stomping out burning weeds.

How will Chysrah react?

The enumerator will have difficulty getting word to Cyad or elsewhere anytime soon, without requesting help from Alyiakal. That will result in a charade by both men, although Alyiakal knows exactly what happened, and Chysrah can only suspect.

Alyiakal keeps walking. He still needs to eat, and he'll hear from Chysrah sooner or later.

He does decide not to accompany third squad on patrol and informs Squad Leader Dettlas before he goes to the mess.

It's not until midday when the duty ranker knocks on Alyiakal's door. "Ser, I have a message from the Imperial tariff enumerator."

"A message?"

"Yes, ser. His clerk delivered it. The fellow handed it to me, then left like he was fleeing the dark angels."

Alyiakal stands and walks toward the ranker, who hands him a folded sheet of paper, sealed with blue wax and holding the imprint of the enumerator's sigil.

"Thank you."

"My pleasure, ser."

Alyiakal returns to his desk, sits down, and studies the sealed message, but finds only the faintest hint of chaos before breaking the seal with the tip of his belt knife. He unfolds the message and begins to read.

> *Overcaptain—*
>
> *Earlier today, I sent my assistant, the magus Khyental, to inquire if you had received orders not to close the Mirror Lancer post here at Luuval . . . or if you had further thoughts on the matter.*
>
> *He has not returned, and, of course, I am concerned about the matter. While I know that he would be perfectly safe at the post, his absence is disturbing. Can you shed any light on the matter?*
>
> *I remain, respectfully,*
> *Chysrah'mer*
> *Imperial Tariff Enumerator*
> *Luuval*

After reading the short note, Alyiakal goes to the duty ranker's table desk in the entry to the headquarters building.

"Ser?"

"I just received a note from Enumerator Chysrah saying that he'd dispatched his assistant to see me, but that the assistant never returned. Has anyone presented themselves or come in besides lancers?"

"No one's been here at all, except Squad Leader Dettlas, early this morning, to say that third squad was leaving on road patrol. I saw Squad Leader Khenn look in about a glass or so ago."

"Thank you. If anyone is looking for me, I've gone to find Squad Leader Khenn."

Alyiakal finds Khenn in the tack room, talking to one of the ostlers.

"Could I have a moment?" Alyiakal gestures for the squad leader to join him, away from the ostler.

Once they're several yards from the tack room door, Alyiakal stops. "I just received a note from Enumerator Chysrah claiming that he sent his assistant to see me, but that he never returned. The duty ranker says no one approached him. I'd like you to ask all the rankers if they saw him. Since he is a mage and wears white, they should know if they did. I'd like to know what you can find out as soon as possible."

"Third squad is still out on patrol."

"I know, but they left early, well before anyone would have come to see me."

Khenn nods. "I'll let you know shortly."

"Thank you. I'll be in my study."

Alyiakal walks back across the courtyard and to his study, where he resumes working on his map of Luuval.

Little more than a quint later, Khenn appears in Alyiakal's doorway. "Ser, not a single ranker recalls seeing anyone like the magus assistant. Most of them saw no one. A few saw fishermen."

"Thank you. That's what I needed to know."

Once Khenn leaves, Alyiakal takes out paper and pen and begins to write—carefully. When he finishes, he rereads his words.

> *Enumerator Chysrah—*
>
> *Although you dispatched Magus Khyental to see me, I can say that he never came to my study, nor did I see him anywhere else. I have had every lancer present in the fort questioned as to whether anyone saw him. None of them did. One squad left early this morning on road patrol. Even though they rode out before I would have expected anyone to come see me, I will pose the same questions to all of those lancers when they return, and should any of them have seen Magus Khyental, I will certainly let you know.*

After rereading the reply, Alyiakal writes out a copy as well, after which he signs and seals the original. *What you wrote is accurate. No one has seen Khyental, not even you.*

Then he takes the sealed reply to the duty ranker. "Have the duty messenger carry this to the enumerator's building and deliver it to the clerk. He's not to wait for a response. Have him report back to you immediately upon his return."

"Yes, ser."

Alyiakal returns to his study and the map of the Luuval area.

In less than a quint, the duty ranker appears at Alyiakal's door. "The messenger delivered the letter, ser. He gave it to the clerk."

"Good. Let me know if the enumerator or his clerk should come to the post." Not that Alyiakal expects any response from Chysrah soon.

Reluctantly, after considering his earlier observations, he puts away the atlas and goes to examine the inside of the south wall to estimate the damage to the barracks when the wall collapses and afterward.

The south end of the barracks stands less than fifteen yards from the wall, and the morass is encroaching on the post more quickly than before. Should he consider only making three trips with the wagons because staying longer might well endanger the lancers? He takes a deep breath and heads back to his study to determine the least important items that could be left behind.

When third squad returns, Alyiakal meets the squad leader outside the stable and instructs Dettlas to question each lancer about whether anyone had seen the missing mage. Then Alyiakal returns to his study.

Two quints later, Dettlas reports to Alyiakal that no one has seen anyone, and certainly not a mage.

As Alyiakal has expected, Chysrah does not contact Alyiakal later that afternoon or evening.

XVII

Shortly after midmorning on sixday, the duty ranker knocks on Alyiakal's open door and says, "Ser . . . Enumerator Chysrah is here to see you."

"Escort him in, if you would, Froyst."

"Yes, ser."

When Chysrah appears in the study doorway, his gray eyes are cold.

While Alyiakal can sense a cool fury beneath Chysrah's calm-looking face, he stands momentarily and gestures to the chairs before re-seating himself.

Chysrah sits, then says calmly, "I presume you're going to tell me that no one has seen my assistant."

"I've had every single lancer questioned. Not a one has seen your assistant in the last two days. Neither have I."

"I find that hard to believe."

"It happens to be the truth. I've never seen your assistant except when I came to your main building and when the two of you came here. Few of the lancers have seen him either. I made sure he was described when the lancers were questioned." After Alyiakal speaks, he discerns a slight puzzlement from Chysrah, which quickly dissipates.

"Then where is he?" presses the enumerator.

"You'd know that better than I would. I do know that he never entered the post, and that no one here saw him, including the lancers who were on gate duty." Alyiakal waits.

After several long moments, Chysrah says calmly, "Are you not required to support the tariff enumerators?"

"There is no specific requirement in either my orders or Mirror Lancer regulations, except for the requirement to abide by the laws of Cyador."

"You've actually read the regulations?"

"That's a requirement for post commanders. We receive a personal copy. I've seen what happens when officers don't." *Not in the way I'm implying, but it's still true.* "That's why I tend to be cautious. Most post commanders are."

"Then I'd like to request that you convey immediately my dispatch to the Senior Enumerator in Cyad reporting the disappearance of my assistant and my request for a suitable replacement."

"I'll be happy to convey your request with the next dispatch run or through a naval cutter, should one arrive sooner."

"I believe that the situation is urgent enough to warrant an immediate dispatch, Overcaptain."

"Enumerator Chysrah, I fail to see the urgency. You are a qualified enumerator. You have Mirror Lancers to support you. In the more than two eightdays I have been here, I have yet to see a trader. Oldroad Post saw more traders than that, and for a time, I functioned as both enumerator and post commander. When an enumerator was finally sent, the Palace of Light and the Senior Enumerator felt that a single enumerator was more than sufficient. Surely, you're not saying that you lack the capabilities to handle an occasional trader?"

"Once you close the post, I will need an assistant, and getting one with Khyental's talents will take time."

"How do you know you'll need one? He's only been missing a day."

"He's not the kind to wander off, as you should know."

"I've met your assistant twice. He barely spoke the first time, and not at all the second. For all I know, he could have gotten too close to the boggy morass and had the ground crumble under him. The morass south of the post continues to expand toward the wall, and that could be the case elsewhere.

"Besides which, road brigands are a greater threat than your not having an assistant, as the incident last eightday demonstrated. The company here is severely understrength, and it takes a squad to escort and transport the equipment the Captain-Commander has required us to move to Fyrad. That leaves only thirty men to carry out patrols and carry out the duties necessary for post operation. We're short on effective firelances as well. Given the possibility of road and swamp brigands, I can't send even a routine dispatch or correspondence with less than three lancers, and a spare mount, and I'll be short those men for an eightday. They'll need effective firelances because of the brigands. I didn't create these problems. I inherited them. Besides that, a naval cutter could show up at any time, with dispatches and payroll, and sending your request with it would get your message to Fyrad much sooner."

"What if there is no cutter in the next eightday or so?"

"Next threeday or fourday first squad will return, and within a day, second squad will escort the wagons back to Fyrad with your message and any letters and dispatches I'll be sending to Fyrad."

"That's absurd!" snaps Chysrah. "Overcaptain, this is urgent. I must insist that you send a messenger to Fyrad. Immediately."

"Beyond what you have already told me, why exactly is reporting the disappearance that urgent?"

"I cannot reveal that," replies Chysrah.

"Then I cannot even consider your request. From what you have told me," says Alyiakal deliberately, "you are overreacting. You have one man who is missing. He is not critical to your job as a tariff enumerator. If you were the one missing, there would be a greater argument for urgency. Second, I am under orders to complete the closure of this post by a specific date. Sending an urgent dispatch will impair and possibly delay that closure. It will place more effort on the men remaining here. There have been far too many delays already, as headquarters has made most clear."

Chysrah stands.

While the enumerator's face is calm, Alyiakal senses Chysrah's fury, but Alyiakal only stands and says, "I will inform you when we can accommodate your request."

"I think you will find you have not served the Empire of Light well," says Chysrah pleasantly.

"I am carrying out my orders to the best of my ability, Enumerator. That is how I serve the Emperor of Light."

"Good day, Overcaptain." Chysrah turns without nodding and leaves the study.

Once Chysrah has left the building, Alyiakal walks to the small window, not really looking out, and thinks over the brief meeting. *Even when company officers are killed, we don't send urgent dispatches. Why is he so insistent? And angry?*

No doubt one of the reasons Chysrah is angry is because he suspects Alyiakal had something to do with Khyental's disappearance when Alyiakal was the one who was supposed to vanish. Chysrah is also upset because he has to ask Alyiakal for a way to get a message to the Senior Enumerator in Cyad, possibly one about his failure to remove Alyiakal. Another reason might be that Chysrah hoped to lure Alyiakal into a mistake that could get him removed from command before the post could be closed.

Beyond all that, something about Chysrah's words before his departure nags at Alyiakal.

You have not served the Empire of Light well. Alyiakal frowns. Usually, people talk of serving the Emperor well, or the Mirror Lancers. That might mean something . . . or it might not.

In the meantime, he will have to tread carefully. *As if you don't have to already.*

XVIII

Over the next five days, very little changes. No naval cutter appears, not that Alyiakal has expected one, and Chysrah has not contacted Alyiakal. The road patrols see no signs of brigands, and the southern wall now definitely leans to the south. The air remains damp and heavy, with seldom much of a breeze, which makes Alyiakal wonder what the attraction of Luuval had been.

Or did the collapse of the headland change everything? He has no idea, and since most of the lancers currently at the post arrived after the collapse, they wouldn't know, either.

When first squad returns late on the first fourday of Harvest, Alyiakal walks out to the rear courtyard, looking to Aaltyn even before the captain dismounts. "You didn't lose any lancers or wagons."

"We didn't, but we did have to have two wheels replaced in Fyrad, and I persuaded the supply officer to lend us a spare just in case." Aaltyn grins. "I did have to point out that he'd end up with all four wagons, but only if they lasted for six more trips, one way, that is."

"No trouble with brigands?"

"I'm sure two riders we saw sixty kays east of here were scouts, but they must have decided not to take on a squad fully armed with firelances. We did get all the firelances replenished."

"Excellent!"

Aaltyn dismounts, then unfastens and hands a messenger bag to Alyiakal. "This is for you. Since there wasn't a cutter being dispatched in the direction of Luuval for another two eightdays, if not longer, the Fyrad post commander sent all the correspondence and directives."

"That way he wouldn't have to send couriers to a post that won't exist in less than a season." *Unless Chysrah and the Merchanters can disrupt things again.*

"There are dispatches, several letters for you, and a packet of letters for men in the company. I did take the liberty of handing out those letters addressed to men in the squad."

"As you should."

"Is there anything else I should know, ser?"

Alyiakal offers a wry smile. "The morass is closer to the south wall, which is definitely leaning and will likely collapse before we can close the post. Also, the Imperial Enumerator's assistant is missing, and the enumerator is angry because I wouldn't send couriers immediately to report the disappearance." Alyiakal provides more of the details about what Chysrah said, then adds, "You'll have to carry his dispatch to Fyrad when you leave on sixday with second squad. We can talk more at dinner. Take care of your mount and anything else you need to do."

After leaving Aaltyn, Alyiakal returns to his study, where he goes through the message bag, sorting the letters for the squad leaders and rankers and setting aside letters from Saelora and Hyrsaal. Then he looks at the official letters and directives. The first is from Mirror Lancer headquarters, signed by Commander Dahlvor. Alyiakal scans the directive quickly, taking in the key points.

> . . . *procedures for lancers due for normal home leave will remain in force. Those lancers who have served two years or more at Luuval will be granted the normal home leave prior to reassignment. Those with less service than that at Luuval will be granted between one and two eightdays' leave based on the time served at Luuval* . . .

Alyiakal opens the next envelope, containing an expanded reiteration of the closure procedures previously given to Alyiakal by Majer Bekkan. One part is definitely expanded:

> *All materiel and supplies at the post will be handled in accordance with current Mirror Lancer procedures. Specifically, all weapons will be transported to Fyrad. All weapons-related equipment that can be physically transported will be sent to Fyrad; equipment of this nature that cannot be transported will be destroyed or rendered unusable.*
>
> *Furnishings and other items unable to be transported will be inventoried and made available to the Imperial tariff enumerator in Luuval. A copy of that inventory will be sent to the Captain-Commander. The post and its buildings will be turned over to the Imperial tariff enumerator for whatever use he may deem, including the sale of brick and other materials, and a signed copy of that transmittal will also be transmitted to the Captain-Commander.*

A few concerns about the probity of the tariff enumerator . . . or just an emphasis on procedures?

The third envelope holds the Fyrad supply officer's receipt of the trader's wagon and its contents under the regulations covering recovered property.

The next letter Alyiakal opens is from Hyrsaal, and he begins to read.

> *. . . I just got my orders for my next posting. I'm being sent to Inividra, where I'll be one of the senior captains. I'll be detached from Lhaarat during the fifth eightday of Harvest, and I get one eightday of travel to Fyrad or Geliendra. Catriana and I are allowing about an eightday to prepare for the consorting. We're hoping to schedule the ceremony on the seventh eightday of Harvest. If that's not possible, then on the next eightday . . .*

Alyiakal frowns. He can't attend the consorting ceremony, given Hyrsaal's timing, but should be able to see Hyrsaal and Catriana during his own home leave. He's still thinking about that when Aaltyn knocks on his door. "Are you ready to eat?"

"I am." Alyiakal stands. "I was going over the official correspondence, including receipt of the recovered property."

"The overcaptain in charge of supplies handed it to me. He said he'd kept a copy and that what he sent was for your personal records."

"He doesn't trust enumerators, either." Alyiakal dons his visor cap, and the two walk to the rear courtyard. "Did you hear anything about Luuval . . . or our enumerator?"

"Nothing about the enumerator. The supply overcaptain did ask why it had taken so long to close the post. I told him about the problems with getting a post commander. He shook his head, said the post should have been closed years ago, and that the only traders who stopped there were ones with baubles for the consorts and widows of wealthy Merchanters."

"So Luuval was where wealthy Merchanters sent unwanted consorts . . . and possibly their widowed mothers?"

"I got that impression. He did say it once had been a pleasant place."

When the two reach the small mess, they seat themselves, and the mess orderly fills their wineglasses and returns with two platters, each containing slices of roast pork and sliced boiled potatoes, both covered with brown gravy, and with sliced pearapples on the side.

Alyiakal lifts his wineglass. "To your safe return."

"Thank you, ser." Aaltyn lifts his glass. "And to an uneventful closure of the post."

"I can definitely drink to that."

The two do not speak for a time.

Then Aaltyn asks, "Is there anything else that I should know?"

"Outside of the enumerator complaining and pressing me to disobey orders and keep the post open, nothing of any import."

"Why is he so adamant? Won't the Senior Tariff Enumerator just post him elsewhere?"

"I'd think so, but there's obviously something we don't know." *And may never know, given how closemouthed enumerators seem to be.* "Tomorrow, we need to go back over the next cargo going to Fyrad. The way the ground is collapsing by the south wall, part of the barracks might collapse before we have time for a fourth trip."

The rest of the conversation deals with post-related topics.

After eating, Alyiakal returns to his study, jots a few thoughts on changes to wagon loads, then picks up the letter from Hyrsaal and the still-unopened letter from Saelora and repairs to his quarters, where, after bolting the door, he slits open the envelope from Saelora, extracts the missive, and begins to read.

I can't believe that you'll be here in less than a season. I want to see you and show you what I've done with the factorage and the house . . . and the expansion of the distillery.

I'm sure you've heard about the consorting. From what you wrote, you'll have to miss the ceremony. That's sad, but we all knew that might happen. Gaaran and Charissa can't come, either. I know Hyrsaal wants to see you and Catriana wants to meet you, after all she's heard . . .

All she's heard. Alyiakal frowns. He's been careful not to mention any real details about his duties or what happened in the battles that led up to the creation of Oldroad Post.

Catriana's sister Elina will host the dinner after the ceremony. Everything will be in Fyrad.

Alyiakal nods. Still, it's too bad that Gaaran can't come, since he is Hyrsaal's older brother, but that's understandable. Catriana's in the same position, if not worse, because her sister Elina will be her only relative at the ceremony.

Catriana finally finished the cottage on the land Faedyrk granted her adjoining Elina and Dyrkan's holding . . .

Faedyrk? Then Alyiakal recalls that Faedyrk is the father of Elina's consort.

. . . she claims she couldn't have built it without what I've paid her to represent Loraan House in Fyrad, but she earned every copper. I worked it out so that she's an apprentice enumerator under the supervision of Haansfel, the factorage from which I rented the space for Loraan House . . .

Alyiakal smiles. *Trust Saelora to work out things.*

It's hard to believe that Gaaran and Charissa are expecting their second. Gaartyn has only been walking a year, but both Charissa and Mother dote on him.

Alyiakal keeps reading, taking in every word.

XIX

Alyiakal wakes early and finds a gray mist has filled his quarters, a mist smelling of the morass and the Grass Hills in Winter. He rises quickly, fearful that the morass has undermined some of the post overnight, but when he leaves his quarters and steps into the courtyard, the mist is so thick he cannot even see the post walls. He takes one step, then another . . . and then the paving stones give underfoot, and he drops into bone-chilling muck.

He tries to turn and grab the stones he knows must be behind him, but there are no stones, just straggly grass, and dirt. Even so, he manages to crawl out of the mucky water and get away from the morass, but when he stands up, the mist disperses some, and he sees a woman in brown, standing by a dirt-heaped grave.

She turns, her face indistinct in the mist. "You killed him. You didn't even know who he was . . . or how hard he worked to keep us alive . . . and then you left me and the children . . ."

The mist thickens, and turns to acrid smoke, and Alyiakal finds himself riding around the corner of a hut toward a girl with a bow. Before he can think, his firelance flares, and turns the girl to ashes . . .

He tries to swallow but his mouth is filled with warm and vile muddy water, and he is back in the morass again, slowly being dragged under . . .

"No!!!"

Alyiakal bolts awake, instantly sitting on the side of his bed, shivering in a cold sweat, despite the heat in his quarters.

So real . . . felt so very real . . . again.

He takes a deep breath and wipes the sweat off his forehead with the back of his hand. Then he takes another deep breath. The shivers slowly subside.

What was that all about? A warning to close the post before it swallows you? But the barbarian woman from the valley? Or the girl archer that you never really even saw . . . You didn't have any choice . . .

Once he's gathered himself together after the unsettling nightmare, Alyiakal washes up, dresses, then visits the ground outside the south wall. He has to stop several yards short of the middle because he can see that farther west there's less than a yard of solid ground between the morass and the base of the wall, and very little ordered substance beneath the morass and not much beneath the ground next to the wall. The wall doesn't lean any more than it had the day before, but there's no doubt that the wall will begin to collapse within days, if not sooner.

That part of the nightmare was definitely telling you something.

He walks back to the gate and says to the lancer on duty, "Keep everyone away from the south wall. There are places there where the ground will give way underfoot."

"Yes, ser."

Alyiakal goes to his study, where he jots down notes for the report he will send to both the post commander at Fyrad and the Captain-Commander at headquarters about the imminent collapse of the south wall and the possibility that the company may only be able to make three trips with weapons and materiel before the post is unsafe. Then he makes his way to the mess, where Aaltyn already waits.

"I'm sorry I'm a little late," says Alyiakal. "I was checking the south wall. It's about to collapse, at least in the middle. The morass seems to be expanding more quickly."

"That's not surprising," replies Aaltyn. "From the lay of the land west of the post, I'd wager they built that part of the post on less solid ground."

Alyiakal almost asks why but realizes that the location was determined by wealthy Merchanters who wanted the post between the more and less affluent sections of Luuval. "We may have to close the post earlier than planned."

Aaltyn frowns. "What will headquarters say?"

"They've left it to my discretion as long as it's closed by the end of the eighth eightday of Harvest. The enumerator won't be happy, but once the south wall collapses, I can certainly claim that the safety of the lancers is more important than a predetermined date. So . . . after we eat and after morning muster, we need to go over the loading plans and make sure the most valuable and useful items and materiel are loaded out on the wagons leaving tomorrow."

"That makes sense," agrees Aaltyn.

After breakfast, Alyiakal accompanies Aaltyn to morning muster, where he takes a moment to address the assembled lancers.

"Some of you may have noticed that the swamp that swallowed much of Luuval has been creeping closer to the south wall. That's one of the reasons Mirror Lancer headquarters decided to close the post. What headquarters did not anticipate was the quick expansion of the swamp. Because the swamp has begun to undermine the foundations of the south wall, you are not to approach the south wall from outside, and all lancers are to remain at least five yards from the wall while inside the post. The wall might collapse tonight. It might last an eightday, but it will collapse, and none of you want to be anywhere near when it happens." Alyiakal remains silent for a moment, then nods to Aaltyn. "Carry on, Captain."

Aaltyn nods in return, and Alyiakal heads back to his study. There, he writes a very pleasant note to Chysrah, informing him that Captain Aaltyn and second squad will be departing for Fyrad early on sixday morning and that the captain will be happy to convey any correspondence, official or otherwise, received before departure.

Two quints later, Aaltyn joins Alyiakal, and the two begin to go over the loading plans for the wagons. A glass passes before Aaltyn departs with the revised plans to begin loading.

Alyiakal returns to the notes he had written earlier and begins his report to the Mirror Lancer Captain-Commander about the state of the post, a copy of which will go to the post commander at Fyrad as well. He has finished a rough draft when the duty ranker appears.

"A message from the enumerator, ser. His clerk brought it."

Alyiakal stands and takes the envelope. "Thank you."

Once the ranker has left, Alyiakal studies the envelope, again with sight and senses, before opening it and beginning to read.

> Overcaptain—
> My clerk will deliver a sealed messenger bag to Captain Aaltyn just before the squad leaves for Fyrad.
> My appreciation for the notification.
>
> *Chysrah'mer*
> *Imperial Tariff Enumerator*

Alyiakal smiles wryly. The response is close to what he has expected. Then he sets it aside and returns to working on his report.

XX

Alyiakal rises even earlier than usual on sixday and hurries to the mess to meet with Aaltyn, arriving a few moments before the captain.

"I haven't seen any messages from the enumerator," says Aaltyn as he seats himself.

"I'm guessing that Chysrah's clerk will hand you the messenger bag as you ride out the gate."

"I'd be surprised if it were otherwise," agrees Aaltyn.

"Don't try to open the messenger bag," says Alyiakal. "I'm certain that the way it's sealed will reveal that it's been opened, and that will not reflect well on either of us. I'd deliver it personally to whomever it's addressed. If it goes by fireship to Cyad—"

"Get a receipt saying it was delivered sealed from whoever I hand it over to?"

"Exactly."

"What do you think it says?"

"It will report factually what I said and did in a way that will attempt to discredit me without ever mentioning my name. Beyond that, I wouldn't want to guess."

Aaltyn laughs softly. "I wouldn't, either. It makes me think that he's hiding something."

"It might be a ploy to get us to open it in order to discredit us," replies Alyiakal. "Enough of idle speculation. We need to eat, and you've got two more eightdays of riding."

"In some ways, it's more pleasant than staying here. The post never gets breezes, except when there are storms at sea, and there aren't many of those. Late fall and Winter are the most comfortable seasons."

"I can see that." Alyiakal takes a sip of ale, and then a bite of the cheesed eggs.

After the two finish eating, Alyiakal accompanies Aaltyn to the rear courtyard where second squad and the wagons are forming up, observes as Aaltyn takes charge, then walks to the east gate to watch as the wagons go by.

Just outside the gate stands the gray-clad clerk of Imperial Tariff Enumerator Chysrah.

As Alyiakal has predicted, the moment Aaltyn rides up, the clerk approaches him and offers the messenger bag, which Aaltyn carefully fastens in place. The clerk walks swiftly down the causeway, keeping abreast of the captain.

As the last of the four wagons heads down the causeway, Alyiakal hears another set of sounds, part rumble, part splintering wood, and part muffled shriek, accompanied by a slight shifting of the paving stones under his boots.

He knows exactly what has happened even before the lancer on gate duty calls out, "Ser! The middle of the south wall is gone!"

"Stay where you are! More of it might come down." Alyiakal glances toward the departing squad, but Aaltyn has kept the lancers and wagons moving.

Alyiakal walks around the small headquarters building on the south side, letting his senses range over stone pavement, which still seems ordered and solid near the building. The middle third of the wall has toppled into the murky waters, and for the moment sections of brick masonry protrude above the surface. Both the east and west thirds of the wall remain standing. Alyiakal edges forward to within five yards of where the center of the wall used to be. The top of the stone footings leans to the south, and two or three courses of masonry remain fixed to it.

Alyiakal presses his awareness below the tilted footings, but all he can sense is a swirling of warm diffuse chaos. After a moment, he steps back, and turns as Squad Leader Maert hurries toward him.

Before Maert can utter a word, Alyiakal says, "I underestimated the speed at which the morass is undermining the walls and ground. We should be able to close the post and transport the most valuable materiel to Fyrad before it destroys the barracks."

"How is it happening?" asks the squad leader. "Do you know?"

"I don't know. I do know that the Mirror Engineers couldn't do anything. Given that the water remains murky and muddy, something must be stirring it up. If I had to guess, I'd say there's a deep current of warm water eroding everything except rock, and everything hard sinks into the depths. That's just a guess, though." He pauses. "We'll need to build a fence across that end of the courtyard, something that can be moved as the morass advances. If you'd get the men to working on that, Maert."

"Yes, ser, but where—"

"You can cannibalize anything nonstructural from the upper level of the barracks. We can't take the building with us, and it'll sink anyway."

"Yes, ser. We'll get on it."

Once the squad leader turns, Alyiakal heads back to his study, shaking his head. *Regardless of what Chysrah wants or thinks, the next trip with the wagons will be the last. Staying here any longer risks disaster.*

That means he needs to make Chysrah aware of the situation, in writing, and finish the documentation to turn over the post and materiel that cannot be transported to Fyrad to the enumerator.

A quint later, Alyiakal reads over the letter that is the first step.

> *Enumerator Chysrah—*
>
> *As you will notice, this morning the morass destroyed much of the southern wall of the post and is about to expand into the courtyard. In the very near future, far sooner than anyone anticipated, the post will be uninhabitable.*
>
> *For that reason, I'd like to request your presence at the post tomorrow at your convenience to discuss the process to transfer the post and all remaining materiel so that you may begin to arrange for its sale and disposal.*

After rereading, Alyiakal makes a copy, signs and seals the original, and then has the duty messenger deliver it.

Two glasses later, Chysrah's clerk returns with an envelope that the duty ranker hands to Alyiakal. The response is brief.

> *Overcaptain—*
>
> *While discussion over these matters should have begun earlier, I will join you around midmorning.*
>
> *Chysrah'mer*
> *Imperial Tariff Enumerator*

How could it have begun much earlier when Chysrah didn't want to accept closure? And what is there to discuss?

The Mirror Lancers transport what they can, and the tariff enumerator gets everything left and sells or disposes of it as he can.

Provided the post lasts that long.

XXI

True to his word, Chysrah arrives at the post and enters Alyiakal's study slightly after midmorning on sevenday.

Alyiakal stands to greet him and gestures to the chair before seating himself. "I appreciate your coming so quickly."

Chysrah sits down and seems to compose himself before saying, "You realize that these matters should have been discussed earlier."

"I was reluctant to bring them up," says Alyiakal, "given your apparent opposition to the closure. Since I've been here a little over three eightdays, I had no way to judge how fast the swamp would expand. According to the more experienced lancers, it's only been in the past eightday that the rate of expansion has increased. It now appears that we will only be able to make one more trip with wagons before we'll have to close the post."

"Only one more trip?" Chysrah sounds appalled.

"That's all the time we have for what I've been ordered to do, Enumerator Chysrah. I've moved as quickly as possible, but there has only been so much I can do in the three eightdays I've been here." *And it's more than previous commanders have done in three years.*

"I see." Chysrah pauses for several moments, then asks, "What do you expect me to do with all these . . . materials under the present circumstances?"

"We're both in a difficult position. I have to follow my orders, and your position requires you to do the best that you can."

"And what will you do if I fail to accept the materials?"

"Then we will close the post and leave a copy of the inventory with you. We will send a copy to both the Majer-Commander of the Mirror Lancers and the Senior Tariff Enumerator with the observation that you felt that there was insufficient time to deal with the post and its remaining contents, but that the unsafe condition of the post left me with no other choices in complying with the directives of the Majer-Commander."

Chysrah nods slowly. "You obviously feel you have no choice. I do appreciate your understanding the difficulties this creates. Since you seem reasonable about *this*, Overcaptain . . ."

Alyiakal hears the slight emphasis on the word "this," but says nothing as Chysrah continues.

". . . I will accept the transfer of the post and the remaining materials with a notation in the transfer documentation that says, because of the various delays, much of the value of what remains is unlikely to be realized."

"I would suggest a slight rephrasing," says Alyiakal. "I would suggest, in your acceptance, that you note that the great majority of the value cannot be realized because of unstable ground and the recent increased and unforeseen speed of the expansion of the morass."

"You'd accept such wording?"

"It's the truth. We're here, and we have to deal with what's happened."

Chysrah nods, then says, "You realize that I cannot just take your word for what you will leave?"

"We know that. We have an inventory of what we planned to take and to leave, but because we can't make a fourth trip, we'll have to make changes. We might have to make a few more once the wagons return, especially if we lose a wagon or if Fyrad can send another wagon. We'll make a revised draft of both inventories, but we may have to make small changes once the wagons return."

"When will that be?"

"In a little less than two eightdays, depending on the roads, the weather, and the wagons. I just wanted you to have as much time as I could provide."

"In this, you're being most accommodating, Overcaptain."

"I try to be when I can, Enumerator. Like you, my accommodations are limited by my orders and Mirror Lancer requirements."

"We do what we can." Chysrah stands.

"Indeed, we do," returns Alyiakal, rising to his feet.

After the enumerator departs, Alyiakal considers what he observed. While he doesn't trust Chysrah, he feels any treachery or difficulty won't lie in the transfer of property. *How Chysrah represents it to others may be another question.*

Alyiakal has no doubt that his documentation and records need to be complete and accurate and that he needs to have copies of everything.

He takes a deep breath.

XXII

Over the next several days, Alyiakal works with Maert and Dettlas to revise the wagon-loading plans to assure the most valuable and useful items will fit in four wagons. The sooner the company leaves, and the post is abandoned, the happier he'll be, and headquarters will just have to accept twelve wagons' worth of equipment instead of sixteen.

The three finally complete the revised wagon-loading plans late on oneday, and Alyiakal hopes they'll work out as well in practice as on paper, but he knows that won't happen.

After Alyiakal sees third squad off on road patrol on twoday morning, he and Maert begin the tedious task of reviewing the post inventory and creating two lists. The first list itemizes equipment too heavy to remove, such as the massive ovens and stoves. The second list contains usable items of lesser individual value which could not be transported with the wagons and time available, including wooden bunk frames, trestle tables from the mess hall, old straight-backed chairs, and several large table desks.

By midafternoon, it's clear to Alyiakal that finishing those lists will take another day or so, longer than expected, but given Chysrah's veiled anger and attitude, Alyiakal wants to account for as much as possible, even though he has a suspicion that that morass may swallow the post before Chysrah can do much to sell or otherwise deal with what Alyiakal turns over.

Since his eyes burn from going over the lists, when Alyiakal senses third squad returning in late midafternoon, he leaves his study and walks to the stables, where he finds Dettlas.

"How was the patrol?"

Dettlas smiles. "Like you suggested, we went about three kays farther west. We saw three riders heading east, toward us. There might have been a fourth. They looked real surprised to see us. Then, they turned and rode south down a trail. It wasn't much more than a path, but they rode as fast as they could. We didn't see any signs of brigandage, but I still say that's what they were."

I wonder where they got the idea we were already gone. Someone here in what's left of Luuval? "Did they yell anything?"

"Not that I heard, ser." The squad leader shakes his head. "Feel sorry for the folks living here once we're gone."

"I do, too," replies Alyiakal. "But the frigging morass could be a bigger problem for them than the brigands." Even as he finishes speaking, it strikes him that Chysrah should know that as well. *Why was he pressing for you to keep the post open? It can't be about you. He doesn't really know anything about you.* "At least you scared them off."

"They'll be back. That kind always is."

"We can only do what we can, Squad Leader. And we both know that sometimes it's sowshit. That's pretty much true in everything, unfortunately." Alyiakal pauses. "I'll need your help in the morning with the inventory for the Imperial tariff enumerator . . . and tell Maert about those brigands, in case they're out tomorrow."

"Yes, ser."

As Alyiakal walks back to his study, he continues to ponder why the Senior Imperial Tariff Enumerator or the Merchanter clans want the post to stay open. *Or do they just want the post open long enough for everything in the post to be swallowed up so they can blame the Mirror Lancers? Is it all part of an overall plan to weaken the Mirror Lancers?*

Alyiakal shakes his head. *They can't be that corrupt. Can they?*

Except Overcaptain Tygael, during Alyiakal's first posting, had not only implied that they'd been behind the death of the fourth Emperor of Light, but strongly hinted that saying much about Merchanter schemes could cost an officer his career—if not his life—especially in Cyad.

And in Fyrad as well.

XXIII

For the next eightday, nothing unusual occurs, except that first squad sights possible brigands at a distance on oneday, and the brigands flee, and that the morass brings down the southeast corner of the post wall and that all the masonry comprising the southern wall has vanished into the murky water.

Additionally, Alyiakal provides the tentative inventory of what will be left to Chysrah and has received the draft acceptance document in return. He reads the document three times, slowly, and can find no fault. *But then, it may be what's not in the document or some act or directive you know nothing about.* Those possibilities worry him.

Late on threeday, Aaltyn and second squad return, and Alyiakal goes out to meet the returning lancers. He instantly notices that Aaltyn has returned with five wagons. "Another wagon?"

Aaltyn smiles sheepishly as he dismounts. "I told the supply overcaptain the way the morass was swallowing the post that the next run might just be the last." He looks to the south at the temporary fence and where the south wall had stood. "Looks like I wasn't exaggerating as much as I thought."

"You weren't exaggerating," replies Alyiakal. "The post is getting too unsafe. The next trip will be the last."

"Can't say I'm unhappy about that. The Imperial tariff enumerator might be, though."

"He knows. I couldn't keep him in the dark," Alyiakal says. "Anything the wagons can't carry goes to him for sale or disposal. I gave him a provisional inventory, but we'll have to change that now that we have an additional wagon. It's good to see you back. Do you have any letters or dispatches?"

"No dispatches, but some letters. There's one for you. They also sent the payroll for the next four eightdays."

"The men'll be happy about that."

"So am I," replies Aaltyn, "even if there's nowhere to spend it." He unfastens the messenger bag and a second heavier canvas bag from behind the saddle and hands both to Alyiakal.

"Nothing for Enumerator Chysrah?"

"Not a thing. There is a letter of receipt from a Captain Kaern for the enumerator's letter. When Kaern asked what was in the bag, I said we were not informed and did not insist. He just said, 'Wise of you.' The letter of receipt was the best I could do because the fireship that will take it to Cyad wasn't scheduled to port until after we departed."

"What about the firelances?"

"We got the empty spares replenished, and we didn't have to use the ones we carried."

"Good. I won't keep you." Alyiakal turns and carries the payroll bag to the armory, placing it in the strongbox in the hidden armory room. Then he takes the messenger bag back to his study. All the letters except two go to rankers in first and third squads. He places the letter from Captain Kaern in the file that holds the papers, dispatches, and other material dealing with the post closure.

The second letter is from Liathyr. Alyiakal hoped there might be one from Saelora. He'd like to read it, but he writes a quick message to Chysrah first.

> *Enumerator Chysrah—*
>
> *As you may have noticed, Captain Aaltyn returned from Fyrad with an extra wagon. While this will require changes to the inventory, we should have a revised copy of your inventory by midafternoon tomorrow.*
>
> *I suggest that we plan to complete and sign the transfer documentation as soon as possible after that.*

Once he signs and seals the message, he has the duty messenger carry it to Chysrah.

He also knows that he and Aaltyn and the three squad leaders need to go over the inventory following the evening meal.

In the meantime, he decides to take a moment to open and read the letter from Liathyr.

> *Alyiakal—*
>
> *Your letters always cheer me up. They remind me that there are far worse billets than being a company commander in a port town that most of Cyador has never heard of. Most officers posted here never want to hear of it again once they leave. I can't say I envy you for your last two postings, and if that's the fast way to make overcaptain, I prefer a slower path.*
>
> *I just found out that I've been extended for one year here. I suspect my next posting will be to a larger port post, hopefully with a promotion, but that's in the hands of headquarters. I won't be able to attend Hyrsaal's consorting because my undercaptain was disabled in an accident dealing with Austran smugglers. I'm allowed home leave before the extension takes effect, but not until I get a replacement undercaptain. Right now, I have no idea when that will be . . .*
>
> *I'm sure you remember Ghallyr from Kynstaar . . .*

Alyiakal could scarcely forget, given that Ghallyr had always been Baertal's toady.

> *. . . Jhoald wrote me. He found out that during Ghallyr's home leave in Cyad, he had his throat cut. He died right there. They never found out*

who did it, but it happened outside a tavern in the merchanting quarter.
That sounds just like Ghallyr. He wasn't even from Cyad. He was from
Wendingway. He probably only went to Cyad because Baertal told him
to . . . have no idea where Baertal is . . .

Alyiakal knows where Wendingway is, but there's another reason he should recall the small town: two of Saelora's uncles live there. His thoughts return to Baertal, because, like Liathyr, he has no idea where Baertal has been posted, or for that matter, Vordahl, but he's certain he'll encounter both sooner or later.

Assuming you all survive.

XXIV

In the gray before dawn on fourday, Alyiakal inspects the southern end of the fort. Less than five yards from the barracks, the paving stones are beginning to sink. Alyiakal goes to his study, adds those observations to what will be his last report on the post's condition, then joins Aaltyn for breakfast.

After eating quickly, the two officers meet with the three squad leaders to review the inventory to determine what else they can now take to Fyrad. It's well after noon before they finish and turn the revised inventory over to the two ranker clerks, while the five then work on revising the wagon-loading plans.

By the fourth glass of the afternoon, Alyiakal has two copies of the inventory of what will be turned over to the enumerator and the revised wagon-loading plans.

Two quints later, Chysrah arrives, and Aaltyn ushers him into Alyiakal's study, then follows him in.

Even before Chysrah seats himself, he looks to Aaltyn and asks, "Before we begin, might I ask about the message bag I sent with you, Captain?"

"There were no fireships ported at Fyrad. I turned the message bag, unopened, over to the senior aide to Subcommander Quellyt, a Captain Kaern, and received a letter of receipt in return, which assures the overcaptain that the message bag will be transmitted unopened to the Senior Tariff Enumerator in Cyad." Then Aaltyn sits down.

"I appreciate the care you have taken, Captain. Thank you."

While Chysrah's voice is pleasant, Alyiakal senses disappointment. *Because he can't accuse us of tampering with his official correspondence? Or because of the delay in getting the message to Cyad?*

Either or both are possible, Alyiakal knows, but the post will be closed before any response can reach Chysrah. While Alyiakal will be on home leave before any Mirror Lancer headquarters response could reach Fyrad, that doesn't mean that he won't face a thorough "debriefing" by Subcommander Quellyt once he gets to Fyrad or that any adverse repercussions won't follow him to Lhaarat.

Alyiakal clears this throat. "I have two copies of the inventory of property and items that will remain and become the responsibility of the tariff enumerator."

"You expect me just to accept this?" asks Chysrah. "Without even looking through the post?"

"We'll be happy to escort you through the post, but the fact is that I'm under orders to take certain items to Fyrad and leave everything else for you. The inventory is for your use. The only inventory that will be scrutinized is what we take to Fyrad, because all that will go into the Mirror Lancer supply warehouse there, and I'll be held accountable for it. I can have one of my squad leaders take you through the post with the inventory of what we'll be leaving. If you feel more comfortable, I can give you a statement that, as ordered by the Captain-Commander of the Mirror Lancers, everything remaining in the post, including the structures, is yours to dispose of according to your procedures and prior agreements between the Senior Tariff Administrator and the Majer-Commander of the Mirror Lancers."

"A signed statement to that effect will suffice."

"I presume you would like a copy of the inventory. We've tried to make it as accurate as possible, but there may be some smaller items that are not listed."

"The inventory will prove useful, especially since I do not yet have an assistant and may not for some time. I only have four guards and a clerk, and they'll be rather busy." Chysrah looks as though he might say something more, but refrains.

"Then we'll have to delay signing and sealing the final papers until tomorrow so that I can draft that statement for you."

"That would be for the best." Chysrah stands. "If you would inform me."

"We will."

Once the enumerator has left, Alyiakal turns to Aaltyn. "He raised the question of the inventory as if he wanted to pick a fight. Then he dropped it once I said everything that was left was for him to handle. I can't help thinking that he's up to something, but I can't see what it might be. Do you have any thoughts?"

"Is there something here that's valuable that he doesn't want to show up on the inventory?" Aaltyn pauses, then says, "Or maybe he's figured out something that he can sell privately on the side."

"The most valuable parts of the fort are the bricks, or the slate roofing, but it would take an angel-fired lot of work to break the bricks out of the masonry without smashing them. Most of the furnishings we're leaving aren't worth shipping. They might fetch a few coppers each in a prosperous town, but not here."

"What about nails?" asks Aaltyn. "He could have his guards burn the interior of the barracks, claim that lightning started the fire and collect the nails."

"That's a lot of work for little return. What are nails worth?"

"In a prosperous hamlet fifty nails might get you a copper."

"Even if there were ten thousand, they'd only be worth two hundred coppers, and it would take a lot of time. Worth it for a poor smallholder, but not for an Imperial tariff enumerator. I'm wagering on the bricks," says Alyiakal dryly. "I'll keep thinking about it, but I have to draft that statement for Chysrah." And he needed to draft it very carefully.

"If you don't mind, ser, I'm going to walk through all the buildings, just to see what might be valuable that we haven't thought of."

"I'd appreciate that. We can talk over anything you come up with over dinner. I'll see you then."

When Aaltyn leaves, Alyiakal begins to adapt the form he'd received from Bekkan to fit the situation at Luuval. By the time he leaves for the evening meal, he has a final version pieced together.

Dinner is pleasant, and Aaltyn admits that he couldn't find anything of great value or large numbers of small items that could add up to significant value. After eating, Alyiakal returns to his study.

By midmorning on fiveday, Alyiakal has the documents, and the necessary copies, ready and sends a messenger to inform Chysrah.

Once the messenger leaves, Alyiakal says to Aaltyn, "I wonder when he'll arrive."

"About a glass. Long enough to indicate that he's not at your beck and call, soon enough that you can't claim that he's being difficult," replies Aaltyn wryly.

A quint more than a glass passes before Chysrah reappears in the doorway of Alyiakal's study.

Before the enumerator can say a word, Alyiakal gestures to the documents laid out on the front of the desk. "They reflect what we discussed earlier. We'll be in the front entry while you look them over. When you're done, or if you have any questions, let us know."

Chysrah just nods and pulls a chair over next to the desk, then seats himself.

Two quints later, the enumerator walks out to the front entry. "I only have one question. I notice that the property does not become the possession of the Senior Tariff Enumerator until a glass after sunrise tomorrow."

"That's to avoid having you sign the document tomorrow at a glass after sunrise," replies Alyiakal. "If you'd prefer that . . ."

Chysrah offers an amused laugh, something that Alyiakal hasn't expected. "I can accept that."

The three return to Alyiakal's study to sign and seal all copies of the documents.

When they finish and Chysrah slips his two copies into a leather folder, he turns to Alyiakal. "Might I ask why you are giving up some valuable material by not making another trip with the wagons? You have enough time for that."

"Because the morass is moving more quickly every day, and the footing near the edge is uncertain, as I've discovered. I fear the barracks would collapse if we took the time to make a fourth trip. That would mean that everyone would lose. I might have injured lancers, and I'd end up transporting less equipment and goods, and you would have less time to remove what you find valuable. There are times to proceed quickly and times to hold back. The morass has made it clear that this is not a time to hold back."

"Spoken like an experienced combat commander," says Chysrah dryly.

"We each have our strengths," returns Alyiakal, adding, "As we discussed earlier, tomorrow morning a lancer will deliver to your building the keys for those door locks remaining, and we will leave the front gate open half a yard."

"I appreciate your care, Overcaptain. If I do not see you in the morning, I wish you a safe and uneventful journey to Fyrad."

Once Chysrah has left the study, Alyiakal turns to Aaltyn. "Now we need to inspect the wagons." *And hope nothing else comes up.*

XXV

Alyiakal does not sleep well, with assorted dreams, in one of which he finds his bunk slipping into the morass and carrying him with it. In another, Saelora's mother Marenda is demanding that he never see Saelora again. In another, he sees the stunned face of a Kyphran mage in light green before chaos consumes him. In the last, Subcommander Quellyt berates him for not saving more equipment. He's relieved to rise before dawn to make his final preparations, and to eat a necessarily cold breakfast, since the kitchen gear was packed the night before.

Then he checks the rear courtyard to see how much more of the courtyard has been claimed, about a half a yard, before returning to his quarters for his duffels and carrying them to the stable. He readies the mare and fastens his gear behind the saddle, then obtains a firelance. The last item is the strongbox that Alyiakal and Aaltyn remove from the armory strongroom and load into the lead wagon.

As the sun peers over the trees on the rise to the east, Alyiakal leads the company out through the post's gate, and a lancer rides down to the enumerator's building to deliver the keys. Aaltyn moves to the gate with several lancers to assure the gate is left as promised.

A glass later, Alyiakal and Aaltyn ride at the head of the company, except for the scouts several hundred yards farther west on the road.

"You think we'll see any brigands?" asks Alyiakal, not that he believes it's remotely likely.

"We might see their leavings, but that's about it," replies Aaltyn. "Did any of those orders and instructions you got mention postings for those in the company?"

"They only said that everyone in the company would get leave." Alyiakal goes on to explain, then adds, "Orders will come to Fyrad for those who haven't already received them. Mirror Lancer headquarters will get my next-to-last report about the time we get to Fyrad, no later than fiveday of the fourth eightday."

"That's a bit earlier than your orders, isn't it?"

"My orders said 'no later than' eightday of the eighth eightday. If I'd waited until then, we'd have been bivouacking in abandoned houses. In less than two eightdays, the barracks will be swallowed." *Getting the post closed earlier might just foil whatever plot or reason the Merchanters might have had to deal with you and force the Mirror Lancers to keep the post open longer.* Alyiakal chuckles, a sound both bitter and wry. "Sometimes, accomplishing orders better or earlier than expected is good for an officer. Sometimes, it's a disaster."

"How do you think this will turn out?"

"Everyone will have to spend more time in Fyrad, possibly being shifted through chores and duties the regular lancers there dislike. Even so, it will turn out better for everyone in the company, regardless of how headquarters feels. It won't make much difference for you. For me . . ." Alyiakal shrugs. "The best I can hope for is a notation that I accomplished the post closure as required."

Over the next three glasses, Alyiakal neither sees nor senses anyone except those in the company. He often senses the order/chaos patterns of various creatures, but none approach the road.

Several quints later, he senses a horse and rider concealed behind tall bushes down a lane heading south, possibly the same lane that company squad leaders reported being used by suspected brigands earlier. Once the company passes the lane, Alyiakal senses the rider turning south.

Probably reporting the Mirror Lancers are leaving.

There's nothing Alyiakal can do about that . . . or the road becoming more dangerous for travelers.

XXVI

The next two days repeat the first—long glasses riding along a rough road encountering a few local people, passing isolated groups of houses with too few dwellings to be considered hamlets, slowing the wagons to avoid or fill potholes that would break wheels, and always watching for the unexpected.

Slightly after noon on oneday, Alyiakal senses something larger and far more ordered ahead, and he finally says to Aaltyn, "What's ahead?"

"Shouldn't be that far to the Lower Ford bridge over the Great East River. We're making good progress."

To Alyiakal, it seems as slow as when he escorted wagons over the east pass into Kyphros, but he nods.

Another glass passes, and the road slowly descends. The trees become more scattered, with occasional clumps of reeds to the south, beyond which more trees, close to the size of those in the Great Forest, suggest it once stretched to the ocean. Before long he sees the Lower Ford bridge, an order-reinforced whitestone causeway that stretches almost a kay, with the Great East River flowing under the middle third.

Alyiakal easily senses the order-reinforced stone piers sunk a good fifteen yards into solid rock. While the causeway is wide enough for four wagons abreast, it has no side walls or railings, and the roadbed is only two yards above the water. "It's rather low. What about floods?"

"The water flows over it," replies Aaltyn. "Sometimes the Mirror Engineers have to rebuild the approaches to the causeway because they wash out, but that's usually in the Spring."

The First built the causeway but never bothered to finish the road? Or did they just build what they knew those who followed couldn't?

As Alyiakal nears the middle of the near-indestructible causeway, he discerns the order/chaos patterns of creatures in the water, including a stun lizard. He says nothing, although he worries about the lancers and wagons until they ride along the graystone road, past the causeway and well to the west.

The stun lizard reminds him of the Great Forest . . . and Adayal, and he wonders how she fares, even though he has no safe way to write. *Besides, she never once wrote you, and said you had a different life to live.*

Late on twoday, the company reaches the Great Canal, crosses it on a high bridge, and overnights at a waystation beside the ordered whitestone of the canal—a waystation with actual, if stark, barracks, clean water, and corrals for the mounts. The stone towpath makes the ride on threeday much easier, with another towpath waystation for overnight lodging.

Late midafternoon on fourday, Alyiakal and the company near the main north gate of the Fyrad post shared by the Mirror Engineers and Mirror Lancers.

"I've only been here briefly, less than a glass," Alyiakal says to Aaltyn. "Where do we go once we're inside the gates?"

"We turn right and follow the road inside the wall until we pass the main part of the harbor. There's another gate on the post's northwest side, but this is the way for wagons."

"That makes sense. Is Overcaptain Kymml the head of supply for the entire post or just the Mirror Lancers?"

"I don't know," replies Aaltyn. "He's definitely in charge of supply for the Mirror Lancers."

The company follows the supply road for a kay before Aaltyn points to a large graystone building ahead on the north side of the road. "That's where we're headed. The loading docks are on the west side. We unload everything to the dock, and the warehouse clerk checks it against the inventory. Then he gets an officer—sometimes it's the overcaptain, sometimes not—and he signs an acceptance, noting that everything's there or noting what wasn't delivered." Aaltyn grins. "After that, I don't know, but I imagine you have more papers to deal with."

"More than a few," replies Alyiakal. "The mounts go to the transfer stables, and there will be a tack room for the company's gear. An armorer will take custody of the firelances. While you're taking care of those details, I need to report to the subcommander's office, wherever that is."

"You can't miss it. The headquarters building is the big graystone building behind the circle with the statue."

"And the circle's right behind the northwest gate?" asks Alyiakal.

"Where else would it be, ser?" says Aaltyn wryly.

Alyiakal smiles in return. Every post headquarters building is located directly behind the post entry square or circle, except, of course, for Oldroad Post.

As soon as Alyiakal and Aaltyn rein up at the northern end of the loading docks, a Mirror Lancer squad leader appears at the end of the dock.

"Sers . . . Overcaptain Kymml will be here in just a bit. If you'd bring up the first wagon to about where you are . . ."

"We'll take care of it, Squad Leader," replies Alyiakal.

"If it's all the same to you, ser," says Aaltyn, "I'll have the squads move back and deal with the wagons, and you can go over the procedures with the overcaptain."

"I'd appreciate that." Alyiakal eases the mare just slightly north of the end of the loading dock and waits.

After a fraction of a quint, a trimly muscular overcaptain with gray hair and a weathered face steps out of the small building door beside the dock. "Overcaptain Alyiakal . . . it's good to see you made it."

"We've returned the wagon you were so kind to make available to us."

Kymml offers an amused smile. "It helps you, and we end up with four more wagons. A supply officer can't ever have enough wagons. Your captain said you had to close the post earlier than expected."

"The morass that took over most of Luuval has expanded. It swallowed the south wall of the post and began to undermine the barracks. It seemed foolish to risk men and materiel. There wasn't much more we could do, and, if you need to, you can put what we've brought to use sooner."

Kymml chuckles. "Those are words a supply officer loves to hear. You have the loadout inventory?"

"Right here."

"Good. If you'll hand over both copies, you and I can go over it as your men unload each wagon. My crew will take it from there."

Alyiakal ties his mount to the nearest hitching post, and for the next two glasses, he and Kymml check off each item.

When the last item is delivered to the loading dock and checked off, Kymml looks to Alyiakal. "Good clean job. You even included the wagons. We'll both sign each inventory and keep our copies. I'll have the final acceptance of all the goods from the post for you in the morning." Kymml then glances to Aaltyn and back to Alyiakal and says, "Until further notice, your company will be doing morning muster at the west end of the courtyard behind the transfer barracks. We don't need anything more from your men."

Both Alyiakal and Aaltyn nod, and Alyiakal says to Aaltyn, "If you'd take care of the horses and the billeting."

"Yes, ser."

After Aaltyn leaves to lead the company to the stables, Kymml says, "After you report to the subcommander, you've got space in the senior officers' quarters. I'm sure I'll see you at the evening mess."

"Thank you."

"No thanks necessary. Pleasure when things are done right."

As Alyiakal mounts the mare and guides her toward headquarters, he wonders if matters will go that smoothly with Subcommander Quellyt. When he reaches the building, he dismounts and ties the mare to the hitching rail at the side of the entry. He removes the leather folder with his orders, directives, and other documents from one of his saddlebags before making his way inside to the duty desk.

The duty squad leader looks up. "Yes, ser?"

"Overcaptain Alyiakal to see Subcommander Quellyt."

Alyiakal sees the confusion, and adds, "I'm not reporting. I was the post commander sent to Luuval to close the post. I'm here to report to the subcommander that all the weapons, mounts, equipment, and wagons have been successfully transferred. I think he'd like to hear that from me."

The squad leader tries not to swallow. "Yes, ser. This way, ser."

Alyiakal follows the squad leader to another anteroom, where a senior squad leader sits at a table desk.

"The overcaptain is here to report the closure of Luuval Post and the transfer of materiel."

"Just a moment, ser." The senior squad leader stands, walks to the door, and raps on it. "The overcaptain from Luuval, ser."

Alyiakal senses the surprise, but after a moment, he can half hear, half sense the words, "Have him come in."

"Ser." The senior squad leader opens the door and gestures.

"Thank you." Alyiakal keeps a pleasant expression on his face as he enters the study, slightly larger even than that of the subcommander of Southpoint Post.

As Alyiakal steps into the study and the squad leader closes the door behind him, Subcommander Quellyt stands. He is roughly the same height as Alyiakal, with blond hair holding a few silvered strands, but slenderer. His gray eyes are pleasant but intent, and Alyiakal has the instant impression that the subcommander is one of those officers who always seem in command of every situation. *That's one reason he's a subcommander.*

Alyiakal inclines his head respectfully and says, "Alyiakal'alt, ser, reporting on the successful closure of Luuval Post."

"Welcome to Fyrad, Overcaptain." Quellyt gestures to the center chair in front of his desk.

"Thank you, ser." Alyiakal seats himself.

"I was more than a little surprised to hear from you and from Overcaptain Kymml last eightday that you were moving so swiftly to close the post. What prompted that decision?"

Alyiakal senses a feeling of concern, but not irritation, behind the subcommander's words. Still, he replies carefully, "As I wrote in my last report, the size of the area subsiding south of the post began to increase rapidly. When we left the post last sixday, the subsidence had already undermined the entire south wall, and all of it had vanished into the morass, in addition to fifteen yards of the east and west walls. The unsafe area about to collapse was less than a yard from the south end of the barracks. Since the Captain-Commander had already ordered the closure, I saw no point in subjecting the men to the possibility of the same sort of sudden collapse that previously destroyed the city and killed thousands. It seemed both prudent and necessary to remove all the equipment and materiel as soon as possible, and to give the Imperial tariff enumerator as much time as possible to sell or otherwise dispose of what we could not remove."

"Your last report didn't indicate that such a collapse was that imminent."

"The speed with which the ground was collapsing has been increasing on a daily basis since I made that report."

"You're known as an officer who carefully documents his actions, Overcaptain. Am I correct in assuming that I would get a similar report from Captain Aaltyn or any of the squad leaders?"

"They all saw the walls and the southern part of the courtyard slowly fall into the morass, ser."

"Why did you put it that way, Alyiakal?"

"They saw what happened. I'm the one who made the judgment that the rate of destruction would continue and possibly increase."

Abruptly, Quellyt chuckles, then shakes his head.

Alyiakal waits, keeping a pleasant expression on his face.

After a long moment, the subcommander says, "Captain Kaern told me about your captain's insistence on an acceptance and transmittal letter for a sealed messenger bag purportedly from the Imperial Tariff Enumerator in Luuval. Why was that necessary?"

"Enumerator Chysrah was most insistent that I not close the post. So was his assistant, a magus Khyental, who seemed reluctant to let me meet with the enumerator. Khyental vanished, and Chysrah sent a note asking about him. I replied that I hadn't seen the enumerator. Then Chysrah appeared in my study and wanted to know what I knew. I'd only seen the magus twice: once when I tried to pay a call on Chysrah and Khyental told me he wasn't available, and later when they both came to my study to insist that I disobey orders and keep the post open. Outside of those two instances, I never saw the magus again."

"What do you think happened to him?"

"If I had to wager, I'd say he got careless and stepped on the crumbling ground at the edge of the morass. That almost happened to me when I checked on its progress toward the post. That's the only thing that makes sense."

"Is it that deep close to the edge?" asks Quellyt.

"I didn't try to measure it," replies Alyiakal dryly, "but a wall four yards high toppled into it, and most of it was underwater in a fraction of a quint and gone in a glass."

"What did the enumerator do?"

Alyiakal describes Chysrah's insistence on a special dispatch run and his reasons for not doing so.

"Do you think it was wise to deny his request?"

"I felt that carrying out my orders and protecting my men was more important than indulging him, especially since it would have made closing the post more difficult and since no traders were landing in Luuval and hadn't for more than a season, according to Captain Aaltyn."

"Saving your men." Quellyt frowns. "Yet, in the battles against the Kyphrans, if I read the reports correctly, you led your company against a thousand troopers. Was that to save your men?"

"Yes, ser. Any other action, in my opinion, would have resulted in greater losses. I might point out my companies have taken higher risks with fewer casualties."

Quellyt's voice remains calm. "So, if you'd care to tell me, why did you effectively delay whatever message the enumerator wanted to send?"

Alyiakal decides to gamble, by telling the truth. "Because of what I've observed. First, before I was ordered from Oldpost Road to Luuval, and at Luuval, the Merchanters and possibly the Imperial Tariff Enumerators have been involved in effectively levying tariffs higher that those posted."

"Why should that concern a loyal Mirror Lancer officer?"

"I worry that the excess funds aren't benefiting the Emperor or the Empire of Light, ser, or might even be being used to his detriment."

"Do you have any evidence of this?"

"Only what I learned from outland traders during my time as acting enumerator at Oldroad Post." Alyiakal begins to explain.

After Alyiakal finishes, Quellyt offers a wry smile, then says, "Why have you told me this?"

"Because lying would be worse in the long run."

The subcommander shakes his head. "You see too much for an officer as young as you are."

"That might be because I listened to my father."

"Possibly, but you're far from the only officer born of a talented senior officer."

"My mother died when I was young. I got to spend the last three years before Kynstaar with him. I sparred with him most nights, and he tried to teach me everything he could." *And got me tutors I shouldn't have had.*

"Interesting. That's not in your record. Then, there's no reason why it would be, but it explains your skill with arms . . . and perhaps more." Quellyt pauses. "You knew I'd question you, didn't you?"

"Yes, ser. I thought you'd want to know why I closed the post early."

"Since you're here earlier than expected, and since I doubt you'll want to burn all the home leave you've accrued, you'll be on duty here until oneday of the last eightday of Harvest. Unless you have any objection?"

"No, ser. I would like to request two days' leave during that period to attend the consorting ceremony of my best friend. It will be here in Fyrad. I don't know which two days yet, though."

"That didn't figure into closing the post early, I trust."

"No, ser. I wrote my friend that I couldn't attend but hoped I could see him after he was consorted when I got to Fyrad."

"Two days won't be a problem." Quellyt stands. "We'll talk about your duties tomorrow. I'll see you at evening mess, I trust?"

Alyiakal stands as well. "I'll be there, ser."

As Alyiakal hurries to find the visiting officers' quarters, he thinks over the brief meeting. He's definitely suspicious about being retained, if only temporarily, for "duties" at Fyrad and wonders why. Had Quellyt been ordered to keep him at Fyrad for a time or was the subcommander doing it on his own initiative? The latter possibility is unlikely, but the former would mean the Senior Imperial Tariff Enumerator and someone high in Mirror Lancer headquarters acted quickly. *Very quickly, and that's more than a little concerning.*

The officers' quarters are to the east of headquarters, and to the west of the stables. Alyiakal drops off his duffels at the quarters' entry and rides the mare to the officers' section of the stable.

"Ser," asks the ostler, "begging your pardon, but does your mount go to the main stables for reassignment?"

"Not for another four eightdays. I've been temporarily assigned to headquarters duties."

"Yes, ser. Thank you, ser."

Alyiakal returns to the officers' quarters to find he's been assigned a two-room suite. The sleeping room is rather small, but he'll enjoy the perquisite that goes with being a very junior senior officer. He shaves, washes up, and changes into a clean uniform, then makes his way to the officers' mess.

Entering the mess, he sees Aaltyn standing beside the junior officers' table talking to another captain, but before he can ask how matters went with the company after the unloading, Overcaptain Kymml gestures to him. Alyiakal moves to join Kymml, who is talking with a majer and a sub-majer.

"Alyiakal . . . I thought you should meet Majer Maerl and Sub-Majer If-lyn. Majer Maerl is the deputy post commander for the Mirror Lancer half of the post. Sub-Majer Iflyn runs operations."

"That's a fancy title," adds Iflyn, a narrow-shouldered man with a broad smile. "It means I keep the Engineers from planning things that won't work for lancers and persuading them that horses and lancers aren't made just of order and chaos."

"He does more than that," says Maerl, "but we'll leave it there. I heard you managed to close the post in Luuval . . . and early as well. Mirror Lancer headquarters should have assigned a real combat officer in the first place." He pauses. "You know why headquarters picked someone like you, don't you?"

"Senior enough to be a post commander, junior enough that those who wanted to keep it open had no idea who I was, and motivated enough to get the job done and get on with my next posting—something like that?"

Maerl laughs softly and adds, "And smart enough not to voice suspicions about those who wanted to keep it open."

But not smart enough to avoid some scrutiny, which is why you're stuck here on temporary duty. "There have been similar incidents, I take it?"

"Rumors only," says Iflyn sarcastically. "Just unfounded rumors."

Maerl winces. "Iflyn . . ."

"Alyiakal knows or he wouldn't have asked the question," replies Iflyn. "If anyone asks, you can say I mentioned the rumors. I'll never make subcommander, likely not even full majer."

Before either officer can speak again, Kymml says, "Here comes the subcommander."

When Subcommander Quellyt enters the mess, the officers stiffen, particularly those gathered around the junior officers' table.

"As you were," commands Quellyt. As the officers take their seats, Quellyt remains standing behind his chair and adds, "You may have noticed an unfamiliar face. This is Overcaptain Alyiakal, on temporary duty here for the next few eightdays before he leaves to become the deputy post commander at Lhaarat." Quellyt inclines his head to Alyiakal, then takes his seat at the head of the small senior officers' table.

As the most junior of the senior officers, Alyiakal is seated across from Kymml and to the left of Iflyn.

Quellyt lifts his wineglass and takes a small perfunctory sip, clearly to allow the others in the mess to drink. Then he smiles and says to Alyiakal, "I see you've met the other senior officers."

"Briefly. I had to stable my mount and put my gear in quarters . . . and make myself presentable after several days on the road."

"How long is the ride from Luuval?" asks Maerl. "It's one of the few posts I've never seen . . . and, of course, none of us have been to Guarstyad."

"With wagons, it takes a bit less than a full six days. That's if the Great East River isn't in flood."

"Alyiakal and Captain Aaltyn turned in the best wagon-loading plans and inventory I have ever seen," volunteers Kymml.

"And you've seen a lot," adds Iflyn.

"Captain Aaltyn is quite accomplished in dealing with records, and he was most helpful in getting the post closed," replies Alyiakal, wondering, just a bit, about why Kymml and Iflyn are so complimentary. He's not about to protest, but he remains wary.

The senior table is served first, and the fare is a white fish, in a white lemon sauce, accompanied by scalloped cheesed potatoes, and green beans served with small, white, buttered onions.

Alyiakal can't help smiling after several bites. "If this is any indication, you have good food."

"We do, indeed," says Quellyt. "It helps that we can get good fresh fish. You must have had some good fish at Guarstyad."

"We did, but with both Guarstyad and Oldroad Posts being newly established, outstanding fare wasn't exactly a priority with the Kyphrans mounting attacks."

"We heard that you found devices from the First," says Maerl. "Is that true or another rumor?"

"It's true. We did. After the fighting, some Magi'i came and took them. They likely brought them here, but I don't know. They said there was nothing new about them, and that they were similar to what the Mirror Engineers use today."

For the rest of the meal, Alyiakal answers questions between bites, about the dissidents and the forgotten road.

After dinner, he returns to his temporary quarters. He thinks about writing Saelora, but he feels exhausted, as much by dinner as by the long day, and one day won't make that much difference.

ALYIAKAL'ALT,
OVERCAPTAIN
Fyrad, Vaeyal

XXVII

Before breakfast on fiveday, Alyiakal arranges for all but one of his uniforms to be cleaned, threadbare as two of them are—and notes, again, that those two and possibly two others need replacement, something he should be able to do while he's in Fyrad. Given that he's had little chance to spend his pay, he can afford the expense of new uniforms, even the heavier winter uniforms he'll need in Lhaarat. After that, he writes a letter of commendation to Aaltyn and makes a copy to dispatch to Mirror Lancer headquarters, signing and sealing both.

Only then does he make his way to the mess, where the conversation is pleasant, polite, and sparse, and he learns the post tailor is better, and less expensive, for new uniforms, than any of the tailors in Fyrad.

Near the end of the meal, Subcommander Quellyt looks to Alyiakal. "We need to go over your duties. I'll see you in a glass. That should give you enough time for a final muster of your complement from Luuval."

"Thank you, ser," replies Alyiakal, realizing that he's been effectively transferred to Quellyt's command.

After leaving the mess, Alyiakal makes his way to the transfer barracks, where Aaltyn and the three squad leaders begin to muster the company.

"Good morning, ser," says Aaltyn.

"Good morning, Captain. When I leave after muster, you're in command." *At least until Quellyt or Mirror Lancer headquarters breaks up the company or reposts it elsewhere.* "Since we closed the post earlier than expected, I've been moved to another temporary duty, reporting to Subcommander Quellyt for the next few eightdays. I'll address the company briefly and then turn command over to you."

Once the company is mustered, Alyiakal steps forward and speaks, using a touch of order to strengthen and carry his voice. "All of you have worked hard and effectively during the last eightdays. Shutting down a post is not a glorious duty, but at times it is necessary. For your effectiveness and diligence at a time when the post lacked a full complement and several different commanders, especially while the post physically collapsed around you, I commend you for a task well done. I was assigned temporarily to close the post, and since that task has been successfully completed, I have been reassigned to other duties. I now officially turn command over to Captain Aaltyn, whom I personally commend for his efforts during a very challenging time." With that, Alyiakal turns to Aaltyn and hands him the sealed letter of commendation, adding quietly, "I'll be sending a copy to Mirror Lancer headquarters." Then he declares firmly, "You have command, Captain." After that he turns and walks away from the company.

Two quints later he arrives outside Subcommander Quellyt's study.

"You can go in, ser," says the squad leader at the desk, gesturing to the slightly open door.

"Thank you." Alyiakal opens it, finding both the subcommander and Majer Maerl in the study, with Maerl seated in one of the chairs in front of the desk. Behind him, the squad leader closes the door.

Quellyt gestures to the vacant chair. "Have a seat, Overcaptain."

Alyiakal seats himself.

Quellyt smiles pleasantly, then says, "Majer Maerl and I have been discussing possible duties for you. You're obviously one of the most experienced overcaptains in terms of combat, and it's clear that any group of Mirror Lancers would benefit from that kind of training under you. But . . . outside of the company from Luuval, which has already benefited from your training, most of the lancers here at Fyrad won't be in a combat situation soon, and Fyrad doesn't train recruits or junior officers."

"That won't change in the near future," adds Maerl.

"On the other hand," continues the subcommander, "you have a potentially bright future in the Mirror Lancers, and you clearly write well and effectively, but your administrative experience with larger posts is nonexistent. Majer Maerl could use some assistance in that area, and a short period of handling administrative matters should give you greater familiarity with how larger posts need to function and to respond to directives for maximum effectiveness."

"Thank you, ser," replies Alyiakal. "I appreciate the opportunity to gain that experience." He turns to Maerl. "And I appreciate your willingness to help me gain the necessary understanding." *Even if it may be a ruse to keep me under close surveillance and away from direct contact with most of the Mirror*

Lancers posted at Fyrad while someone reevaluates whether sending me to my next posting is a good idea.

"You've had considerable experience," continues Quellyt, "where you necessarily had to decide matters quickly and on your own initiative. You did so efficiently and effectively." His tone turns wry as he continues. "There are, unfortunately, instances where such effectiveness needs to be modified or delayed because of other imperatives required by either the Emperor or the Captain-Commander, or the Majer-Commander. Sometimes, those modifications cannot be spelled out, and a senior officer needs to be able to read between the lines of those directives."

"Yes, ser," replies Alyiakal. "More experience in learning to read between those lines is clearly a necessity for those in command of larger posts and commands." *Especially if they want to get promoted.*

"How did you interpret your orders to take command at Luuval?" asks Quellyt, almost idly.

"As a compromise," replies Alyiakal. "In order for the post to be closed, a senior officer had to be post commander. Headquarters chose one of the most junior overcaptains in the entire Mirror Lancers, suggesting that there were some other administrative concerns about the post. I had the impression that my task was to close the post as late as possible before the deadline in my orders. That was the way I planned the initial transportation of equipment. Unfortunately, the swamp bordering the post didn't care about implied imperatives, and when it destroyed part of the post, it became clear that I'd have to expedite the closure. I chose the safety of the lancers and preservation of supplies and equipment over a possible concern that was never revealed to me."

Quellyt nods. "That's what I thought, but I wanted you to make that clear. Situations you might encounter in the future may not be that clear-cut."

"I've had that feeling, ser."

The subcommander looks to the majer. "Is there anything you'd like to add?"

Maerl offered an amused smile. "Only that much of what you'll be reading and doing will seem dry and boring. It's definitely dry, but it's less boring if you understand it."

Alyiakal has a slightly more favorable impression of Maerl than of Quellyt, but first impressions can sometimes be misleading. *Sometimes, but usually not.* He'll just have to see.

Quellyt stands. "Then, Alyiakal, I'll leave you in Maerl's capable hands."

Alyiakal stands as well and inclines his head. "Thank you, ser." He follows the majer out of the study into the anteroom and then into the smaller adjoining study. The desk holds several boxes for papers, two partly filled, and one empty.

"Take a seat."

Alyiakal does.

"You've read the Mirror Lancer regulations for post commanders? Thoroughly?" Maerl's words are more statement than question.

"Yes, ser."

"I thought as much." Maerl pauses, then adds, "There's an empty study down the hall, the first door on the right. It was Captain Kaern's, but he's on home leave before reporting to his next posting. The desk has two stacks of papers. Read the shorter stack first. Take your time. I'll want to go over each one with you and get your recommendation. Don't rush. Consider each carefully. A glass past midday?"

"I'll start immediately. Does the study have writing materials?"

"It does."

"By your leave, ser?"

Maerl nods, a faintly amused expression on his face that matches what Alyiakal can sense. Although Alyiakal can't discern the source of that amusement, it might be the anomaly of an overcaptain slated for deputy command undertaking the duties of a second-posting captain.

After Alyiakal settles behind the empty desk, he picks up the first set of papers in the shorter stack, entitled "Recommended Disciplinary Action: Lancer Emaelt, Second Maintenance Company, Mirror Lancer Post, Fyrad." The key section regarding the offense reads:

> . . . *Lancer Emaelt was knowingly and willfully absent from his duties and did not return to the post until morning muster. He offered no explanation for his absence. There being no factors in mitigation, the recommendation is two eightdays in custody at hard labor, followed by discharge . . .*

Alyiakal rereads the recommendation, which bothers him, and then writes down a series of questions on a separate sheet and picks up the next set of documents, dealing with the failure of a produce factor to supply edible potatoes to the post. That document also raises questions, which he writes down.

Four glasses later, as he prepares to return to Majer Maerl, he gathers the documents he has reviewed and his questions and observations about each.

He can't help but be puzzled about the documents, which deal with a range of matters over the past two seasons.

"Do you have any general comments about what you've read?" asks Maerl.

"The documents span two seasons. As they're written, all seem to represent problems that were not fully described and where, without other information, the decision reached would seem problematical at best."

"Why don't you go through some of them and explain why you think that might be the case?"

Alyiakal nods, then begins, "There is no background on Lancer Emaelt. None. I've read more than a few disciplinary reports, and a single unexplained absence of less than a day in a noncombat situation shouldn't merit confinement at hard labor and discharge. Someone is hiding something, and I don't have the background knowledge to know what it is or the reasons for the concealment."

"You wouldn't approve of the sentence?"

"Not without knowing more. I'd be skeptical even if a senior officer insisted on imposing such a sentence."

"Why?"

"Because it's a bad precedent that undermines support of command authority." Alyiakal can sense a certain surprise from Maerl.

"Do you care to explain further?"

"Ser . . . lancers know life isn't fair. They know that at times command decisions seem arbitrary, but they're willing to accept decisions if there are reasons, even reasons they don't agree with—at least if that's not a pattern—but what they have trouble with is decisions that not only seem unfair, but that are handed down with no reason or rationale. Every time that occurs, a commander loses a bit of respect and authority."

"Surely, you're not saying that the lancers know what's right."

"No. I'm saying that the appearance of unfairness undermines authority." Alyiakal pauses, then adds, "And it's unwise to unnecessarily undermine your authority."

"Let's go on to the next one," says Maerl.

Again, Alyiakal can't sense any strong emotion. He continues, "In the instance of the produce factor, the settlement reached was that the factor had to provide another suitable shipment or repay the silvers he was paid. Perhaps I'm missing something, but that seems to send a message that the factor can get away with supplying unacceptable produce unless he's caught, and that he faces no real penalty for attempting to defraud the Mirror Lancers."

Maerl merely says, "What are your thoughts on the next set of documents?"

A glass later, after Alyiakal has offered his last observations, Maerl leans back slightly in his chair. "You don't miss much. Only a few things that you'd have no way to know, especially since you've never been posted to Cyad." He smiles wryly. "Forget about the remainder. Take the rest of the afternoon off and deal with personal things you need to do, like ordering new uniforms. Yours look a bit worn."

"They are. It's been three years since I was posted somewhere I could replace them."

Maerl stands. "Tomorrow, you'll start on real work. A number of reports need to be rewritten and improved. That will help me, and you'll learn a few things in the process. I'll see you at the mess tonight?"

"Yes, ser." Alyiakal stands, knowing that Maerl's expectation is a command. *Not that you have any intention of going anywhere else to eat.*

"Bring those papers back to the anteroom and give them to the squad leader." The majer smiles and adds, "They're real reports . . . or were before I went through them the way you did."

Alyiakal manages to conceal a wince. If he'd turned in reports like that, at Pemedra or Guarstyad or Oldroad Post, he'd certainly have heard about it . . . and not pleasantly.

"Until later," adds Maerl.

Alyiakal returns to his temporary study, and removes the sheets of paper he used for notes, tearing each sheet to shreds. Then he returns all the documents to the command squad leader, after which he leaves the headquarters building and heads to the base tailor's shop. There he arranges for six sets of uniforms, three of them summer and three winter.

With that taken care of, he returns to the headquarters building, since it's on the way out of the post, and stops by the headquarters duty desk.

"Ser?" asks the duty squad leader.

"I'm newly posted here, but I heard that a local factorage has some interesting goods. It's called Haansfel. Do you know about it?"

"I know it's on the harbor market square, ser."

"How would I get to it from the northwest gate?"

The squad leader smiles. "Just walk five blocks north, ser."

"Thank you." Alyiakal leaves the building, heads for the northwest gate, and continues walking north. The harbor market square extends half a kay on a side and is twice the size of the main market square in Geliendra, the largest market square Alyiakal has previously seen.

Alyiakal makes his way along the east side of the square, then starts along the north side when he catches sight of a signboard proclaiming HAANS-FEL FACTORAGE. The building is a third wider across the front than Vassyl's Factorage—except he realizes belatedly that factorage is no longer Vassyl's but is now Loraan House.

On the lower left corner of the front window Alyiakal catches sight of a small placard sign that proclaims:

LORAAN HOUSE
DISTRIBUTOR OF GREENBERRY SPIRITS

He smiles and makes his way inside.

A young man appears, catches sight of the uniform, and, after a moment, frowns.

Alyiakal guesses. "No . . . I'm not Captain Hyrsaal, but I am looking for Catriana." He can tell his words startle the young man.

After a moment, the youth says, "I'll take you to her stall." He turns.

Alyiakal follows him.

"Catriana . . . I have a visitor for you," says the youth cheerfully.

The petite young woman who turns from the shelves in the rear of the stall doesn't look anything like Alyiakal had visualized. Above the Merchanter blues she wears, her short hair is a silvery blond, and her eyes are black.

Alyiakal senses the stunned surprise, and quickly says, "We've never met. I'm Alyiakal."

Her mouth opens. Then she shakes her head. "Hyrsaal said you wouldn't be here until after the consorting." Her words are warm, but firm and some-how crisp.

"It's a long story. Circumstances changed my orders, and I got to Fyrad earlier. It appears that I will be there."

"Hyrsaal will be so pleased!"

The warmth and excitement in her voice is more than supported by the emotion Alyiakal senses.

Then she asks, "Can you come to dinner? At my sister's?"

Alyiakal shakes his head. "Not tonight. I have to eat with my new command-ing officer, but I wanted to let you know as soon as I could. I arrived in Fyrad last night." He pauses, then asks, "Do you know when Hyrsaal will arrive?"

"Only that it will be during the sixth eightday of Harvest. I'm guessing it will be sevenday or eightday."

"So . . . roughly two eightdays from now. I *should* be here, but nothing has gone as planned for the last two seasons."

Catriana raises her eyebrows.

Alyiakal briefly explains his assignment in Luuval.

Catriana is smiling even before he finishes. "Both Hyrsaal and Saelora have written that you're destined for an eventful life."

"Saelora has made her life meaningful and eventful. I've just tried to avoid disaster and stay alive."

"I doubt Saelora would accept that description," replies Catriana.

Alyiakal chuckles. "I fear she thinks too highly of me."

"You two make a perfect pair. She thinks the same of you."

He shakes his head. "I'm a third-generation Mirror Lancer. She's become a full Merchanter with her own house through her own ability." Before Catriana can reply, he goes on. "Congratulations, by the way."

For a moment, she looks confused, then replies, "For what?"

"Becoming a junior enumerator. Saelora wrote that you were an apprentice enumerator, but you're wearing the blues of a junior enumerator. That must be recent."

"Thank you. It was two eightdays ago." She gives him a wry smile. "Saelora was right. You don't miss much."

"More than you'd think," he says. "Now . . . if you'll excuse me, I need to get back to the post. Being late would be unwise."

"Alyiakal . . . thank you for coming. Hyrsaal would be pleased, and so am I."

"I'll be back when I know more."

"I'll be here, until Hyrsaal arrives."

Once he leaves the factorage, Alyiakal considers visiting the market square to look for a gift for Saelora, since he has more time than he'd suggested to Catriana, but decides against it. He'd rather not risk being late. Besides, he needs to finish unpacking.

After walking back and dealing with various chores, Alyiakal arrives at the mess half a quint early. For a brief time, he is the only senior officer, but Overcaptain Kymml soon joins him.

"Alyiakal, I hear you got the other job that falls to overcaptains."

"Besides supply, you mean?"

Kymml laughs. "The Mirror Lancers need three things: good combat officers and rankers, good supplies, and a flow of paper and directives. Most people think the only important posts are combat commands."

"Supplies," replies Alyiakal. "Without the extra firelances, we would have lost to the Kyphrans. That's why the Mirror Engineers rebuilt the old road. That way we could get supplies from Guarstyad in a day."

"Was it that close?"

"When it was all over, we had less than three companies and most of the lancers had no chaos left in their firelances."

"Word is that you didn't take many prisoners."

"Anyone who surrendered or who was captured and laid down their arms."

"How many Kyphran survivors?"

"Possibly a company."

"Out of fifteen hundred?" asks Kymml quietly.

"They didn't give us much choice. They kept attacking. They wanted the devices the First left in the ruins."

"Sending you to Luuval makes more sense, now." Kymml's laugh is sardonic.

"What makes more sense?" asks Sub-Majer Iflyn as he joins the two overcaptains.

"Alyiakal's assignment to Luuval and as the majer's de facto administrative officer," replies Kymml. "He doesn't have much exposure to high volumes of directives, forms, and other administrative trials."

Alyiakal senses that Kymml's reply isn't what he might have said in Iflyn's absence, but he offers a wry smile.

"We all need that experience," says Iflyn, "dry drudgery as it is." He glances toward the mess entry. "Here come the majer and subcommander."

Alyiakal and Kymml follow Iflyn to the senior officers' table, where they stand behind their chairs until Subcommander Quellyt says, "As you were."

After accomplishing the formalities, and all five have full wineglasses and platters of shellfish in a red wine glaze over rice, with a side of roasted squash slices, Quellyt asks, "Are you getting settled in, Alyiakal?"

"Yes, ser."

"A bit different, I'd wager."

"Fyrad's the largest post I've experienced."

"Where else have you had duties?"

"Syadtar, Pemedra, Guarstyad, Oldroad Post, and Luuval."

"Syadtar?" muses Quellyt.

"I had a little more than an eightday of training duty there before Pemedra."

"Just enough to get a feel of the post?"

"A very little bit, ser."

"Have you been on or passed through other posts?" asks Kymml. "Not waystations."

"Geliendra and Northpoint."

"Northpoint?" asks Quellyt.

"In the last years before Kynstaar, my father was in command there. My mother died when I was young, but I was close to going to Kynstaar, so that was allowed."

"You've had a wider range of post experiences than most junior overcaptains," says Maerl.

"But not in Cyad or, until now, in Fyrad," Alyiakal points out.

"The next few eightdays will help with Fyrad," says Maerl. "I saw you heading out toward the tailor's shop."

"I took care of that as soon as I could."

"Do you have any friends here?" asks Iflyn.

"No, but I hope to meet a friend from Vaeyal. He's taking his home leave here and getting consorted."

"If he's your age, that's a bit young," says Iflyn.

"It all depends on the woman," says Kymml. "Naarlyn and I consorted young, and it worked."

Iflyn frowns for an instant, looking as if he wants to speak, but doesn't.

Alyiakal feels certain that the sub-majer thought about pointing out that Kymml had been a ranker, possibly a squad leader, and had no idea he'd become an officer when he consorted.

Before anyone else speaks, Quellyt interjects, "As Kymml put it, it all depends on both, not just the woman." Then he looks to Alyiakal. "I wish your friend well."

Then Maerl cuts in, "I didn't realize we were getting the blue crabs tonight." He looks to Alyiakal. "Enjoy them. They're tasty, and we don't get them often . . . unlike the clams."

"You can say that again," adds Kymml. "If you were here for a full tour, you might not ever want to taste clams again." Then he looks at Iflyn and grins. "Except a very few officers *are* partial to clams."

From that point on, Alyiakal knows, the conversation will be light. He wonders why Quellyt wanted the others to know Alyiakal's posts, because he doubts the subcommander had just been making conversation.

XXVIII

For the next two days, Alyiakal reviews and comments on every single piece of administrative and disciplinary paperwork coming to the Fyrad Mirror Lancer post.

A glass before midday on eightday, he saddles the gray mare and rides out through the northwest gate, following the carefully written directions to Catriana's sister's house. The first kay takes him past the port-related shops and trades between the post and the docks, and through the harbor market square. He continues past another trade and craft section into a welter of small houses and cots, bordered by higher ground, where he catches glimpses of large houses and several mansions.

In time, the avenue becomes a road. After another kay, he turns down a lane flanked by roughly trimmed hedgerows. Several hundred yards past a narrow lane leading to a dwelling—larger than a cot, but barely a house—and a small outbuilding, perhaps a stable for a few horses, he finally reaches a gate, unlocked as Catriana has promised.

Alyiakal closes it behind him and the mare, and follows the brick-paved drive toward a modest two-story brick dwelling nestled between a stable and a substantial barn.

Alyiakal knows that Catriana's sister married a successful smallholder, but from the look of the lands and the buildings, the smallholder is more than merely successful. Alyiakal concentrates to remember their names—Elina and Dyrkan. Then, belatedly, he realizes the small house he passed just before the gate has to be the cot Catriana has built.

Hyrsaal's definitely fortunate in her.

As Alyiakal nears the house, he sees Catriana on the covered porch that wraps around the entire dwelling. She points to the stable, then walks toward it to open the door as Alyiakal rides up. She wears the Merchanter-blue vest and trousers, but a white shirt rather than full blues.

"You're early. Saelora wrote that you're always early. Hyrsaal never is, but he's seldom late, either. The first stall is for visitors. Dyrkan says, that way, if he doesn't have time to clean the rest of the stable, most visitors won't notice."

Alyiakal dismounts. "I'd still wager that the stable is clean most of the time."

"You'd be right."

"Have you heard anything from Saelora?" asks Alyiakal. "Since I had to close the Luuval Post early, anything she wrote recently is either lost or hasn't caught up with me. I couldn't even post my last letter to her until this last fourday. At best, she might get it tomorrow."

Catriana smiles. "I haven't heard from her in an eightday. That was about Loraan House, but she did say she looked forward to seeing you."

"I'm looking forward to seeing her." *More than a little.* "This time . . ." Alyiakal breaks off the words.

"This time you won't have to deal with Marenda?" asks Catriana in a tone both understanding and amused.

"I had thought that," Alyiakal admits, "but you've had to deal with her for years."

Catriana shakes her head. "I don't deal with her, and I won't. She's welcome to come, but Elina and I—and Hyrsaal—are paying for everything. It's our consorting, not hers. I can see why Saelora bought her own house and moved out."

"I saw it right after she got it, and I want to see what she's done."

"I'm sure it is both practical and tasteful." Catriana gestures toward the stall.

Alyiakal smiles sheepishly and leads the mare in, following Catriana to a side porch after settling the mare.

There, a slightly older woman, who can only be Elina, joins them. She has the same silver-blond hair as her younger sister, but her eyes are gray. She stands several digits taller, with broader shoulders. "I'm so glad you could come."

"I'm honored you and Catriana asked me. You don't know me at all."

Elina smiles. "You're Hyrsaal's friend. That's enough."

Alyiakal laughs softly. "Only because he's very careful making friends. Meeting Hyrsaal on the way to Kynstaar was one of the best encounters in my life."

"He's said the same thing about you," replies Catriana.

"You haven't heard more about when he'll be here?" asks Alyiakal.

"No. His last letter said I probably wouldn't, since by the time he found out, he'd get here faster than another letter."

"And letters are expensive," adds Elina.

"Anything worthwhile is," says Dyrkan, standing in the doorway and looking to Elina. "You're needed in the kitchen for a moment . . . and then the nursery."

Elina laughs cheerfully. "Even with help, there's scarcely a moment's peace." She turns and hurries inside.

Alyiakal is struck by how high Dyrkan's order and chaos levels are, and yet how balanced. He radiates a sense of solidity and stability, although he's only a digit or two taller than Elina.

"We should all go inside to the parlor," Dyrkan says. "In case you haven't guessed, I'm Dyrkan." Then he holds the door open.

"And I'm Hyrsaal's friend Alyiakal." He gestures for Catriana to precede him, then follows her. Once inside, he glances around the parlor, which holds sturdy but well-crafted dark oak furniture, including two small chairs, one on each side of a small table.

"That's where Kandara and Dyrkyl sit when they mind their manners and listen," says Dyrkan. "That occurs less often than I'd hoped and more than Elina believed possible. Would you like something to drink? We're limited to dark lager, pale ale, and passable red or white wine."

"You should try the lager or ale," says Catriana. "They're both from Dyrkan's brewhouse, and they're good enough that the Harbor Inn features them."

"Then I'll have the pale ale," replies Alyiakal, preferring a lighter brew over those that require chewing to swallow.

"That's Elina's choice," says Catriana, "and mine, too."

By the time Dyrkan provides two beakers of the pale ale, Elina returns, with an ale, while Dyrkan has a lager so dark it looks black, confirming Alyiakal's choice. Alyiakal takes one of the cushioned wooden armchairs, as do Elina and Dyrkan, while Catriana perches on one side of the settee.

Alyiakal finds the ale light, smooth, and subtle, although he'd be hard-pressed to describe the flavors. "This is the best ale I've ever had."

Dyrkan starts to reply, "Then you must not—"

"*Dearest*," says Elina firmly, but warmly. "It may not be your very, very best, but even the dark angels couldn't deny how good it is. The Harbor Inn wouldn't be paying you what they do if it weren't."

"Do you have other secrets besides creating excellent brews and being one of the most successful smallholders in or around Fyrad?" asks Alyiakal.

"None except having the best consort I could possibly have," replies Dyrkan in a cheerful tone that understates the deep conviction behind the words.

"The brews are a secret," says Catriana. "His success in reclaiming and rebuilding what everyone else thought were worn-out lands isn't secret at all."

"Too many people still think he uses order and chaos," adds Elina.

"It's all about replenishing what's in the soil by what you plant," says Dyrkan, "and where you plant it, tilling as little as possible and planting radishes and groundnuts regularly. You want as little bare ground as possible. That way, good soil doesn't get blown or washed away. There's more to it than that, of course."

"Groundnuts?" Alyiakal has never liked their taste, even roasted.

"I mix them with the other food I give the hogs."

"We can continue over dinner," says Elina dryly. "I can't count on Kandara and Dyrkyl behaving for too long, and that's not fair to Maerthe."

"She's Dyrkan's cousin," adds Catriana, standing.

In moments, the four sit at the table, and a serving girl appears with platters of sliced roasted chicken with a brown sauce, cheesed lace potatoes, and pickled strips of quilla.

"You must try Elina's quilla," insists Catriana. "It's wonderful, and I hate most quilla."

"Dyrkan's mother taught me," Elina says.

"After practically forcing it on you," replies Dyrkan.

Alyiakal cuts a small morsel of the quilla and tastes it. While he doesn't find it wonderful, it's pleasant enough, unlike most quilla, which he finds close to inedible. "I have to say that it's the best quilla I've ever had." Which is absolutely true, and Alyiakal will be able to eat the rest without forcing it down.

"I told you!" exclaims Catriana.

Dyrkan clears his throat. "If I might, I have a few questions, Alyiakal."

"Of course," agrees Alyiakal.

"You were in Guarstyad, and a little bird suggested you might know something about a certain mushroom growing on the roots of certain trees."

"They grow on or around the roots of mountain holly oaks, but I was led to believe other oaks might do as well. Other than that, I don't know much more, except traders from Fyrad buy them from the one hamlet where they're grown. Oh . . . yes, they take a certain amount of care and don't travel far very well, which may be why only traders from Fyrad are interested."

Dyrkan nods, then says, "They have a different kind of oxen, don't they?"

Alyiakal relates what he recalls about the mountain musk oxen.

"It doesn't sound like either would do well here. That's a pity . . ."

For the rest of the meal Alyiakal answers Dyrkan's questions, largely on grower-related matters, and touching only lightly on Alyiakal's lancer career, which is fine with him.

When it is time to leave, Alyiakal tenders his thanks, remarking to Dyrkan, "I really don't know how to repay you and Elina for such a good dinner."

"Oh," replies the smallholder cheerfully, "you already did. I seldom get to ask someone well-traveled about possibilities or grower practices in other parts of Cyador or Candar." He lowers his voice, adding, "The few lancers I've talked to don't notice a fraction of what you do. Next time, I won't take all your time with my questions."

Alyiakal smiles. "You can ask all you want, but you've exhausted all I know about growers elsewhere."

"Then I'll wait until you're posted somewhere new." With a parting smile, Dyrkan turns, leaving Alyiakal with Catriana by the door to the porch.

"I have to thank you, especially," Alyiakal says to her, "for arranging everything."

"I didn't have to arrange anything. I just told Elina you arrived earlier than expected, and she said you had to come to dinner." She pauses. "If you come by the factorage around mid-eightday, I might know more about when Hyrsaal will arrive." She grimaces. "Except if I know, it will mean he'll be later."

"I doubt he'll be that much later," declares Alyiakal, "but I'll stop by."

"Good. I'll see you then."

While Catriana walks back to the stable with Alyiakal, neither says much, and before long he rides back to the post, thinking over what he's seen and heard.

XXIX

Over the next ten days, Alyiakal spends most of his time reviewing and rewriting various documents. He picks up and pays for his new uniforms and stops by the Haansfel Factorage twice, but Catriana has not heard from either Hyrsaal or Saelora. Nor has Alyiakal.

After breakfast on threeday morning, Alyiakal sees that Aaltyn is free and joins him, asking, "Do you know where you'll be posted?"

"Majer Maerl says I'll get orders any time, but I'm supposed to meet with someone in the next few days. He didn't know who, just that someone was coming from Cyad and wanted to talk to me about the condition of the post."

"I'm more than certain some commanders in Cyad are having trouble believing my report. They'll be even more surprised, I'm afraid."

"You think the post will disappear like the main part of Luuval?"

"Sooner or later. Sooner, I suspect."

"You knew that all along, ser. How?"

"Because there was no trace of anything that collapsed into the morass after a day or so. That means the morass is deeper than anyone thought. Also, the Mirror Engineers couldn't create a clear channel." Alyiakal pauses. "I'd like to know where you'll be posted, whenever you find out."

"I'll let you know, ser."

"Thank you."

As Alyiakal heads for headquarters, he has no doubts whoever is coming to talk to Aaltyn won't stop with the captain. He does wonder why Maerl would tell Aaltyn and think Alyiakal wouldn't find out. *Or did Quellyt instruct Maerl not to tell you?*

If that's so, then Maerl's not happy with Quellyt or he's setting it up to reflect badly on the subcommander. *If not both.*

In less than a quint, Alyiakal is at his desk looking at more paperwork, a directive from Mirror Lancer headquarters to reduce the amount of firelance training in areas not subject to attack or not dealing with smuggling or road brigandage. The note on top is from Maerl and simply says, "Your thoughts?"

Alyiakal's first thought is it's a good idea if it makes more chaos replenishment possible for border posts, but he's skeptical of making replenishing firelances harder. His second thought is that he should only mention the border posts—and that's what he writes in his short reply.

Then he reads about replacing the sewer line from the mess hall to the covered cesspit, realizing that, while the document details the necessary steps and estimated cost for replacement, there's no explanation of why it needs to be replaced.

More than a glass later, a ranker knocks on the half-open door. "Ser, I have a letter for you."

Alyiakal stands and walks to the door, where he takes the letter from the messenger. He sees that it's from Saelora by the envelope, but he does not smile, not yet, and only replies, "Thank you."

"My pleasure, ser." The ranker does not flee, but his departure is quick, and Alyiakal can sense wariness.

Is that because you're an unknown senior officer . . . or has he overheard something? Alyiakal suspects both. He closes the study door and walks back to the table desk. He does smile as he slits open the envelope and begins to read.

> *Alyiakal—*
>
> *I'm so glad you can come to Hyrsaal and Catriana's consorting! I got your letter and one from Catriana at the same time. There's so much I want to tell you, but I wanted to get this off to you.*
>
> *Catriana was stunned when you showed up at Haansfel. She had no idea who the handsome overcaptain was until you gave your name. She wrote that I'd never said just how good-looking you were. You are, you know, but it's in a quiet way, and I find that most appealing.*
>
> *Since I'll be coming to Fyrad for the consorting, I've arranged for canal passage for my wagon and two guards. That way I can bring more brandy to Fyrad in a less costly way—since I have to come anyway. I can also bring back any goods I find might to sell here. I don't know if you can travel back to Vaeyal with me, but I'd like it if you could.*
>
> *Mother won't speak about the consorting. I fear that Hyrsaal will get a cold welcome when he stops here on the way to Fyrad. I wrote him a season ago about Mother's feelings. He wrote back that he'd still stop by to see Gaaran and . . . and Mother, if she'll see him. She will, and she'll try to make him feel guilty. She doesn't ask about you anymore. That's for the best . . .*

After finishing the letter and thinking about Marenda, Alyiakal wants to shake his head. *If Mother were still alive, she wouldn't be like that.* But then, that's easy to think. Hyrsaal has to deal with his mother as she is.

He slips the letter back into the envelope and looks at the stack of papers in the inbox. Then he picks up the next one.

XXX

When he wakes on sevenday morning, Alyiakal wonders when he might see or hear about Hyrsaal. If Hyrsaal left Lhaarat as planned, and no later than eightday of the fifth eightday of Harvest, he should reach Vaeyal in the next few days. However, it's two days by firewagon from Vaeyal to Fyrad, and Hyrsaal *is* stopping in Vaeyal first. Even with the way Marenda feels, Alyiakal doesn't see Hyrsaal spending less than a few days there.

But you never know.

After breakfast, Alyiakal is finishing the last of the paperwork from the majer when Maerl appears in his doorway.

"I thought you'd like to know that you were right about Luuval Post," Maerl announces in a matter-of-fact tone.

"In what way, ser?"

"The post is gone. The *Kief* arrived in Fyrad last night, and the subcommander got a report that the bog swallowed everything, including the Imperial tariff enumerator's buildings. Those locals who survived said it happened late at night five days after you left. Apparently, the enumerator and his staff did not escape."

"That was over two eightdays ago," says Alyiakal, "and he just found out?"

"The *Kief* arrived there this past twoday. The ship spent two days looking into the situation, then headed here."

Alyiakal feels unsettled, especially since Maerl is definitely hiding something. He suspects Cyad sent the fireship directly to Luuval in response to whatever message Enumerator Chysrah sent.

"The subcommander is being briefed right now. It might be best if you remained available to answer any questions after the briefing."

Alyiakal considers asking who might be briefing the subcommander, then decides against it, instead gesturing to the short stack of papers. "I didn't have any other plans."

"How are you coming?"

"I'm about done."

"Good. Your work has been most helpful. I hope you've gained a certain insight that will prove useful in future postings."

"I'm sure it will."

"Until later, then." Maerl leaves the door ajar when he departs.

Alyiakal extends his order/chaos senses and finds a higher level of free chaos in the subcommander's anteroom and even more behind the closed door of Quellyt's study. He smiles wryly, checking his shields before returning his attention to the document before him.

Two quints pass before the subcommander's squad leader raps on the door. "Ser, the subcommander would like you to join him."

Alyiakal stands, unhurriedly, then follows the squad leader back to the anteroom.

The squad leader knocks on the closed study door and says, "Overcaptain Alyiakal, ser."

"Have him come in."

The squad leader opens the study door, closing it as soon as Alyiakal enters.

Seated at the side of the desk, facing the empty chair, is a magus with the silver starburst signifying one of the senior Magi'i.

"Overcaptain, this is Senior Magus Kharlt. He's here to follow up on events at the Mirror Lancers' Luuval Post."

"And a few other aspects," adds the round-faced magus in a pleasant voice that carries a slight edge. "You don't look surprised to see me, Overcaptain. Why is that?"

"When I was in command of Luuval Post, Enumerator Chysrah's assistant was a magus. He vanished, and Enumerator Chysrah sent a sealed message bag to Cyad. While I believe the assistant's carelessness around the morass caused his disappearance, I'm scarcely surprised that the Magi'i would want to look into it."

"Did you have anything to do with his disappearance?"

"As I reported and as I've told Subcommander Quellyt, I didn't even see the magus on the day he disappeared. Nor did any lancer or officer in the post."

"Then why did you delay the sending of the message bag?"

"I didn't delay it. I refused to send a special dispatch, which would have required additional troopers at a time when the post was understrength, and I was under orders to expedite its closure." Alyiakal provides, essentially, the same explanation and details he'd earlier provided Quellyt.

For a glass, the magus interrogates Alyiakal, going over and over the questions previously asked by the subcommander. Alyiakal answers patiently and consistently.

Abruptly, Kharlt says, "According to your records, you have slightly higher order levels and are an accomplished field healer."

"I was fortunate to get additional training at Kynstaar and at Syadtar, and I've learned from experience."

"Healers don't have shields. You do."

"The two Magi'i with whom I worked in building the Oldroad Post buildings also told me as much. They said I had strong natural shields. Two years prior I was interviewed, along with every other officer at Geliendra Post, by the Third Magus of the Magi'i."

Quellyt looks to Kharlt. "You already mentioned that."

"I wanted to hear what the overcaptain said."

"Is that a problem?" asks Alyiakal.

"So long as you only have shields, it's not," says Kharlt. "However, if you can handle and manipulate any significant amount of chaos, then you're a mage, and you could be a danger to yourself or others."

"I've been a lancer for nine years, counting Kynstaar, going on ten. If I could use chaos, wouldn't it have showed up before now?"

"It should have, but one never knows."

"Wouldn't the Third Magus certainly have known?" asks Alyiakal evenly.

Kharlt does not speak.

Quellyt looks to the senior magus. "Overcaptain Alyiakal has an exemplary record as a combat officer. He's been given orders as deputy post commander in Lhaarat. We need officers like him to deal with the problems on the borders. He's been examined by Magi'i for years. Now, you're implying he's somehow a problem because he saw a possible danger and closed a post before the Merchanters wanted it closed."

Again, Kharlt is silent.

From the increased churning of the chaos around the senior magus, Alyiakal suspects that Kharlt isn't pleased with Quellyt's statement.

Finally, the magus says, "The First Magus is always concerned when a magus disappears, just as the Captain-Commander of the Mirror Lancers should be concerned about officers who are far more effective than could be reasonably expected."

"Most honored Senior Magus," replies Quellyt, his tone cool, "I don't believe it is in your purview to suggest what the concerns of the Captain-Commander should be. Also, I do not appreciate your efforts to raise suspicions of an officer with an unblemished record at a time when good and effective combat commanders are needed more than ever. Unless, of course, you have hard evidence with which to back those suspicions."

"It's often said, and true, that where there is smoke, there is flame," says the magus.

"I'd agree," declares Quellyt, "but I'd say that you're looking in the wrong place for the flame. First, no one in an entire company saw your magus. Second, that morass swallowed most of a town without warning, and all the buildings of a closed post and of the Imperial Enumerator just as suddenly. Third, Overcaptain Alyiakal warned the Imperial tariff enumerator about the possible danger before he closed the post and removed the company. He was not anywhere near when all those happened."

Alyiakal can sense the subcommander's growing irritation.

Apparently, so can Kharlt, who abruptly stands and says, "I've conveyed the information to you. I leave the matter in your hands." Then he turns and leaves the study, closing the door firmly.

Surprisingly, Quellyt laughs, then shakes his head, before looking at Alyiakal and asking, "What in the name of the Rational Stars did you do to get the Magi'i so concerned?"

"I don't think *all* the Magi'i are concerned, just those close to certain Merchanters. Do you honestly think that I'd be here after being examined in person by the Third Magus, if he'd thought I'd be a danger to anyone?"

"That thought had crossed my mind. You didn't finish answering my question, though."

"Let me tell you what happened in my last season at Oldroad Post." Alyiakal recounts what he learned from the traders and what he suspects about the Imperial tariff enumerators overtariffing outland traders and funneling the golds elsewhere. When he finishes, he simply waits.

"I don't doubt it," says Quellyt, adding wryly, "but there's no way to prove it."

"That's why I only reported what I did," replies Alyiakal. "I know what the outland traders said, but I didn't know if they'd confirm it if questioned."

"Probably not, but their choice of where they entered Cyador speaks for itself." Quellyt pauses, then continues, "A solid few years as a deputy post commander in Lhaarat and no one will recall a missing magus, especially when an entire town, a complete post, an enumerator's building, *and* the enumerator all got swallowed by a frigging swamp. When does your friend get consorted?"

"The eightday after the one tomorrow, or the one following, depending on when he gets here from Lhaarat."

Quellyt nods. "We'll end your temporary duty an eightday from now, and you can begin your home leave the next day."

"Thank you, ser."

"Majer Maerl will have a few more documents for you to review, but I doubt they'll tariff you unduly." With that, the subcommander stands.

Alyiakal inclines his head respectfully, then turns and leaves the study.

He senses Kharlt waiting outside the door to his temporary study but continues down the corridor until he reaches the senior magus. "You have a word for me, Senior Magus?"

"I cannot prove what I know, Overcaptain, but I believe you are more than you present. Perhaps I am wrong, and you are not. Either way, you're treading a dangerous path."

Alyiakal has known that for years, but asks, "Why do you say that?"

"Because I've never encountered natural shields as strong as yours, with an exception or two among healers."

"I've been told by one healer that I was close to being a healer." Alyiakal isn't about to mention that Vayidra had really said that he could be more than that.

"Oh, there's no doubt of that. You carry enough order that your touch will at least blunt wound chaos. I suspect you could be approved as a healer—if, of course, you were a woman, but everyone is suspicious of men who are healers."

"I'm only a field healer."

"And that is how matters should remain, Overcaptain. If you think it over, I'm sure you will agree." Kharlt offers a cold smile, then turns and strides down the corridor.

Alyiakal would like to have followed the magus under a concealment, but using one, which any mage could sense, would have shown Kharlt that Alyiakal had at least some abilities as a mage—something Alyiakal can't afford. Instead, he steps into the study and walks to the single narrow window, looking out without seeing anything. Both the subcommander and the senior magus had given him the same advice—be a good combat commander and a field healer and don't do anything involved with magery.

In some ways, the subcommander's reaction to Kharlt surprised Alyiakal. Then again, Kharlt essentially told Quellyt to get rid of a good officer for no reason beyond the disappearance of a magus. He had also been more than slightly condescending, which grated on the subcommander. It's not lost on

Alyiakal that terminating the temporary duty on the subcommander's projected date meant that Alyiakal would be effectively unreachable until he reported to Lhaarat. *Which is where everyone wants you.*

Vayidra had warned him in no uncertain terms, and the fact that the Third Magus mentioned Alyiakal to other Magi'i is more than merely concerning. Vayidra could have provided good advice, but writing a Magi'i healer would alert higher Mirror Lancer officers, just like writing Adayal would . . . if he even had any idea where to write.

Lhaarat definitely looks like a good post for the next few years.

XXXI

A knock breaks Alyiakal's concentration in late midafternoon on fourday.

"Yes?"

"There's someone to see you, ser. A Captain Hyrsaal."

Alyiakal jumps to his feet, heading toward the door, which he opens to see a surprised ranker standing there. "Where is the captain?"

"At the duty desk, ser. Since he's not posted here . . ."

"I understand. Thank you." Alyiakal hurries to the duty desk.

Hyrsaal's flame hair is unchanged, but there are circles under his eyes, and he looks tired, not surprisingly, if he spent six days traveling, two days with Marenda, and then two more in a firewagon. When he sees Alyiakal, the tiredness vanishes with his infectiously warm smile.

Alyiakal can't help smiling back. "You saw Catriana first, I hope."

Hyrsaal's smile becomes a momentary grin. "I did. She said it would take a glass for her to turn everything over to the girl she's been training. So I thought I'd find you."

"You've had a pair of long eightdays, haven't you?"

"The two days in Vaeyal were longer, but we can talk about that later. I can't believe you're going to be here for the consorting."

"Sometimes these things even out. The last time we hoped to meet in Fyrad didn't happen. This time, because of a bog, it did."

"You're coming for dinner on eightday. Fourth glass of the afternoon. At Elina and Dyrkan's house. We can talk there. By then, I should know everything that Catriana and Elina have planned." Hyrsaal offers a wry expression.

"I'll be there." Alyiakal pauses. "Do you know when Saelora will arrive? She wrote me that she was bringing a wagon full of goods, mostly brandy, I gathered."

"Why do you think we're having a dinner on eightday? She's supposed to arrive on sixday or sevenday. I offered to come with her. She told me, very politely, that she had no intention of delaying my getting to Fyrad."

"That's Saelora, always thinking about others."

"In more ways than one." After the slightest hesitation, Hyrsaal asks, "When does your duty here end?"

"This sevenday. My home leave starts on eightday, but I can stay at the officers' quarters until after the ceremony. I'd thought I might accompany Saelora back to Vaeyal. Or, I could take a firewagon to Geliendra and stay there. That depends on what Saelora has planned."

"I could be wrong," says Hyrsaal with a smile, "but I don't think you'll need to use a firewagon until you leave for Lhaarat. I didn't tell you that, though."

"Just in case, I won't make any arrangements just yet."

"It's good to see you," says Hyrsaal, "but—"

"You don't want to keep Catriana waiting. Go!" Then Alyiakal adds with a wicked smile, "You've kept her waiting long enough."

"I'll see you on eightday." Hyrsaal turns and hurries off.

Alyiakal walks back to his study, thinking about Hyrsaal and Catriana, and about Saelora, wondering whether her feelings about life and about him have changed in ways that do not show in letters. What the two of them will say, do, and decide in the eightdays ahead.

XXXII

Late on sevenday afternoon, the squad leader from the subcommander's anteroom appears at Alyiakal's soon-to-be-vacated study, shortly after Alyiakal has finished reviewing the last of Maerl's documents.

"Ser, the subcommander would like to see you."

"Thank you. I'll be right there." Alyiakal picks up the leather folder holding his personal documents and follows the squad leader.

The door to Quellyt's study is open, and the subcommander motions for him to enter. Alyiakal does, closing the door.

"Majer Maerl has your orders as well as the endorsements of your temporary duty here at Fyrad. I wanted to compliment you on your handling of a difficult situation and wish you well at Lhaarat. I know you'll be staying at the post for a few days, but I might not have the opportunity for a private word before you leave."

"Thank you, ser. I appreciate having the opportunity to gain the experience."

"You're quite welcome." Quellyt stands. "After you get your orders from the majer, would you tell him that I'd like to see him for a moment?"

"I'll pass that on, ser. And thank you again." Alyiakal inclines his head respectfully, then walks from the study, leaving the door open.

Then he stops at Maerl's open door, knocking on the frame.

"Come on in, Alyiakal. I have your orders. We'll need an eightday notice on your travel." The majer stands and hands an envelope to Alyiakal, who slips it into his leather folder. "Overcaptain Kymml has your pay through tomorrow."

"Thank you, ser."

"You're welcome. I assume we'll be seeing you at the mess for the next few days."

"Yes, ser. Then I'll be going to Vaeyal and possibly Geliendra for the rest of my home leave."

"Friends, I assume?"

Alyiakal nods.

"Before you go, might I ask what you thought of Senior Magus Kharlt?"

"He is a senior magus, ser. He was ordered here. By whom"—*precisely*—"I have no idea, but I have strong doubts those orders would benefit the Mirror Lancers. That is only a feeling, however."

Maerl merely nods. "I wish you well."

"Thank you, ser." Alyiakal pauses, then adds, "Subcommander Quellyt would like to see you once we're finished."

"I won't keep you." The majer smiles. "Thank you for the message."

Alyiakal inclines his head and steps out of the office, moving to one side of the open doorway and glancing toward the squad leader's table desk. The squad leader nods to Alyiakal, then returns his attention to the papers before him.

Alyiakal takes two steps, then raises a concealment. Earlier, he hadn't used a concealment around Senior Magus Kharlt because Kharlt could have sensed his presence. There's also always the possibility that a magus or a talented Mirror Engineer might sense magery, so he's been wary of using any magery at all in Fyrad. *But neither are present in the headquarters building and this might be your last chance to hear something more . . .*

He eases quietly back into Quellyt's study and waits. The subcommander doesn't even look up until Majer Maerl arrives and closes the door.

"What do you think of the overcaptain, Maerl? No polite sowshit, either."

"He's much more competent as a combat commander than his record shows."

"His record shows a high level of competence. You're saying he's better than that?"

"I'd wager on it."

"What makes you think that?"

"What's not in his records. He was promoted to overcaptain extremely early after being chosen to command a border post, but there's only a standard letter of commendation. Five companies destroyed over a thousand Kyphran troopers. The Kyphrans had a magus and even a half score firelances. Two companies lost their captains and half their complement. Alyiakal lost maybe a fifth of his men and his wounded all survived. Yet his company engaged the Kyphrans more than any of the other companies."

"How did you find out all of that?" asks Quellyt.

"A few notes from someone who knew."

"One of your contacts in Cyad, I assume? Why did they tell you?"

"Because they want him in Lhaarat. Matters there could get worse."

"Good as he may be, I doubt that's the only reason," declares Quellyt.

A long silence follows, but, under a concealment, Alyiakal cannot see facial expressions and neither officer's body position changes.

Finally, Maerl speaks. "The Emperor is said to have recovered from his last illness, but he sees very few and holds no audiences. The whereabouts of the heir are not known."

"Not known to whom?"

"Both the Captain-Commander and the Majer-Commander have said they do not know . . . more than once."

"What in the name of the Rational Stars does this have to do with an accomplished but very junior overcaptain?" asks Quellyt, tapping his fingers on the desk.

"I have no idea. Those were the observations I received when, at your direction, I inquired about the overcaptain."

"He's very junior to have acquired enemies and supporters among the seniors of the Triad," says Quellyt evenly.

"He is *very* junior."

"You really don't know, do you?" Quellyt laughs softly. "Neither do I."

From the feelings and the order and chaos around each officer, Alyiakal surmises that both men are concerned, but more about the unsettled state of the Imperial succession than the puzzle of a junior overcaptain catching the attention of the seniors of the Triad.

"Leave the door open when you go," says Quellyt matter-of-factly.

Alyiakal slowly and carefully eases out of the subcommander's study, leaving space between him and Maerl. He does not drop the concealment until he is well away from the anteroom, and he senses no one nearby. He makes his way from the headquarters building, still thinking over what he heard.

The only officer in Cyad who knows about him is Commander Laartol. Possibly Commander Dahlvor, but Dahlvor seemed more interested in his own son and Baertal, both of whom might be overcaptains by now, although Alyiakal has no way of knowing. Laartol made sure Alyiakal was promoted early without overt signs of favoritism.

Rather, he'd decided on the facts—not favoritism—and made sure both you and Kortyl were promoted.

Still, Alyiakal can't help but worry—and trust nothing else interferes with his leave. He needs to get to Lhaarat without any more complications. In the meantime, he needs to pick up his pay.

XXXIII

Alyiakal tries not to hurry on eightday. After returning from breakfast, he writes a letter to Liathyr, from whom he hasn't heard in close to a season. While Liathyr has never been the most reliable of correspondents, and his posting at Chaelt isn't considered particularly dangerous, Alyiakal still worries. Then he spends time adding details to the map in his atlas depicting the area between Luuval and the Great Canal.

He leaves the post stable in early midafternoon, hazy and hot, as befits late Harvest, riding the gray mare past the harbor market square, far busier than he has seen before. As he continues north toward Elina and Dyrkan's not-so-smallholding, he sees fewer people out or on the road.

When Alyiakal rides up the stone-paved lane to the house, he's unsurprised to see Saelora on the side porch in her Merchanter blues. She hurries toward the stable and the high-sided enclosed wooden wagon outside the stable door. Painted on the side facing Alyiakal are the words LORAAN HOUSE, under which are VAEYAL, CYADOR in smaller letters. Alyiakal smiles, then calls out, "Handsome wagon!"

"Handsome officer!" she replies.

Alyiakal reins up outside the open stable door. Even before he dismounts, he can see and sense the warmth and love from Saelora. He looks at her, taking in her strikingly handsome face and figure and her short-cut, mahogany hair and warm brown eyes.

He barely has both boots on the ground, still holding the mare's reins in one hand, when Saelora's arms are around him and her body is tight to his.

"I can't believe you're here," she murmurs without releasing him in the slightest.

"I wondered . . ."

"Wondered?"

He holds her even tighter, then kisses her, with all the longing he hasn't realized he held. After a time, he whispers, "Not any longer."

In return, she kisses him, fiercely, yet with an underlying gentleness. When she releases him, keeping him in her arms, she asks quietly, with a trace of humor, "Wondered about what?"

"If you were really here. Seeing you . . . you were . . . you are . . . so alive, so real . . . that it felt unreal. That sounds strange . . . but . . ."

"It's not strange at all. When I see you . . . that feels unreal, too." She eases back from him, then says, "That scar on your forehead . . . ?"

"From the last battle with the Kyphrans."

"You never wrote that you were wounded."

"It wasn't serious. There wasn't any point in worrying you." He smiles. "I ought to stable the mare. She shouldn't stand out in the sun."

"Neither should we."

In less than half a quint, Alyiakal has the mare unsaddled and stalled, and the two leave the stable.

As they walk toward the house, he asks, "What's in the wagon?"

"Very little. I stopped and unloaded at Haansfel first. The way the good roads run, it worked better, since I'm staying here."

"Giving the about-to-be-consorted time together?"

"They wouldn't even notice I was here. The consorting is a necessary formality." Saelora's last words are wry.

"Did anyone else come with you?"

"Karola can't come, not with the children, and Mother's not about to. She says she's too old to travel that far for such a short time."

Alyiakal is certain that Marenda's words had been uttered with a degree of chill appropriate to the Roof of the World, but he only says, "What about your guards?"

"I hired canal guards. They stayed with me until I unloaded the wagon at Haansfel."

Alyiakal nods. "That makes sense, but then, you always do."

"Not always," she replies with a glint in her eyes. "There is a certain overcaptain very few have ever seen . . ."

Alyiakal leans toward her and brushes her cheek with his lips. "Just as there is this successful Merchanter no one has ever heard of."

When the two step onto the porch, Elina says, "That was quite a reunion."

"Three years is a long time," replies Alyiakal.

"I couldn't do what you two do." Elina shakes her head.

"People are all different, sometimes a lot," says Dyrkan from where he sits on a bench, a child on each side. He turns to the girl, whose white-blond hair looks just like her mother's. "Kandara, say 'Greetings' to Overcaptain Alyiakal."

"Greetings," says Kandara, giggling.

"We won't try that with Dyrkyl," explains Dyrkan. "He's a little young for conversation."

"We hope you don't mind," says Elina. "Dinner is a bit much for them, but we're trying to get them used to family first, and after your . . . reunion, Alyiakal, you definitely qualify as family."

Alyiakal finds himself blushing.

Saelora laughs, a low sound of warm amusement.

Not knowing what else to say, Alyiakal asks, "Are Hyrsaal and Catriana here yet?"

"They're in the kitchen," replies Elina. "Catriana did most of the dinner, with Luzza's help, and Hyrsaal managed not to get in the way."

"At times, I don't know what we'd have done without Catriana," says Dyrkan.

"You'd have starved, and I'd have died," replies Elina, with a smile, adding, "It seemed like that, anyway."

Those words explain, even more, to Alyiakal why Dyrkan's father had gifted the adjoining plot of land to Catriana.

"She's been a great help to me as well. I couldn't have done much in Fyrad without her," declares Saelora.

"You two also increased Haansfel's sales," says Dyrkan. "I've heard that from more than one person."

"That's what happens when people work together," replies Saelora.

Dyrkan laughs. "No. That's what *you* made happen. Too often, the greater the number of people involved, the greater the chance for mistakes and failure."

"Unless they agree on the objective and the way to achieve it," suggests Alyiakal.

"Too much of life isn't like the Mirror Lancers," counters Dyrkan.

"True," replies Alyiakal amiably. "Most times people don't die when they make stupid mistakes."

"You're not saying there aren't stupid officers, are you?" asks Dyrkan.

"Some," admits Alyiakal, "but most of the really stupid ones don't live to make captain or overcaptain. From what I've seen, bad decisions involving senior officers mostly come from conflicting objectives or imperatives mandated by headquarters."

"You sound like you have some experience with that," says Elina.

"If you're interested, when Hyrsaal and Catriana join us, I'll tell you about my temporary duty at Luuval."

"Until then, what can I get you two to drink?" asks Dyrkan, standing and then carrying young Dyrkyl to his mother.

At that moment, belatedly, Alyiakal realizes how much taller he and Saelora are than Dyrkan and Elina, something he hadn't even thought before. *That might be because Saelora wasn't here, and she's so much taller than most women.*

"The pale ale," says Saelora.

"The same," adds Alyiakal.

Elina stands and motions for Kandara to join her. "I'll be back in a few moments."

"Nap time?" asks Saelora.

"Quiet time, anyway, but Maerthe can deal with any unhappiness. Every once in a while, it's nice to have an uninterrupted meal. By the way, we'll stay out here until it's time to eat. The porch is cooler."

When Elina leaves, Alyiakal looks to Saelora. "Just the two of us for the moment. You look so good in those blues." He grins. "I like the bracelet, too."

"Someone with good taste gave it to me. I wear it everywhere. More than a few women have looked at it with envy. It's puzzled a few factors, Merchanters, and outland traders."

"Why? Because you're not consorted, and there's no man visible in your life?"

"It's also not delicate, while being striking and tasteful."

"I was fortunate to find it."

"You didn't just find it."

"I was looking for something special."

"How many shops did you visit?" she asks with an amused smile.

"A few."

Dyrkan's return spares Alyiakal from further interrogation.

The smallholder sets a tray on the side table next to the brick wall of the house. On it rest six beakers—four pale ales and two dark ales. "Catriana and Hyrsaal will be here shortly."

Saelora takes a pale ale, and Alyiakal another. Dyrkan takes one of the dark ales.

Hyrsaal appears next, picks up the remaining dark ale, looks at Alyiakal, and smiles sheepishly. "They banished me from the kitchen."

"So that Catriana might be able to concentrate on finishing fixing dinner?" asks Saelora in mock surprise.

"Elina won't let me set foot in the kitchen if she's in a hurry," Dyrkan says. "Neither will Luzza."

"For good reason," interjects Elina as she steps out onto the porch. "If it were possible, you'd burn water." She picks up the next to last pale ale and takes a healthy swallow.

"See what you have to look forward to," Hyrsaal declares to Alyiakal, unsuccessfully trying to sound doleful.

Saelora laughs. "Until you met Catriana, the only time you got near the kitchen was to snitch something. Usually something you weren't supposed to have."

"There are times," Dyrkan tells Hyrsaal, "when I'm glad that I never had sisters."

"That's because you never had any, until you consorted me," says Elina.

"And aren't you glad you did?" asks Catriana, as she steps out onto the porch, lifts the last beaker off the tray, and takes a small swallow.

"That was the best thing of all," says Dyrkan with an amused smile. "I got a charming and helpful sister without having to watch her grow up."

Saelora looks at Alyiakal, then takes his hand and squeezes it gently, before letting go.

She understands so much.

"Was having two sisters too much?" Saelora asks her brother.

Hyrsaal grins. "Not anymore."

The banter and light conversation continue for a quint before Catriana says, "We should go have dinner."

The six leave the porch and follow Catriana through the parlor to the dining room, where they seat themselves—Dyrkan at the head of the table, Elina at the foot, with Catriana on Dyrkan's right, Saelora on his left, Hyrsaal on Elina's right, and Alyiakal on her left.

Luzza appears and refills all the beakers, after which Dyrkan lifts his. "To the happy pair, Catriana and Hyrsaal."

"Catriana and Hyrsaal."

Luzza then serves, beginning with Dyrkan and then Elina.

The plate Luzza sets before Alyiakal holds sliced pork strips covered with a translucent green sauce, sautéed brown mushrooms, small new potatoes in butter and parsley, and green beans.

"That wouldn't be a greenberry-based glaze, would it?" Alyiakal looks first to Catriana and then to Saelora.

"It is," confirms Catriana.

"Wait until you taste it," adds Saelora.

Alyiakal doesn't wait long, only until Elina and Dyrkan lift their utensils, and cuts a small sliver of the pork. The taste is different but enhances the already tender meat. "That glaze . . . I can't describe it exactly, but the taste is outstanding." He pauses, then adds, "Maybe you should sell that as well."

"We've thought about it," admits Saelora, "but right now we're selling all the brandy we have. I bought some more land adjoining the swamp, but it will be another year or two before it's that productive."

"Maybe you should charge more for the brandy," says Dyrkan.

"We are, but I'm a little wary of raising prices enormously all at once."

Dyrkan nods. "There is that."

"Ah . . ." Alyiakal clears his throat. "You all know something I don't. When and where is the ceremony?"

Hyrsaal laughs boisterously. "Of course, you wouldn't know. We only got it worked out yesterday. We had to settle on next sevenday. Third glass of the afternoon. Lots of couples wanted to be consorted on a Harvest eightday. Would have been three eightdays to have a consorting in the Recording Hall, and Catriana deserves that."

"The people we wanted most are already here," adds Catriana, glancing from Saelora to Alyiakal.

"I've never been to a consorting ceremony," say Alyiakal. "Where is the Recording Hall, and what do I need to know?"

"The Recording Hall is two blocks north of the harbor market square," says Hyrsaal. "There's space for wagons and mounts in back."

"You don't need much," adds Catriana. "Just be at the Recording Hall two quints before the glass. I'd say appropriately attired, but Hyrsaal tells me that you're never inappropriately attired. The ceremony is short, less than two quints, and then we all come here for the consorting dinner."

Left unsaid, Alyiakal can tell, is that most of those at the dinner will be from Dyrkan's family.

After a momentary silence, Elina turns to Alyiakal. "You were going to tell us about your time in Luuval."

"Something about conflicts over priorities," says Dyrkan, adding, "Didn't most of Luuval fall into the ocean three or four years ago?"

"It did, and more since then." Alyiakal summarizes the difficulty in finding and keeping post commanders, dealing with the tariff enumerator, and closing the post. "I can't prove it, but I'm guessing that both the Merchanters in Cyad and the Senior Imperial Tariff Enumerator are working together to keep tariffs as high as possible. The tariff enumerators skim off the excess, and the Merchanters can charge more for their goods. Even after most of the city and the harbor were destroyed, both were concerned about smugglers using the remaining wharf. The Mirror Lancer high command wanted to close the post, but the—"

"The Merchanters and the mage who disappeared had something to do with the death of the post commander before you, I'd wager," interjects Hyrsaal, "and headquarters chose a junior combat officer barely senior enough to close the post. That's scarcely surprising. At Summerdock, there were certain patrols we weren't allowed to make because we might have caught Cyadoran Merchanters smuggling in goods that would have been highly tariffed."

"Smuggling by Cyadoran traders is tacitly allowed," says Dyrkan, "but not by outlanders. And those smuggled goods are priced almost as high as those that are tariffed, and the Merchanters make outlandish profits?"

"It would seem that way," suggests Alyiakal.

Dyrkan turns to Saelora. "Do you know anything more about this?"

Saelora offers a wry smile. "I'm selling to outland traders, not buying. Several complain about the high tariffs. They say that nowhere else charges as much. One said that in the Summer he sells various goods to Suthyan traders in Rulyarth. They sell them to Jeranyi smugglers who find ways to get them into Cyador."

"Is that why shimmersilk is so expensive?" asks Catriana.

"One of the reasons," says Alyiakal. "Also, the Hamorians don't allow outland traders to buy the cloth, only scarves or garments made from it. Hamorian traders alone can sell the cloth outside of Hamor. That's what outland traders told me."

"Someone knew that whoever commanded that post might be in danger," Hyrsaal continues. "Did anyone convey that to you?"

"No. I did discover that a senior overcaptain refused orders to Luuval. I didn't find out how the sub-majer before me died until I got there."

"Refused orders? That's unheard of," says Hyrsaal. "Especially to a non-combat post in a port town."

Particularly when an officer is allowed only one refusal in his entire career.

"Saelora," asks Dyrkan, "what do you think about it?"

"From what I've heard, it's dangerous to cross the more powerful Merchanter clans in Cyad. Even the established factors and traders here try to avoid them. That's why I've tried to sell directly to outland traders."

"It helps that no one in Cyador thought about greenberry brandy," says Catriana. "Most of the outland traders have never heard of greenberries. All they care about is what it tastes like and how strong it is."

"You should have something else unique," says Dyrkan. "Relying on just one thing—that's not a good idea."

"The factorage in Vaeyal is doing well," Saelora points out. "But I'd be happy to have another good that no one else has." She offers a warm but amused smile. "Do you have any ideas?"

Elina laughs quietly.

Dyrkan frowns thoughtfully. "I'll have to think about that."

"And he will," declares Elina. Then she turns to Alyiakal. "How long before you have to leave for your new post?"

"About four eightdays."

"That's the longest leave you've had, isn't it?" asks Hyrsaal quickly.

"I didn't have much choice when I was posted to Guarstyad . . . unless I wanted to refuse the orders. For a captain that wouldn't have been wise. This time, I'll have the chance to spend time with those I want to without every day feeling rushed."

"And?" presses Elina.

"I think it's obvious to everyone how I intend to spend my time, as much as I'm allowed."

"Allowed?" asks Catriana with a wicked smile.

"Allowed," affirms Alyiakal sonorously. "I'm just a mid-rank Mirror Lancer officer, not a prosperous Merchanter with her own house and distillery." He looks to Hyrsaal. "And one with two brothers who are lancer officers. Since I respect the lady Merchanter and her brothers, 'allowed' is the proper term." He grins. "Hope, however, springs eternal."

Saelora, trying to keep a straight face, begins to laugh, as do Elina and Catriana, followed by Hyrsaal, whose boisterous laugh is the loudest of all. Dyrkan smiles as he shakes his head.

As the laughter dies away, Catriana stands. "It's a very good time for dessert, I think."

In moments, Luzza clears the table and places a pearapple tart in front of each diner, a tart with a greenberry glaze, similar to the one Saelora had served Alyiakal at her house three years ago.

He finds the tart as before, with the glaze providing a sharpness that makes the pearapple intense without it being excessively sweet, but he waits to see what others may say.

Dyrkan is the first to speak. "Can't say as I'm all that fond of pearapple, but I'd have this again anytime."

"This is the only pearapple I'll ever eat," says Hyrsaal, "at least willingly."

"It's Laetilla's creation," explains Saelora. "Cooking and baking aren't among my accomplishments."

"You have many others," replies Hyrsaal instantly, "and I'm not the only one here who knows that."

Both Alyiakal and Catriana nod emphatically.

The remainder of the dinner conversation is pleasant.

As everyone rises at the end of dinner, Hyrsaal says, "I need a few moments with Alyiakal to let him know what he's getting into at Lhaarat."

"Lancer talk?" asks Saelora.

"Exactly, sister dear," replies Hyrsaal with a broad smile.

Alyiakal follows Hyrsaal into the parlor, where the two stand in the corner farthest from the dining room.

"First off," says Hyrsaal worriedly, "you're getting a sowshit stew. Don't tell Saelora. She'll worry enough about you anyway. The post is small and it's a fourday ride from Terimot, which is the closest town the firewagons can reach. They don't go there regularly, either. The post isn't as small as Oldroad, but not much bigger. Just three companies."

"That's all?"

"For now. They were talking about adding another, but I didn't see anything happening when I left. The post commander is Majer Byelt. He likes results, but he wants them in the traditional way."

"Like not splitting the company or, the Rational Stars forbid, squads? Or ambushing them to reduce casualties."

"It's better to avoid detailed explanations. As much as you can. He doesn't like questions. He also likes 'ser' in every sentence when he's talking to you . . . more like lecturing . . . Till recently, the mountain bandits were mostly an annoyance. We only had a few raids the first year, and there weren't many brigands involved. On my last patrol we ran into nearly a squad's worth of raiders, and half had those short horn bows. Lost two men and had three wounded. The majer was pissed. Wanted to know how that happened, then didn't want to hear why. I didn't tell him about you. Figured that might give you an advantage in dealing with him."

Hyrsaal continues with a brief description of the remaining two company officers, the senior squad leaders, and the general outline of the post.

A quint later, Hyrsaal concludes, "Don't say I didn't warn you. Probably better you don't mention my name."

"The majer couldn't have been too upset if you're being posted to Inividra."

"Could be headquarters saw that I actually had experience in fighting brigands and barbarians. Besides, captains are disposable."

"Don't let yourself be disposed," replies Alyiakal. "I do appreciate the warning. Very much. We'd better rejoin the others now."

A quint later, when Hyrsaal and Catriana have withdrawn to her small house, and Dyrkan and Elina are dealing with their offspring, Alyiakal and Saelora sit side by side on the bench in the twilight on the side porch.

"That was an excellent dinner," he says.

"Catriana is an excellent cook."

"We all have different strengths. You're better at other things."

"You don't mind?"

"Why in the Rational Stars would I mind?"

"Women are supposed to cook."

"As Elina put it, Dyrkan could burn water, and no one thinks the less of him. I love you for what you are, as you are."

"That's good. I'm not likely to change," she replies wryly.

"And you shouldn't." After a moment, Alyiakal asks quietly, "What's the appropriate gift to a just-consorted couple?"

"You've already given the best gift you could, just by being here."

"What about the next-best gift?"

"Would you mind helping me with a gift? I didn't realize it, but Catriana won't get a wedding chest."

For a moment, Alyiakal is puzzled. Then he recalls the chest that had been his mother's that had vanished sometime after her death, possibly because his father couldn't bear to look at it. "Her family didn't give her one?"

"Her mother hasn't spoken or written to her in more than three years."

"You've been looking here in Fyrad?"

Saelora nods. "I found one, but . . ."

"You hadn't planned on it?"

"I hadn't. I brought some linens, but I'd like to add a few more things. She shouldn't get an empty chest."

"How much do you need? Will five golds be enough?"

Saelora just looks at him.

"Do you need more?"

She shakes her head. "The chest was four golds. It's beautiful. I've already paid for it. But linens, towels, blankets, they're all expensive, and Catriana doesn't have—"

"It's for both of them, really. I'll match you. Four golds for you to get linens, or we could get them together?"

"I'd like that."

"Tomorrow?"

"That would be best. It might be hard to find everything I'd like to get on such short notice, but I didn't know. Even Elina got an empty chest from her mother."

"Was she the one who told you?"

"Who else? I didn't find out until I got here. Elina just found out that their mother had actually written Catriana saying that the inheritance from her aunt was more than enough. Elina doesn't have that many silvers, let alone golds. She couldn't ask Dyrkan, not after all he and his family have already done for Catriana." Abruptly, Saelora turns and hugs him tightly, murmuring, "Thank you."

Alyiakal savors the closeness for a time before asking, "When tomorrow?"

"What if we meet at Haansfel at two quints before noon? There's no sense in your riding out here just to ride back with me."

"That's true. There are a few other things we should talk over."

"What few other things?"

Alyiakal dislikes the hint of wariness in her voice and quickly says, "You wrote that you'd like me to go back to Vaeyal with you. I'd like that as well." He pauses. "It might even save you a few silvers."

"About a gold, and you're far better company."

"Now, as for where I stay—"

His words are stopped by a finger to his lips. Then she says, "You're staying with me. When we enlarged the distillery last year, I added another small bedroom and bathroom, totally separate from Laetilla's quarters. Officially, they're for when we need someone else full-time at the distillery. You can put all your things there." She leans toward him and kisses his cheek. "That will satisfy the proprieties. After all, your rooms are in a separate building." She offers a wicked smile. "What actually happens is up to us."

He can't help smiling. "You do plan ahead."

"Oh . . . and one other thing. I ended up buying two more horses, because we've needed one full-time for the wagon."

Alyiakal stands, then takes her hands, but Saelora is on her feet before he has a chance to help her stand, and their arms go around each other.

Much later than either of them has expected, Alyiakal rides the mare back to the post stables.

XXXIV

After making travel arrangements for a firewagon to pick him up in Vaeyal on oneday of the first eightday of Autumn, Alyiakal takes his time and arrives at Haansfel early, three quints before noon. He decides to wait outside. Saelora rides up within half a quint.

"No wagon, I see."

"I wouldn't want to leave it unattended. We can use Haansfel's stalls in the rear for the next two glasses. That's where I was."

"And I thought I was early," replies Alyiakal.

Saelora smiles. "You still are. Follow me." She leads the way to the northeast corner of the harbor market square and turns north, but thirty yards later, turns west down a paved way too narrow to be a street and too wide to be an alley.

A young man waits by an open door barely large enough for a single mount. Saelora dismounts and leads her horse through. Alyiakal lets his senses precede him, but finds nothing amiss and settles the gray mare, although the stalls are small and suited only for brief use, in his opinion. Then he closes the stall door.

Saelora emerges from the adjoining stall carrying a canvas square.

Alyiakal looks at it.

"Two folded carrying bags," she explains. "They're larger than they look. I just hope we can find everything."

"Does Haansfel have anything Catriana needs?" asks Alyiakal.

"Not much, but I haven't had a chance to look closely. We might as well start here, though. I brought two sets of bedsheets and blankets, but Catriana should have more than that for the future. She could use other linens. She doesn't need much in the way of pots. Besides the small inheritance from her great-aunt Ilsyen, she also got a set of porcelainware that was practically unused."

"What about glasses and beakers?" asks Alyiakal.

"Definitely. She has all of two glasses and two beakers in her house." Saelora gestures toward the door into the factorage.

"Lead the way." Alyiakal opens the door, following her into the cavernous warehouse at the rear of the factorage. An open space beside the east wall leads to the front display area, which holds the stall for Loraan House.

Alyiakal follows Saelora from counter to table to stall. Most goods only get a cursory glance from her, but Alyiakal sees a small table and turns toward it. As he suspects, it holds soaps of various types and sizes. "What about these soaps?"

"She'd like them, but they can't go in the chest. The oils and fragrances might harm or discolor the sheets and linens."

"Could we give them these and anything else like them in one of the canvas bags?"

"We can do that."

"You pick out the most appropriate ones." Left unsaid is that he's paying for them.

The soaps Saelora selects, ranging from a block of laundry soap to individual perfumed soaps, come to three silvers, and go in the canvas bag Alyiakal carries. The only other item that Saelora finds suitable is a set of iron kitchen knives, which cost nearly a gold.

The set of bronze knives costs a third as much, but Saelora just shakes her head and says, "They're not even worth that, and if you could get cupridium you can't sharpen them."

"But I can cut anything with my belt knife." *Or sabre.*

"They don't put the same quality into kitchen knives, and the blade is thicker."

Alyiakal isn't about to dispute her on that.

From Haansfel, Saelora and Alyiakal make their way around the square, ending up back where they started more than two glasses later.

As Saelora carefully arranges the goods into one canvas bag, which she and Alyiakal fasten behind her saddle, she notes, "We didn't get everything I'd like, but she can use what we did get, especially the beakers, glasses, and wineglasses. I'm glad we could get the glass-smith to pack them. You were sweet to pay the extra."

"It wasn't that much more." And in fact, he'd ended up spending four golds and two silvers for what he and Saelora had picked out, but that amounted to half a season's pay for a Mirror Lancer captain such as Hyrsaal. Alyiakal smiles. "Besides, that way they'll have glasses for us at their house. I only had to buy the glassware once. You'll have to supply the greenberry brandy for years."

"I can do that." After a moment, Saelora adds, "The ride back to the house will be slow."

"That will give us more time to talk."

Saelora unstalls her mount, and Alyiakal makes sure that the canvas bag doesn't bump into anything as she guides the horse out and into the alley. He's equally careful with the mare, and before long, they're riding north out to Elina and Dyrkan's house.

"I assume the chest is somewhere at the house."

"She'd see it there. It's locked in the wagon. It would be perfectly safe without being locked, but that's to keep Catriana from snooping. We'll put everything else there as well. We can present it to her just before the dinner. You and Dyrkan can carry it in while I keep her distracted."

"You don't think she suspects?"

"I doubt it, but it doesn't matter if she does. She can use everything we've gotten, and she'll be pleased, even if it's not customary for the sister of the man in a consorting to come up with the chest and its contents—especially not for the best friend of the man to contribute."

"What you're saying is that she deserves a pleasant surprise," says Alyiakal. "I agree. Have you told Elina?"

"I only told her that I had a few things for Catriana. Elina might suspect, but she won't ask or say anything. They both have had too many disappointments with their family."

"Just because they left Vaeyal?"

"I'm very fortunate that Gaaran and Charissa are willing to deal with Mother."

"That's the price they pay for getting the house? And since Elina consorted Dyrkan, as the youngest daughter Catriana was supposed to forgo getting consorted to take care of her mother?"

"That was the expectation."

"I can't see Catriana doing that . . . or you."

"If necessary, I'll help Gaaran and Charissa with silvers, or even golds, but I won't ever live under the same roof with Mother again."

When the two turn onto the brick-paved drive, Alyiakal doesn't see anyone on the porch or around the stable, and no one comes out when they rein up outside the stable beside Saelora's wagon.

Alyiakal ties the mare outside. Then he helps Saelora get the canvas bag off her horse, and they carry what they bought to the wagon. Saelora opens the rear and climbs inside, while Alyiakal hands each item up to her, waiting as she carries them forward. She motions for him to join her and goes forward, where she unlocks the space directly behind the teamster's seat.

"Here's the chest. What do you think?"

Alyiakal studies the brass-bound golden oak chest: three cubits long with a flat top so a cushion placed on top can turn it into a padded bench, usually at the foot of the bed. "It's a handsome piece of work, solid but not plain, or too ornate. You did well."

"I thought so, but I'm glad you agree. If you like it so will Hyrsaal."

While the chest will be Catriana's, Alyiakal understands Saelora's concerns. A chest that Hyrsaal doesn't like will end up out of the way, at best.

"Now," says Saelora, "if you'll hand me things one at a time, starting with the glasses . . ."

In less than a quint everything purchased is either in the chest or alongside it, and Saelora locks the inner compartment. Then they leave the wagon, stall both horses, and walk to the house.

Elina steps out onto the porch just before they reach the door to the parlor. "I saw you two putting things in Saelora's wagon."

"We did some shopping," replies Saelora. "At times, even for a Merchanter, some things are hard to find in Vaeyal."

Elina's laugh is harsh. "You're being charitable to Vaeyal."

"It has its good points," replies Saelora.

One of which, Alyiakal understands, is that Saelora would have found it far harder, if not impossible, to have become a full Merchanter in a larger town, or especially in a city like Fyrad or Cyad. He merely says, "And someone there makes quite good greenberry brandy."

Elina turns to Alyiakal and asks, "Can you stay for dinner?"

Alyiakal senses that she is offering out of courtesy. "Not tonight. Though I would like to sit on this shady porch and spend some time with Saelora before I head back to the post."

Elina smiles. "You're more than welcome to stay as long as you like."

Alyiakal smiles back. "Only as long as Saelora wants."

After Elina goes back inside, Saelora looks at Alyiakal warmly and raises her eyebrows.

"She felt she had to ask, but she has enough to deal with besides having an unplanned guest to dinner."

"For someone who had no sisters, you read women well." Saelora takes one of the wooden armchairs.

Alyiakal takes the chair facing hers. "The healing talent helps. I can't always sense exactly what people feel, sometimes only that they feel ordered or chaotic."

"But most of the time you can?"

"Let's say often," Alyiakal admits.

"More with people you know or have seen often?"

"Not necessarily. Except with me now, you keep your feelings tight to yourself. That was one reason why I was very cautious when we first met."

Saelora gives him a thoughtful look. "Even more now, I have the feeling that you're more of a mage than you're saying."

"The senior magus implied as much when I came to Fyrad. The other night I didn't mention it." Alyiakal outlines his conversation with Senior Magus Kharlt and his guess as to why Kharlt was sent to Fyrad.

"The senior Merchanters, the Magi'i, and senior Mirror Lancer officers don't want any officers who are mages? Why?"

"I have suspicions, and I've been given reasons, but none of them make sense. A firelance can throw more chaos than most mages. Most mages carry too much chaos and are vulnerable to iron weapons. Some mages can conceal themselves, but when they do, they can't see; they have to use their order/chaos senses to find their way. They can sense people and larger objects, but they can't discern facial expressions. Of course, others can hear or smell them if they're not careful."

"Hmmmm." Saelora frowns, then asks, "So they're not nearly as powerful as people say?"

"I'm guessing that the highest of the Magi'i are quite powerful and impressive. I met the Third Magus when I was in Geliendra—"

"You mentioned that when you spoke with Vassyl. Is there more that you didn't tell us?"

"He could sense my healing abilities from a distance; most of the Magi'i I've encountered can't. From what I learned from the ruins at Oldroad Post, some of the First could have stood up to a company of lancers, but from the handful of Magi'i I've encountered, most don't seem that powerful. That's why I don't understand why they keep sending Magi'i to study me or why senior officers worry about officers having *any* magely ability beyond healing. But that seems to be the way it is." Alyiakal shrugs.

"People often fear the wrong things."

"Like strong women Merchanters?" asks Alyiakal.

"How about *any* strong women?"

"You have a point. I got the impression that Healer Vayidra was as much a magus as a healer, but she never demonstrated anything beyond healing. There aren't any women who are recognized as Magi'i. That might be another reason why Adayal would never leave the Great Forest for long. I saw her do things that only Magi'i do . . . concealments, taking on the likeness of a great black panther cat."

"You were fond of her, weren't you?"

"I was, but she told me that our lives were too different and that she could never leave the Great Forest."

"Have you ever heard from her?"

"No." Alyiakal pauses. "Before I met you," *and even after,* "I thought about writing her, but the only way I knew to contact her was through Magus Triamon."

"The magus who vanished?"

Alyiakal nods.

"And she's never written you?"

"No. Not that I know of."

"That sounds like she was very clear about different lives."

"Quite clear," says Alyiakal with a short wry laugh.

"We also have different lives," Saelora says quietly.

"Merchanter and Mirror Lancer, you mean? Or something else?"

"No. Merchanter and Mirror Lancer. Hyrsaal is consorting Catriana. It's unlikely he'll become even a sub-majer. He knows that." Saelora offers an amused, but sad, smile. "He told me he'd be fortunate to make anything beyond overcaptain, even if he didn't consort her. He also said you could easily become a subcommander or commander." She pauses. "If you don't consort too young."

"I doubt he said it that way."

"No, but we both know what he meant." She holds up a hand. "You know how I feel about you, and there's no doubt in my mind that you feel strongly about me."

"But?"

"No 'but's right now. Let's just see how the next eightdays go. I just wanted you to know that I've thought about our different lives, and, if you haven't, I'd like you to think about it as well. Now, not another word on that, and no speculations about the eightdays ahead."

"No speculations, but one logistics question."

"Logistics?"

"When are we leaving for Vaeyal? I have to notify the supply officer at the post."

"I've already booked the wagon on a barge leaving Fyrad at midday on the eightday right after the ceremony."

"Thank you. And now, I'll follow your instructions, dear lady." Alyiakal isn't quite sure what else he can or should say.

"Good. Oh, before I forget: After Hyrsaal arrived in Vaeyal, he told me there were more and more mountain brigands east of Lhaarat, but that the post wasn't getting any more lancers. Is it like that everywhere?"

"I don't know. They cut back the number of lancers in Guarstyad and Old-road Post by two companies, and they closed the Luuval Post. I'm not aware of where they might be adding lancers, but that doesn't mean they aren't. I might learn more once I get to Lhaarat." *And then again, you might not.* "I have a question for you. What do you really think about the possible ties between the high Merchanters and the Imperial Tariff Enumerators?"

"I didn't know as much as you. There are only a handful of Merchanters in Vaeyal, and this is the first time I've been to Fyrad. After what you've said, though, I'll keep my eyes open."

For the next two glasses, the two talk. But eventually, Alyiakal knows it's time for him to go. "I should be heading back to the post."

Saelora stands. "I can't help Elina with dinner, but I can take care of Dyrkyl and Kandara, but before you go . . ."

Her arms go around him, and her lips seek his.

XXXV

The next five days follow the same pattern as oneday. Alyiakal meets Saelora in Fyrad and accompanies her as she looks for goods to sell in Vaeyal. Sometimes, he escorts her to various factorages and trading houses, and lingers nearby while she meets with whoever she needs to and transacts whatever business she can. Then they ride back to Elina and Dyrkan's smallholding and spend time together talking.

On sevenday morning, as Alyiakal enters the officers' mess at the post, he glances around, noticing Aaltyn standing near the head of the junior officers' table. Alyiakal is about to go over to ask Aaltyn if he has orders when Majer Maerl motions and says, "Alyiakal?"

"Yes, ser?"

"You'll be leaving us tomorrow."

"I will. Hyrsaal's consorting ceremony is later today, and the dinner is this evening. I'll be in Vaeyal with friends for the next three eightdays, and then I'll take a firewagon from there to start the trip to Lhaarat."

"I've heard that you've been seen with a woman Merchanter here in Fyrad."

"I have. She's Hyrsaal's sister, and she has her own trading house in Vaeyal. We've corresponded for years."

"A friend?"

"She's a friend. She's spending her efforts in expanding her factorage and distillery. It's Greenberry Spirits, which makes an exceptionally good and distinctive brandy. If you're interested in getting any, Loraan House has a stall in Haansfel, on the harbor market square."

Maerl smiles politely. "I might give it a try." He nods toward the senior officers' table as Subcommander Quellyt enters the mess.

Hoping he'll have a chance to talk to Aaltyn after breakfast, Alyiakal follows Maerl and seats himself after the subcommander takes his place.

Once the senior officers are served, Quellyt looks to Alyiakal. "Overcaptain, how have you found your time here?"

"Everyone has been most professional and cordial, and the time here has been most instructive. I'm looking forward to my next post. Have you heard anything recently about Lhaarat?"

"There have been reports of more brigands. You'll be back to defending the borders. That's always the case at such posts." Quellyt's smile is both sardonic and wry.

"Thank you." Alyiakal takes a swallow of ale and then a mouthful of slightly overcooked egg scramble.

"That's a bit of a change for Lhaarat, isn't it, ser?" asks Overcaptain Kymml.

"Whenever we quash the barbarians in one place, trouble turns up somewhere else," replies Quellyt, "or so it seems."

"What about the company from Luuval?" asks Alyiakal. "Has it been determined where the officer and the lancers will be posted?"

Quellyt looks to Maerl.

"After the required leave," says the majer, "the majority of the company will be posted to Inividra. Those due for transfer to another company will be posted to Chaelt, as will Captain Aaltyn, as replacements for the casualties there."

It has to be Liathyr! Is that why he didn't write back? Alyiakal opens his mouth, but Sub-Majer Iflyn speaks first.

"Casualties in Chaelt? That's a small port where there's seldom much trouble."

"Apparently some smugglers lured part of the company and its commander into a trap and detonated cammabark explosives," replies Maerl.

"They must have been Hamorians," declares Kymml. "They're the only ones crazy enough to deal with cammabark."

"Or someone who wanted everyone to think it was Hamorians," replies Iflyn.

"Whoever it was," says Kymml, "has to be mad . . . or desperate."

"It sounds like the company captain was too effective," says Alyiakal, with a calm he doesn't feel.

"He got himself killed," replies Maerl. "That's not exactly effective."

Alyiakal knows that an officer and a squad pursuing smugglers don't expect explosives and a military ambush, and such an ambush would take golds and planning. No mere smuggler would try that, which suggests to Alyiakal that Cyadoran Merchanters are the smugglers in question. But he only says, "I've seen very good and effective officers get killed."

Maerl looks annoyed but doesn't respond.

Interestingly enough, Subcommander Quellyt says, "It happens. Less to the best prepared and most effective, but I've seen what Overcaptain Alyiakal pointed out. The best we can do is slant the odds in our favor as much as possible."

"Sometimes that's not enough," adds Iflyn.

"Sometimes, it isn't," agrees Quellyt.

Alyiakal returns to eating, taking a bite of the fresh-baked bread.

After a time, Kymml, sitting across from Alyiakal, says quietly, "Three border postings, with only a season's temporary duty?"

"That's about it," replies Alyiakal pleasantly.

Kymml nods.

After the subcommander and majer finish eating and leave, Alyiakal stands. As does Kymml. "You pissed off Maerl a bit."

"If I'd said what I wanted to, I really would have upset him."

"Good thing you didn't. He'll make subcommander. He's the kind that does. Good thing for us that Quellyt keeps him in line." Kymml pauses, then adds, "If I don't see you again, best of fortune."

"Thank you. I appreciate it."

After Kymml turns, Alyiakal hurries to catch up with Aaltyn.

"Ser?" asks the captain when Alyiakal approaches him in the corridor outside.

"I just wanted to wish you well. Do you have orders yet?"

"Yes, ser. I'm to take over a port company in Chaelt. I heard the captain there was killed because he wasn't as careful as he could be."

"That might be," says Alyiakal pleasantly. "Or it might be that he tried to do his duty without fully understanding certain smuggling efforts need to be approached with far more care."

"Ser?"

"A friend of mine was a port company captain in Summerdock. He had some interesting observations, as perhaps you did." Alyiakal pauses, adding, "I do wish you well and hope you can avoid difficult situations without compromising your future."

"Thank you, ser. Best of fortune in Lhaarat."

Alyiakal senses that Aaltyn means what he has said, and that he understands what Alyiakal has implied. *That will have to do.* "These are quietly challenging times, no matter where we're posted. Take care." He smiles and steps back.

"You, too, ser." Aaltyn turns and proceeds down the corridor.

Alyiakal returns to his quarters, thinking about Liathyr, and wondering if Maerl could have been mistaken, but if the undercaptain had arrived and been killed, headquarters wouldn't just be sending a very senior captain to Chaelt. *It had to be Liathyr.*

He shakes his head.

Shortly before second glass of the afternoon, he dons his dress uniform and makes his way to the stable, saddling the mare and setting out. He rides along the east side of the harbor market square, turning west two blocks later. The Recording Hall stands in the middle of the block's north side, a single-story, white, stone building rising ten yards above the stone pavement surrounding it.

Since another consorting is ending, Alyiakal reins up well short of the hall. Two quints pass before the group departs and Alyiakal can ride to the rear of the building.

An attendant gestures to the bronze hitching rail, saying, "A copper a horse, ser."

Alyiakal provides the copper and has just tied the mare in place when Dyrkan drives up an open carriage holding Elina, Saelora, Hyrsaal, and Catriana.

Once the carriage is secured, Saelora joins Alyiakal. "I've never seen you in a dress uniform."

"And I've never seen you in such formal blues."

"You're not quite as cheerful as you might be," says Saelora.

"I'm glad to see you, and everyone else."

"Something's bothering you, isn't it?"

"Not about you or the consorting. This morning I got some news from Subcommander Quellyt that wasn't the best. It doesn't affect me, you, or Hyrsaal," *not directly, anyway,* "but it was something more about unsettling aspects of smuggling. I'd rather not talk about it until later." Alyiakal looks closely at Saelora and smiles. "You look gorgeous."

Saelora grimaces. "I'm not the gorgeous type."

"How about handsomely beautiful?"

She offers a warm, if wry, smile. "That's still exaggerating, but since they're your words, I'll accept them, thankfully." She pauses. "You will tell me everything?"

"I will, all of it, but later. When we can commiserate about the stupidity of Mirror Lancers and Merchanters without casting a pall on the happy day." *And especially on Hyrsaal, who has always been close to Liathyr.* "Now . . . where do we go?"

"We just have to follow behind Hyrsaal and Catriana."

Alyiakal abruptly realizes he hasn't actually looked at the consorting couple and turns his eyes to them.

Catriana is attired in Merchanter-blue flowing trousers and formal tunic, with a matching scarf, her white-blond hair held in place by gold and lancer-green clips, while Hyrsaal wears his formal green-trimmed cream uniform.

"Shall we go?" asks Hyrsaal in his infectiously warm way, looking at Catriana lovingly.

Her smile is radiant as she nods.

Alyiakal and Saelora follow several steps behind the couple.

He leans toward her and says in a low voice, "They look so happy."

"They've waited years," replies Saelora in a quietly amused tone.

When the four reach the front of the Recording Hall and climb the four wide and low steps up to the open doors, the white-clad attendant gestures for them to halt. "Just a moment, please. The recorder is readying the book."

While the four wait, Alyiakal takes a better look at the whitestone building, its walls devoid of any adornment, the tall white oak doors without any symbols, and the polished white marble floor.

In less than half a quint, the attendant says, "You may proceed."

Hyrsaal and Catriana step through the doors. Saelora and Alyiakal follow as the doors close behind them. Inside, the hall stretches some ten yards from the doors to the rear wall, and perhaps seven from side to side. Each side wall holds three narrow windows glazed with azure glass. There are no wall sconces, sculptures, or other adornments.

Alyiakal sees Dyrkan and Elina, and a few other couples standing on each side of the hall, the oldest pair most likely Dyrkan's parents. Since Alyiakal and Saelora are the only ones connected to Hyrsaal, the others represent a statement of support from Dyrkan's family, because close family members are usually the only ones who attend consort recording ceremonies. All of them watch Catriana and Hyrsaal as they walk across the polished white marble floor toward the white sunstone pedestal holding the recorder's open book.

Alyiakal and Saelora stop several yards short of the pedestal, behind which stands the recorder, wearing a brown tunic and trousers, and a wide white shimmersilk scarf. The recorder looks at the two and intones. "I am Reynaek, recorder of consortings in Fyrad. Approach the book."

Hyrsaal and Catriana step up to the open book.

"Do you, Captain Hyrsaal of the Mirror Lancers, and Catriana, Merchanter enumerator, declare your intentions to take each other as consorts?"

"I do," says Hyrsaal warmly.

"I do," says Catriana.

"Then each of you inscribe your name in the book before you, signifying that such is your choice of your own free will, in the prosperity of chaos and light and under the oversight of the Emperor of Light." Reynaek extends a shimmering white pen.

Catriana takes the cupridium-tipped pen, dips it in the inkwell in the pedestal, and signs her name. Then she hands the pen to Hyrsaal, who signs.

Reynaek takes the pen from Hyrsaal, replaces it in the ceremonial holder of the pedestal, and then declares for all to hear, "As entered in the book of Fyrad, you are hereafter consorts. May you always be fulfilled in the light and in the fullness of time."

Hyrsaal completes the rite by placing a single shiny silver in the book just below their signatures. Then he turns and kisses Catriana, gently, but firmly.

After the tender kiss and embrace, the consorted couple turn and begin to walk back toward the doors as they are opened by the attendant. Alyiakal and Saelora step to the side, then follow Catriana and Hyrsaal.

In less than a quint, Alyiakal rides alongside the carriage on the road back to Elina and Dyrkan's smallholding, with another carriage and two open wagons following.

When he nears the house, he sees two long trestle tables set end-to-end on the side porch, flanked by backless benches. When Dyrkan halts the carriage beside the porch, Alyiakal rides on to the stable and quickly stalls and unsaddles the mare. By the time he's finished, Dyrkan's relatives have arrived, let off their passengers, and are on their way to the stable area.

Saelora reaches Alyiakal before the other conveyances are secured and motions for him to join her at the rear of her wagon, which she opens. She climbs up inside and returns with one of the canvas sacks, nearly full. As she lowers it to Alyiakal, she says, "Careful. It's heavy."

When he takes it, he realizes just how heavy. "This weighs more than two stone."

"It's what won't fit or can't be in the chest. It's much heavier."

Once Saelora is on the ground, she says, "I left the compartment unlocked, and I'll have Dyrkan join you shortly."

Alyiakal hands her the canvas bag, then watches as she walks toward the side porch, carrying the weight of the gifts easily. Not for the first time, he admires her athletic grace and strength.

Shortly, Dyrkan appears, smiling as he nears Alyiakal. "Saelora said you have a surprise for Catriana."

"Saelora planned and carried it all out. I just helped a bit at the end."

"From what I've seen of you two, you did more than that. What do you need from me?"

"Just stand there for the moment." Alyiakal climbs up into the wagon and moves forward to the compartment that now only holds the chest. He carefully eases it into the open area of the wagon and then carries it to the tail, where he sets it on the edge and then drops to the ground.

"That's a fine chest, really fine," declares the smallholder.

"Saelora had to search for it."

"I'm sure she did."

"We should wait until the others are all back on the porch," Dyrkan says. "They won't be that long. All the fellows want to get to the ale."

"I could use one myself," replies Alyiakal. "The ride back was dusty."

"Always is near the end of Harvest."

A quint passes before they lift down the chest. Carrying it isn't that hard for the two of them, but Alyiakal wouldn't have wanted to carry it the whole way by himself. As they near the porch, he hears Saelora say to Catriana, "Close your eyes."

"Why?" asks Catriana.

"Because I'm your consort's sister," replies Saelora with a light and amused tone. "It's time for surprises, and you don't want to waste them."

"Especially since there're few enough good ones in life," adds Elina.

Particularly if you're consorted to a Mirror Lancer officer. Alyiakal can't help but think that after what he'd learned about Liathyr at breakfast.

All the others on the porch watch as Dyrkan and Alyiakal carry the chest and put it at the base of the gift table.

"Not a word," says Saelora.

"What have you done, now, Saelora?" asks Catriana.

Alyiakal looks to Hyrsaal, who appears and feels stunned.

"Open your eyes."

For a long moment, Catriana is silent. "Oh . . . oh . . . you . . . you shouldn't have . . ." Tears begin to stream down her cheeks. "I never thought . . ."

Hyrsaal looks to his sister and then to Alyiakal. "You never said a word."

"You can't keep secrets, not from Catriana," says Saelora with a broad grin. "Besides, it was her surprise, not yours."

Hyrsaal's eyes go to Alyiakal. "And you never let on."

Alyiakal laughs and looks to Saelora. "I didn't dare."

Chuckles and laughs run through those gathered around the gift table.

"Now!" declares Dyrkan. "It's time for some good ale!"

As the assorted relatives head for the tray of beakers filled with pale and dark ale, Catriana, her cheeks still wet, puts her arms around Saelora. "You've been so good to me . . . so good."

"You've been so good for Hyrsaal . . . and for me," replies Saelora. "That's the way family should be."

"The chest . . . it's beautiful. But you really shouldn't have." Catriana lets go of Saelora and steps back.

"Alyiakal split the chest and what's in it with me."

Catriana's mouth opens, and more tears appear. "The chest alone . . ."

"In years to come," says Saelora, "it will be your turn. Enjoy the day and the people who care for you."

Catriana embraces Saelora again. When she steps away, she looks to Alyiakal. "Thank you. You didn't have to, either."

"You've made Hyrsaal happy and helped Saelora. It was my pleasure." Alyiakal finds his eyes burning. "Just enjoy it all."

"I will . . . I will . . ."

At that moment, Hyrsaal hands Catriana a beaker of pale ale. "I think you need this." He leans forward and kisses her cheek.

Alyiakal eases away from the couple, as does Saelora. Then he says to her, "That moment was worth everything."

"She deserves it. She's worked long and hard and never asked for anything."

"Hyrsaal's sent her part of his pay all along, hasn't he?"

"I've never asked. That's between them, but I'm sure that he has."

"I'm very glad I'm here."

She takes his hand and squeezes it. "So am I."

Following the first round of ale comes dinner. The fare is simple, but good—rosemary roasted lamb, with sliced buttered potatoes and green beans amandine, along with baskets of rosemary-garlic bread and platters of pickled cucumbers, beets, mushrooms, and quilla. Alyiakal avoids the pickled quilla. Hyrsaal and Catriana sit at one end of the joined trestle tables, flanked by Dyrkan and Elina, while Alyiakal and Saelora sit at the far end.

"You're the officer who's Hyrsaal's friend," declares the wiry weathered-faced man seated beside Alyiakal. "Afraid I don't recall your name."

"Alyiakal."

"I'm Gheston, Maerthe's father."

"I'm pleased to meet you," replies Alyiakal.

"You're the farrier, then," says Saelora quickly.

"That I am. Good-looking mare you're riding, Alyiakal."

"Most lancer mounts are. I've been riding her for about a season, but today will be the last day. From tomorrow on, someone else will have the pleasure." Before Gheston can reply, Alyiakal goes on. "You've had a great deal of experience in working with horses. What would you say is the most rewarding part of what you do?"

Gheston chuckles. "The horses. They'll try to hide where they're hurt, but they don't offer tales or excuses . . ."

Alyiakal listens, occasionally prompting the farrier with questions.

"Now!" announces Dyrkan loudly. "Seeing as most folks don't like the traditional seedcake—and I don't either—Elina and Luzza have fixed cherry-almond tarts."

No sooner has he finished than Luzza places one tart in front of Catriana and another in front of Hyrsaal.

Within a fraction of a quint, everyone has a tart, including Alyiakal, who looks to Saelora and says, "Why not greenberry almond?"

"Because you don't serve things people haven't had before at consorting dinners. Catriana and Hyrsaal might serve greenberry almond tarts at a consorting dinner for one of their children." Saelora grins.

Alyiakal tries to counterfeit a mournful expression, then shakes his head. "I'll have to make do with this."

"You'll eat every bit of it," she replies, "and enjoy it."

Alyiakal does.

The sun is dropping behind the hedgerows to the west by the time the last of Dyrkan's relatives have left the smallholding and Hyrsaal and Catriana have withdrawn to her small house.

Alyiakal and Dyrkan have broken down the trestle tables and carried them to the stable and dealt with other matters, while Elina, Luzza, and Saelora have taken care of dishes, platters, and cleaned up the house and kitchen. Predictably, there's little food left.

Alyiakal and Saelora sit in the wooden armchairs on the porch.

"Now . . . what was bothering you this morning?" asks Saelora.

"The subcommander made some comments about my leaving and wishing me well, and in the course of the conversation, I asked if he knew where the officer and lancers I'd brought from Luuval would be posted . . ." Alyiakal quickly comes to the point that the officer killed in Chaelt had to have been Liathyr and that it had to have been planned.

"I see why you didn't want to tell Hyrsaal today," she says wryly. "Liathyr and you are his closest friends. He had hoped Liathyr could come here as well, but Liathyr wrote that it wasn't possible."

"He wrote me that as well, but I was worried because he never answered my last letters." Alyiakal pauses, then asks, "What do you think about it all?"

"Liathyr upset someone's smuggling. Whoever planned it had to be from Cyador, but that doesn't mean that it was planned by one of the Cyad clans. It's more likely, but without knowing more . . ."

"There's not much we can do, except tell Hyrsaal. I'll ride out here early tomorrow."

"It's stupid for you to ride out here and then ride back," declares Saelora. "I'll just drive the wagon to the Mirror Lancer gate."

"But then, I won't be able to tell Hyrsaal."

"I'll tell him that you didn't have a chance to say goodbye, and that he needs to accompany me anyway because I won't have any guards until I meet you."

"I hadn't thought of that. I should have because you'll have all the goods you got here."

"Sometimes, dear man, you don't have to think of everything."

"Not with you," Alyiakal admits.

"In a little while, I'll need to see you off. I have a few things to take care of." Saelora stands.

"Then I'd better be going." Alyiakal gets to his feet.

She steps toward him. "I said in a little while."

XXXVI

On eightday morning Alyiakal carries his two duffels to the Mirror Lancer post gate so that he is there early. Even so, he doesn't have to wait long before he sees Saelora driving the high-sided, single-horse wagon toward the gate, with Hyrsaal riding beside her.

As soon as she brings the wagon to a halt, Alyiakal opens the rear doors and lifts his duffels up into the wagon.

"Put them forward, next to the compartment door," calls Saelora.

Alyiakal climbs into the wagon and does so, noting various goods are fastened securely in place. After that he closes the rear doors and walks forward until he stands below Saelora, wearing her Merchanter working blues.

Hyrsaal rides up to join the two. "Saelora says you have something to tell me."

Alyiakal looks to Saelora, who nods. "I thought it would be best coming from you."

"That sounds like something I don't want hear," says Hyrsaal.

"When I found out, I didn't want to, either." Alyiakal repeats Maerl's comments from sevenday morning, adding, "He didn't know the name of the captain, but from what Liathyr wrote me, and the fact that he never responded to my last letters, I can't see how it could be anyone else."

"I haven't heard from him in eightdays," says Hyrsaal slowly.

"You can see why I didn't want to say anything yesterday."

"I appreciate that. Catriana and Elina will appreciate it even more." Hyrsaal hesitates, then says, "I should have written him about what I knew from Summerdock, but I was only guessing at the reasons."

"It's dangerous to put guesses in writing," says Alyiakal.

Hyrsaal raises his eyebrows.

"The seals on some letters I've received have been tampered with."

"By whom, do you think?"

"It doesn't matter," replies Alyiakal. "It's not good no matter who it is."

Hyrsaal frowns and nods slowly. "I see what you mean." After a moment, he adds, "I appreciate your coming. You two didn't have to get the chest and everything in it for Catriana."

Knowing that Saelora felt she *had* to, Alyiakal says, "How could we not? Catriana deserves it, and you deserve to have her happy."

"She was still talking about it this morning. You two made her very happy."

"She deserves it," insists Saelora.

"I know that," says Hyrsaal with a smile, "but you two made it happen."

Saelora glances around, then says, "We need to move. There are lancers coming out the gate."

"I won't keep you," says Hyrsaal. "You have a barge to catch." He looks back to Alyiakal. "Thank you. I can't tell you how much your being here meant to both of us." He eases his horse back from the wagon.

"I'm glad I could be here, and seeing you two together was special." *In so many ways.* "I hope it won't be so long before we see each other again."

"Me, too," replies Hyrsaal, offering his broad smile, and adding, "Take good care of Saelora."

"She's more likely to be taking care of me."

As Hyrsaal turns his horse, Alyiakal climbs up beside Saelora, since she's on the left, as are all teamsters, and she simply says, "Go." The horse starts forward.

"Voice commands?" he asks.

"Just for starting. The lines are mostly for everything else. It took me a while until I didn't have to think about it, but Vaeyal's a quiet enough place that I got enough practice. Vassyl helped me."

"You're your own teamster, too?"

"Only for now. Vassyl and I have been training Gaaran. Driving doesn't put that much stress on his leg. I don't need a full-time teamster, not yet. He can use the silvers."

"What does your mother have to say about that?"

"I haven't asked, and she hasn't said." Saelora guides her wagon around a stonemason's cart halted beside the post wall. "We don't see each other much these days. Only when I go to see Gaaran, Charissa, and Gaartyn. Mostly, they come to see me. I try to have them for dinner at least every other eight-day. I gave up on inviting Mother. She's never seen the house."

"That's her loss."

"It's mine, too. But living there . . . you saw how she is."

"I did. It's sad that she can't accept you and Hyrsaal for who you are." Alyiakal isn't sure which is worse, having a loving mother and losing her, or having a mother who continually undercuts and minimizes. *But at least you have good memories, and both your parents loved you.*

Less than half a kay east, Alyiakal sees the whitestone tow-road of the Great Canal, only a few hundred yards from the east gate to Fyrad Post. "Where do we load the wagon on the barge?"

"About a hundred yards north of where we get on the tow-road."

Once Saelora drives the wagon onto the tow-road, Alyiakal sees a line of wagons next to two linked barges.

Before he can ask, she says, "We go to the rear barge. That's the one with upper deck."

As they near the barges, Alyiakal understands. The forward barge has an open well-deck with barrels, pallets, kegs, and other canvas-covered objects already stacked deep. The aft section of the rear barge has a flat deck with a waist-high bulwark, designed to handle wagons and other items unsuited to being stacked or lashed in place.

A squat wagon drawn by two draft horses moves across a loading gangway as Saelora brings her wagon to a stop.

The loading clerk approaches, and Saelora hands him her loading sheet. The clerk takes it, looks at it, then at her, and finally at Alyiakal. His eyes widen as he takes in the officers' insignia.

"I'm family," says Alyiakal. "On leave."

The clerk turns back to Saelora. "Six silvers."

She hands over the coins and waits while the clerk signs and seals her loading sheet, then returns it, saying, "Once the wagon in front is positioned, the loader will signal you. He'll assign a stall for the horse. You're responsible for getting the manure to the animal waste bin. There's a fine if you dump in the canal."

"I know," replies Saelora. "I came down on sixday."

As the clerk moves to deal with the next wagon, Saelora grins and asks, "Family?"

"Elina did say I was family."

Saelora raises her eyebrows and declares, mock-archly, "Neither of you asked me."

"You didn't mean it when you told me to write you as if you were my sister?" Alyiakal counters in a doleful tone.

Saelora shakes her head, then turns her full attention to the loader.

Unlike the clerk, the loader barely looks at Saelora or Alyiakal as he signals and positions the wagon, finishing up with a matter-of-fact "Stall number one," before heading back to the gangway for the next wagon.

Once the Loraan House wagon is positioned next to the starboard bulwark, Alyiakal says, "I can help with stalling."

Saelora shakes her head. "You stay here and guard the wagon."

Alyiakal laughs. "Duties understood, Lady Merchanter."

She smiles, then proceeds with unhitching the gelding and leading him to the assigned stall.

Alyiakal concentrates on sensing the area around the wagon. The other wagons being loaded were set close enough together that it would be possible for a thief to get to the back of the wagon unseen. The open wagon inboard of Saelora's has sideboards about half as high, and is filled with barrels, with a heavy canvas tarp spread over the load and lashed in place. The wagon bears no name. The muscular teamster wears a sabre, as does the guard.

The guard looks to Alyiakal, nods politely, and murmurs something to the teamster, who laughs while he unhitches the horses. Like Alyiakal, the guard remains with the wagon.

When Saelora returns, he says, "All secure. Are you going to lock the rear doors?"

"Not yet. Besides, the accomplished thieves could pick the lock in a fraction of a quint. That's why we'll sleep in the wagon, and why everything is packed over the locked compartment or against the side. The doors also bar from inside." She climbs back up to the teamster's bench.

"Those are rather close quarters."

"Did you have something else in mind beside sleeping?"

"You'd said that we need to take matters a day at a time." *Or words to that effect.*

She gives an amused headshake. "You didn't answer my question."

He smiles ruefully. "Unless I'm mistaken, we both want each other. But we have some time, and I want it to be right." *Especially for you.* "I have some doubts about a cramped wagon on a barge with all sorts of . . . travelers . . . rather close."

"If I hadn't felt the way you've embraced me, I might think you're having second thoughts."

Alyiakal recognizes the glint in her eyes and the hint of teasing. "No second thoughts at all. If you prefer . . ." He turns and gestures to the wagon behind the bench.

Saelora shakes her head. "I appreciate your doubts, especially while they're still loading the barge."

"Do you have any idea what's in those barrels?" Alyiakal motions to the adjoining wagon, less than a yard away.

"You're changing the subject."

He grins. "I thought you already had."

She laughs. "Fair enough."

"The barrels?" Alyiakal prompts.

"I'd guess they hold wine for the taverns and inns north of the Great Canal. Palatable wine. If it were for inns along the canal, they wouldn't be on the barge. Using the canal saves wear on the draft horses and the wagon, and it's quicker than driving."

They sit on the bench and talk, on and off, for two glasses, but Alyiakal remains alert, although no one comes particularly close to Saelora's wagon.

Then, a deep bell rings and two crewmen remove the loading gangway. A firetow rolls past the rear barge, and in another quint the barge begins to move, at barely a creep.

"This is the first time I've been on a barge or on the canal," Alyiakal says.

"The second time for me," replies Saelora.

"Was bringing the wagon worth it?"

"For Hyrsaal and Catriana, definitely. For Loraan House, I'll find out in time. It was good to meet with the people at Haansfel and the other factorages. I gave out a few bottles of Greenberry brandy. It might lead to more sales."

"You're worried about not having enough?"

"Some days I worry about not selling enough. Other days I worry about not having enough to sell."

"I can see that." Alyiakal shifts his weight on the wooden bench seat, much harder than any saddle, then looks eastward beyond the swamp forest separating the Great Canal and the Great East River, noting its similarities to the Great Forest. "Did Dyrkan ever come up with an idea for another unique good for you?"

"Not yet, but Elina says he'll keep thinking about it. He's very patient."

"Good holders have to be, I'd imagine."

After a short silence, Saelora says quietly, "Can you tell me what really happened in Guarstyad? There's no one else around, and you don't have to rush through it."

"I wrote you—"

"Hyrsaal said you had to have done more than you wrote to get promoted to overcaptain years early, but you couldn't put it in a letter."

"It has to stay between us. Not even to Hyrsaal. Not now, anyway. When the right time comes, I'll have to be the one to tell him."

"You're serious, aren't you?"

"I'll tell you, and you can tell me if I'm wrong, but you still have to keep it between us, unless you can persuade me otherwise."

"That's fair."

Alyiakal clears his throat, then adjusts his visor cap, glad for it with the white sun beating down through a clear green-blue sky. "I told you about the road and the dissidents, and the devices they left hidden in the ruins, but I didn't tell you everything. Since we have time, I'm going to retell what happened and fill in a few of the missing pieces." *Including my encounter in the Great Forest and how that affected everything.* "Some of it begins with something that happened when I was here before." He begins with what happened in the Great Forest and the visions and images he received.

A glass later, he completes the full story of the battle against the Kyphrans, including his gathering and use of chaos. "I still don't know why the Great Forest gave me those images and insights."

"Because you recognized and respected it, I'd guess."

"I worry that it has a purpose for me, something that I can't even imagine."

"Maybe it wants to keep Cyador strong to protect itself, and by helping you, it's helping itself as well."

"It didn't need people before the First came," Alyiakal points out.

"Before the First, people didn't have weapons that concentrated chaos."

Alyiakal fingers his chin. "That's true."

Saelora looks at him fondly. "I knew you were a magus of some sort. Thank you for trusting me enough to tell me."

"Do you think I'm wrong in keeping it between us?"

"No . . . although Hyrsaal has said that you're no ordinary Mirror Lancer officer. Right now, he suspects, but he can deny actually knowing."

"He's going to Inividra." Alyiakal pauses as a crewman walks by in the narrow space between the wagon and the bulwark, but the man is inspecting the hull and doesn't even look up. "That's one of the most dangerous border posts."

"That's where your father . . ."

Alyiakal nods. "After all he'd been through, it still seems so wrong. He was riding a routine patrol, with no barbarians anywhere around, and his heart stopped. It just stopped. Even a great healer like Vayidra couldn't have saved him."

"You've never heard from her, have you?"

"There's no reason I would. I did wonder why she was recalled to Cyad. I do have a suspicion, though."

"Oh?"

"I didn't mention this, but right before I left Guarstyad, Majer Bekkan told us that the Emperor was failing and might not live. Apparently, that hasn't happened," Alyiakal interjects dryly. "I got the impression that his health has been problematical for some time, and I have to wonder—"

"If that was the reason she was recalled to Cyad?"

He shrugs. "It might just be coincidence. She was recalled over three years ago, but it was sudden, and no one at Syadtar knew why. If it happened to be for the Emperor, no one would say anything."

Saelora frowns. "Why did the majer bring up the Emperor's illness? What does that have to do with a Mirror Lancer post in Guarstyad?"

"Apparently, there's concern about the succession." Alyiakal goes on to explain.

When he finishes, she says, "You're implying that the Captain-Commander of the Mirror Lancers may not agree with the Majer-Commander."

"I've seen small signs that there *may* be differences between them. The reactions of both the Imperial tariff enumerators I've dealt with suggest they and the Merchanters in Cyad favor the Captain-Commander. Majer Bekkan implied that the Majer-Commander favored Kaartyn as Taezyl's successor. I have no idea whether my impression is correct or what view, if any, Mirror Lancer headquarters has on the succession."

"Either way, it could get very messy when the Emperor dies." She turns more toward him and says, "Lhaarat might be less dangerous than Cyad in the next few years."

"And Vaeyal is far less dangerous than either," he replies with a smile, taking her hand.

XXXVII

For Alyiakal, sleeping in the wagon turned out to be more comfortable than sleeping in the dissident ruins or in the grasslands south of Cerlyn, but not by much. The Harvest air along the canal is hot, damp, and still. Lying close to Saelora on the thin pallets she'd brought, Alyiakal thought more than occasionally of making love to her, but thoughts were as far as he went. From the way she kissed and embraced him, he had no doubt he'd know when she was interested in greater physical contact. *And pressing anything will destroy everything you have.*

At the hint of first light, Alyiakal is fully awake.

So is Saelora, and she turns on her side to face him. "How did you sleep?"

He stretches, carefully, and sits up. "Adequately. The company was superb, but the air was hot and damp. From what you've told me, the quarters are better than most inns along the way."

"Certainly fewer insects and no mice or rats." Saelora moves to a kneeling position. "We also have a tolerable breakfast."

"Tolerable?" asks Alyiakal warily.

"Some travel pastries that Elina made for us. Half for this morning, half for tomorrow morning. Dyrkan gifted us a small keg of pale ale. And I have a case with beakers."

Alyiakal chuckles. "That makes the best travel breakfast I've ever been offered. Remind me to travel more often with you."

After the two wash up, sparingly using some of the water from the wagon's keg—which Alyiakal dusts with order—they sit on the teamster's bench as the sun begins its climb into a hazy green-blue sky and sample the almond-paste rolls and the pale ale.

"Elina baked these?"

"She did . . . Elina and Luzza. Catriana found Luzza. She was an orphan, little more than a girl. Most end up in the brothels or on the streets. She'd been beaten for not accommodating one of the alehouse patrons. Catriana found her in the alley behind Haansfel and took her to Elina's to heal. That was more than two years ago. Luzza needed a mother as much as a friend, and Elina needed help."

"Sounds like it's worked out for both," replies Alyiakal.

"For all three. That way Catriana could do more of what she wanted without feeling like she was abandoning Elina, who couldn't handle the children, the house, and Dyrkan without help. Luzza feels safe for the first time in her life, with a room of her own and decent clothes, and she's paid better than a scull."

Alyiakal takes another bite of the large almond-paste roll, then says, "Catriana's a bit like you, isn't she?"

"How did you ever guess?"

Alyiakal mock-frowns, cocks his head, then says, "I haven't the faintest idea." Then he laughs.

"I'd wager you don't say that on duty."

"Not off-duty, either, not around other officers."

"What if you really don't know?"

"I just say that I don't know. In the long run, it's the safest answer. The few moments after I've said that can be uncomfortable, especially if I should have known."

Saelora gives Alyiakal a puzzled look. "What's the difference between the two?"

He smiles wryly. "I always have some glimmer of an idea. It might be half wrong or all wrong."

"I should have guessed."

This time, Alyiakal's the one who's puzzled. "Why?"

"You don't lie." She pauses. "It might be better to say that you don't utter anything that's untrue. I've seen you mislead with statements that are true, but I don't recall you actually offering a straight-out lie."

"I'm not good at straight-out lies."

"You don't like doing things you're not good at," declares Saelora. "That's why you work so hard to be the best at whatever you have to do."

"I've never heard you lie, either. Might be another reason why we're good together." *One of quite a few.*

"I'm not as good as you are at misdirecting. I'd rather say nothing."

"One of the reasons your mother calls you her recluse?"

"She used to call me her little recluse, until I got bigger than her."

"Was that when Karola became more polite to you?"

"How . . ." Saelora shakes her head. "Sometimes, I forget how much you see."

"Only if I know what to look for. Sometimes, I don't see what I should."

Saelora finishes the last morsel of her pastry and licks her fingers. "That was good."

"I told you it was the best travel breakfast I've ever had . . . by far."

The two sit quietly for several moments before Saelora speaks again.

"I was wondering . . ."

"About what?" asks Alyiakal cheerfully, after swallowing the last drops of pale ale in his beaker.

"You've spoken cautiously about all the Magi'i you've met, except for Healer Vayidra."

"It's wise to speak cautiously about the Magi'i," Alyiakal replies dryly.

"You don't care much for most of them, do you?"

"No. Except for Magus Triamon."

"The one who first taught you? What was he like?"

"He was stern and very precise. Behind that sternness, he was kind, and more perceptive than I realized at the time."

"Go on," she prompts.

"At first, I thought Triamon was being unfair when he said I shouldn't be a magus. At the same time, I also felt relieved. I was also disappointed, but more so for my father. I think he wanted an easier life for me. He felt I could go further as a magus than as a lancer officer. But Triamon looked out for me. He said that I was more aligned with order. Looking back, I suspect he felt that too many Magi'i are corrupted by the power of chaos, and because I was different, they wouldn't take well to me, and might try to destroy me before I could really develop. He was right. I suspect he was in Jakaafra because he was different as well."

"Do you think the Magi'i came after him because of you?"

Alyiakal shakes his head. "That would be vanity. Triamon never named names. He wouldn't even tell me Adayal's name. If the Magi'i knew he'd taught me, they'd have been after me while I was still in Kynstaar. No, they went after him because he believed in teaching what he felt a student needed to know, regardless of Magi'i strictures. I can't think of another magus who would have taught either me or Adayal. I didn't even think about that at the time. The Magi'i don't want mages they can't control. I've never heard it said, and it's more a feeling on my part. I don't have anything to back that up except my few encounters with some, but not all, Magi'i." He pauses, then adds, "And from Healer Vayidra's warnings."

"Those encounters were more than suggestive, from what you told me yesterday. Why did she warn you?"

"I don't know, not really. Perhaps because she felt I could do some good as a healer."

"And perhaps more. She sounds like someone I'd like to meet."

"I'd like to meet her again, but that's unlikely. The only way I might is if I'm posted to Cyad. That won't happen for years, if ever, especially if I don't get promoted into the senior ranks. She might not even be alive by then."

"You'll get promoted. They can't afford not to."

Alyiakal raises his eyebrows. "I've seen too many good officers not get promoted."

"Were they as effective in dealing with barbarians or Kyphrans?"

He laughs harshly. "That means I'll spend my time as a border commander and be stipended out as a subcommander at best, if I survive."

"You don't know that," she says gently. "Hyrsaal believes you're destined for greatness. About people, he's seldom wrong."

"He said that?"

"He did."

Alyiakal shakes his head, then says, "I worry about him going to Inividra."

"I do, too. I worry about your going to Lhaarat." She pauses. "Now that we've said that, it's time to go. Is there anything you'd really like to do that you haven't mentioned?"

"I'm sure there is. At the moment, I can think of one," *besides the unspoken obvious.* "That's for you to take me through the distillery, step by step, and explain exactly how it works and why you chose to do it that way."

"I'll bore you to death."

"You won't. I can assure you of that."

The remainder of oneday passes as did eightday. Alyiakal and Saelora continue talking as the firetow tirelessly pulls the two linked barges north past towns and loading docks set irregularly along the relentlessly regular whitestone canal and towpath. Because large holdings fill the rich bottom-land between the canal and the Great East River, Alyiakal notes the absence of the tall trees that fill the delta to the south and the Great Forest to the north, an absence that inexplicably saddens him.

XXXVIII

In late afternoon on threeday, after the barge moors at the loading dock in Vaeyal, Saelora drives the wagon over the loading ramp, onto the tow-road, and then onto Canal Street heading north.

"Are you going to stop at . . . Loraan House?" Alyiakal almost says "Vassyl's," even though the factorage has been Saelora's for well over a year.

"Only for a moment to tell Vassyl that we're back, and that I'll deal with anything tomorrow."

"He didn't mind taking over for an eightday?"

Saelora smiles broadly. "He's still part owner, remember? He doesn't want to work all the time, but he'd feel left out if I didn't keep him involved. Besides, I still have things to learn."

True to her word, Saelora halts in front of the factorage, where the signboard reads LORAAN HOUSE, and hands the drive lines to Alyiakal, who surveys Canal Street as he waits for Saelora. Several carts pass, and the drivers barely look in his direction, though he doubts a lancer officer seated on a teamster's bench is all that common in Vaeyal.

Then, maybe they really weren't looking at all, except at the wagon.

Saelora returns less than half a quint later and lithely swings up to the teamster's bench. "Nothing that can't wait until tomorrow. Vassyl's glad you came back with me. He hopes you'll come in with me tomorrow."

"You told him about the Imperial tariff enumerators?"

"No. I told him that you had some information he should hear. I'd like his views after he hears it." She takes the lines and says, "Go."

"I'd like to hear what he has to say as well," replies Alyiakal. "Is everything all right with the factorage?"

"Nothing out of the usual."

"We'll unload the wagon tomorrow?"

"I like the way you said that. Yes, except for your things and a few items I got for the house."

"What's the plan for the rest of the day?" ask Alyiakal. "I'm in your hands."

"I hope so," she replies with a mischievous smile. "Once we get to the house, we get your duffels in your quarters, and we each get a bath—separately. Then you admire everything I've had done before we have a good dinner."

A block up Canal Street, a woman in brown trousers and a tan tunic waves and calls out, "I'm glad to see you're back. I'll stop by tomorrow."

"Not too early, Cheslya. We'll need to unload first thing."

"That's fine."

Once they're past the dark-haired woman, Alyiakal asks, "Friend, customer, supplier?"

"Friendly acquaintance and customer. She runs the only reputable brothel in Vaeyal. She asked me if I could pick up some things in Fyrad. I got some of what she wanted."

Reputable brothel . . . interesting wording. Alyiakal's not about to say that, though.

"What couldn't you get?"

"Tri-spice and vanilla. Except you can always get them, but not at the prices she was willing to pay."

"She a recent customer?"

"She occasionally came in before the factorage became Loraan House, but she's been more regular since."

"Has it worked the other way?"

"Not so far. That could be because I let it be known Vassyl still has an interest in Loraan House. A few older men come in looking for him, but they'll tell me what they're seeking if he's not there."

When Saelora turns onto the older graystone road leading to the distillery, the swamp, and her house, Alyiakal realizes he's forgotten just how far her land is from Canal Street—more than two kays. When they get there, he notices that the distillery is a good third longer, and the addition to the east end reaches close to the stone-paved drive running from the road to the stable. There's also a door flanked by windows on the side facing the road.

Then he takes in the house and says, "You added to the end of the stable, I see. For the wagon, I take it?"

"And two additional horses." She slows the wagon to a stop in front of the door on the east end of the distillery. "Those are your official quarters. I thought you might like to drop off those heavy duffels there before we drive to the stable."

"I'd appreciate that." Alyiakal vaults down and hurries to the rear of the wagon, where he unloads both duffels, closes the wagon doors, and carries his gear to the door.

"It should be open," declares Saelora.

Alyiakal tries the door. It opens, and he steps inside, finding himself in a modest stone-floored chamber containing an actual bedstead with a side table and a lamp, a writing table with a chair against one wall. A lancer-green quilt covers the bed. Through an open doorway is a bathing and dressing room, with a built-in wardrobe, a copper tub, and a side table for a bowl and pitcher.

He shakes his head, impressed with the care displayed before him, yet hoping he doesn't spend every night in his "official" quarters.

But then, she could certainly show them to anyone . . . even Marenda, although Marenda's never been here and probably never will be.

He sets the duffels beside the bed and walks back outside, closing the door. "Those are very impressive quarters, especially the quilt, and the private bathing chamber." He rejoins Saelora on the teamster's bench.

"I tried to prepare for all the possibilities," she replies. "I had the addition finished a year ago."

"I'd kiss you right now, but . . ."

She laughs softly. "The only person anywhere close is Laetilla."

Alyiakal kisses her cheek and squeezes her hand. "Anything more up here could get awkward."

"Excuses, excuses." But she grins, before easing the horse and wagon forward. "After I get my personal things, we'll just lock the wagon and the stable. We can unload in the morning. I'm ready to get cleaned up and have a good dinner."

After the two get the wagon into the stable, unhitch the gelding, and settle him in his stall, Alyiakal follows Saelora from the attached stable into the kitchen.

Laetilla turns to greet them. "Good. You're both here. I'll have warm water in your bath chamber in a quint, Overcaptain." Laetilla turns to Saelora. "No problems with the distillery. Your water is hot and on the stove." Then she looks back to Alyiakal. "Would you like a pale ale to take out to your room while the water's getting hot?"

Alyiakal smothers a smile. "Very much, thank you."

In moments, Alyiakal walks back to his "official" quarters, a bemused smile on his face and a beaker of pale ale in hand. When he gets to his room and actually walks into the bath chamber, he discovers that the copper tub is already half full of warmish water. He can't recall when he had a warm bath.

A quint later Laetilla arrives with an enormous kettle of boiling water that she pours into the tub. "Take your time. Then join Merchanter Saelora in the parlor."

"Thank you."

"She thinks you're special. I hope you are."

Although Laetilla's voice is pleasant, Alyiakal senses the woman's willingness to do anything to defend Saelora.

"She's special," he replies, "and she deserves the same. I wouldn't have it any other way."

"You go off and get yourself killed, and you'll kill a part of her."

While Alyiakal knows the depth of Saelora's feelings, Laetilla's words are like liquid ice.

After a long moment, he says, "Thank you. She's fortunate to have you, and I'm fortunate you're here."

"At least you didn't say you'll try."

"Trying isn't doing. We both know that."

"Don't be too long. It's her favorite dinner."

"I won't be."

Laetilla departs, carrying the empty kettle, whose heat Alyiakal feels from several yards.

Still thinking about Laetilla's words, Alyiakal adds hot bathwater to the bowl and uses it in shaving. Then he enjoys a warm bath and dresses in a clean uniform. He does take a little time to empty the tub, hang up his clean uniforms in the wardrobe, and put an order lock on his personal strongbox before leaving his "official" quarters and walking to the house.

Saelora opens the front door as he approaches. "Come in and see!"

Once inside, Alyiakal stops dead in his boots. The parlor doesn't even look like the room he recalls, a chamber that had held little more than two simple, wooden armchairs and a low table. Now there's a pale blue settee, flanked by two larger upholstered armchairs set in an oval arc around a low, dark golden-wood table. Each of the two wooden armchairs, still with their blue cushions, fills a corner. The oak floors have been sanded clean and sealed with a clear varnish. The pale blue plaster walls brighten everything.

"I like it! It's brighter and yet . . . still you."

"Still me?"

"The brightness of you with a touch of the formal, the reserved."

"I'd like a large blue carpet, but they're expensive."

"And all this wasn't?" asks Alyiakal.

"They're all pieces I picked up and refurbished or paid to have refinished."

Alyiakal shakes his head. "You're amazing, but I've known that for years."

Saelora gestures. "Pick a chair. I'll be back in a moment."

Alyiakal moves to the armchair closest to the hearth but is barely seated when she returns carrying a tray with two blue-tinted wineglasses.

"It's Alafraan white." She presents the tray.

He takes the nearest glass and smiles warmly. "I haven't had wine this good since the last time I was here."

Saelora takes the other matching armchair, wineglass in hand.

Alyiakal lifts his wineglass. "To you."

"To you," she returns.

Alyiakal does not drink but raises his glass again. "To us."

She smiles. "I can drink to that."

They both sip from their glasses.

"You've turned a plain and worn-out room into an elegant parlor. I can't wait to see the dining room . . . or your study."

"I haven't done much with the study. I don't use it much right now. I do most of that work at the factorage."

"I'm looking forward to seeing what you've done there, too."

"You won't see much change. I did most of that for Vassyl."

"What do Gaaran and Karola have to say about the house?"

"Karola and Faadyr have only been here a few times. I've never been to their house or holding."

Over three years? Alyiakal doesn't quite know what to say to that. Finally, he manages, "Because it takes so long to get here?"

"Partly."

"And partly because it's so elegant? Haven't things turned out as well for them as she'd hoped?"

"Faadyr does well for a smallholder."

"But not nearly so well as Dyrkan, perhaps?" He pauses. "Is she jealous of what you've done?"

"Disappointed by comparison, I'd say."

Alyiakal shakes his head. "I'm sorry."

"We don't need to go there, especially tonight. Some things are going to be what they are, no matter how we'd hope they'd be different."

"Then you're doing well with Gaaran and Charissa?"

"Charissa's a dear. They're so good together, especially now that Mother's cottage is finished."

"You helped with that?"

"Vassyl, really. We got a small stove and a good sink and a few other things. I paid some of the workers. Mother actually likes it. She can see them both when she wants, and she no longer has to take care of such a large house." Saelora laughs softly. "I have the feeling that Gaaran and Charissa are going to fill the place. She's expecting again in late Autumn."

Before Alyiakal knows it, Laetilla appears in the archway from the kitchen. "Dinner is ready."

Alyiakal stands, as does Saelora, and the two enter the dining room, which holds the same table as before, with the same blue crystal, silver utensils, and Merchanter-blue tablecloth, but the walls are now cream, and a Merchanter-blue chair rail has been added. The three candles of the single candelabrum shed a warm light in the increasing twilight.

They seat themselves, and Laetilla sets a plate before Saelora and then one before Alyiakal, before refilling their wineglasses and withdrawing.

"I hope you like this," says Saelora. "It's one of my favorites, but it's not as elegant as what you've had before."

Alyiakal looks at the casserole on his plate, accompanied by thin slices of apple and thin wafery flatbread. "What is it?"

"Lamb emburhka . . . but Laetilla fixes it the way I like it, not the way the alehouses do. It has a touch of chili, just enough for the flavor. The alehouses use too much and large flat noodles, because it's cheap that way and they want to disguise the taste of the meat."

"Some officers' messes do the same," says Alyiakal dryly. He tries a small morsel of the emburhka, which consists of rice, cheese, and tender lamb with spices he does not recognize. "This is excellent." He takes a much larger mouthful the second time, followed by a bite of the flaky-crispy flatbread. "I can see why it's a favorite. Did you like it before you had Laetilla's version?"

Saelora shakes her head. "My first bite was just like yours—tentative."

Alyiakal winces. "You don't miss much."

She smiles. "I was watching closely."

"As always . . . in everything."

After several more bites of the emburhka, he asks, "What do you have in mind for tomorrow?"

"Breakfast, and I'd hoped you'd come with me to the factorage."

"Of course. I meant after that."

"You could ride one of the horses while I take the wagon so that you could do something else after we unload and you talk to Vassyl."

"Would that be best for you?"

"I'll have to catch up on things."

"Then I'll follow your suggestion."

When they finish the emburhka and flatbread, Laetilla clears away the dinner plates and brings in two smaller plates.

"Greenberry-pearapple tarts!"

Saelora smiles. "I could say that we're having them because you missed them at the consorting dinner, but we'd already planned on them before I left for Fyrad. I wanted to make the dinner here special."

Just your being here makes dinner special. "A very good idea." Alyiakal waits for Saelora to take a bite before he does. He forces himself to take his time and enjoy each and every bite.

A glass later, long after Laetilla has cleared everything away, Saelora and

Alyiakal are still talking, this time about the mystery of the dissidents, when Laetilla appears in the doorway.

"Everything's cleaned up, and I'm going to bed."

"I'll make sure all the lamps and candles are out," says Saelora. "Thank you so much. Everything was delicious."

"More than that," adds Alyiakal.

Laetilla smiles, then turns and leaves.

"You're fortunate to have her," says Alyiakal. "She cares a great deal for you."

"It's been good for both of us." Saelora shifts her weight in the chair, then stands, trying to stifle a yawn.

"You're tired." Alyiakal gets to his feet and moves around the table toward her, taking her hands.

"The last days have been long," she admits.

Much as he'd rather not have the evening end, he says, "You need some sleep."

"I want to make one thing clear, dear man," she says quietly.

Alyiakal can sense the calm and determination behind her words and replies, "I'm listening, but I worry, given the way you said those words."

Her lips quirk into an amused smile. "I'm glad. It shows you care."

Alyiakal waits.

"I love you. There's no point in pretending that I don't or that you don't know. But even if you ask me, I won't consort you. Not now. I'm not interested in anyone else, and I won't ever be. Not after you. For both our sakes, consorting now would be wrong. I won't do something that will keep you from doing what you must . . . and from . . ." She pauses. "I think you have a destiny. I'll be with you, but I won't consort you. Not until . . . I can't say what, but we'll both know." She lets go of his hands, steps even closer, and wraps her arms around him. Her lips are warm on his for a long time before she murmurs, "You need to think everything over." Then she eases slightly away from him. "I'll see you to the door."

They walk to the front door, where he opens it, then turns and holds her once more, kissing her gently, but fervently, before stepping back. "Until breakfast."

"Until breakfast."

XXXIX

Despite trying to think over what Saelora said, Alyiakal falls asleep on the comfortable bed in his quarters, but he wakes early on fourday, worried and feeling uneasy. He appreciates her concerns that, if they consort, his chances of promotion beyond majer are almost nil. *Possibly even beyond sub-majer.* He also worries that she has unrealistic expectations of him, both professionally and personally.

He might have one senior officer in all of Mirror Lancer headquarters who has any interest in him, and he'll soon be a deputy commander at a post where, because of the poor reputation of mountain brigands, an outstanding performance will rate as merely competent, and a competent performance as substandard. *Then what? A posting as deputy commander somewhere else, followed by command at a smaller border post like Isahl or Pemedra?* Or will he not advance even that far and spend years chasing smugglers and worrying about Merchanter corruption and intrigues?

As for disappointing Saelora personally, he worries that she has an image of him far beyond what he is, especially since his romantic experience is minimal, if that.

Rather than lie in bed and stew, he rises and prepares himself for the day, including making his bed and straightening up the room.

When he sees smoke rising from the kitchen chimney, he makes his way to the house. He thinks about entering through the stable and the kitchen door, but the stable doors are barred from inside. So he knocks on the front door.

Saelora opens it, fully dressed in working Merchanter blues.

"I waited until I knew someone was up. I didn't want to be intrusive."

"I can't imagine your ever being intrusive . . ."

Not with you.

"You're just in time. Breakfast is ready. I was about to go knock on your door."

"You look rested . . . and beautiful."

"Not this early in the morning," Saelora replies dryly, opening the door wide.

Alyiakal steps inside, then gives her a hug and kisses her cheek. "You are beautiful, and I'm very glad to be here."

"Thank you."

Alyiakal follows her to the dining room since there's definitely no other place to eat.

Saelora gestures to the table. "Breakfast is simple—just biscuits with jam, eggs, and ham strips. And Dyrkan's pale ale."

"And that's more than you usually have, isn't it?"

"A bit more."

Alyiakal shakes his head. "Do you even eat breakfast most mornings?"

"I have to, or I don't feel well."

"Bread, cheese, and ale . . . and maybe a slice of leftover meat?"

"Most mornings we do have simple pastries with fruit and ale."

"Then we should do that from now on. Guests," and Alyiakal grins before he adds, "even guests considered almost family, shouldn't impose too much upon working lady Merchanters." Before she can protest, he goes on. "Don't tell me that you aren't having Laetilla do more because I'm here."

"We can do simpler breakfasts," declares Saelora as she seats herself, "but we will have good dinners."

"I'll appreciate and be thankful for every tasty morsel," replies Alyiakal, settling himself across the table from her.

"The biscuits are a little heavy," says Laetilla as she sets the pitcher of ale on the table between them.

"They'll be lighter than those I've gotten at the mess, and warmer."

"I would hope so," returns Laetilla.

Alyiakal does indulge himself at breakfast, enjoying the warm biscuits with mixed-berry jam, and freshly fried eggs and ham strips. When he finishes, he looks to Saelora. "That was the best breakfast I've ever had." *But eating that much and that well every morning might not be the best idea.* Not that he's about to say so, because Saelora or Laetilla might take it the wrong way.

"Then you're ready to unload a wagon?"

"Absolutely. Is there much that stays here?"

"Not that much, but I didn't feel like dealing with it last night, except for the ale and some of the cheeses."

In less than a quint, the two unload the items and goods for the house, which Saelora stacks on the end of the wagon and Alyiakal carries into the kitchen. Then Alyiakal helps Saelora ready the wagon, before he introduces himself to the roan, talking a bit and projecting a touch of order warmth before he saddles the gelding. Before that long, they head for the factorage, with Alyiakal riding beside Saelora.

"You're more than a field healer, more like a real healer, aren't you?"

"I'm more than a field healer, more like an apprentice healer. Why?"

"Could you look . . . or however you do it . . . at Vassyl? I don't think he's as well as he claims. I worry about him."

"I can sense his order and chaos balance, and if he's got wound or injury chaos. If it's not bad, I can help some."

"Thank you."

Just before they reach the turn off Canal Street to the alley behind the factorage, Alyiakal sees a white-haired man stop and watch them. Alyiakal knows they've met, then nods. "That's Charissa's uncle, isn't it? Does he still come to the factorage?"

"Mostly to talk to Vassyl. Occasionally, he orders something."

As he rides closer, Alyiakal calls out, "Good morning, Rhobett!"

For a moment, the older man looks puzzled. Then his eyes go to Saelora before returning to Alyiakal. "Good morning, Overcaptain. You're on leave?"

"For the next few eightdays. It's good to see you again."

Rhobett nods and replies, "And to see you. Enjoy your leave."

Once Saelora turns the wagon around the corner and then heads south down the alley, Alyiakal says, "He wasn't quite sure who I am."

"He'll be in the factorage asking Vassyl before we finish unloading."

"I'll stall the roan, first, and then help with the unloading, if that's all right. What do you do with the horse and wagon?"

"Stall the horse and block the wagon against the wall."

The two have just finished unloading the wagon when Vassyl appears.

"I would have been here earlier . . ." he begins.

"Except Rhobett came in and wanted to know who Alyiakal was," finishes Saelora.

"He was surprised and impressed that you're already an overcaptain," Vassyl tells Alyiakal, then looks to Saelora. "There haven't been any senior officers in Vaeyal since your father died. He also wanted to know if a consorting was in the works."

"What did you tell him?" Saelora's voice holds a slight edge.

Vassyl chuckles. "I told him that I didn't know one way or the other, and that he should ask you. He said that he wouldn't think of asking about such a delicate matter."

"After he just did?" Saelora shakes her head, then turns to Alyiakal. "Everyone in a small town wants to know everything."

"He could ask your mother," says Alyiakal, his voice deadpan.

Saelora looks hard at him, then smiles wryly. "That was evil."

Vassyl chuckles again and turns to Saelora. "I'll be in front if you need me."

Once the older factor leaves, Saelora grins. "That really was evil, and Vassyl might even tell Rhobett that if he asks again."

"Your mother and Vassyl?"

"They're polite to each other. She blames him for my independence, and he doesn't see why she's not proud of me."

"She doesn't want you to outshine her, and you've done it by yourself, not by consorting. That's important to you."

"I'm glad you understand. Hyrsaal does, and so do Gaaran and Charissa."

"And Catriana. Most of your family understands." Alyiakal isn't about to comment on the omission of Karola, although he suspects Karola knows, but is jealous of how well Saelora has done.

"We need to get back to unloading."

"At your service, distinguished Lady Merchanter."

Saelora feigns a swing at Alyiakal.

"Careful there. I don't want to turn up at Lhaarat injured."

"You're more durable than that," she retorts.

"I'd rather not test that," he counters.

After all the goods are on the warehouse shelves and the wagon is blocked in place, Alyiakal turns to her. "You need to catch up on things with Vassyl, I imagine."

"I should."

"I'll walk around, then I'll come back and talk to him . . . and see what I can sense about his health."

The two walk through the rows of shelves, past the area with the two desks and the small circular conference table, and through the door into the front area, where Vassyl stands behind the counter.

"Until later," Alyiakal says. He exits and takes the stone steps down onto Canal Street, where he glances around. Finally, he crosses the street and walks to the edge of the tow-road, where he concentrates on sensing the ordered structure of the whitestone comprising the canal walls and the tow-road.

On his previous visit, he'd gotten the impression there were two conflicting, yet ordered structures—the canal and tow-road, and a deeper structure. In less than half a quint, he confirms his earlier feeling that the canal and tow-road had been built over the Great Forest, when it was larger, because the deeper ordered area feels much like the forest. He still can't discern why the First would have built like that unless it was the only way they could.

With that minor mystery as resolved as it ever likely would be, he walks north on the tow-road, almost as far as Marenda's house, before heading back, taking his time. Every adult he sees looks quickly at him and then away. Several of the children stare, as if they'd never seen a lancer uniform.

When Alyiakal returns to the factorage, Vassyl stands alone behind the counter.

"Saelora said you'd hoped I had time to talk with you." Alyiakal studies Vassyl, sensing that the older man's order level is low, but Alyiakal can't discern a single cause.

Vassyl gestures vaguely around the front area. "Do you mind talking here? That way she can go through the manifests and invoices undisturbed."

"That's fine."

"I'll be blunt, Alyiakal. Saelora is like a daughter, maybe more my daughter than Elinjya is. I don't want to see her hurt."

"Neither do I."

"She's told me that she won't consort you now. Was that idea hers or yours?"

"Hers. She told me last night after dinner. She said not to ask her. Saelora isn't manipulative."

"No. But she might tell you what she thinks you want to hear."

"I don't think that's what she's doing. I'm guessing, but she wants to establish Loraan House as more than it is before she'll consider consorting. She didn't say we *wouldn't* consort. She said, 'Not now.' I have to take her at her word."

Vassyl frowns.

Alyiakal waits.

"She doesn't want you to give up your future for her," the factor finally says.

"I don't want her to give up her dreams of what she wants before she consorts."

"Have you slept with her?"

"No," replies Alyiakal. "We slept together but separately in the wagon on the way back from Fyrad. Anything more has to be her choice. I can't conceal how I feel, but if I even hint . . ."

"You're both playing with chaos, you know."

More than you have any possible idea. But Alyiakal just nods. "I have to trust her."

"She's trusting you."

"I know. I can't break that trust."

"Fate and the barbarians might."

"That could happen whether we consort or not."

"Tempting chaos." Vassyl sighs. "By the Rational Stars, you two are stubborn."

"Maybe that's why we fit," replies Alyiakal.

"Makes sense in a strange way. Anyway, I've said my piece."

"She respects you," says Alyiakal. "So do I." He pauses. "There is one other matter."

Vassyl looks warily at Alyiakal.

Alyiakal smiles. "Not about Saelora. I've run into some odd situations with Merchanters and Imperial tariff enumerators. I told her, and she said I should tell you. She wanted to be here when I did so that the three of us could talk it over."

Vassyl laughs briefly. "She thinks I have more wisdom than I do."

As Vassyl talks, Alyiakal has been studying him more intently, noticing small bits of chaos all through his body, but he cannot find any source, and that bothers him.

"Alyiakal?" prompts the older man.

"I'm sorry. I was just thinking. If it's all right with you, I'll ask her if she wants me to tell you now."

"She's in charge now."

Alyiakal opens the door to the private study area. "Saelora . . . do you want me to tell Vassyl about the Merchanters now . . . or later?"

She looks up from her desk, clearly thinking, then says, "Now is better. I'll be right there."

Once Saelora joins them behind the counter, in case customers arrive, Alyiakal outlines his experiences with the traders coming through Oldroad Post and continues through the Luuval Post closure and Liathyr's death, but does not mention the interrogation by Magus Kharlt.

When he finishes, Saelora looks to Vassyl. "What are your thoughts?"

"I'm not surprised. Smuggling by Cyadoran traders has been going on for a long time. I hadn't realized the extent of extortion by the tariff enumerators or that it might involve the Emperor's Merchanter Advisor. It makes sense, though. Emperor Taezyl has seldom been interested in trade. Emperor Kieffal was, and that may have had something to do with his death."

"Because his plan to take over Cerlyn would have resulted in lower profits in the copper trade?" asks Alyiakal.

"That's a rumor, if well-founded," replies Vassyl. "But Kieffal was also concerned about the excessive costs of tariff enumerators."

"Did he think that too many younger sons of Merchanters were given enumerator posts?" asks Saelora. "Or posts they weren't qualified for?"

"That was my opinion, but no one wanted to say much."

"Because unfortunate events occurred to those who spoke out?" presses Saelora.

"There are reasons why many of us avoided trading with the Clan Houses out of Cyad," says Vassyl dryly. "And sometimes with certain houses in Fyrad."

"Is that why you recommended I approach Haansfel?"

Vassyl nods.

"They've been honorable," says Saelora.

"They should be," replies Vassyl. "You've increased their profits."

At that moment, a burly man in a brown tunic enters the factorage.

"Good morning, Vaartol," says Vassyl cheerfully.

Saelora turns to Alyiakal. "I'll see you at the house for dinner, after fourth glass."

"Until then." Alyiakal leaves through the door behind the counter, making his way to the rear of the factorage, where he unstalls the roan and leads him out.

After mounting, he rides south down the alley, then to Canal Street, where he continues south, since he's never explored that section of Vaeyal. Four blocks later, Canal Street ends at a low stone wall. South of the wall, a pearapple orchard extends as far as Alyiakal can see.

He smiles, thinking about where Saelora likely obtains her bruised pearapples, then turns the roan north again.

XL

After exploring all the side streets and back streets of Vaeyal, Alyiakal returns to Saelora's house, where he unsaddles and grooms the roan. Back in his room, he spends more than a glass updating the map of the area around Geliendra, then leaves to walk up the gentle slope in the old road to where he can see the swamp that swallowed the original road decades before.

He pauses, thinking about the morass at Luuval. *Are the causes the same?*

Thinking about the possibility, he walks down the remainder of the road, past where a pile of stones used to be. He stops well short of the softer-looking ground and extends his senses. As he suspected, there is more chaos than order, but not the swirling bottomless chaos he had sensed at Luuval. Beneath the chaos before him is the same layer of order that undergirds the depths beneath the Great Canal. *That must make the difference.*

He walks slowly back toward the house but sees no sign of Laetilla. Because he's not about to enter Saelora's house uninvited, he returns to his quarters and works on his maps. Slightly before third glass, he hears hoofs on the stone drive and looks out the window to see Laetilla ride up to the stable, with two paniers fastened behind the saddle. He hurries after her, catching up as she reins in the horse.

"Can I help unload those?"

"Thank you." Her pleasant expression holds a hint of amusement. "I won't tell anyone I had an overcaptain carrying supplies."

"I don't mind. You're the one cooking, and cooking very well. Which panier first?"

"It doesn't matter."

"Is the door from the stable unlocked?"

"It is."

"After I carry them in, I'll unsaddle and groom the horse. That way, you can get on with whatever you need to do."

"I appreciate that. It took longer than I'd planned."

"Will you need any more help?"

Laetilla shakes her head.

He smiles and says, "In other words, the best help is not getting in your way."

She doesn't speak but smiles in return.

Alyiakal slides the heavy stable door open, then lifts the first panier and carries it into the kitchen. When he finishes his self-imposed chores, he returns to his quarters.

A quint later, he discerns the horse and wagon, partly because he's been actively sensing, hoping Saelora would be early. He's out the door and waiting by the drive as she slows the wagon and turns onto the drive.

"You're early," he says cheerfully, walking alongside the wagon.

"I'd hoped to be even earlier, but a Hamorian trader showed up. He made a special trip from Fyrad. He wants some of the brandy when he returns next year."

"Next year?"

"We've sold all we have this year." She reins up short of the stable door.

"Would you like me to take care of the horse and wagon?"

"I'd rather we do it together. There's not much to do now that I'm here." She climbs down from the wagon and gives him a brief but emphatic hug.

Neither speaks, but once the horse is stalled and groomed, the wagon blocked in place, and the heavy stable door closed, Saelora turns to Alyiakal. "Thank you. I'm sorry I was so long at the factorage."

"I didn't expect anything else. I thought so much about seeing you that I didn't plan on what I'd do when you were busy. Is there any place like an old quarry or a sand pit or a rocky cliff nearby?"

Saelora frowns. "If you head north out of town on the road past Mother's house, there's a hill about four kays farther out. On the east side they used to dig out clay, but it's been abandoned for years. Hyrsaal and Gaaran used to hunt waterfowl in the pond at the bottom."

"Waterfowl . . . what for? I can't imagine they taste that good."

"They're awful to eat, but the males have bright feathers, and there was a trader who'd buy the feathers for a milliner in Cyad. Then feathers went out of fashion." Saelora pauses. "Why do you want to know?"

"I'd like to practice a few things while you're working, somewhere not connected with you."

She raises her eyebrows. "Magery?"

"More like attempted magery," he says ruefully. "Things I've thought about but don't dare try on or near a post."

"Well . . . there's no one there . . . or wasn't the last time I rode that way."

"I'll ride out there tomorrow after you leave."

"Until you leave, what if I work until the second glass of the afternoon, and then we spend the rest of the day together, except on eightdays, when we have all day."

"Can you afford to do that?"

"Gaaran's been helping some, and he can watch the counter."

"And he and Charissa can use the silvers?"

She nods, then says, "We've needed someone for a while. Vassyl shouldn't be working as much as he has been, but even without the consorting I needed to go to Fyrad. It made sense to combine the two."

"Speaking of Vassyl, you're right to be worried. He's got little specks of chaos all through him, not exactly like wound chaos, but it's worrisome."

She shivers slightly. "The way you say that—it's so matter-of-fact. You're like a real healer, aren't you?"

"I sense more than many healers, but I don't know anything about surgery, except dealing with wounds."

"Can you do anything for Vassyl?"

"I can try, but it might not help much. The bits are tiny, and they're scattered. Each one I remove causes heat. The number I can remove safely at any one time is limited."

"What happens if you remove too many?"

"That will be worse than the chaos."

"You'll try?"

"Quietly. I can do it while you're talking to him. Then I can see how he is the next day."

"That won't interfere . . . ?"

"No. I can only do so much at a time. I'll just ride in with you the way I did this morning."

"You're sure."

"I'm very sure."

"Why don't you have a glass of that Alafraan in the parlor while I talk to Laetilla and wash up quickly?"

"That would be good, especially when you join me." Alyiakal follows her into the kitchen.

"Alyiakal's going to have a glass of Alafraan while I wash up."

"I thought you'd have some for dinner," says Laetilla. "I'll bring you a glass, ser."

"Thank you." Alyiakal follows Saelora only as far as the parlor, where he takes the armchair that offers the best view of the kitchen archway and the hall.

Laetilla arrives with a wineglass in moments, which she offers and Alyiakal accepts.

"You never came into the house today, ser," says Laetilla quietly, "except to help me."

"It's not my house. I wasn't invited, and it wouldn't have been right."

Alyiakal senses her surprise, but he only says, "Thank you for the wine."

"You're welcome, ser." Laetilla inclines her head and returns to the kitchen.

Alyiakal takes a sip of the wine, then sets the glass on the table, and smiles as he looks at it, because the blue glass hides the wine so the wine seems to have vanished.

"You're thoughtful," says Saelora as she leaves the hallway some time later. "I'll be right there after I talk to Laetilla."

Alyiakal immediately sees that while she still wears Merchanter blues, the fabric is lighter-weight and a touch more formfitting without clinging.

When she returns, holding her wineglass, he stands. "You look wonderful."

"I feel better. How was your day, besides helping Laetilla?" She settles into the other armchair.

"I only carried a few things." Alyiakal sits down, summarizing his few activities, then asks, "What about your day?"

"Except for the Hamorian trader, I worked on invoices, manifests, organizing the goods we brought back for those customers who ordered them, and persuading Vassyl to let Gaaran at least watch the counter so that he can rest more at the factorage."

"He worries about you."

"He needs to worry more about himself. I knew something wasn't quite right."

"You were right."

"We can't do anything about Vassyl now." She pauses. "Are you going to tell me what you plan for tomorrow?"

"Some of what I'm thinking about will depend on what that place is like. I promise to tell you after I've done it. Why don't you tell me more about how you make the brandy? The good things . . . and those not so good."

Saelora takes a sip of wine, then says, "The good thing about working with greenberries is that the bushes produce from early Summer all the way through Harvest. That way we can make the wine continuously. You can't do that with grapes. Making the wine is the easy part. We crush the berries and pearapples separately and then mix the two. They ferment for two eight-days, and the barrels have to be stirred daily. After the first fermentation, the must—"

"Must?" asks Alyiakal.

"That's the term vintners use. I don't know if we should call a greenberry-pearapple mix that, but it's as good a word as any. The must goes into sealed oak barrels, where more fermentation goes on for about two seasons. Good grape wines usually take longer than that, but more aging at this stage really doesn't improve the wine that much. We add more pearapple syrup to the raw wine before we distill the brandy . . ."

Alyiakal listens intently.

"As for the more difficult aspects, we still have a tough time getting enough barrels, but the hardest part was the copper tubing. Vassyl found ways to get it." She smiles. "A few times, he said it wasn't against any law but wouldn't say more."

"So, you're limited to what you're producing now?"

"More like what we'll be producing by the end of the year. Dyrkan was right about needing another unique product." Saelora turns her head as Laetilla enters the parlor. "Is dinner ready?"

"It is."

Both Alyiakal and Saelora stand.

"You haven't told me what dinner is."

"You'll see," Saelora replies as she walks into the small dining room, where the candles in the candelabrum are already lit, although the sun is just beginning to set.

Once the two seat themselves, Laetilla sets one plate before Saelora and the other before Alyiakal.

"They're fowl breasts of some sort," says Alyiakal.

"Boneless fowl breasts stuffed with cheese and herbs and covered with an apricot glaze that has just a touch of greenberry brandy, with brown rice and buttered diced mushrooms," Saelora says, adding sweetly, "Laetilla suggested quilla as another accompaniment, knowing your fondness for it."

"I would have eaten it."

"But not enjoyed it."

"Not the way I'll enjoy this."

Enjoy it, he does, leaving not a morsel, as he asks Saelora questions about Loraan House in between bites.

When Laetilla clears away the empty plates, Saelora says, "We're having a different dessert."

"Another surprise?"

"You deserve some surprises."

Laetilla places before each of them a small plate holding a smaller circular steep-sided shallow bowl and a sweet biscuit, then leaves, although Alyiakal senses that she stops just out of sight.

"What is it?" he asks.

"It's a baked, glazed egg custard."

"With a hint of greenberry?" asks Alyiakal hopefully, because Areya, who had fixed all the meals for him and his father at Northpoint, had been fond of a completely tasteless custard.

"Of course. Laetilla tries out all sorts of my ideas. She makes most of them work."

"Have you tried this?" asks Alyiakal teasingly.

"I wouldn't serve anything we haven't tasted, and Laetilla wouldn't let me."

"I hope you're paying her well. She deserves it."

"She does, and I am. At least, I hope I am."

Alyiakal can sense that Laetilla doesn't disagree, or at least that she's not disturbed by Saelora's words.

Saelora lifts the small spoon and takes a mouthful. She smiles. "Now you try it."

Alyiakal dips the small spoon into the custard and eases a small portion into his mouth. What he tastes is smooth and silky, yet firm, and the glaze brings a depth to the taste. "That's good . . . very, very good." He takes another bite. "Excellent, in fact."

"Why were you so dubious?" asks Saelora.

"I've had too many tasteless egg custards in my life." He pauses. "This is anything but tasteless. It's exactly right, but I can't explain it any better than that." Alyiakal smiles, not only at the taste, but also because he senses Laetilla's satisfaction as she withdraws to the kitchen. He takes another small spoonful, trying to determine the combination of flavors. Finally, after finishing the last bit of the custard and the sweet biscuit, he asks, "What's in it that makes it taste that good?"

"Mostly egg yolks and cream with sweet syrup. It's not just the ingredients, but how it's prepared." Saelora shifts her weight in her chair and smiles ruefully. "Good cooking takes a light touch and patience. I'm short of both."

"You've shown a light touch and patience in trading."

"That's different from the kitchen."

Alyiakal is about to say that she certainly knows what makes a good meal but closes his mouth abruptly as another thought strikes him.

"What were you about to say?"

"My second thought was that your mother complained when you did something in the kitchen, and the way to avoid that was to be terrible at cooking."

For a moment, Saelora looks stunned. Then she bursts into laughter. "You're right! I knew that I really didn't like cooking. I like food. You know that, but cooking . . ." She shakes her head.

"I'll wager you actually cook fairly well when only Laetilla's around. Or at least help her a lot."

Saelora smiles in rueful amusement. "With you around all the time, I wouldn't have any secrets at all."

"I think you'd manage. You don't like secrets."

"There you go again."

A glass passes, during which time the sun sets, deep twilight settles over the house, and Laetilla removes the dishes, cleans up, and announces that she is retiring for the evening.

Alyiakal finds himself staring at Saelora. "You know, you're even more beautiful in candlelight."

"That's just because you can't see me as clearly."

"I see you clearly in sunlight and in shadow, and I love you in both."

"Why?"

"Because you know what you want. Because you don't like pretense. Because you're loving and kind. Because you stand up for yourself. Because you're as fair as you can be in an unfair world . . ."

"Dear man, you're expecting too much of me."

"I'm not expecting. That's what you are." Alyiakal senses that the cold certainty of his words silences her, if momentarily, and he asks softly, "Why do you love me?"

"For many of the same reasons you gave, and you know that." She stands. "Wait here. I'll be right back."

Alyiakal gets to his feet but doesn't leave the small dining room.

In moments, Saelora returns with an unlit candle in a brass candleholder, which she lights off the end candle in the candelabrum, before snuffing all its candles. "There's no sense in wasting candles. Now . . . you've never seen the rest of the house, unless you sneaked a peek."

"I haven't seen anything but the kitchen, parlor, and dining room."

Saelora laughs. "Laetilla said you wouldn't come inside without being invited. That impressed her."

"I try not to intrude in people's personal lives, unless invited."

"'Try'?" she asks teasingly.

"Sometimes I've had to . . . as a lancer officer." Alyiakal still remembers the barbarian holder woman and the two children whose consort he'd had to kill, the gray-haired part-mage woman whose brother he'd also killed, the girl archers he'd turned to ashes, and too many young barbarians forced into raiding by others.

"I'm sorry. I didn't mean . . ."

"I know."

"You have to live two separate lives, don't you?"

Alyiakal smiles ruefully. "I hadn't thought of it quite that way, but this part of my life . . . you especially . . . is what gives meaning to what I have to do."

"Have to do?" she asks gently.

"I've seen other lands and the way they treat each other and feel about us. Cyador's far from perfect, but from what I've seen, it's better than anywhere else. I'd like to make it better, but so far all I've been able to do is defend it." He adds wryly and self-deprecatingly, "Maybe that's all I'll ever be able to do. But I can try and hope."

"You've done more than try, dear. Now . . . let me show you what you haven't seen yet. We'll start with the study. I haven't done much there, but you can see that I'm not always as neat as you think."

Alyiakal knows the brief tour will either be brief, or be much more than that. *It's her choice . . . and yours as well.*

Saelora leads him from the dining room across the short hallway to a door that she opens, revealing a table desk piled high on one side with papers, a straight-backed chair, and a three-shelf bookcase with the top shelf the only one holding volumes, and nothing else, unsurprisingly, since the room is barely large enough to contain the desk and a narrow single bed.

"Definitely a small study," observes Alyiakal.

"I told you so."

"Shall I close the door?"

"Please."

As Alyiakal does, Saelora turns toward the double doors at the end of the short hall. "This is the only real change to the house. There were two small bedrooms. I had them turned into one with a small bathing chamber."

She opens the left-hand door, and Alyiakal realizes that the right-hand door is just secured to the wall and leads nowhere. He follows Saelora through the door, which she closes before turning and saying, "What do you think?"

Alyiakal's first thought is that he doesn't know what to think, not ever having been in a grown woman's bedroom before, that he can recall. He takes in the chamber, which has a double bedstead with its headboard between two windows to the left, flanked by two small night tables. A chest, topped with an oblong cushion, sits at the foot of the bed. Directly back from the door are a dressing table and stool, and to Alyiakal's right is an armoire. The quilt on the bed is Merchanter blue, as are the window hangings and the cushion. A door splits the middle of the wall to the right, leading to the bathing chamber.

"It's beautifully done. Tasteful, well-organized." He smiles. "Like you."

"Do you like it?" Saelora moves to the side and sets the candleholder on the nearest night table.

"I do."

Before he can say more, Saelora takes his hands, her eyes meeting his. "I said I wouldn't consort you. I didn't say I wouldn't make love to you."

Then her arms are around him, and his around her, and their lips meet.

XLI

Alyiakal wakes in the wide bed to see Saelora lying on her side beside him, looking at him fondly in the early-morning light.

Before he can speak, she places a finger across his lips. Then she kisses him and puts her arms around him. "Just hold me."

"That's going to be hard," he murmurs.

"Not yet. We have time."

For now . . .

"I'm not crystal," she murmurs in his ear.

"No . . . you're far more precious . . ."

Much later, Saelora eases slightly back from him. "I've wanted you for so long."

"I wanted you from the moment I saw you and realized that you were the woman who wrote me."

"That's a strange way of putting it."

"No. I loved the woman who wrote me, but I wanted to make sure that the woman I met was the woman who wrote."

She frowns for a moment, then nods. "I didn't think of it that way. Maybe because Hyrsaal had told me so much about you."

Alyiakal smiles dryly. "He said very little about you except that you were special. He was right, but I needed to find out." He laughs quietly. "You've told me that Hyrsaal is always right about people."

"So are you."

Alyiakal shakes his head. "I can sense what people feel when I'm near them. But I often don't know what's deeper inside them. That means I have a good sense about people I've known for a while, but not as much about those

I've just met. Hyrsaal knows what people are instantly." He smiles. "You said you'd wanted me for a long time. Why now?"

"Because I don't have to have you. I can want you because I want you, not because I need you."

He nods slowly. "You're quite successful in your own right, possibly more successful than a very junior senior officer."

"We're not comparing," Saelora replies warmly, but firmly. "Also, consorting now would be wrong for both of us. If I were a Magi'i healer, and not an unknown Merchanter, or one unknown in Cyad, that would be another matter."

"It's better right now that neither of us is known in Cyad."

"After the battles with the Kyphrans, I doubt you're unknown."

But little regarded, I suspect. "You're right, but the less known for now, the better."

"Much as I'd like otherwise," declares Saelora, "I do need to get to the factorage." She sits up in the bed.

Alyiakal just looks at her, marveling.

"Enough of that, dear. For now, at least." But her smile is warm as she stands and says, "I told Laetilla that I wouldn't need her for breakfasts any longer while you were here, as long as she keeps us supplied with some sort of morning pastries and fruit."

"I imagine she was dubious."

"She's very protective," says Saelora.

"I saw that. She told me in no uncertain terms that I was not allowed to get myself killed."

"She said that?"

"Close to word for word, and she was far less worried about me than you." Alyiakal's not about to repeat the exact quote.

"She respects you, but she doesn't have a high opinion of most men."

"I imagine that's based on experience."

"You need to get dressed," says Saelora firmly, "and so do I. You're hungry, too." She pauses, then adds, "And I don't mean that way."

Alyiakal thinks about embracing her again but catches the look in her eyes. Offering a sheepish smile, he quickly pulls on the uniform he wore the day before and withdraws to his official quarters to shave, wash up, and don another uniform—an older one—and then returns to the house, where he finds beakers and half fills two. He's about to start searching for pastries when Saelora joins him in the kitchen.

"I poured ale."

"Then sit, and I'll bring the pastries."

Alyiakal half obeys and walks to the dining room but does not sit. When she enters with two plates, he waits until she sets them on the table, then sits when she does.

"You could have seated yourself."

He grins. "If you won't let me seat you, then I won't let you serve me."

"You can be stubborn, dear."

He just raises his eyebrows.

She laughs, and they both sit down.

Alyiakal looks at the apple slices and pastries on his plate. "What are they?"

"Almond rolls. You and I like them. They're not too hard to make, and they keep better than most sweet pastries."

Alyiakal manages to wait until she takes a bite of her roll before he picks up his. Neither speaks until both plates are empty.

Then he looks at her. "Don't say it. You were right."

In return, she offers an amused smile before she finishes the last of her ale and stands. "We need to be leaving. I don't need the wagon today."

He stands as well.

Before that long, they're both riding toward the factorage.

Since they arrive before Vassyl, Saelora unlocks the front door and heads for the back of the factorage to unbar the doors, while Alyiakal rides to the alley entrance, leading her mount. While she readies the factorage for the day he stalls both horses and unsaddles hers. Then he closes the rear doors and makes his way to the front.

Since he can hear and sense that she is talking to someone—not Vassyl—he waits until the possible customer leaves before joining her.

"Anything important?"

"He was looking for black wool."

"Natural black wool? Not dyed?"

"I've heard that you can find it west of Lydiar. I've never seen any."

"That could be unique."

Saelora shakes her head. "I'd rather deal with greenberries. Sheep are smelly."

"Here comes Vassyl," says Alyiakal as the front door opens.

"You two are early," comments the older factor.

"You've been here early while I was gone," replies Saelora, giving the slightest nod to Alyiakal. "Khulkor just left. He was looking for black wool."

Alyiakal begins to sense Vassyl, locating and removing some of the tiny bits of chaos he'd discerned the day before.

"He always wants the impossible and never has the silvers for it, even if we had it." Vassyl's words convey resigned dismissal.

"What else has he asked for?" Alyiakal doesn't care but wants to keep Vassyl distracted. He locates several chaos bits, and destroys them with equally tiny bits of order, trying to move to separate areas of the older factor's body so that the small bits of heat aren't close together.

"He wanted a set of cupridium tableware," says Vassyl, "as if the Magi'i or Mirror Engineers could be bothered with tableware."

"Every town has someone like him," Saelora adds, "but you have to be polite, or word gets around."

"I thought you said that there were cupridium kitchen knives," says Alyiakal, returning his attention to Vassyl.

"Knives, but not tableware," says Saelora.

As Saelora and Vassyl talk, Alyiakal concentrates on the older factor. After a short time, he steps back. "I need to let you two get on with factoring."

"You're going exploring?" asks Saelora.

"More like investigating, the way we talked about. Second glass?"

"As close as I can manage. I'll walk back to the stalls with you so I can bar them after you go."

Once the two are well away from Vassyl and walking through the warehouse shelves, Saelora asks, "Could you do anything?"

"I removed more than a score, but there are scores. If they don't increase, I might be able to remove them all, but I have the feeling they might keep appearing. I'll have a better idea tomorrow."

She squeezes his hand. "Thank you."

"We'll just have to see." Far from the first time, Alyiakal reflects on how much he dislikes that phrase, accurate as it is.

When they reach the back of the warehouse, just short of the stalls, he stops and embraces her tightly, and she kisses him, then murmurs, "I could get very used to this."

"So could I."

Reluctantly, they separate, and she watches as he unstalls the roan, leads him out into the alley, and then mounts.

After turning north on Canal Street, Alyiakal takes a deep breath, knowing he needs to sharpen his order/chaos skills and see what other possibilities he can discover while still wishing that second glass would arrive sooner. Since he's going to need a fair amount of chaos, he creates a large invisible order funnel to collect the tiny chaos bits flowing from the sun.

When he rides past Marenda's house—or Gaaran and Charissa's—he doesn't see anyone outside, and he wonders if Gaaran will work out in helping with the factorage. Pleasant as Saelora and Hyrsaal's older brother is, Alyiakal doesn't see the determination evidenced in Saelora and Hyrsaal. *Maybe he suffered more than just the loss of his leg.* Judging people without knowing them well is not one of Alyiakal's better skills.

Less than a kay later, Alyiakal rides past the last of the houses and into an area of smallholdings interspersed with woodlots. After another kay, the road turns northwest. Ahead, on his left, a misshapen hill rises above low rolling lands that look ill-tended, as if they'd once been tilled and later abandoned.

Shortly, he comes to a broken gate, and a lane half overgrown with bushes and intermittent clumps of grass leading toward the east side of the hill. A mixture of grass and bushes covers most of the hillside, except for the bare earth bluff that remained from the removal of clay. Scattered young trees dot the ground near the base of the hill. He guides the roan around the gate and along the lane that shows no traces of recent use. The lane ends at the edge of a pond, continuing into the water. At the far side of the pond is the bluff, and piles of dirt lie at its base, clearly having fallen there over time.

As Alyiakal reins up, a waterfowl rises from the pond with a flurry of wingbeats, followed by a second, and then two more. Although he hasn't time to look closely, Alyiakal thinks the bird has teal and golden feathers.

He looks at the water, clear, but deep enough that he cannot see the bottom distinctly. He rides back to a young tree a good thirty yards from the water, where he dismounts and ties the roan, then walks back to the pond, stopping some five yards from the edge.

First, he compresses all the chaos bits he has gathered on his ride, then looses a quick blast of coiled chaos at the edge of the pond. A column of steam spurts from the water but disperses quickly, not enough to conceal riders or movement. *So much for that idea.*

Next, he walks closer to a sapling with a trunk about as thick as a man's wrist, stopping some ten yards away. This time, he compresses some of the remaining chaos into a blade, a blade that he swings into the trunk.

Hssst! While the bark flares and turns to ashes, the chaos merely blackens the green wood beneath.

Alyiakal compresses the chaos even more tightly and tries again, aiming for a point higher on the trunk, where he can see the results.

Hsst! When the smoke and ashes clear, the tree still stands, albeit with a gouge on one side of the trunk.

A third attempt with an even thinner "blade" results in a partial slash into the tree trunk.

For his fourth try, Alyiakal compresses the chaos even more tightly, forming it into a line no thicker than a fingernail . . . and wielding it like a shimmering blade. It slices through the trunk, and the sapling topples.

Alyiakal nods. *That could be useful, especially since there was no chaos lightflare.* At the same time, he realizes that he's exhausted all the chaos he gathered, and he shakes his head.

While he can gather more, it will be a long and tiring day.

XLII

Alyiakal and Saelora reach the factorage on sixday morning—the first there, again. Alyiakal deals with his mount and stalling the horse that drew the wagon, since Saelora needs the wagon for Gaaran to collect greenberries from various women on smallholdings around Vaeyal. He also blocks the wagon in place.

After finishing, he joins Saelora in the front behind the counter. "No Vassyl yet?"

Saelora shakes her head. "We were early, though, and it's not a short walk from his house."

"There's one thing I don't understand," says Alyiakal. "You said Vassyl sold his house north of town and gave you the set of porcelainware, and he was living above the factorage here when I first met him."

"When I bought the factorage, I told Vassyl he could keep the quarters here. After all, he is a part owner. He insisted he didn't want to. He said that he tired of climbing the steps and having to carry water up there. That's why he tore down an old house and built a small place that has just what he needs. That was two years ago."

"He's only gotten tired in the last season or so?"

"It's come on so slowly I didn't notice it until just before I left for Fyrad. Maybe I was so caught up in everything that I didn't see it as soon as I should have."

"You saw it sooner than anyone else did. I'm a field healer and—"

"You're a real healer."

"I didn't notice anything until you mentioned his tiredness. Even then it took a while to discern anything."

"I still wish I'd noticed sooner."

"I understand that. He's been good to you and given you the opportunity to become a full Merchanter."

"I wouldn't be a Merchanter without him."

"There's someone coming. I think it's Vassyl."

Within a few moments, the door opens.

"Took me a little longer to walk here from my place," says Vassyl, breathing heavily.

"You're still early," replies Saelora cheerfully.

"Not as early as I'd like, especially since you'll be gathering greenberries today."

"Not today. Gaaran'll be here later to do the gathering. There are still things I need to catch up on."

Alyiakal starts sensing Vassyl to see if he can discern any change in the amount of chaos bits within the older factor.

Vassyl frowns. "Thought you'd just about finished."

"I thought I was, until Haayal came in late yesterday, and Cheslya decided that she wanted more of that cloth than we have. I'll need to send some letters to Haansfel about it . . ."

As the two continue to talk Alyiakal scans Vassyl, but the amount of chaos bits seems little changed from the previous day. *Maybe it takes time.* He goes to work removing chaos bits.

After a quint, he steps back slightly.

Saelora pauses, then asks Vassyl, "Do you think Doerst will have those barrels ready?"

"He should have unless someone wanted slack cooperage. With him you never know."

"Alyiakal could go with me early next oneday or twoday, and we could also take care of the other items the goldsmith is interested in. That way I wouldn't need to hire a guard, who might not even be trustworthy."

Vassyl turns. "You willing to do that?"

Alyiakal smiles. "If that's what you need."

"You won't have a firelance," Vassyl points out.

"I'll manage."

Vassyl smiles wryly. "I believe you will."

"You're still out of breath," Saelora says to Vassyl. "Why don't you sit down in back for a bit while Alyiakal and I figure out the rest of the day?"

"You sure?"

"I'm sure."

Once Vassyl leaves the front area, Saelora turns to Alyiakal.

"He's still got about the same amount of chaos as yesterday before I removed all those bits. I removed even more today. All I can do is try for the next few days and see what happens."

"Do some people have those chaos bits . . . just because they're different?"

Alyiakal hesitates. "I don't know. All those I've seen were ill."

"How ill?"

"Very ill," he admits quietly. "But they had thousands of chaos bits. Vassyl only has hundreds."

"Could he get worse?"

"I don't know . . . but I don't think it's good."

"I was afraid of something like this." Saelora sighs softly. "He's always been so active. Will removing the chaos bits hurt him?"

"It might help some, as long as I don't overheat him, but I can watch that."

"Can you do that for the next few days, then? And we can see?"

Alyiakal nods. After a moment, he asks, "What are those 'items' you mentioned?"

"Old gold and silver jewelry and other pieces Vassyl's accepted as payment over the years, most of them broken or damaged. A goldsmith in Geliendra said he'd buy whatever Vassyl had for the value of the metal."

"And you'll negotiate?"

"It won't hurt to have an overcaptain with me."

"It might," he says, "but I'm no expert on Merchanter negotiations."

"It won't hurt to have a more senior officer with me."

"Then that's settled. Is there anything else I can do?"

"Not right now."

"Then I should let you get on with what you have to do." Alyiakal turns, then stops as the factorage's front door opens and Gaaran appears.

"I wasn't expecting you until later," declares Saelora. "I'm glad you're here. Vassyl's not feeling that well. He's in back resting. Would you man the counter here while I see Alyiakal off? I'll be right back."

"Of course," replies Gaaran.

"You're looking well," Alyiakal says.

"Being consorted to a good woman helps." Gaaran turns to Saelora. "Before I forget, Mother's having everyone for dinner on eightday, Karola and Faadyr, you and Alyiakal, and us."

Alyiakal sees Saelora's resignation as she says, "Let me see Alyiakal off and you can give me the details. I won't be long."

Saelora takes Alyiakal's arm for a moment. "You go first."

He follows her instructions and opens the door to the study-like section of the factorage. Saelora follows and closes the door.

Vassyl looks up from his chair with a worried look.

"Gaaran came in early," says Saelora. "He's at the counter, and I'll be back in a moment. You just take it easy for a little longer. Gaaran will call you if he needs help."

Although he leads the way through the rows of shelved goods, Alyiakal has no trouble sensing Saelora's agitation.

When they reach the stalls, he turns. "You're not exactly pleased, but you said the other night that she'd invite us for dinner."

"An invitation is one thing. A command conveyed by Gaaran is another. I know he doesn't have a choice, but I don't have to like it. And I don't."

He takes her hands, then decides to embrace her as he says, "All that is why you have your own house and factorage."

Saelora shakes her head. "I shouldn't let it get to me, but it does."

"I'll be there," Alyiakal reminds her.

"Thank the Rational Stars." Her arms circle him for a long moment. Then she says, "We need to get you on your way. Vassyl will worry if I'm not back soon."

"I can see that."

Alyiakal quickly unstalls the roan and leaves the factorage, heading for the abandoned clay quarry, hoping that he can make more progress in gathering the tiny bits of sun-chaos and in handling coiled and compressed chaos.

Like Saelora, he can't say that he's looking forward to dinner on eightday.

XLIII

On sixday, and again on sevenday, Alyiakal enjoys only moderate success in finding new ways to employ chaos, and, unfortunately, Vassyl shows no change in the amount of chaos in his body, despite Alyiakal's efforts.

On eightday morning, Alyiakal wakes before Saelora, worrying, not so much about his dwindling time with Saelora, but about the afternoon dinner at Marenda's house.

He's still thinking about it when she turns, kisses him, then asks, "You're worrying about dinner, aren't you?"

"And about Vassyl. I don't see much change."

"You're doing your best. We can only hope that he's better tomorrow. Maybe a day without you trying to remove those chaos bits will tell you something."

Most likely that you don't know what you can do to help him.

"You don't need to worry about me today, and you don't know enough about your next post to really worry. Don't worry about dinner. It's only for two glasses, and Mother can't do anything to you."

"No, but she can be cruel to you and Gaaran and Charissa, and possibly Karola and Faadyr."

"That's true, but she did ask us, even if it was a command. I don't want to live under the same roof with her, but I don't want to cut her off. It will be harder for her to be too cutting because Karola and Faadyr are coming. Also, it's easier with you there."

"But not next eightday, please. That's our—"

"I wouldn't do that to either of us. If she asks us for then, or even issues another command, I'll tell her that we already have plans. If she asks you, since she might not address the question to me . . ."

"I'll tell her that we already have plans," Alyiakal confirms. *Even if the plans only consist of not having dinner with her.* For a long moment, he just looks at Saelora. "I suppose we should get up and have some of those almond rolls. Plain lancer bread won't ever taste the same." He sighs deeply with a doleful expression and swings into a sitting position on the edge of the bed.

"Good!" declares Saelora. "I want to make sure there's plenty for you to miss."

"All it takes is you."

She stands, and Alyiakal follows her with his eyes as she throws on a robe, wondering how he ever could have been so fortunate. He stands and dons his robe—one of lancer green she had waiting for him, even if he hadn't noticed the first night—and they walk to the kitchen.

When they sit at the table, with sweet pastries, ale, and sliced pears, Alyiakal asks, "Is there anything new about the family I should know?"

"I told you Charissa's expecting."

"In late Autumn, yes." He bites into the almond roll, not too big a bite, because he wants it to last.

"She's beginning to show, and she gets tired. I worry about Gaartyn. Mother spoils him, and that will make things harder for Gaaran and Charissa."

"I won't say a word about that." *Except to you later.* "What about the consorting?"

"I told Gaaran about it when he came to the factorage on threeday. He said he'd tell Charissa and Mother. She may not ask about Hyrsaal. She certainly won't mention Catriana."

"What about Charissa's family? Anything I shouldn't ask or mention?"

Saelora shakes her head. "They're pleased that Charissa's happy and getting along with Mother."

"It sounds like all Vaeyal knows about your mother."

"How could they not?"

"That means everyone knows about us."

"They know I'm interested in you. Half of them think I'm being foolish, and the other half doesn't much care, at least as long as you're not around."

"That half doesn't care much for lancer officers?"

"They don't care for those with power who they don't know or trust. They'll give the benefit of the doubt to Hyrsaal and Gaaran because they grew up here. Other officers, not so much."

"And to your father, because he consorted your mother and settled down here."

Saelora nods.

"That's all understandable," says Alyiakal, finishing off the last morsels of the almond roll. "What would you like to do after we get dressed and before we leave for your mother's?"

"I'd like you to bring your book of maps in here on the table and show me exactly where you've been. I want to learn more about why you have to do what you do and where." She lifts her glass and empties it. Then she stands.

"A pleasure." He rises and takes her in his arms.

After several moments and a long kiss, she murmurs, "Later."

"Promise?" he asks with a smile.

"You're impossible." She smiles back, then says, "I do want to know more about where you've been." Then she eases out of his arms.

Alyiakal follows her to the bedroom, hangs the robe in the armoire, then throws on his uniform before returning to the quarters he's slept in only once.

A glass later, cleaner, shaved, and wearing a fresh uniform, he returns to the house carrying the map atlas to find Laetilla in the kitchen.

"Good morning."

"Good morning to you, ser."

"More of those delicious almond rolls?"

Laetilla turns from the worktable and says, "They're easy enough to make, and you both like them."

"How could I not?"

"People have different tastes."

"What pastries do you like best?"

"Whatever I'm baking."

"That's why everything you cook is good."

"Has anyone ever cooked for you before?"

"You mean anyone besides lancer mess cooks?"

Laetilla nods.

"For three years before I went to Kynstaar, I lived with my father, and Areya cooked for us. She was good. You're much better."

"Thank you. Do you treat all women so well?"

"There aren't any other women, not since before Saelora first wrote me."

"Why not?"

"I'm not interested in anyone else."

"Neither is she."

Alyiakal manages not to wince at the not-so-veiled warning not to hurt Saelora. "I know."

Laetilla offers a pleasant smile. "I'm glad you like the almond rolls. I'll make sure you have some to take with you when you leave."

"Thank you. I'd like that very much."

Laetilla looks at the volume he carries.

"It's a book of maps of Candar. Some of the maps aren't that good, and I

update the ones in the places I've been posted. Saelora wanted to see them."
Alyiakal wonders what else he can say and how to leave the kitchen without
seeming abrupt when Saelora appears.

"Is that your book of maps?" she asks. "It doesn't look like the maps are
very big."

"They fold out on each side. I can show you." Then he looks to Laetilla.
"Thank you for everything."

"You're welcome, ser."

Alyiakal smiles. "I'm grateful for all you do, especially all you do for Saelora."
He can sense a certain surprise.

"I'll be with you in a moment," says Saelora. "I need to go over a few things
with Laetilla."

"Take whatever time you need," says Alyiakal warmly, before making his
way to the small dining room, where he opens the atlas to the map containing
Pemedra.

Half a quint later, Saelora joins Alyiakal.

"Everything settled?"

"We needed to talk over what we'll be eating for dinner the rest of the
coming eightday. Would you mind if we had Vassyl for dinner on threeday?"

"Not at all. He'd enjoy Laetilla's fare." Alyiakal can also see that she doesn't
want any appearance of impropriety with the older factor, which means Vassyl
only gets asked when others are present, usually family, Alyiakal suspects.

Saelora studies the opened map. "I see what you mean. You added most of
the places here, didn't you? That's your hand."

After that, he points to all the places he's patrolled, and where his company saw action, but he doesn't detail that action.

When he finishes, two glasses later, Saelora looks at him. "You don't like
talking about the fighting, do you?"

"No. A company officer doesn't have much choice about whether to fight,
only about how, and sometimes not even that. Some fights will continue, year
after year, because nothing changes what's behind them. All a good company
officer can do is drive off or kill attackers with the loss of the fewest lancers
while inflicting the greatest damage, in the hopes that will delay the next
attack."

"You'd like to do more, wouldn't you?"

"I'm not in a position to." He shrugs. "I think what the Merchanters in
Cyad do creates more unnecessary deaths and problems on the border, and
in the port cities, like what happened to Liathyr. I think that the Emperor

Kieffal saw that, but when he tried to do something . . . well, I doubt that his death was the accident that was announced." He carefully folds the last map, that of the area between Luuval and Fyrad, into the atlas and closes it gently.

Just before third glass of the afternoon, as Saelora and Alyiakal ride north on Canal Street, Alyiakal sees a hint of darkness just above the horizon to the northwest. "There's a chance we might get rain later."

"Usually, we don't get much in Harvest. The heavy rains are in early Spring and Autumn."

"It looks like we're going to get one of those Autumn rains early then." He grins at her. "If it looks like a heavy rain, we might have to leave early."

"Don't even say it. Mother will insist we stay until it passes, and that might not be until tomorrow."

"Then I'll hope it doesn't become a downpour until we get back home."

"I like the way you said that."

Said what? "Home"? "Maybe that's because your house feels more like home than any place I've lived, at least since my mother died. Even then we didn't stay in one place long."

"I'm not planning on moving," replies Saelora.

"You shouldn't. Your house is tasteful and welcoming."

"Even with its patchwork slate roof?"

"I have to say I never noticed that. I wasn't interested in the roof." Saelora laughs.

When they near Marenda's house and turn down the drive, Alyiakal gets a better look at the cottage to the rear of the east side, which isn't visible from Canal Street. The small dwelling stands even with the barn to the west and is close to the same size. "That's a good-sized cottage."

"Gaaran and Charissa—and her family—wanted Mother to be comfortable."

"Good of them."

"And very practical, dear—as you know."

When Saelora and Alyiakal near the barn, Gaaran limps from the side porch to meet them, calling out, "You two are the first!"

Once he and Saelora rein up and dismount, it doesn't take long to stall the two geldings, since Alyiakal's not about to unsaddle them.

As the three walk toward the house, Gaaran says, "We're all in the parlor because it's easier to listen for Gaartyn there—he's napping—and that way Charissa or Mother can look in on the kitchen and how dinner is coming. I do hope Karola and Faadyr won't be long."

"Karola will make sure they're not too late," says Saelora, "if only so that it doesn't give Mother an opportunity to comment."

Alyiakal has the feeling that Marenda will find a way, if that's what she has in mind.

Saelora leads the way onto the porch and into the parlor, but the moment Alyiakal steps into the parlor, he looks to Marenda, whose hair now shows more gray strands among the flame red. She remains in the same chair from which she had presided the last time Alyiakal visited. He inclines his head respectfully to her. "Thank you for the invitation."

Marenda smiles pleasantly. "It's one way to get the recluse away from her retreat, and we all might learn something of interest from beyond Vaeyal."

Gaaran says quickly, "We have some white Alafraan, or a very good pale ale." He glances toward Charissa, seated on the settee.

"The ale, please."

"If you'd been here past eightday," adds Marenda, looking to Alyiakal, "you could have had that delicious red Fhynyco—but I forgot—you were both still in Fyrad."

"I had temporary duty there after finishing my assignment to close the post at Luuval early," Alyiakal says easily, looking to Gaaran and adding, "The Alafraan, please."

"The same," says Saelora.

As Gaaran leaves to get refreshments, Charissa asks, "Wasn't that where the whole town fell into the ocean?"

"Most of it. After we closed the post and left, the morass swallowed the entire post."

"It appears that your timing was impeccable, again," says Marenda smoothly. "You appear to be most fortunate."

"Merely vigilant," replies Alyiakal. "When the morass swallowed the south wall, we cut short the closure period, packed up what we could and left. Less than an eightday later, the morass swallowed the post and everything close."

"Was anyone hurt?" asks Charissa.

"Only the Imperial tariff enumerator, his staff, and guards. They all died."

"They didn't believe Alyiakal," adds Saelora.

"I have everyone's refreshments," declares Gaaran, returning with a tray containing wineglasses and beakers. He presents the first wineglass to Marenda, who sets it on the side table as if it were her due, and offers a long-suffering look as Gaaran serves the others, then says, "Here come Karola and Faadyr."

At Gaaran's announcement of his sister, Marenda offers a not quite inaudible sigh.

"I'll see them in and be back in a moment," declares Gaaran.

"Of course, dear," replies Marenda too sweetly.

Karola is the first to enter the parlor, followed by the lanky Faadyr. Alyiakal is once more reminded of how much Karola resembles her mother, although her flame-red hair has no gray and is cut shorter.

"How are the children?" Marenda asks Karola in a tone conveying little interest.

"Karmara looks more like you every day," says Faadyr before Karola can speak. "She's not quite three, but she definitely has a mind of her own. It's a bit early to tell about Daarfyn."

"He looks like you," declares Karola, turning to her consort. "It's obvious."

"I suppose that's the way it should be," replies Marenda.

"Of course it is," adds Gaaran cheerfully as he enters the parlor behind Faadyr. "Pale ale or white Alafraan?"

"The Alafraan," says Karola.

"The same," says Faadyr with a nod.

Gaaran leaves the parlor but returns with two half-filled wineglasses moments after Karola seats herself on the settee beside Charissa.

"It's good to have *almost* the entire family here for eightday dinner," says Marenda pleasantly, "as well as the distinguished overcaptain." She inclines her head to Alyiakal.

"I'm not distinguished yet," replies Alyiakal with a smile. "I have a way to go before reaching the accomplishments of your consort, but I appreciate the encouragement."

"As you are finding, Overcaptain, officers not from Cyad seldom gain full recognition for their accomplishments. He should have been at least a subcommander, and you, like him, will be fortunate to become a majer. But we shouldn't devote conversation to what we cannot change." Marenda turns to Saelora. "Did you sell any more of that green liqueur in Fyrad?"

"All that I took, and I have orders for the next batch of greenberry brandy."

"Mostly from outlanders, I'd imagine. They'll drink anything as long as it's strong." Marenda abruptly stands. "We should start dinner. That way, Charissa might actually get to eat it."

As Charissa awkwardly rises from the settee, Alyiakal sees that she is definitely with child and senses the order/chaos patterns within her, suggesting that the child is healthy.

Marenda directs the seating. She sits at the head of the table, with Gaaran at her right and Charissa at her left. Karola is to Gaaran's right and across from Faadyr, while Alyiakal is on Karola's other side and across from Saelora.

In moments, the serving girl appears and provides plates, beginning with Marenda. On each dish are two healthy slices of ham with fried apples, cheese scalloped potatoes, and boiled quilla strips.

Alyiakal glances from his plate to Saelora, who gives a quick amused smile.

"To family," says Marenda, lifting her wineglass, "even to those who carry it on from afar."

"To family."

Everyone at least sips their drink, and then, after Marenda lifts her utensils, begins to eat.

"When do you have to leave, Alyiakal?" asks Gaaran.

"An eightday from tomorrow."

"Seems like a short leave."

"I've a long way to travel to get to Lhaarat."

Gaaran nods. "Not quite as far as Isahl or Pemedra, but still a long journey."

Alyiakal returns to eating, finding the ham tasty, if slightly drier than he prefers, aided by the fried apples, the potatoes good, and the quilla barely edible, although he eats it all.

Karola clears her throat. "Do you think you and Hyrsaal will ever be at the same post at the same time?"

"There's nothing that says we can't be, but with all the border posts, the port posts, and other assignments, the odds are against it."

Abruptly, Charissa rises from the table as the sound of a crying child carries into the dining room. She turns and says, "It was good to see you, Alyiakal . . . in case you have to leave before I get Gaartyn settled."

"It was good to see you."

"She almost got to finish dinner," says Gaaran.

"Mothers seldom do," comments Karola, "unless their consorts don't." She glances fondly at Faadyr.

"That's not exactly traditional," Marenda points out.

"Times change," counters Karola.

"Not as much as younger people think," replies Marenda. "Traditions have their reasons."

"Both good and bad," says Alyiakal.

Marenda raises her eyebrows.

Alyiakal merely smiles.

"I take it traditions don't run strongly in your family, Overcaptain."

"Oh, two of them do. Do whatever you do right and do it well. My father was very clear on that. Oh . . . he also said to make sure that you know why people do something before you try to change it."

"That sounds like Kayral, but then they were both majers." Marenda lifts a small bell and rings it, and the serving girl appears and begins to clear.

"Dessert?" asks Karola.

"Dessert is simple," declares Marenda. "Just a sweet lemon cake."

In moments, each diner has a small plate with a slice of unremarkable-looking yellow cake, except for Charissa, who has not returned.

Marenda takes a bite and cocks her head. "Not bad."

Alyiakal notices the momentary frown from Gaaran and wonders. Then he takes a small bite. The cake is moist with a pervasive taste of sweet lemon, although he thinks that it would be better if it were slightly moister. *But it's better than any dessert you've had besides those fixed by Laetilla . . . or Catriana and Elina.*

Another half glass passes before Marenda rises. "We shouldn't keep Karola and Faadyr any longer. They have a long drive home." She looks more to Faadyr than Karola and says, "I do appreciate your coming," then focuses cold eyes on Alyiakal, "and you as well, Overcaptain."

"I appreciate your hospitality," replies Alyiakal, "and am glad for the opportunity to see everyone. It was thoughtful of you to do this, and I thank you."

Saelora says, "Thank you, Mother, and please convey my thanks to Charissa."

"That I will."

"I'll see you all out," declares Gaaran.

A quint later, Saelora and Alyiakal ride slowly south on Canal Street.

"What did you think about dinner? Honestly?" she asks.

"Well . . . that toast your mother offered was . . . rather enigmatic."

"Pointed, I'd say, especially at the bottom of the table. What about the food?"

"Good, but nothing compared to what comes out of your kitchen. Does your mother have a fondness for quilla?"

"You try to hide it, but it's not your favorite. Mother noticed that. She's good at annoying little details."

"I wondered. But she was almost complimentary about the dessert. Was that because Charissa made it?"

"How did you know that?"

"Gaaran frowned when your mother said, 'Not bad.'" Alyiakal pauses, then asks, "She can't even compliment Charissa?"

"That's about as close as she comes." She smiles wryly. "It could have been worse."

"It has been," Alyiakal says wryly.

Saelora laughs.

XLIV

Early on oneday morning, Alyiakal rides beside the Loraan House wagon that Saelora drives east along the graystone road to Geliendra. He has already extended his order/chaos funnel to gather sun-chaos bits, partly for practice and partly in case they run into brigands.

"How do we get to the cooperage?" he asks.

"Just before we get to the edge of town, there's a lane on the north side. It's not very long. Doerst is at the end. He mostly does slack cooperage, but years ago Vassyl persuaded him to do tight cooperage for linseed oil because no one else did. We still ship some, but not many flax growers are left, and he agreed to make tight barrels for us so long as it didn't interfere with his dry barrels. Sometimes he'll clean and retoast old barrels, too."

"Most coopers don't do both, do they?"

"Not in places like Fyrad or Cyad."

It's late midmorning when Saelora turns down a narrow lane, barely wide enough for two wagons, to Doerst's cooperage. As Saelora brings the wagon to a halt with the rear doors in the middle of the small loading dock, a burly, white-bearded man appears.

"Didn't expect to see you today," he says, looking from Saelora to Alyiakal. "Especially not with a Mirror Lancer officer."

"Alyiakal is a friend of my brother's. He'll be leaving for his next post shortly," says Saelora. "I persuaded him to accompany me. Since we were coming to Geliendra anyway, I thought it wouldn't hurt to stop and see how you were coming on the barrels."

"I've got a half score done. The early wheat crop wasn't that good, and the millers didn't need as many dry barrels for the flour."

"Then we'll take them. That's about all I'd want to carry right now."

Alyiakal wonders if they'll fit in the wagon, but says nothing, knowing that Saelora must have that figured out.

"I'll roll 'em out," says Doerst.

Alyiakal dismounts and ties the roan to a post to the right of the loading dock, glad that he'd had the foresight to bring riding gloves, since he'd felt he might end up loading or unloading things. In the end, the wagon holds eight barrels upright, and two lashed sideways on top of the eight.

Once Saelora has paid the cooper and drives back down the lane, she says to Alyiakal, riding beside her, "We could have taken two more, but that wouldn't leave much space."

"Are we getting much more?"

"Probably not, but it doesn't hurt to have a little space just in case."

"Where is this goldsmith?"

"He's the only one in Geliendra," she says with a smile. "That's why I wore the bracelet."

Alyiakal isn't about to point out that she always wears it when she's in Merchanter blues. "Have you met him before?"

"Twice, with Vassyl. He knows who I am, not much more."

By the time Saelora maneuvers into a space before the goldsmith's shop, it's nearly midday. After Alyiakal ties up his mount, she secures the horse and wagon and sets the brakes, then retrieves a leather case, and says, "If you'd come with me while I meet with Draesyl but keep an eye—or your senses—on the wagon. Now that I have this, there's not much to steal easily, but you never know."

The same muscular, middle-aged man Alyiakal met three years earlier looks up from the counter and frowns, then smiles. "I didn't recognize you at first, Lady Merchanter. You're here about the broken jewelry and the like?"

"I am." Saelora sets the case on the counter.

The goldsmith's eyes widen as he glances at the bracelet on Saelora's wrist, and he looks to Alyiakal. "Overcaptain . . . have we met?"

Alyiakal smiles. "Not since I was a captain. I did tell you that you wouldn't have to worry."

"I can see that." Draesyl looks to Saelora. "I beg your pardon, Lady, but the piece on your wrist . . . I had no idea."

"Neither did she when I purchased it," says Alyiakal, "but I believe you two have certain matters to discuss." He steps back to where he can survey both the wagon and the counter.

"Factor Vassyl said we'd be discussing the value of the metal and stones."

"Mostly," replies Saelora. "There are a few intact pieces. There's no obligation on your part."

Alyiakal turns his full attention to someone who slows his mount and studies the wagon as he rides past, a rider with a short sword, or a long knife, at his waist, and a long leather case that just might hold a bow and a quiver.

Perhaps half a quint later a second armed rider passes the wagon at a slow walk. While he doesn't vary his pace, Alyiakal senses his interest as well, and he has a very good idea what the two have in mind, although neither rides past the goldsmith's shop again.

Several people look to enter the shop, but when they see both the wagon and Alyiakal, they hurry past.

Close to a glass later, Saelora closes the case and waits as the goldsmith checks the list that she wrote as the two went through the items in the case, not all of which were to Draesyl's liking or interest. Another quint passes before the goldsmith counts out golds into a leather bag, and Saelora signs and seals a receipt for the coinage.

"Thank you, Lady. These days it's often hard to get enough gold of any sort, and I cannot sell what I cannot make." He looks to Alyiakal. "Thank you, Overcaptain, your presence kept us from being interrupted."

"You're welcome."

Saelora slips the leather bag into the case, then moves toward the door.

Alyiakal steps outside first and scans the area. He sees no sign of the two riders. *Not yet.*

Once outside, Saelora locks the case in the secure compartment through the small door concealed behind the teamster's seat.

"I take it there's a lot there," says Alyiakal.

"Close to forty golds. Most of it for the gold in the broken jewelry and rings. Three golds' worth of silver. The silver and gold were worth more than that, but Draesyl will have to melt it down."

"How long has Vassyl been accepting broken, damaged, or unwanted jewelry for payment?"

"Some of it his father took in. Not that much in a given year, but it adds up."

"We're likely going to have company on the drive back." Alyiakal explains about the riders. "They'll either follow or precede us to a more deserted section of the road. I'd guess it will be two or three kays after the road to Vaeyal splits off from the road to Fyrad."

"Can you deal with them?" she asks worriedly.

"Yes, but it would be better in a deserted place. I'll unblock the wheels and untie the horse. We might as well get this over with." He shakes his head. "I was going to ask if you wanted to see the Great Forest, but with brigands following us, that wouldn't be the best of ideas."

In less than half a quint, Saelora has the wagon headed west on the avenue that turns into the road to Vaeyal and Fyrad.

Riding beside her, his unseen order/chaos funnel still fully extended, Alyiakal senses her unease. "Don't worry about it."

"How can you be so calm?"

"Because a few brigands aren't anything to worry about compared to Kyphran mages and firecannon."

Saelora shivers slightly.

Alyiakal keeps gathering chaos bits while sensing in all directions, but especially behind them, although he suspects at least one of the brigands is already in front of them, since the brigands had taken a good look at the wagon and discerned that it was from Vaeyal.

Once Saelora and Alyiakal pass through the outskirts of Geliendra and the avenue becomes the whitestone road to Fyrad, Alyiakal senses two riders well back from the wagon, just out of sight. "Two of them are following us. I'd guess that there will be two or three waiting ahead, where there aren't any dwellings close by. They'll order us to stop. Do what they say."

"Then what?"

"Do what I say," he replies good-naturedly.

The two proceed for several kays farther west until they reach the fork in the road, where Saelora turns the wagon onto the graystone paving of the road to Vaeyal.

Three kays farther along, two riders emerge from the trees ahead to block the road. Both carry bows. "Stop the wagon!"

Saelora slows the wagon to a stop, and Alyiakal extends his shields to cover her and the wagon horse.

The two riders edge closer, but remain some thirty yards away, close enough for Alyiakal. Neither rider says anything as the two wait for the trailing riders to join them.

As the other two riders slow to a walk ten yards behind the wagon, one of the riders with a bow says, "Sorry about this, officer." Then he looses a shaft aimed straight at Alyiakal, and the shaft snaps against Alyiakal's shield.

Alyiakal fires a thin, compressed, and coiled chaos bolt at the archer that cuts through the middle of his chest, followed in quick succession by three others. Four cold black death mists drift across the road. Two of the dead brigands have been unhorsed and their mounts shy away. The other two horses back off slightly, but don't flee.

"Just hold the wagon," Alyiakal says to Saelora, as he rides slowly toward the nearest mount, projecting a sense of reassurance. When he gets close enough, he manages, using order to nudge the other mount, to unhorse the dead brigand, and tie the mount to a nearby tree. He does the same with the other mount bearing a dead brigand. Then he uses more chaos to destroy all four bodies, before dismounting and gathering all the metallic items that survived the chaos bursts and scattering them into the bushes away from the road. Then he remounts and rides up beside Saelora.

She looks at him. "They would have killed us both."

He nods.

"You could sense them. Couldn't we have avoided them?"

"We could," Alyiakal admits, "but that would have left them free to rob and kill other travelers. This way, it's mysterious. Known brigands vanish, but their mounts don't. Sooner or later, they'd be caught and executed. If they weren't, then more travelers would have died." He looks at her. "I didn't want you to be one of them after I leave."

"You set it up so that no one but me would know how it happened?"

"It was that or avoid them and let them kill others. This way the road will be a little safer." *For a while.* "We should get moving."

"What about the horses?"

"I couldn't catch two. Someone will find them, and horses are valuable. They should be all right. At least as all right as being a brigand's mount." *Which may not be wonderful, but that's the best you can do.*

Saelora eases the wagon forward, clearly thinking. Finally, she says, "You had it all planned, didn't you?"

"I had several plans, depending on what they did."

"You weren't really in danger, were you?"

"*We* weren't in danger. I had you shielded."

"Can you do that . . . when you fight?"

"Only for a short time. I spent the whole trip to Geliendra gathering chaos. I used most of it dealing with the brigands, and there were only four of them. I almost didn't survive against the Kyphrans."

Saelora shivers once more but keeps her eyes on the road. "So you have a better chance of surviving than Hyrsaal."

"Probably," he admits, "but I'll always be assigned to more dangerous posts. That evens it out a bit."

"You seemed so cold . . . so efficient."

"I'm sorry, but it's better you know. I've never liked hiding what I have to do from you. I've told you what I've done, but seeing it is different."

"It is." She swallows but doesn't look in his direction.

Alyiakal continues to ride beside her but says nothing.

After half a quint, she asks, "What should we tell Vassyl?"

"That's up to you, except if you do tell him, please leave out exactly how I dealt with the brigands."

Saelora frowns. "He has enough to worry about. You will check him before we leave, since he wasn't at the factorage when we left?"

"I will."

Another quint goes by, and they pass the side road that used to be the main road to Vaeyal.

Saelora finally says, "How do you feel about . . . the brigands?"

"About killing them? It doesn't bother me. They had no problem with robbing, injuring, or killing people. That's evil."

"That's true . . ." Saelora leaves her words hanging.

"But it still bothers you?"

"It does. I can't say why."

"Because it seems so final? They would have kept doing that, just like the ones who killed the salt and spice traders I told you about. The attack was planned from the moment they saw your wagon. I had more problems in killing the Kyphran troopers. They weren't evil. They were just following orders. Killing them was necessary for us to survive. If we didn't stop them, a lot more people would have died." *Of course, that's a rationalization as well, but it's got some basis in fact.* "I don't have much sympathy for men who kill and take what others earn through hard work."

"I can see that," says Saelora dryly.

"Do you think I'm wrong?"

She shakes her head. "It just happened so quickly."

Alyiakal can tell that she's still disturbed, but at the moment he doesn't know what else he can say. *Perhaps later you can talk about it.*

They arrive at the alley behind Loraan House just before the third glass of the afternoon.

"You want the barrels to stay in the wagon, I take it," says Alyiakal.

"Yes, please."

"I'll take care of the horses and block the wagon in place, while you talk to Vassyl."

"You're sure?"

"Very sure. You need to get those golds locked away."

Even so, Vassyl and Saelora are still sitting and talking at the conference table in the study area of the factorage after Alyiakal finishes with the horses and wagon.

Saelora gestures to an empty chair and says, "Gaaran's out front."

Alyiakal sits down at the table and begins to sense Vassyl for bits of chaos.

"I was telling Vassyl about what Draesyl didn't want. They were all undamaged pieces. He was definitely looking for what he could melt down or reset."

"I hear you surprised him," says Vassyl.

"Some, anyway."

"Vassyl's been arguing with me," says Saelora. "He claims that the golds from Draesyl should go into the factorage accounts."

"She bought the factorage," declares the older factor. "That broken jewelry belonged to the factorage, not to me."

Saelora laughs. "You brought that case from your place. I didn't even know about it, and I certainly didn't buy it."

"But it all bought goods from the factorage," insists Vassyl.

"You still own a fifth of the factorage."

"Only for now." He pauses. "I suppose I could take a fifth. I refuse to take all the golds."

"Half and half," counters Saelora, "and if you won't take it, I'll give what you won't take to Elinjya."

"You are stubborn," says Vassyl. "I'll take half, then, but it will stay in the hidden strongbox here with Elinjya's name on it. She doesn't need it now, but her daughter might in time."

"Done." Saelora sighs. "You're the stubborn one." After a pause, she stands. "Let me take care of that now." She turns to Alyiakal. "If you wouldn't mind telling Gaaran he can leave, and you can stand behind the counter for a few moments."

Alyiakal stands.

"I can do that," Vassyl insists.

"You've been here long enough today," declares Saelora.

"You're acting like my daughter," grumbles the older factor.

"Hardly," replies Saelora cheerfully. "She'd never tell you what to do."

Vassyl looks to Alyiakal and says, "You see what you're getting into?"

"I've known that from her first letter."

Vassyl stands and smiles. "You're as stubborn as she is. I'll see you both tomorrow."

Alyiakal follows him through the door to the front of the factorage but stops behind the counter. When Vassyl leaves, Alyiakal turns to Gaaran. "Saelora says that you can go now. We'll take care of things."

"She did?"

Alyiakal nods.

"Tell her I appreciate it."

"She appreciates what you do."

Once Gaaran leaves, Alyiakal waits for half a quint before Saelora returns.

"Thank you," she says.

"No thanks are necessary. I like being here with you."

"What about Vassyl?"

"It's not looking good. There are more of those chaos bits. I removed what I could."

She purses her lips. "I think he knows something isn't right."

"Why? Because he gave in too quickly on the golds for Elinjya?"

Saelora nods. "He's usually more stubborn, especially since Elinjya has never liked the factorage. She still comes by every eightday or so, sometimes with the children. She'd rather see him at his house, but she can't get away in the evenings so it's usually here. She's happy being a mother and the consort to a landholder."

"Doesn't she have any interest?"

"In the factorage? No. She even told me, quietly, that my buying it was the best thing for everyone, because her father didn't have to work as hard, and she didn't need to feel guilty about the future of what he'd built."

"You are one of his daughters, you know."

She smiles wryly. "I know. We're a bit alike. We both want to create something, even if it's only a strong factorage."

"Or trading house," adds Alyiakal. "You wanted it to be more than just a factorage, and it already is."

"Barely."

"You've done wonders in less than three years." He laughs softly. "And not another word about how much there is to do or what you haven't done, stubborn driven woman."

"It takes one to know one, and I will need someone strong and stubborn to unload those barrels at the distillery." Then she grins.

But Alyiakal senses something behind the grin, and he's afraid he knows what it is.

XLV

Twoday morning Alyiakal is awake early, trying not to disturb Saelora when she turns and looks at him.

"You didn't sleep well last night. Don't deny it."

"I didn't. I admit it."

"It sounded like you had nightmares. Do you want to tell me why?"

Alyiakal doesn't answer immediately. Finally, he says, "I remembered yesterday . . . and you. You looked stunned after I dealt with the brigands. I tried to explain, but last night I had the feeling that all the explaining . . . somehow . . . didn't . . . and that you were upset . . ."

"You didn't say anything about it last night." Her voice is even, not judgmental.

"I couldn't."

"Couldn't?" She frowns slightly.

"Maybe it's more accurate to say that I didn't know what else to say. Anything besides what I did would have been worse for everyone. It's . . . I do what has to be done. I don't think much about it. The feelings, and the nightmares, come later." *Sometimes much later.*

For a moment, Saelora says nothing. Then she nods slowly. "The perfect combat officer . . . doing what has to be done . . . and the feelings come later."

"I'm not that perfect. I don't have nightmares about everyone I've killed." *Thank the Rational Stars.*

"Not that you remember," she says gently. "But you had nightmares last night, and that was after you dealt with brigands who you felt deserved to die."

"One way or another, if I hadn't killed them, there would have been more deaths, either theirs or those of others they robbed and killed. Removing brigands has been one of my duties."

"Dear, you don't have to convince me. They shot at you before you said or did anything."

"Then why . . . ? I could tell that something about yesterday . . . that even after I explained, you moved away . . . that's not it . . . not exactly . . ."

"You're right," she says softly. "I was . . . stunned, I guess. You've been so thoughtful, so considerate, so loving . . . and then . . . there's this . . ."

"Other side?" he asks.

"Something I knew had to be there, but I didn't realize . . . I couldn't understand how the man I love could seem so cold, when I know you're not. I know you and Hyrsaal have to do what you do. But you were so cool . . . as if . . ."

"As if?" he asks quietly. "As if the brigands were just an obstacle to be removed?"

She nods.

They were. "I can't pretend to have much feeling for them. They would have killed us both without a thought."

"But you had nightmares about them." She looks at him directly. "Do you have nightmares like that often?"

Alyiakal isn't sure how he should respond but realizes that there's only one way to answer. "More than I'd like." He pauses. "Always within days of a skirmish, but also at times when there's no apparent reason." After a moment, he adds, "Sometimes, the Great Forest gets into them."

At her expression of surprise and possibly annoyance, he says, "Not like it's dictating the dreams or telling me what to do, but sometimes I get flashes of scenes or things that might have been in the times of the First, and when I wake up from those dreams, I always wonder why I dreamed that."

"I'm surprised you don't have more nightmares," replies Saelora thoughtfully. "I can see why you worry about the Great Forest having a purpose for you."

Alyiakal is relieved not to sense judgment or displeasure, but he still worries. Finally, as the silence drags out, he says, "I worry that I've disappointed you, that somehow . . . that I could have found a better way . . ."

"You haven't disappointed me. You couldn't have done anything any better with the brigands. It's just . . ."

"That I should have said more last night . . . and before?"

"It doesn't matter now. You've told me." She eases closer to him and holds him tightly. "Just don't shut me out."

Alyiakal senses the words are as much command as plea, and he puts his arms around her, feeling her tears against his face, her last words echoing through his thoughts. *Don't shut me out.*

XLVI

After spending the late morning and early afternoon of threeday at the abandoned clay pit working with coiled and compressed chaos, Alyiakal rides back to Saelora's house, where he finds Laetilla well into dinner preparations.

"Can I help?" he asks as he enters the kitchen from the stable door.

"You could bring me half an armload of stove wood."

"The wood stack just inside the stable door?"

"The same. Put it in the copper bin beside the stove."

In moments, Alyiakal returns with the stove wood and carefully stacks it in the bin. "Can you tell me what we're having for dinner?"

"I'd rather not." Laetilla smiles and adds, "No quilla, though."

Alyiakal shakes his head. "Saelora will have you knowing all my bad points."

"Far as I'm concerned, your only bad point is that you're seldom here."

"Right now, any other choices are worse."

"Least you didn't say you don't have a choice. How long will you be gone?"

"It's a three-year posting that can be extended another year or even two. Depending on how it's extended, I might get home leave before the extension."

"So three years again this time?" Laetilla's tone is quietly sardonic.

"Most likely."

"Thank you for the stove wood."

Alyiakal understands that Laetilla needs to get on with making dinner and his presence is unnecessary. "My pleasure." He inclines his head and leaves the kitchen for his quarters, knowing that Vassyl and Saelora won't get to the house anytime soon.

As he approaches the distillery building, he smiles faintly, recalling the afternoon before when Saelora had taken him through the distillery, and he thinks how far she's come from the girl who had first written him so many years before.

Rather than work on maps, Alyiakal turns and walks east along the old roadbed to the edge of the swamp, more than three hundred yards from the distillery building. There he stops and studies the patterns of order and chaos beneath him, marveling once again at the two separate yet conflicting structures of order.

As he considers what he senses, he realizes that the two structures aren't parallel to each other, the way they are beneath the Great Canal. *Could that be what caused the chaos that undermined the old road?*

Alyiakal turns and walks slowly back to his quarters, pondering the possibilities.

He is still pondering when he senses the approach of Saelora's wagon, but in moments, he's out of his quarters and standing at the end of the drive, waiting.

"You must have good ears," calls Vassyl, sitting on the teamster's bench beside Saelora as she turns the wagon toward the stable.

Alyiakal walks alongside the wagon.

"All his senses are excellent," says Saelora.

Once she halts the wagon, she turns to Alyiakal. "If you'd show Vassyl to the parlor."

"I will, but once he's settled, I'll be back to help you."

Even so, it's more than a quint before the three are seated in the parlor, each with a glass of white Alafraan.

Vassyl raises his wineglass. "It's amazing what you've done here, Saelora. Five years ago, the house was falling apart. Now it looks like a small mansion."

"Hardly that," she replies. "It's now an older house in good repair with moderately tasteful rooms."

"You also made the factorage much more welcoming as well," says Vassyl, "and more important, more profitable."

"I used your experience and built on what you'd done."

"It looks to me," says Alyiakal quickly, "that it's worked out well for everyone, including the whole town."

Vassyl nods, then turns to Alyiakal. "It's a shame you've got to depart so soon."

"I wish I had more time, but I took most of my allowable leave. I left a little on the books for unforeseen circumstances, just in case."

"Wise of you," says Vassyl dryly. "There are always unforeseen circumstances, even at my age. You just can't predict everything, no matter how hard you try." Then he looks at Saelora and then Alyiakal. "Don't put things off too long." He chuckles wryly, then adds, "None of my business, but you two belong together. Clear as the Rational Stars in Winter."

Saelora looks toward the kitchen and rises from the settee. "Dinner is ready."

Alyiakal stands and follows her and Vassyl into the small dining room, where she seats herself at the head of the table, with Alyiakal at her right and Vassyl at her left. Before he sits, Alyiakal quietly refills the wineglasses.

"I'm sure you recognize the porcelainware," says Saelora.

"I'm happy you have it. It needs to be used and appreciated, and there's no one left in my family who's able to use it, at least publicly, and it shouldn't be hidden away. Elinjya feels the same way. You're like her sister."

"I'm glad she feels that way," replies Saelora.

Laetilla begins to serve, and Alyiakal wonders what might be on the plates, then sees that each diner has a boneless fowl breast stuffed with some kind of cheese, along with crispy lace potatoes, and green beans and mushrooms in a butter sauce, as well as a small loaf of fresh-baked bread for each person.

"This is what you'd expect in the Palace of Light," says Vassyl.

"I imagine the surroundings would be quite a bit more lavish," replies Saelora, "but thank you . . . and Laetilla. She's outstanding."

Alyiakal nods to that, then lifts his wineglass. "To Saelora . . . and Laetilla."

"To them both," returns Vassyl, raising his wineglass and then taking a sip before setting it on the Merchanter-blue tablecloth.

For a short time, no one says much, given how tender and tasty the cheese-herbed fowl breast is, complemented by the just-crispy-enough lace potatoes. But after another mouthful and a sip of Alafraan, he looks to Vassyl. "I don't believe I've ever heard how you and your family got into factoring."

Vassyl chuckles. "It's a very boring story, but it's short, and you haven't heard it." He clears his throat and takes another sip of wine. "My grandfather was a cobbler, and he was always complaining that he couldn't get decent nails here in Vaeyal. The two smiths were more interested in horseshoes and more profitable ironwork, because shoe nails and tacks take more effort than regular nails. There were also other small goods folks didn't want to travel four glasses to Geliendra to get. By themselves, they didn't add up to much, but my father didn't want to be a cobbler. So he borrowed from his father and others and bought an old mule and started making trips to Geliendra and other places. People were willing to pay a bit more, especially if they didn't even know if they'd find what they needed in Geliendra.

"Once I was old enough, I did the traveling and buying, and that's how it started. Nowadays, some merchants send goods by barge because they know us." The older factor shrugs. "Like I said. Simple and boring."

"You left out all the hard work," says Alyiakal.

"To accomplish anything worthwhile takes hard work," replies Vassyl. "What about you? Why a Mirror Lancer?"

Alyiakal laughs. "Even simpler. My father was a lancer officer. I never thought much about being anything else, although I did have some instruction from a magus, but he and my father decided my talents weren't suited to the Magi'i. What little I could do was too order-based."

"Sounds like they thought you were too honest and straightforward," says Vassyl. "Just as happy I've never even met a mage. Saelora said you had to deal with some at your last post."

"Mostly at Oldroad Post. Two Magi'i and two Mirror Engineers. The Magi'i were more interested in the chaos-cutter and the old firelances we found. The Mirror Engineers rebuilt part of the road so it could be used again. I crossed paths with a magus at Luuval and another in Fyrad. That's about it." Alyiakal pauses. "Oh, the last time I was here, the Third Magus visited the post at Geliendra, and he spent a few moments with every lancer officer."

"Sounds like you've seen more of them than most folks. What do you think of them?"

"They're like people with power. Some are pleasant; some aren't; most are condescending."

Saelora winces, if slightly.

"You have power," says Vassyl evenly.

"I try very hard not to be condescending. I'm aware many people have more power than I do. I'm about the most junior senior officer in the Mirror Lancers, and any full magus likely has more power." Alyiakal has some doubts about the last statement, given that he has more ability than the most junior mages, but it would certainly be true for most overcaptains. "We all will die . . . and anyone can be killed in certain circumstances, no matter how powerful they are." He smiles wryly. "That's far too pedantic for dinner conversation, which should tell you how few I've had."

"I'm not sure most of us are that honest," replies Vassyl.

"From what I've seen, you're more honest than most people, and you've also accomplished more. Do you think honesty and accomplishment go together?"

Vassyl shakes his head. "I've known honest men who've accomplished nothing and lying schemers who died wealthy. I do think that honest men— and women—who accomplish something are more likely to be at peace with themselves . . ."

For the next glass, Alyiakal tries to say as little as possible and to get Vassyl to do most of the talking.

After a pause, Vassyl clears his throat, then says, "You two were pretty fortunate on oneday."

"Oh?" returns Saelora. "In what way?"

"Remember how I told you that folks were talking about brigands along the roads out of Geliendra?"

"That's why I asked Alyiakal to accompany me."

"Well, it seems like something strange happened on oneday." Vassyl takes a sip of the Alafraan white. "One of the smallholders there found four horses along the road. Two of them tied up neat like, and two running loose. All four were saddled, with no sign of the riders."

"You're thinking that brigands robbed the riders and got rid of the bodies?" asks Alyiakal.

"That's what Traybett thinks," replies Vassyl. "He's the one who told me. Only problem is that no one who's well off enough to have horses is missing. No one's missing horses. Traybett said that there wasn't any sign of blood, but two of the horses had empty bow cases fastened to the saddle. There was a wallet with a few silvers and some coppers stashed in one saddlebag."

"That's definitely strange," says Alyiakal agreeably.

"That's what I told Traybett."

Alyiakal can see the hint of a twinkle in the older factor's eyes.

"I'm guessing those horses belonged to brigands, and they picked the wrong folks to rob." Vassyl shrugs. "There's no trace of the brigands and no sign of who they tried to rob. Seems like whoever it was didn't want it known."

"It would seem so," replies Alyiakal.

"Well, it's best that way. Might even make other brigands wary, least for a while."

"We can certainly hope so." Alyiakal means every word.

"It's really time for me to go." Vassyl rises from the table. "I appreciate the dinner and your listening to me prattle, and the extra effort to get me here and home."

"After all you've done, it's little enough," replies Saelora as she and Aly-iakal stand.

In half a quint, Alyiakal rides alongside the wagon in the late twilight as Saelora drives the more than two kays to Canal Street before heading north then turning west. She brings the wagon to a halt at the fourth house, a dwelling that looks roughly similar to the others on the street, but is far newer, with solid brick walls and a slate roof.

Vassyl climbs down carefully and walks to the front, where he turns. "Thank you again! I enjoyed the dinner and the evening."

"We'll see you tomorrow," Saelora calls back.

The two wait until Vassyl is safely inside before Saelora eases the wagon away from the house. The ride back is slower, given that twilight has given way to full night, but Alyiakal neither sees nor senses anyone following or lurking about.

Once they return and take care of the wagon and horses, they repair to the parlor, and, since Laetilla has retired to her quarters at the other end of the distillery, he pours them each another glass of Alafraan, then sits down in the other armchair.

"How was Vassyl tonight?" asks Saelora.

"You mean his chaos? There were more chaos bits than there were after I removed what I could this morning, but a few less than before I did."

"Then he's slowly getting worse, in spite of what you're doing," says Saelora. "He's getting weaker, but he doesn't want to talk about it, and I don't want to bring it up, except to insist that he get more rest and not be on his feet too long."

"I don't know what else I can do. I saw this once before with Healer Vay-idra. She knew much more than I did, and she couldn't do anything then, either. Even if I stayed here . . ."

"It wouldn't change anything, except destroy your future."

"I still don't like it."

"Neither do I, dear."

Alyiakal takes a slow deep breath, then says, "He knows, or suspects, about the brigands. That was clear."

"He doesn't want us to confirm it," replies Saelora.

"That's to protect you."

"And you," she points out.

Mainly because I protect you. But Alyiakal only nods.

XLVII

Eightday morning comes all too soon, and when Alyiakal wakes, he can't help but think that in just one more day, he'll be on a firewagon starting the long trip to Lhaarat. He turns toward Saelora, and her eyes open.

"How did you know?" he asks.

"When we're close, I can feel when you're looking at me. Sometimes, it's enough to wake me." She yawns, then takes a deep breath.

"That sounds like you've got a bit of the Magi'i in you."

She shakes her head. "It's you, not me."

"I'll take your word on that."

She smiles. "What would you like to do today—besides have a special dinner tonight?"

"Just be with you. Beyond that, what would you like?"

"Let's have breakfast, and then we can decide."

Meaning that you'd better have an idea by then. "I am hungry."

"You're hungry every morning."

"And you're not?" he teases as he pulls on his robe, still surprised that she'd had one made of lancer green. *But then she could always claim—and probably did—that it was for one of her brothers.*

She mock-glares at him as she ties the cloth belt on her robe—of Merchanter blue.

"Did you get a robe like this for Hyrsaal as well?"

She smiles. "I had two made. One for him as a consorting gift, and one for you, but I just said they were for family."

"You plan ahead for everything."

"Some of it's also hope."

He steps toward her and embraces her gently. "I'm so glad."

"So am I."

In a fraction of a quint, they sit across the table from each other, eating almond rolls, accompanied by ale from Faadyr, not quite so good as Dyrkan's brew, but far better than the ale available at any lancer post.

"Is there any place you'd like to ride together?" Alyiakal asks. "Just to be riding, not having to go somewhere?"

Saelora purses her lips. "No . . . I don't think so."

"What if we just spent the day together?" He smiles. "I could show you how the lancers roll bones . . . unless Gaaran or Hyrsaal or your father already taught you."

She laughs. "Father said officers shouldn't do that, and never with rankers. He pretended he knew nothing about it, but he taught Gaaran and Hyrsaal all the tricks so that they'd know all the ways rankers could cheat."

"And you beat them at it?"

Saelora blushes. "They wouldn't play with me after a while."

"Then I wouldn't be much fun."

"You've never played?"

He shakes his head. "Do you play Fyrr?"

"I haven't in years, but I do have a deck of pastecards and a board."

"That would make us about even. I played some with my father."

"Do you play the way you fight?" she asks cautiously.

"No. What would be the point?"

She offers a slow smile. "Then, I'd like that. Just to talk and play occasionally." She stands. "After we clean up and get dressed. I don't want to look slovenly on your last day here."

Alyiakal gets to his feet. "I don't think you could look slovenly if you tried. No matter what you wore." *Or didn't wear.*

Saelora laughs. "I saw that look."

This time, Alyiakal flushes. "I love you no matter what you wear."

"Go wash up and put on a clean uniform." But her voice is warm.

Roughly half a glass later, Alyiakal returns to the house and sits down in the parlor, thinking . . . and hoping Saelora won't be too long.

A quint passes before she appears in the parlor. "I have the board and pastecards in the dining room."

Alyiakal stands and surveys her. "You look so good."

"Even fully dressed?"

He shakes his head ruefully.

"You look good, too," she says, adding mischievously, "Even fully dressed."

Alyiakal can't help laughing.

As they sit on adjoining sides of the dining room table, and Saelora shuffles the pastecards, Alyiakal asks, "Did you play Fyrr with your father?"

"I was the only one. Mother said he was too competitive. Gaaran didn't like losing, and Hyrsaal felt Father took the fun out of the game. Karola never liked games."

Alyiakal frowns. "Your mother strikes me as competitive. Why would she say that?"

"What she meant was that she seldom won." Saelora deals six pastecards to each of them.

"How did you fare?"

"I won when I really wanted to. The rest of the time I asked him leading questions. Mostly about the places he'd been and what he'd seen. I never asked him about battles or fighting."

"And?" asks Alyiakal, arranging the pastecards in his hand and noticing that Saelora does not arrange hers.

"He was much more interested in geography and buildings than in people."

Alyiakal nods. "The map of Biehl was only one of a number."

"He had several others at one time, but he sent a number to other officers after he was stipended."

As they played, Alyiakal quickly realizes that Saelora is far better and can mentally calculate the likelihood of his holding certain pastecards. Nonetheless, he enjoys the game, even as he loses nearly every hand.

At fourth glass of the afternoon, Laetilla walks into the dining room. "I need to prepare for dinner."

"We've played long enough," says Saelora.

"Long enough that she's now winning all the time," adds Alyiakal, his tone amusedly doleful.

Saelora stands. "We'll go to the parlor." After gathering the pastecards and board, she turns toward the study. "I'll be back in a moment."

Once she returns, each takes an armchair, and she says, "I shouldn't have won so many hands."

"I was enjoying talking with you, especially listening, and watching you calculate the likelihood of what pastecards I might have. I'm more interested in you than in winning."

"You're more complicated than that."

"I'm fairly simple," says Alyiakal. "I just try to be as effective as I can be."

Saelora laughs softly and shakes her head. "You're anything but simple . . . except maybe on the surface. My father was a Mirror Lancer majer, and my brothers are officers. No matter what they claimed, they all wanted to win at Fyrr or bones or any game. Warm as he could be, Father wanted to dominate the conversation. You're a more effective, and more deadly, officer than any of them. Yet I seldom see that—except . . . on oneday." She glances toward the kitchen, then back to Alyiakal. "Vassyl said that you remembered more about trade and people than any officer and more than most traders and factors. You can hate brigands, but you hold no anger against troopers trying to kill you. You put up with a great deal of quiet abuse from Mother. None of that's simple. Very few men think the way you do, especially military men."

Alyiakal smiles wryly. "You're right, but they should. Often a small victory is only the beginning of a disastrous defeat." He turns from Saelora as Laetilla steps into the parlor.

"Dinner is ready."

Both Saelora and Alyiakal stand, and he asks, "What are we having?"

"It's special and a surprise for the moment." Saelora leads the way to the dining room.

The three candles in the candelabrum are lit, and there is wine in both glasses. Saelora takes her place, and so does Alyiakal. Laetilla serves Saelora, then Alyiakal, and slips away.

Alyiakal looks at the fare upon his plate—roasted game hens with a wine and herb glaze, rice and raisins with a thicker version of the glaze, and green beans with crushed nuts in butter. Then he laughs. "This is the first dinner I had with you, right here."

"Sometimes, firsts need to be remembered."

Alyiakal lifts his wineglass. "That's a toast. To a well-recalled first."

They both sip their wine.

Then Alyiakal says, apologetically, "I'd meant to bring you a gift, another surprise, but I never could find anything special enough for you."

"I don't need any more surprises. You've given me two."

"Two?"

"More than that, really. You wrote me for years before we met, and you've always kept your word. You gave me this." She lifts her arm to let the sleeve fall away from the electrum and blue zargun bracelet. "That doesn't include always being supportive, helping with Catriana's consorting chest, and saving my life." She smiles and adds, "We should enjoy the dinner . . . and the rest of the evening."

XLVIII

At a glass past sunrise, Alyiakal paces in front of the waitstop, little more than a roofed three-sided hut with a backless bench, on the far side of the Great Canal from Vaeyal proper, looking for the firewagon from Geliendra to Ilypsya. He can't see Loraan House from the waitstop but knows Saelora is there, as is Gaaran, who insisted on seeing him off, more to make sure his sister would be safe so early in the morning after dropping Alyiakal off.

Another quint passes before the firewagon rolls to a stop and the lancer ranker who handles passengers steps out of the small front compartment. "Overcaptain Alyiakal, ser?"

"The same." Alyiakal shows his seal ring and travel pass.

"There's only two of you in front for now, ser. Rear compartment's full. Ten candidates for Kynstaar."

"Thank you." Alyiakal puts one duffel behind the empty seat on the right that faces forward and the other under it, then eases into it.

The lancer closes the door behind him.

"Good morning," offers the other officer, also an overcaptain, who at first glance looks to be a good ten years older than Alyiakal. "I'm Khaan, headed to Dellash."

"Good morning. Alyiakal, on my way to Lhaarat." Alyiakal shifts slightly in his seat as the firewagon begins to move.

"Better you than me." Khaan looks at Alyiakal more closely, then asks, "Recent promotion?"

"Comparatively. Two years ago."

"Combat postings?"

"Pemedra and Guarstyad, then temporary duty as post commander closing Luuval."

"I heard that the whole place collapsed right after it was closed. That right?"

"Less than an eightday after we transported the last gear and equipment to Fyrad."

"You remind me of someone. We haven't met, have we?"

"I don't think so. Are you headed to a new posting or on leave?"

"Both. Home leave. Last post was logistics at Chulbyn."

"Did you know a Majer Kyal?"

"Kyal?" Khaan frowns, then nods. "Yes, must have been ten years ago, maybe longer. I headed supply at Geliendra. He commanded Northpoint, occasionally came to Geliendra. Why?"

"He was my father. Several other officers have noted the resemblance."

"That might be it. How is he?"

"He died several years ago. On duty, but not in combat."

"I'm sorry to hear that."

"It's rare, but it happens." Alyiakal hesitates, then asks, "Are you headed to Dellash to unscramble some sort of mess?"

"No one's said, but it's possible. What's your assignment at Lhaarat?"

"Deputy post commander."

"If I'm treading heavy, let me know, but . . . as an overcaptain? That's usually a sub-majer or majer's billet."

"Lhaarat's a smaller post, and I have some experience in dealing with brigands, barbarians, and Kyphran troopers."

"Then you're one of the ones who destroyed the Kyphran invaders. That explains it." His smile is sympathetic as he adds, "I don't envy you. Word is that the Kyphrans are supplying some of the mountain brigands. After what happened at Guarstyad, I wouldn't be surprised if they even started sending their own patrols along the border."

"I had that feeling, but how did you find out?"

"In logistics, it's all bits and pieces, but sometimes the pieces fit together. In the last season we had to send more firelance replenishments to Lhaarat, and the number of recruits and replacements went up. Had to schedule some special firewagon runs to Terimot. Played hob with scheduling. Lhaarat's the backside of nowhere."

"So I've heard." *But so are Pemedra, Guarstyad, and Oldroad Post.*

In time, their conversation lapses, and Alyiakal sits back in the not-too-comfortable seat, thinking, partly about Lhaarat, but mainly about Saelora, wondering when they could consort, not at all liking the possibility of having to wait for posting after posting.

Maybe Hyrsaal has the right idea. There's no guarantee you'll make it through combat post after combat post.

Then again, Saelora's not ready. *Not yet, especially after the brigands.*

ALYIAKAL'ALT,

OVERCAPTAIN

Lhaarat

XLIX

Late on the afternoon of sixday, Alyiakal sits in the front compartment of yet another firewagon as it heads down a narrow whitestone road toward Terimot, a town that apparently exists for little reason besides maintaining a supply warehouse, stables, and a waystation serving Lhaarat.

The rear compartment contains ten lancers, and the only other officer with Alyiakal is Paersol, a recently promoted captain originally from Sollend, a town near Cyad that Alyiakal has never heard of. Paersol served two years as a company officer at Westpoint, patrolling the Great Forest, before being posted to Lhaarat.

"Ser? What do you think patrols at Lhaarat will be like?"

Alyiakal does not sigh, much as he would like to, since Paersol has asked similar questions at least twice before. "Most patrols will be tedious. Only a few turn dangerous, and you never know which ones will. Because Lhaarat is at the north end of a mountain valley, the terrain will be more rugged than around the Great Forest or even than the Grass Hills. Other than that, I really can't say as I've never been here before. What I do know is that the raids have become more frequent in the past year."

"Begging your pardon, ser, but why do you always call it the Great Forest instead of the Accursed Forest?"

"I lived at Northpoint when my father commanded there. It's a Great Forest. It has creatures that are dangerous and deadly, but so do the Grass Hills and the Westhorns. I don't know of any magus cursing it. I respect it but remain aware that it holds creatures that can easily kill. Most people don't kill other people blindly, and neither do most animals, but both are dangerous in the wrong situation. If the animals could talk, they might consider us the accursed lancers." *I'm not so sure that the Forest doesn't regard the great magus of the First exactly that way.*

"Most lancers don't see it that way, ser."

"Some don't. Respecting creatures or others who can kill you isn't weakness. It's common sense, and it might keep you from underestimating them."

"Begging your pardon, ser, but is this your first combat duty?"

Alyiakal laughs softly. "Outside of a half-season temporary assignment, I've never had anything but combat duty."

Paersol shrinks into his seat.

Alyiakal senses the captain's puzzlement but sees no point in more explanation, because Paersol believes that adversaries are always enemies. *Some are, but you have to know which are and which aren't.*

He takes out the sheet of paper listing the names of the ten lancers in the rear compartment, eight recruits and two barely experienced lancers recovering from injuries. After going over the names and their homes of record for a time, he sets the sheet aside and turns his thoughts back to Saelora, his eyes absently taking in the same rolling hills, mostly tree-covered, through which they have traveled since leaving Ilypsya at dawn, with occasional hamlets close to the road. At some point, he drifts into a doze, waking perhaps a glass later. When the firewagon slows, Alyiakal looks out the window. While they've passed more steads and holdings in the last half glass, he still hasn't seen anything resembling a hamlet.

Abruptly, the firewagon passes small houses on each side of the whitestone road, followed by several shops and a modest alehouse. After the alehouse there's only bare ground for fifty yards, at the end of which the whitestone road runs through a pair of gates flanked by brick walls little more than two yards high.

The firewagon creeps through the gates and comes to a halt in front of a two-story brick building possibly fifteen yards across the front. The ranker assistant to the firewagon driver opens the side door. "Terimot, sers."

"Thank you," replies Alyiakal before getting out and reclaiming his two duffels, followed by Paersol.

An officer steps forward, a gray-haired and weathered undercaptain who clearly has come up through the ranks. "Undercaptain Hurzt, sers. Welcome to Terimot supply depot. You two must be replacement officers." He hesitates as he sees Alyiakal's insignia, seemingly repressing some amusement, then continues, "And you must be the new deputy post commander."

"That's right. Alyiakal, from Guarstyad."

"Paersol, from Westpoint."

"Good thing you both have combat experience. We hear Lhaarat's getting more raids." As the undercaptain speaks, a squad leader appears and takes charge of the lancers disembarking from the rear compartment. "We'll get you settled, and then we'll open the mess. We don't have an officers' mess, just a table in the lancers' mess."

"Just you, squad leaders, and squads?" asks Alyiakal.

"Just one squad and squad leader. Along with a farrier and a trainer, some teamsters, and a few local women who clean and cook. We purchase the horses from the locals and train them. Occasionally, we even train a few recruits. I'll show you your quarters, such as they are."

Alyiakal's quarters are located at the rear of the front building and consist of a tiny room with a single narrow pallet bed, a chair and a table usable for writing, and a row of wall hooks.

Hurzt glances at the two duffels. "You're carrying a bit more gear, ser."

"Extra winter uniforms and boots. Also maps."

Hurzt nods. "Mess'll be open in a quint, ser."

"Thank you."

After the undercaptain leaves, Alyiakal washes up, stretches, and places an order block around the duffels before leaving the room to survey the supply depot. He takes the rear door and steps out into the cool air of early evening, far cooler than it would be at either Oldroad Post or Pemedra. *But then, it's a good thousand yards higher than Pemedra.* And Lhaarat is even higher.

Behind the main building to one side is a warehouse with two loading docks. To the other side is a large stable, and behind it are several training corrals. A road leads to the east gates of the depot. Alyiakal has no doubt that beyond those gates lies the road to Lhaarat.

Once he's studied the supply depot he heads to the ranker barracks, which holds the mess hall. Hurzt is already there, standing to one side of a table set for four. Two long tables stretch behind that table, and every space is filled.

Half of the rankers there have to be replacements or additional lancers for a fourth company, if not both.

Both rankers and officers stiffen as Alyiakal enters, which momentarily surprises him, but he quickly says, loudly, "As you were." Then he joins Hurzt, Paersol, and a senior squad leader, who looks as old as Hurzt. The presence of the senior squad leader isn't usual, to say the least, but Alyiakal can see that it makes sense in a unit as small as the supply depot.

"Overcaptain," says Hurzt, "Senior Squad Leader Bhaarn."

"Good to meet you, Bhaarn. Please be seated."

Once Alyiakal is seated, he picks up the beaker, since it's clear no wine is available, and says, "For your hospitality."

"To hospitality."

Then Hurzt says, "Most people at this table in a season."

"Not many officers coming or going?"

"Just one officer leaving in the last season, red-haired captain. Can't remember his name. He was going home to get consorted, then heading to Inividra. Pleasant officer." Hurzt shakes his head. "Going from Lhaarat to Inividra is going from the skillet to the spit."

Because of Hyrsaal's warning, Alyiakal hasn't mentioned Hyrsaal to Paersol, and he's not about to now. "That'd be true of Pemedra and Isahl as well."

A ranker appears and serves the table, beginning with Alyiakal. On the plate are two healthy slices of mutton, covered with brown gravy, with a glop of cheesed potatoes, and overcooked green beans. *Definitely lancer cooking.*

When all four are served, Alyiakal takes a bite of the potatoes, not wanting to make anyone wait.

Then Hurzt turns to Alyiakal. "You said you'd come from Guarstyad. You happen to be there when the Kyphrans attacked?"

"I was."

"I heard that there were fifteen hundred Kyphrans and only five lancer companies."

"That's about right."

"You one of the company officers?"

Alyiakal nods and takes a small swallow of ale.

"True that most of two companies and their officers were wiped out?"

"First and Third Companies. Less than a hundred Kyphrans survived."

"That was two years ago. How did you fare?"

"Cuts and bruises. Mirror Lancer headquarters ordered the old road between Kyphros and Guarstyad to be repaired and a new post built at the east end. They gave me command."

Alyiakal senses Paersol's apprehension, as well as concealed amusement from Hurzt and the senior squad leader, and asks the undercaptain, "Did you happen to know anyone involved?"

"Matter of fact, I did. Former senior squad leader like me. He's an undercaptain on his way to Kynstaar as an instructor. He wrote me about it."

Alyiakal laughs. "Torkaal! You knew all along. I'm glad he got the posting to Kynstaar. When I left, he thought he would, but his orders hadn't come through."

"He said he owed it all to you."

"He deserved that and more." After the slightest pause, Alyiakal asks, "Is everything ready for us to ride out tomorrow?"

"Yes, ser. Everything's ready. You've got thirty rankers, two squad leaders, and two scouts from Lhaarat as guides, not that you'd need them. The road doesn't go anywhere else."

"Have there been any raiders close to Terimot?"

"No, ser. Not until you get close to Lhaarat."

As he eats, Alyiakal does his best to learn what he can, but Hurzt can't tell him much about the replacement rankers or squad leaders.

When dinner is over, Alyiakal takes his time after he stands and overhears Paersol say to Hurzt, "Do you have a few moments, Undercaptain?"

Perhaps it's vanity, but Alyiakal wants to know what Paersol has to say to Hurzt. So he lags in heading from the mess, but as soon as the two officers step outside, he glances over his shoulder, raises a concealment, and follows them, calculating in the dim light no one will see the door opening and closing. Then he moves closer.

". . . never said much on the firewagon from Ilypsya . . ."

". . . felt he couldn't say much, ser. Be like bragging."

"He was one of the surviving captains, and he got promoted for that?"

"He's the one whose company destroyed close to a thousand Kyphrans. The Kyphrans call him the Lance of Fire. Torkaal said he did it with the fewest casualties of any company. Came close to dying twice. You see that scar on his forehead? You don't get those unless you're in close combat . . . reason why he's here . . ."

The two enter the main building.

After several moments and making sure no one can see, Alyiakal removes the concealment and takes his time getting to his quarters. He stifles a yawn.

L

Alyiakal rises at the first hint of light on sevenday, dresses, and meets with Hurzt to talk over the arrangements for departure and make sure that the wagon teamsters will be ready. Then he heads for the stables to find a suitable mount. There's only a single ostler present, who looks slightly puzzled as Alyiakal asks, "Which horses are for the replacements?"

"Ah . . . all those in the larger part of the stables, ser. That's past the black ceiling beam."

"What about tack?"

"We set out tack at each stall."

"Thank you."

"Ah . . . ser . . . the best mounts are nearest the east end."

Alyiakal strides to the east end of the stable, followed by the ostler. He studies more than a half score mounts before he notices a dark chestnut gelding that appeals to him and that has no physical faults he can sense.

"That one's high-spirited, ser."

"That shouldn't be a problem, but we'll see." Alyiakal turns his attention to the gelding. "They say you're high-spirited, fellow." He continues to speak in a firm but soothing voice as he enters the stall, letting a reassuring feeling of warm order precede him.

As the ostler said, the gelding is edgy and spirited, and it takes Alyiakal longer than anticipated before the chestnut decides to accept him. Abruptly, he laughs, as he realizes that, somehow, he's drawn to chestnut geldings. *Well, so long as it works for both of us.*

He returns to letting the gelding get comfortable with him. In time, he sees several more ostlers in the stables. He decides to head for the barracks, but before reaching them he sees two squad leaders walking toward him.

"I see we have the same thing in mind," he says as they halt and stiffen. "As you were. I'm Alyiakal, and my orders say I'll be the deputy post commander at Lhaarat. I've had previous full postings at Pemedra and Guarstyad."

"Yes, ser," says the taller and younger-looking squad leader. "Rhemsaar, from Syadtar."

"Chaaltyn, ser, from Isahl."

"Then you've both had experience with barbarians and brigands."

"Yes, ser."

"Have you had a chance to work with the replacements? I only arrived last night."

"Just basic drills, ser," answers the shorter Chaaltyn. "And only with the squad that's been here a few days." He hands Alyiakal a sheet. "That's the roster, ser. Five men with at least one posting, three with partial postings, and twelve just out of recruit training."

"What do you think about handling the ten men who arrived with me and getting them to work together on the ride to Lhaarat, while Rhemsaar takes over the larger group." Alyiakal's words are not a question.

"Yes, ser. Might work better that way."

"Eight of the ten who arrived with me are just out of training. Two recovered from injuries." Alyiakal offers a wry smile. "Have you met the scouts from Lhaarat?"

"Yes, ser," replies Chaaltyn. "That is, we know who they are."

Alyiakal doesn't like the sound of that, but only says, "Let's go find them."

The two scouts—Riiks and Maaetz—wait outside the mess. Both exchange glances as they see the overcaptain and two squad leaders. Then they stiffen to attention.

"Ser."

"As you were. I thought you should know that we'll be mustering the replenishment group in a little over a glass. I'll be early at the muster, and you can brief me and the squad leaders on what to expect then. Is that clear?"

"Yes, ser."

"You're dismissed to finish your preparations."

"Yes, ser."

After the scouts hurry off, Alyiakal says, "We'll meet again before muster."

"Yes, ser."

Alyiakal enters the mess and walks to the officers' table, where he sits down and turns to Paersol. "Have you picked a mount?"

"Not yet, ser."

"You'd better eat quickly, then. Officers and squad leaders will be meeting in three quints and leaving as soon as possible after muster."

"Yes, ser."

As Alyiakal eats, he studies the two roster sheets.

When he leaves the mess hall, the two squad leaders follow and then join him outside. Alyiakal hands the appropriate roster to each squad leader. "Right now, you need them more than I do."

Both Rhemsaar and Chaaltyn nod politely.

"We'll also be escorting three wagons. One carries replenished firelances. The other two have an assortment of supplies." From there, he explains what formation training he expects on the ride to Lhaarat, including formations to maximize the impact of the firelances, which he concludes by saying, "I don't plan on having them firing chaos bolts for practice, since it may be more difficult to get firelance replenishments than in the past."

"Why might that be, ser?" asks Rhemsaar.

"I don't know why, but noncombat posts have been ordered to minimize the use of firelances, and that suggests difficulties in getting replenishments. Do either of you have any questions?"

"Begging your pardon, ser," says Chaaltyn, "but it sounds like you're expecting more trouble here. Could you give us an idea what we could expect?"

"I can't tell you exactly. I do know that the Duke of Kyphros is not happy with Cyador, and recently the mountain brigands attacking this part of Cyador seem to have acquired more weapons."

After several more prosaic questions, Riiks and Maaetz arrive, and Alyiakal's first question to the scouts is, "How much forage is there along the road to Lhaarat?"

"This time of year, ser," replies Riiks, "there's enough for a company's mounts, with plenty to spare. By early Winter, there's nothing."

"What weather can we expect?"

"Right now," says Maaetz, "we won't see rain. By mid-fall storms are more common."

"Did you two ride here alone from Lhaarat?" Alyiakal knows that was unlikely but wants to know the circumstances.

"No, ser. We accompanied the supply wagons and several lancers being injury-stipended or posted elsewhere."

After that, Alyiakal runs through his mental list of questions quickly, then says, "We'll start with standard scout spacing, unless you have another recommendation."

The two exchange glances. Then Riiks replies, "Near here that makes sense, but once we start the climb to the east valley, you could lose sight of us."

"Thank you. I'll keep that in mind."

Once he dismisses the scouts to muster, Alyiakal looks to the two squad leaders. "Any further thoughts?"

Chaaltyn frowns, then says, "The post commander only sent two scouts and teamsters for the return trip. Usually, there are a few lancers and a squad leader."

Rhemsaar nods.

"It does seem unusual," replies Alyiakal, "but every post is a bit different. It may be that the post commander didn't think additional lancers were necessary because they haven't had raider attacks on supply runs. Or they could be shorthanded. I'm sure we'll find out." Even without trying, he can sense doubt from both squad leaders, a doubt he shares.

LI

On sevenday, and for the next two days, Alyiakal leads his mostly inexperienced replenishment force and three supply wagons eastward along a dirt road around low hills mostly covered with trees and through small hamlets ten to fifteen kays apart and indistinguishable from each other, with log walls and shingled roofs and with exterior privacy screens. Even the barns and outbuildings are log-walled.

All along the way, Chaaltyn and Rhemsaar conduct various drills, and Alyiakal watches, sometimes offering suggestions—but only after an evolution is complete. Every day, after they bivouac, Alyiakal leads various drills.

Early on twoday morning, Alyiakal meets with Paersol, Chaaltyn, Rhemsaar, Riiks, and Maaetz, first asking the two scouts, "How far before we start the climb to Lhaarat?"

"Around three kays," replies Maaetz. "You can see the river gap and the hills ahead. They separate the lower lands from the high valley."

"How wide is the river where it goes through the hills?"

"No more than ten yards, sometimes less. But it's deep and cold."

"And once we get to the high valley?" presses Alyiakal.

"The road doesn't wind as much, but it keeps getting higher, gradually, all the way to Lhaarat. The post is at the east end of the town, on the south side of the river."

All that matches what Hyrsaal told Alyiakal, but Alyiakal's still worrying when he and the group resume the ride. Given what Riiks has said, and the cool of the Autumn morning, Alyiakal's taken out his riding jacket and fastened it on top of the duffel behind his saddle.

He's certainly not prepared for his first view of the River Lhaar when he rides over a rise and the road turns right along a ridge. More than ten yards below him on the left, white-foamed water tumbles down a narrow gorge that angles to the northwest, although Alyiakal knows that somewhere west of Terimot the river turns south and eventually joins the Great East River.

Alyiakal wonders how high the water gets in the Spring, but from the looks of the rocky gorge and the lack of vegetation on either side of the road, he doubts that the water ever reaches the road.

"Wouldn't want to end up there, ser," says Paersol.

"Not as cold as that water looks and where it came from," replies Alyiakal.

As Riiks had suggested earlier, Alyiakal repositions the scouts, Maaetz only a hundred yards before Alyiakal and Riiks a hundred yards forward of Maaetz.

The road winds up the steep slope in a series of switchbacks, and it's well past midday when Alyiakal reaches the top of the west pass, the river still on his right. From there, the road heads due east, sloping down for a kay before rising again, while the river angles more to the north.

The valley before him appears slightly smaller than Guarstyad's valley had been, perhaps eight kays wide, seemingly flat, but rising upward toward the east as if it had once been a lake that had been tilted and drained. The river, if the trees along it are any indication, meanders through the valley. The hills on each side get progressively higher the farther east they are and seem to merge into the lower Westhorns somewhere beyond the far end of the valley. Alyiakal gets the impression that raiding the valley from either the north or south would be more than a little difficult, but there might be gaps in the hills farther east.

He keeps riding, and perhaps a kay farther along, he notices a dirt track leading south from the main road.

Little more than a kay later, the group rides past a hamlet—Westyll, according to Riiks—located on slightly higher ground on the south side of a bend in the river. The fields outside Westyll show bare ground, and the outbuildings look as sturdy as the log-walled houses, but the hamlet is not walled, nor do the dwellings have exterior privacy screens.

Another glass goes by, and Alyiakal rides past two side roads leading to other hamlets, judging from the thin lines of smoke rising into the hazy green-blue sky. Before that long, the group passes through the middle of another hamlet, also without walls. In time, after passing through two more hamlets, and noting the smoke from two others, he sees, near the end of the valley, a grouping of houses and other buildings that have to be Lhaarat.

From the number of hamlets, Alyiakal gets the definite feeling that ground is fertile and that there's plenty of rain or other water, which suggests, in turn, that Lhaarat Post has no trouble obtaining food and fodder. *And of better quality than what we got at Pemedra.*

Just before Alyiakal and the replenishment group reach the first outlying houses in Lhaarat, he sees a crossroad that branches north on one side and leads to a stone bridge over the River Lhaar. Beyond the stone bridge are several structures beside the river and another hamlet. On the other side of the main road, the crossroad heading south is clearly less traveled but looks to go to the lower hills on the south side of the valley.

Alyiakal nods. What Hyrsaal had told him now makes more sense. The post is on the south side of the river, but there are roads on both sides, and the river is deep enough and wide enough that crossing—or bridging it—in the hills and low mountains east of Lhaarat and the post is problematic, if not impossible.

The town itself is smaller than Terimot, although it does have two ale-houses and a factorage, as well as two other shops, and an unidentified building Alyiakal suspects is a brothel. Unlike the hamlets Alyiakal had earlier passed, the houses and buildings here are walled with heavy planks.

The post sits beside the road leading into the foothills of the Westhorns, half a kay north of the last dwelling in the town, with rock walls over four yards high at the west but only three at the east end, because the eastern end has been dug into the ground to keep the courtyard and the top of the walls level. Because the east-west walls are twice as long as the north-south walls, Lhaarat is the first oblong post Alyiakal has seen. That makes sense, given the rapid narrowing of the mountain valley east of the town proper. The south wall of the post is within a few hundred yards of the southern bluffs, but because of the way the bluffs angle east, the eastern end of the post is more than half a kay from where the road enters the hills. The distance between the road in front of the post and the river is well over a kay.

There are two gate guards, as well as two wall guards, all watching when Alyiakal, Paersol, and the scouts ride into the post.

Once the group comes to a halt between headquarters and the stables, both squad leaders ride up to Alyiakal and hand him the rosters of their lancers.

"Thank you both. They all look much sharper than when we set out."

In moments, a squad leader appears. "Overcaptain, ser. Majer Byelt would like to see you once you're finished here."

"Thank you. I'll be there as soon as I can."

The squad leader looks to Paersol. "Captain, the majer will see you after the overcaptain."

"Thank you."

Alyiakal turns back to the squad leaders. "I'd like a little time with both of you after the evening meal. By then I should have a better idea to which companies you'll be assigned." He smiles wryly. "And if you find out before I do, you can tell me."

"Yes, ser." They both smile.

After settling the chestnut in the stable, Alyiakal leaves his duffels in his quarters and hurries to the majer's study, his orders and accompanying documents in hand, along with the replacement rosters.

When he enters the anteroom, he notices two doors in the far wall, one closed, and the other open, with a desk and a ranker set midway between and well forward of the doors.

The ranker in the anteroom says, "You're to go inside, ser."

"Which door?" asks Alyiakal, although he can sense that there is no one behind the closed door.

"The open door, ser."

Alyiakal nods, then enters the study, closing the door behind him. "Overcaptain Alyiakal, reporting, ser." He places his orders and endorsements with the rosters on the desk.

The dark-haired but balding Byelt does not rise, but gestures to the chairs. "Have a seat, Overcaptain."

Alyiakal seats himself and waits, looking attentively at the majer, who appears calm as he quickly scans what Alyiakal presented.

After a time, the majer says, "I didn't ask for a deputy post commander, but headquarters sent me one. Since they sent enough lancers for a fourth company, I'm not going to complain. But I'd like to know why you think you're here."

"No one told me that, ser. My guess is that there have been increasing raids by the mountain brigands which might have been instigated or supported by the Kyphrans and possibly even by the Cerlynese."

"I haven't seen any Cerlynese around."

"They don't work that way, ser. They supply weapons and sometimes horses, and occasionally women they find troublesome, to the barbarians and brigands."

"Who told you that?"

"I saw some of that in Pemedra, and I interrogated the barbarian survivors from a group of raiders supplied by the Cerlynese."

"Then why don't I know that?"

"Ser, I can't tell you that. I reported everything to my commander, and I know the report went to Mirror Lancer headquarters."

Byelt shakes his head.

Alyiakal waits.

"According to a directive from the Captain-Commander, you're to have physical command of a company. That's why we didn't get an additional officer."

Alyiakal doesn't even have to feign surprise. "Ser?"

"You didn't know, either?"

"No, ser."

"You're supposed to be an outstanding field commander. Are you?"

"I get the task accomplished, and, in the past, I've done it with the fewest casualties from my company."

"You didn't answer my question, Overcaptain."

"Ser, at Guarstyad, I was the most effective company officer. How that compares to other officers at other posts, I have no way of knowing."

"Is there anything in your record to support that?"

"Only that I was made commander of the new Oldroad Post and promoted to overcaptain four years early, despite being the most junior captain at Guarstyad, and that I was detached early and sent to close Luuval Post before reporting here."

Byelt laughs harshly.

Again, Alyiakal waits.

"You're also a field healer, and apparently most of your wounded alive a day or so after fighting recover. Are you part Magi'i?"

"I have no known Magi'i relatives. I've been examined multiple times by Magi'i, including the Third Magus. All they discovered was that I have a high order level and a slight talent for healing."

"I wonder what I did to deserve you," says Byelt acidly.

Less than I did to be posted here. Alyiakal keeps that thought to himself. "Headquarters must have thought it necessary for both of us."

"You must have evaluated the two squad leaders that came with you. Is one of them suited to be a senior squad leader?"

"They're both suited, but Chaaltyn has more experience."

"What about the replacements?"

"All but a handful are essentially just out of recruit training. On the ride here, we worked on formation riding, the basics of using a firelance—without discharging—and blade skills." Alyiakal explains briefly the way he'd divided the replacements.

"I've already talked with Captain Dhaerl and Captain Vaarkas. Each of them will transfer one squad to your company. Since you've already worked with the replacements and the incoming squad leaders, you'll keep the squad-sized group and both squad leaders, and you'll get a junior squad leader with one of the two existing squads. You'll have final rosters late this evening."

"If it's not a problem, since the new company has never patrolled together, I'd like a few days to work with the company squad leaders and rankers on some training. That way, the squads will get used to working together."

"I'd thought about that. Your company will be First Company, and your first patrol will be on sevenday."

"I'd like to read through the patrol reports for the last year, to get a feel for what the companies encountered."

"I'll have those to you in the next day or so."

"For the next few eightdays, I'd like to be able to take single squads on short local patrols when they're not scheduled for regular patrols."

The majer frowns. "Local."

"Within the valley or very close."

"Just for the next two eightdays. After that, ask me."

"Ser, where exactly have these raids occurred? Or have patrols encountered armed groups on patrols east of the valley?"

"Most of the larger skirmishes have been on or near the east road that leads to and through the Westhorns. There have been a few raids on the hamlets west of here, usually involving a handful of riders. Nothing serious. We killed a few and the others fled."

"How far east of here does Cyador extend?" asks Alyiakal. "Is there any definite border?"

"Was there one at Pemedra, Overcaptain?"

"Not that I knew of, but there was at Guarstyad."

"Here, it's like it is at Pemedra. Kyphran territory ends at the eastern base of the Westhorns, and Cyadoran territory at the end of this valley, which is considered the western base of the Westhorns. We're free to patrol—or not—on this side of the summit lines. The same for the Kyphrans and Gallosians on their side. There are scattered hamlets strung out in various locales. Most mind their own business. A few have walled themselves off. We don't bother the walled lands. So far, they haven't bothered us. The others . . . well . . . it's like the northern borders."

"The small walled lands essentially rule themselves and keep order?"

"That's the idea."

"Are there any of those walled lands near Lhaarat?"

"There's supposedly one to the southeast somewhere. We haven't had any trouble there, and there's no point in creating any."

Alyiakal decides not to ask the majer more about the raiders until he talks to the other officers, without Byelt present.

The majer continues, "As you'll discover, your quarters will be the former visiting officer's quarters. That won't be a problem since we've never had a visiting officer. Your study is adjacent to the officers' study."

"Yes, ser." Alyiakal wonders why Byelt isn't giving him the adjoining study, but has the feeling that Byelt doesn't want Alyiakal close by.

"Now . . . there's the problem of your duties, besides leading patrols."

"If I might, Majer . . . for the next few eightdays, I'm going to have my hands full. So will the other captains. That might give you some time to determine what duties I could take off your hands while I get accustomed to the post and its unique features."

"You don't sound enthused about being deputy post commander."

"I'd like to do the job right, ser, and that requires knowing how you operate and how you want things done. That should allow you to see what I can do and how."

Byelt frowns again, and Alyiakal notes that what he said was unexpected in some fashion.

"Are you unsure of something, Overcaptain?"

"Not of my abilities, ser. I've been commander of two smaller posts, but this is your command, and I have no idea of how you operate. I'd rather not do something that inadvertently conflicts with what you expect."

"Apparently, you respect authority," says Byelt. "That's rare in young successful combat commanders."

"One of the first officers I served with made the observation that there are bold officers and old officers, but no bold old officers—and no cowardly old officers, either."

"How have you been successful without being bold?"

"Something well thought out and executed as planned, but unexpected, looks far bolder than it is."

"How did you manage that?"

"By listening to and working with experienced senior squad leaders and discussing what I had in mind."

"Did you always do what they recommended?"

"No, ser, but I never did anything that they violently opposed after I'd explained what I had in mind."

"Well . . . we'll see how this idea from headquarters works out. Welcome to Lhaarat, Alyiakal. I'll see you at the mess." Byelt stands.

So does Alyiakal. "Yes, ser."

When he leaves, Alyiakal feels that Byelt is less wary, but reserving judgment, and that's all that Alyiakal can expect.

He returns to his new quarters, quickly washes his hands and face, then unpacks some of his gear before making his way to the officers' mess, a modest chamber at the east end of the building holding officers' quarters.

On his way to the mess, he passes the officers' study and then a closed door, which he suspects might be his study. He stops and opens the door. The chamber holds a desk and chair behind it with one other chair, an empty three-shelf bookcase, a file chest on a low stand, and an oil lamp on the corner of the desk. There are no windows.

Alyiakal smiles wryly and reaches the mess door, where a wiry captain possibly fifteen years older turns to him and smiles. "Overcaptain Alyiakal, I'm Dhaerl. Pleased to meet you."

"I'm pleased to meet you, Dhaerl. I take it you're the senior captain."

"For now, anyway."

"I suspect you'll remain so, but I don't know yet. Is Captain Paersol in the mess?"

"No, ser."

"He should be along shortly. He had to meet with the majer after I did."

"The majer said you came from Guarstyad."

"Not quite directly. I was ordered from Oldroad Post to complete the closure of Luuval Post."

"You've been a post commander?"

"Twice. Small posts," says Alyiakal wryly.

Dhaerl looks momentarily puzzled, then nods, and glances past Alyiakal. "Here comes Vaarkas."

Alyiakal turns to see a gangly black-haired captain approaching.

"Overcaptain," offers the captain, "I'm Vaarkas."

"Good to meet you. Majer Byelt told me there will be some shuffling of squads."

"Not as though there's any alternative," replies Vaarkas with a good-natured smile. "Is it true you'll be personally commanding the new company?"

"A mandate from Mirror Lancer headquarters," confirms Alyiakal, "since headquarters hasn't indicated any more officers are being posted here."

"Sounds like they're short of junior officers," suggests Vaarkas.

"Or that they've forgotten to count the complement again," says Dhaerl sardonically.

Alyiakal senses someone entering the building and glances back to see Paersol. As the captain approaches, Alyiakal discerns undercurrents of swirling personal chaos around Paersol. *Feels like the majer disconcerted him . . . if not more.*

Rather than say anything, he moves toward the doorway into the mess, and the others follow.

The four have just entered when Byelt arrives and motions to the table. Alyiakal sits on the majer's right, with Dhaerl on his left, and with Vaarkas beside Alyiakal, indicating that Paersol is the junior captain, not that Alyiakal had thought otherwise.

"For the record, since you all have met, if barely," says Byelt, "the new faces are Overcaptain Alyiakal and Captain Paersol. The overcaptain has a dual role, both as a company officer and the deputy post commander. He'll command First Company, and Captain Paersol will have Fourth." He raises his wineglass. "To our new arrivals."

The mess orderly serves the majer and Alyiakal, followed in order by Dhaerl and Vaarkas, and then Paersol. Alyiakal examines the fare for a moment, trying to decide what it is, before realizing it's essentially beef pounded thin, layered with something, and then rolled up and baked before being covered with brown gravy and served with fried potato spears, green beans, and bread.

Once Byelt lifts his knife, Vaarkas slices off a bit of the beef roll and begins to eat. Alyiakal follows his example, if with a much smaller chunk of beef and filling. He's pleasantly surprised to find the filling between the layers of beef is largely buttered parsley, or something similar, with small chunks of a pungent cheese—far better than the trail food of the previous days.

After eating several bites, Alyiakal asks, "Do the mountain brigands or raiders have any different weapons or tactics?"

"Depends on what you mean by different," replies Dhaerl. "Most of them carry smaller horn bows. Some have spears. Most have blades. Range from large knives to sabre-length."

"Shields?" asks Alyiakal.

Vaarkas looks puzzled.

"Some of the barbarians we ran into at Pemedra had polished metal shields," explains Alyiakal. "The Cerlynese I observed carried the same kind of shields. They're of some use against firelances."

"Haven't seen anything like that," says Dhaerl.

"Do they have any favorite attacks—besides ambushes and setting off landslides?" asks Alyiakal dryly.

"Landslides, ser?" asks Paersol. "Isn't that a little far-fetched?"

"It might be far-fetched, but the Grass Hills barbarians killed my predecessor in Pemedra that way."

"Hasn't happened here recently," says Dhaerl, "but Second Company reports mention an attempt four years ago."

Alyiakal continues to ask questions throughout the meal, and the majer and the two senior officers are pleasantly forthcoming, even the majer.

Once the majer leaves the mess, Alyiakal turns to Dhaerl and Vaarkas. "I have a few more questions about patrols and procedures. What if we meet in my study tomorrow a glass before evening mess?"

"That's a good idea," declares Dhaerl.

Vaarkas just nods emphatically.

"Good. Now . . . if you could tell me where the senior squad leaders' study is."

"The last door at the far end of the corridor," replies Dhaerl.

"Thank you." As the two captains leave the mess and head in the direction of their quarters, Alyiakal follows and makes his way to where Chaaltyn and Rhemsaar wait outside the door.

Chaaltyn offers an amused smile and asks, "How did you know, ser?"

"I didn't, but I thought you both *might* be in the new company. What I didn't know was that I'd be the company officer as well. Who told you what?"

"The duty squad leader just said that we'd be in the new company under you and that rosters wouldn't be available until later this evening. That's all."

"I can add a bit to that. Chaaltyn, you'll be the senior squad leader. Rhemsaar, you'll be squad leader of a squad transferred from the one of the existing companies. We'll also get a squad with a junior squad leader from the post complement. We'll have four days before we make a patrol, and we'll start some intensive training after muster tomorrow. Let's walk back to my study and see if the rosters have been delivered. If they haven't been, we'll work on the training plan until they arrive, but we'll have to go over that with the new squad leader as soon as possible."

From what Alyiakal senses, both squad leaders are agreeable . . . and relieved. But he knows that four days won't be enough time to get First Company in the shape it should be.

LII

Alyiakal rises very early on threeday morning, since it had been late on two-day before he received the rosters and finished working out a tentative schedule for First Company for the next four days. After dressing, he hurries to his study, where Chaaltyn, Rhemsaar, and Taenyr, assigned as third squad leader, stand outside the door.

"It's good to have you here, Taenyr," Alyiakal says warmly as he studies the squad leader whose boyish face contrasts with his stocky muscularity.

"It's good to be in First Company, ser," replies Taenyr in a sincere tone matching the order/chaos flows that Alyiakal can sense.

Alyiakal opens the study door, steps inside, picks up a striker, but lights the lamp with a bit of chaos, although it would appear that he used the striker.

"We have a draft training plan here," he begins, "partly because first squad is largely inexperienced and partly because none of the squads have worked together. We'll go over it quickly, and I'd like any comments you might have about anything I might have overlooked, especially from you, Taenyr, since you know the post, terrain, and locale far better than the rest of us."

For the next quint, Alyiakal goes over the plan.

Taenyr makes several suggestions for additions or changes, but after Alyiakal finishes, he says, "Begging your pardon, ser . . ."

"You're wondering about my sparring with every lancer?" asks Alyiakal with a smile.

"Yes, ser."

"First, we'll use wands, even if we have to make them. There's no point in casualties from training. Second, we'll all get a sense of each lancer. Third, they'll know a bit more about me."

Taenyr frowns.

"I tell you what," says Alyiakal. "I'll spar with each of you. Then you can tell me what you think."

"Fair enough," agrees Taenyr. "I even know where there are some wooden wands."

While Taenyr gets the wands, Alyiakal chooses a spot to the north of the stables that's shielded from direct view from either the officers' quarters or the administrative building.

Both Rhemsaar and Chaaltyn stand back as Alyiakal and Taenyr take their positions.

Alyiakal raises his wand, enough to counter or slip a high attack, but low enough to deal with a thrust, given that Taenyr is close to a head shorter than Alyiakal.

Taenyr begins with a thrust that turns into a rising backslash. Alyiakal senses that and slides the squad leader's wand away from his own body, then steps inside and taps Taenyr on the shoulder before stepping back. Taenyr twists to bring the wand into a thrust, and Alyiakal brings his wand up under the squad leader's wand with enough force to knock it out of Taenyr's hand.

Taenyr shakes his blade hand and grins ruefully. "You're not only fast, but strong."

Alyiakal turns to Chaaltyn. "Would you like a turn?"

Chaaltyn shakes his head. So does Rhemsaar.

"Has anyone bested you in sparring?" asks Rhemsaar.

"Not since my father did when I was sixteen. He was a majer."

Taenyr straightens. "Ser, I withdraw my objection. A quick sparring with the overcaptain will forestall a number of problems."

At least the ones where rankers complain that they could handle a blade better than their commanding officer. "I have a question for you, Taenyr."

"Ser?"

"Have the companies made many patrols through the valley, or have most of them been to the east of the valley?"

"The only patrols I know in the valley were when hamlets reported raiders."

"How did the raiders get into the valley?" asks Alyiakal.

"They might have come down the east road and gone north at the base of the hills and followed the river to the bridge. Or they might have come some other way."

"Didn't anyone check the roads for tracks?"

"Captain Hyrsaal checked once that I know of. He reported to the majer. He never checked again."

Hyrsaal hadn't mentioned that to Alyiakal, but Alyiakal just nods, even as he senses the disbelief from Chaaltyn and Rhemsaar, and says, "Then you were a squad leader from the old Third Company before you were moved to First Company?"

"Yes, ser."

"What sort of casualties have the companies suffered over the past year or so?"

"Maybe ten men, half of them from wounds that didn't heal."

Alyiakal poses several more questions, then asks, "Is there anything else you'd like to go over right now?"

"No, ser," answer all three squad leaders.

Once the three leave, Alyiakal takes a deep breath. *The more you learn, the less sense anything makes.* He still doesn't understand why Byelt went to the trouble of moving the study furnishings from the study in the headquarters building to what had likely been a storage room in the quarters/studies building. *A message to the captains about who's in command?*

After those brief thoughts, Alyiakal leaves his study and heads for the mess, where he's pleasant and cheerful, but says comparatively little, but learns that Vaarkas and Third Company will be patrolling the east road after breakfast.

Immediately after morning muster, Alyiakal and Chaaltyn begin the blade training with first squad. Alyiakal explains the need for the training and that he'll be sparring with every lancer to determine what they need to improve. While he works with individuals in first squad, the other two squads practice formation riding so that the lancers and squad leaders get more accustomed to working together. Then Alyiakal works individually with second squad, while the other two practice mounted drills. He then works with third squad.

He's definitely tired by the time all the training exercises are completed, but he's getting a much better feel of First Company.

When he returns to his study, he finds a stack of patrol reports in his box, and he begins to read through them. It's clear from the very first reports that most patrols don't venture more than ten kays into the hills east of Lhaarat. It's also clear that there aren't that many serious raids.

So why are you here as a deputy post commander? Because no one could figure out where else to post you because you're too young and too junior? Or because headquarters thinks there will be more trouble here?

He keeps reading.

He's not surprised that both Dhaerl and Vaarkas arrive at his study on time.

"How was your patrol?" Alyiakal asks Vaarkas.

"About the same as usual. We saw two traders and their wagons, a logging wagon, some mule carts lugging firewood, and some hoofprints near the river overlook that could have belonged to brigands or raiders. Wind was pretty stiff on the way back."

"Who uses the roads, besides lancers, that is?"

"The locals do, for logs and firewood," replies Vaarkas. "Some traders from Kyphros. Even a few from Hydlen and Gallos. Maybe other places. We don't ask."

"Traders? Is there an Imperial tariff enumerator here?"

"There's one in Ilypsya," says Dhaerl.

"But not here or in Terimot?"

"Not that I've heard," replies Dhaerl.

No tariff enumerator? That makes no sense to Alyiakal. Not when the Imperial Tariff Enumerators are fighting to have one everywhere along the coast. Or is it because traders can't make that many silvers in Lhaarat and Terimot, and, thus, neither can enumerators?

"Have you run into any brigands or raiders lately?"

"Not in the last eightday or so," says Vaarkas.

"I'm curious about attacks and raids," says Alyiakal evenly. "Where have most of them occurred?"

"Biggest one recently was over at Gairtyn," says Dhaerl. "That's the mill hamlet. They hit there about a season ago in the middle of the night. Stole a wagon and ten barrels of flour. Took three women. Tracks headed south, but we never found them."

"Why not?" asks Alyiakal.

"Rain and wind washed out the tracks, and the majer's standing orders are not to pursue when firelances can't be used."

"He says peasant lives aren't worth as much as lancer lives," adds Dhaerl dryly.

"He said that?"

"More than once," confirms Vaarkas.

Alyiakal decides to pursue another tack. "Who buys all that flour?"

"A lot of the mountain folks do. They stock up for the Winter in late Harvest."

"Isn't that a bit early?"

"Not for them," says Vaarkas. "They don't live close. Almost no one lives in the hills east of the valley. The soil's poor, and there's not much game. There's a lot more in the lower Westhorns, and the folks there build small forts."

"So where do the raiders and brigands come from?"

"The raiders look to come from the southeast," replies Dhaerl, "and maybe folks to the northeast. The brigands are mountain folk who didn't plan well enough or came on hard times."

Alyiakal wants to shake his head. The more he hears, the less it makes sense. *Which means you either don't understand or don't know enough—or both.*

He switches to questions about stables, feed, the general patrol schedule, and the weather patterns. A quint later, he thanks the two captains, excuses them, and then sits in his study thinking until the evening meal, still concerned that Byelt clearly has reservations about Alyiakal, given that his study should be somewhere in the headquarters building.

LIII

For Alyiakal sevenday comes far too soon.

Over the previous four days, he'd stepped up the training started on the ride to Lhaarat, with more work on blade skills, squad drills, full-company drills, and short patrols into the nearby foothills with Alyiakal and the squad leaders meeting afterward and discussing the various evolutions.

In the evenings, Alyiakal takes out his chestnut gelding and accustoms him to riding under a concealment, which involves far more glasses than he hoped, but he feels strongly that he might need that ability in the eightdays ahead. He also studies the rosters of the other three companies and works on learning the names of all the squad leaders. After studying the available maps of the area, because he's again struck more by what Mirror Lancer maps don't show than what they do, he begins to sketch out his own map of the valley and the surrounding area.

When the scouts lead Alyiakal and First Company out through the north gate on a chill sevenday morning that requires riding jackets, if not yet full winter uniforms, Alyiakal is definitely concerned, although the chance of encountering brigands or barbarians on any given patrol is low, and, unlike at Luuval, all the firelances are replenished. Since the sky is clear, Alyiakal spreads his order funnel to gather sun-chaos bits.

As the squad turns east on the road leading into the lower reaches of the Westhorns, Alyiakal turns to Chaaltyn. "Your thoughts?"

"Second and Third Company haven't seen any signs of raiders this eightday. The longer we don't see signs, the more likely the next company on patrol will. It's good that the scouts are familiar with the roads and trails."

Especially since few of us are. Alyiakal only nods, although he's glad that Maaetz and Raayls are the First Company scouts, because he had been uneasy with Riiks for reasons he cannot explain, even to himself.

Alyiakal's eyes flick northward to where the river emerges from the hills and where the sawmill and the gristmill stand on the north side of the rapid water, then back to the road ahead.

First Company travels less than a kay before the gravel-surfaced road becomes plain dirt when it reaches the gap in the low hills and begins a gradual climb. The undergrowth near the road is more than knee-high, and at least half the low bushes are turning winter gray. The trees on the slopes farther from the road are a mixture of evergreens and broad-leafed trees, also with leaves turning gray.

While the exercises and short patrols of the previous days have given Alyiakal a good sense of the area near Lhaarat, he hasn't taken the company more than a kay into the eastern foothills that eventually give way to the lower reaches of the dominant peaks of the Westhorns.

The only recent tracks Alyiakal sees are those of the scouts ahead, but that's not surprising so early in the morning. He also notes blurred hoofprints from earlier patrols and the deeper tracks of a log wagon, to be expected when the best timber lies in the foothills and even higher.

The road slowly angles east-southeast before turning back eastward. In two quints, the company nears the first fork, where a narrower road goes southeast, and on that road are the untouched traces of the log wagon.

Alyiakal signals to Raayls and when the scout rides back, Alyiakal asks, "Where does that road go?"

"Not really anywhere, ser, except to the timber they're cutting. Every year, I'm told, the road gets a little longer."

Alyiakal dismisses Raayls to scouting and continues to study and sense each side of the road as it continues mostly eastward, rising slowly but continually. Maaetz has moved some two hundred yards ahead of Raayls, who rides a hundred yards in front of Alyiakal. He only senses small patterns of chaos in the undergrowth and in the trees farther from the road, but nothing the size of a mountain cat or a red deer, and certainly nothing that could be a person or a horse. He observes the few definite trails or paths lead south from the road.

The undergrowth is thicker than in the Grass Hills, or along the east pass road from Guarstyad, but much thinner than in the damp forests between Luuval and the Great Canal, which means that most of the time Alyiakal can sense farther than he can see.

Less than a glass has passed when Maaetz signals.

In a fraction of a quint, Raayls rides back to report. "Ser, fresh hoofprints of a single rider. Looks like he turned and headed back east. Maaetz doesn't see anyone on the road ahead or to either side."

Alyiakal extends his senses as far as he can, slightly beyond Maaetz, but can't sense anything except small creatures, then says to Raayls, "You move to where Maaetz is and have him scout farther."

"Yes, ser." Raayls turns his mount back east and heads off.

Alyiakal turns to Chaaltyn. "We'll keep moving, to where the hoofprints are. Anyone who'd turn back this close to Lhaarat is a raider scout or someone who doesn't want to be noticed for other reasons."

"Smugglers?" asks the senior squad leader.

"Possibly, but not likely." *Not with a four-day ride to Terimot and another three days to anywhere they could sell anything. Then again, a lot of what you think doesn't seem to fit.*

In less than half a quint, Alyiakal reins up beside Raayls, and the company halts. Even before examining the road and the tracks, Alyiakal stretches his senses as far as he can. There might be a large creature to the east, beyond his limits, but it could be a red deer or mountain cat as easily as a raider or horse. The road continues to rise ahead, turning slightly southward.

"Raayls, according to the maps, the road meets the river again roughly eight or ten kays ahead. Could raiders follow the river west and come out in the valley near the mills?"

"Don't think anyone could follow the river on our side. It's cut a gorge through the hills. The north side looks easier, but I don't see any way to cross where the road nears the river. Or anywhere close by."

"Thank you. You can resume scouting. We need to see more."

"Yes, ser."

Roughly a kay and a half farther along, after the road circles back to leading north-northeast, Alyiakal notices a side road, apparently disused, on the right and signals to Raayls, who rides back.

"Where does that go?"

"Nowhere, ser. Except to a collapsed hole or tunnel in the side of a hill.

A few weathered pieces of wood left. Not much else, except a little stream. You can see that the hoofprints keep heading up the main road."

"Could raiders use it as a camp?"

"There's water, but it's rugged and rocky and without much cover. There's no easy way out, not by horse, except by the road there."

"Riders couldn't reach it another way?"

"You can reach anything another way in these hills if you want to risk your mount or your neck, ser. Wouldn't be easy."

Alyiakal nods and orders the company to proceed. The mild breeze feels more chill, and he pulls on the riding gloves he's brought.

Over the next glass, as the company follows the road, with its gentle climb, Alyiakal sees that the single rider continues to retrace his tracks. Alyiakal can't help but wonder if they're being led into an ambush, but the scouts see nothing. He neither sees nor senses anything but two red deer and a mountain cat, and all three move away from the road at their approach. In one instance fresh deer prints cross the road, but the only hints of side paths are narrow game trails.

In time, Alyiakal notices a break in the trees that seem to rise endlessly on the north side of the road, that appears as though it will meet the road several kays ahead. The road continues to rise, and at the end of a slightly steeper incline the road flattens, and there are no trees directly ahead.

When Alyiakal reaches the flatter section, he reins up and calls a halt. On his left, fifteen yards below, the River Lhaar runs through a gorge some forty yards wide. Beyond the gorge, to his left and east, smooth expanses of rock angle upward. Beyond them, Alyiakal sees the snow-and-ice-covered peaks of the Westhorns. The gorge continues due east, and Alyiakal discerns that it gets shallower the farther east it goes, but the rocky slopes on the north side get steeper. Alyiakal can certainly see why Raayls thinks brigands or raiders can't cross to the north side of the river.

He gestures to Raayls, and the scout rides over and reins up.

"How much farther do patrols usually go?" asks Alyiakal.

"Some stop here. I don't know of any that have gone more than five kays farther east."

"Then we'll go a few kays farther. You and Maaetz lead."

"Yes, ser."

Within a hundred yards of the river overlook, the road turns slightly south and continues to rise, but the undergrowth thins. Alyiakal senses several strong order/chaos patterns close together and uphill and to the north, well away from the road, and suspects they're red deer. Even farther away he discerns a single, stronger pattern. *A mountain cat stalking the red deer.*

After another kay, the road swings back more to the east. Two kays farther on, Alyiakal sees a road angling southeast and signals for Raayls to rejoin him.

As he does, Alyiakal calls a halt. "That road there. What do you know?"

"We've seen raider tracks on it. Runs southeast. The old First Company followed it nearly ten kays. Never saw any sign of anyone living there, but the tracks kept going. Has to be something there, but I don't know what or where."

Belatedly, Alyiakal realizes three things: the chestnut is breathing a bit harder; it's a lot colder, uncomfortable even in a riding jacket; and the trees are all evergreens. As far as he can see, the road continues to climb, as do the retraced tracks of the single rider. He looks to the northeast, where he sees a hint of dark clouds.

After a moment of looking around and mentally marking a large red boulder on the north side, he nods and says, "Signal Maaetz to return. We've gone far enough for today."

While Raayls summons the other scout, Alyiakal turns to Chaaltyn. "Your thoughts, Senior Squad Leader?"

"That rider has to be a raider or a barbarian, ser."

"You think he was trying to lead us to an ambush?"

"It's possible, but I don't think so. There would have been tracks closer to Lhaarat. He might have been sent to see what the lancer companies were doing or just to see if we still made patrols as Winter gets closer."

As First Company heads back toward Lhaarat, Alyiakal doesn't relax his scrutiny of the road or the areas on either side. He also thinks about what he's seen—and what he hasn't.

And he's also gathered a fair amount of chaos, only some of which can he safely force into his firelance. He'll have to quietly disperse the rest. In a way, it seems a waste to gather chaos all day, not use it, and quietly release it every night. The only way to keep it while he sleeps, though, would be to link it to himself, which is what too many Magi'i do, and that slowly erodes their order/chaos balance.

LIV

On eightday, after morning muster, Alyiakal rides out of the post with first squad and the two scouts.

"West on the main road," Alyiakal orders.

"Squad left!" Chaaltyn orders.

As the scouts, only five yards in front of Alyiakal, lead the squad through the town, Alyiakal senses that the few townspeople out early on eightday are surprised by the riders.

Is Lhaarat so secure that lancers never have to come this way? Or they're wondering if there's been a raid they don't know about?

Once the squad clears the town, Alyiakal orders them onto the side road leading to the stone bridge over the River Lhaar. He studies the road and notices that, like the road through Lhaarat, it is surfaced with gravel with no significant ruts or depressions in the roadbed, and the road is slightly higher than the surrounding currently bare fields.

The bridge is not entirely stone but consists of two massive stone abutments, which extend several yards into the water, with a short stone and mortar causeway on each side. The timbered roadbed between the abutments runs roughly ten yards. The lower and flatter land flanking the road on both sides of the bridges, particularly on the south side, suggests to Alyiakal that there's significant Spring runoff.

The sturdy timbers don't give as Alyiakal rides across, and he looks toward the hamlet some three kays away, just north of the gorge that discharges the river into the valley.

The road eases away from the river as it nears the dwellings, out of necessity, since the two mills and their stone foundations stand within yards of the north bank. Less than a score of houses and their outbuildings stand on the north side of the road where the ground is higher. They have visible stone foundations as well, but the walls are of heavy timber planks, as are the shutters. As he nears the hamlet, he also sees that the closest dwelling on the northwest side looks as though it has been recently completed, with both a privacy screen and a barn where two men work to apply long, thin, wooden shingles.

The few people outside pay little attention as first squad trots into the hamlet toward the north end. There, Alyiakal studies the two mills. Judging from the covered lumber-drying racks north of the easternmost mill, it must be the sawmill, while the one closer to the hamlet proper is the gristmill.

Alyiakal takes first squad to the end of the graveled road alongside the sawmill's drying racks, where he calls a halt to study the path leading from the end of the road up the steep hillside to the left of the rocky cleft of the river gorge. He senses only rodents and birds in the nearby hills. Then he beckons to Maaetz.

"Ser?"

"Go check the tracks on the path."

"Yes, ser."

While he waits, Alyiakal looks northward along the irregular base of the hills comprising the east end of the valley north of the River Lhaar. He sees no obvious tracks or paths, but the few yards below the beginning of the hills, where the straggly evergreen bushes bordering the fields end, look wide enough for first squad to follow.

Maaetz returns in less than half a glass. "Ser, there are footprints on that path, but no hoofprints. It's too steep for a mount. Safely anyway."

"Do you know if any squads have ridden north along the base of the hills recently?"

"Not that I know, ser. The old First and Second Companies didn't, but I never scouted for Third Company."

"That was Captain Vaarkas's company?"

"Yes, ser."

"Thank you." Alyiakal turns to Chaaltyn. "We're going to see if we can find anything interesting."

"You think there are tracks coming out of the hills?"

"There are tracks. The question is whether animals or people made them and what's using them now." Alyiakal turns. "First squad! Forward on me!"

He eases the gelding forward on a path barely wide enough for two mounts abreast. When he reaches the largely bare and uneven ground between the underbrush and the rocky hillslope, he turns the gelding north, at a slow walk, both eyes and senses alert for anything large.

For the first half kay north, Alyiakal and the scouts only come across small animal tracks or footpaths. For the next two kays, there are traces of rodents, but no animal trails at all. Some three kays north of the hamlet, Maaetz gestures to Alyiakal.

"Ser . . . there might be a trail or path about half a kay ahead above that low hill that sticks out from the steeper slope."

"Keep an eye out as we get closer."

"Yes, ser."

As first squad nears the low rise, Alyiakal strains to sense any sign of life, but when the squad circles around the hill what they find is a brook running into a small pond hidden by the hill. After riding another kay, Alyiakal is about to give the word to turn back when Raayls gestures.

When the squad reaches the scout, it's clear that Raayls has found an old road. It hasn't been used in some time, because old, fallen limbs cover parts of the road leading up to a depression between two outcrops. Yet it's clear to Alyiakal that, in the past, the trail had been used frequently. He turns the gelding west from where the old road emerges from the hills and rides closer to the underbrush, beyond which are low rocky hillocks and scattered scrawny trees. He finds only years-old traces of ruts that might have been made by wagons.

Then he turns back. "We're done for today." He's found enough to be convinced there are other ways raiders could enter the valley besides the main road. The unused road, however, raises other questions.

He's still considering those when first squad returns to the post.

After dismissing the squad, he leads the gelding to the stable, where he grooms him and settles him into his stall. He's finishing up when he senses someone approaching, and that someone turns out to be the duty messenger.

"Ser, Majer Byelt would appreciate seeing you at your earliest convenience."

"Thank you. I'll be there shortly."

As the ranker turns and leaves, Alyiakal shakes his head. Whatever Byelt wants, it's not likely to be good, and if Hyrsaal was right, it won't even be politely unpleasant.

He doesn't dawdle, but he also doesn't rush, and a quint later he enters the majer's study. "Ser?"

"Close the door and sit down."

Alyiakal complies.

"Exactly what did you have in mind by parading a squad through the town this morning, Overcaptain?"

"First squad is the most inexperienced squad in the company, ser. They need all the experience they can get. Also, the lancers and I both need to know where the roads around Lhaarat go and what condition they're in. The existing maps don't show any access to the valley other than the main road, but when I asked whether there were other trails or paths that raiders might use to enter the valley, the scouts didn't seem to know."

"That's because there aren't any."

"Begging your pardon, ser, but we did find what appears to be an unused road some three kays north of the mills."

For an instant Byelt's face shows surprise, before he replies, "It's doubtless unused because it's unusable."

"That may be, ser, but when I asked, the scouts told me that it's been some time since any squad has surveyed the edges of the valley to see whether smugglers or raiders have been using other routes to avoid the main road. As I'm sure you can appreciate, I don't like getting unpleasant surprises, like raiders appearing where they've never been seen before."

"The raiders are to the east, not to the north and south."

"I was informed that raids are increasing here, ser. Was I misinformed?"

"There have been increasing attempts and attacks on patrols."

"Just along the east road or within the valley?" asks Alyiakal in a pleasantly mild tone.

"Both."

Alyiakal manages a puzzled look. "I'm afraid I don't understand, ser. If the only access to the valley is by the east road, which passes in front of the post gates, how could brigands or raiders possibly get into the valley without being noticed until they started raiding?" Even before Alyiakal finishes the question, he can sense Byelt's increasing agitation and/or anger.

"That's for you to find out. That's why you were foisted off on me."

"Then, with your permission, that's what I'll address myself to, which has to include finding any other access trails or roads into the valley."

"So long as First Company also takes scheduled patrols, Overcaptain."

"Yes, ser."

"That's all, Overcaptain."

"By your leave?"

Byelt doesn't speak, but gestures for Alyiakal to depart.

Alyiakal inclines his head politely, then turns and leaves the study, quietly closing the door.

Once he's in the corridor, he glances around, and seeing no one, he raises a concealment and waits. Half a quint passes, and neither the duty ranker at the table outside the majer's door nor the majer has moved. So Alyiakal moves to where he can remove the concealment without being seen and heads to his study. On the way, he sees that Paersol is in the officers' study talking to Vaarkas.

He enters his own study, again conceals himself, and opens the door. Sensing no one nearby, he steps into the corridor and eases into the officers' study, getting close enough to eavesdrop.

". . . don't know why headquarters sent me here," says Paersol. "From what everyone's said, not much is happening . . . don't see the need for four companies and an overcaptain . . ."

"The overcaptain might not be here for that reason at all . . ."

"Then why?"

"You hear what happened in First Company on threeday?"

Alyiakal thinks Paersol shakes his head.

"Overcaptain sparred with every lancer in First Company. Not one could touch him. How many officers even have that strength and stamina? He's training them in battle formations I've never seen. Rumor is that one captain pretty much destroyed the Kyphrans at Guarstyad. You like to wager who that might be?"

"What's he doing here, then?"

"I haven't the faintest idea, but I wouldn't get between him and the majer."

"But he's only an overcaptain."

"You roll the bones any way you want, but I'm not playing in that game . . ."

". . . doesn't make sense . . ." mutters Paersol.

Not to me, either. But Alyiakal wants to hear Vaarkas's response.

". . . wager it makes sense to headquarters . . . not a good idea to get crosswise with them, either . . ."

Alyiakal listens a little longer and eases back to his study, where he steps behind the door and drops the concealment. Then he works on updating his map of the valley.

When it's time for the evening meal, Alyiakal times his arrival slightly before that of the majer, who has little to say until after the wine, a weak red, is poured and everyone is served.

"Alyiakal, how did your scouting patrol go this morning?" Byelt smiles pleasantly, and Alyiakal now only senses a hint of irritation, which concerns him.

"Interestingly, ser. We found an old logging road, and I suspect in time we might find a few ignored or concealed ways into the valley. Of course, I could be wrong, but, either way, we'll have a better idea of exactly where to patrol to cut off the raiders. In the meantime, I'm using the most inexperienced squad in the additional short patrols to bring them up to the level of the other two trained squads First Company received."

Byelt nods. "Good idea." The majer glances at Dhaerl, then Vaarkas.

"You'd mentioned that the Cerlynese made trouble when you were posted to Pemedra," says Vaarkas. "I heard that it was the Jeranyi."

"They both did. First it was the Jeranyi. They supplied blades and specialized shields to the west branch barbarians. After we took them out and fired their town, Imperial fireships fired Jera. That stopped the Jeranyi problem. Then the northern barbarians stepped up their raiding. We removed most of the raiders, and in the process discovered the Cerlynese supplied them with blades, horses, and sometimes troublesome men and women. The Cerlynese also tortured any outsider who tried to trade with the barbarians."

"How civilized," declares Dhaerl sarcastically.

"Why didn't you deal with them then?" asks Paersol.

Alyiakal catches Vaarkas's momentary wince, then says, "My company was dispatched to deal with the barbarians. We took care of the barbarians. I thought that crossing into Cerlyn and attacking them was not only a bad idea but might be regarded as excessively presumptuous. I reported on the matter to my commanding officer, and a copy of my report went to headquarters. Shortly after, I was posted on schedule to Guarstyad, so I don't know what happened later."

"That, Captain Paersol," says the majer evenly, "is what any good officer should have done."

"And which a few, in the past," adds Dhaerl, "have not."

"Because Cerlyn's been a problem and is closer to Lhaarat than is Kyphrien," adds Alyiakal, "that's why I wondered if the Cerlynese were behind the increase in raids here."

"How could you even tell?" asks Paersol.

Vaarkas doesn't bother to hide his headshake.

From Byelt's glance, Alyiakal knows he has to answer. "By changes in the weapons, or gear they use, possibly new tactics, and by interrogating captives."

"They lie," says Paersol.

"But knowing *when* they lie will tell you a great deal," replies Alyiakal.

"Of course, it does help if you happen to be a field healer with higher order levels who can discern those lies," adds Byelt smoothly.

"There is that," agrees Alyiakal.

All three captains are momentarily silent.

Then Dhaerl laughs. Vaarkas nods, and Byelt exudes satisfaction. Paersol looks and feels confused enough that Alyiakal feels sorry for him, if briefly.

"I'm a field healer, Paersol, and I did the interrogations," Alyiakal explains quietly.

Paersol swallows. "My apologies, ser."

"Now that we have all that out of the way," says Byelt cheerfully, "we might have some dessert, such as it is."

Alyiakal understands exactly what the majer has done. Not only is Alyiakal now effectively responsible for "solving" the raiding problems, but he's also the one the captains need to watch. *But isn't that usually the case with deputy post commanders?*

LV

On oneday, Alyiakal takes Taenyr and third squad for another short search for possible trails used by raiders, beginning where first squad halted. The search covers another five kays, and as Alyiakal suspects, third squad discovers little more than narrow animal tracks, largely for red deer browsing the more succulent vegetation on the valley floor. On twoday, second squad covers another five to six kays, with the same results. On threeday, Alyiakal has the squads working on blade skills.

Fourday dawns with heavy high clouds and a moderately chill wind out of the northwest. Alyiakal leads First Company on another patrol of the east road. This time the company wears winter riding jackets with gloves and winter caps because there's no doubt the lancers will need them, especially on the road above and beyond the river gorge. Alyiakal ensures his water bottles are filled with ale, and he has some trail biscuits.

The scouts find cart tracks to and from the valley and the deeper tracks of another lumber wagon turning onto the logging road, about which Alyiakal briefly wonders, until he realizes that the sawmill is building up log supplies for late Autumn and early Spring, when there will be enough water to run the mill but little access for logging.

Beyond the road to the mining site, if that indeed was what the collapsed tunnel was for, the only tracks on the section of road leading to the river overlook are those of previous lancer patrols. This doesn't surprise Alyiakal since none of the recent road patrols reported any tracks. The leaves of the broadleaf trees have either fallen or turned winter gray, and by the time First Company reaches the river overlook, the wind is stronger and colder, and Alyiakal has only sensed one animal at a distance.

Still, he feels First Company should go farther east.

"Half a quint break. Then we'll go farther east."

After relaying the break order, Chaaltyn asks, "Do you think we'll find anything?"

"If we go where we're not expected, we might."

Once everyone remounts, First Company continues eastward for half a glass when Alyiakal and the scouts sight a wagon accompanied by two riders.

"Have to be traders, ser," declares Chaaltyn.

"The traders generally went unmolested in Pemedra," replies Alyiakal. "Is that true here?"

"Most times, ser."

The wagon does not slow until it nears First Company, when the teamster calls out, "Is there trouble ahead?"

Alyiakal rides closer, and the teamster halts the wagon, and the two mounted guards rein in as well.

"No trouble so far, trader. Have you seen any other riders?"

"None today, save you, Captain."

"What do you have in the wagon?" asks Alyiakal.

"Not much of interest to you. Mostly hides and fur."

Those words ring true to Alyiakal, but he suspects the trader isn't revealing everything. "Any weapons besides your own?"

"No."

"What else?"

"Now, that'd be giving away what people pay for."

"I asked politely. You can answer or we can search." Alyiakal pauses and adds, "For a time I was an Imperial tariff enumerator."

The trader sighs, deeply. "I'd ask that you keep my words among you and your senior officers."

"That, we can do."

"Salt and peppercorns, Captain."

Those words also ring true.

Are spices that dear here? "Anything else?"

"A bit of burnet and brinn, and knitbone."

"What else?"

"That'd be it."

"We wish you well, trader," says Alyiakal, easing the chestnut back and calling out, "Give the wagon passage."

Once the wagon and riders are past First Company, Chaaltyn asks quietly, "Was he telling the truth?"

"He was, and he wasn't happy about it."

"That makes sense, ser," adds Maaetz, who has moved closer to Alyiakal. "Some of the desperate mountain brigands might kill for salt. It's likely hidden under a false wagon bed."

"There isn't any in the mountains here?" asks Alyiakal, thinking of the salt mines east of Geliendra.

"No, ser."

For the next kay, the only recent tracks on the road are those of the trader and his guards, and First Company reaches the side road to the southeast, which shows partial tracks of several mounts leading onto the main road, where they're lost.

"Those are days old, maybe older," says Chaaltyn. "Too few prints for a raider band."

After checking them, Alyiakal orders the company to keep riding. While the chill wind hasn't strengthened, it also hasn't decreased. After another two kays, Alyiakal recognizes the large reddish boulder on the north side.

"This is where First Company turned back last time," he tells Chaaltyn. "We'll ride a few kays farther."

Close to three kays farther east—and at least a hundred yards higher—Raayls signals, and Alyiakal rides ahead to join him, extending his senses and discerning nothing.

Raayls waits where the road's surface shows a welter of hoofprints.

"Half score riders?" asks Alyiakal.

The scout nods. "More or less. They came this far and turned back."

"We'll follow them back a ways."

For the next half kay, the company follows the double tracks before reaching a section of the road that's several hundred yards of solid rock, with a steep treeless drop-off to the south.

At the far end of the rock section, Raayls halts. As Alyiakal rides up he notices the only tracks are single—and heading west.

"See that, ser?" asks Raayls. "After they turned back, you have double tracks, one set coming and one going, but after that last part of the road, there's only a single set."

Alyiakal's first thought is that they're about to be ambushed, but he senses no one close by—in any direction. The slope to the north is far too steep, and there's no cover on the equally steep southern side. Also, the tracks must have been made much earlier in the day because the wind has carried road dust over some of the hoofprints.

"Let's go back and see if we can find where they turned." Alyiakal turns the chestnut back west and rides past the company on the south side of the road.

From the end of the rock section of the road and as far as Alyiakal can see, the undergrowth appears solid except for a few substantial evergreens, and there are no tracks on the narrow south shoulder of the road. Then he notices faint marks in the dust on the shoulder, and he nods as he slowly rides west to two massive evergreens standing close together. In the dimming light south of the trees he senses what may be a trail. Alyiakal reins up and looks back to Raayls. "Look closely at the shoulder. I'd say someone's dragged an evergreen branch along it."

"Might be, ser."

"Why don't you look closely between those two trees?"

Raayls eases his mount onto the shoulder and toward the trees. "There's a narrow path here."

"See if you can follow it," orders Alyiakal, knowing full well the scout can, for at least several hundred yards.

A quint passes before Raayls returns and reports. "They went down that way. There are prints and other traces. It's narrow and steep for the first fifteen to twenty yards and not much wider for the next hundred. Then it joins another road, most likely the one that the old First Company followed."

And I'd wager that there's another hidden trail off that road that leads to another way into the valley.

"We're going to follow that trail and see where those tracks lead us," says Alyiakal.

"Ser?" asks Chaaltyn.

"We won't get many chances like this, Chaaltyn. Raayls will lead, and I'll follow with first squad. Once first squad is on the lower road, the other squads can follow. Pass the word back."

"What about an ambush?"

"We know there's no one along the trail. If they attempt an ambush, they'll have to try on the lower road because they can't get close enough to use blades in the trees and brush, and they can't get decent shots with bows. There's a slight risk when we come out on the lower road, but these tracks are glasses old, and I don't see raiders waiting glasses to see if someone penetrates their concealment."

"Yes, ser."

A half quint later, first squad forms up on the lower road, and Alyiakal takes several long swallows of ale while the other two squads make their way down the trail and form up. The raiders' tracks lead west, as Alyiakal suspected, but he has the feeling following the tracks will eventually lead to another road, possibly an old logging trail, that provides hidden access to the valley.

First Company turns back west on the road.

At least, we're not getting farther from Lhaarat. At the same time, he wonders why others haven't done what he has. Or weren't there enough raids that anyone felt the necessity? *There are too many unanswered questions, and too much you don't know, which limits what you can ask.*

A kay and a half later, the tracks turn off the road onto a trail between two bushes, possibly a game trail until raiders began using it. After perhaps half a kay, the trail runs into an old logging road, but unlike the old logging road north of the sawmill, fallen branches and limbs have been dragged off the road, wide enough that the lancers can ride two abreast again. The road also has a more gradual slope and angles west-northwest. *Where it just might come out on the south side of the valley at least a kay or so south of the town.*

Another half glass passes, and the afternoon light dims even more under the still-cloudy skies, suggesting that sunset is approaching.

Ahead, Alyiakal senses a hint of chaos/order patterns just at the edge of his abilities. He turns to Chaaltyn. "Silent riding. Pass it back."

Then he signals for Raayls and Maaetz to join him.

"Ser?"

"There's something ahead, and we need to move the whole company closer quietly. Flank me and let me know anything you hear or see."

Alyiakal slows the advance to a slow walk. He senses the area ahead, a slope angling down toward a flat area that had been logged over years before now filled with younger evergreens only five to ten yards high. The road continues in a gentle curve to the north into the previously logged area, an area Alyiakal estimates as close to two kays south of the south side of the valley. To the west side of the logging road is a cleared area, where Alyiakal senses both horses and men in separate groups.

First company keeps moving slowly.

"Smoke on the wind," murmurs Maaetz. "From the northwest."

"Ready firelances," orders Alyiakal. "Pass it back."

As First Company draws nearer to the logged area and the clearing, Alyiakal tries to sense a sentry ahead, but the only man away from the group is posted to the north, obviously to warn if any lancers showed up from the post. *Interesting, but not surprising . . . unfortunately.*

He also senses more chaos/order patterns than there are horses, suggesting the raiders have captives.

He quietly passes the information to Chaaltyn, then says, "Once we attack, detail three men to take care of the sentry. Capture him or kill him, but he's not to escape. When we charge, have third squad spread out beyond both sides of the road to make sure no one gets by."

"Yes, ser."

First Company is within fifty yards of the group when someone yells, "Lancers!"

"Company! Forward!" orders Alyiakal, urging the chestnut forward. By the time he can clearly see the concealed raiding camp, one of the raiders is about to loose a shaft from a short bow.

Alyiakal drops him with a firelance bolt, and the raider behind him. Another shaft shatters against his shield. Most of the raiders in the camp are dead in moments, including one who, instead of fleeing or fighting, slits the throat of a captive woman before Alyiakal, or another lancer, can bring him down.

Moments later, Rhemsaar appears. "We caught one, ser."

"How did you manage that?"

"After seeing the others die, he made a run for the horses. I got him in the back of the head with the flat of my sabre. Didn't break his skull, and he's still breathing. Cormaar's tying him up. What do you need from second squad?"

"Gather the mounts and load the bodies on them. Save two for the captives. Put all the spoils in one bag."

"We're taking bodies back?"

"We're too close to the valley to just leave them. They'll draw mountain cats too close to the hamlet." *And Byelt's too skeptical and might not trust you all that much.*

As Rhemsaar rides away, Chaaltyn appears with a ranker cradling his arm. Alyiakal looks at the man but can't recall his name.

"Ser, Crendaak here . . . I think his arm's broken."

"How did that happen, Crendaak?" asks Alyiakal.

"Didn't see a branch, ser."

"Let me take a look at it. We'll have to dismount."

Before he gets close to the lancer, Alyiakal can tell there's a fracture, but a clean one. By the time he has Crendaak's arm splinted and infused with a touch of order to forestall severe wound chaos, second squad has loaded up the raider mounts, tying bodies over several, and gathering arms, as well as packing everything taken from the locals on two of the raider mounts.

Then he tells Rhemsaar, "The women get to keep the mounts they're on, and the hamlet gets the mounts that carry what the raiders stole."

"Yes, ser."

With that done, Alyiakal rides to where the two surviving women sit uneasily on separate mounts. "Which hamlet are you from?"

"Southtyll," says the older woman, who looks ten years younger than Alyiakal.

"That's the one on the south end of the mill road?"

"It is. Why couldn't you come sooner? Then Pemina would still be alive."

"We did the best we could." *Until now, from what I've heard no one's caught anyone, just killed a few and driven the others off.* "If we hadn't attacked as quickly as we did, all of you would be dead." *But if we hadn't attacked, you all would be alive and headed for a life you wouldn't like.*

Neither woman replies.

"We're taking you back to Southtyll," says Alyiakal.

"And Pemina?"

"And Pemina," Alyiakal confirms, then asks, "Who is the Southtyll headman?"

"Rhuust . . . for the little he's worth, always saying things could be worse."

"Each of you can keep the horse you're riding." Then Alyiakal moves to the head of the company.

Raayls and Maaetz lead the way along the old logging road sloping unevenly downhill toward the valley floor. Raayls rides around the large pile of brush at the road's end and calls out, "It's mostly clear beyond the brush, but it's narrow."

Alyiakal follows, noticing that the path between the trees beyond the pile of brush looks like an animal trail for the fifty yards or so before he emerges from the wooded slope and undergrowth.

If we'd only started on this side of the valley. He shakes his head.

In the dimming light, he can only see uneven ground ahead and no obvious tracks in the bush-dotted grass, but he follows Raayls for another half kay before coming to a path of sorts leading to a hamlet that must be Southtyll.

When First Company reins up in the open center of the log-walled houses of Southtyll and the two young women dismount, a handful of men and women appear and surround them.

Two men walk toward Alyiakal. The younger man halts, while the older, taller, brown-bearded, and broad-shouldered man steps forward and asks, "Why couldn't you—" Then he breaks off speaking for a moment. "You're not the same officer who was here earlier."

"No, I'm Overcaptain Alyiakal. We tracked the raiders from the roads to the east to where they were holed up in the woods uphill and south of here. We managed to save two women. One of the raiders killed the third. We killed most of them, except one. No one got away."

"They'll be back."

"Not this group," says Alyiakal. "Are you Rhuust, the hamlet headman?"

Rhuust nods.

"How many times have you been raided? I'm asking because I've only been here a little more than an eightday."

"They raided us last Spring two eightdays after the east road opened. They raided the Spring before. They took food and lambs, not women."

"This time, did they kill anyone? Or hurt anyone badly?"

Rhuust shakes his head, and Alyiakal gets the impression that those in the hamlet didn't put up much of a fight, if any. "Were these raiders different?"

"Who can tell? Raiders are raiders."

"Where did they come from?"

Rhuust shrugs. "They just appeared. They must come from the hills or the mountains. They don't come from the valley."

Alyiakal can tell he won't get more from the headman. "I'm sorry for your losses. Each of the women can keep or trade the horse she rides. Pemina's consort or family can have the mount that carries her, along with the saddle and tack. I'll be very unhappy if I later find out otherwise." Alyiakal projects a touch of order and a sense of power.

Rhuust shudders. "I understand . . . Overcaptain."

"Good." Alyiakal smiles politely.

Alyiakal turns to Chaaltyn. "Has the raider we captured recovered enough to talk?"

"He's conscious."

"Then I need some time with him before we leave the hamlet." Since Alyiakal definitely wants to learn as much as he can before reporting to Byelt, he turns the gelding and rides back to the dark-haired captive, standing beside a

mounted ranker. He's tied with his hands behind his back and what amounts
to a rope harness around his arms and chest, which is tied to a longer rope
held by the lancer.

"What's your name?"

The captive doesn't speak.

"Does he have all his fingers?" asks Alyiakal.

"Yes, ser."

"We'll save those for later, if necessary." Alyiakal turns back to the captive. "I'm not in the mood to be kind." As he speaks, Alyiakal slowly tightens
a vise of unseen order around the captive's head, until he can see the panic in
the young man's eyes. Then he releases it. "Now, what is your name?"

Again, the man says nothing.

"Tie another rope around his foot, tightly. We'll drag him for a kay or so
and see if he wants to talk."

"It's Dietro, you ill-used sow."

"Your blades and arrows. Did you get them from the Kyphrans?" Alyiakal
hesitates, then adds, "Or from the Cerlynese?" From what Alyiakal can sense,
the young man doesn't react to either name, "Or perhaps the Gallosians?"
Still no reaction.

"Or the Grass Hills barbarians?"

Alyiakal gets a definite reaction.

"The horses, too, I take it. You poor bastards couldn't afford mounts that
good, and that tack looks like it came from armsmen somewhere. It all looks
alike." *Very similar if not identical to what those Cerlynese armsmen use.* "So
where is the other band of raiders holed up? Somewhere on the north side of
the river ten or twelve kays out?"

Neither of the last two questions seem to register with the captive.

Alyiakal senses desperation behind the silence. "Of course, the Grass Hill
barbarians taunted you because you don't have women the way they do . . ."

That also fails to elicit an emotional response, and Alyiakal turns to the
two lancers in charge of the captive. "Put him on a mount, and if he tries
anything yank him off. He can walk to the post."

Even so, it's another quint before First Company leaves Southtyll and another glass before Alyiakal makes sure the captive is securely locked in the
post's seldom-used brig. He then stables the chestnut, unsaddles, and grooms
him, examining him closely to make sure that he has no injuries, no matter
how small. He pats the gelding on the shoulder with a touch of reassuring
order and leaves the stables.

The majer's messenger waits for him outside.

"The majer wants a word?"

"Yes, ser." The ranker doesn't quite meet Alyiakal's eyes.

"I'm on my way."

Once in the headquarters building Alyiakal raps lightly on the majer's open door and without hesitating enters.

"You returned rather late from your patrol, Alyiakal." Byelt's tone is pleasantly measured. "While you were gone, brigands attacked one of the hamlets and got away before Fourth Company got to the hamlet."

"We were ordered on a road patrol to the east," replies Alyiakal. "But we found recent tracks and followed them back along one of those old roads that no one thought anything about. We caught them and killed all but one of the ten. We had one injury. The lancer rode too close to a branch during the attack and broke an arm. Simple break, it should heal. We saved two of the women they took. One of the raiders killed the third before we could stop him. We returned the two women to the hamlet." Alyiakal can sense Byelt's hidden consternation but continues, "I questioned the single captive. From what I could get from him, they got blades, mounts, and tack through the easternmost of the Grass Hills barbarians. The saddles appear to be Cerlynese, and all ten blades, saddles, and bridles are identical, and they don't look Kyphran."

"You'd know that." Byelt stands. "We might as well head to the mess. You can give a short briefing on what happened at dinner."

The three captains turn when Alyiakal and Byelt enter the mess together, and Alyiakal senses a mixture of surprise and concern hidden behind professionally pleasant expressions.

"As you were, Captains," says Byelt. "After we're served, Overcaptain Alyiakal has some interesting news."

Once the wine is poured and the mess orderly finishes serving, Byelt offers no toast, but just lifts his wineglass slightly and says, "If you would, Overcaptain."

"Thank you, Majer." Alyiakal summarizes the day's events concisely without omitting anything he thinks is critical. When he finishes, he nods to the majer.

"Very thorough without dragging it out." Byelt pauses, then says, "If you'd pass back the salt, Paersol."

"Yes, ser."

"How did you know you'd find them?" asks Vaarkas.

"I didn't," replies Alyiakal. "I was fairly certain we'd find how they were getting into the valley without coming near the post. There are only so many ways to get somewhere around here, and I thought we'd either find them or discover another way to and from the valley."

"How could you be so sure?" asks Paersol.

"I've spent a fair amount of time during my first posting studying and making maps of where I've been. I've gained a better understanding of terrain and geography from that. I also have some acquaintances, through my friendship with another officer, who are traders and factors in small towns. Talking to them when I've been on leave has taught me more about trade and traders, as did my short stint acting as an Imperial tariff enumerator."

"I don't believe you mentioned that," says Byelt.

"That was a collateral duty when I was in command of Oldroad Post. After a year or so, the Emperor's Merchanter Advisor or the Senior Imperial Tariff Enumerator sent a tariff enumerator."

"The Senior Tariff Enumerator," says Byelt. "No one else would have the authority."

From there on, the conversation turns to far more mundane matters, including how soon it might be until the first snow.

LVI

When Alyiakal wakes on early sevenday, his dreams haven't been the best, although he has only a vague memory of them, for which he's more than grateful. He's glad that he'll be riding, which helps clear his head.

After morning mess, Alyiakal takes out third squad, partly to explore the edge of the eastern hills behind the post and for several kays to the west, more as a precaution, while having the squad practice various maneuvers. The reconnaissance finds no large animal trails and no abandoned or concealed trails, and by early afternoon Alyiakal leads the squad back, picking up the narrow road from Southtyll a kay north of the hamlet and taking it back to the main road.

Third squad is only a few hundred yards from the main road when two Mirror Lancer dispatch riders appear, riding toward the post.

Routine directives, news, and mail . . . or something more urgent, like the continuing illness or even the death of the Emperor?

Alyiakal shakes his head. From what he's heard and overheard, the death of the Emperor will result in unrest and turmoil. He hopes for a letter from Saelora along with the official directives and correspondence.

More than two glasses pass before third squad returns, gets debriefed by Alyiakal and Taenyr, and Alyiakal grooms and settles his chestnut. Then he makes his way to his study, where he finds a single document on his desk and three letters: one from Saelora, one from Hyrsaal, and one from . . . Kynstaar? *Torkaal . . . it has to be from him.*

Alyiakal decides the letters can wait, especially if he wants to enjoy them, and picks up the document, with an attached note, which states:

> *Read this, initial below, and pass it on to the next junior officer. The last to read it should return it and this initialed note to me.*

Underneath the text is an elegant "B."

Alyiakal turns his attention to the Majer-Commander's directive, entitled "Responsibility and Duty: Mirror Lancer Officers":

> *Commanders will remind all subordinate officers that the Emperor of Light has placed special trust and confidence in each officer. This trust and confidence presumes and requires integrity, good manners, sound judgment and discretion on the part of each and every officer, and the understanding that such trust is conveyed by the institution and position of the Emperor of Light, not upon any specific individual who holds that position . . .*

As Alyiakal reads those words, he whistles softly to himself. Headquarters is all but declaring that a succession struggle is about to occur. *And warning officers not to take sides.*

The rest of the short directive merely expands on the opening statement, as is often the case, as Alyiakal discovered in reading all the directives crossing Majer Maerl's desk. After reading the statement, he initials the note, then stands and makes his way to the adjoining officers' study, where he places it in Dhaerl's inbox.

Vaarkas looks up from his desk.

"It's a directive from headquarters that Majer Byelt wants all of us to read and initial."

"Must be serious. He doesn't do that often."

"I'd say so, but you can read it and see what you think." Alyiakal smiles wryly and heads back to his study.

Once there, he picks up Hyrsaal's letter, which he senses . . . and nods, noting the seal has been heated by chaos, removed, and replaced, presumably after someone read the letter. Then he slits the envelope, avoiding the seal, and extracts the single sheet.

> *Alyiakal—*
> *I just wanted you to know that I arrived safely in Inividra. We've already had two encounters with barbarians, but they decided against getting closer or engaging when they saw they were outnumbered . . .*
>
> *I also wanted you to know how happy Catriana was with the consorting chest and all that came with it. She couldn't believe it. I can. I know Saelora, and I know you. Together the two of you could go far. I know Saelora says it's not the right time. It's never the right time. If you wait too long, there won't be any time. I won't nag, again. But those are my thoughts.*
>
> *The weather here is better than at Lhaarat, but it looks like there are more barbarians . . .*

When Alyiakal finishes Hyrsaal's letter, he sets it aside and picks up the letter from Kynstaar, slitting it open, and noting its seal has also been chaos-tampered, and it is from Torkaal.

> *Overcaptain—*
> *I promised I'd let you know. I'm in Kynstaar, and they decided to put me in charge of blade training. Good thing someone had me working with blades for the past two years. None of the officers here are as good as you.*
> *Also wanted to thank you for everything.*

Alyiakal smiles as he replaces the letter in the envelope, then turns to Saelora's letter. He smiles as he slits it open, avoiding the Merchanter's seal, partly out of habit and partly because it reminds him of how hard Saelora worked to earn the right to use such a seal.

I can't tell you how relieved I was to get your letter. I know traveling is much safer than your usual duties, but I still worry. Silly, I know, with all the dangers you've faced. I also appreciate your letting me know how long it can take for our letters to get to each other. It helps.

But Alyiakal knows she still worries.

We're now busy with fermenting the last of this year's greenberries. The must looks and smells promising, but, as someone often says, we'll have to see.

Alyiakal smiles at that affectionate reminder, then resumes reading.

Vassyl is getting weaker. It's slow, but we all can see it. He can, too. He says he realizes how much your presence helped while you were here. Elinjya comes by more often now. We've talked several times, and she told me every time that I'm as much his daughter as she is, and that she never could have gotten so close to him if I hadn't taken on and bought the factorage. I think she feels guilty that she wasn't interested, even before Evaant's death. I've been putting aside coins from the time I bought the factorage so that I can pay her for Vassyl's share, and I owe you for your help in Geliendra, as I've thought about it, I think I understand more about both you and Father.

I'm also glad that you liked the way I've decorated and changed the house so that it now looks appropriate for a Merchanter. According to Catriana, Dyrkan is still thinking about what additional unique good might be suitable for Loraan House . . .

After he finishes reading the letter, Alyiakal smiles, if wistfully, and then writes out the last of the letter he has been working on so that he can send it with the dispatch riders in the morning. Afterward he places Saelora's letter with all the others. He can't help thinking about her and their time together, although he knows he'll soon have to turn to working out upcoming exercises and patrols . . . and Winter evolutions.

When it's time for the evening meal, Alyiakal makes his way to the officers' mess a bit earlier than usual, to see if there's any reaction to the directive Byelt circulated.

Dhaerl and Paersol stand beside the table talking, but both turn to him.

"What do you think about that directive, ser?" asks Paersol.

"I'm guessing, but I'd say that the Emperor is gravely ill, if not dead by now."

Dhaerl nods.

Vaarkas joins the group, and Alyiakal goes on, "The Emperor has been in poor health for years, according to some senior officers—" Alyiakal pauses as Majer Byelt enters the mess and walks toward the group, then continues, "And his sole heir is considered by many not to be fit for the Malachite Throne, while his son by a previous . . . liaison is apparently regarded by some as more capable."

"There's more to it than that," says Byelt, "but so far as it goes, the overcaptain is accurate. I'll fill you in on that at dinner." He gestures toward the table.

Once the five officers sit and are served, Byelt lifts his glass. "I'd offer a toast to certainty, but at times, certainty can be very unwelcome." Then he takes a small swallow and goes on. "Overcaptain Alyiakal is correct about the situation, but there are complications. First, the woman with whom the Emperor Taezyl had his liaison is the youngest daughter of the former, and now deceased, Second Magus. Her older sister was the second consort of the Emperor Kieffal. She died in the accident that killed Kieffal. His first consort died of something that caused uncontrolled chaos in her body. I'm skeptical of that, but you might know more." Byelt looks to Alyiakal.

"Ser, it does happen. When I got some training from a noted healer at Syadtar, she showed me a lancer dying from that. He wasn't much older than I was. It's something only *very* experienced and good healers can sense. Even they can't do anything except prolong life a little."

"Hmmm. I didn't know that, but it makes matters more interesting. In any event, Taezyl's . . . less legitimate son is consorted to a daughter of the Third Magus while the presumptive heir is consorted to a Magi'i healer of a less distinguished heritage. I've been told there are other complications, but I don't know them." Byelt looks once more to Alyiakal.

"No, ser. You know more than I do."

"How great is the Magi'i interest in who takes the throne?" asks Paersol.

Byelt laughs harshly. "Only the Magi'i know. Whether they act on that interest, and how, is what affects us."

"So the directive," says Dhaerl slowly and deliberatively, "says that we're to be loyal to whoever becomes Emperor of Light and that we're not to get involved." He pauses, then adds, "Since there's no way we *could* be involved, the Majer-Commander issued a general directive as a warning and a veiled threat to those who might be without having to reveal who they are."

If he even knows for certain. Alyiakal merely nods.

"Exactly," replies the majer. "If you wouldn't mind passing the bread around."

Alyiakal knows the discussion is closed.

LVII

When he wakes on eightday morning, Alyiakal still wonders about the raider band First Company surprised on sevenday. He goes to the small infirmary, and, after checking Crendaak's arm and deciding the arm has stabilized with comparatively little internal wound chaos, he replaces the splint with a plaster cast.

"How long will I have to wear this, ser?" asks the ranker.

"Until the fracture in your arm heals. That could be as little as five eightdays or as long as eight. You won't be doing any combat-related duties for the time being, but there are other duties you'll be able to handle." Alyiakal can think of several, but Crendaak will need a few quiet days, and Alyiakal prefers to talk to Byelt before assigning any duties. "Don't bang the cast into anything. You could make the break worse."

That's unlikely, but the fact that Crendaak broke his arm in the first place suggests that the ranker's not as careful as he might be.

"Yes, ser. Thank you, ser."

"I'll be checking your arm every so often, and I'll let you know about other possible duties when the time comes."

"Yes, ser."

Alyiakal hurries to the mess but arrives just after Byelt.

"Where have you been, Alyiakal?"

"The infirmary. I put a plaster cast on Crendaak's arm to keep it immobile while the fracture heals."

"I still don't see . . ." Byelt shakes his head. "Not even a barbarian blade, but a frigging branch."

"He'll be fine well before Spring."

Byelt shakes his head again, then takes his seat, as does Alyiakal.

None of the three captains say anything, even after all the officers are served, and Byelt turns to Dhaerl. "What do you think about raiders this time of year?"

"They've only got three eightdays left or thereabouts before we start getting snow. They lost the whole band. According to the overcaptain, most of them were young. The older raiders might not want to chance another raid." Dhaerl shrugs. "Just my best guess, Majer."

"Vaarkas?" asks Byelt.

"They might send scouts to see what they could find out. It's possible they might send a larger group, but I wouldn't."

"Paersol?"

"Ser, I've never dealt with barbarians or raiders before."

"Your judgment, Overcaptain?"

"I'd agree with Vaarkas, but we can't count on that."

Byelt nods. "With barbarians and raiders, you can't count on anything . . . except that they often don't think; they just react to their animal urges."

Alyiakal doesn't agree with Byelt's last observation but refrains from comment. Because the barbarians often don't have many choices, they seem less rational than they are.

"Don't most men?" asks Dhaerl. "At least now and again."

"The barbarians do most of the time," replies Byelt. "That's the difference."

Alyiakal just eats quietly, and a quint or so after breakfast, he goes to the majer's office.

"Do you have a moment, ser?"

"I've got more moments than I know what to do with right now." Byelt motions for Alyiakal to enter.

Alyiakal closes the door and approaches the desk, then stops. He doesn't sit down. "I've been thinking . . ."

"I'm glad at least one of my officers is."

"I'd like to talk to Dietro—"

"The worthless barbarian captive?"

". . . and see if I can learn more from him."

"What is there to learn? He won't say anything. But be my guest. Just don't waste too much time. If you do discover anything, let me know."

"Yes, ser."

Alyiakal leaves the majer's study and makes his way to the brig, which occupies the end of the stable building.

"Ser?" asks the ranker on duty.

"I'm here to talk to the prisoner," says Alyiakal, looking past the guard to the heavy, iron-banded oak door to the first cell, at the barred opening a hand in width and height set at eye level.

"Ser . . . he's rather violent. Let me call Stefant, just in case."

"That's fine. I doubt I'll need backup, but you never know."

Once the two lancer guards are ready, one unbars and unlocks the door and says, "Mind your manners, Dietro. You've got a visitor."

As the iron-banded door opens, Alyiakal senses Dietro will attack instantly, and, as Alyiakal steps into the small cell, the young man lunges. Alyiakal expands a section of his personal shield with enough force that the raider is thrown back hard against the stone wall.

"I wouldn't try that again," says Alyiakal pleasantly, before saying to the lancers, without taking his eyes off Dietro, "Close the door."

The captive straightens up, looks at Alyiakal in the dim light, and then slumps.

"We need to talk about a few things, Dietro. Sit down on the edge of the bed." Not that the bed is much more than a thin pallet over wooden planks.

Dietro doesn't move.

"Do you want to get hurt even more?" asks Alyiakal, order-projecting a sense of cold implacable force.

Dietro remains standing.

"So, you think that you're already dead?"

"I failed. They will kill me. You will kill me. I am already dead."

"Then what do you have to lose by talking?" Alyiakal asks kindly.

Alyiakal senses the young man's confusion and waits.

Dietro remains standing. "You . . . you're not like the others."

"No, I'm an overcaptain. Most senior officers don't lead patrols." While that doesn't really answer Dietro's question, Alyiakal knows Stefant and Yosert are listening closely at the opening in the door. "Why did you raid the hamlet?" He projects a sense of interest and sympathy, some of which is not feigned.

"No choice."

"Would the others have killed you?"

"They would have left me on the heights without clothes or weapons."

"That's a cold death."

Dietro does not reply.

"It's a long ride to Southtyll."

"Southtyll?"

"The hamlet you raided. It's a long ride."

"Twenty kays. Maybe more."

"Do the Kyphrans leave you alone?"

"The easterners? They are cowards."

"Are the Grass Hills barbarians cowards?"

Dietro shakes his head. "We are stronger. They sneak through the grass, and give us mounts and blades to leave them alone."

Alyiakal senses that's not precisely true. "Have you seen the warriors who live to the north of the Grass Hills barbarians?"

"They do not show themselves. They are cowards also."

"It's a long ride to the Grass Hills barbarians. Five or six days, isn't it?" Alyiakal exaggerates, hoping that Dietro will correct him.

"None of us would take that long. Four days, at most, on the high road."

The high road? Alyiakal nods. "I'll talk to you more later." He raises his voice. "Yosert, if you'd open the door." Then he looks to Dietro. "Don't be foolish. You'll only hurt yourself." He pauses, then adds, "I'm usually addressed as 'ser.'"

Dietro remains standing but doesn't move as Alyiakal leaves, and the door closes behind him.

Both lancers just look at Alyiakal.

"I'll be back to talk with him more." He turns and heads back toward his study, where he'll write a brief report for the majer, and a recommendation about what to do with Dietro. Since the raid hadn't killed anyone, and neither had Dietro, there are possibilities for him, but Alyiakal doesn't know enough yet.

And you need to find out more.

LVIII

For the next two eightdays, Alyiakal continues the same general pattern: training, investigating the edges of the valley for other concealed or abandoned roads, and patrolling the east road with First Company. Crendaak's broken arm continues to heal. None of the squad-level explorations find additional roads or any new raider tracks. Nor does Alyiakal learn much more from Dietro, except to narrow the location of the raider hamlet to someplace more than fifteen kays and less than thirty from Lhaarat. That leads Alyiakal to wonder why they don't move, and the only conclusion he can reach is that it's the safest place they can find and far enough away from lancer patrols. The fact that the raider hamlet hasn't yet been found by lancers tends to support that conclusion.

On fiveday, Alyiakal leads second squad out, heading west on the main road past the crossroad leading to Gairtyn and the mills to the north and Southtyll to the south. Northward, the sky is cloudless but hazy, with a light wind. Alyiakal feels a storm might be on the way by evening, but he hasn't been at Lhaarat long enough to be certain. Since the encounter with the raiders, the post has only seen one storm—if scattered light snow flurries for two glasses could be called a storm. Even so, the days are chilly, the nights close to freezing, and the lancers ride in winter gear.

"You think we'll run into any more raiders before the snows close the east road?" asks Rhemsaar, riding beside Alyiakal.

"I have no idea. If there are raiders to the north and east of the Westhorns, we could have raids until early Winter." Alyiakal pauses. "Do you have any idea why no one seems to know much about the raiders?"

"There weren't many raids until last year, and then some of the raiders had those horn bows. Captain Hyrsaal tried to point that out. That was what I heard . . . and then he got posted to one of the north border posts."

"Were the raiders we took out different from the ones several years back?"

"Don't know as they're different, ser, but they had better weapons. If they'd known we were coming, we might have had more casualties."

"That's true with anyone you have to fight," replies Alyiakal dryly.

Second squad continues west for another six kays until it nears another hamlet, with narrow roads leading both north and south.

"Do you know the name of this hamlet?" asks Alyiakal.

"Midtyll, ser."

Alyiakal wonders if every hamlet in the valley has a name ending in "tyll," but belatedly recalls that Gairtyn doesn't.

Several men and women watch as the squad reaches the middle of the hamlet and turns onto the side road that curves north-northeast beyond the hamlet proper.

Less than half a kay farther Alyiakal sees a narrow timber bridge over the

Lhaar. As the squad nears, he understands the bridge's location. The southern span connects the south bank to a rocky islet in the middle of the river, and the second span stretches from the islet to the northern bank.

"Single file!" Alyiakal orders. "Maaetz, check the span."

The scout slowly rides across, then calls back, "No more than two mounts at once."

When Alyiakal and the chestnut cross, he feels the span vibrate, but doesn't sense a lack of order in the timbers, which look comparatively new, and he wonders how often the span gets damage from Spring runoff. *Or damaged enough that it has to be rebuilt.*

On the north side of the bridge, the road angles back to the northwest. Little more than a kay later, the squad reaches a much smaller hamlet, little more than a half score of log-walled houses and small barns. The hills bordering the valley on the north are about a kay away. While the road proper ends on the north side of the hamlet, there's a well-worn path through the fields and grassland to the wooded lower slope of the northern hills.

The dirt of the path shows hoofprints, but not as many as a raider band. Still, Alyiakal focuses his senses on the wooded slope as second squad draws closer to the trees, but he discerns only small animals and birds. He glimpses a traitor bird on a gray-leafed branch at the edge of the wooded area, but the bird is silent, a fairly good indication that neither people nor possible prey are nearby.

"Take a look, Maaetz," Alyiakal orders. "Don't go too far."

"Yes, ser." The scout slowly rides onto the narrow trail that slopes upward.

Alyiakal follows him with his senses for perhaps a hundred yards before the scout turns his mount and heads back, finally reining up before Alyiakal.

"Ser, it gets narrower, but it leads to a little spring, and there are bushberries along one side."

"That explains the trail. Did you see anything else?"

"Not sure, ser. There might be something farther west, or it just might be a seasonal streambed. Too rocky to ride to it."

"Then we'll head that way and see." Alyiakal turns the chestnut west and proceeds at a slow walk behind Maaetz, with the rest of the squad following.

More than a hundred yards west, Maaetz reins in and points ahead on the right to a slight depression in the slope. "Seasonal stream."

The squad has continued along the base of the hills for more than a kay when Alyiakal notices a definite gap in the hills to the northwest. "Maaetz? Do you know anything about that lower point in the hills?"

"No, ser. I don't recall seeing it before."

A scout not seeing something like that? "It looks like it's two-three kays as the vulcrow flies. Could be farther." Alyiakal makes an effort to mentally place it on the maps he's been drawing of the valley, then says, "We've done enough for today. Time to head back."

When they reach the hamlet, Alyiakal looks toward the gap, but it's barely perceptible. Intermittently, he looks back, but when second squad reaches Midtyll, Alyiakal can barely locate the gap, which means it's only visible from the east and close to the north edge of the valley.

He nods. That just might be worth a closer look.

LIX

Sixday dawns gray. When Alyiakal makes his way to the mess, he studies the clouds with special interest, both the higher gray clouds over Lhaarat and the valley and the heavier and darker gray clouds hanging over the Westhorns, because First Company is scheduled to patrol the east road and it's too cold for rain.

From what Alyiakal can discern, the clouds overhead move slowly southwest, but he can't tell much about the darker clouds shrouding the Westhorns to the north and east, except that he can't see any snow. *For now, anyway.*

He reaches the mess early. Only Dhaerl has arrived, and Alyiakal says, "Did you see the clouds to the northeast?"

"They're like that in late Autumn and in Winter," replies the captain. "Sometimes, they mean snow. Sometimes they don't. Sometimes, we've gotten snow for days, and it piles up. The big snowfalls are in the upper hills, mostly above the river overlook."

"I wondered. We had thundersnows in Pemedra—"

"I got caught in one of those years ago, when I was a ranker just out of training." Dhaerl shakes his head. "Nothing like that here, although snow can come down fairly hard in the upper hills. Sometime in the next few eight-days, we'll get snow. Might be a few digits. Might be more. Then it just keeps coming. By Winterend, snow might be close to two yards deep." He offers an amused smile. "Clearing it out of the post keeps the rankers busy. Keeps 'em from trouble, too. They don't like the extra snow duty."

"Most don't, anyway," adds Vaarkas as he joins the two. "You have patrol today, Overcaptain?"

That's a courtesy question, because the schedules are posted, but that's not what Vaarkas is asking, Alyiakal knows. "We do. We'll have to see what it's like when we pass the logging road."

Dhaerl nods. "Good point to make a decision. Road gets treacherous above there if there's more than a few digits of snow."

Paersol hurries into the mess just before Majer Byelt, and with the majer's arrival, the officers all seat themselves, and the mess orderly serves them. Breakfast consists of fried oatcakes with a berry-pearapple syrup, ham strips, and egg scramble.

All the officers eat for a short time before Byelt turns to Alyiakal. "If you do get some snow, just patrol as far as it's reasonably feasible."

"I've been talking to Dhaerl and Vaarkas about how snow affects the road. We'll have to see what weather the day brings."

Byelt nods and takes a mouthful of oatcake.

Alyiakal mixes the ham and oatcake and follows it with a small swallow of ale.

Before that long, he dons winter riding gear, since a standard patrol will take them a thousand yards higher than Lhaarat, to where the ground has already begun to freeze in places. After saddling the chestnut, Alyiakal gives him a small carrot he'd gotten from the kitchen, then leads the gelding out into air almost Winter cold, where he mounts and then rides to join Chaaltyn.

As First Company forms up, Chaaltyn turns to Alyiakal. "The weather looks like snow coming in from the northeast."

"The majer left it up to me as to how far we go into the hills. We'll just have to see what the day brings." Alyiakal has no intention of going far enough that the company will have to slog through heavy snowfall to return to the post, especially after Dhaerl's words, but he also doesn't want to return too soon if there's no snow at all.

Especially since it's not certain how much snow will fall.

When First Company rides out through the gates, Alyiakal checks the wind—steady out of the northeast and not gusting. The road is dry and firm. He tries to sense the clouds overhead, but they're too high for him to discern the order/chaos flows.

Raayls takes the forward scout position, with Maaetz equidistant from Raayls and Alyiakal as First Company leaves the metaled road and starts up the east road that leads through the hills, up farther through the Westhorns and, eventually, to Kyphrien. For the first three kays, the wind remains steady and chill. When Alyiakal rides past the logging road, the air feels colder, but the clouds over the Westhorns to the northeast don't seem to have moved closer, although they're uniformly dark enough to make it difficult to see how much closer they might be.

By the time First Company reaches the dead-end road to the collapsed tunnel, the wind rustles through the evergreens bordering the road, and light intermittent snowflakes begin to appear.

Alyiakal studies the darker clouds to the northeast, realizing that they're approaching faster than he has realized. He turns to Chaaltyn. "It's time to head back. Call in the scouts. First squad will be rear guard, and I'll move to lead from third squad."

"Yes, ser."

The snowflakes remain light, even after First Company reverses direction and rides back down toward Lhaarat—until the company approaches the logging road. Then, the intermittent snowflakes become flurries.

Another quint passes, and a light, steady snow replaces the flurries, and by the time First Company reaches the metaled road at the base of the hills, the snow is heavy enough that Alyiakal can barely make out the outline of the post. While the intensity of the snow is nowhere near that of thunder-snow, it's heavier than Alyiakal expected, and he's more than happy when First Company is within the post walls.

Dealing with mounts and gear takes longer than usual, and it's midafter-noon when Alyiakal makes his way from the stable toward his study to write up the report on his snow-shortened patrol. He pauses outside the stable to sense the clouds above, as their base is far closer to the ground than when First Company had begun the patrol.

The order and chaos flows within the clouds are stronger and more intense than he guessed, if not nearly of the intensity within a thundersnow cloud, and the clouds move much faster than before.

Because they gain speed once they're past the peaks of the Westhorns and there's less to impede them? Alyiakal shakes his head, knowing he should have consid-ered that possibility.

He resumes his walk toward the building that holds officer quarters, stud-ies, and the officers' mess, while the snow continues to fall. Already a good four digits covers the untrammeled parts of the post courtyard.

Once in his study, Alyiakal quickly writes out the patrol report, very brief because First Company had encountered no one and seen no new tracks. He is finishing his copy when the Crendaak, who has become the usual duty messenger, raps on his half-open door with his good hand.

"Yes?"

"The majer would like to see you, ser."

"I'll be right there." Alyiakal signs and seals the report, noticing that Crendaak waits outside the door. *He doesn't want to report back without me close behind.* Then he picks up the report and follows Crendaak out of the building and through the snow to headquarters.

Once he reaches the majer's study, he knocks on the open door. "You asked for me, ser?"

Byelt nods and gestures for Alyiakal to close the door.

Alyiakal does so, then lays the report on the desk. "Since I had just finished this when the messenger arrived, I thought I'd bring it with me."

"I'll read it later. I'm sure it's accurate." Byelt pauses. "The lookouts spotted First Company just before it began to snow heavily. How far did you get before turning back?"

Alyiakal senses no anger, and no untoward chaos, and says, "Just above the side road to the collapsed tunnel."

"Why did you decide to turn back then?"

"It had started to snow, and the wind picked up. I could see heavier snow to the northeast, and the clouds there were far darker. I'd been cautioned that traveling the road above the fork to the logging area was dangerous with more than a few digits of snow on the road. Since there were no signs of anyone on the road, it made sense to turn back."

"Have you ever been caught in a heavy snow?"

"Once, ser. At Pemedra. I'd prefer not to repeat the experience."

Byelt nods slowly. "That's all, Overcaptain. I'll see you at dinner."

Alyiakal nods politely and leaves the study, wondering what Byelt had in mind or what he might have been looking for. *Or was he just reminding me that he's in command?*

The last is certainly possible, even though Alyiakal has never considered being insubordinate or going around Byelt. He decides to return to his study and write a bit more on his current letter to Saelora, although it could be days before another dispatch run.

LX

The snow ends sometime in the night, but there's more than six digits on untrammeled ground on sevenday morning, and high gray clouds cover the sky. No tracks mark the east road, and Alyiakal suspects that there's close to half a yard of snow on the higher part. A slight hint of wind blows out of the north, but not enough to cause drifts in the snow.

The sky remains cloud-covered for most of the next three days before the sun returns on threeday, with enough warmth to melt the snow off the east road in the valley around the post by the end of the day.

On fourday, Alyiakal leads first squad up the east road, following the tracks of the logging wagons, but there are no tracks in the snow on the main road after the point where the logging wagons turn off. Less than half a kay farther east Alyiakal calls a halt when the snow gets more than knee-deep, and he can sense the chestnut's uneasiness. Once back at the post, he writes a brief report to Byelt describing the short patrol and the road conditions. He also turns in the latest report on his interactions with Dietro, who has become more respectful, if also more depressed.

The majer doesn't make any comment on either report, either in writing or at the evening meal.

On sixday, Alyiakal and third squad leave the post early, heading west on the main road to Midtyll, where Alyiakal orders the squad to head north through the hamlet.

After the squad leaves the hamlet and as Alyiakal and Taenyr approach the two-span bridge over the River Lhaar, the squad leader asks, "Do you really think we'll find another way in and out of the valley out here?"

"Today, who knows?" replies Alyiakal. "Experience tells me that there are more ways to get to and from places than most people know. The last raiders we dealt with had weapons and tack that had to come from Cerlyn. Cerlyn is closer than Kyphrien, and the Cerlynese have caused trouble before. I'm wagering there are trails raiders could travel from the north into the valley, yet no one in the Mirror Lancers seems to know about any. I could be wrong. Or I could be half wrong, and there's a trail farther west of where the road climbs up to the west end of the valley." Alyiakal offers a sour smile. "If we can't find one, at least the men will have a better sense of the valley, and they and their mounts are getting exercise."

"That's true. If the weather's like two years back, the only exercise anyone will get is moving snow and keeping the snow packed down on the road."

While Hyrsaal hadn't mentioned that, Alyiakal senses that Taenyr believes it.

When he rides across the bridge, Alyiakal checks the level of the river below, but it seems only slightly higher than before.

Once the squad rides into the small hamlet at the end of the narrow road, Alyiakal tells Taenyr, "Straight ahead until we reach the foot of the hills. You can see a few tracks. There's a spring out there. Likely has better water."

After the squad reaches the base of the hills and heads west, Alyiakal sees that very little of the snow under the trees has melted, but that there is a path in the snow up to the spring. The squad continues west past the snow-covered depression that looks like a seasonal stream. Two quints later, Alyiakal sees the point where he'd turned second squad back on the previous patrol.

He keeps looking ahead and north where the gap between two hills seems to be getting wider, or at least his ability to see the gap is increasing, wondering when and if Taenyr will notice it.

Then he frowns, because the gap appears smaller. "Squad! Halt!"

After a moment, he nods. The gap appears smaller because there's a larger rise in front of it. That presents a problem. If there is a road or trail, does it circle around the rise to the east or to the west? "Raayls!"

The scout rides back to join Alyiakal. "Ser?"

Alyiakal explains, then asks, "If there is a road, where would it be?"

Raayls pauses. "On the west side. Smugglers'd want to get as far from the post as possible."

"You're probably right, but I'd like you to go up through the trees a bit and see what you can find."

"Yes, ser."

Once Raayls leaves, Alyiakal turns to Taenyr. "What do you think?"

"I'd go with the scout, ser."

A quint passes before Raayls returns. "No sign of anything, ser. It's steeper and even rockier starting about a hundred yards uphill."

"Then we'll keep heading west until we find something or until it's clear there's nothing to find."

After riding another four kays, with Raayls making periodic rides up the tree-filled slopes, Alyiakal is about to turn back when he sees a depression in the tree-shaded snow ahead. As he rides closer, he notes that the depression extends north to a wide gap between the trees at the base of the hill. Turning the chestnut toward the gap, he reins in just short of the trees. From there he studies what lies beyond them, with both eyes and senses.

There's definitely a trail wide enough for a horse, possibly even a small cart, and that trail angles northwest along the hill shielding direct view of the gap in the hills behind it, but Alyiakal is more than certain that it turns north farther uphill and leads to the gap.

He signals for Raayls to join him, then gestures toward the trail. "See what you can discover, but don't go more than half a kay."

"Yes, ser."

As Raayls rides onto the trail and uphill, Alyiakal keeps sensing as the scout moves northwest and then north-northwest. After a quint Raayls turns back, and another quint passes before he reins up beside Alyiakal, offering a wry and amused smile.

"Looks to be pretty much what you thought, ser. Trail circles up and around this hill. There's a vale halfway up in the back, and it looks like the trail turns north and runs through that gap. Too deep for me to go much farther, but the slope's even enough for a cart."

"Thank you." Alyiakal turns to Taenyr. "Now we'll see where that path goes."

"Path?"

"I wager that the snow here is covering a path or narrow road that eventually reaches the east road somewhere near Westyll." Alyiakal smiles wryly. "We'll have to see."

He turns the chestnut south and begins to ride. Within fifty yards the snow gives way to flattened brown grass and what is either a very wide path or a narrow road angling southwest.

A half kay farther southwest Alyiakal sees a grouping of five houses and outbuildings ahead, not even a hamlet, with several chimneys trailing smoke. A single figure pauses, turns in the direction of the lancers, then hurries into one of the dwellings.

None of the inhabitants appear as the lancers ride through.

Some three kays farther south, the road leads to a timber bridge over a narrow section of the Lhaar, a structure of such dubious appearance that Alyiakal has the lancers cross one at a time. While the bridge vibrates, it holds, but Alyiakal sighs in relief once the last lancer is on the south side of the river, where the land is higher than on the north. Less than a hundred yards from the bridge is the first dwelling of Westyll.

Taenyr looks to Alyiakal. "You suspected this all along, didn't you, ser?"

"I did. There are always smugglers. This part of Cyador doesn't get as many, but the question is what roads or paths they take. Often those are the same ways that raiders, barbarians, or brigands use." *And barbarians supplied by Cerlyn just might use this way.*

When the lancers enter the hamlet, Alyiakal looks for larger barns or buildings that seem somehow out of place and might be used by smugglers, but he sees none. The log-walled buildings look solid, but how long the doors would last against a raider ax is another question. Once more, the few inhabitants who are outside quickly enter their dwellings, although Alyiakal can vaguely sense that a few watch as third squad turns north on the main road.

While there is no road or trail heading south from the hamlet, Alyiakal recalls, when coming to Lhaarat, he had ridden by a trail that appeared to head south about half a kay west of Westyll. *Another possible route for raiders or smugglers? Or just another dead end to be investigated?*

That patrol may need to wait, depending on the weather.

Four long and uneventful glasses later, Alyiakal leads the chestnut into his stall, where he unsaddles and grooms him before he heads to his study to write up the patrol report he won't be able to finish until after the evening meal.

Alyiakal is the next-to-last officer to enter the officers' mess, and Majer Byelt follows within moments.

Once the officers are seated and served, the majer says, his tone of voice more casual than the feelings he conceals, "You had a rather lengthy patrol for just a single squad, Overcaptain."

"Yes, ser. We finally located a trail smugglers have been using to bypass the post. Possibly smugglers coming from Cerlyn, but we won't be able to determine where else that trail may lead until Spring."

"Where did you discover this?"

"A little more than four kays north-northeast of Westyll. There's also a group of dwellings, too small to be a hamlet. I'll have a full report for you in the morning."

"I look forward to reading it."

"A smugglers' trail?" asks Paersol.

"It appears to lead in the direction of Cerlyn," replies Alyiakal. "Since the last group of raiders we encountered had weapons and tack from Cerlyn, it's possible that the barbarians east of the Grass Hills might use it or other raiders might use it in order to avoid our patrols on the east road."

"We haven't seen any raiders in Westyll before," says Vaarkas.

"We might not in the Spring, either," replies Alyiakal. "Or we might next Summer, or not until the following year. Since the number of attacks has increased, with the majer's agreement," *or lack of disagreement,* "I've used the time to train what amounts to a new company and to investigate possible ways raiders could use."

Byelt nods grudgingly, and Alyiakal isn't looking forward to meeting with the majer on sevenday. He smiles and turns his attention to the section of rolled stuffed beef flank steak on his plate.

LXI

Although Alyiakal finishes the patrol report on sixday evening and leaves it in Byelt's box that night, at the morning mess, Alyiakal offers pleasantries and waits for what he knows is coming. Just as the officers have finished eating, the majer says, "Overcaptain, we need to go over a few matters. After breakfast, if you would."

"Yes, ser." Alyiakal senses a certain resolve, but no obvious anger. He can also sense the curiosity of the three captains, but neither Byelt nor Alyiakal says anything further.

When the majer leaves the mess, Alyiakal and the others stand.

"Is there anything we should know, ser?" asks Dhaerl.

Alyiakal offers a pleasantly amused smile. "Not yet, but if there is, I'll let you all know."

Then he turns and follows the majer from the building and through the frigid air to headquarters and Byelt's study. He closes the door.

"Take a seat, Overcaptain."

Alyiakal does and waits for the majer to speak.

"You've stretched out the training time you requested far longer than we had agreed upon."

"Yes, ser, I did. I was trying to investigate points of access before Winter snow precluded that. I worry that we may see more attacks in the Spring."

"Attacks are a fact of life at border posts."

"Yes, ser."

"Are you through with such investigations?"

"There's one more possibility, but it's far less probable."

"Why is that?"

"Because it's in the southwest corner of the valley. It's likely still a route for smugglers, but there wouldn't be much advantage for raiders to use it."

"I'm glad to hear you've finished with problematical investigations. It's past time to take up your duties as deputy post commander. You'll be going through all the directives the post has received over the past four eightdays. I'd like your written comment on each, including what it entails or might entail for the post. Your comments can be brief, but I would like your views. Since you've had some administrative experience, you should be able to get up to date on them in the next eightday. In addition, I'll be giving you any new directives when they arrive, and I'd like your comments on those within a day."

"Yes, ser."

"You'll still be leading First Company on patrols, although those will obviously be limited by weather."

"I wouldn't have thought otherwise, ser."

Byelt frowns, then asks, "Do you really believe that we'll see attacks from the north any time soon?"

"I don't know, ser. Like you, I doubt we'll see much in the way of large attacks until Spring. It's always possible there might be attacks on individual houses by a few brigands. As for attacks by larger bands, I know that the tack and weapons and some of the mounts used by the last raider group came from Cerlyn. I have doubts that the Cerlynese provided them out of the goodness of their hearts, as I've noted little goodness or generosity evidenced by Cerlyn. Also, I've seen a certain contempt of Cyador by some Cerlynese armsmen."

"Why haven't I heard this from other officers?"

"As far as I know, I'm one of the few to have had any direct contact with Cerlynese armsmen, and unless headquarters circulated my report, only the other officers at Pemedra would have heard."

Byelt snorts. "That information would be useful. If you weren't here, I wouldn't even know. Then again, that might be another reason why you're here. Now, have you found any more information on the raiders from Dietro?"

"Not really. He doesn't have that much more to tell. He's younger than most ranker recruits. He doesn't even know his birthday, only that he was born fifteen or sixteen years ago. His parents are dead."

"What would you recommend we do with him?"

"He hasn't killed or wounded anyone yet, although that may be by chance. I'd send him to Terimot for ranker training and tell him that it will give him the ability to use weapons, get well fed, and make a few honest coins. We would have to stipulate that he'd have to be posted anywhere besides Lhaarat, but I'm certain there's empty space in firewagons leaving Terimot. If you agree, I'll make certain he knows that trying to escape is a death sentence."

"I'm inclined to agree. We have gotten more than a few good lancers from young barbarians. It's worth a try. Let me think about it. We'd have to send an extra lancer, and one who's willing to flame Dietro if he tries to escape." After a moment, the majer goes on, "I never asked why you didn't mention acting as a tariff enumerator."

"It seemed to me that I'd appear to be exaggerating my abilities, ser. It was very much a small part of my duties until the last season, when outland traders started coming through Oldroad Post in increasing numbers."

"Did you find out why?"

"Some of them discovered I followed the tariff regulations."

The majer frowns, then barks a laugh. "Likely the only time any of them had kind words for a Mirror Lancer officer." He pauses. "I can see why you're wary of the Imperial Tariff Enumerators and the trading clans in Cyador. What about those in Fyrad?"

"I don't know. Several of the outland traders landing at Stonepier and coming through Oldroad Post indicated they'd done so to avoid Guarstyad, Luuval, and Fyrad. They didn't seem to be lying, but other than what they said, I don't know."

"You're a very dangerous officer, Alyiakal."

"Ser?"

"You know I didn't want you here. Not you in particular, but not a deputy commander. I've watched you. You don't lie. I can count on that. But you don't always tell everything, do you?"

Alyiakal smiles wryly. "If I told you everything, our meetings would be much, much longer. All officers omit details. They either forget some, or they don't report what doesn't seem necessary or relevant. I make an effort to mention anything of possible relevance. That's also why I've investigated other entry points in the valley."

Again, Alyiakal has the feeling that his words have discomfited Byelt.

Byelt smiles abruptly, and Alyiakal senses both rue and amusement. He points to the stack of papers in the outbox. "That's all for now, Alyiakal. Those are the directives I mentioned. You might as well take them on your way out."

"Yes, ser." Alyiakal stands and nods respectfully before taking the directives and leaving the study.

As he walks out of the headquarters building, Alyiakal has the feeling that Byelt is more comfortable with him, but he smiles wryly as he thinks about the documents he'll have to read and comment on over the next eightday.

But it might be interesting to see if there's anything Byelt hasn't relayed.

LXII

By the following threeday, the weather is warm enough to melt most of the snow in the valley and has turned the east road beyond the metaled section into mud that not even the log wagons will try, and the side roads in the valley aren't much better.

Since the weather has precluded much in the way of patrols or reconnaissance, Alyiakal uses the time to make his way through the directives, and to attach a sheet with his comments to each. He has just finished the last set of comments and is about to leave the quarters building to take them to Byelt when he sees two lancer couriers ride into the post, tie their mounts outside the headquarters building, and carry the dispatch pouches inside.

Because Byelt will want to see the urgent messages or directives immediately, Alyiakal returns to his study and turns his attention to planning Winterweather exercises, which he bases on those used at Pemedra and Guarstyad.

Two quints pass before Crendaak knocks on Alyiakal's study door. "Ser, Majer Byelt requests your presence at your earliest convenience."

"I'll be right there, Crendaak. We can walk back together." Alyiakal picks up the dispatches and comments, closing the study door as he leaves.

As the two cross the courtyard to headquarters, Alyiakal says, "Couriers don't usually give any indication of dispatch contents. Were these two any different?"

"No, ser. They did say that it was still much warmer in Terimot."

"That's because we're really partly in the mountains."

When Alyiakal reaches the anteroom, the ranker at the desk says, "You're to go in, ser."

Alyiakal does so, closes the door, and walks to the desk. "Ser, here are the past dispatches with my comments, as you requested."

"Thank you. Just put them in the box. They can wait." Byelt pauses. "As you surmised earlier, Emperor Taezyl has died. He died this past sixday. The First Magus, the Majer-Commander, and the Emperor's Merchanter Advisor have announced that Kaartyn'elth is now the Emperor of Light, due to the ongoing and continuing illnesses of the former heir."

"Just a brief announcement, then? Nothing more?"

"Not so far. The Majer-Commander is obviously following his own earlier directive."

So far as we know.

"There's one other matter."

"Dietro?" asks Alyiakal.

Byelt nods. "I'd like to get him out of the post, and out of Lhaarat. Do you think he'll behave well enough to send him back with the couriers to be trained at Terimot? We'd still have to send two responsible rankers to go with them."

"Let me talk to him first. Then I'll give you my thoughts."

"The sooner the better."

"I'll talk to him immediately."

Byelt looks at the stack of directives that Alyiakal has returned. "I'll go through these as I can. When I'm finished, we'll talk."

"Yes, ser."

After leaving the majer, Alyiakal heads for the brig. The duty guards nod and open the cell door, then close it behind Alyiakal.

Dietro stands when Alyiakal enters his cell. "Ser?"

Alyiakal motions for Dietro to sit on the bed, waiting until he does. "We've talked about your becoming a lancer ranker, and that you wouldn't ever be posted here. What are your thoughts?"

"I have no real choice, do I?"

"We all have choices, but sometimes they're all bad. Being a lancer, in my opinion, is much better than any other choice you have. If you work in your training, you'll get paid to do something like you did before. You'll have decent food almost all the time—"

"Almost?"

"On long patrols, you'll have trail rations and hard biscuits."

"And if I don't?"

"There's no other choice," Alyiakal says bleakly. "I think you could become a good lancer. I don't want you to waste your life."

"Then I will become a lancer."

"If that is your decision, you will leave here in the next day or so. You will still be a prisoner until you get to Terimot, but you'll wear a plain uniform. That's a town four days' ride to the west. The undercaptain and the rankers there will train you. Then you will be sent to a post somewhere else." Before Dietro can speak, Alyiakal holds up a hand. "If you try to escape on the ride, the lancers escorting you will turn their firelances on you." He projects absolute certainty. "Now, there is one other thing you need to know."

"Yes?" Dietro's voice is wary.

"After four years as a lancer, if you don't get into trouble, you will have a choice. You can remain a lancer until you cannot be one any longer, and you will receive silvers every eightday for the rest of your life. Or . . . you can leave the lancers with any coins you have saved."

"You would give me that choice?"

"Every lancer has that choice after three years. You would spend four years because you fought against us."

"I will become a lancer . . . and in four years, I will see."

"Remember what I said. If you try to escape . . ."

Dietro shivers, then says, "I will not escape."

Alyiakal can sense the resolve . . . and the hope. He adds, "I might even see you again, but it wouldn't be for a while."

For the next half quint, Alyiakal does his best to answer Dietro's questions.

When he leaves the cell, the two rankers secure the door and look at him. One asks, "Can you trust him, ser?"

"I think so. He knows he's dead if he tries to escape. We also know that he'll fight, and we'd rather have him fighting with us, and not against us. Besides, I'd hate to waste a possibly good recruit."

When he steps out into the chilly courtyard, he's fairly certain Dietro will not be stupid, if only because the young man has received better treatment as a captive than as a raider. *But you never know.*

In less than half a quint, he's knocking on Byelt's study door.

The majer motions him in. "Close the door."

Alyiakal does so. He remains standing and says, "I spent some time with Dietro. It's dawned on him that he's effectively dead if he does anything else but become a lancer." Alyiakal relates the interchange.

Byelt nods. "That's as close to certain as we'll get. I will personally make it clear to his escorts that he's to be treated well, unless he tries to escape." He pauses, then shakes his head.

Alyiakal understands. The choice is up to Dietro, not the Mirror Lancers. *Of course, it's a forced choice, but it's the best we can do for him.*

"Prepare all the documentation for my signature, with a copy for the files."

"Yes, ser."

Alyiakal heads back to his study, where he looks up the provisions in the post commander's manual he's kept from Oldroad Post, drafts the documents, and returns them to the majer.

Only then can he return to his study, to find a letter from Saelora in his inbox, which he opens with both hope and trepidation.

> *I got your latest letter yesterday. I'm glad to know that everything at Lhaarat is close to what you expected, and that you are well.*

> *Vassyl is much weaker. He's so thin you wouldn't recognize him, but he always tells me to give you his best wishes. Elinjya now comes by every day to spend time with him. Most days she also draws me aside and asks about him because Vassyl always tells her that he never felt better. In some ways, I've gotten closer to her and Catriana than to Karola . . .*

Alyiakal can understand that, especially since Karola has never reached out to Saelora.

> *I just heard from Catriana. Some of the traders with contacts in Cyad are saying that the Emperor is ill and not expected to live. They're all worried about who the next Emperor will be because the heir is also very ill.*

Which suggests that the Merchanters are behind Kaartyn. That concerns Alyiakal, given what he's seen.

> *I haven't heard from Hyrsaal since his letter saying he'd arrived at Inividra, but Catriana has, and he's fine, but Winter can't come too soon because that means fewer raiders and fewer patrols in the cold.*

Alyiakal nods. He's known that Hyrsaal has never been fond of cold weather from the time he and Alyiakal were at Kynstaar.

When he finishes reading Saelora's letter, he turns to finishing his latest letter to her, telling her, in general terms, about his recent activities, and predicting any letters he writes during Winter will be delayed because of the heavy snowfall.

Then he takes the letter to the duty desk to send with the couriers on their return to Terimot.

LXIII

First thing on fiveday morning, Alyiakal dons his winter uniform and riding jacket and heads for the mess kitchen, absently hoping that Dietro is keeping his word and will arrive at Terimot safely.

Once he enters the kitchen and stops just inside the door, one of the mess boys approaches, grins, and asks, "A carrot, ser?"

"If you can spare one," returns Alyiakal warmly.

The mess boy leaves and returns shortly and extends the single carrot. "You're not spoiling him, are you, ser?"

"Only a little, but he's worth every carrot." Alyiakal smiles, turns, and leaves the kitchen, stepping into the courtyard, where a fierce and bitter wind blows out of the clear northeast sky, although Winter won't arrive by the calendar for another three eightdays. Despite his winter uniform and riding jacket, Alyiakal shivers as he hurries to the stable.

The chestnut turns his head as Alyiakal enters the stall, then nuzzles the overcaptain.

"Not yet, fellow. Not yet." Alyiakal senses the area around the stall and, sensing no one, raises a concealment around himself and the gelding. "We have to keep you accustomed to the darkness." He pats the gelding on the shoulder. "I'm afraid we're going to have a busy time of it come Spring."

Alyiakal talks quietly and holds the concealment for a good half a quint before releasing it. When the dim light of the stable reappears, the chestnut nuzzles Alyiakal insistently. Alyiakal grins and offers the carrot. The gelding makes short work of the carrot and nuzzles Alyiakal again.

"Just one. You'd eat every carrot in the kitchen." He pats the gelding again, then leaves the stall, walking swiftly through bitter wind back to his quarters, where he hangs his winter jacket, then leaves for the officers' mess.

Dhaerl stands alone in the mess. "Good morning, ser. Did I see you coming from the stable?"

"You did. I check on my mount more when we don't ride."

"Might I ask if you knew a Captain Faaryn?"

"I knew an Undercaptain Faaryn. That is, he was an undercaptain when I last saw him. I take it that you know each other."

"Yes, ser. We were at Isahl for a year at the same time. He said that you should have graduated first, but there were political necessities. He also sends his best."

"He was the best of all the instructors at Kynstaar, while I was there, anyway."

"I'm not surprised." Dhaerl hesitates. "He said that as a raw recruit you sparred with him and disarmed him in moments."

"I had the advantage of not looking terribly prepossessing."

Dhaerl laughs. "He wrote the same thing."

"I hope he's well."

"He is. He took his stipend and consorted the younger daughter of a successful cooper in Kynstaar."

Alyiakal smiles.

"You two look cheerful," says Vaarkas as he joins them.

"Just discovering someone that we both know, happily," replies Alyiakal.

"Much better than discovering you both knew someone, unhappily," returns Vaarkas in a cheerfully sardonic tone.

Paersol's arrival, followed by that of Byelt, spares Alyiakal the need to reply. The five officers seat themselves.

"Alyiakal," says Byelt casually, "before it slips my mind, a quint after breakfast?"

"Yes, ser."

Alyiakal takes several bites of the ham strips and over-browned toast before he asks Dhaerl, "Just when were you in Isahl?"

"From Autumn 90 to Harvest 93."

"I take it that was a busy time?"

Dhaerl chuckles sardonically. "From what I saw and keep hearing, all times at Isahl are busy."

"And at Inividra," adds Vaarkas.

Paersol looks as though he might speak, but then takes a sip of ale.

After breakfast, Alyiakal returns to his room and spends half a quint there before donning his winter riding jacket and walking through the still-bitter wind to headquarters and the majer's study. He closes the door as he enters, then sits down.

Byelt nods to the papers before him and says, "I've read your comments on the directives. You're perceptive, and mostly diplomatic. I don't disagree with any of your observations. From now on, you'll get the directives first and comment on them before I see them. Just as you did on these." Byelt pauses. "On another matter, what are your observations on Captain Paersol?"

"Even for a junior captain, he has a certain lack of perception."

"You put it more diplomatically than I would, but there's almost nothing in his record to indicate that."

Almost? Alyiakal considers what he knows, and then says, "He was a company officer at Westpoint. Was he assigned to patrol from Westpoint to Southpoint?"

"Interesting question, Alyiakal. Why do you ask?"

"That's the section of the wall with the fewest incidents with trees or Forest creatures, ser."

"It is. How did you know that?"

"My father was a commander at Northpoint."

"And your conclusion?"

"I'm only guessing, but my guess would be that he had a slightly higher number of injuries and/or deaths than average."

"More than just slightly."

"That would suggest ties to someone with influence," says Alyiakal. *A great deal of influence . . . and that he was posted here before an "accidental" firelance bolt hit him during an incident along the Great Forest wall.*

"Any thoughts on who it might be?"

Alyiakal shakes his head. "I've met one of the headquarters commanders briefly, and the subcommander who commanded at Guarstyad was promoted to commander and posted to headquarters."

"Before or after you got orders here?"

"We got orders pretty much the same time."

"Have you heard from either commander?"

Alyiakal senses unease in Byelt, but replies, "No, ser. I've never written them, either."

"You don't have any other contacts in Cyad?"

"No, ser. The only other person I know from the Mirror Lancers who might be in Cyad is the Magi'i healer I studied with briefly in Syadtar. She was older, and that was more than six years ago."

Byelt's unease vanishes, and he nods. "Then we'll just have to schedule

Captain Paersol's patrols carefully from now on. If you were planning patrols for the next few eightdays, what would you do?"

"Short patrols up to the logging road, so long as it's passable, and squad-sized patrols and riding and formation drills on the main and side roads while it's possible." Alyiakal goes on for a little longer, then stops.

"I concur. From now on, you draft the patrol schedule and give it to me. If I have any changes, I'll let you know, along with my reasons."

"Thank you, ser."

"Well, now that I have a deputy, I might as well use him." Byelt actually smiles, if briefly. "That's all for now."

"Yes, ser." Alyiakal stands, nods, and turns, hoping that matters between him and the majer remain cordial.

LXIV

Four days later, on oneday, it snows, dropping only a few digits on the valley, but doesn't get cold enough to freeze the mud for another two days, just after the lancers escorting Dietro to Terimot return, reporting that all went well with the young man. They also return with dispatches and letters. There are none for Alyiakal, but he hardly expects any, since Saelora might not even have received his last letter.

That night, it snows again, adding a few more digits to what remains on the valley floor, but three times that falls in the lower hills, and doubtless more in the upper hills and lower Westhorns.

Alyiakal continues to schedule the patrols, although the majer issues and signs the schedule. Alyiakal leads First Company's individual squads in rotation on short patrols over the next two eightdays as the depth of the snow on the valley floor slowly increases, along with the piles of snow outside the post walls—snow that the lancers continually remove. Clouds shroud the upper peaks of the Westhorns much of the time, occasionally giving way to the cold sun that turns them shimmering white.

On sixday of the last eightday of Autumn, the dispatch couriers bring more routine reports and directives, as well as two letters for Alyiakal, one from Hyrsaal and one from Saelora. Hyrsaal's is comparatively brief, and Alyiakal chuckles as he reads the opening lines.

Alyiakal—

    You may have already heard this from Saelora, but I never thought I'd be glad to see Winter arrive. First, right after I arrived, we got an early Autumn grass fire so bad that after it died down some of the local holders who lost late crops were raiding the holdings that weren't burned. Then came the barbarian raids, and a bunch of Jeranyi troopers who claimed they were just chasing brigands. There weren't any brigands, and not many Jeranyi after we finished with them. Then we got three days of downpour . . . and more mud than even in Lhaarat . . .

The rest of Hyrsaal's letter outlines what Catriana has done, including her hopes of becoming a full Merchanter like Saelora in the next few years, since Saelora has added another stall and more merchandise to her space in the Haansfel Factorage.

Another stall? That sounds promising.

Alyiakal opens Saelora's letter and begins to read. He has to reread the opening lines.

Alyiakal—

    I cannot make this gentle. Vassyl died four days ago. I just couldn't write about it then . . .

How could she after all he's done for her, and I couldn't help unless I stayed, and that would only have prolonged his life a little. He still feels guilty, even as he shakes his head and continues reading.

You know how much he did for me. I'd still be a poor scrivener without him. It seems so unfair I couldn't do more at the end. Both Elinjya and I stayed with him. That helped a little.

Earlier today, once things were more settled, I gave her all the golds for his share of Loraan House . . . and his share of the golds from the broken jewelry. She couldn't believe it. She thought the whole factorage was mine when it became Loraan House. Vassyl never told her. I had to show her the documents. We both cried again. She really is sweet. She kept thanking me for making the last years of his life happy in a way that she just couldn't. She kept asking if everything Vassyl left her was hers. How could it not be?

Elinjya asked me to keep half for when her daughter is older. Her son will get all the lands since her consort had no children from his first consort.

Also, Charissa had her daughter yesterday. She wasn't due for another two eightdays, but the baby seems fine. They don't have a name yet.

Alyiakal winces. With Vassyl's death, and Gaaran tied up with Charissa, Saelora has to be struggling to keep everything together.

I'm leasing two stalls at Haansfel and that's already increasing our sales. One of the experimental barrels of must looks like a dismal failure, but the other is promising . . .

The remainder of the letter is about the distillery and Loraan House, except for the closing lines, which Alyiakal lingers over.

I know that I do not write as well as you do, but I wanted to tell you I treasure every word you pen, as well as the words you have written by your actions and care. Use that same skill and care in your duties for your sake, for our sake, and for the sake of Cyador.

Although he appreciates Saelora's words, the very last phrase concerns him because she's never said anything like "the sake of Cyador" before. That wording suggests she may have found more amiss with the Merchanters than what she learned from him but dares not be more explicit in a letter that may be read by others. Yet there's little he can do except follow her advice.

LXV

Even before Winter officially begins, most of the valley is effectively snowbound except the main road and Lhaarat, Gairtyn, Midtyll, and Westyll. At times, the post sends out horse-drawn snow rollers to pack the snow on the road, which not only keeps the main road passable but also makes it smoother and firmer for sleighs and sledges.

Alyiakal spends a fair amount of time improving his maps. He also tries to come up with better tactics to use in the hills and woods, because he hasn't yet fought in terrain with trees and thick undergrowth, except for his short time at Luuval.

On the third fourday of Winter, Byelt summons Alyiakal, something that has happened less and less; if Byelt wants to see Alyiakal, he usually makes a comment at breakfast or dinner.

When Alyiakal enters the majer's study, Byelt gestures for him to close the door. "There are a few things we need to talk over, Alyiakal."

Alyiakal nods and waits, wondering what those might be, since Byelt's manner and order/chaos flows don't indicate anger or distress.

"I don't know if Dhaerl's mentioned it, but he's put in his papers to retire and take his stipend at the beginning of Summer. He could have done that a year ago, and headquarters has accepted and approved his request."

"I wondered if he might be due," replies Alyiakal. "He'd mentioned an officer he'd served with years ago had recently taken his stipend."

"Headquarters indicated that we'll be getting an undercaptain to replace Dhaerl in late Spring." Byelt frowns. "I don't know the details yet."

"Getting an undercaptain in Spring. I'd have to wonder . . ." Alyiakal lets his words fade.

"We could be fortunate and get a former senior squad leader, or I could recommend someone here to be promoted to undercaptain." Byelt looks to Alyiakal.

"In several years, Chaaltyn will be a possibility, but not yet."

"I thought that might be the case, but I wanted your thoughts. That's the same with the other companies as well, except possibly for Baarth, Captain Paersol's senior squad leader."

"Would you like me to talk to Chaaltyn quietly and see what he can tell me?"

"That might be helpful. There's also the fact that Vaarkas is due for reposting in Autumn."

Which would leave Paersol as the senior captain unless headquarters sends a seasoned captain. Alyiakal doesn't like even to think about Paersol as the senior captain. "It's too early to know anything about that, I take it?"

Byelt snorts. "We'll be fortunate to know by Harvest."

Alyiakal smiles wryly. "In that case, I'd suggest that I accompany Paersol and any new officers on occasional patrols, especially in early Spring."

"That might not be a bad idea." Byelt offers an ironically amused smile. "Especially if any of them fail to take your advice."

In short, document your observations thoroughly and word them carefully. "Is there anything else?"

"I think having your study in the quarters building has served its purpose. I'd thought to have your study returned here in early Spring, but with current matters, it makes more sense to make that move over the next eightday." Byelt offers a cheerful smile. "I'm sure you can handle the details."

Alyiakal can't say he's surprised, but he's relieved that Byelt's finally accepted him as deputy post commander. "I'll take care of it. Do you have any specific use in mind for the space I'll be leaving?"

"Given the surprises that headquarters has sprung on us in the past, we'd best leave it vacant for the moment."

Alyiakal nods, then says, "We've heard nothing significant from Mirror Lancer headquarters since the death of Emperor Taezyl."

"We haven't. What do you think that signifies?"

"That any dissatisfaction with the new emperor is either under control, is biding its time, or both."

"I'd agree," replies Byelt. "I'd also wager that Emperor Kaartyn is proceeding cautiously. The real dangers will come, if they do, when he begins to exercise his full powers in ways that conflict with the wishes of the upper reaches of the Triad." Byelt adds sardonically, "That time will come; it always does."

"Changes in headquarters, you think?"

"Most likely, once the Emperor ascertains who supported him and who did not, unless the First Magus restrains him. That's always possible, but far from certain."

"So, we'll just keep the raiders, brigands, and barbarians at bay and see what happens?"

"That's the usual role for senior officers on the borders," replies Byelt in a tone of mild sarcasm.

Usual . . . but is it best for Cyador? That question hangs in Alyiakal's mind as he leaves Byelt's study.

The first thing he wants to handle is talking with Chaaltyn.

He finds the senior squad leader in the squad leaders' study, seated at his table, reading a letter, and he motions for Chaaltyn not to stand.

"Ser?"

"If you'd come to my study shortly."

"Yes, ser."

Alyiakal turns and heads to his study. He thinks the letter is cheerful. With the long separations, more than a few lancers receive letters that aren't, but Chaaltyn had been smiling.

When Chaaltyn arrives, with a worried look, he closes the door. "Is there a problem, ser?"

Alyiakal shakes his head and motions to a chair. "No problems this time. I thought it was time for a talk. You've been here at Lhaarat a bit more than a season. How does it compare to Eastpoint and your other postings?"

"Colder, mostly, ser," answers Chaaltyn dryly. "The patrols are like those at Syadtar. Not so many raiders as we had at Isahl."

"You've been around. Your request or headquarters' whims?" Alyiakal has overheard enough to know that rankers and squad leaders seldom have a high regard for Mirror Lancer headquarters.

"Some of each, ser. I requested Accursed Forest duty. One posting was enough."

"You mind telling me why?"

"I'd rather not, ser."

"Might it be that the need to kill animals whose only fault was escaping walls didn't set well with you?"

For just a moment, Chaaltyn freezes, as if stunned by the question.

"It never set well with me, either," Alyiakal adds. "I'm not sure the animals know what awaits them, unlike raiders and barbarians, who know and still persist."

Chaaltyn gives a slight nod. "I've never understood that. Even when the raiders escape, they don't usually get that much."

"Unfortunately, it's more than many of them have. They're kept poor by the Jeranyi, the Cerlynese, and sometimes the Kyphrans, and they're convinced that we're monsters because we fight off and kill raiders. I've heard, but can't confirm, that some barbarians will chase down and kill anyone who takes a horse and tries to leave."

"I've heard that, too."

"You, Rhemsaar, and Taenyr work well together."

"We do." Chaaltyn nods.

"That's usually the way it is in most effective companies, especially when the senior squad leader is good. When I was an undercaptain, I learned a lot from my senior squad leader. The senior squad leaders at Pemedra were close.

They weren't that close at Guarstyad, and they don't seem to be that close here. Or am I missing something?" Alyiakal pauses.

"I get along well with Baarth. He's solid. So are Naltr and Ghastnaar, but they sort of stick together."

"So all the senior squad leaders are solid, but Naltr and Ghastnaar tend to keep to themselves?"

"That's fair to say, ser."

"What about the more junior squad leaders?"

Chaaltyn frowns. "Except for Rhemsaar and Taenyr, I'm not close enough to say. You'd do better talking to their senior squad leaders."

Which is exactly what he should say. "I've heard that Baarth is quite good, and it's good to know you think that as well."

Chaaltyn smiles wryly. "He's the kind of senior squad leader who ought to be an officer before long. Be a good company officer after another year or two, especially if he stays with Fourth Company." Chaaltyn stops. "Sorry, ser . . . I didn't mean . . ."

Alyiakal knows full well that Chaaltyn meant every word. "I know, and I appreciate your discretion. What about you?"

"No, ser. I'd like to be the best senior squad leader I can. I don't want to do what undercaptains and captains do."

"You're well on your way, Chaaltyn. You've done well with First Company, and first squad." Alyiakal pauses. "Do you have any thoughts on any training that might be helpful over the Winter and early Spring?"

"I'd like to think about that, ser."

Alyiakal stands. "Do that, and we'll get together in an eightday or so and discuss possibilities. I won't keep you longer, but I appreciate your thoughts and observations."

"Thank you, ser."

After Chaaltyn leaves, slightly worried but also relieved, Alyiakal considers what he's learned, and what to convey to the majer. He also needs to embark on organizing the move of his study furnishings and papers to the traditional study location for a deputy post commander.

LXVI

Light snowstorms besiege Lhaarat and most of the valley during the fifth eightday of Winter, and Alyiakal uses the time to move to the deputy post commander's study. Not until late afternoon on sevenday of the next eightday do dispatch riders arrive from Terimot with letters, directives, and other official correspondence. All of what comes from headquarters appears to be routine, but Alyiakal still has to review and comment on each directive. There is also a letter from Saelora, which Alyiakal sets aside for when he can read with his full attention.

Then he scans the official documents, ranging from revisions to procedures for storing firelances to updating sanitary measures in post kitchens. The most interesting of the documents is the announcement of the official coronation of Kaartyn'elth'alt'mer as Emperor of Light, Protector of the Steps to Paradise, and Inheritor of the Keys to the Rational Stars.

Keys to the Rational Stars? Alyiakal can't recall ever seeing that term, and he wonders if there might be actual keys, some ancient device, or whether the words only serve a ceremonial purpose.

He shakes his head, and begins to read the directive on sanitary measures, hoping he can finish before the evening mess.

Despite occasional interruptions, Alyiakal finishes the last comment—on a revision to the documentation required for payments to local holders for procurement of provisions—roughly a quint before the evening meal. He looks at the letter from Saelora, then tucks it inside his winter jacket, before lifting the small pile of papers and taking them into Byelt's study, where he deposits them in the empty inbox.

Byelt watches, and lifts his eyebrows.

"Nothing to get excited about, except possibly the coronation announcement. It's on top. It mentions the three top Magi'i, the Majer-Commander, and the Emperor's Merchanter Advisor, but it doesn't mention the Empress-Consort."

"That might be because she's the daughter of the Third Magus."

Verinaar, as I recall. "So you'd mentioned. Do you think the omission is because the First Magus doesn't want to hint that the Magi'i favored Kaartyn over the direct heir?" Alyiakal has never mentioned the Third Magus by name because he's never wanted Byelt or anyone to know the intensity of Verinaar's scrutiny.

"Most likely, although those in the Triad leadership certainly know. I doubt they care what junior senior officers know, since there's little we can do, one way or the other."

Alyiakal nods. "I'll see you shortly." He leaves the study and makes his way from the headquarters building to the mess, hurrying through the chill wind and low light.

While none of the stone buildings are particularly warm, the one holding the officers' quarters and mess is more comfortable because it contains the kitchens and the lancers' mess hall. It feels even warmer as Alyiakal steps inside.

Vaarkas is already there, along with Paersol, still wearing his winter riding jacket and gloves. Both stand close to the hearth at the end of the room away from the doorway.

"You've never been this far north in Winter, have you?" Alyiakal asks Paersol.

The junior captain shakes his head.

"This is about as cold as it gets," says Vaarkas. "It just doesn't get any warmer until after the first eightday of Spring."

"If then," adds Dhaerl from behind Alyiakal.

"Then it gets muddy," says Vaarkas, smothering a grin.

"Since you seem to like the mud," says Alyiakal, deadpan, "it might be best to schedule Third Company for the mud patrols."

Dhaerl smiles.

"I'm really not that fond of the mud, ser," says Vaarkas. "It's just a lot better than the snow."

Alyiakal has his doubts but says nothing as the majer enters the mess.

Once everyone is seated and served, Dhaerl says, looking to Byelt, "I saw the dispatch riders. Was there anything interesting from headquarters?"

In turn, the majer nods to Alyiakal.

"Not a great deal," replies Alyiakal, "unless you consider changes to sanitary practices fascinating."

Even Paersol smiles at that.

"They've announced the coronation of Kaartyn'elth'alt'mer as the Emperor of Light, with a long list of additional titles, including one I'd never heard before, something like Inheritor of the Keys to the Rational Stars."

Byelt frowns momentarily but doesn't speak.

"Did it mention any changes at headquarters?" asks Paersol. "I'd think there might be some, what with a new emperor."

"There will be," says Byelt, "but those won't be made public until after the coronation. That way, people don't get the idea that everything's changing all at once."

"Do you know what the new emperor is like, ser?" Paersol asks Byelt.

The majer chuckles ruefully. "I wouldn't know him if he walked into the mess. I doubt if anyone in the Mirror Lancers would, except for the Majer-Commander or the Captain-Commander. He has to have some ability as a magus, but there's no standard as to how much. There's no real requirement for him to be in the Imperial bloodline, although that's been usual. Still, the second Emperor had no blood relation to the first."

"He didn't?" asks Vaarkas.

"Not a drop," replies Byelt.

Alyiakal notices Paersol nods to the majer's comment, then asks, "But wasn't he a very powerful magus?"

"Supposedly," replies Byelt, "but history favors those who succeed and those fortunate enough to be in the right place at the right time." Byelt glances to Alyiakal briefly, adding, "That's always been true. Just as the Winters here are always cold."

From there on, the conversation turns to weather.

After the meal, Alyiakal retires to his quarters, where he slits open the letter from Saelora and begins to read.

> *Alyiakal—*
>
>   *Catriana is expecting! She kept it to herself until she was certain, but I'm so happy for her. She and Hyrsaal have wanted this for so long. Elina is excited because she'll be an aunt to a child who's so close. That's good because Catriana and Elina's mother never said a word about Elina's children. She won't about Catriana's, either. We'll see about Mother. I'm guessing she'll be pleased, but she will say nothing. That's sad, but she has Gaaran and Charissa nearby, though their little daughter is colicky and finicky, and Mother doesn't do well with that . . .*

Alyiakal can almost feel Saelora's happiness for her brother and Catriana. Not for the first time, he wonders if she is having second thoughts about waiting to consort and have children. *But we're separated for so long, years, in fact.* But the feeling nags at him, even though he's followed what Saelora said and felt at the time. *Does she still feel that way, though, after seeing Catriana's joy?*

He takes a deep breath and resumes reading.

. . . the trading is going well. Gaaran is able to spend more time here and has been a great help. We made some pearapple butter last Autumn after you left and sealed it in small pots. It didn't sell well here in Vaeyal. I sent what we had left to Catriana, and she sold it all in less than an eightday. People in Fyrad liked it, and so did some of the cooks on the ships and outland traders. We could make a lot more, and see how it goes . . .

Alyiakal nods and keeps reading about her trading ventures, some of which he can't really follow.

You know I've appreciated all that you could tell me and Vassyl about trading and merchanting practices elsewhere and what you heard from other Mirror Lancer officers. Some of the outland traders have said many of the same things, and even some of the smaller Cyadoran traders . . .

She's confirming that, in short, the larger clans and houses smuggle in goods, and Mirror Lancers are being ordered to patrol against outlanders . . . or Cyadoran ships are being told where the Mirror Lancers aren't . . . if not both.

. . . I'm almost finished with getting the house the way I want it. I so want you to see it, but I know it will be longer than I'd like. That makes me think of you. I miss you even more than I thought I would . . . and you know how much that is. Do take care of yourself in every way possible.

The last line is as much warning as it is advice.
Alyiakal rereads the letter, carefully, before adding it to the others.

LXVII

On the second fiveday of Spring, when Alyiakal enters the mess for breakfast only a fraction of a quint before Byelt, the other three officers standing by the table turn, then stiffen as the majer enters.

"As you were," declares Byelt. He seats himself and waits for the others. "I have a few matters to discuss. First, although I mentioned it more than half a season ago, I'll remind you that, upon occasion, Overcaptain Alyiakal will accompany and observe company officers on patrols. Those patrols will not be announced in advance. Second, now that Winter is, in fact, over, Overcaptain Alyiakal and I will conduct a *full* inspection and inventory of all spaces in the post on sevenday."

Dhaerl and Vaarkas merely nod. Paersol frowns uncertainly.

"Third, the horseshoes we were supposed to receive last eightday will not arrive until later this eightday because the high Spring runoff washed out the road north of Terimot. For that reason, the supply wagons will also be delayed."

"But we're getting dispatches . . ." Paersol murmurs.

Dhaerl manages a stoic expression, while Vaarkas rolls his eyes.

Alyiakal thinks, *Heavily laden wagons require roads. Dispatch couriers can find ways around washouts.*

"That's all I have for now," says the majer, turning to Alyiakal.

"Blade instruction and drills will continue for the rest of the eightday. There will be remedial instruction every evening after supper for those who," Alyiakal smiles wryly, "have forgotten the basic skills until they regain those skills."

Paersol does not look in Alyiakal's direction.

As the officers begin to eat, Vaarkas says, "It always feels good to change back to regular riding jackets."

"Here in the valley, anyway," Dhaerl rejoins. "You'll still need winter gear going east until near the end of Spring."

After eating and listening, Alyiakal notices Paersol motioning for Vaarkas to remain as the others leave the mess, then lags slightly, glances around and, seeing no one but Byelt and Dhaerl, who aren't looking, raises a concealment, and returns to the mess.

". . . still don't see why the overcaptain's insisting on blade skills," says Paersol. "Firelances are what we use."

"Until you run out of chaos," replies Vaarkas.

"How often does that happen?"

"Often enough to get you killed if a barbarian makes a flank attack. Or if you get caught in a downpour and the barbarians attack. *You* may not have to worry, but your rankers will."

Alyiakal eases out of the mess, drops the concealment, and walks slowly toward the door to the courtyard.

Vaarkas catches up to him, and Alyiakal asks, "Questions about blade drills?"

"What else?" The captain shakes his head. "Ser . . . Never mind."

"I don't know, either," replies Alyiakal to the unasked question. *I've got a few ideas about why he's here, and none of them speak highly of headquarters.* "We'll just have to deal with it."

Vaarkas shakes his head again.

Alyiakal makes his way to his study, to see if Byelt has anything for him to do before he returns to the courtyard for a long day of blade drills.

In midafternoon, Alyiakal is in the post courtyard working with third squad on blade skills when two dispatch riders enter the post. The appearance and condition of the couriers' mounts confirms to Alyiakal they are once again traveling on dirt and gravel, rather than packed snow or semi-gelid mud. The main road to the east above the logging road, though, will likely remain impassable for at least another two eightdays.

Alyiakal wonders at what may be in the dispatches, but he continues with the drills.

When he returns to his study, now firmly established in the chamber next to the majer's study, Byelt calls out, "We need to talk."

Alyiakal turns and steps into the majer's study, closing the door.

Byelt gestures to the chairs. "We're getting an Undercaptain Staalt as Dhaerl's replacement. He's due to report no later than the tenth eightday of Spring. He's had less than a year in command of a port company at Chaelt, but he's being reposted as part of a reduction of the complement in Chaelt."

Alyiakal can't quite control his surprise, thinking, *The frigging Merchanters want fewer lancers there to allow greater smuggling by Cyadoran traders and clans.*

"From your reaction, you know something about him," observes Byelt.

Alyiakal shakes his head. "I don't know anything about Staalt, except that he didn't have more than a season at Chaelt."

"How do you know that?"

Alyiakal explains about Liathyr's letters and death and Aaltyn's assignment as Liathyr's replacement as well as what he heard from Hyrsaal, although he does not mention Hyrsaal's name, only saying several officers mentioned problems of a similar nature at other ports, including Summerdock. "I already told you about what I learned at Oldroad Post and Luuval."

"It sounds like headquarters is replacing everyone there," replies Byelt. "I can't say I'm surprised, except by the increasing brazenness of the Merchanters. How do you think Staalt fits into that?"

"He had to be commissioned last Autumn. Three different postings under half a year is worrisome. I don't know what to think, except that he can't know much about patrolling."

"Whatever his other posting was, headquarters thinks a tour here will take care of him," says Byelt sarcastically. "He either gets killed or cashiered or becomes a useful junior officer, and it's up to us to determine which." He pauses. "How much of what you've told me do you think headquarters knows?"

"They have to know there were problems with tariff enumerators in Luuval and Guarstyad, but I only reported verifiable facts. They wouldn't know what I learned from Liathyr's letters because I wasn't about to put anything in ink about that."

"Hmmm . . . so they might have an inkling of the facts, and they can't or don't want to say much, because it might prove embarrassing, and that wouldn't be good for those in headquarters with a new emperor on the Malachite Throne. One way or another, you'll have some additional work on your hands getting Staalt ready to lead a company."

"Doesn't every senior officer dealing with a green undercaptain?" returns Alyiakal with gentle humor.

"I'd wager you listened," returns Byelt. "More than a few don't or can't be bothered, or don't seem to understand what they hear—like a certain captain."

"Baarth seems able to guide him, so far."

"You'll still need to spend more time with him in the field. That's why I reminded the captains this morning."

Alyiakal nods. "Is there anything else?"

"Not right now."

After Alyiakal returns to his own study, he considers the brief meeting. Byelt seems genuinely surprised by the situation at Chaelt, but not unaware of Merchanter brazenness, which suggests he'd been apprised of the possibility, either by Hyrsaal mentioning his experiences at Summerdock or from other sources.

How many other senior officers know bits and pieces, but think what they've heard is overstated or just an isolated exception?

He shakes his head, then sees the letter in his box. He recognizes the Merchanter seal and smiles.

LXVIII

With the snow almost gone in the lower hills, Alyiakal can't help but wonder about the resumption of raider attacks. As first squad musters for a short patrol in the valley on sevenday after morning blade drills, Alyiakal sees Crendaak joining the formation and nods, glad the lancer's arm has healed fully, then turns to Chaaltyn. "How soon do you think we'll see raiders?"

"Long, cold Winter. As soon as they think they can find one of the nearer and smaller hamlets to raid."

"Gairtyn's the nearest, and Southtyll's the easiest to reach," Alyiakal observes.

"Gairtyn's close to the post, and there's no easy way to escape once we're alerted." Chaaltyn frowns. "They could take that old logging road, but it'd take forever to get back to where their hamlet is."

"Let's take the squad over there and see if there are any traces of someone scouting the area. It can't hurt."

Chaaltyn nods.

"On oneday, I'll take second squad to look at the old road south of Southtyll. That's a lot easier than the way we followed them."

"Less mud right now, too."

"Unless we have to follow tracks uphill out of the valley or attack in the woods." Alyiakal turns and motions for Raayls, the nearest scout, to join him, and the scout rides over. "We're headed to Gairtyn and then north to see if anyone has used the old logging road. Let Maaetz know."

"Yes, ser."

Once the scouts are in position, Alyiakal orders, "First squad! Forward!"

Maaetz and Raayls lead the way through the gates and turn west toward the crossroad.

Two quints later, Alyiakal and the squad approach the stone causeway leading to the bridge over the River Lhaar, its swirling and fast-moving waters now running less than a yard below the top of its banks. The lowlands to the east and south of the bridge still hold standing water from the Spring runoff.

When Alyiakal reaches the middle of the span, he glances east to the rapids exiting the gorge and to Gairtyn, where the millworks stand east of the hamlet and north and west of the gorge. At first, he sees no sign of anything unusual, but then he notices two new dwellings being built on the northwest side of the small town with accompanying barns.

Two? Border towns seldom grew that quickly, not with the possibility of raiders, and the two houses are in addition to the new one he'd observed last Autumn. As he rides past, he spots five men working with horses and a trestle-like device to lift the wall logs into place. As before, the men give less than a passing glance to the lancers.

The squad rides through the hamlet to the end of the road, then north across the winter-flattened grass and undergrowth that parallels the trees at the bottom of the hills. After three kays, they reach the area west of the old logging road. There, Alyiakal rides over to join Raayls at the tree line. The same fallen limbs cover the lower parts of the trail, but to Alyiakal the section of the old road leading to the depression between two outcrops looks different, although he doesn't sense anyone or any large animals anywhere amid the trees.

He turns to the scout. "Something's changed. Go see what's beyond the fallen limbs."

"Yes, ser." Raayls eases his mount into the trees and around the debris. He reins up fifty yards from Alyiakal and looks down, proceeding slowly for another fifty yards, beyond Alyiakal's sight, but not his senses, then stops.

After a time, Raayls rides back and reins up. "You were right, ser. There are hoofprints in the trail. Not today, but no more than a few days old. Only a single rider. Farther up, some of the deadwood and fallen brush has been moved."

"There aren't any tracks besides yours on this side of the fallen limbs, are there? I didn't see any."

"No, ser."

"I take it the old road looks passable?"

Raayls smiles. "Hoofprints on it as far as I could see."

Alyiakal motions for Chaaltyn and Maaetz to join them, then explains what Raayls has found. "I don't want to take a whole squad up that road, but to be safe, I'd like two more solid rankers to accompany me and the scouts. We can see far enough along the old road that we can't be surprised there, and the trees on each side are thick enough and the ground uneven enough that they couldn't attack easily from the side. Five lancers should be enough."

"So long as you're one of the five, ser," says Chaaltyn dryly. "I'll send Huulz and Jaarkoy to join you."

Raayls leads the other four lancers into the trees and to the old road, wide enough for a logging wagon and not much more, which angles northwest between the two stone outcrops and then along the side of an increasingly steep hill.

After riding half a kay, Alyiakal calls a halt. "We're turning back. The hoofprints keep following the road. If they're going to raid today, they'll need to show up in the next glass. If that's the case, I'd rather face them on the flat at the base of the hill than here." What he doesn't mention is that he senses no one near and not even a mountain cat or a red deer.

Both Maaetz and Raayls nod.

Once the five return to first squad, Alyiakal briefs Chaaltyn as the squad continues riding north for another kay or so looking for other hoofprints but finding none. Alyiakal then orders the squad to return to Gairtyn and from there to the post.

After grooming and settling the chestnut, Alyiakal makes his way straight to the majer's study.

"I saw you took a squad out this afternoon," Byelt says with a hint of curiosity in his voice.

"I wanted to see if anyone had been using that old logging road north of Gairtyn recently." Alyiakal takes the chair in front of the desk. "We found hoofprints. A single mount. Interestingly, the hoofprints came from the east on the old logging road and then returned, at least for half a kay. The rider never got closer than fifty or sixty yards from the edge of the woods. We scouted north another two kays, but found nothing. To me, that looks like someone's scouting approaches to Gairtyn."

"It could be, but we can't put a company or even a squad there all the time, on the chance that raiders *might* attack."

"You're right, but we could warn the headman that we've found signs of scouting and they should be aware. We could post an additional lookout on the walls with the specific order to watch Gairtyn and the tree line from the road to Gairtyn for signs of raiders."

Byelt nods slowly. "That's a possibility. Let me think on it."

"Because of our discovery, I'll be taking second squad out on oneday to look at the road southeast of Southtyll to see if there are any tracks there."

"That can't hurt."

Meaning that he's not convinced. "I'll keep you informed."

Byelt smiles wryly. "You always do." Then he adds, "I'd be happier if those horseshoes arrived."

"So would the farrier." Alyiakal stands. "If you don't have anything else?"

"Go," declares the majer humorously.

Alyiakal leaves and enters his own study, thinking about the old logging road north of Gairtyn and when it will be used. *When . . . not whether.*

LXIX

Eightday morning, Alyiakal arrives early in the mess, followed immediately by Dhaerl.

"Is it true you found barbarian scout tracks in the hills northeast of Gairtyn?" asks the older officer.

"We did. They were on the old logging road we found last Autumn and stopped short of entering the valley. Single mount, came down close to the valley's edge, then retraced the path back, for a kay at least."

"Had to be some sort of scout. But that's a far piece out of the way from where the past raiders have been coming from."

"Maybe it's a different set of raiders or maybe they moved their base after we removed their entire raiding party."

"After *you* did," replies Dhaerl. "I'm just as glad I put in my papers. Have the feeling that the Summer here is going to be busy. Not in a good way, either."

"I do, too, but why do *you* feel that way?"

"The valley's getting more prosperous. Gairtyn's getting bigger."

"I noticed they're building more dwellings, but how can they afford it?"

"The rumor is that they grow tri-spice."

"Here? Isn't it too cold?" asks Alyiakal.

"They do. Angel-fire if I know how."

"What about the timber? Gairtyn's too small for a sawmill."

"They do special woods. Heartwoods, lorken, dark ironwood. Late Summer three wagons come and load up."

Alyiakal represses a shiver. Suddenly, a raid from the north doesn't seem so improbable. Before he can ask another question, Vaarkas and Paersol arrive, and then the majer.

Once all five officers are served and have at least sampled their ale, Byelt clears his throat. "There's going to be an addition to the watch list—a lookout whose duties are specifically to scan the edge of the woods to the north on the east end of the valley, including Gairtyn, the gorge, and the entrance to the east road. He'll be posted in the northeast corner watchtower. The other lookout will move to the northwest tower."

Dhaerl nods, and so does Vaarkas, after a moment. Paersol looks clueless.

"You haven't been here long enough to see what's happened with Gairtyn, Paersol," explains the majer. "It's not really a hamlet any longer, but a small town. It needs more protection, but we're not equipped to post lancers there. The best we can do is be ready to send a force immediately, and we'll need to know as soon as possible." Byelt looks to Alyiakal. "The headman's name is Vhoraal. His house is the one closest to the sawmill on the north side."

"I'll see him today," replies Alyiakal.

At that exchange, Paersol looks even more clueless. None of the other four officers bother to explain.

Right after breakfast, Alyiakal leaves the post with four lancers from third squad, and less than three quints later, he and the lancers rein up outside the house Byelt described. Alyiakal dismounts and walks around the privacy screen to the front door, and knocks.

While Alyiakal expects a burly broad-chested figure, the man who answers the door is white-haired, stoop-shouldered, and frail, but his eyes are as fierce as any vulcrow's.

"Headman Vhoraal?"

"I answer to that, Overcaptain. What brings you to my door so early on an eightday morning?"

"Because of a discovery yesterday, Headman Vhoraal." Alyiakal expresses his concerns about the old logging road, summarizing what the lancers discovered about the raiders killed at Southtyll, where they received their weapons and tack, and about the tracks first squad discovered. "It's likely that the barbarians have found a way to get from their high road to Cerlyn to the old logging road. We found out about the road after Winter closed off any way to search for it."

"Is it not your duty to protect us from raiders?"

"It is, but we cannot be everywhere. We have posted additional lookouts and are increasing our patrols, but we wanted you to be aware. Your houses are sturdy enough to hold off barbarians until we can get here."

"I do not understand. You are here to protect us. But you say you cannot."

Alyiakal refrains from sighing. "I did not say that. I said that it might take us some time to get here to protect you if the raiders attack from the northeast. There are two towns in the valley, three large hamlets, and a half score smaller hamlets. The Mirror Lancer post is located between the largest town and where the barbarians usually attack and is close to Gairtyn, which is the next-largest town. It appears that the raiders have found another possible way into the valley. We're working to prevent that. It takes time, but I thought it only right to let you know."

"That we're in more danger?" Vhoraal spits to the side. "We know we're in danger. Tell me something I do not know."

"I cannot," replies Alyiakal politely. "You seem to know everything. Apparently, my attempt to inform you was a waste of your time and mine. In the future, we'll not trouble you."

Vhoraal stiffens.

Alyiakal can sense the anger, but waits, saying nothing.

"You would abandon us, then?" Vhoraal spits out the words.

"The Mirror Lancers will never abandon you. We will always do our best, even when it's not appreciated. Sometimes, our best is not enough. Since you know everything, you should know that as well."

"You mock me."

"I took you at your word."

"How many raiders have you killed? Personally, Overcaptain?"

"I lost count," replies Alyiakal, infusing his words with truth and cold order.

Vhoraal steps back, clearly shaken.

"Talk to Headman Rhuust of Southtyll, if you will. We could not stop the raid, but not a single raider returned."

"Perhaps . . . I was too hasty, Overcaptain."

"I understand your concerns. I respect them." *Maybe not you, but your concerns.* "I will not lie to you. I cannot promise absolute protection from raiders. I can only promise that we will do our best."

"Are you the new commander?"

"No. I'm the new deputy commander, and I command the patrols against the raiders."

Vhoraal nods slowly. "I wish you well on those patrols, Overcaptain. Do keep us informed." The headman steps back and closes the door, not quite in Alyiakal's face.

Alyiakal turns and walks to where a lancer holds his chestnut's reins, then mounts and turns the gelding toward the bridge. "We're heading back.

I believe Headman Vhoraal finally understood." *And he wasn't all that angry at the end.*

As he rides, he goes over the brief meeting in his mind, trying to think how he could have handled it better. *Maybe you should have started with "I will not lie."* But that implies that he lies often.

He shakes his head.

More than a glass later, back at the post, he enters Byelt's study and closes the door.

"How did your meeting with Headman Vhoraal go?" asks Byelt.

"In the end . . . it went about as well as it could." Alyiakal relates the interchange, then waits.

Byelt smiles wryly. "You're right. That's about as good as you'll get from him, prickly old bastard. He slammed the door in the face of my predecessor."

"Have you ever met with him?"

Byelt grins. "Saw no reason to. You suggested telling him."

Alyiakal laughs.

LXX

When Alyiakal and second squad ride out of the post early on oneday morning, he glances to the northeast corner wall post, and the lookout that Byelt agreed to, then to the north toward Gairtyn. He shakes his head as he thinks about Headman Vhoraal.

"Do you think we'll find tracks in the same place we caught the raiders?" asks Rhemsaar. "Or somewhere close?"

"I have no idea," replies Alyiakal. *Even if we don't find anything, it only means the raiders haven't sent scouts there in the last eightday or so—or couldn't because they're still snowed in on the heights.* But if the raider hamlet somewhere off the east road is still snowed in, who scouted the logging road near Gairtyn? *The Grass Hills barbarians caught between Pemedra and the Cerlynese? Or some other group?*

The main road west of the post is mostly firm, and a glass later, second squad approaches Southtyll. Alyiakal can see low green sprouts in many of the fields, while teams of men and women are planting in fields with no shoots.

"Do you know what the green shoots are?" he asks Rhemsaar.

The squad leader gives Alyiakal a puzzled look, then says, "The green is Winter wheat grain, and they're planting maize."

"There aren't any growers in my family," Alyiakal replies to the unspoken question, "and I've never been posted where there were many holdings growing grains or maize."

"You're not from Cyad, are you, ser?"

Alyiakal shakes his head. "My father was a Mirror Lancer and so was his father. I grew up around the Great Forest. Temporary duty in Fyrad is the closest I ever got to city or port duty. What about you?"

"Smallholder's fifth son from the flatlands near Kynstaar. Didn't like dirt then and still don't." Rhemsaar's chuckle verges on bitter.

"You didn't think about being a naval marine?"

"The only thing I like less than dirt are boats."

"I can understand that," says Alyiakal, "especially after I had to take a fast sail cutter to get to temporary duty at Luuval."

"Better you than me, ser."

Alyiakal just nods, feeling the light and cool breeze at his back.

As second squad rides closer to the dwellings forming Southtyll, several of those planting take quick glances at the riders and then lose interest.

When the squad reaches the end of the narrow road, Raayls continues on the path toward the edge of the hills that form the south side of the valley, slowing as he nears the trees, then turns eastward, which is what Alyiakal recalls, although he's not completely certain.

Maaetz and Raayls confer, then continue east, paralleling the trees.

While Alyiakal uses both sight and senses, all he can sense, besides small animals, are two red deer, one a fawn, which suggests the other is a doe, and they're at the edge of his senses.

Then he senses a narrow gap in the trees ahead to his left, and he calls out, "We're getting close."

In less than a third of a quint, Raayls calls out, "Here!"

As Alyiakal rides closer, he sees the narrow opening that looks like an animal trail, recalling that the trail leads uphill for a time and seems to end in a pile of brush, but that the logging trail begins behind it. He can also sense the brush pile, but no one nearby, except for second squad.

Raayls turns in the saddle as Alyiakal approaches and says, "There are tree rat traces and red deer prints, but no boots and no hoofprints."

"Then you can lead."

The first fifty yards are as Alyiakal recalls, so is the uneven slope of the logging road, which second squad follows for two kays to the southeast before reaching the logged-over area where First Company had encountered the raiders the previous fall. While there are numerous red deer tracks, there are no signs of riders or anyone on foot.

"Maaetz, Raayls," orders Alyiakal, "take the road up about half a kay and see if there are any tracks."

"Yes, ser."

While the squad waits for the scouts to return, Alyiakal senses the area around the clearing in every direction but senses no others except the scouts and second squad.

The scouts return slightly more than two quints later, and Raayls says, "We couldn't see any tracks at all farther uphill."

"Then there won't be any for at least several kays farther southeast." Alyiakal turns to Rhemsaar. "Time to head back to the post."

The way downhill is slower than the climb up had been, but Alyiakal's been up and down enough slopes to know that's always the way it is.

As he rides the chestnut through the last trees and out toward the path leading through the bushes and new grass to Southtyll, the wind is again at his back. The warmer wind has completely shifted and now blows south-southwest.

He glances over his shoulder, but he's too close to the valley's edge to see more than the evergreens with fresh needlebuds at their branch tips, and the new growth and winter-gray leaves greening on the leaf-trees. He really hadn't noticed the Spring growth while looking for the trail to the logging road.

A quint later, when second squad reaches the road, Alyiakal glances south again, nodding as he sees the distant dark clouds. *Likely warm rain.*

He looks to Rhemsaar. "Your thoughts, Squad Leader?"

"There was no sign of anyone. Makes me wonder if the barbarians are still snowed in, or if it's real muddy where they are."

"That's possible. If the wind and clouds to the south are any indication, we're going to get a warm rain."

"More frigging mud, begging your pardon, ser."

"I feel the same way about mud," replies Alyiakal. "Always have."

Rhemsaar laughs softly.

Two glasses later, after returning second squad to the post and dealing with the chestnut, as well as rewarding him with a carrot, Alyiakal enters Byelt's study.

"What did you find?" the majer asks as Alyiakal drops into the chair in front of the majer's desk.

"No one's been that close to Southtyll on that old logging road, possibly not since we took out the raiders last Autumn. They were planting in the fields north of the hamlet, and no one gave us more than a glance. Someone would have if they'd seen raiders or had trouble. I'm wondering if the higher hills to the east had even more snow than we thought."

Byelt nods. "Could be. What do you want to do next with patrols?"

"It looks like we're going to get some heavy rain before long, but once things dry out, I'd like to send Second Company along the east road. They can see if the side road beyond the river overlook is clear, while I take First Company and follow the old logging road northeast of Gairtyn. I'm concerned that the tracks we saw the other day don't belong to the raiders we caught last Autumn. Especially when there's no sign of them and it has to be even harder for them to get to the old logging road north of Gairtyn."

"That's possible," concedes Byelt, "but if the local raiders can't get to the valley, the Kyphrans certainly can't either."

"That means another group of local raiders or possibly the barbarians who live in the grasslands east of Pemedra."

"You don't think it could be Gallosians?"

"This time of year, it would seem unlikely," replies Alyiakal, "but we can't rule anyone out."

"You're in charge of patrols. Go ahead and write up the schedule."

"Subject to change if we get a lot of rain," says Alyiakal.

"Everything here is always subject to change because of the weather, sometimes several times in a day," says Byelt dryly.

Alyiakal stands. "I'll have the official report to you by the end of the day, but I thought you'd like to know immediately."

"I appreciate it." Byelt smiles. "We're having red deer for dinner this evening. One of the hunters from the town brought down two and offered one— for silvers, of course—to the cooks. It will be a change, at least."

Alyiakal nods politely and says, "I've never had any red deer." But then, he's had more than a few dinners of grass antelope, and he can hope that red deer isn't gamier. He also isn't looking forward to scheduling "observational" rides, especially with Paersol.

LXXI

After heavy rains during the third eightday of Spring, which leave mud everywhere, the weather changes, and the next eightday is Summer-like, so that by fifth fourday of Spring, Alyiakal can finally take First Company on patrol to follow the old logging road northeast of Gairtyn, while Dhaerl takes Second Company on the east road, although how far they'll be able to go remains to be seen.

As Alyiakal and Chaaltyn ride out through the post gates, following Maaetz and Raayls, Alyiakal studies the green-blue sky to the northeast, but it remains clear, and the day is warm, but not yet Summer-like. Because the hills will be cooler, the lancers carry or wear riding jackets and gloves. Alyiakal has his water bottles filled with ale, and some trail biscuits in his saddlebags, just in case. By now, all the company lancers make similar provisions.

When Alyiakal nears the stone and timber bridge, he sees that while the river still runs high, the standing water in the fields has vanished. Beyond the bridge, several men work to roof one of the new houses. The locals outside barely look as the company rides through the small town. While men shift planks and timbers in the drying barns, Alyiakal sees no sign of Vhoraal. He wonders if the presence of First Company heading toward the old logging road will allay some of the headman's concerns, but he doubts that.

He's the kind who'll always find something to complain about.

Once the company leaves the path beyond the end of the road, they turn north along the edge of the trees. Alyiakal extends his senses, but discerns little beyond his own force and small animals and birds amid the trees. For the more than three kays to the old logging trail, there's no sign of anything but small animal and red deer tracks coming and going from the trees.

Raayls leads the way along the narrow animal trail through the trees to the fallen limbs and calls back, "No new tracks so far."

Once past the fallen limbs, First Company re-forms two abreast and continues up the old road through the trees to the depression between two outcrops. Again, Raayls reports no new hoofprints on the old road.

Beyond the outcrops, the old road, partly dug out of the hillside, angles northwest. Before long Alyiakal rides past the point where he'd turned back before. Neither Alyiakal nor the scouts can see any new hoofprints as they ride northeast for a kay before the road curves into a relatively flat area between two hills where the evergreens are much shorter, and there are stumps everywhere.

Alyiakal sees that the flat area would make loading the logs easier but wonders if that was the only reason. He doesn't know enough about trees to tell if the stumps are what's left of more valuable timber but supposes that's also a possibility.

Raayls leads the way along a narrow trail between the low undergrowth and the second-growth trees for close to a kay before the ground begins to slope upward. The evergreens on each side of the trail are much larger than those through which First Company just passed.

While Alyiakal can't sense any large order/chaos patterns, barring the occasional red deer and a possible mountain cat, he worries about the company being strung out along the hillside.

The fact that brigands or raiders would be in the same situation and lancers have more effective weapons doesn't comfort him. He notices that the trail has widened enough that two lancers can ride abreast, largely because the older trees are farther apart. He also sees dead, crushed undergrowth at the edge of the trail, from the previous Autumn, and what might be the partial imprint of a horseshoe.

"Raayls! We're going to need more warning if anyone shows up. Move ahead another hundred yards. Maaetz! Take Raayls's position."

"Yes, ser!"

First Company follows the trail another two kays as it curves upward before it ends intersecting a narrow road that appears to run north-northwest and south-southeast with recent hoofprints heading both ways.

Alyiakal calls a halt and motions for the scouts to join him.

"Frig . . ." mutters Chaaltyn.

"I'd wager this might be the high road the surviving raider mentioned," says Alyiakal. "It's definitely a road that's not on any of our maps." He glances to the northwest, where the road slowly climbs and disappears around a curve a kay or so away. Then he looks to the southeast. The road also climbs in that direction, barely, at least for half a kay before it curves east and the trees conceal it.

Which way? Alyiakal has no doubt where the road heading west eventually leads, and he suspects that before long there will be Grass Hills raiders looking to attack the valley. He surmises, from what Dietro revealed, that somehow the eastern end of the road will lead, if circuitously, to some of the raiders plaguing the valley.

Alyiakal turns to the scouts. "How recent are the hoofprints? How many riders?"

"The ones heading north are older, since the rain ended, two or three days. Three riders," says Raayls. "The ones heading south yesterday. Four, five riders. None of them turned the way we came."

That doesn't help much. Finally, he orders, "To the south!" *For now, anyway.* "Scouts out! Raayls forward!"

For the first kay heading south the climb is gentle. Then the road turns east and becomes steeper, and the air cooler with patches of snow higher on the slopes. Roughly two kays farther, the road flattens and runs twenty yards north of and below a long, rocky ridge unsuited to horses.

After a time, Alyiakal glimpses a thin plume of smoke ahead and to his right, but since the ridgetop blocks his view of the terrain, he can't determine how far away it might be. He also feels that they should be nearing the River Lhaar or, at the least, riding parallel to it, although the road slowly rises compared to the ridgetop. Three quints later, Alyiakal and the company reach a flatter area, where the road makes wide curves around the base of the hills, with fewer and fewer trees, that lead to the higher slopes of the Westhorns.

After riding another two kays, Alyiakal can't see any more trees ahead, on either the east slope or close to the road ahead. Then within a few hundred yards, the rocky slope to his left drops away into a small canyon less than fifty yards below, through which runs a narrow river. Ahead is a towering bare rock face, and below it a mass of rock extends to a point on the road roughly a kay ahead.

Alyiakal looks again. The river seemingly disappears into the base of the rocky mass. "That has to be the River Lhaar, but looks like it just goes under the rocks ahead."

The company keeps riding. Then Raayls gestures to his right where the canyon extends westward toward the Lhaarat valley.

Alyiakal sees what happened sometime in the distant past. One side of the low mountain split off and collapsed into the canyon. Either it left space or the hard rock lay over mud or sand, and the river tunneled its way through and continued to flow west. He looks back to the shallow canyon. The area to each side of the water is solid rock. There might have been a lake there for a while, but the force of the Spring runoff over the years created the gorge.

He looks ahead where the road curves south around the half mountain. Then he calls out, "Company! Halt!"

"Ser?" asks Chaaltyn.

"This is probably the high road. It's at least another ten to fifteen kays to the raiders' hamlet, if not longer, and it's well past midday."

Seeing the senior squad leader's confusion, Alyiakal says, "That river below is the Lhaar. We're on the north side. This road likely leads to and joins the road we followed last Autumn, the one with the hidden turnoff. I'm estimating, but we're a good five kays east of the river overlook on the east road. With those hills ahead, I doubt that there's any direct way west to the overlook."

Abruptly, Chaaltyn nods. "I see what you mean. It would take less time to go the other way."

"We don't know that, but I'd like to explore the other way first and find out more." *Why is it that no one knows much here? Because they haven't had many raids until recently? Or because the distances are farther and the climbs steeper?* "Explain it to Rhemsaar, and I'll tell the scouts and then Taenyr."

After calling in the scouts, and briefing them, Alyiakal returns to third squad and explains to the third squad leader.

Some uneventful five glasses later, Alyiakal enters Byelt's study.

"That was a long patrol, Alyiakal. What did you find out?"

Alyiakal seats himself and explains, then waits for Byelt's comments.

"Do you really think that road stretches all the way to Cerlyn?"

"I can't prove it, but the road goes somewhere, and Cerlyn is north of us. I suppose it could go to Gallos, but that would require crossing the Westhorns. If it did, that could be as much of a problem as Cerlyn, and I know it doesn't go to Pemedra or Syadtar."

"That river tunnel explains something else," declares Byelt. "I've always wondered why the Spring runoff on the Lhaar lasted longer and even when it's been really wet, it doesn't get that high."

Alyiakal frowns, then nods. "That tunnel can only take so much water, and when the runoff's high it backs up there. If we'd been there an eightday earlier, we might have seen a lake."

"Anything else?"

"Nothing I can prove yet, but I have the feeling from the trails, that we may be dealing with several groups of raiders."

"Because of the distances? What if there are more trails that connect them?"

"That's possible, but some would have to go through truly rough terrain."

"What do you plan next?"

"To investigate the easternmost part of the east road. We'll have to leave at first light on sixday."

"You're hurrying. Why?"

"Because whoever scouted the old logging road north of Gairtyn wasn't one of the usual raiders."

Byelt purses his lips, hesitates, then says, "He was a single rider, and a single rider would be hard-pressed to do that in a single day?"

"And he was careful not to get within easy sight of the valley. Also, raiders seldom scout." Alyiakal offers a rueful smile. "But that could always change. Things don't always stay the same."

"With barbarians and brigands, betting on change is a poor wager."

"But an intelligent barbarian might figure that out, and that could be trouble." Alyiakal catches himself before he can utter the words, "We'll just have to see."

"When are raiders and barbarians not trouble?"

Alyiakal isn't about to answer that directly. "They're often more trouble when the Jeranyi or the Cerlynese get involved. Or the Kyphrans. That's why I want to scout those roads as early as possible."

"So long as there's a company ready to deal with local raids," replies Byelt. "What are you doing with Paersol?"

"I'm riding with him tomorrow. We'll scout the lower road that heads south off the main east road. We'll see if we can discover any more side roads."

"Best of fortune." Byelt stands. "Time to head to dinner."

LXXII

On a hazy, Spring-like fiveday morning, Alyiakal rides beside Paersol at the head of Fourth Company up the east road. As always, his water bottles contain ale, and he creates an unseen order funnel to collect chaos bits from the sun. He doesn't say much to the junior captain until they reach the point where the logging road branches off to the south.

"Why do you think the loggers never see much of the raiders, Captain?"

"What would they gain, ser? They couldn't use the log wagons. Loggers don't have weapons or coins."

"You're right about that. What else?"

"Draft horses aren't that good for riding, and raiders don't use wagons."

"You're right, most raiders don't. Anything else?"

"I can't think of anything else, ser."

"There are three things I can think of that you didn't mention. One: Axes are valuable to raiders. Do you know why, besides for chopping firewood?"

"Ah . . . no, ser."

"They're useful for breaking down doors so that they can get to young women. Two: Young women are one of the main objects of raids. Which is another reason why raiders seldom attack loggers. No women. Three: Most loggers are at least as tough and strong as the raiders, and up here the loggers don't have to worry about protecting women and children."

Paersol nods.

When Fourth Company reaches the disused road to the failed mining attempt, Alyiakal asks, "Where does that go?"

"An old mining attempt." Paersol continues, giving an adequate explanation.

By the time Fourth Company nears the River Lhaar overlook, the haze has lifted, and the sun feels warmer to Alyiakal. The lancers see no travelers, and no clear tracks in the dirt of the road or along the shoulders. Alyiakal senses several red deer, and one fawn, as well as a mountain cat, but none of them move closer.

"A half-quint break at the overlook, ser?" asks Paersol.

Alyiakal nods.

While the lancers take a break, and drink from their water bottles, Alyiakal gulps a little of his ale and studies the gorge to the east, but he can't see the collapsed mountainside that created the river tunnel.

After the short break, Fourth Company continues south-southeast on the road. Some three kays from the overlook, Alyiakal says quietly to Paersol, "Take the side road just ahead."

"Might I ask why, ser?"

"You might. The short answer is because I ordered it. The long answer is because last fall First Company found raiders using it and because past patrols never bothered to find out where it goes. It's difficult, if not impossible, to stop brigands and raiders if you have no idea where they're based and what roads they use."

"Ser, previous companies never found anything on this road."

"That was the report—more than two years ago. Times have changed." Alyiakal doesn't mention his doubts about the thoroughness of those earlier patrols. Even if Hyrsaal had been one of the captains, Alyiakal has no idea what constraints Byelt or his predecessor might have placed on patrolling.

The company rides some two kays before Alyiakal recognizes the place where First Company had followed the raider tracks from farther east, then taken the game trail that joined the old logging road. He gestures ahead to the small gap between two bushes. "What do you see there, Captain?"

"The space between the bushes and trees is wider. You might get a mount through there."

"Call a halt when we reach the gap."

"Yes, ser."

Once Alyiakal and Paersol are opposite the gap, the captain orders, "Company! Halt!"

"Let's take a look," says Alyiakal.

Once the two officers rein up, Alyiakal asks, "What do you think?"

"It's narrow, but a mount could fit, at least as far as I can see."

"In fact, we did. We followed raider hoofprints down and they led to the old logging road which they used to get close enough to raid Southtyll. Now, I wouldn't have led lancers through that narrow way if we hadn't found the hoofprints, but that's another reason why we're patrolling here." What Alyiakal still wants to know is why the raiders used such a circuitous route. *Was it shorter? Or does it avoid another barbarian hamlet? Or is it something you haven't considered?*

"How did the raiders know about that gap?" asks Paersol.

"Like every good scout and every smart red deer, they were looking for an easier way to get where they wanted to go, or possibly a way to avoid our patrols." Alyiakal pauses. "I wanted you to know that raiders might use that way again. Now, we can continue the patrol." Alyiakal eases the chestnut off the shoulder and onto the road.

Paersol follows, then orders, "Company! Forward!"

Alyiakal recalls that the trail from the higher road connecting to the one they're following is somewhere over a kay to the south. He studies the trees and underbrush as they ride, particularly on the left. He searches for hoofprints or other signs of raiders or travelers, but sees neither, suggesting that the road ahead remains impassable, or that it's recently become so.

He's beginning to think he's missed the narrow trail from the higher road, but then he discerns a red deer ahead and uphill, and smiles—the deer is likely using that very trail. With the sound of the approaching horses, the deer freezes.

"Do you see anything ahead to the left?" Alyiakal asks evenly.

Paersol frowns and turns his head. "No, ser. Well, there's a space between the trees there."

"Have the company stop."

"Yes, ser."

Once the company halts, Paersol rides onto the shoulder, then turns in the saddle. "It looks like a trail."

"It is."

"How did you know that was there?" asks Paersol.

"Because First Company followed raider tracks down on it. The entrance to the trail off the higher road is more obvious. I recalled about where it came out, but I still had to concentrate and look closely to see it. That's why I wanted to point it out." Alyiakal senses only a lessening in Paersol's irritation.

"You expect . . ." Paersol hesitates, then says, "The brush and trees tend to look the same all along the road."

"They do look similar," replies Alyiakal calmly, "but not if you look closely. The only people whose primary responsibility is to study the terrain and the road ahead are you, the scouts, and your senior squad leader. And *you're* the one who will take the blame if they miss anything, especially if it results in casualties."

Paersol nods, but stays silent. Alyiakal *thinks* his words may have had some impact.

Once the company resumes riding, Alyiakal refocuses his attention on the road ahead, trying to sense order patterns, but other than patterns from various small creatures, red deer, and one mountain cat, he discerns neither men nor mounts.

After another three kays, the road curves to the east between two hills covered with evergreens. Halfway around the curve, when Alyiakal sees that the road narrows and begins to descend, he motions for Riiks, the trailing scout, to join him and Paersol.

"Ser?" asks the scout as he eases his mount alongside Alyiakal.

"Have you taken this road this far before?"

"No, ser."

"Do you know if any other company has?"

"I couldn't say, ser. Most patrols before you were posted here seldom went farther than ten kays. Don't know of any that went more than fifteen."

"Thank you. Resume your position."

Once Riiks has departed, Alyiakal turns to Paersol. "That's another thing to remember, Captain. The brigands and barbarians quickly learn if a post has fixed operational patterns. They'll use those patterns against you or to avoid you."

"But if we go fifteen kays instead of ten, they'll just pull back."

"If we go fifteen or even twenty, but only occasionally, it makes it harder for them. It also keeps them guessing." Alyiakal returns his attention to the terrain. The downward slope of the road suggests it leads into a small valley, and the narrowing between the road and the hills concerns him, especially with taller trees and thickening undergrowth.

Then the forward scout reins up, signals, and points left.

Alyiakal strains his senses and can barely make out what might be a road heading east off their current heading.

Riiks rides forward to join the other scout, talks a moment with him, and then rides back to Alyiakal and Paersol. "Sers, there's a wider road heading east and hoofprints going south onto the road we're on. They also head back along the wider road."

Alyiakal looks to Paersol. "Your thoughts, Captain?"

"It sounds like there might be a hamlet somewhere ahead."

As Paersol speaks, Alyiakal wonders if the road leading to the possible hamlet ahead might swing west and provide an exit into the west end of the Lhaarat valley, eventually ending up in Westyll.

"How many riders, do you think, Riiks?" asks Alyiakal.

"Dhaask thinks six or seven. I'd agree."

"Then I'd recommend we proceed," says Paersol. "That is, if you agree, Overcaptain."

"For now," replies Alyiakal.

As the company rides past the road heading east, Alyiakal notes that it is somewhat wider and in seemingly good condition.

Beyond the junction with the road to the east, the road the company travels curves back toward the west, and the tree-filled hills give way to gray rock on both sides of the road as it narrows to perhaps twenty yards across. Less than two hundred yards away, filling the gap between the gray stone cliffs, is a closed timber gate with gray stone walls a good five yards tall flanking it. The ground fifty yards in front of the gate and walls has been cleared, and two watchtowers flank the gate, but Alyiakal senses only a single order/chaos pattern.

Both scouts have reined up.

This has to be the small walled land to the southeast that the majer mentioned. "Halt the company," says Alyiakal, noting that the hoofprints stop a few yards in front of the chestnut, and that the road beyond is unmarked, except by the lancer scouts.

"Company! Halt!" Paersol looks askance at Alyiakal.

"Unless one of these walled communities attacks us, we're to leave them alone. Standing orders because they're not within Cyador's borders." *Unlike the town set on the coastal headlands of Guarstyad.* "The majer informed me of this one. We need to take the other road for at least a little way to see where it may lead."

"To the rear! Ride!" orders Paersol.

In less than a quint, Fourth Company heads east on the wider road that begins to climb. After another three kays, as the road climbs, the company reaches a relatively flat stretch of road, where Alyiakal advises Paersol to call a halt and give the lancers a half-quint break.

"Why did you stop when those other riders went through the gate?" asks Paersol quietly.

"They stopped as well. There weren't any tracks leading to the wall and gate. If there had been, they very well could have been from the walled valley. Since they weren't, I imagine they were young raiders sent out to see if the gate might be open or just to see who might be on the road. That suggests that there's a hamlet farther out, but it's time to turn back. You've found a bit more. That's good, and we're learning more about where the various roads go."

On the long ride back to Lhaarat, Alyiakal keeps his senses alert, but discerns no other riders. Since he doesn't have to handle the company, he settles the chestnut in his stall, talking to him while grooming, then makes his way to the headquarters building.

Byelt motions Alyiakal into his study. "How did the patrol with Paersol go?"

"He's learning."

"Meaning that you're teaching him what he should already know?"

"Some of that. Some things he's never encountered. Also, we found that walled valley hamlet or town you mentioned last fall." Alyiakal describes the location of the walled gate.

"That's good to know."

Alyiakal adds, "Since the hoofprints came from the east, there's likely another hamlet off that road, a long way out, and higher in the hills. Before looking into that, though, I'd like to take First Company on an extended patrol on the higher eastern road to see if it connects with the high road across the Lhaar."

"You're in command of patrols."

"But the commanding officer should always know what's planned and why," says Alyiakal, smiling.

"That's why you're still in command of patrols," replies Byelt lightly. "I won't keep you. We'll have to leave for the mess in less than a quint."

"Until then." Alyiakal turns and leaves the study.

LXXIII

After dinner on fiveday, Alyiakal returns to his study to update and revise his maps, as well as estimate possible distances. Then, early on sixday, he leads First Company out and up the east road. They ride past the logging road just after sunrise.

Once the sun is up, Alyiakal creates a large order funnel to capture all the sun-chaos bits that he can, hoping that he won't need that chaos, but knowing that he'll regret not having the chaos if he happens to need it.

First Company rides past the mine road to the River Lhaar overlook, where Alyiakal orders a short break. Some four quints later, the lancers pass the fork taken by Fourth Company the day before. Two kays farther along, they reach the red boulder to the left, and a glass later, Alyiakal has the company rein up for another break on the section of the road that's mostly hard rock. Since they left the post, Alyiakal has neither sensed nor seen riders or anyone in the woods flanking the road.

He slowly studies the steep rock face on the northeast side of the road. His senses tell him that while the rock face extends about three yards or so above the road, on the far side there's a dip of some sort.

Before he gives the order to resume riding, he motions for Maaetz and Raayls to join him and Chaaltyn. Once they arrive, he asks, "Has either of you ridden beyond this point?" He doubts that they have, since First Company is roughly twelve kays from the post, but he wants to know.

Both answer, "No, ser."

Alyiakal refrains from shaking his head. He grins. "Neither have I, but we need to find out what's here and where the raiders are coming from. Let me know if you see or hear anything out of the ordinary. Mount up. We're about to move out."

"Yes, ser."

When the scouts are in position, Alyiakal calls out, "Mount up!"

As First Company leaves the rocky part of the road, Alyiakal glances back. He confirms his earlier suspicion; he did sense an indentation in the evergreens running northeast to a narrow cut in the rocky ridge joining two treeless low peaks. Alyiakal suspects the low-lying evergreens grow in some sort of depression or gully, maybe a small streambed.

For the next kay or so the road climbs gently, then flattens. Alyiakal senses occasional red deer, as well as two mountain cats, one obviously stalking a deer. He also notes the presence of smaller animals, bigger than tree rats, roughly the size of large dogs, not that dogs are common in Cyador. He has no idea what they might be, except that he's unfamiliar with that particular order/chaos pattern.

The hills to the left of the road, the northeast side, are markedly shorter than those ahead and to the right. Alyiakal can clearly see the peaks of the Westhorns, the tops of which look almost to touch the clouds. After riding another glass, he sees a few wisps of smoke rising from the trees several kays ahead and to the east. It suggests individual holdings or a hamlet, if not both, but he sees no signs of a hamlet over the next several kays.

Then a horse bolts onto the road less than a kay ahead, and the rider races away from the lancers.

"Somebody's not happy to see us, ser," says Chaaltyn.

"That rider's off to warn someone, but from what I've been told," Alyiakal replies, "Mirror Lancers have never patrolled this far from Lhaarat. There certainly aren't any other lancers around here. Is the rider worried because this is where the raiders come from, or is he mistaking us for someone else?" *Possibly from that walled valley?*

"I couldn't say, ser."

Neither can Alyiakal. He doesn't want to order "ready arms," at least not until there's some hint of a danger. The rider was far enough away that Alyiakal saw him before sensing him.

The company rides another half kay before the trees flanking the road on the left end, and a wall of heaped stones, runs around a square field roughly a hundred yards on a side. Alyiakal sees low plants with green leaves everywhere, but senses no one around the field. He looks to Chaaltyn. "Do you know what they've planted there?"

"Looks like potatoes. Short growing season, tolerate late-Spring frosts, and you get a lot of potatoes for the amount of land."

"Thank you." Again, Alyiakal feels a bit stupid. *But how would you know?*

At the end of the field, the trees resume, but within a few moments, he senses another treeless area on the left. "We're definitely nearing some sort of community. Have the company check arms."

"Company! Check arms! Pass it back!"

As First Company rides past the second area, half planted with potatoes and the other half in something else, Alyiakal senses two people hiding behind the heaped-stone wall. A bell or gong sounds from somewhere ahead, a clangor that isn't stopping.

At the edge of his senses, he discerns several small cots and outbuildings; to his right is another stone-walled field, but one that's long and narrow. He wonders why anyone would create a stone wall around a field, then abruptly shakes his head. *The stones come from the fields, every Spring, and they just pile them at the closest edge of the field.*

Before long, the evergreens thin, revealing small log-walled dwellings and outbuildings, all apparently built on mounds walled by stones, which strikes Alyiakal as unusual—until he realizes that must be so that the dwellings and outbuildings don't get buried in the heavy Winter snows, and keeps them from being flooded when the snow melts.

Farther ahead, set back from the road on the left, is a rectangular fort. One side abuts a gray stone cliff, the other three sides being of large logs. Men, women, and children run toward the fort, and riders appear on the road beside it, but Alyiakal doesn't see a gate. What he does see beyond the fort is another road to the north intersecting with the road on which the company advances.

On the far side of what Alyiakal believes is the high road, massive animals, along with much smaller animals, graze on a sloping alpine pasture. Alyiakal frowns, knowing he's seen them. *Of course!* Mountain musk oxen, like the ones in Guarstyad.

As the company moves toward the fort and Alyiakal senses order/chaos patterns more clearly, he discovers at least a score of figures behind the top of the wall, potentially archers.

When First Company is about two hundred yards from the fort, Alyiakal calls out, "Company! Halt!"

"Ser?" asks Chaaltyn.

"They're calling archers to the walls of the fort. I don't see much point in riding into a hail of shafts."

Alyiakal continues watching and sensing the riders forming up. His observations tell him they number more than a score. The front ranks have long spears and bucklers, but Alyiakal can't tell whether they have blades as well.

Much as Alyiakal would like to confirm that the road in the distance is the high road that crosses the River Lhaar, he sees no point in attacking, particularly since First Company hasn't been attacked. *Yet.*

He looks at the width of the road, then says to Chaaltyn, "First squad, five abreast, staggered formation. Ready arms."

Chaaltyn barks out the orders.

Alyiakal eases the chestnut to the right side of the road, almost against another stone wall, in order to be out of the line of fire, and waits.

The riders from the hamlet spur their mounts forward, and a handful of arrows fly from the fort, but all land in the road short of First Company. Once the oncoming riders near the Mirror Lancers, mounted archers behind the charging vanguard loose shafts, which join those from archers moving quickly along the sides of the road, following the riders.

Alyiakal expands his outer shield forward of the first rank of the Mirror Lancers, using some of his gathered and compressed chaos as reinforcement, then orders, "Fire at will. Short bursts!" The firelance bursts should keep his lancers from realizing that he's blocking the archers' arrows.

His first three bursts take out attackers, and in a fraction of a quint, fallen men and mounts litter the road, and the remaining riders and foot archers flee back toward the fort.

"Cease fire!"

For another fraction of a quint, Alyiakal watches the fort with both sight and senses, then turns to Chaaltyn. "What a waste. If we'd tried to withdraw, the same thing would have happened, and we'd have had more casualties." He pauses. "Detail four lancers to come with me. Have another pair pick up a few of those bucklers and some blades."

"Ser, where are you going?"

"To see if there's anyone sensible in that fort."

"Ser?"

"If they start loosing shafts, we won't stay."

While Chaaltyn picks the lancers for both details, Alyiakal studies the terrain and the buildings, keeping an eye on the fort.

As he has suspected, the fort was built to dominate the intersection of the north road and the east road from Lhaarat. The graystone cliff behind it effectively signals the end of a line of high hills running back to the collapsed mountain over the River Lhaar. The hills to the south of the eastern road continue climbing until they merge with the heights of the Westhorns.

Alyiakal nods. The hamlet controls any trade from the east to Lhaarat as well as trade requiring a wagon from Cerlyn and north. The fort, the fields, the rapid response to the Mirror Lancers, even the mountain musk oxen, all suggest the community isn't the kind to support raiders. *So where in the name of the Rational Stars are the raiders?*

"Ser," says Chaaltyn.

Alyiakal turns his head toward the four lancers with Chaaltyn. "Follow me and keep close together." He eases the chestnut onto the road heading toward the fort, riding slowly and avoiding the bodies of mounts and men, and a few women as well.

Alyiakal senses an archer about to draw, and instantly raises his firelance. A single narrow firelance burst turns the archer to ashes and flame. He calls out, "Drop the bows if you don't want the same."

While he can sense that few have dropped bows, no one is raising one.

He calls out again to the fort, using order to boost his voice. "All we wanted was passage. You attacked us."

After several long moments, a gray-haired woman appears, a polished buckler on one arm. "You would deny us our rights. No one passes without tribute."

He aims the firelance at the log wall below and to the right of the speaker, then adds a fair amount of the free chaos he's gathered through the day.

The wood explodes into fire and a spray of ashes, leaving a gap more than a yard wide and two high.

After a moment, Alyiakal calls back. "Our tribute will be to let you live, only so long as you let Mirror Lancers pass."

"Does Cyador covet our lands?"

Hardly! "Not in the slightest. We require free passage to pursue those who try to raid our lands."

"Then look to the north. We permit no raiders here."

"We will. If a single shaft flies as we pass, we will turn this fort to ashes. If any other Mirror Lancers are attacked, the same will happen. Do you understand?"

"Only passage," calls back the gray-haired woman.

"Only safe passage," returns Alyiakal.

"Then pass and trouble us no more."

"Others may occasionally pass as well. Do not trouble them."

"So long as they do not trouble us beyond passage."

Alyiakal returns to First Company. "Is the company ready to ride?"

"Yes, ser."

"I've reached an agreement with those in the fort. We'll ride past and head north on that road."

"Is it safe, ser?"

"As safe as anything in this life," returns Alyiakal. "Once we reach the fort, continue leading and I will slip back to third squad."

Chaaltyn looks as though he might question, but then says, "Yes, ser."

"Company! Forward!" Alyiakal concentrates on the fort, alert for hostile movement, any shift in position, but those in the fort honor their commitment. Once Alyiakal reaches the fort, he slowly drops back to third squad and remains near the rear until the company turns north onto the road and is a good kay past the last dwelling.

Then he rides forward and rejoins Chaaltyn and first squad.

"Ser, how did you manage that?"

"I appealed to their sense of self-preservation. I just wished that they'd asked our business first. It would have been much easier on everyone. Obviously, these mountain hamlets and towns don't talk to each other much. The headwoman said that we needed to look to the north for the raiders."

"Do you think she was telling the truth?"

"She told me what she believes, and that means the raiders have tried to attack from the north. From what we've discovered about these roads, I'd say that any attacks would have to come from the east or north, unless they came from the walled valley. That's always possible, but there was only one sentry in that tower, and that suggests that they don't attack others."

"Or that they're so strong no one dares attack them," Chaaltyn points out.

"Possibly true, but if they did a lot of attacking, I think we'd have heard more. Did you get some of those blades and bucklers? What about the spears or lances?"

"Lances aren't anything special, just iron tips on long poles. There were all kinds of blades. The bucklers are all wood-framed with a thin layer of bronze over the wood. They're all alike."

Meaning they were likely made elsewhere, most likely Cerlyn. Alyiakal nods, thinking over the events in the last hamlet. Although the headwoman declared that the hamlet didn't "permit" raiders, the people had a strong fort—and a system for defense. *Which means attacks occur.* The bronze-faced bucklers are a puzzle. The raiders First Company encountered had no shields at all, but the rest of their tack and blades clearly came from Cerlyn.

Are the Cerlynese just being opportunistic traders . . . or do they have something else in mind? Alyiakal takes a deep breath. *Or are you making up a scheme that doesn't even exist?*

"Ser?" Chaaltyn's voice pulls Alyiakal from his thoughts.

"I'm trying to figure out how things fit together, like why that hamlet has bronze bucklers when they've never attacked lancers before, while the raiders we found, who knew they might encounter us, had no bucklers. Yet both the bucklers and the raiders' blades and tack came from Cerlyn."

Chaaltyn frowns. "See what you mean, ser. It doesn't make a lot of sense."

"We can worry about that later. Call the company to a halt. We need to talk to the scouts, and it's time for a break."

Shortly, Alyiakal addresses the returned scouts. "No one seems to know exactly where these raiders are located, except vaguely to the north. I have the feeling that they may have concealed their hamlet and their tracks. Look closely at the shoulders of the road and the ground beyond."

"You think they've used a pine branch to wipe out their tracks?" asks Raayls.

"Or rocky places that won't show tracks," replies Alyiakal. "Or possibly places where an entire hamlet could be that no one would suspect."

"Couldn't the raiders be farther east? Or north of the Lhaar?" asks Maaetz.

"There could be raiders father north or east, but it's likely there's one closer. Would raiders from farther away have known all the hidden trails south of the river? Also, the one we captured let drop that the hamlet was twenty-some kays from Lhaarat."

"Then you think it's here?" asks Chaaltyn.

"It has to be hidden. No patrol has even come close to finding it. The head-woman in the last town could only say that the raiders came from the north." Alyiakal pauses. "In any case, we need to confirm that this road is the same as the one crossing the Lhaar."

Maaetz looks puzzled.

"That would at least confirm that's how the raiders got the blades and tack from Cerlyn," explains Alyiakal. "Now, we need to move on." As he speaks, Alyiakal again raises his unseen order funnel to gather chaos bits from the white sun.

Despite looking and sensing diligently, for the next five kays, Alyiakal cannot find any trace of raiders or hamlets or even animal trails that would accommodate more than a single red deer. Nor can the scouts. The only sign that anyone else has used the road recently are two sets of hoofprints heading in the same direction as First Company.

Then, abruptly, Alyiakal senses—something—ahead and to his left, beyond his limit for discerning distinct order/chaos patterns. The evergreen forest sloping upward into the rocky crests nearer the River Lhaar seems unbroken. To the southeast, the hills run roughly north-northwest, effectively passing just west of the fort-like hamlet and continuing to the River Lhaar. *Which explains why the eastern road and Dietro's high road don't meet until the fort.*

He examines the left shoulder of the road and the ground, covered with ancient trees, that climbs to within a hundred yards of the rocky upper section of the ridge. Then he sees a crevice in the middle of that ridge, and recalls that he's seen the other side of that split, but from the natural rock-paved section of the eastern road earlier in the day.

Would that offer access to both roads?

He recalls the depression on the other side that seemed to lead to the narrow gorge and looks for something similar, but he finds nothing.

He keeps riding and searching, then almost reins up as he realizes whatever he has been sensing, barely, has vanished.

"Company! Halt!"

Chaaltyn looks to Alyiakal.

"I want to check something, and the men and their mounts could use a break." Alyiakal turns the chestnut toward the rear of the company and rides slowly, studying the thinner underbrush. By the time he reaches the last rank in third squad, he can, once again, faintly sense distant order/chaos patterns.

He sees no trails or hidden roads, nor even sense red deer anywhere on the slope, and he's sensed red deer everywhere. For a moment, he stiffens, then nods. *Why else would red deer avoid an area?*

Yet, a more thorough examination of the roadside and underbrush several hundred yards back yields nothing, not even game trails.

Maybe what you're sensing can't be accessed from here.

Alyiakal turns the chestnut and returns to the head of the company, where he addresses Chaaltyn. "We'll ride north a little farther."

Once the lancers remount, Alyiakal and the scouts continue.

A half kay later the road curves east, around the end of a low ridge, and then curves back west. Halfway around the curve, the road surface turns to gray rock lightly covered with dirt, that vanishes after another fifty yards, leaving only rock. At the end of the curve, where another low hill begins, a thin sheet of water flows over the rock and into a streambed on the northeast side of the road.

As he rides past the part of the hill closer to the water, which obscures the forest and ridge, Alyiakal looks to the southwest, directly toward the gap. There's definitely a slight depression in the trees leading to the gap, created over time by the small stream he's approaching.

Just short of the water, Alyiakal calls a halt and motions for Raayls to join him. While he senses nothing more than small animals in the trees, he thinks—and hopes—that there's the beginning of a trail.

"Ser?" asks the scout as he reins up.

"We're going to take a look at where the water comes from."

The roadbed is solid stone, with occasional sand, less than a digit deep, at the edge of the water. The water has eroded the soil, leaving an uneven stretch of stone sloping upward from the road into the trees flanking the tiny stream.

"Don't see how you could ride up the streambed, ser."

Alyiakal has to agree and shifts his study to the stream's far side. There's no sign of a trail, though there's more than enough space under the evergreens. Beyond the low brush bordering the road, uphill there's little undergrowth due to the thick carpet of evergreen needles.

Alyiakal guides the chestnut into the thin flow of water, over the calf-high brush on the other side, and under the evergreen canopy, moving parallel to the stream. Immediately he notices depressions in the needles. With Raayls behind him, he only rides another twenty yards before reining up short of a narrow trail worn into the soil beyond two ancient evergreens. A trail that angles toward the narrow gorge kays away. In the dirt, there are hoofprints.

He carefully turns the chestnut and eases past the scout to allow Raayls the space to turn his mount.

"Ser, how did you know?"

"I didn't. But the raiders have to be somewhere, and they've used rock to hide their tracks before. There can't be many other places for them to hide."

When Alyiakal and Raayls return to the road, Chaaltyn looks to Alyiakal.

"There's a trail. It must lead to something because it's been traveled, but we don't know what lies along the trail. We don't have any proof that it even leads to a raider hamlet, although I suspect it does. I'm not about to string out the company on an unknown trail. It's also been a long day and even longer before we get back. Besides which, until we reach the Lhaar we don't know for certain if this is the high road."

Chaaltyn nods.

Alyiakal can sense the senior squad leader's relief. "Company! Forward!" He doesn't say what he suspects: that there's another way to the hidden hamlet, and it's quite a bit closer to Lhaarat.

Over the next two glasses, First Company rides along the high road. Alyiakal sees no one, and the only hoofprints are the same set seen earlier by the company. Then Alyiakal catches sight of the edge of the collapsed mountainside.

"You were right, ser," says Chaaltyn, the relief evident in his voice. "Now what?"

"We'll follow the road back to the old logging trail. That's faster than going back the way we came." *Not by much, but we'll be able to see if there are more tracks coming down the logging road to the valley.*

Once First Company rides around the curve to the stretch of collapsed rock and the road running across it, Alyiakal breathes a little easier. The two sets of hoofprints continue as well. The road turns out to be more irregular than it had looked from the other side; the earlier road builders had simply filled spaces with rock and anything else, providing firm, if uneven, footing.

Beyond that, the road remains relatively level with wide curves for several kays, then sloping downward along the ridge Alyiakal recalls. Close to five kays later, the slope gets steeper as the road turns west. After another two kays, the road descends more gradually, and Alyiakal begins to look left for the trail down to the logged-over area and the old logging road into the valley.

As Raayls rides around a westward curve, he reins up and signals, calling something back to Maaetz, who turns his mount and rides back to Alyiakal.

"Ser, there are five riders at the foot of the grade."

"Have Raayls wait, and we'll ride down together."

Even before Alyiakal joins Raayls, he can barely sense the riders, since they're a kay away.

As the full company appears, the riders, moving at a fast trot, take the road north. They're far enough away that trying to catch them would exhaust already tired mounts. Alyiakal, squinting, can't make out whether they wear uniforms, but doesn't see any bright colors. *Which isn't much help, since the Kyphrans wear a light blue that looks gray at a distance, the Cerlynese wear dark green and brown, and the raiders don't wear bright colors.*

Alyiakal turns to Raayls. "Go ahead, carefully. See what you can learn from their tracks."

"Yes, ser."

Alyiakal checks the sun, lower in the sky than he'd like, and orders First Company forward while Raayls and Maaetz move farther ahead.

When First Company nears the trailhead where it meets the road, Raayls joins Alyiakal and Chaaltyn. "Ser, the hoofprints head down toward the logging road and come back. I'm pretty sure it's the same number, but it's hard to tell. The tracks are mixed up on the trail."

Alyiakal nods. "Just be careful on the way down to the start of the logging road."

"Yes, ser."

When First Company reaches the logged-over area, the hoofprints spread, indicating that all five riders have ridden the two kays down to the brush pile, but only a single rider appears to have gone farther. He, or she, stopped several yards short of leaving the trees before turning back.

By the time First Company reaches the valley floor and heads south toward Gairtyn, it's twilight, and almost full dark by the time Alyiakal rides into the post. He wants to make sure that the lancers' mess has held some sort of dinner for his men, so he postpones grooming the chestnut.

He's met short of the kitchen by Drassyl, the head cook. "Nothing to worry about, Overcaptain. The majer sent word that First Company might be late."

"Thank you. Especially for the men."

"We'll get something to the officers' mess now that we know you're back."

"I appreciate it. Don't hurry, though. We need to settle the mounts."

"Understood, Overcaptain."

Alyiakal returns to where he tied the chestnut, leads him to the stable, grooms him, and then heads for the mess, where a dinner of some sort of hash and hot gravy awaits him, as does Majer Byelt.

"I thought we could talk while you eat," says the majer conversationally.

"We found the high road that Dietro mentioned."

"Dietro . . . the captive. I'm not surprised. You did him a favor, and possibly the Mirror Lancers. Undercaptain Hurzt sent me a message that he did well in training and that he left on a posting for Inividra last eightday."

"I suspect he'll do well."

"At least he knows what to expect, if from the other side," replies Byelt dryly.

Between bites, Alyiakal describes the long day's events. He keeps his suspicions about the hidden trail to himself, only mentioning that they found a concealed trail, but didn't have the time to explore it, given its narrow nature.

When Alyiakal finishes, Byelt says, "You think that hidden trail leads to a hideaway for raiders, don't you?"

"It's possible, but the biggest surprise was a fortified hamlet that attacked without ascertaining who we were."

"To me," says Byelt, "that sounds like they fight and feud with each other and we're only incidental."

"That seems likely, except for the raiders. They may try to strike here more, especially with the precautions some of the outlying hamlets are taking. Even so, I worry more about the riders from the north. They've been scouting three times."

"From Cerlyn, you've suggested."

"I don't know that they're Cerlynese. More likely that they're supplied and armed by Cerlyn."

"What do you have in mind next?" asks Byelt.

"On oneday, I'd like to take another patrol out the east road to investigate a section of the road on the opposite side of that gorge through the ridge."

Byelt raises his eyebrows.

"It would take any raiders far too long to ride from the hidden trail to strike Southtyll when they did, especially with no sign they'd bivouacked overnight."

The majer nods slowly. "You're in charge of patrols."

In other words, some of the credit is yours—and all of the blame if it fails. "Tomorrow, I'll revise the local maps so that the other company officers have an idea of where and how the various roads and passable trails connect."

"That will be helpful, especially for Undercaptain Staalt. He can use all the help we can provide." Byelt stands. "I'm glad you accomplished what you had in mind. I'll see you at breakfast."

"Until then, ser." Alyiakal doesn't stand.

LXXIV

As planned, on sevenday, while Dhaerl and Second Company patrol the east road, and Paersol patrols west all the way to Westyll, Alyiakal revises his map, and makes copies for the majer and other company officers. He assigns one of the duty rankers to make copies, but after one look at an attempt, he decides that he'd better do it.

Then he reviews the various instructions and directives Lhaarat Post received while he was on patrol and makes his comments and recommendations to the majer. After that, he quietly inspects the post, making a few "suggestions" along the way, since any orders of that nature should come from Byelt. While inspecting the stables, he stops and spends a little time with the chestnut. He also visits the northeast lookout, who has seen nothing out of the ordinary.

Eightday dawns misty, and that's about the only unusual aspect of the day.

On oneday, First Company leaves right after breakfast, heading up the east road. While there are new tracks on the logging roads, and scattered hoofprints on the east road, all appear to be from individual riders or carts.

All that means is that the tracks don't belong to a raider band. Some tracks could belong to raider scouts or raiders getting supplies.

Once more, Alyiakal makes a point of quietly and invisibly collecting sunchaos bits as he can.

First Company stops briefly at the river overlook, but Alyiakal sees little difference in the water levels. The south road, branching off to the walled valley and possibly beyond, shows a few hoofprints, but little else. By midday First Company nears the rock-hard section of the east road which would only reveal hoofprints as smudges in the scattered sand, if at all.

Alyiakal calls in Raayls and Maaetz and says, "Study the left side of the road carefully. If there's anything at all unusual, let me know."

"Yes, ser."

As the chestnut carries Alyiakal closer to the rock face to the left of the road, he only senses small animals in the forest. The trees extend to the far side of the small ridge, possibly even to the narrow gorge in the northeast and the suspected raider hamlet. Then he turns his senses to the steep rock face.

Surprisingly, he discerns faint patterns of chaos some five yards ahead, but only in an area some six yards wide where there's slightly more chaos than in the surrounding sections of the face.

"Ser!" calls Raayls.

"Company! Halt!" Alyiakal orders, then rides forward to join the scout, who has reined up fifty yards farther, where the ridge is lower and the edge of the road is a mixture of rock and soil.

Raayls points to a small dead evergreen, apparently squeezed to death by the massive trees on each side. "Ser, this evergreen . . . the trunk down here isn't right. They usually spread where they enter the ground, and the dirt's not quite the same."

Alyiakal smiles wryly. The dead evergreen is over two yards high, small only in comparison to the nearby trees. "Well, let's see if we can move it."

"I'll do it, ser, if you'd hold my mount's reins."

"Go ahead." After Raayls dismounts, Alyiakal takes the reins.

Raayls wrestles with the dead tree, staggering backward as the tree comes loose.

The dead tree's removal reveals a hole in the rock, as well as a narrow trail leading uphill, deeper into the woods.

Chaaltyn rides closer, looking from Raayls to the tree to the trail and then to Alyiakal. He shakes his head. "I'm not sure I want to know."

Alyiakal shrugs, then says, "I had a feeling."

"Begging your pardon, ser, but I wouldn't want to bet against your feelings."

"Let's see where it goes. Raayls, just go a few yards and call back."

The scout remounts, then eases his horse between the trees, calling out, "It only goes a little over ten yards. There's a bunch of big rocks piled up to the left, just past the first two or three big trees. Wait. The path turns left . . . Ser . . . maybe you'd better come see. I think it's a road."

A road? Not a path or trail?

Alyiakal eases the chestnut between the two trunks, following the path past the rocks and left. When Alyiakal sees the smooth, narrow road cut into the stone, flanked by old-growth evergreens, he has trouble keeping his mouth closed—because only the First or Mirror Engineers could build this sort of road. To his left, a mass of irregularly shaped boulders covers the road. Alyiakal guesses that, at one time, the road went through the ridge to the eastern road, as little sense as that makes to him.

Why in the name of the Rational Stars would anyone build such a road here?

He looks closely and sees that dirt and moss have crept over the edges on both sides of the road and that some twenty yards to the northwest, branches, cut at the end by an ax, are heaped to the side.

"Ser?" asks Raayls. "What is it? I mean, yes, it's a road, but I've never seen one like this. What's it doing in the middle of a forest?"

"I'm guessing, but it looks like it was built by the First. I have no idea why it's here." Alyiakal glances to his left, where it appears, in retrospect, as though a higher hill had been cut down in such a way as to block the road. *Then whoever blocked it smoothed over the side facing the eastern road.* After a moment, he says, "We might as well follow this to see what's at the other end. I suspect raiders found it, maybe years ago, and have been using it as a base. It's wide enough for two abreast, three in a pinch, and I doubt the raiders will be expecting us—if this, indeed, leads to their hamlet."

In less than a quint, First Company forms up on the old road. As the company rides northeast toward the narrow gorge in the ridge, Alyiakal can't help but notice a lack of tree stumps on either side of the road, and in places the trees look younger. Not young, but younger. *Whoever built this meant for the road not to be seen, even when it was built. Dissidents who escaped from Guarstyad? Or another group that didn't like being controlled by Cyad?*

For the first two kays or so, while Alyiakal sees dirt on the road and more than a few hoofprints, he still can't sense large animals or people. Then he discerns quite a few large animals, but not the patterns of people. He chuckles to himself as he realizes that he's sensing horses, and the horses are being kept ahead on the right side of the road, a good kay or more away. After riding another few hundred yards, he finally senses a single person, but definitely northeast of the horses. Then, that order/chaos pattern fades—and vanishes.

Into the gorge, behind a mass of rock?

"Ready arms," Alyiakal says to Chaaltyn. "Pass it back."

Chaaltyn repeats the order.

After riding more than a half kay, Alyiakal not only clearly senses the horses ahead on the right, but also sees an irregular, wooden fence running from tree to tree. "Horses ahead on the right."

The location of the horses surprises Alyiakal, but there must be a reason, which he suspects he'll discover soon.

The trees that overarch the stone road thin over the next hundred yards, and for the first time, Alyiakal can see the top of the gorge clearly, far narrower than he'd judged. He doubts the two sides of the gorge are even twenty yards apart. Ahead, the road makes a gentle turn eastward heading directly toward the narrow gorge, where the trees flanking the road end, revealing the opening.

The road surprised Alyiakal, but what he sees above the road stuns him.

Cut into the north wall of the narrow gorge are dwellings, some windows containing actual glass, with stone staircases leading down to the road, and recessed entries. Alyiakal can see a score of doorways with stairs, and there must be internal staircases because some of the windows are a level above the doors.

Although he cannot see anyone, he senses order/chaos patterns appearing, then disappearing, and appearing again, obviously partly shielded by the stone into which the dwellings have been cut.

When Alyiakal is about a hundred yards from the gorge, a handful of raiders appear on a long balcony cut into the stone on the western end of the gorge, a good four yards above the old road. All have horn bows, and one immediately looses a shaft.

Alyiakal expands his shields, raises his firelance, and pulses three quick order-guided bolts.

Three figures on the balcony flare into ashes.

The others either duck behind the chest-high stone wall or flee. Alyiakal can't tell which. Then he calls out, "If you don't attack, we won't. We're mapping the old roads." The first statement is true, and the second at least partly true.

He waits, but no one appears.

"If someone in charge doesn't show themselves, we'll just take your horses and leave." Alyiakal hopes someone will appear because, without horses, some members of the hamlet will die, later if not sooner.

A silver-haired woman appears on the balcony that had held archers.

Alyiakal rides slowly forward then reins up on the stone road perhaps fifteen yards from her.

"What do you want from us?" the woman asks.

Alyiakal can sense enhanced order within her frame and also realizes that while she is older than he is, she is not old.

"Information and your pledge to stop raiding the lands of Cyad."

"Haven't you done enough already?" replies the woman. "You killed a half score of our young men."

"They raided a hamlet in Cyador, killed one woman, and took two others. Then they attacked us when we tracked them down."

The woman looks long at Alyiakal, and he can see her slump.

Alyiakal continues to regard the silver-haired woman. "Since we didn't catch anyone in a raid," *and since your whatever-this-is lies beyond the borders of Cyador,* "we'll leave you with a warning. If we catch or track you from a raid in Cyador again, there won't be another chance." He reinforces the last words with cold order. "Is that clear?"

Frustration, anger—and especially fear—from the silver-haired woman reaches Alyiakal. He can also sense a certain order focus.

"You're most clear, Firstborn. We have no choice."

"How did you find this . . . refuge?" asks Alyiakal.

"My great-grandmere lived here when it was truly a refuge from the tyrants of Cyad. She was out riding when the evil ones came and killed or kidnapped all who lived here and destroyed part of the road to hide it. When it was safe, she came back. Others joined her." She pauses. "That was what I was told. Are you going to destroy us, for all your words?"

"No. So long as you do not attack us on our patrols or raid the lands of Cyador. Whether we destroy you is your decision, not mine."

"As if we have any choice."

"There are always choices. Sometimes, they're not the best."

"Leave us, Firstborn. Leave us to survive as we can."

"We will leave. Others may come to view your hamlet. If you harm them, you will not survive." Alyiakal turns to Chaaltyn. "Take a very good look at those dwellings cut into the rock." Alyiakal turns to the scouts. "You two as well."

After several long moments, Alyiakal orders, "To the rear, ride."

Chaaltyn relays the order and turns his mount, then asks, "You're not going to do more, ser?"

"We don't need to. It would create more problems than it would solve. I'll explain when we're away from the hamlet." Once First Company rides back to the east road, Alyiakal continues, "We rode down a road in lands outside of Cyador and were attacked because the attackers thought we were going to destroy them. We repulsed the attack, and in the process killed three attackers. We warned them against raiding. So . . . if they raid again, we can attack to remove the problem. Besides, we may have to escort Mirror Engineers there."

"Ser?"

"It's likely the dissidents built the road."

"Dissidents?"

"Opponents of the First. The First destroyed their post or community near Guarstyad. The Mirror Engineers may want to view the hamlet. It would be better if we didn't destroy it." *Not that firelances would do much to the road or the dwellings.*

Chaaltyn opens his mouth, then closes it.

When First Company reaches the east road, Alyiakal turns to Raayls. "Replace the tree. They'll need the concealment. They've lost a good many young men. Apparently, everyone in these hills fights everyone else."

"Yes, ser." Raayls shakes his head.

The ride back to Lhaarat is uneventful, and Alyiakal is still thinking about the raiders and the dissident refuge built into the gorge when he walks into Byelt's study and closes the door.

"You don't look pleased, Alyiakal. Didn't you find your raiders?"

"We found them, all right, and we found more trouble." Before Byelt responds, Alyiakal takes a chair in front of the desk and begins to explain what happened.

The majer shakes his head long before Alyiakal finishes, but says nothing until then. "I'd ask how you knew it was built by the dissidents, but you know more about that than anyone. Do you think there are any devices or artifacts?"

"I have no way of knowing, but I doubt it. Certainly, nothing working, or they would have used it against us. How it was built and where suggests a desire to remain hidden. First, the dissidents used most of what they had to build a refuge in a remote place. Second, the First didn't want anyone to know that there were any dissidents left."

"So why didn't they destroy it?"

"Because even then Cyador had a limited number of fireships and chaos towers. Firelances won't even scar the walls. The effort to destroy it would have required bringing large chaos equipment hundreds of kays, and that was before we had all the sunstone roads. Just blocking off the road likely required more of an effort than the Emperor of Light would have liked."

Byelt nods. Then he frowns and asks, "You didn't tell them that Cyador doesn't care what they do so long as it doesn't happen to us or our people, did you?"

"No. I suspect that's the effective policy, but that would be an untoward assumption on my part. Besides, saying something like that would eventually get around and give them the idea that they could fight with each other all they want."

"What do you suggest we do?"

"I'll write up a patrol report, and you review it. When we agree on a recommendation, we send it to headquarters, and let the Majer-Commander decide. In the meantime, we keep a close watch on the hamlet."

"What's your recommendation?"

"To leave the hamlet alone unless there are future raids from there. There's no point in removing them because another group will find it and use it, and the place can't be destroyed without using a large firecannon and a great amount of chaos, but that decision, of course, is up to headquarters."

"As it should be," says Byelt sardonically. "I'll see you at dinner."

Alyiakal stands. He needs to write the patrol report, but he really doesn't even want to think about what Mirror Lancer headquarters will think or say about him finding *another* old road and structures created by the dissidents.

LXXV

After working more than a glass on his report, Alyiakal leaves it unfinished and heads for the mess. When he enters, slightly early, the three captains standing beside the table all turn, looking expectantly toward Alyiakal.

Then Dhaerl grins. "Word is that you had an . . . unusual patrol."

"We did. Starting with finding a hidden entrance to the raider hamlet." Alyiakal summarizes what happened in three long sentences.

"There's more to it than that, ser," declares Paersol.

"There is indeed," says Byelt as he approaches the table. "You can ask about it after we're seated."

After all the officers are served, Dhaerl says, "You mentioned dissidents. I've never heard of them."

"From what I learned at Oldroad Post," replies Alyiakal, "they didn't want to be part of Cyador, and some of them had to be mages. The ones here had chaos stonecutters. They couldn't have cut dwellings into a sheer rock face or built several kays of stone road without them. They might have had firelances. The First captured and removed almost all of them and took any of their chaos-powered weapons or tools. A few of the dissidents eluded the First and later returned to the gorge."

"Makes sense that they're raiders," declares Vaarkas. "They can't have much love for Cyador."

"Why did the dissidents put their refuge so close to Cyador?" asks Paersol.

"When they created it close to a hundred years ago, Cyador hadn't grown to what it is now," replies Alyiakal. "That refuge was close to nowhere. They even concealed the stone road." Alyiakal suspects that the original end of the road, before it was covered in rock, had also been hidden, possibly with a magely concealment of some sort.

"Do you know anything more about these dissidents?" asks Vaarkas.

Alyiakal shakes his head. "There was nothing about the dissidents at the Kyphran border site, just old weapons and a stonecutter, and headquarters reported only finding a few fragmentary references to dissidents in the Mirror Lancer archives."

"Why didn't you just get rid of them?" asks Paersol. "They're raiders, and they're descended from rebels."

"We already removed the raiders we found last Autumn," replies Alyiakal. "Only three of them attacked us on this patrol, and they're dead. No one else attacked. The headwoman agreed that other lancers could enter their land."

"Their lands?" questions Paersol. "Those are our lands."

Alyiakal is about to answer when Byelt says, evenly but coldly, "Captain Paersol, currently Cyador only claims the lands to the base of the Westhorns. That base is defined as the east end of the valley. Cyador has the rights to patrol lands all the way to the midpoint of the line between summits of the Westhorns, but those lands are *not,* as you put it, our lands."

Before Paersol can speak, Alyiakal adds, "As a result of the short war with Kyphros, Cyador's eastern border along the southern part of Kyphros is now set ten kays east of the base of the Westhorns, but that border ends roughly even with Geliendra. The border north of that point is the same as here."

"How do you know that, ser?" Paersol's tone borders on being snide.

"When I was in command of Oldroad Post, I was responsible for patrols of that border. I do believe I mentioned that to you previously."

Dhaerl smiles faintly and sadly. Vaarkas winces.

"Do you have any other questions, Captain?" asks Byelt in a tone that suggests that Paersol should think before asking.

"No, ser."

Alyiakal not only senses Paersol's smoldering anger but sees the tension and tightness in his face and upper body. Not for the first time, he wonders if Paersol comes from an elthage or high altage background, where he was never questioned or rebuked. *More likely elthage. Angry that he lacks magely abilities and has to be subordinate to comparatively low-ranking Mirror Lancer officers.*

For the rest of dinner, the conversation returns to speculations about the dissidents and why they built the retreat where they did.

When Alyiakal returns to his study to finish the patrol report, he can't help wondering about the dissidents. *What were they like? Were they such a threat that all evidence of their existence needed to be expunged or was that the result of personal affront on the part of the Emperor of Light?*

He ponders for a moment, then realizes he doesn't even know when, precisely, it happened, which Emperor reigned, or whether it was Kief or Kiedral—it could have been either.

There's still so much you don't know.

Speculation, however, won't finish the patrol report, so he picks up his pen and begins to write.

LXXVI

Alyiakal finds himself riding down a long, smooth, graystone road, with black raised curbs, under tall evergreens that keep the sun from even touching the seamless stone pavement. As he rides, he keeps thinking the pavement should be whitestone, not graystone, and that he needs more chaos than he's gathered.

The road curves toward a cleft in a hill, and light from the white sun reflects off windows cut into the stone of the gorge. Before long he sees the balcony at the end of the gorge facing the road. Out of nowhere, three men in shimmering black, carrying short firelances in one hand, appear on the balcony. Short blasts of flame skitter off Alyiakal's shields, and he lifts his firelance, loosing a line of tight-coiled chaos that slices the three men, flaring them to ash.

Another figure in black appears, and Alyiakal looses another bolt, only to see the figure of a silver-haired woman with open hands, who vanishes in flame and ashes. Alyiakal's chaos bolt strikes the stone behind where she stood and angles back at Alyiakal, slicing through his shields, bathing him in thousands of fire-needles.

Alyiakal struggles to guide the gelding out of the hail of fire, and he plunges into a dark forest, trees catching fire as he passes, struggling to reach the raiders just ahead. When he reaches the edge of their encampment, he sees three men. Each holds a young woman bound with black rope. The three turn as one, and before Alyiakal can use his firelance, each slits the throat of his captive. Alyiakal fires three quick bolts. When the chaos strikes, it transforms each raider into a giant vulcrow, which all swoop toward Alyiakal, penetrating his shields, and ripping into him with claws and beaks that burn and freeze simultaneously . . .

Alyiakal wakes, drenched in sweat, thrashing out of his bedclothes, and gasping for breath.

For a time, he just sits on the edge of the bed, trying to recover from the all-too-vivid nightmare, inchoate fragments of thought swirling through his head.

Finally, he takes a slow deep breath.

Why was he killing everyone, even the innocent women?

Because you would have, if you'd had to?

He takes another deep breath, as other questions come to mind.

Given the hidden nature of the retreat, how did they get weapons from Cerlyn? Alyiakal can't see the headwoman revealing the location of the hamlet, and that means trade elsewhere, even if indirect, trade possibly subsidized by Cerlyn.

He also doesn't see much point in punishing the hamlet's dwellers further. Given what he saw and sensed, there aren't enough young men to undertake any more raids, and now that Alyiakal and the Mirror Lancers know their location, they can't escape retribution for further raids.

He stands, blotting the remaining sweat off his forehead.

Getting through the rest of the day will be easier than getting through the night. *At least, you hope so.*

LXXVII

When Alyiakal rises on threeday, more than an eightday after dealing with the putative descendants of the dissidents, he wonders if he's been overly worried about raiders from the north and supplied by Cerlyn. So far, the patrols on the east road for the past eightday have seen no signs of mounted groups, something Alyiakal scarcely finds strange after the skirmish outside the wooden fort, but it raises other questions.

His worry about raiders from the north prompts him to assign each of the other three companies a patrol going through Gairtyn, up the old logging road to the high road, and then north, just to give them familiarity with the trails and roads—and in case there might be raiders. At the very least, those patrols should keep Headman Vhoraal from complaining too much.

When Alyiakal walks into the mess, Dhaerl is the only other officer there. "Good morning."

"Same to you, ser."

"Your time is getting short."

Dhaerl smiles ruefully. "I try not to think about it. Had a friend who kept thinking about it. A barbarian shaft got him on his last patrol."

"I'm sorry I mentioned it. Let me take your mind off it. I've been worried about attacks from the north. What do you think about the possibilities?"

"I don't know, but I wouldn't trust the Jeranyi or the Cerlynese as far as I could throw my mount. Probably a good thing you're taking First Company that way today." Dhaerl grins. "Leastwise, you're making a solid trail up to the high road. Might bring a few more traders, in time." The grin fades. "Any word on the new undercaptain's arrival?"

"Nothing so far. Undercaptain Staalt is supposed to arrive no later than this eightday, but, if he doesn't, I'll take Second Company on patrols until he does. Unless, of course, the majer prefers to do that."

Alyiakal senses others approaching and turns to see Paersol and then Vaarkas enter, followed by the majer, and in moments, all five officers seat themselves.

"It looks like a pleasant day for patrols," says Byelt, looking to Paersol, who will be taking Fourth Company to patrol the side road that leads to the walled valley. "Clear and warm, but not hot."

"At least for now," adds Alyiakal dryly.

"It's still a touch early for raiders," adds Dhaerl. "Usually, we don't see them until the first or second eightday of Summer. Unless Spring gets warm early, and that didn't happen this year."

"You never know," cautions Byelt.

Alyiakal nods and continues eating the cheesed egg scramble.

After breakfast, he makes his way to the stable, where, as usual, he talks quietly to the chestnut as he readies the gelding for the day. He also spends a brief time under a concealment, just to keep his mount used to the total darkness. Then he leads his horse out, mounts, and rides to join Chaaltyn, Rhemsaar, and Taenyr.

"Anything special today, ser?" asks the senior squad leader.

"Not unless we run into raiders or trouble," Alyiakal replies genially, studying the rankers and their mounts as First Company forms up.

"You think that's likely?"

"Sooner or later. We haven't seen many riders or traders on the high road, but it doesn't look abandoned. We'll see tracks or travelers, or both, before long."

Less than a quint later, First Company rides west on the east road, and Alyiakal spreads his unseen order funnel to collect chaos bits. The company passes a logging wagon headed north, but no one looks at the lancers after they cross the bridge and ride through Gairtyn. A glass later, the company reaches the logged-over area. Since every company has ridden that way over the past eightday, all the scouts only look for recent tracks or hoofprints, and neither Raayls nor Maaetz sight any there, or later, on the trail to the high road.

Alyiakal calls a short break when the company gains the high road but sends Raayls north and Maaetz south to see what they can discover.

"No sign of anyone but us, ser," Chaaltyn says.

"So far," replies Alyiakal, before taking a swallow of ale from his water bottle and dismounting.

Before long, Raayls rides back and reins up beside the chestnut. Looking down at Alyiakal, he reports, "Hoofprints, ser. Four riders. All four mounts recently shod. Looks that way to me, anyway."

"Which way are they headed?" asks Alyiakal. "Are there return tracks?"

"South. I'd guess they passed here early today."

"What about two riders, each with a spare mount?"

"It's possible, but the tracks look like four riders."

"Anything else?"

"No, ser."

"Take a quick break."

"Four riders . . . in the morning . . . coming from the north," muses Alyiakal. "I can't see them riding all night." He looks to Chaaltyn. "Wonder what we'll find heading north."

"So do I, ser."

Almost immediately, Maaetz returns with the same report as Raayls. Alyiakal lets another half quint pass before motioning for the scouts to join him.

"Ser?" asks Maaetz.

"We're about to mount up. In addition to everything else, I'd like you both to keep an eye out for places where travelers might have left the road to make camp."

"Yes, ser."

Once the scouts have moved out heading north, Alyiakal orders First Company forward.

For the next glass or so, the only recent signs of travelers are the hoofprints of the four riders. Then Raayls signals and calls back to Maaetz who rides back to Alyiakal.

"Just ahead, there's a rider with a pack mule. No sign of anyone else."

"I'd like to talk to him."

"Yes, ser."

While Alyiakal suspects that the man is a trader, given the pack mule and his appearance, a weathered face, a ragged beard, and brown hair shot with gray, he still asks.

"What else would I be, Overcaptain?"

Alyiakal senses the truth, and replies with a hint of humor, "I'm glad to hear it. You could have one of quite a few other less desirable occupations."

"Not for me."

"What's loaded on the mule?" asks Alyiakal.

"White fox pelts."

"White fox?"

"Their coats only turn white in Winter."

"Not ermine pelts?"

"The white foxes are rarer. I pay the mountain folk for them. I cure them and sell them to outland traders."

"Why outland traders?" asks Alyiakal, honestly curious.

"Because this is the only place in the world with winter-white foxes, and the outlanders'll pay more, especially the ones from Nordla. Gets cold there, and the consorts of those with gold love them. No one in Candar with golds lives where it gets that cold. Leastwise, none that I know of."

"Isn't it risky?"

"Everything's risky, Overcaptain, but the mountain folk want my coin and no one else'll pay for pelts. They leave me alone."

Alyiakal senses a certain unease and says, quietly, "And since fox pelts aren't on the Imperial tariff schedule . . ."

The trader stiffens.

"Don't worry. I have no interest in telling anyone." He pauses. "You'll take the high road another twenty kays south and then come down through Lhaarat?"

"Any reason I shouldn't?" asks the trader warily.

"No, not at all. Right now, things are quiet." After a moment, Alyiakal asks, "You didn't see four riders heading south earlier today, did you?"

"No, ser. I saw their tracks when I got on the road earlier today."

Alyiakal nods. "I won't keep you. Best of fortune."

"Same to you." Then the trader frowns. "Never seen Mirror Lancers on the high road before."

"We're patrolling farther out due to raiders."

"Might help . . . might not. Least it'll cut down on some of the brigands."

Once First Company has left the fur trader behind, Chaaltyn asks, "How truthful do you think he was?"

"He didn't lie, but he didn't tell us everything either."

A good glass later, Alyiakal wonders about the white foxes, and who else, besides raiders and traders, might be using the high road, not to mention his continuing amazement at absolutely no mention of the high road in any Mirror Lancer patrol reports. Then Maaetz signals again and rides back to report.

"Ser, there's a rough sort of waystation ahead. From the hoofprints and the fresh droppings, it looks like it's where the four riders spent the night."

"How big is it?"

"Not big enough for even a squad, and it's not much more than partial shelter."

Maaetz leads the way, and Alyiakal senses the area, finding small animals in the hills nearby, but no sign of people or red deer. When Alyiakal stops at the edge of what passes for a waystation, he agrees with Maaetz.

The campsite is little more than a cleared flat area on the west side of the road, with a spring several yards to the left of the rough structure partly dug into the hillside. Water flows from a small cleft into a rock-lined basin, and trickles over a rock lip before heading downhill between two hills. A log palisade on the north side angles into the hillside on one end, with a roof of hide-covered saplings topped with branches and enough space for a few people and several mounts. The logs in the palisade wall have been replaced over the years and so have the stones bracing the base of the logs.

Alyiakal rides closer, and glances in from the open end. Soot on the stone above the rough stone hearth suggests decades of use, if not more as does the neat semicircle of stones holding the ashes of a recent fire. The small stack of chopped branches and sticks to one side of the raised hearth conveys another meaning.

A custom to leave fire-starters for the next traveler.

While Alyiakal hasn't seen signs of other travelers besides the four, he asks, "Can you tell if others have used this recently?"

"There aren't any traces of others, but . . ." Maaetz shrugs.

After searching intensively, Alyiakal has the company continue along the road.

First Company rides north another glass before Alyiakal allows a break. Then he gives the order for the company to return to the post.

After a quint, he looks to Chaaltyn. "Your thoughts about the road, Senior Squad Leader?"

"We've scarcely seen anyone, but the road is passable. People have to be repairing it at times, but we haven't seen any hamlets near the road on this side of the river."

"You think there might be a hamlet or town not that far ahead?"

"I'd almost wager on it, ser, but there's too much I'd have wagered on around here that didn't turn out that way."

"That's true for both of us."

"Do you think we'll see raiders from the north soon?"

"I don't know. I have the feeling we will, but it's more feeling than fact, and I certainly don't know when."

Chaaltyn just nods.

As Alyiakal leads First Company back toward Lhaarat, he finds it hard to believe that the post commanders at Lhaarat had no knowledge of the high road or the hamlets and roads farther into the hills. *Simply because there weren't that many raids, and the losses weren't that significant?*

But that suggests another unpleasant possibility—that Alyiakal was posted to Lhaarat because no one at headquarters knew what to do with him, and they thought he couldn't upset matters in a comparatively quiet border post.

LXXVIII

Late on sixday afternoon, Majer Byelt walks into Alyiakal's study. "The lookouts sent word that we've got supply wagons coming, hopefully with our new undercaptain."

"That's cutting it a bit close," replies Alyiakal, "but it may not have been up to him."

"We'll find out, not that it changes things." Byelt pauses. "I'm going to have him report to you first. You brief him on patrols and make sure he knows you're in charge of scheduling and training."

"I can do that, ser."

More than a glass later, Alyiakal hears through the open doorway, "Undercaptain Staalt, reporting."

"Ser, you're to see Overcaptain Alyiakal first. He's the deputy post commander. That door."

Staalt appears in the doorway.

"Close the door, Undercaptain." Alyiakal does not stand.

"Undercaptain Staalt, reporting for duty, ser." Staalt stiffens. Staalt himself is of average height, neither slender nor muscular, with undistinguished brown hair and hazel eyes, and a dusty uniform and boots.

Alyiakal gestures to the chairs before his desk and waits for the undercaptain to seat himself. "I understand you had a very brief posting to Chaelt. Where were you posted prior to that?"

"At Klehl, ser. Assistant port company commander."

"What were your duties?"

"There was only one company at Klehl, but it had four squads. I was in command of third and fourth squad."

"That's an unusual arrangement. Were you given any rationale for it?"

"Yes, ser. The post is responsible for dealing with smugglers for roughly a hundred kays along the coast. Fifty to the south and fifty to the west. There's not that much smuggling, but the distance is considerable. I was told that headquarters felt one company had too few lancers to cover that distance and that having two companies would be a waste of lancers."

"How did you fare in catching smugglers?"

"Poorly," replies Staalt. "We usually didn't find out until after they'd vanished into the grasslands. Unless there was a storm. The seas are treacherous offshore in bad weather. We caught more smugglers when their ships were driven aground."

"Usually outlanders, I imagine." Alyiakal can sense Staalt's surprise at his comment.

"Ah . . . yes, ser."

"What about Chaelt?"

"I was supposed to have a position similar to the one in Klehl, but I reported there after an ambush by smugglers killed the company commander. Not long after I reported, a senior captain arrived, and I was given orders to Lhaarat."

"Sometimes, that sort of thing happens." Alyiakal smiles pleasantly. He's heard enough for the moment, and in time he'll find out more. "Your duties here will be rather different in some ways and very much the same in others. You'll be in command of Second Company, and I'll accompany you on at least your first patrol. I'm in charge of scheduling and assigning patrols, and determining what additional training is necessary." Alyiakal briefly summarizes Staalt's duties and responsibilities, the quarters and mess arrangements, the problems patrols may face, and the names of the other officers. "Do you have any questions?"

"Ah . . . you ride patrols, ser?"

"I do. I was posted here by Mirror Lancer headquarters to be in charge of patrols and directed to ride patrols as well." Because Alyiakal can tell that Staalt isn't quite sure what to say, he asks, "Do you have any other questions?"

"Ah . . . no, ser."

"If you think of others, you can always ask." Alyiakal stands. "You need to meet Majer Byelt." He escorts Staalt into Byelt's office. "Undercaptain Staalt, Majer."

Then he eases away, closing the door as he leaves, and returns to his own desk, leaving his door ajar.

Staalt is roughly what Alyiakal expected. His presence and what Alyiakal has encountered over the past half year, however, reinforce the questions he's posed to himself more than once. Does Mirror Lancer headquarters have more than a minimal interest in Lhaarat Post? Is the post one to which officers are assigned when no one knows what to do with them? *You, Paersol, and now Staalt—none of you are exactly highly regarded by headquarters . . . and Dhaerl was assigned for what was his last posting before he could be stipended.*

Or does Lhaarat train rankers to be sent to border posts in the future? *Or are you trying to find a reason that doesn't exist?*

Alyiakal shakes his head, waiting for Byelt to dismiss Staalt and come ask him what he thinks.

Less than half a glass passes before the majer enters Alyiakal's study. He closes the door but doesn't seat himself. So Alyiakal stands and waits for Byelt to speak.

"Not quite as green as some." Byelt grins. "You still scared him stiff."

"I just told him his duties and responsibilities and a bit about the post and patrolling."

"In a way that makes him wish that he'd never have to explain anything to you, except for the fact that he'd know that failing to explain would be worse." Byelt pauses. "There's no word from headquarters about that dissident hamlet. It'll be interesting to see who headquarters sends to look at it."

"They didn't send anyone from headquarters at Guarstyad, just two Magi'i and some Mirror Engineers."

"You said there were some references to that dissident ruin. I'd wager there aren't any mentions of this one. That will concern headquarters. They'll send a commander." Byelt offers a lopsided smile. "That'll give him something to do besides fretting and drafting directives, or maneuvering to become Captain-Commander or Majer-Commander." With a shrug, the majer adds, "Who knows? He might find something useful."

"When do you think someone will arrive?" *Assuming headquarters thinks sending a commander is worth it.* While Alyiakal remains dubious about someone coming from headquarters, he *knows* that a senior magus will at least want to look at the hamlet in hopes of finding something of interest or value.

"Not for another two eightdays. It could be a little sooner. In the meantime . . ." Byelt looks to Alyiakal.

"We need to get Staalt used to riding patrols and ready for raiders."

"There will be raiders," replies Byelt. "More likely fewer, but you've seen evidence that someone from the north is interested."

"I'd say raiders moving south from the grasslands, encouraged, or pushed by the Cerlynese, and possibly by increased patrols from Pemedra."

"Or all of them. I'll see you at mess." Byelt nods and heads back to his own study.

Once Byelt leaves, Alyiakal smiles sardonically. The Summer is looking more and more interesting. Then he picks up the draft patrol schedule.

Later, as time for the evening meal approaches, Alyiakal leaves early and makes his way to the mess, entering, and, with no one else around, raising a concealment to wait, standing to the side.

Staalt enters the mess first, looking around, followed quickly by Paersol.

"It's not exactly impressive," declares Paersol. "The fare's not bad for a border post, though."

"I wouldn't know," admits Staalt. "But it couldn't be much worse than at Chaelt. Fish with a side of fish."

"Here it tends more toward mutton. Some fowl and beef. Every so often, red deer. That's a bit gamy for me. What do you think of Lhaarat so far?"

"I'm not sure what to think," replies Staalt. "Is this a typical post?"

"I'm not the one to ask." As another figure enters the mess, Paersol says, "Dhaerl would have a better idea."

There's a silence for a moment, and Alyiakal wonders if Dhaerl is smiling, chuckling, or just considering.

"It's pretty much like other border posts in most ways," says the most senior captain. "Most have three or four companies and a majer or subcommander in charge. We get fewer raids, but that seems to be changing."

"Do overcaptains usually command companies directly?" asks Staalt.

"Never heard of it before. But then, never seen an overcaptain like him."

"What do you mean? Isn't an overcaptain an overcaptain?"

"There are lots of different overcaptains. You'll see. He's black-angel scary at times. Sees things no one else does. Finds things. Never misses with a firelance."

"So why is he here?"

"Headquarters decided that. My guess is that they put him here as an easier posting and to get him prepared to command one of the smaller and more dangerous border posts."

"Easier posting?"

"His previous postings were at Guarstyad and Pemedra," says Dhaerl laconically.

Alyiakal eases toward the door to the mess and into the corridor and out of sight, waiting until Vaarkas arrives and making sure that Byelt isn't nearby. Then he drops the concealment and waits a few moments before entering, saying, "As you were," followed by, "I see you've all met Undercaptain Staalt."

"If barely," declares Vaarkas with a smile.

Paersol just nods.

"Even with Undercaptain Staalt's arrival," says Alyiakal, "the patrol schedule will be the same, but I'll be accompanying Undercaptain Staalt on his first patrol." He turns to Dhaerl. "Since you're leaving on eightday, I'd appreciate it if you'd brief the undercaptain on as much as you can tomorrow."

Dhaerl offers a broad smile. "I'd be happy to."

"Listen closely," says Alyiakal cheerfully, "Dhaerl's forgotten more than most captains ever learn."

"Exactly," adds Byelt as he steps into the mess and gestures to the table. When the other officers have seated themselves, he raises his wineglass. "To our new arrival."

After the toast and after everyone has been served, Alyiakal turns to Staalt. "Where are you from originally?"

"Deuvor. It's up the river from Cyad. It's where most of the whitestone comes from."

"Your family still there?" Alyiakal prompts.

Staalt nods.

"I'm not at all familiar with the area around Cyad," Alyiakal says, "but Paersol is from Sollend. Is that far from Deuvor?"

"They're across the river from each other," Paersol says quickly. "There's a good bridge connecting the two, but the towns are definitely different."

Staalt again nods but doesn't speak.

Alyiakal suspects that means that Sollend is more of a Magi'i retreat from Cyad, while Deuvor is Merchanter-dominated.

"How did you end up in the Mirror Lancers?" asks Vaarkas.

"If you're from a Merchanter family, don't want to be a Merchanter and don't have magely abilities, what else is there?" replies Staalt in a cheerful tone.

Alyiakal senses the tone doesn't reflect what Staalt feels, but he asks, "What part of your training at Kynstaar did you like the best?"

"Riding, by far."

The instant response matches what Staalt feels, and that affords Alyiakal a certain amount of relief. Alyiakal smiles. "Well, you'll get a lot of riding here. Some of the necessary patrols entail a long day in the saddle, and some of that will be on trails, as well."

"Trails, ser?"

"Some raiders don't limit themselves to roads."

"Most of them, anymore," adds Vaarkas. "Or so it seems."

"Did you have a long trip?" Alyiakal asks Staalt.

"The longest part was getting to Kynstaar. After that, it wasn't too bad. I was a bit surprised when the firewagon stopped at Terimot. I'd never heard of it."

"Stay in the Mirror Lancers, and you'll encounter more than a few places you've never heard of," says Vaarkas.

"And some you'll wish you never had," adds Dhaerl dryly.

Alyiakal smiles wryly but from that point on lets others do most of the talking. He also realizes that he'll miss the levelheaded and often laconic Dhaerl, who reminds him of Torkaal.

But that's part of being a Mirror Lancer.

LXXIX

On twoday morning, under a hazy green-blue sky that promises a warm day, although it will be cooler higher in the hills, Alyiakal rides up and joins Staalt as the undercaptain musters Second Company for patrol along the main east road.

"Good morning, Staalt." Alyiakal looks him over, checking that the undercaptain has two water bottles, which he does, unlike Alyiakal, who has made a habit of carrying three, all filled with ale slightly diluted with order-infused water.

"Good morning, ser."

"You're in command of the company. If you miss something, or if I want the company to do something, I'll tell you, and you'll give the orders."

"Yes, ser."

"I will also emphasize again: Trust and rely on your senior squad leader."

"Yes, ser."

Once Second Company rides north from the post, Alyiakal creates his order funnel, then senses ahead, finding only the order/chaos patterns of birds and small animals as the company begins the long slow climb into the hills.

"Ser," begins Staalt, "how often do patrols encounter mountain cats?"

"Almost never. The same is true of red deer. Both mountain cats and red deer can hear and smell us, so they avoid patrols. That's why, if you do hear a traitor bird, there's a good chance there's a person nearby."

Staalt nods thoughtfully.

As the company proceeds, Alyiakal points out the logging road.

"How much timber do they take from there, do you know, ser?"

"I have no real idea. I've been told that they especially look for rarer woods, like black lorken and goldenwood, and that perhaps once a year wagons come to Gairtyn to buy those."

"That has to be good, or traders wouldn't come that far," says Staalt quietly.

"My guess as well," replies Alyiakal.

Alyiakal also points out the side road ending in the collapsed tunnel.

"These hills don't look like they'd have ores of much value," says Staalt.

"Not here, anyway."

"Apparently not," Alyiakal chuckles. "No one else has tried."

When the company nears the River Lhaar, Alyiakal says quietly, "The overlook is usually a good place to call a break. The area is wide enough and flat enough that you and the scouts can see anyone approaching for a fair distance."

"Yes, ser."

After a break at the overlook, Second Company continues on the east road. When they near the next branching road, Alyiakal says to Staalt, "The road to the right has been used at times by raiders, as well as connecting side trails. About twenty kays south, the road dips into a valley extending south-southwest. A wall and a gate block the road there. So far, no one in that valley has conducted raids into Cyador. Unless or until they do, we're to leave them alone." Alyiakal suspects that those in the valley trade with hamlets in Cyador using roads or trails from the valley's south end, but since no raids have ever been traced to the valley, the majer has suggested learning more is not a priority. Alyiakal, however, is not about to get into that with Staalt.

"Walled off and you leave them alone?"

"At present, those lands are not considered a part of Cyador. If a hamlet isn't in Cyador and it doesn't harbor brigands or raiders, we leave them alone."

"But . . ." Staalt breaks off his words.

"Undercaptain, every time that we attack a hamlet or kill someone from a hamlet, we make enemies. There's no point in making enemies unnecessarily. We do insist on the freedom to travel the main roads and have had to fight to assert that right. We try to use as little force as necessary, when *and only when* it has been required."

"How often have you personally had to exert that right, ser?"

"Three times, so far. Twice here, and once at Guarstyad. It's unlikely you'll have that problem here, but it could happen if you're posted somewhere else in the future. Usually, troublemakers remember for a few years."

When Second Company reaches the rocky area, and the dead evergreen that conceals the hidden entrance, Alyiakal has Staalt call a halt. Then he points to the dead tree. "Behind that tree is the trail to the dissident hamlet. You're not to go there unless you've been attacked by raiders, and you actually track them to this point."

"Ser?"

"The Magi'i, and possibly officers from Mirror Lancer headquarters, will likely want to investigate the hamlet. They might not appreciate any of us destroying anything."

"Do you really think they'll even travel this far for something that old?"

"I think so. I could be wrong, but we should know in an eightday or so. Until then, the order stands."

"Yes, ser." After a moment, Staalt asks, "Do you think there's anything valuable left?"

Ah, there's the Merchanter background. "Besides the structures and the road, I doubt it, but if the Magi'i want to investigate, they'll make that determination."

"Did you find anything at Guarstyad, ser?"

"Old firelances, some mirror shields, a chaos-powered cart, and a chaos stonecutter. But they'd all lost their chaos over the years."

The undercaptain nods.

"Today, this is where the patrol will end. As I told you before, you need to become familiar with the road so that you can instantly tell if something is different." Alyiakal gestures. "Another ten kays to the east, this road joins the high road. That's where the log-walled fort is. I pointed that out when we went over the maps, but what you see is often different from what you see on a map." After a moment, Alyiakal asks, "Do you have any questions?"

"Not right now, ser."

"Then let's head back."

On the return ride to the post, the company passes two carts heaped with firewood, and an empty logging wagon returning to Gairtyn. Along the way, Alyiakal points out a few more items that Staalt should know.

Having dismissed Second Company to duties, Alyiakal grooms and stables the chestnut and walks back to his study. Before he can enter, Byelt calls, "How did it go?"

Alyiakal steps into the majer's study, closing the door. "He rides well, seems to pay attention to details. He does comment a bit on value."

"His Merchanter background, no doubt. What else?"

"He probably doesn't know as much as he thinks, but that was true of all of us, I suspect."

Byelt barks a short laugh.

"No dispatch riders?"

"It'll be another eightday, at least. Headquarters might even want to know more before deciding."

"They did at Guarstyad."

"Then again, seeing as you're the one who found this place, they might not need more information."

"I won't second-guess headquarters."

"Good. Because there's no point. That's all I wanted to know." Byelt smiles. "How are you coming with the directives that arrived with Staalt?"

"You should have my comments tomorrow morning."

"Good. I'll see you at mess."

Alyiakal walks from Byelt's study to his own and settles behind his desk. While he wonders what sort of patrol report Staalt will turn in, his pressing concern is finishing the comments on the latest directives, at least one of which seems meaningless.

LXXX

Alyiakal is about to leave his quarters before morning mess on the second fiveday of Summer when there's a rap on his door. He opens it on the duty ranker.

"The north lookout saw riders to the north of Gairtyn early this morning. Only for a bit."

"Thank you." *So much for breakfast.* "Run to the kitchen and tell the cooks I need trail rations for First Company in two quints, sooner if they can manage it. Then let the majer know First Company is heading out." Alyiakal grabs his visor cap, riding gloves, and jacket—and his water bottles—and hurries for the senior squad leaders' study, hoping to find Chaaltyn there.

The senior squad leader isn't there, but Alyiakal finds Chaaltyn in the courtyard on his way. "First Company needs to mount up and head out immediately. The lookout saw riders north of Gairtyn. It might be nothing, but we can't afford to gamble on that. I've already told the cooks to get us trail rations."

"Yes, ser. We'll have the men ready."

Alyiakal walks swiftly to the kitchen door and steps inside.

Drassyl hurries toward him with a pitcher of ale. "The boys'll have water and trail rations in the stable courtyard in less than a quint. Thought you might need this."

"I will, thank you."

After filling the three water bottles and stuffing some hard biscuits into his riding jacket, Alyiakal makes for the stable, where he saddles the chestnut and leads him into the courtyard to mount. While he's one of the first there, in a fraction of a quint, lancers appear and begin to form up. Two of the cooks' boys appear and hand out trail rations, while a third cook begins filling water bottles.

In little more than a quint, First Company rides out of the post and heads west to the crossroads where the north road leads to Gairtyn.

"You think it's raiders, ser?" asks Chaaltyn.

"It could be more raider scouts, raiders, Cerlynese, a holder after an escaped horse, or nothing at all. But the exercise won't hurt. We may have to do this again." Although the sun hasn't cleared the hills and mountains to the east, Alyiakal, nevertheless, deploys his order funnel, collecting what chaos bits he can.

Early as it is, more than a handful of people work outside the small town, and several men ready a logging wagon as First Company reaches the end of the road and continues east to the end of the valley, before heading north for the old logging road. Alyiakal worries about the possibility that the raiders—or the Cerlynese—might have told the scouts to be sure they were seen as a way to lure Mirror Lancers into an ambush. But Alyiakal senses only small animals in the trees, and possibly a red deer moving away from the valley.

When Raayls nears the trail up to the logging road, he reins up and signals, and when Alyiakal nears, he calls out, "New tracks. Two riders. Came down and headed back up."

Alyiakal still can't sense any riders, and shouts, "Scouts! Lead the way!"

Followed by Maaetz, Raayls starts along the animal trail through the trees, more passable now because of all the patrols. Alyiakal and First Company follow, re-forming two abreast past the pile of fallen limbs. From the old road to the depression between two outcrops, the only recent tracks are those of two riders. Alyiakal still senses no one else.

Not yet, anyway.

As Alyiakal rides up the logging road northwest, he begins to sense fleeting order/chaos patterns and signals Raayls and Maaetz to halt.

"What is it, ser?" asks Chaaltyn.

"Call it a feeling. Raayls, post yourself a hundred yards ahead, Maaetz fifty. If you see anything, halt, and signal. Don't make a sound."

"Yes, ser."

Alyiakal waits until the scouts are in position before ordering First Company forward. The company rides uphill for a kay before he senses the faint order/chaos patterns of mounted figures. Ahead of him, the road flattens as it curves left, then corrects slightly to the right, entering the flat logged area, but the patterns are higher up.

Alyiakal turns to Chaaltyn. "We'll start through the flat area ahead, but if I give the order to flank me, first squad is to spread out evenly on me, each lancer behind a tree, as much as possible, lances ready. They're not to use them until I give the order. Pass those orders back."

"Yes, ser." Once Chaaltyn relays the order to the lancers behind him, he asks, "Do you think someone is coming?"

"I think it's likely, and I don't want the company outflanked in the middle of the trees. If we're spread first, with some cover, we'll have the better position." *Even if the raiders have horn bows.*

First Company enters the reforested area, following the path widened by previous patrols, and rides close to half a kay before Alyiakal clearly senses a score of riders moving down the narrow trail above.

After riding several hundred yards farther, Alyiakal senses when Raayls halts, before Maaetz relays Raayls's signal. Alyiakal waits until he sees Maaetz's signal before motioning for the scouts to pull back.

"Riders entering the flat area, less than a half kay away," reports Raayls when he reins up beside Alyiakal. "Couldn't see much more than that."

"Scouts, flank me," orders Alyiakal, adding to Chaaltyn, "First squad flank as ordered. Ready arms. Silent riding."

The flanking movement seems hardly silent to Alyiakal, but he hopes the oncoming riders are far enough away that the sounds of horses and the occasional cracking of small branches will not carry to them.

Then the waiting begins. Alyiakal worries, knowing that he hasn't gathered much chaos, and hopes First Company can surprise the attackers and disperse them without too many casualties.

While Alyiakal can sense the raiders' approach, he doesn't see them until a raider appears on the trail directly in front of Alyiakal, little more than thirty yards away. The raider nocks and looses a shaft that breaks on Alyiakal's shield. Another shaft follows the first.

"Mirror Lancers in the trees ahead!" shouts someone. "Spread out!"

Sensing when the first raider moves to loose another shaft, Alyiakal guides a quick firelance bolt into the man, leaving a smoldering patch on the tree trunk.

"Get 'em from the sides!" yells another raider.

Alyiakal barely understands their words, but definitely grasps the intent.

For close to a glass, firelance bolts flare in one direction and arrows fly in the other.

Alyiakal senses death mists, mostly in front of him, but at least once to his left.

The raiders loose fewer and fewer shafts until they stop abruptly. No more shafts fly toward Alyiakal, and he senses a handful of raiders turning and withdrawing. "First squad, forward! Form up behind me on the trail. Second and third squads! Re-form and follow!"

He urges the chestnut forward, trying to close the gap between himself and the retreating raiders.

None of the raiders slow, but Alyiakal begins to catch up with the four riders once he enters the older growth higher on the slope, where the larger trees are farther apart. He's less than half a kay behind the last raider when, up ahead, he sees where the trail widens and joins the high road. The four remaining raiders reach the high road, hesitate, and turn east.

The trailing raider slumps in his saddle, and his mount halts.

Alyiakal puzzles over that as he continues up the trail, until he senses a squad or more of riders to the north on the high road. *Mounted archers! From the north?* Strangely, the riders aren't moving. Alyiakal has an uneasy feeling; those riders aren't acting like raiders.

Given the trees and the terrain, the archers among the new band of riders won't be able to see or target first squad until the squad reaches the high road.

Do you want to try it?

Alyiakal nods to himself.

He turns slightly to Chaaltyn. "There are more raiders ahead." *Just a slight misidentification.* "They won't see us until the moment we reach the high road. Just before we reach the road, we'll go to a fast trot. When we hit the road, we'll turn left and charge the raiders. Keep a tight two-abreast formation behind me. Pass it back."

"Yes, ser."

Alyiakal turns his concentration to the trail ahead.

Even when he nears the high road, the riders, less than fifty yards to the west, do not move.

Alyiakal shifts his shield into a large wedge, then urges the chestnut into a fast trot over the last few yards to the high road, turning north, but holding back until most of first squad is directly behind him, when he orders "Charge!" and immediately looses a series of chaos bolts into the first ranks of the riders.

For several moments, shafts fly at first squad, but flare away from the charging lancers as they strike Alyiakal's shields. Each impact is a needle on the skin of his chest and upper arms.

In moments, the riders arrayed on the road attempt to turn and flee, exposing them to the firelances. In less than a third of a quint the riders, and often their mounts, are ashes or strewn across the road. Somewhere, a horse screams.

A single rider remains, and turns his mount north, flattening himself against its neck. Alyiakal raises his firelance, boosting the firebolt with the remainder of his gathered chaos. The last rider flares into ashes, along with his mount. Tiny lightnings of pain knife through Alyiakal's skull, and he shudders in the saddle. *Shouldn't have pushed that far.*

"Angel-fired blast," mutters Chaaltyn.

"I didn't want him to get away. Not after something this cruel." Each word vibrates in Alyiakal's skull. His hands tremble as he fumbles open a water bottle and slowly drinks the ale.

After a time, Alyiakal says slowly, "Collect all the weapons and tack. See if they look like they're from Cerlyn. Then drag the bodies and everything else into the woods, out of sight. In a bit, I'll need to look at the wounded. Ours first."

Chaaltyn looks at Alyiakal, then looks away.

More than half a quint passes before Alyiakal feels steady enough to look at the wounded. He turns to Chaaltyn, who has just returned. "How many did we lose?"

"Just one—Paawl. Shaft through the neck."

Alyiakal winces. "Wounded?"

"Three of ours. One of theirs. He was fortunate, if you want to call it that. Unhorsed by a tree branch, knocked out, and broke his arm. Ghaan took a shaft in his upper arm, stayed to help the other two wounded, and heard the raider. They brought him up the trail."

Alyiakal begins by dealing with Ghaan's arm, cleaning, dressing, and binding it. "I'll need to see you every day for a while. Otherwise, it might fester."

"Yes, ser."

Both Fhraanz and Kael have shoulder wounds from shafts, which should heal. Then Alyiakal turns to the wounded raider, noting that he barely looks seventeen, if that.

He checks the youth's head, which has a set of shallow gashes, but senses no wound chaos inside the skull. The break in the arm is simple, requiring a temporary splint, and Alyiakal says, "You'll get a plaster cast in a day or so."

"Why bother? You killed everyone else."

"Consider yourself fortunate." Alyiakal looks up to Chaaltyn, still mounted. "Were all the raiders young?"

"Couldn't say for sure. No signs of any graybeards, though."

That supports Alyiakal's suspicions. He turns back to the injured raider. "You're from the grasslands west of the Grass Hills and south of Cerlyn, aren't you?"

The surprise in the youth's eyes and body is more than evident.

"The Cerlynese came and took a score of young men and escorted you here. They said the only way you could escape was to go down the trail and into the valley, and they'd kill you if you tried to return." *Or something like that.* As he finishes, Alyiakal senses Chaaltyn's surprise, as well as that of the other three wounded.

The youth does not speak.

"Suit yourself." Alyiakal steps back and walks to mount up, talking to Chaaltyn as he does. "There's no point in chasing the three who escaped. They have bows, without shafts, and old blades. They'll be fortunate to survive an eightday unless they persuade someone to take them in. We need to head back to the post. Do we have enough horses for the tack and weapons?"

"Yes, ser. We caught five mounts, and there's Paawl's, also, if necessary."

"What about the weapons, a uniform or two, and the tack?"

"Only about half the bodies weren't totally charred or turned to ashes. The riders up here all wore dark green uniforms. The tack looks similar to the other raiders'."

Alyiakal wants to shake his head, but given how much it still aches, he doesn't.

"I'll get the company formed up, ser."

"Good." Alyiakal takes a long swallow of ale from one of the water bottles, followed by a hard trail biscuit, knowing that he needs to regain some strength.

Once First Company starts down the trail to the logged-over area, Chaaltyn asks quietly, "How did you know the Cerlynese were there, ser?"

"I didn't know who it was, but the surviving raiders turned east, and one took a shaft or more in the back. That meant someone was to the west preventing them from going that way, and that suggests Cerlynese to me."

"That makes sense."

Except it doesn't, not to Alyiakal. He knows the Cerlynese don't like Mirror Lancers or Cyador, but why would they capture and force barely trained barbarians to ride more than a hundred kays to get them largely killed by Mirror Lancers?

He ponders this until First Company nears the end of the old logging road. Another thought crosses his mind, and he calls Raayls back.

"Ser?" asks the scout.

"Before the company gets there, go ahead, and check any hoofprints that the raider scouts left on the ground beyond the trees—see if you can find any untouched. Raiders don't usually send scouts ahead to move in the open long enough for someone to see them."

"See what you mean, ser. I'll look close." Raayls turns his mount downhill again.

Little more than half a quint later, when Alyiakal rides out of the trees, Raayls rides up alongside him.

"Were you able to find anything?"

"Not much, but one of them even rode up on that little rise over there," says Raayls, pointing to his right.

"What about the hoofprints?"

"They all look pretty much the same, ser."

Suggestive that all the horses came from Cerlyn, but not definite proof. "Thank you. I appreciate it, Raayls."

Raayls nods, then rides ahead, as Alyiakal orders the company forward, to the post.

More than two quints later, as First Company rides through Gairtyn, Alyiakal almost wishes Vhoraal would peer out, but there's no sign of the town headman, and most of the townspeople who are out barely note the lancers. Alyiakal does notice that the two new dwellings are complete, and the smoke rising from one of the chimneys suggests that it's occupied.

The company has to wait short of the bridge over the River Lhaar to allow a timber wagon to cross, but then rides unimpeded to the post.

Once he orders First Company to a halt, Alyiakal turns to Chaaltyn. "Unload the tack, weapons, and uniforms in a clear space in the stables where the majer can look at it." *If he chooses to.* "Put the raider in the brig. I'll deal with him later. I can't put a cast on his arm until tomorrow anyway. The three wounded go to the infirmary. I'll need to check them again after I report to the majer." *When I'm steadier and can use more order.*

"Yes, ser."

"Company!" orders Alyiakal. "Dismissed to duties!"

Then Alyiakal rides to the stable, where he dismounts, carefully, and leads the chestnut to his stall, unsaddling and grooming him, and making sure he's settled before leaving the stables and walking across the courtyard in the afternoon sun to the headquarters building.

He doesn't even try to enter his study, instead going straight into Byelt's.

"You left in quite a hurry this morning," says the majer evenly. "Was there anything to it?"

"Some fifteen very young raiders and some thirty troopers from Cerlyn," replies Alyiakal dryly, settling into the chair opposite the center of the majer's desk.

When he finishes outlining the morning's events, Byelt remains silent for several moments, then says, "So you killed most of the raiders and all the Cerlynese troopers? Was killing them all necessary?"

"We didn't have much choice, and we didn't kill all the raiders. We took out ten; the Cerlynese killed one; three escaped; and we brought back one wounded captive. We lost one lancer to an arrow through the neck, and have three wounded, who should survive."

"You have this tendency not to leave many survivors, Alyiakal."

"When people try to kill me or my men, I don't want to have to fight them again. I'm not indiscriminate. We only killed three when the raiders attacked us in the dissidents' hamlet, and only the barbarians who attacked us at the log fort." Alyiakal pauses, adding, "Besides, the Cerlynese deserved it and then some. They essentially kidnapped young grassland barbarians, set them up—"

"Set them up?"

"They sent two scouts down to parade around where our lookouts could see them, then forced the barbarians to go down the trail. Then the Cerlynese patrolled that stretch of road to make sure the barbarian youth rode down into the valley. We reacted faster than the Cerlynese expected, but even if we hadn't, some of the barbarians, if not all, would have ended up dead. I very much doubt they would have laid down their arms." Alyiakal shrugs. "In fact, the moment they saw us, they loosed shafts before we used a single firelance."

"I believe you," says Byelt earnestly, "but none of this makes sense. The closest part of Cerlyn is well over a hundred kays from here."

"With what we know now," replies Alyiakal, "it seems bizarre. I don't know whether the idea was to claim we murdered innocent young men or to get everyone on the border angrier at Cyador or to divert attention from Cerlyn to Lhaarat, or something else entirely." He pauses. "But we've found Cerlynese tack and blades before. That means there's some kind of trade taking place using the high road. I wondered about that earlier, but what happened today makes me think it's more than trade." *And that's an understatement.*

"Write it up, even more carefully than you usually do. Facts only. None of the surmises you've laid out. I'll send it to headquarters. The Majer-Commander can draw his own conclusions, and that's definitely as it should be."

"Yes, ser." Alyiakal nods and leaves the majer's study, heading to the infirmary to check more closely on the lancer wounded. After that, he'll go to the brig.

LXXXI

When he wakes early on sixday morning, Alyiakal sits up in bed, winces, and looks down at his chest, taking in the scattered identical bruises. *You need to carry heavier shields.*

Then his thoughts return to the question that he'd been pondering since his return to the post. *Why did the barbarians attack?* The young barbarian facing Alyiakal had nocked and loosed his shaft well before Alyiakal or any lancer used a firelance. Had they been told that the Mirror Lancers would kill them on sight?

He shakes his head. Lancers respond to force with force, but the only time the Mirror Lancers attacked first was in response to a raid or if attacked a second time by the same force.

He washes and shaves hurriedly, trying to spare himself the cold air in his quarters, then dresses and heads across the courtyard through the light but biting wind to the brig.

Yosert stands as Alyiakal enters the small antechamber that accesses the three cells.

"I thought you'd be here early, ser."

"How is he?"

"How are any of the young and stupid barbarians?"

"Can you and whoever else is here get him to the infirmary right away? I need to put a cast on his arm."

"We can do that, ser. He won't appreciate it."

"Not now. He might later. Dietro did."

"I'll give you that, ser."

"Thank you."

From the brig, Alyiakal hurries to the infirmary, where he checks Ghaan's wound first. As he had suspected, there are small bits of orangish-red-white wound chaos in several places. He hadn't been at his sharpest after the fighting.

"This might hurt," Alyiakal reassures Ghaan, as he gently touches the dressing above each area while simultaneously easing order around each spot.

"Doesn't hurt. Feels a bit warm, though, ser."

"You'll stay here for another day or so. Then we'll see."

Alyiakal then looks at Fhraanz, whose shoulder wound has more chaos than Ghaan's. "I'm going to have to re-dress this."

"Whatever you need to do, ser."

While there are bits of wound chaos around the wound entry, Alyiakal is more concerned about where the arrow point gashed the bone. After using order-infused spirits to clean the wound externally, Alyiakal applies order to the deeper wound chaos.

Fhraanz stiffens but says nothing.

"You're going to be here for a few days," Alyiakal says. "That wound's a bit nastier than I thought."

"Ser?"

"You should be fine. Healing will just take longer."

Kael's superficial wound contains less wound chaos.

Alyiakal leaves Kael and turns to the captured raider youth and says pleasantly, "It would help if I knew your name."

"Does it matter?"

"I'm Overcaptain Alyiakal. I'll heal your arm regardless of whether I know your name."

"Why bother, if you're going to kill me?"

"Who said anything about killing you?"

"You killed all the others."

Alyiakal shakes his head. "Four of you tried to escape from us and the Cerlynese. They killed one of you. The other three escaped east on the high road. They might survive if they throw themselves on the mercy of the local hamlets. We killed those of you who attacked us. We didn't use our firelances until you fired at us. Now, let's look at your arm. Sit on that stool and rest the splint on the table."

The youth looks puzzled.

"I don't want you to move it. After I remove the splint and look at your arm, I'll see if it's safe enough for a cast. That's plaster and cloth that holds the broken bone together while it heals and will protect it."

Abruptly, the youth says, "Taaryan."

"Thank you, Taaryan."

A quint passes before Yosert and another lancer escort Taaryan back to the brig. During that time, Alyiakal does not question the youth; he only explains his medical actions and why—but nothing about the unseen order healing.

Then he hurries to the mess.

"You're a little late," observes Byelt.

"I was checking on the wounded lancers, and I had to put a cast on the prisoner's arm. All that took a little longer." Alyiakal slips into his seat.

"Why didn't you put a cast on yesterday, ser?" asks Staalt.

"Sometimes the arm swells. You need to wait until the swelling subsides so that the cast holds the bone in place."

"How did you get to be a field healer?" asks Staalt.

"When I was in training at Kynstaar, a magus noted I had higher order levels and suggested that I be trained as a field healer if I got through training. I did, but I had to wait for an eightday before the supplies and replacements were ready to go to Pemedra. I worked long glasses every day under a Magi'i healer, who taught me everything she could in that time."

"Was she attractive, ser?" asks Vaarkas, with a smile.

"Very, and she was also fifteen years older and probably had enough talent to have been a magus. I wasn't about to do anything except what she told me to."

Byelt smiles. "Wise of you."

"Do women of the Magi'i really have chaos powers?" asks Staalt.

"At least a few do," replies Alyiakal. "Beyond that, I couldn't say. But then, not all men born into the Magi'i have those abilities, either."

Paersol nods slightly but does not speak.

"Do you think we'll see more of the Cerlynese?" asks Vaarkas, looking to Alyiakal.

"The Cerlynese are up to something, but that's just a feeling. I'm hoping the disappearance of some thirty troopers might give them pause, but anyone willing to set barbarians up is certainly capable of doing more. I just can't predict what it might be, or when."

Alyiakal also can't help wondering about how the hamlet with the timber fort ended up with bronze shields capable of deflecting firelance chaos bolts, or the trade between the dissident/raider hamlet and Cerlyn. *Mere trade? Something more?*

After breakfast, Alyiakal returns to his study and takes out his maps: from Pemedra, those he's created, and his atlas. Since there are no detailed maps of much of the intervening area, he needs to discover how the roads and geography might link the two areas—at least theoretically.

LXXXII

The days after the skirmish with the grass barbarians get increasingly hotter, particularly in the valley, so that patrols into the hills east of Lhaarat afford some relief from the still heat blanketing the post. Not a single company encounters raiders or even tracks of large groups of riders, let alone Cerlynese armsmen. Nor are there any raids on hamlets in the valley. Alyiakal checks on his wounded, imparting small bits of order to remove wound chaos. He also talks to Taaryan about his options, much as he had with Dietro.

After two eightdays, headquarters has yet to respond to the finding of the dissident structure or Alyiakal's report of the Cerlynese involvement in a barbarian attack, nor has Saelora answered his latest letter.

In midafternoon on sixday of the fourth eightday of Summer, Alyiakal has just returned to his study after conducting a training exercise in the woods to the south of the post, designed to improve First Company's operations in that terrain. He's not particularly satisfied with the results and is considering how to improve the company's effectiveness when a dispatch rider hurries into Byelt's study.

Even as the dispatch rider leaves, the majer calls out, "Alyiakal!"

Byelt's tone of voice alerts Alyiakal, and he swiftly enters the majer's study, closing the door.

"Yes, ser?"

Byelt gestures for Alyiakal to take a chair, then says, "An investigation team from headquarters will arrive late on eightday. It's headed by Commander Laartol, and a team of two Magi'i, a senior Mirror Engineer . . . and, of course, a squad of lancers."

"Do you get any word beyond their arrival?"

"Only that the commander and his party will be looking into a number of matters, including the reputed dissident dwellings and the apparent Cerlynese intrusion."

"That wording suggests a certain doubt on the part of some at Mirror Lancer headquarters."

"I have my thoughts," says Byelt. "What are yours?"

"First, I hope the Cerlynese don't show up while the commander's here, but there's not much we can do about that. We should increase patrols to the north, so we're not caught unaware. It'll have to be Vaarkas and Paersol."

"Makes sense. The commander's going to want to talk to you and your squad leaders. What else?"

"There's never been much said about the dissidents."

"They certainly didn't let me, or anyone I know, find out," interjects Byelt. "I had to learn it from you."

"The new post was named after the old road, and I don't think much was conveyed to officers or others in the Mirror Lancers. I'd say that they want anything about the dissidents buried. As for Cerlyn, there's always been something about the copper trade that hasn't been right. After Emperor Kieffal built the post at Pemedra and talked about gaining control of Cerlynese copper mines . . . well . . . we know that outcome."

Byelt nods slowly. "Unfortunately. Do you know anything about the commander and the others in his party?"

"Laartol was the subcommander picked to set up the post at Guarstyad, and he was in command of the effort against the Kyphrans. Thiaphyl and Ataphi were the mages, and Mirror Engineer Skaarn investigated the dissident ruins and artifacts. I'm guessing some of them will be here because they already know about the dissidents, but that's only a guess."

"The commander knows you."

"For better or worse," replies Alyiakal dryly.

"For better, I'd judge," says Byelt. "You *are* an overcaptain."

"Both Kortyl and I were promoted with the same date of rank."

Byelt frowns for a moment, then nods. "That means you both did a good job of handling a difficult situation. Headquarters likes that."

"Let's hope they like what we've done here," replies Alyiakal.

"What do you suggest about quartering the group?"

"Give Laartol my quarters. Put the two Magi'i in my old study. I can double up with Vaarkas, and Paersol and Staalt can double up. The Mirror

Engineer majer gets the other officer's room. We have some spare beds, and there's more than enough space in the lancer barracks. Some might have to do with pallets."

"I'll leave it to you to take care of that."

"I'll get right on it." Alyiakal pauses. "Did the messenger deliver anything else?"

"He said all the regular dispatches and letters would arrive with the commander and his party."

"Thank you, ser." Alyiakal leaves in search of the senior squad leaders. He'll also need to let Drassyl, the head cook, know, as well as the ostlers. He'd hoped for a letter from Saelora before anyone from Mirror Lancer headquarters arrived, not only because he enjoys and appreciates every letter, but also in the event she could pass on anything about Cerlyn and trading.

But that will have to wait.

LXXXIII

In late afternoon on eightday, half a glass after Paersol and Fourth Company return and report no signs of large numbers of riders on the northern high road, the lookouts sight a short column of riders heading toward the post. Alyiakal and Byelt ensure they're standing in front of the headquarters building when Commander Laartol and his party ride in.

Laartol looks much as Alyiakal remembers—wiry, with silver-shot black hair and hazel eyes—but his face looks thinner and slightly drawn, and his hair has more silver than black.

"Welcome to Lhaarat Post, Commander," declares Byelt.

"Thank you, Majer . . . Overcaptain," replies Laartol. "It seems you've had an interesting Summer, but we'll talk about that later."

"We've arranged for quarters for your party."

Even before Byelt can say more, Laartol declares, "Whatever you've done will be fine. We're well aware Lhaarat is a border post and not accustomed to having excess officers or lancers. We're just glad to be here." He offers a rueful smile. "It's been a while since I've spent this much time in the saddle. I'm certain I'll feel it even more tomorrow."

Alyiakal senses the commander's genuine warmth, at least for the present.

"Before we ride to the stables and dismount, I'd like to introduce Senior Magus Thiaphyl and Magus Kiel"—he gestures to the white-clad, if dusty, Magi'i—"and Mirror Engineer Majer Skaarn." Laartol then adds, "Majer Byelt is the post commander, and deputy post commander Overcaptain Alyiakal discovered the ruins."

From Skaarn's resigned expression, Alyiakal gets the impression the Mirror Engineer would rather be anywhere but Lhaarat. *He knows that there's likely nothing new to be discovered and feels that his time is being wasted traveling to a backwater of Cyador.*

Alyiakal accompanies the party to the stable on foot, then escorts the officers and Magi'i back to the officers' quarters, where he directs each to their chambers.

Thiaphyl looks at Alyiakal questioningly when shown Alyiakal's former study.

Alyiakal replies, "This is the best we can do. Except for the post commander, all the post officers are doubling up to make space available."

Thiaphyl shakes his head. "I suppose there's no help for it." He carries his small duffel into the chamber, followed by Kiel.

As Alyiakal is about to return to his study, Laartol steps out into the corridor and motions.

"Yes, ser?"

"Do you have a moment, Overcaptain?"

Alyiakal smiles. "As much time as you require, ser."

Laartol smiles wryly in return. "You still have the ability to be perfectly obedient without being subservient. We need to talk." He gestures toward the open door.

Alyiakal enters his, temporarily, former quarters, and the commander closes the door.

"Alyiakal, how did you find this dissident ruin, honestly?"

"At the time, I was tracking raiders who seemed to be close enough to raid and didn't seem to be in any of the known hamlets or those not on the maps. From the outside, it doesn't look all that ruined, but I didn't press the issue of inspecting it at the time. I said that other Mirror Lancers might come to inspect."

"You were rather concerned with maps, as I recall."

"As much for refreshing my own memory as anything."

"I have the impression that patrolling here, until your arrival, anyway, was, shall we say, somewhat limited."

"From past patrol reports and what I learned, patrols were seldom conducted farther than ten to twelve kays from the post. I found several hamlets not on existing maps as well as a high road that may well run all the way to Cerlyn."

"How far from the post have you personally patrolled?"

"Somewhat more than twenty kays."

Laartol nods. "Thank you. I appreciate the background. We'll go over the details with the others in the morning."

"Yes, ser."

"I'll see you at the evening mess."

Alyiakal closes the quarters door as he leaves. That Laartol had questions does not surprise him; what does, however, is that he has so few, and none regarding the Cerlynese. *The commander has his reasons.*

He makes his way back to the headquarters building and begins to enter his study when Byelt calls. He turns and enters the majer's study. "Yes, ser?"

"Did the commander ask you about anything?"

"He only asked how I happened to discover the dissident community. I told him it was the result of trying to find out the raiders' origin. He said that we'd go over the details with the others in the morning."

"He ask anything else?"

"If I still had a fondness for maps. That was all."

Byelt frowns. "Why would he ask that?"

Alyiakal manages a rueful smile. "I wasn't discreet about the lack of maps when I was posted to Guarstyad."

"It sounds like he doesn't forget much."

"No, ser. I don't think he forgets anything."

"Did he give any hint of why he's here?"

"Besides asking how I discovered the dissident community? No." Alyiakal pauses. "He's very deliberate. At least he was at Guarstyad. You could never tell what he had in mind until it was announced, and sometimes not until it was accomplished."

"When did you last have any contact with him?"

"Personally, more than three years ago. He sent a letter slightly after that, confirming my promotion to overcaptain."

Byelt shakes his head. "What do you make of it all?"

"I honestly don't know." While Alyiakal has suspicions, he certainly doesn't *know*. "Maybe he'll give some indication at dinner."

"We'll see." Byelt gestures vaguely in dismissal, but his eyes are unfocused.

After Alyiakal returns to his study, he wonders if Laartol's presence has more to do with the Cerlynese and the high road than the dissidents, or if the commander is in Lhaarat because there are too many loose ends.

Then he notices the letter in his box and smiles as he recognizes the familiar blue Merchanter seal. As he carefully slits open the envelope, he also senses that Saelora's seal bears a touch of chaos and shakes his head.

> *For some reason, your last letter was delayed longer than usual . . .*

Alyiakal has no doubts that's because his letters are being read.

> *but I enjoyed it all the same. In some ways, I was surprised to hear about your discovering another ruin dating back to the First. Perhaps not completely surprised, though. You have a knack with seeing things others overlook. I hope your superiors appreciate that talent, but sometimes people don't want to know things.*
>
> *Sometimes, things are forgotten quickly—even here in Vaeyal. Someone asked me the other day who had owned the factorage before me. She was serious.*
>
> *Charissa and Gaaran's new little one was colicky when she was born, and she still isn't sleeping well. Some mornings Gaaran looks like he hasn't slept much. Mother insists that none of us were that way. She's probably remembering what she wants to . . .*
>
> *Some of the outland traders have asked Catriana if she knows where they can obtain cheaper copper. The clans in Cyad have raised prices because the war between Austra and Nordla makes traveling there dangerous . . .*

Alyiakal frowns. He's heard nothing about such a war. *Well, why would you, as far from Fyrad and Cyad as you are?*

He continues reading, smiling at her closing words.

> *. . . as always, I miss you. I'd write that you don't know how much, except that I do know the depth of your feelings.*

After a moment, he replaces the letter in the envelope and tucks it inside his uniform.

Well before the time he usually leaves for the evening mess, Alyiakal slips away. He's not surprised to find Vaarkas waiting outside the mess door.

"I thought you might be early, ser." Vaarkas pauses. "Isn't it a little unusual to send a commander to a border post?"

"It is, but it's unusual to find a surviving dissident structure, and, I suspect, concerning to hear of Cerlynese troopers using a previously unknown road. Speaking of that, when you patrol tomorrow, look very carefully for any signs of Cerlynese troopers."

"Yes, ser. Do you think they might attack?"

"I have no idea, but, with a commander here, we don't want to be caught unaware. I'm sure you understand."

"Yes, ser."

Paersol and Staalt appear, and Alyiakal gestures to the door. "We might as well go in."

A fraction of a quint later, Byelt and Laartol arrive, along with Skaarn and the two Magi'i. Once everyone is seated, Laartol sits at the head of the mess table with Byelt at his right and Skaarn at his left. Sitting beside Skaarn, Thiaphyl sits across the table from Alyiakal, with Kiel and the more junior officers farther down the table.

Alyiakal wonders whether it's the first time the table has been filled and whether there were times in the past when the post held more officers.

Laartol lifts his wineglass. "With thanks for your hospitality."

In return, Byelt toasts, "To your arrival."

Once everyone is served, Byelt asks, "Besides long, how was your trip?"

With an infectious smile, Laartol replies, "Long . . . and warm, but not excessively so. Thankfully, there's not much happening in Cyad, or there wasn't when we left. Emperor Kaartyn is being very deliberate. Rumors suggest he may pick a new Merchanter Advisor, and possibly a new fleet commander, but no one seems to know for certain. The most recent interesting news has been your discovery of a possible dissident community, but we'll defer discussion on that until you and Overcaptain Alyiakal can brief me after breakfast tomorrow. Other than that . . ." Laartol shrugs.

In the momentary silence that follows, Alyiakal looks across the table at Thiaphyl. "When you were at Oldroad Post, Magus Ataphi worked with you."

"He's currently assigned to other duties at Fyrad," replies Thiaphyl, clearly studying Alyiakal. "I'm still amazed you can carry so much order, with no signs of chaos, yet remain strong and vigorous. Usually, someone so order-bound ages more rapidly."

"I am bit young for my rank."

"Young, but deserving," interjects Laartol, in a warm tone, but his eyes fix on Thiaphyl for a moment while he continues, "as the Kyphrans discovered."

"I'm certain of that, Commander," replies Thiaphyl evenly, although Alyiakal can sense irritation.

"Ser?" asks Paersol, looking to Laartol. "Have other dissident ruins been discovered besides Guarstyad and now this site?"

Alyiakal notices a momentary wince from Vaarkas.

"Not that headquarters records show," replies Laartol mildly, "but this discovery may shed some light on that. For now, there's nothing more to say."

From that point, the conversation ranges from subdued to nonexistent, and Alyiakal makes a mental note to let Chaaltyn know that First Company should be ready to ride out in the morning.

LXXXIV

Alyiakal is already up on oneday when the duty ranker raps on the door of the room he temporarily shares with Vaarkas.

"Overcaptain, ser, Majer Byelt wants you to know that First Company should be ready to ride out after the morning briefing."

"Thank you. I'll take care of it."

Alyiakal smiles wryly, glad that he'd informed Chaaltyn the night before. Still, he needs to confirm it with the senior squad leader before mess. He finishes dressing and goes in search of his senior squad leader.

After meeting with Chaaltyn, he makes his way to the mess. Breakfast conversation is subdued, at least until everyone has eaten and the captains and the sole undercaptain are excused. Commander Laartol wishes to have all the senior personnel at the briefing, and the mess is the best suited to hold all those involved.

Laartol remains at the head of the table and begins, "Overcaptain Alyiakal, would you please relate the circumstances leading up to your discovery of the dissident community?"

Alyiakal does so, beginning with the raid which captured Dietro, relating briefly the subsequent patrols leading to the discovery of the high road, his observation of the hidden entrance and trail, and then the discovery of the second entrance leading to the stone road and the rock-face dwelling in the gorge. He includes the brief exchange with the silver-haired presumptive headwoman.

When he finishes, Laartol simply says, "Very thorough, Overcaptain." He turns to Byelt. "Very perceptive of you to insist on a full report." He looks to Thiaphyl. "Do you have any questions for the overcaptain?"

"Did you see any evidence of recent use of chaos-based devices?"

"I did not, Magus Thiaphyl. Everything I saw did not appear recent. Moss and grass had grown over the edge of the stone road. I can't speak to anything inside as we're under standing orders not to infringe on people outside the borders of Cyador unless attacked, impeded, or specifically ordered by headquarters."

"But they attacked you," returns Thiaphyl.

"Only when they thought we might attack them. When I declared who we were, they set aside their arms. I thought it best not to press the point."

"But they could be removing useful items," says Thiaphyl.

"That's rather a moot point at the moment," says Laartol. "Does anyone else have any questions?"

"Not at the moment," says Skaarn.

"Excellent. We'll be riding out in less than a quint, escorted by Overcaptain Alyiakal and First Company." Laartol stands.

Somewhat more than a quint later, Raayls and Maaetz lead as First Company rides out and turns onto the east road. Laartol and Alyiakal follow the scouts, with Magus Thiaphyl and Majer Skaarn next, followed by Magus Kiel and Chaaltyn, and the rest of the company.

Alyiakal briefly describes to Laartol each road they pass and where each leads, along with any encounters with raiders. He refrains from creating an order funnel, knowing that Thiaphyl would notice that immediately.

After a brief break at the River Lhaar overlook, the group continues southeast. When they reach the road leading to the walled-off valley, Alyiakal explains.

Laartol frowns, then asks, "You didn't pursue entering that community?"

"No, ser. They lie outside Cyador, and they've caused no trouble. At that time, we were tracking down the raiders."

"Can you tell me," Laartol lowers his voice, "why you seem to be the only officer dealing with raiders?"

"I'm the one who has ridden beyond the past restrictions regarding patrol distances. I'm also the most experienced, and I knew what to ask the scouts. I've tried to pass those skills on to the other company officers. Recently, both Captain Vaarkas and Captain Paersol have gone on more extended patrols and tracked raiders, or possible Cerlynese scouts."

"That doesn't exactly answer my question."

"Ser, I was given explicit orders to lead patrols. I've led the best way I know how. I've given all the companies additional instruction and drills, far more than I received as an undercaptain, or a junior captain. I've rotated the patrol schedule so that all company officers have equally shared patrols."

"I'd expect no less." Laartol offers an amused smile. "But you still haven't answered my question."

"The only answer I can give is that I try to learn everything I can. I've drafted all the usable maps of the area and given a copy to each officer. When I first arrived, I took squads on individual patrols along the valley's eastern border to seek out possible ways in and out."

"And?"

"That's why we were able to stop the raiders and the Cerlynese." Alyiakal explains how he found the old logging road and where it led. He adds, "I couldn't have done it without the scouts and good squad leaders."

"All of whom you essentially trained, I understand."

"They were good before I worked with them."

Laartol smiles wryly. "I looked at the rosters. We'll leave it at that." After several moments, the commander laughs softly, then says, "You don't accept anything you can't verify, and you're always looking to learn more." He pauses. "Just remember: Sometimes there's nothing more to learn and you still have to act. Not acting is also an action."

Once Alyiakal reaches the rocky part of the road, he says, "The hidden entrance is just ahead."

"Well-hidden, because I don't see any sign of anything resembling an entrance," replies Laartol.

When Raayls is almost abreast of the dead evergreen, Alyiakal calls out, "Scouts hold!"

Alyiakal then halts the company when he and Laartol are just short of the dead evergreen, then orders Raayls to remove the tree and scout the entrance all the way to the old road.

Laartol says nothing.

Raayls returns shortly and reports, "Trail is clear, and there's no one in sight on the road."

"Good. Lead on." Alyiakal urges the chestnut forward. He senses slight apprehension in Laartol, and considerably more in Majer Skaarn.

Once on the road, Alyiakal continues for a hundred yards, reining up to allow First Company to re-form behind him.

"I see what you meant by the road," says Laartol, "not that I doubted your report."

"What's been cut into the gorge is more impressive," replies Alyiakal.

A half a quint passes before Chaaltyn reports, "Company re-formed, ser."

"Two lancers forward, to join the scouts," Alyiakal orders.

"You don't trust the locals?" asks Laartol.

"I trust the word of the headwoman, but five men with firelances should be sufficient if someone else has taken charge." Alyiakal offers a lopsided smile. "I wouldn't want to lose a commander or senior Magi'i." Then he orders, "Company! Forward!"

As with the previous approach to the gorge, the first large order/chaos patterns Alyiakal senses are horses. "We'll see a fenced area for horses ahead to the right. The gorge is too narrow to keep them there."

The commander nods, taking in everything.

Alyiakal senses someone running from the horses toward the gorge but says nothing. He and Laartol ride past the first part of the fenced area. After they ride another half a kay, the trees begin to thin, revealing the top of the gorge.

"I see what you mean by the gorge being narrow," says Laartol.

Raayls, now only fifteen yards ahead, leads the company around the turn to the east, and the riders head directly toward the narrow gorge. The trees on each side of the road end, revealing the dwellings cut into the wall, with windows, stone staircases, and recessed entries.

Alyiakal senses the commander's surprise—and even the majer and the Magi'i are momentarily stunned.

"This is . . . quite something," says Laartol.

While Alyiakal senses traces of order/chaos patterns, even as the company nears the end of the gorge, no one appears on the road or on the long stone balcony at the west end of the gorge's north face.

Then, when the scouts are less than thirty yards from the balcony, the silver-haired woman appears.

Alyiakal calls the company to a halt and waits.

"Firstborn, why do you return? Are you here to drive us out?" asks the silver-haired woman.

"I told you others might come. We're here so that some Magi'i and engineers can look at what was built here. That will determine what happens."

Alyiakal senses her resignation, but her posture remains erect. *Defiant but resigned.* He waits.

"Must we beg to be left alone?" she finally asks.

"Do you have any tools left by those who built your dwellings?" asks Laartol.

The silver-haired woman shakes her head. "Those were all taken when our forebears were driven out. All that is left is what is cut into the stone, and some of the windows that were not destroyed."

"We'd like to look into each dwelling cut into the cliff," says Laartol. "One at a time. We're not interested in harming anyone. If whoever is inside leaves while we look, they can return immediately."

"How do we know you will honor those terms?"

"We'll enter the doorways one at a time. When we leave, they can return." Laartol smiles openly. "After one doorway, you can see whether we honor those terms."

Alyiakal can tell neither Magi'i nor Majer Skaarn is pleased with Laartol's proposal.

The silver-haired woman looks to Alyiakal. "What will your armsmen do?"

"Nothing, so long as no one lifts arms against those looking into the dwellings. If anyone uses force against those looking, then all of you will suffer." Alyiakal doesn't want to be more specific, especially since he doesn't want to turn firelances on the innocent.

The woman turns her eyes on to Laartol. "When you are done, will you trouble us no more?"

"If we find something that others wish to look at, we'd like to be able to have them see it," says Laartol. "As long as you do not raid others, we will not trouble you."

"We have no choice. We cannot stand against the flames of death. I can only beg your kindness."

"Thank you, Headwoman," says Laartol.

Alyiakal eases his mount to the side and beckons to Chaaltyn, who rides forward.

"Detail two lancers to accompany the Magi'i and the majer. Two with good blade skills. They'll enter any area first."

Chaaltyn nods.

"Also, dispatch third squad to ride to the far end of the gorge and stand by until the Magi'i and the Mirror Engineer finish their inspection. Second squad remains here to ensure no one attempts any violence. First squad will follow the Magi'i and the Majer as they examine the spaces."

"Yes, ser."

After Chaaltyn leaves, Laartol looks to Alyiakal. "Blade skills?"

"We do blade training and testing, ser. Chaaltyn knows who has those skills."

"Who is the very best?"

"Besides me, Squad Leader Taenyr, ser."

Laartol merely nods, returning his focus to the first doorway in the gorge. There, the silver-haired woman steps out and walks down the stone steps to the road. Two others follow her: a frail-looking older woman in a shapeless long brown garment, and a boy of, perhaps, ten. The woman gestures to the open door.

Alyiakal moves the company forward. The two lancers selected by Chaaltyn dismount and enter the doorway. They reappear shortly and stand outside while the two Magi'i and Majer Skaarn enter. A much longer time passes before the three emerge.

Laartol looks to Alyiakal. "Overcaptain, we might as well take a look as well."

"Yes, ser." As Alyiakal dismounts, he nods to Chaaltyn to take command.

Alyiakal lets the commander lead the way up the four, smooth-cut, stone steps. The door is sturdy, if crudely shaped of wood planks, and the doorframe fits irregularly inside stone grooves. Leather hinges attach the door to the frame. To the right of the door is a narrow window little more than a handspan wide but two yards high. Inside, the room opens into a single large chamber. A set of steps, cut into the stone, leads to an upper level. Centered in the rear wall, also cut into the stone, is a fountain from which water bubbles and flows into a basin with a slightly elevated drain. A raised hearth, with a chimney cut into the rock, dominates the rear left corner. Forward of the hearth stands a small worktable, and a trestle table with a backless bench on each side sits closer to the window. Against the wall beside the worktable is a set of wooden shelves with pots and plates, and a few utensils.

Under the stone staircase is a door, behind which is a stone jakes over a circular opening, presumably to some sort of sewer below, given the odor.

Laartol starts up the steps, and Alyiakal follows. Above are two chambers, forward of a narrow hallway that leads, Alyiakal can tell, to the balcony from which the headwoman had spoken. Each chamber has two narrow windows looking out on the gorge. The furnishings are simple—raised pallet beds and several chests.

Before Laartol starts down, he says, "Simple, but impressive."

Once outside, the commander turns to the Magi'i and Majer Skaarn. "We'll leave you three to inspect each dwelling. Unless you find something differing from this dwelling, I don't need to see it. I'd like to finish here as soon as possible . . . unless, of course, you find something additional of real interest."

"It doesn't seem that likely," says Thiaphyl, "but we won't know until we've looked."

Majer Skaarn's face is impassive, but Alyiakal gets an impression of disinterest.

Laartol turns to the silver-haired woman. "Thank you. I am a little surprised that you stayed after we discovered your . . . retreat."

"Where else could we go? There's nowhere else better. Those who live in the hills avoid us because they fear the spirits of those who built Lestroi."

"Also because your people appear and disappear mysteriously?" asks Alyiakal.

A hint of a smile crosses the woman's lips and immediately vanishes. "That does make matters a little easier."

"Is Lestroi the name of your community?" asks Alyiakal.

"It has always been Lestroi."

The name, while completely unfamiliar to Alyiakal, catches a glimmer of interest from Thiaphyl, who looks away.

After the Magi'i and the majer turn to the second doorway cut into the stone, and the silver-haired woman gestures for the boy and the older woman to reenter their quarters, Laartol quietly addresses her. "I'm Commander Laartol, and this is Overcaptain Alyiakal. Might I ask your name?"

"Kiefala."

"I'm hopeful we won't have to trouble you again," Laartol continues, "but for certain reasons, we were sent to see if some . . . tools . . . might have remained here from the time Lestroi was built."

"Nothing from that time remains, except the walls and the water."

"If that is so, you won't see us again, provided that you do not raid Cyador."

"I have seen what you of the Firstborn can do." She looks to Alyiakal, adding, "And what you hold. We will not raid Cyador. The price would be too great." Then she steps back and climbs to the top step before her doorway, where she continues to watch.

Alyiakal worries about Kiefala's words to him, considering what he might say if Laartol asks him.

The commander only comments, "We might as well remount. I don't think this will take all that long."

In the end, closely inspecting the contents of forty-two dwellings, by Alyiakal's count, takes slightly more than two glasses, and another two quints pass before First Company rides beyond the hidden entrance, replacing the dead evergreen, and west back toward Lhaarat.

Laartol is largely silent, if pleasant, when he speaks on the ride back, and Alyiakal decides not to intrude.

As Alyiakal and the commander dismount outside the stable, Laartol says, "We'll have an all-officers meeting in the mess right after we eat. That way, we can leave early in the morning, and everyone will hear the same thing." He smiles wryly. "Not everyone will understand it in the same way, but that's the best we can do." He pauses. "I'm just as glad we found nothing except, as the headwoman put it, the walls and the water. That should close out the concerns about the dissidents."

"It's been a rather long trip for you, with so little to show for it."

"I got to see a border post and cross off a nagging matter, and it didn't take an eightday here in Lhaarat. As far as I'm concerned, those are worth it. I'll see you at mess."

"Yes, ser."

Alyiakal spends a little extra time with the chestnut, then goes back to his temporary quarters, where Vaarkas asks, "What happened?"

"Not much, but the commander is calling an all-officers meeting right after supper to brief everyone."

"If he's doing that so soon, then there's not much to it."

"I did say that not much happened," replies Alyiakal.

Vaarkas shakes his head.

"Did you find anything interesting on your patrol?" asks Alyiakal.

"Two traders with carts, and no tracks that would indicate raiders or Cerlynese troopers."

"Well, that's good." *At least for the moment.*

Alyiakal washes up, brushes off his uniform, and heads to the mess.

Once everyone is seated, Majer Byelt declares, "Immediately after we eat, there will be an all-officers meeting. Commander Laartol and those with him will brief us on their discoveries. Save your questions until then."

Once more, the meal is largely silent.

When the dishes are cleared away, Laartol eases his chair back and clears his throat. "The entire mission today was the kind we prefer—ordered and routine. Overcaptain Alyiakal had informed the headwoman of the possibility of a Mirror Lancer inspection of the community and the dwellings. The inhabitants were cooperative, and Magus Thiaphyl, Magus Kiel, and Majer Skaarn inspected every space cut into the stone of the gorge. I'm going to let Senior Magus Thiaphyl explain what they found and any significance those findings may have." Laartol inclines his head to Thiaphyl.

"Thank you, Commander Laartol. I'll summarize our findings, and what it indicates." Thiaphyl clears his throat. "Lestroi is what the inhabitants call the community. It was definitely built at the time of the First. The location and design strongly suggest construction methods only available to the First because all chambers, as well as air channels, were smoothly cut into the stone. Water and sewage conduits were also cut in a way that rendered them impermeable. The local lore states the First later attacked Lestroi, taking everything that could be removed. The condition of the dwellings supports this. At the same time, I will point out that everything cut into the rock still functions as designed. The water lines and fountains work. The sewage conduits work. We found no devices or any sign of them, unlike what was discovered several years ago in the ruins adjacent to Oldroad Post near Guarstyad." Thiaphyl turns to Skaarn. "Majer, would you like to add anything?"

Skaarn frowns. "Not so much an addition as a question. Today, we can still cut into the stone in the same fashion, but it's clear that whoever designed that retreat knew exactly where to make the cuts. There's no sign of recutting, or if there was, they concealed it in ways we can't detect. Can you explain that?"

"They may have had a geomancer—an earth mage. We know at least one of the First had that talent," replies Thiaphyl.

"Would that have allowed Lestroi greater concealment?" asks Laartol.

"Definitely," replies the senior magus. "It could easily explain why the retreat was located where it was and why it went undetected as long as it did." He pauses, then adds, "That's only one possibility based on circumstantial evidence."

"Are there any geomancers who could examine Lestroi?" asks Laartol.

"To my knowledge there are none among the Magi'i at present," replies Thiaphyl.

For an instant, Alyiakal freezes, thinking of how he'd seen the conflicting order patterns beneath the Great Canal—and those in the stone blocking the road entrance to Lestroi. *No geomancers at present? If a group including a dissident geomancer created Lestroi, that would also explain the positioning and strength of the old road from the post to Guarstyad.* He, however, decides to keep both thoughts to himself.

A silence falls across the mess.

After several long moments, Laartol stands. "Then the meeting is over. I'd like to thank you, Majer Byelt, and all your officers for your hospitality and support. It's made this investigation less onerous and much quicker than it could have been. For that, you not only have my thanks, but my appreciation. We will be leaving after breakfast tomorrow."

"Thank you, Commander," replies Byelt.

Alyiakal does not move until the commander and his party leave, but he doesn't get far. Byelt motions to him. "A moment, if you will, Alyiakal."

Alyiakal smiles and joins the majer, who doesn't speak until the other officers have left the mess.

"How do you read what the commander said?" asks Byelt.

"You have a better idea than I do, ser. Ultimately, I think he had to come here for reasons that aren't known or obvious to me. He seems more than happy to discover that the dissidents have left no usable devices or traces, which will allow him to quietly close the book on the dissidents. He's also pleased he could do it quickly."

"I think there's something more," muses Byelt.

So does Alyiakal. "You're better than I am at reading headquarters' officers."

"Well," says Byelt, drawing out the word, "whatever it is, we won't find out for some time, if at all. I'll see you in the morning."

"Until then, ser." Alyiakal follows the majer from the mess and then heads toward his temporary quarters.

LXXXV

On twoday morning, Alyiakal is again up early, checking the wounded and making sure that arrangements for Laartol's departure are taking place as planned. He also visits the brig.

Taaryan looks up warily as Alyiakal enters his cell. "You are early . . . ser. What is it?"

"I talked to you about your choices."

"Those choices weren't the best."

"Can you come up with a better one? The Cerlynese will kill you if you try to return home. You can't stay here forever."

"Do I have to choose now?"

Alyiakal considers, then shakes his head. "But you'll have to within two or three eightdays."

"Thank you, ser."

Alyiakal really doesn't want to send Taaryan to Terimot yet, not until his arm heals more fully, but he does want the youth to think matters through carefully. He just nods and leaves the cell.

He hurries to the mess, but he is one of the last to enter, arriving just before the commander and Majer Byelt.

Commander Laartol's toast is simple. "Thank you all for making this a swift and effective investigation. I can't tell you how much that has meant to me and for the Mirror Lancers."

Swift? questions Alyiakal. *Possibly because he was sent here to get him away from Cyad on the pretext that he'd know the most about the dissidents? Or for some other reason?*

"We were glad to host," declares Majer Byelt, "and we wish you a swift and smooth return to Cyad."

"Thank you," replies Laartol.

After several moments of silence, Staalt asks, very respectfully, "Ser, can you tell us anything about the new emperor?"

"I haven't met Emperor Kaartyn. I only saw him at a distance at his coronation, but I understand he's a talented magus with a great understanding of the complexities of managing the Triad," replies Laartol. "The Majer-Commander has met with him on several occasions but has not yet shared anything beyond that. That may be because various trade matters have been a major concern, and because the Mirror Lancers have the borders under control."

"What about the Empress?" asks Vaarkas, with a grin.

Laartol flashes a warm and amused smile. "She was quite striking at the coronation. I imagine she's more so in person."

"The commander has a long ride ahead," says Byelt before anyone else can speak. "We should let him eat his breakfast now."

Alyiakal has hoped that Laartol might give some indication of headquarters' feelings on the Cerlynese, but since deputy post commanders don't go around their superiors, the only thing he can do is ask Byelt privately if the matter came up.

He takes a swallow of ale before Thiaphyl turns to him and says, "For someone who's discovered two dissident structures no one else came close to locating, you've been remarkably quiet, Overcaptain."

"Both structures speak for themselves, Senior Magus. In both instances, I was following my orders."

"That's very clear. But what do you think about them?"

"They both appear to have been well designed and engineered, and they obviously represented a threat of some sort to the First. That seems clear from the destruction of the buildings at Oldroad Post and the almost total hiding of Lestroi." After the slightest hesitation, Alyiakal asks, "Do you know what 'Lestroi' means?"

"I understand that it's a degraded version of an Anglorian word meaning 'ruler' or 'emperor' or something similar."

"That would suggest—"

"Exactly, a power struggle among the first," replies Thiaphyl. "That is why it's best Lestroi be left to itself."

"I see." Alyiakal nods.

"I believe you do, Overcaptain." Thiaphyl returns to eating the rest of his cheese-egg scramble.

After breakfast, while Alyiakal makes certain they depart smoothly, he does not talk to Laartol or Thiaphyl further, nor does either seek him out, and that's for the best, as far as Alyiakal is concerned.

Once Laartol and his party are well away from the post, Staalt and Second

Company depart on another patrol up the old logging road north of Gairtyn with instructions to look for signs of scouts or horsemen using the high road.

Then Alyiakal heads back to his study, expecting at least a few documents from Mirror Lancer headquarters for him to review. He's hardly surprised when Byelt motions for him before he can enter.

Alyiakal steps into the majer's study and closes the door. "Ser?"

"Take a seat."

Alyiakal does and waits for Byelt to speak.

"For a visit from a headquarters commander, the past several days have been a pleasant surprise. What are your thoughts?"

"Magus Thiaphyl suspected there was nothing new to find and was glad, if a little annoyed. Young magus Kiel didn't know what to make if it. Majer Skaarn thought it was a waste of time, but unfortunately necessary. I suspect Commander Laartol felt relieved on several counts. First, he hoped the community was real, because it would have looked bad for the Mirror Lancers if it weren't. Second, he didn't want to deal with any devices or surprises and was glad he didn't have to. Third, and this is just a guess, from the way he didn't answer the question about Emperor Kaartyn, he's worried about what's happening in Cyad and wants to return as quickly as possible."

"Did he mention any of this?"

"No, ser. About the only thing he said about Lestroi was that it was impressive and simple."

Byelt frowns. "What do you think he meant?"

"He didn't say. My guess is he saw how well-designed Lestroi was and that everything still worked, and that impressed him. It was also simple, because it was designed to work without magery, and discovery would be less likely as well."

"But the First still found it."

"Several years later, I'd guess."

Byelt frowns. "Why?"

"The ruins and the road near Oldroad Post weren't concealed at all, and the destruction of everything except the road was close to total. Lestroi was carefully hidden, suggesting that it may have been built later. Also, the interiors were looted and gutted, but the actual chambers weren't damaged. The only major use of chaos at Lestroi blocked and concealed the road. To me, that suggests that the attack on Lestroi came *after* the First had lost much of their initial ability for brute-force destruction, *or* perhaps the distance from Cyad just made it more difficult."

"I don't suppose we'll ever know." Byelt pauses. "Do you still think the Cerlynese might attack?"

"An attack makes absolutely no sense, but I still think it's possible. There have been too many Cerlynese on the high road, and there's too much evidence of trade and weapons coming from Cerlyn. Neither can be coincidence."

"Mounting an attack from over a hundred kays away seems improbable."

"Ser, did Commander Laartol say anything about the Cerlynese situation?"

Byelt's smile is sardonic. "I asked. He said the matter was still under discussion."

"Meaning part of his visit was to take a personal look?"

"I'd judge that was a large part of his reason for being here. He asked about the reports and wanted to know what we didn't put in them. I told him we omitted no facts but didn't engage in suppositions. He replied that headquarters appreciated that, and we'd hear in due time."

"That definitely sounds like someone didn't trust our report, or found it hard to believe." Alyiakal shakes his head. "I think it's time for a longer patrol to the north."

"That's up to you," replies Byelt, smiling.

"I'll keep you informed." Alyiakal stands.

As Alyiakal leaves the majer's study and enters his own, he starts to consider how the Cerlynese might attack. Moving a large Cerlynese force from the high road, through the logged area, then down the old logging road would invite disaster. Taking the high road to the log fort and coming down the east road would be easier, except for possible opposition from Lestroi and the log fort.

But why would they oppose Cerlyn when they've been trading with them for years?

Alyiakal shakes his head. He needs to make that patrol.

In the meantime, after he reviews and comments on the handful of directives in his box, he can spend some time on his reply to Saelora, although it will be at least several days before any dispatch riders arrive and he can send a letter.

LXXXVI

First Company leaves the post in the cool of first light of threeday morning, and by sunrise, the company is on the old logging road north of Gairtyn. Alyiakal suddenly senses a single rider farther northwest, coming down the road. The rider halts. Almost simultaneously, Raayls relays Maaetz's signal that he's seen something.

Alyiakal senses the rider turning and heading back up the slope.

Raayls rides back to Alyiakal. "Ser, there's a rider ahead. Possibly from Cerlyn, wearing brown and green. He's headed back uphill toward that logged area."

"Back to the high road, no doubt. Keep an eye out. If you sight more than a single scout, let me know." While Alyiakal doesn't want to fight another skirmish, he also doesn't want to pull back if there's only a scout. He'd much rather deal with any Cerlynese force on the high road.

In under half a quint, Alyiakal can no longer discern the rider, and neither scout signals anything over the next glass or so as First Company reaches the high road. There, Alyiakal calls for a break while the scouts check the road for several hundred yards in both directions. He blots his forehead with his kerchief. Although the day is only moderately warm, so far, the cloudless, green-blue sky holds Summer sun intense enough for him to collect more chaos than usual.

When the scouts return, Raayls says, "Can't tell much from the road, ser. Most of the hoofprints look to be from Second Company. A few small wagons. That rider headed back north."

"Anything useful heading south?" Alyiakal asks Maaetz.

"No, ser. Same as Raayls said, except for any sign of that scout."

Alyiakal takes a swallow of slightly watered ale, checking his order funnel, then remounting and ordering the company north. He wonders if the crude waystation will hold any signs, but a glass later as Alyiakal rides up to the waystation, he sees no indications of recent use or occupation.

Past the waystation, the road curves through the hills for the next several kays without climbing or descending much. Alyiakal notices several paths winding up into the hills, wide enough for a single mount, and most show hoofprints, if not particularly recent.

Another glass passes, and then Raayls signals and rides back to report. "Ser, there's a road to the west. It twists out of sight, but appears to head into a valley to the northwest. The valley also shows trails of smoke."

Another frigging hamlet that no one's investigated? While the possible hamlet is close to fifty kays from Lhaarat by the "known" roads, by taking the east road to the high road and then north, Alyiakal wonders, again, why no one in the Mirror Lancers seems to know about it. It certainly isn't on any maps. While those thoughts flash through his mind, he replies, "Thank you, Raayls. I'll take a hard look at it. We may need to follow the side road."

When Alyiakal reins up at the side road, he can tell they need to investigate. The single rider's tracks lead in that direction and a plethora of hoofprints to and from the north turn onto the side road. Given the number of riders, it's clear far more have used the side road, which is every bit as wide as the high road.

Alyiakal turns to the scouts. "We'll take a break here, but I'd like you to ride north to make sure there's no one coming in the next half kay or so."

"Yes, ser."

Once the scouts ride north, Chaaltyn turns to Alyiakal. "Can't say I like what I'm seeing, ser."

"It's a bit concerning." *More than a bit concerning, like black-angel sowshit concerning, especially that no one seems even to know about this place.*

"Begging your pardon, ser . . ." Chaaltyn lowers his voice. "Except for what you've discovered, no officer seems to know anything about anything more than fifteen kays from the valley."

"That's understandable for Paersol and Staalt," Alyiakal says evenly. "I can't speak for the others, but I haven't seen anything to dispute what you're saying." He offers a lopsided smile and adds, "It looks like we're about to learn more."

Raayls and Maaetz return, reporting that while the tracks continue to the north, there are no other signs of riders, nor are there any in sight. There is, however, a fairly new wooden bridge over a small stream half a kay farther north.

"We'll give you two a small break, and then see where the side road leads."

A quint later, Raayls and Maaetz usher the way down the side road, which gradually descends for several hundred yards before turning due west between a rocky hillside and a straggly evergreen forest. The trees end at a slope covered with irregular, sharp-edged chunks of black rock, as well as larger boulders of the same rough rock, extending down to the valley. The road skirts the boulder field and leads to a hamlet, of sorts.

Alyiakal calls a halt at the top of the boulder field and surveys the valley, counting roughly twenty scattered dwellings, each surrounded by fields of what might be potato plants. Then, well past the first dwellings partly hidden by a slope, stands a log structure. It suspiciously resembles a barracks, with another building behind it and a large, fenced pasture. Alyiakal sees a handful of horses. Farther to the west are more fields.

Alyiakal shakes his head, then blots his forehead with the back of his hand.

"Ser?" asks Chaaltyn.

"What do you think of the large, long building partly shielded by the hillside . . . and what lies beyond it?"

"Where . . . oh." After a few moments, the senior squad leader says, "All that looks like a post."

"That was my impression as well, and I'm certain that it lies inside Cyador."

"Are we going to attack it?"

"Not right now. Possibly not at all."

"Ser?"

"Overcaptains don't get to start wars without approval from higher authority." *Not if they want to remain Mirror Lancers.* "We will head back to Lhaarat, but we'll need scouts to the rear as well until we're well clear."

Chaaltyn lifts his eyebrows.

"We can defend ourselves if threatened, and in those circumstances, at times, an attack is the best defense."

"Do you think they will?"

Alyiakal shrugs. "At the moment, I don't know what to think." *Except that we could be in the middle of a large pool of sowshit.*

For all of Alyiakal's concerns and precautions, the ride back to Lhaarat Post is uneventful. They encounter only two traders. A red deer bounds across the high road just before First Company rides off the road and down the trail past the logged area and onto the logging road.

Because the company returns so late, Alyiakal goes straight from the stable to the mess. Both he and Byelt arrive at the mess door at the same time.

"How was the patrol?" asks the majer.

"We have a complicated situation. If you don't mind, we should talk after dinner."

Byelt raises his eyebrow. "That bad?"

"Not yet."

"After we eat, then, in my study."

Once everyone is seated and served, Vaarkas asks, "How was your patrol? You went farther north, didn't you?"

"Long," replies Alyiakal. "We saw signs of more trails into the higher hills."

"Higher than the high road?"

"They seemed to be. I've noted the positions on my map, but they were trails, not roads, and we didn't have the time to follow them."

"You think there are more hamlets to the north?" Vaarkas presses.

Alyiakal laughs. "I'm sure there are, especially if you go far enough."

The remainder of conversation centers more on how hot late Summer and early Harvest will be and speculation on whether there might be any raids after what's already happened. Alyiakal refrains from commenting beyond saying, "We'll just have to see."

After dinner, Byelt and Alyiakal walk back to the majer's study. Although the ranker in front has left for the day, Alyiakal still closes the door, then sits down.

"What is it?" asks Byelt.

"There's an indication that someone has built a small post some twenty-plus kays to the north." Alyiakal explains his thinking, including his observations about the amount of goods and weapons from Cerlyn that the lancers have already found. "Since that post is within the lands of Cyador, it shouldn't be there. But Cerlyn isn't just a hamlet, and while the Cerlynese have pushed and encouraged raiders to attack us, they've only attacked us once, and I doubt there's much evidence of that remaining."

"I wouldn't think they would admit to an attack. What are you asking, Alyiakal?"

"I'd like to remove all the barracks and posts they've built along the high road, up to the point where it enters the actual border of Cerlyn, but that's a lot for a post commander to approve, let alone a junior deputy post commander."

Byelt laughs, briefly and sardonically, then says, "Write up the situation and offer two courses of action."

"To allow the Cerlynese to continue to encroach on Cyadoran lands and encourage raids, but remove only actual raiders . . . or to remove both raiders and Cerlynese posts and installations?"

"Something along those lines," agrees Byelt.

"I'll have it to you tomorrow."

"Is that minor little problem all you had in mind?" asks Byelt in a tone of gentle sarcasm.

"For now, ser." Alyiakal refrains from smiling.

LXXXVII

Although Alyiakal finishes his patrol report by midmorning on fourday, Byelt doesn't finish reading it until later. By the time Alyiakal receives the majer's comments and makes the necessary revisions, the report doesn't leave Lhaarat Post until sixday morning. That allows Alyiakal to finish his letter to Saelora and to send it off with the dispatch riders.

For the next two eightdays, Alyiakal schedules patrols and regularly rides out with First Company. There are no raids, no signs of raiders, but there are traces of Cerlynese hoofprints on the high road, though not in large numbers. Two sets of dispatch riders arrive and depart over the next two eightdays, but none bring more than routine correspondence and directives.

Then, late on twoday of the last eightday of Summer, another set of dispatch riders arrives. Two quints later, Byelt requests Alyiakal's presence.

Once Alyiakal closes the majer's door, he asks, "A definitive response from headquarters, ser?"

"It's a response," replies Byelt, handing a single sheet of paper to Alyiakal.

Alyiakal takes the sheet, embossed with the letterhead of the Majer-Commander, and addressed to the majer, and begins to read, concentrating on the words following the introduction and procedural niceties.

> *Cerlyn's establishment of posts for armsmen in Cyadoran lands needs to be addressed expeditiously and effectively, especially after the earlier reports indicating Cerlynese support of raiders.*

Alyiakal understands the unstated implication that he and Byelt should have done something sooner, even when it's taken seasons just to determine the situation.

> *You are to take the requisite action as swiftly as possible and complete all efforts before inclement weather makes resolving the situation impractical.*

At the same time, any and all measures to remove those armsmen and posts should minimize the impact on those families and individuals located in such areas who are not associated with the Cerlynese and allow them to become more a part of Cyador in the future.

And how are we supposed to determine that? Alyiakal can see who will be blamed for any civilian casualties. No matter how hard he works to "minimize" the impact, there *will* be casualties and ill will.

. . . particularly traders and factors who may have long-standing associations with well-established Cyadoran trading and commercial establishments . . .

While the content of that line doesn't surprise Alyiakal, such wording in an official document does. *More than a little.*

We look forward to timely reports on accomplishing these ends.

The signature appears to be that of the Majer-Commander, although Alyiakal has no way of knowing if it is. He hands the letter, which is in fact a directive, back to Byelt.

Byelt takes the sheet, laying it on the desk and smoothing the edges. "Your thoughts?"

"I'll need three companies, all the spare firelances, and all the wagons. Second Company will have to patrol within ten kays of the post until we return. We should be able to ride out on fiveday."

"Do you really think . . . ?"

"There's no good way to ride out, remove one post, ride back, then ride out again . . . and do it all over again . . . and again. I'm guessing that there are Cerlynese outposts at least every twenty kays, possibly even closer together. Eliminating them one by one would take at least a season. In addition, it would give the Cerlynese time to bring up reinforcements, and that would mean more deaths on both sides."

"And if I don't approve your plan?"

"Then I'd do it the hard, slow way, post by post. If I read that directive correctly, those are the only options." Alyiakal pauses, then adds, "Unless I've overlooked some other strategy; that's always a possibility."

Byelt's laugh is harsh. "With you, unlikely, especially in matters of arms."

He shakes his head. "Besides, your plan is the only one that might leave us with a future in the Mirror Lancers."

Alyiakal can't argue with that assessment. "Then I'd better get started on organizing this small campaign."

"In the end, one way or the other, it won't be small."

Alyiakal can't disagree with that, either.

LXXXVIII

Just after first light on fiveday, following a quick breakfast, Alyiakal meets in the mess with Vaarkas and Paersol.

"I know I've said this before, Vaarkas, but your immediate task is to take the east road to the high road and get the wagons headed north with as few delays as possible. That's why Third Company will head out first. Try not to use force, but if the people at the log fort give you trouble, just clear the way with firelances and get past the fort as quickly as possible. I don't like splitting forces, but there's no way we can take wagons up the old logging trail." *And if I'm still a deputy post commander after this, we're going to turn that path into a road, one way or another.* But that could take seasons, and Alyiakal doesn't have seasons.

"Have to wonder why someone didn't think about turning that trail into a road before," replies Vaarkas.

"Traders take the easiest route, even if it takes longer. We're the ones who need the better shorter roads, but the Mirror Engineers aren't interested in building those here, even if good roads and the Great Canal are part of the reasons why Cyador's powerful." Alyiakal turns to Paersol. "Do you have any questions?"

"No, ser. Not now, anyway."

"Then it's time to mount up and head out." Alyiakal gestures to Vaarkas, and the senior captain leads the way from the mess.

Three quints later, Third Company and the wagons start into the hills on the east road, and First Company heads toward the bridge over the Lhaar, followed by Fourth Company.

By midmorning, First Company is past the old logging road and riding through the northeastern end of the logged-over area. Alyiakal senses some red deer to the northwest, but no riders or scouts on the trail leading to the high road.

All the same, he's relieved when the last riders of First Company reach the high road without incident. He calls a halt so that Fourth Company can catch up, and sends Raayls north and Maaetz south to see what they can discover. He doesn't worry about raiders or Cerlynese armsmen being too close, since he senses only birds and small animals.

Slightly less than a quint later, the two scouts return.

Raayls reports first. "A few cart wheels, ser, and some hoofprints. A handful could be Cerlynese. No large parties or formations."

"Four riders from the south stopped just short of this position and then turned back," says Maaetz. "The rest is just like Raayls reported."

Alyiakal turns to Chaaltyn. "Send a lancer north and another south as temporary scouts. Just two hundred yards."

"Yes, ser."

Alyiakal blots off the sweat oozing out from under his visor cap, and takes a swallow of his slightly watered ale. While the high road is slightly cooler and drier than the valley, the day is warmer than on any previous patrol, and it's not even midday.

When Fourth Company reaches the high road and stands down for a break, Alyiakal walks the chestnut to meet with Paersol.

"Any problems coming up?"

"Not so far, ser."

"Good. We'll mount up in a bit less than a quint." Alyiakal walks the chestnut back to the head of First Company. He's just mounted when Chaaltyn calls out, "There's a wagon coming from the north, with two mounted guards."

"I'll go out and meet it. If you'd detail two men to accompany me?"

"Yes, ser."

Alyiakal nears the wagon more than a hundred yards north of First Company, then reins up and waits for the teamster to approach. The wagon, moderately high-sided but not roofed, has a canvas over the load. A guard with a small crossbow sits on the wagon seat beside the teamster.

As the wagon comes to a slow halt, one of the riders reins up several yards from Alyiakal and says, "You're the first Mirror Lancers we've seen. We heard you were patrolling more."

"But not the first armsmen, I'd wager," replies Alyiakal.

"Well . . . the first in a while."

"You mean, since very early this morning," replies Alyiakal, guessing the wagon belongs to a trader and that the trader spent the night at the hamlet with the Cerlynese barracks.

The rider's eyes narrow, but he replies, "Might be."

"You'd be foolish not to stop where there are armsmen. That is, if you trust them."

"I've been traveling this road for years," says the rider. "First time I've seen lancers."

"There's a first time for everything. What are you trading?"

"Whatever we can."

Alyiakal senses unease, but any trader would be uneasy to run into Mirror Lancers or other armsmen. "And that might be . . . ?"

"We're headed back."

"To where?"

"Kyphrien," admits the trader, uneasily.

"Salt and spices on the way out?" asks Alyiakal.

"Some. Also, honey, candles, and cotton."

"And what did you get in return?" From looking at the very sturdy wagon and the two horses, and the impressions of the wheels, Alyiakal suspects there are more than a few copper ingots in the wagon or something equally weighty.

"Officer, would you strip a trader of his living?"

"So long as you're not carrying goods that might strip my men of their lives," returns Alyiakal, concentrating on the rider who has to be the trader.

"Some do trade in arms," says the trader, "but I'm not carrying any."

While Alyiakal can sense the truth in the words, he suspects that the trader is no stranger to arms-trading. "Then you wouldn't mind showing me that you're not?"

"If need be," says the trader sourly, nodding to the man with the crossbow, who sets aside the weapon, carefully, steps down, and unfastens the rope on one side of the wagon so that he can pull the canvas back.

Alyiakal sees more than a dozen half barrels behind the teamster. He points. "Those?"

The trader smiles. "Evergreen nuts."

Alyiakal glances over the cart, not seeing or sensing anything like weapons, but several cheese wheels, and a stack of animal hides as well as several blocks of salt. Then, recalling what he'd seen before, he asks, "You're hoping for mountain musk oxen wool at the log-fort town?"

"If there is any to be had."

Alyiakal refrains from smiling, sensing that the trader is more than hoping. "We'll escort you past the lancers ahead and you can continue south."

"Thank you."

Once the trader passes, Alyiakal has both companies mount up, then turns to the two First Company scouts.

"It's unlikely, but if you see a large group of Cerlynese riders, pull back and see if you can lure them toward us."

"You don't want us to take them out by ourselves, ser?" asks Raayls, with a smile.

"I thought about it, but the rest of the company should have a chance."

"We wouldn't want to deprive them," adds Maaetz.

In moments, the scouts are in position, and Alyiakal orders, "Company! Forward!"

Despite the white sun's heat, Alyiakal finds his order funnel collecting only slightly more chaos bits than in the past. First Company reaches the crude waystation in less than a glass and continues past it into the section of the curving road. Several paths leading from the high road show recent hoofprints, while others appear unused. Alyiakal senses a horse and rider up one path, but the rider retreats uphill.

A glass and a half later, First Company and Fourth Company reach the road to the post, and Alyiakal notices very few recent tracks leading to or from the hamlet below. While he ponders that, he has the companies proceed to the small stream north of the side road, where the horses can be watered, and the lancers can take a break.

While the horses are being cared for, Alyiakal sends for Paersol and his senior squad leader.

"Ser?" asks Paersol. "Has something changed?"

"Not so far, but sooner or later, it will," says Alyiakal, with a touch of wry amusement, before describing the terrain and the side road to the hamlet. "First Company will ride into the hamlet. Fourth Company will halt and take a position at the top of the slope covered with black rock. There may not be any Cerlynese armsmen here right now, but if there are, your task is to make certain none of them escape, and to protect our rear. The less the Cerlynese know about us, and the longer they take to find out, the better."

Especially since you have no firm idea of how many hamlets there are or how many armsmen they hold.

After watering the horses, the lancers mount up, and First Company leads the way back to the side road and down to the hamlet, past the slope filled with the odd black rocks, while Fourth Company halts at the top.

When First Company reaches the bottom, Alyiakal motions the scouts to fall in, then orders, "Ready arms!"

Then he and the lancers continue along the road past the first dwellings. Several men and women working in the field behind them stop and look up as the lancers ride past.

But as Alyiakal nears the suspected barracks, two things strike him. First, the building is new, possibly only a year or so old; and second, he can only sense a few people nearby. Only six or seven horses graze fenced pasture on the far side of the small stream separating the first building from the second, which feels empty.

Alyiakal reins up in front of the closed door at the end of the building. The few windows are shuttered.

"Doesn't seem like anyone's home," says Chaaltyn.

"Not today," replies Alyiakal dryly.

"Detail someone to examine the building—carefully."

Alyiakal senses no one inside but studies the dwellings nearby, waiting in the midafternoon sun for the scouts to return, noting the dwellings are older than the building, but only by perhaps ten years at most.

He turns his attention to the four lancers who walk back toward him.

"It's a barracks, ser," reports Maaetz, "except it's more like a waystation. Pallets but not much else. Might hold a full company, but it'd be tight. There's no glass in the windows, just shutters, inside and out."

"No sign of supplies, either," adds Raayls.

"Thank you. I'm going to take a look at that second building. Maaetz and Raayls, with me."

"Yes, ser."

Once the two ride up and join him, Alyiakal heads toward the second building, guiding the chestnut toward a solitary man in faded brown trousers and shirt, digging at the side of the stream, possibly deepening an irrigation ditch.

The man looks bewildered as Alyiakal reins up. Finally, he asks, "Who are you, ser?"

"Who were you expecting?"

"The green riders. They said they wouldn't bother us so long as we helped build the quarters and looked after the horses."

"Last year sometime?"

"After harvest."

Alyiakal senses both honesty and confusion, and replies, "The green riders are trying to invade the lands of Cyador. We won't bother you, either, but we will be staying here tonight. How many riders usually come here?"

"I never counted. Twenty, I'd guess, maybe thirty, sometimes just a handful or so."

"They're armed, I take it?"

"Yes, ser. They have long blades and shiny metal shields. Some have bows, the short kind they can use when they ride."

Alyiakal frowns, then asks, "Have they always had shields?"

"You know, ser, I can't say as I recall. This Spring and Summer, mostly. Before that . . ." The man shrugs.

"Have you seen any wagons?"

"Not with them. Only with traders."

While Alyiakal questions the man for another half quint, the responses don't add anything to his initial words. He finally thanks the man and rides across a simple, if sturdy, log bridge to the second building, only to find its doors and windows shuttered—and little inside except open space.

He rides back to the empty barracks and shares the man's information with Chaaltyn and a description of the unfinished empty building.

"You think this is an overgrown waystation for Cerlynese armsmen, then?" asks the senior squad leader.

"It's at least that. We'll have to see what we find farther north. We'll stay here tonight. Send word for Fourth Company to join us, but to post four men at the juncture of the side road with the east road—both to warn us if a Cerlynese force is headed this way and to direct Third Company here."

"Yes, ser."

For the next two glasses, the two companies settle in and take advantage of the fenced pasture for the horses. Accompanied by a pair of lancers, Alyiakal rides from dwelling to dwelling, trying to learn more about the hamlet and how closely they're linked to the Cerlynese.

Once Vaarkas, Third Company, and the supply wagons arrive, Alyiakal gathers both captains and all three senior squad leaders in the cooler, late-afternoon shade on the east side of the waystation barracks.

Alyiakal turns to Vaarkas. "Did you have any trouble with the log-fort people?"

"They all retreated into the fort, but they didn't bother us. That stretch above the river slowed us down a great deal. We didn't see any riders, and only one trader with two mounted guards. He said you'd looked into the wagon."

"I did. I wanted to see if he was Cerlynese selling arms. He wasn't, but I wouldn't be surprised if he has in the past. Did you see anything else?"

Vaarkas shakes his head, then asks, "What happened here?"

"Nothing." Alyiakal summarizes their arrival and his conjectures about the barracks. "I spent some time talking to the settlers. They're a mix. Some came from the Grass Hills east of Pemedra, but most are the younger sons of the mountain families south of here. Fertile land is scarce, and it takes a fair amount for a single family. The oldest dwelling was built eight years ago. The barracks was finished in early Autumn. The locals think that the next hamlet is more than thirty kays north."

After summarizing his findings, Alyiakal concludes, "We'll leave at first light tomorrow. Leave the buildings clean. We'll need them on the way back."

Much later, as Alyiakal lies on one of the hard pallets—still more comfortable than the rough stone floor—he wonders how everything will turn out. He has a fleeting thought that perhaps the Cerlynese are less brutal than he thinks, but that thought pales against his experience at Pemedra, and the recent appearance of polished bronze shields.

Still . . . you never know . . .

LXXXIX

All three companies—and the supply wagons—leave the unnamed hamlet at first light, heading north on the high road well before the sun clears the Westhorns. Alyiakal has debated firing the barracks building but sees little point. Once they remove the Cerlynese armsmen from the high road—or the portion that falls within Cyador—Mirror Lancer patrols can use it to extend their range.

As Alyiakal looks to the northeast, he can see the jagged peaks clearly, with no mists or clouds, something that's not possible from the Lhaarat Post, where the foothills block the view. The air is comfortable, but not cool, suggesting that the day ahead will be at least as hot as fiveday, but not so hot as Pemedra's late Summer and early Harvest.

The high road shows no new tracks or hoofprints. *Not yet, anyway.*

Alyiakal adjusts his visor cap, then creates his order funnel to gather more chaos as the sun creeps over the Westhorns. In a way, it still seems a waste to gather chaos all day, only to release it in the evening, but the alternatives are worse.

As he crosses the log bridge over the stream running through the small valley, he wonders whether the next hamlet will be like the last, with little more than a waystation for Cerlynese armsmen. Perhaps it will be a permanent post or fort of some sort. Given the orders from Mirror Lancer headquarters, the eightday ahead is going to be a long slog, one way or the other, even if it's not especially brutal. Alyiakal's past experience suggests that, before it's over, a lot of blood will be let, and chaos loosed.

For the next two glasses, the three companies encounter no riders or traders, not surprisingly given their location and how early it is, but then Raayls signals and rides back to report.

"Ser, there are four or five cots on the hillside to the left up ahead. Some fields, but mostly trees. Wide paths leading to them, not really roads. Two or three men in the fields, but they didn't even look in our direction."

"Five cots on a hillside aren't what we're looking for. There aren't any real roads, are there?"

"No, ser."

Alyiakal turns to Chaaltyn. "Send back word to Captain Vaarkas and alert the squad handling rear guard, just in case someone decides to follow us."

The companies ride past the hillside without event, but in less than a kay, the terrain around the road becomes rockier and more rugged, so much so that few trees grow on the hills and the white sun seems hotter. That has to be an illusion, Alyiakal knows, because there's no change in the amount of chaos he's collecting.

Illusion or not, he finds sweat oozing from under his visor cap and wipes it away with his kerchief. He understands why there's no hamlet some fifteen to twenty kays north of the one where they spent the night.

The rugged terrain continues for another ten kays before the road turns northwesterly and winds through lower hills forested with evergreens.

Alyiakal has the companies stop at the next steam to water the horses and give the lancers a break. According to the sun, it's already midafternoon.

After the break, Alyiakal orders the companies forward once again, wondering just how far ahead the next valley or hamlet might be.

Two quints later, Maaetz rides back and reports, "There's a bigger valley ahead, ser. You can see it from the top of the next rise. Might be as big as Lhaarat. The road looks to go through the middle of it. Hard to tell much more from here."

"If there's a large flat valley, there'll be people and a hamlet," replies Alyiakal.

Less than a quint later, Alyiakal reaches the top of the rise and looks north. From there, with its sweep of grass showing the touches of gold that will come with Harvest, the valley looks more like it belongs in the Grass Hills, rather than the hills below the Westhorns. *But then, we're getting close to the southeast part of the Grass Hills.*

A thin and intermittent line of trees marks the course of a small stream, and the hills on the north side of the valley remind Alyiakal of the Grass Hills, even with the Westhorns looming on the eastern horizon.

The road angles through the grass to a small town near the far side of the valley, beside the line of trees marking the stream, but Alyiakal sees other brownish spots that might be hamlets, with one or two near the road or the stream.

He looks to Chaaltyn. "I'd wager there's a permanent garrison in that town, and that there's a much larger town somewhere beyond the hills on the far side of the valley."

Chaaltyn smiles. "I don't think I'll take that wager, ser."

Alyiakal estimates the distances. While the companies could probably reach the town by early evening, he doesn't like the idea of getting that close to a possible garrison after a long, hot day on the road. He turns back to Chaaltyn. "We need to see if one of those hamlets near the road would be a suitable place to bed down before we move on the town."

Chaaltyn nods.

Over a glass later, First Company reaches the valley floor, where the grass beside the road is tall enough to reach his boot tops. Rather than the tan of the tallgrass around Pemedra, the stalks are starting to turn gold. Alyiakal has already sensed two grass cats stalking the scattered antelopes that bolt at the approach of the lancers.

As the lead scout, Maaetz now rides half a kay ahead of First Company, with Raayls midway between him and Alyiakal. The air is moister and hotter than it had been in the hills, and Alyiakal hopes they'll reach a suitable hamlet to rest men and mounts.

He also worries about dealing with the Cerlynese in the grasslands. Remaining in formation on the road will make it easier for Cerlynese archers to target lancers, but if the lancers spread into the tall grass flanking the road, they'll be slowed and hampered and still remain good targets.

If there were only some way to ambush them, but there's nothing tall enough to hide lancers.

While a concealment would allow lancers to remain unseen, Alyiakal doesn't want to reveal that ability. He also doesn't want unnecessary casualties. He's still pondering options, when suddenly he shakes his head, thinking about his very first use of magery, when he created a massive flame.

Images! An image could deceive both Cerlynese armsmen and lancers and still be useful.

For the next glass, while he rides, Alyiakal concentrates on creating images of the tallgrass, impinging on the road, enough to force Raayls to ease his mount farther into the middle. None of the rankers appear to notice the appearance or disappearance of the illusory grass, and creating illusions is far easier than expanding and holding shields.

Alyiakal's estimates of distance turn out to be optimistic, and the sun is just above the hills to the west when Maaetz sends back word of a small hamlet ahead.

Another quint passes before the tallgrass partly thins to reveal fields and plots. Crude mud-brick dwellings, with walls shorter in the front and taller in the back, sit beyond the plots. Woven grass-thatch roofs slant between the two walls, and most of the thirty or forty scattered dwellings have a mud-brick chimney roughly in the middle of the back wall.

Two tired-looking children, half-heartedly weeding a small garden, look up, then run screaming to the nearest dwelling. A woman appears in the narrow doorway, steps aside as the children run inside, and firmly closes the door.

Just like the last time you neared Cerlyn.

As First Company nears the center of the hamlet, little more than packed dirt that passes for a square and a single building that might be a chandlery, the various people who are outside move quickly away.

After the companies halt, Alyiakal addresses Chaaltyn. "Send scouts to find the best site for a camp and have a pair of lancers check the chandlery. I'd like to talk to whoever's there."

"Yes, ser."

In short order, two lancers enter the one-story building and return. "Just one man and a boy, ser."

"Haelsyn, you can accompany me," Alyiakal says to the older lancer, then dismounts and hands the chestnut's reins to the lancer behind Chaaltyn.

Alyiakal and Haelsyn walk to the chandlery and enter, where Alyiakal senses only two order/chaos patterns, but the boy has obviously been ushered into a back room. The chandler stands alone in front of a simple wooden counter. He looks to be only a few years older than Alyiakal.

"Good afternoon," says Alyiakal politely.

"Ah, good afternoon to you, ser."

"This is your chandlery?"

"It is."

"How long have you been here as a chandler?"

"Just six years, ser. I don't own it. I run it for the family."

"Then your family has a chandlery or factorage in the town on the north end of the valley?"

"Yes, ser. Would you like to buy anything?"

"Not at the moment. Does this hamlet have a name?"

The chandler offers an amused smile under which is worry. "Lastop."

"Because it's the last stop before the wilds of the high road?"

"I imagine so."

"What's the name of the town to the north?"

"Kraaslaen."

"There's a post or fort holding Cerlynese armsmen there, I take it?"

"Unless they've left in the last few eightdays."

"A brick-walled fort, then," Alyiakal half asks, half states.

"I didn't tell you that."

"They've been bringing in more armsmen in the last few years, haven't they?"

The young chandler says, "I haven't counted, ser."

Alyiakal senses that his surmise is correct. "How far is it from Kraaslaen to the next town beyond the hills?"

"Depends on how you go."

"Where does the road split, then?"

His question has upset the chandler, who's trying to answer the questions without giving Alyiakal any more information than he has to.

Alyiakal gambles, "Then the high road ends just beyond the hills to the north and splits into a low road eventually leading to Clynya and a northwest trail to the grasslands?"

"Pretty much, ser."

"And your family has chandleries or factorages in Clynya as well as in several towns along the way?"

"Not that many," protests the chandler.

Alyiakal smiles pleasantly. "We'll find out more when we get to Kraaslaen."

"You're not going to—" The chandler breaks off his words.

"We're not interested in destroying hamlets or towns. We're very interested in stopping Cerlyn from causing trouble on the borders. You're not allowed to trade with the grassland barbarians, are you?"

The chandler clearly doesn't know how to answer.

"Not if you want to remain whole and healthy, anyway," adds Alyiakal.

The chandler smiles wanly and sadly. "You're asking questions as if you already have the answers."

"Some I do. Do you have any for me?"

"Why are you doing this? After you leave, they'll just come back, and things will be worse."

Alyiakal almost denies that the Mirror Lancers intend to leave, but realizes he can't make that commitment, especially since the chandler revealed that the high road crossing the hills on the valley's north side roughly marks the boundary between Cyador and Cerlyn. Instead, he replies, "We all do what we have to. My task is to remove Cerlynese armsmen from the lands south of the high road to the point where it enters Cerlyn."

"Unless you remain, they will return."

"I'll do what I can," replies Alyiakal. "Thank for you making matters clear." He turns and leaves the chandlery. He doesn't shake his head, but instead turns his focus to determining the best place for an encampment.

In the end, after going over the scouts' discoveries, Alyiakal selects an area north of the stream and east of the road to Kraaslaen.

Once the camp is set, with sentries posted, mounts watered and picketed, lancers detailed to cut grass for forage, and meals being prepared, Alyiakal summons Vaarkas and Paersol to join him in the vanishing late-afternoon shade cast by one of the supply wagons.

"There's more we don't know than what we do," Alyiakal begins, "but we know Cerlyn has been causing trouble along lands on the west side of the Westhorns from east of Pemedra all the way to somewhere southeast of

Lhaarat. We've found some evidence of that in the waystation barracks where we stayed last night. The town on the north side of the valley is Kraaslaen, and the Cerlynese have a brick-walled fort there. We don't know how many arms-men they post there. Since we haven't seen any traces of large groups, and it's almost impossible for a large group to have gotten around us, it's a fair wager that most of the Cerlynese armsmen south of Cerlyn are in that fort."

"Do you have any idea how many, ser?" asks Paersol.

"No, but I doubt that it's much more than two companies, if that." Aly-iakal smiles coldly. "Whatever the number, our job is to make certain that all of them are captured or dead."

Paersol swallows; Vaarkas nods.

"That may sound callous," Alyiakal continues, "but remember the Cerlyn-ese torture and kill traders who trade with anyone the Cerlynese don't like. They send weapons, tack, and horses—and sometimes women—to those who raid other lands, especially Cyador. If we don't remove those armsmen in Kraaslaen, we'll be spending most of our time spread over something like seventy kays of high road."

What Alyiakal doesn't say is that that will still happen, in a year or so, unless Mirror Lancer headquarters builds a post in Kraaslaen or sends more compa-nies to Lhaarat. Alyiakal strongly doubts that headquarters will do either.

After a pause, he adds, "If we don't get rid of them, headquarters won't exactly be pleased, because those are our orders."

"Sowshit, as usual," says Vaarkas. "How do you think we can do it?"

Alyiakal says, deadpan, "I'll let you know after I see what their fort looks like."

XC

Alyiakal leads First Company onto the high road toward Kraaslaen just be-fore sunrise under a cloudless but hazy green-blue sky that promises a miser-ably hot day.

"What kind of fort do you think they'll have?" asks Chaaltyn.

"*If* they have one, it will be stone-walled or mud brick. My wager is on mud brick. They'd have to bring logs or timber from the hills to the east or stone from the hills to the north. Timber burns. Stone and mud brick don't. I'm guessing, though, just like everyone else."

Two glasses pass before Raayls signals from the top of a low rise in the road ahead. Alyiakal signals for him to hold, then orders, "Company! Halt!"

"Ser?" asks Chaaltyn.

"Raayls sees something. If it's Cerlynese approaching, I don't want them seeing us yet. I'm riding to join him, and I'll be back immediately."

"Yes, ser."

When Alyiakal reaches Raayls and the rise, he sees that the center of the town lies more than two kays away and the Cerlynese fort dominates a low hill on the northeast side of Kraaslaen. The dull brown mud-brick walls look more like an extension of the hill, without obvious watchtowers or crenellations for archers.

"Dust ahead," says Raayls, almost simultaneously with Alyiakal's observation. "Has to be a squad, maybe more."

"They must have had scouts watching from a distance," replies Alyiakal, "maybe even got word from someone in Lastop." *If not both.* "Both you and Maaetz ride back to First Company with me."

Once back with First Company, Alyiakal says to Chaaltyn, "Possibly a company headed toward us. They'll start loosing shafts as soon as they're in range. Then they'll either charge or withdraw so that they can repeat a fast attack." He studies the grass ahead, finally sighting a slight rise slightly more than two hundred yards ahead. "I'm going to try something. The grass ahead on that little rise to the left just might be tall enough to hide a squad." *With the help of an illusion.*

Alyiakal pauses, looks to the rise, then adds, "You're in command here. I'll take first squad there, and we'll rake them from the side. Then the rest of First Company can charge while they're disorganized, if necessary. The road's wide enough for four abreast. If a charge isn't necessary, move to join first squad."

"You don't want to spread lancers into the grass, then?"

Alyiakal shakes his head. "No. That will just give the Cerlynese more targets." Besides which, Alyiakal can shield the column from shafts, if only for a little while. He turns in the saddle. "First squad! On me. Fast trot!"

Within fifty yards of the rise, Alyiakal concentrates on creating the illusion of taller grass there and slightly lower grass in front, where he intends to position first squad.

He calls a halt short of the rise and orders, "First file, follow me into the grass. Second file, close behind, staggered formation." Alyiakal eases the chestnut off the road and into the grass.

As the lancers move into position, Maaetz trots by with a slightly puzzled expression, possibly because he may have seen tallgrass seem to grow a yard or more, but that's not something that Alyiakal can help. *Hopefully, with all the fighting to come, he'll forget that little oddity.*

Once first squad is in position, Alyiakal moves slightly farther to the left and says, "When I order you to fire, make your first burst very quick, and keep it level. The riders will be even with you, and that first quick burst should burn away enough of the grass that you'll have a clear second shot. Make it count."

"That grass looks pretty thick, ser," says Haelsyn.

"Just trust me," replies Alyiakal dryly. "Now, silent riding, or silent waiting."

He concentrates on sensing the Cerlynese riders, now less than half a kay away. The rise is just high enough to keep them from seeing the main body of Mirror Lancers until they top the rise. Alyiakal suspects they'll get just past that point before loosing arrows. If so, first squad should be able to disrupt the attack before the Cerlynese shafts fly.

If not, Alyiakal will have more work cut out for himself.

Only a quint passes, which feels more like a glass, before the Cerlynese riders near the rise. Alyiakal senses roughly forty armsmen, with a suspicion that half are archers.

A single scout precedes the riders by about fifty yards, riding past the illusory grass without a hesitation, but slows and then stops less than fifteen yards past the lancers' concealment, before turning his mount and heading back to the top of the rise, where he stops, and shouts back to the oncoming force, "Mirror Lancers, a little over two hundred yards!"

"How many?" shouts someone in return.

"More than a company!"

In a fraction of a quint the first squad of Cerlynese rides over the rise and halts. While the first ranks in the column bear circular bronze shields, the armsmen hold those shields facing the larger Mirror Lancer force.

Alyiakal immediately orders, "Fire! Now!" He uses two quick blasts on the lead riders, then drops the illusion to his right, leaving it in place to his left to block the view of the armsmen in the rear of the column, then orders, "Fire at will!"

In moments, most of the first Cerlynese squad is either ashes or dead, and

Alyiakal drops the rest of the concealment and turns his firelance toward the rear of the force, flaming one armsman.

"Ambush!" yells someone belatedly.

Alyiakal picks off three more riders before the Cerlynese turn and struggle to withdraw. He extends his shields momentarily in case archers in the Cerlynese rear loose shafts, but if they do, none strike his shields, and he contracts them.

"Cease fire!" His order is unnecessary, because there are no Cerlynese left in range, only ashes, partly burned bodies, mostly of horses, and two mounts screaming in agony.

A single armsman staggers along the side of the road, unhorsed by a startled mount in the initial ambush, a bronze-faced shield on one arm.

"Haelsyn! You and Fuast take that man captive! Unharmed!" Alyiakal orders, looking around for others, but there aren't any. That's not surprising given the closeness and intensity of the firelance barrage. He shifts his attention to the road to the north, but the squad of remaining Cerlynese, already close to half a kay away, shows no signs of slowing.

Someone behind Alyiakal says, "How'd he manage that?"

Alyiakal ignores the comment and orders, "First file, clear the road, and stack all the bows and blades in one place, and the shields. Especially the shields. Hanskyn! Deal with any spoils." *Not that there'll be many from these poor bastards.*

The remainder of First Company rides to join first squad, followed by Fourth and Third Companies.

As the scouts approach, Alyiakal calls out, "Post on the rise there and let us know if anyone else is headed this way."

"Yes, ser."

Then Alyiakal turns to Chaaltyn. "Send messengers to request that Captain Paersol and Captain Vaarkas join me."

While he waits for the captains, Alyiakal force-funnels the sun-chaos bits he's gathered into his firelance, replenishing most of the chaos he expended, then returns the funnel to collecting more chaos, knowing that he'll need all he can gather.

Paersol arrives first, and scans the road ahead. He looks to Alyiakal for explanation.

"A Cerlynese company attacked. I'll fill you in when Vaarkas arrives."

When the senior captain arrives, Alyiakal briefly outlines their ambush, adding, "I doubt we'll be able to surprise them like that again, but we'll continue once the road is clear and see how to deal with their fort."

Even with the help of second squad, given the number of fallen horses, it takes longer than Alyiakal anticipates to gather the usable tack and weapons, and drag the dead horses off the road. So Alyiakal calls for the captive.

The Cerlynese armsman still appears slightly stunned when the two lancers bring the now-unarmed man before the three officers.

"Your name?" asks Alyiakal, looking down from the saddle.

"Chaudyl," stammers the man.

"Where are you from?"

Chaudyl doesn't answer.

"Kraaslaen?" When there's no response, Alyiakal adds, "Not there, then. Clynya? Or some half-forgotten hamlet?"

Chaudyl stares sullenly at the road beneath his feet, but says nothing.

"How many companies are in the fort in Kraaslaen?" Alyiakal waits, then asks, "Two?"

Chaudyl's order/chaos patterns suggest to Alyiakal that there are indeed two companies assigned to the Kraaslaen fort. He turns to the lancers. "Truss him up and put him in one of the supply wagons. Give him some water first."

After the lancers march Chaudyl to the supply wagons near the end of the column, Paersol asks, "What about the fort?"

"You'll see it when you ride over the rise. It's moderately large, mud-brick, and sits on a hill overlooking the town. The hill is next to a stream."

"We don't have any siege gear," says Paersol.

"We don't," agrees Alyiakal. "But we might not need it. That depends on how that fort is built and what's inside it. It's time to go find out. You can return to your companies. I'll let you know when I know more."

Less than a quint later, Alyiakal rides over the rise behind the scouts, leading the three companies north toward the town. He rides another kay before reaching the first of the mud-brick dwellings flanking the road. They don't look markedly different from those in Lastop, although those nearer the fort are set closer together. There are no dwellings or other structures on the hill with the fort, and the road appears to run past the base of the hill and over a bridge before angling to the northeast as it climbs the hills on the north side of the valley.

As First Company leads the way into Kraaslaen, where the high road turns into the main street, Alyiakal can't help but notice doors and shutters closing as people catch sight of the lancers. *Why are the lancers so feared, when they haven't entered this part of Cyador in years, if ever? Because the Cerlynese have told everyone they've come to protect the people from the terrible Mirror Lancers of Cyad?*

Before long, Alyiakal rides into Kraaslaen's central square, containing a simple fountain with a circular basin at its base. Anyone getting water has vanished before First Company rides into the square. A line of small shops borders the west side of the square and a modest inn sits to the east. The whitewash coating the inn's mud-brick walls has worn thin in places, and Alyiakal struggles to make out the image of a copper bowl on the signboard over the door.

He then looks at the shops—a chandlery, no doubt run by the same family as in Lastop; a tinsmith; a cooperage; another shop that likely offers dry goods; and three others without identifying marks. All are shut tight.

Turning to Chaaltyn, he says, "We'll proceed to the fort, or close enough to study it without being in arrow range from the wall."

Another kay brings Alyiakal to where the high road crosses the bridge and begins a slow climb to the northeast, where an equally broad road branches off and runs straight to the gate of the Cerlynese fort.

Alyiakal reins up fifty yards from the base of the hill, out of easy bowshot, and studies the fort and the ground around it.

With mud-brick walls three yards high and each fifty yards long set in a square, the fort isn't that imposing, especially given a single wooden gate that is two and a half yards high and barely that wide that serves as the only entrance. While the gate has wide iron hinges, it isn't iron-bound. It's also firmly closed at the moment. Alyiakal nods and works on sensing what lies within the walls. Horses are the first and most obvious set of order/chaos patterns, either penned or confined in some fashion in the northeast quarter of the open courtyard. Although Alyiakal cannot be absolutely certain, he feels the wooden structure backed by the west wall is a combination of quarters and mess areas.

The east end of the hill is a large, fenced pasture, currently empty, indirectly confirming that the Cerlynese arms-commander brought all the horses into the fort. That will create other problems after a while, not that Alyiakal intends to play a waiting game. At the same time, he knows a direct attack on the fort is impractical; the open ground would make lancers easy targets for archers on the wall before they could get close enough to use firelances. He's already learned, however, that there are ways around that problem.

Alyiakal turns his mount and sends lancers to summon Vaarkas and Paersol, while he considers the possibilities and practicalities.

Once they join him, Alyiakal begins, "We'll alternate companies so that one company is always ready to attack anyone leaving the fort."

"Do you really think we can lay siege to them and wait them out?" ask Paersol.

"What are they seeing?" asks Alyiakal. "First, we brought supply wagons. Second, we control the town, and there's certainly enough forage for our mounts. We can keep them from being able to feed their horses. While there are reasons we can't stay too long," *like raiders closer to Lhaarat finding out that three-quarters of the companies are elsewhere,* "they don't *know* that for certain. What we need to do is to make them think we're here indefinitely."

"How do we do that, ser?" asks Vaarkas.

Alyiakal tells the pair; that is, he tells them what they'll see before dawn on eightday.

"That's risky," says Vaarkas dubiously.

"If it doesn't work," replies Alyiakal, "it won't cost us much, and we can try something else. In the meantime, we need to set up as if we're here for a while and make sure they can't leave the fort."

XCI

Alyiakal rises in the darkness well before dawn, partly because he must and partly because he didn't sleep well. He is keeping all the sun-chaos he collected on the previous afternoon linked to him, rather than quietly discharged, but he knows he'll need all of it before the morning is over.

He has several swallows of order-infused water and some trail biscuits before meeting briefly with Paersol and Vaarkas, cautioning them to ready their lancers quietly, which shouldn't be a problem, since only one squad from each company will be mounted. Then he saddles the chestnut and meets with Chaaltyn and the two lancers who will accompany him—Haelsyn and Fuast.

"First Company ready and standing by, ser," says Chaaltyn.

"Good. Don't move forward until you see flames or hear shouts from the fort, and keep the company spread in the darkness. They're not to use firelances until I give the command or it's clear that the Cerlynese are leaving the fort."

"Yes, ser."

What Alyiakal is attempting requires fairly accurate timing. He wants the Cerlynese scrambling from the fort in early light so that they can be picked off easily, but he needs to stir them up before most would rise and while it's still dark.

Alyiakal mounts the chestnut, and the two lancers quickly mount up as well and follow him as he rides through the darkness to the fort.

Just in case there are sharp-eyed sentries on the wall, Alyiakal creates an illusion of fuzzy blackness in front and to the right of the three of them as they ride up the hill road. Given the small size of the fort and the range of a firelance, Alyiakal doesn't need to be directly under the walls, only within twenty yards of the southwest corner. However, that means covering close to two hundred yards, largely relying on his order/chaos perceptions. While he senses sentries on the wall beside the gate and at each corner of the wall, none of them act as if they hear the three riders, at least not until Alyiakal reins up perhaps fifteen yards from the southwest corner.

"Something's out there."

"Always something out there."

Alyiakal forces himself to be thorough as he readies his firelance, then releases a large burst of chaos in an upward arc, which he guides down to the wooden roof at the rear of the large barracks building. Five more bursts follow—then a sixth when he senses that the flames he's triggered may not be strong enough in one part of the building.

Cries of "Fire!" and "Fire in the barracks!" come from within the fort.

"Turn right," Alyiakal says to Haelsyn and Fuast, "toward the gate." As he rides, he releases two more firelance bolts, each guided to take out a gate guard.

Then, when the three stand roughly fifteen yards in front of the gate, he orders quietly, "Fire the gate and keep at it."

While the two lancers direct their bolts at the gate, Alyiakal gathers his stored chaos and adds it to a firelance bolt aimed squarely at the gate's center.

Flames explode outward from the impact, turning the gate into a mass of flames.

"Withdraw now!" snaps Alyiakal. "Stay close!" He wheels the chestnut around and away from the fort, toward First Company's advance. Third Company covers their right flank and Fourth Company their left. Alyiakal drops the dark illusion and extends his shields to cover the two lancers just in case some archers have gained the walls.

Alyiakal glances back to the fort, where he can now see tongues of flame above the walls. While the gate still burns brightly, there's one dark area, and he turns in the saddle and points his firelance in the general direction of the gate, guiding the chaos bolt to the darker area.

Then he looks right, to the east, where light oozes over the Westhorns, a bit later than he'd hoped. Even so, there's enough light for First Company to move close enough and pick off any archers on the walls—there are a handful, because Alyiakal can sense incoming shafts.

When he reaches the spread line of First Company, on foot, he turns the chestnut and orders, "Company! Forward! Targeted fire! Targeted fire!" He glances at the burning gate, but it remains in place, even as it burns.

First Company advances within sixty yards of the fort before Alyiakal sees Cerlynese armsmen scrambling down the east wall of the fort. "Cerlynese on the east side!"

Even as he calls this out, he targets one, two, then three of them. Other lancers follow his example, and the mounted squad from Third Company rides toward the fleeing armsmen.

Alyiakal vaguely senses some Cerlynese climbing the rear wall and escaping northeast, behind the fort. "Third Company mounted! Sweep the east side and move to the north."

He looks at the still-burning gate. While it's burned through in places, it hasn't yet collapsed.

"Fourth Company! Mounted squad to the bridge!" Alyiakal watches to ensure the squad blocks access to the stream bridge to the fort's northwest, then returns his attention to the Cerlynese fort. Only a few armsmen now climb down or jump from the east wall.

Then there are none, and the lancers on foot return and form up, waiting to see if they're needed, while the three mounted squads comb the ground behind the fort. Alyiakal takes a moment to do what he quickly can for the few lancer wounded.

Three quints later, as full sunlight spreads across Kraaslaen, the screams from inside the fort, most from horses, have ended. Small fires continue to burn or smolder within the fort, and the main gate has not so much collapsed as slumped off its iron hinges into a heap of still-burning coals. The three mounted squads have returned.

The only Cerlynese armsmen alive are those who fled or were captured, and all of those captured are wounded. Alyiakal sees little point in trying to chase the handful or so who escaped Third Company. They have few weapons and no mounts, and based on the chandler's words and his own experience, he doubts that they'll get much sympathy from the people of Kraaslaen.

As for the handful of injured Cerlynese troopers, Alyiakal will heal those he can, but sees no sense in dragging them back to Lhaarat. He turns the chestnut to the supply wagon on the far side of the high road from the fort, glancing to the bridge, guarded by Fourth Company's third squad, and then to the east and the center of Kraaslaen, where he sees several scattered groups of locals gathered and pointing at the fort.

When he reaches the middle wagon, he dismounts and hands the chestnut's reins to a lancer, saying, "Don't go far. I'll need him shortly."

"Yes, ser."

Alyiakal turns to Chaaltyn. "Did we have any deaths?"

"Only one. Vhaelyt—second squad—took a couple of shafts. He was dead before anyone noticed."

Alyiakal winces. *As much a casualty of a night attack as of the fight.* "Any other wounded?"

"No one else in First Company, ser."

"Thank you."

Alyiakal then joins Vaarkas and Paersol. "You both did well."

Paersol nods briefly in acknowledgment.

"So did you, ser," says Vaarkas. "I never asked, but how did you come up with this?"

"We faced a similar situation against the Kyphrans several years ago. I just changed some of the details."

"Begging your pardon, ser," says Vaarkas, "but was it the wisest decision for you to set those fires?"

"Probably not," replies Alyiakal, "but it made sense at the time, and I didn't have time to find out if anyone else could do what I knew I could." He offers a wry and apologetic smile. "There are ways to use a firelance that aren't taught, and perhaps I should have done so."

"Like burning people alive, ser?" asks Paersol.

"Every time you kill a raider with a firelance, Captain, you burn him alive. I'd thought the gate would burn to ash and that the Cerlynese would attack that way, but the gate held and everything else went up in flames. In any event, an officer's duty is to accomplish the mission with the least loss of lancers and materiel. I'd be very interested to hear if you can think of a better way to accomplish what we did this morning." Alyiakal pauses. "We'll be leaving early tomorrow morning. After you collect all the weapons and usable tack, I'll leave you to begin preparations for departure."

Then he walks around the wagon, and, after glancing around, and seeing no one looking his way, raises a concealment around himself. He senses either Paersol or Vaarkas coming around the wagon.

Alyiakal eases back to where he can hear.

"He's gone," says Paersol, "the ice-blooded bastard."

"You know," says Vaarkas, "he could get you cashiered for insubordination."

"I did everything he ordered. I don't have to like it. He set that up to kill as many of them as he could. I could hear screams. Some of them burned to death . . . and the horses . . ."

"You itching to die, Paersol?" asks Vaarkas, quietly, but intensely. "We got two-three dead and a few wounded. The way I figure, he wiped out three companies and destroyed their post. You're the one who pointed out that we couldn't take the place, and we couldn't wait them out."

"It's so cold . . . as if their lives didn't matter."

"Dead is dead. Doesn't matter if it's by blade or firelance or by a frigging fire. This way we're the ones going home. You want to be bled to death raid after raid?"

Alyiakal has heard enough and slips away quietly.

He has a great deal to do, including dealing with the wounded, before he can even think about organizing the ride back to Lhaarat.

After taking time to calm himself, Alyiakal makes his way to the stable behind the fort, where the tack rooms have been cleared out and pallets laid down for the wounded who cannot stand and benches for those who can sit. The first and smaller room holds the lancer wounded, most of whom he's already seen. As Alyiakal has ordered, there are now lengths of wood as well as cloth, effectively requisitioned from the local chandlery, that he can use for splints and dressings.

The one lancer Alyiakal hasn't seen earlier lies on a pallet, definitely pale, with a dressing on one side below his ribs. Alyiakal senses wound chaos beneath the dressing, but not so much as he would expect. He struggles for a moment to recall the man's name, then asks, "What happened to you, Ashaar?"

"Don't know, ser. One moment I was moving forward . . . just taken down a green bastard. Then something hit me, and I was on my chest. Felt like something stabbed me . . . woke up here."

Alyiakal carefully senses the wound, but all he can discern is some sort of puncture wound. He's never sensed anything like it, and he has no idea what will happen. Out of caution, and partly because he doesn't know what else to do, he infuses order around the internal chaos. While he has considerable doubts about how effective the order will be with a wound that close to the gut, there's no sense in not trying.

He turns to the lancer caring for the wounded. "Move him as little as possible for now."

Aerek is the next lancer, with a shoulder wound from an arrow, not particularly serious, except there's more wound chaos than there should be, and definitely more than Alyiakal would like after initial treatment. He makes a mental note to check the lancer's wound chaos carefully in the days ahead.

For the remaining lancer wounded, Alyiakal has little to do, but he wants to check. His earlier efforts had been hurried, and there had been a broken arm he didn't have the material to splint, which he now does.

Then Alyiakal enters the larger tack room.

The first Cerlynese armsman has burns covering the right side of his body, including a third of his face, as well as a broken arm, and he moans incessantly. Alyiakal just offers a touch of order, even as he wonders if he should remove enough order to let the man die more easily and quickly rather than possibly suffering for days.

The next man sits on a bench, cradling a broken arm. He looks up at Alyiakal and freezes. "We just followed orders. We just followed orders."

Alyiakal wonders what he did that the mere sight of an officer spurs those words.

Still, Alyiakal sets and splints the arm. After he does, he says, "You'll need to keep that splint on for at least five eightdays, longer if you can." There's little more he can offer, given that he's not staying in Kraaslaen.

"We just followed orders," the Cerlynese says as Alyiakal moves away. "That's all we did."

The next Cerlynese, a hard-faced man, has a burn down his entire left arm, and any cloth that had been there either burned away or was cut off. The man's skin, though, is red—not blistered or charred—although there is a dusting of wound chaos in places. The larger problem is a clearly broken wrist.

"I'll have to splint this."

"Do what you will. It likely won't heal right."

"It'll have a better chance. Besides, that will allow you to help the others."

"For what? Be slaves?"

"These lands belong to Cyador, not Cerlyn. We allow the people to do what they want. We remove those who don't belong. We don't care if you stay or go, so long as you don't bear arms for Cerlyn if you stay. Now, try not to move while I set, splint, and wrap your wrist."

Alyiakal actually uses order to immobilize and move the bones back in place, but doubts the armsman even notices, given the pain. He also adds a bit of order.

The armsman looks at Alyiakal's uniform as if for the first time. "You're an officer, not a healer."

"I'm both. Try not to bang that against anything. I'd suggest keeping it splinted for the next four or five eightdays."

Alyiakal moves to the next armsman.

"Why do you bother?" asks an older Cerlynese, as Alyiakal splints his leg, doubtless broken by jumping from the wall and landing wrong in the dark. "All of you were trying to kill us two glasses ago."

"The fighting's over," replies Alyiakal. "When this heals you can at least limp back to Cerlyn."

"Have to limp into Cyador. The Duke isn't charitable to those who fail him."

"What's the name of the Duke?"

"Does it matter? He's the Duke."

Alyiakal doesn't pursue the question, giving the same advice about the splint before moving on to the next wounded man.

Another glass passes before he leaves the makeshift infirmary and walks down the hill past the still-smoldering fort toward the supply wagon that has become an unofficial headquarters.

Thoughts and mixed feelings swirl through his head. *Could you have dealt with the fort another way without losing more lancers? How could you not have done it, given the way the Cerlynese treat people? Will it change anything without endless days of patrol or another post here in Kraaslaen? And with the Merchanters trading with Cerlyn to obtain copper, how will headquarters respond to what you've done—even if you were ordered to resolve the problem?*

When Alyiakal nears the supply wagon, he finds a middle-aged bearded man in brown trousers, a tan shirt, and a brown vest standing near Chaaltyn and clearly waiting for him.

"Ser," says Chaaltyn, stepping forward, "this is Headman Nauraal."

"You're the headman of Kraaslaen?" inquires Alyiakal, rather than asking what Nauraal wants, because it's obvious from the man's agitation that he definitely wants something.

"Overcaptain, ser?"

"Yes?" replies Alyiakal politely.

"Your . . . squad leader, he says that you do not plan to stay."

"We do not. Our job was to remove those who do not belong in Cyador and to leave you in peace."

"You must stay, or the evil ones will continue to harm us."

"There are less than a score left, and most of them are injured. They have neither weapons nor horses."

"Others will come. The evil Duke Taartyn will send more," insists Nauraal.

"You don't know that," replies Alyiakal, "but if he does, we will remove them as well. If more armsmen come, send a messenger to the Mirror Lancer post at Lhaarat."

Alyiakal wishes he could promise more, but he knows he can't, *especially as a mere overcaptain and deputy post commander.* He can only hope Mirror Lancer headquarters and the Emperor of Light will inform the Duke Taartyn of Cerlyn, assuming that indeed is his name, that Cyador will act as necessary against further intrusions.

"Is that all?" Nauraal asks, scandalized.

"No. We will send patrols along the high road to deal with raiders and others who threaten the peace and well-being."

"Just the high road?"

"Does the high road not extend to that bridge?" Alyiakal points to where Fourth Company lancers still maintain guard.

Nauraal nods, then finally says, "That is not enough . . . but it is something."

Alyiakal gestures to the fort. "Anything you and your people find there is yours." That isn't so much a gift as a recognition of reality. *But you might as well take credit for it.* "Leave the stable. We will need it when we come to Kraaslaen."

"Yes, honored ser."

"Is that all?" asks Alyiakal.

"Yes, honored ser." The headman backs away, then turns.

Alyiakal watches him for a moment, then turns to Chaaltyn. "All that means is that we've got another problem. Leaving the wounded Cerlynese here will either get them killed or get locals killed, sooner or later, maybe both." He pauses, then says, "See how many horses survived. There were some in the stable. Look for a wagon or a cart."

"You're thinking of bringing them back to Lhaarat, ser?"

Alyiakal shakes his head. "They'll have to go back across the hills to Cerlyn. At least half of them can ride. It won't be comfortable, but that's the best we can do, under the circumstances. We'll have to stay here another day or so to take care of that." *Something else that you didn't think about.*

XCII

Alyiakal's sleep on eightday night is troubled, even as tired as he is. His exhaustion leaves him with the images of flames, and the silent dream-sounds of screaming horses and dying men are only an inchoate jumble when he struggles into wakefulness on oneday morning. He has no doubts he will dream clearer and more disturbing images in the future.

Once he is fully awake, Alyiakal makes his way to the makeshift infirmary, where he checks on the handful of lancer wounded in the smaller room, making certain that splints are firm and wound chaos is diminishing. It is, except in Ashaar's case, where, from what Alyiakal can recall, there's a bit more.

"How are you feeling, Ashaar?"

"About the same, ser. Still hurts, but not any worse." The lancer hesitates, then says, "Gut wounds are bad, aren't they, ser?"

"No wound is good, but gut wounds are among the worst. So far, you're doing better than most." As he talks, Alyiakal eases small bits of order into the worst areas of chaos around the wound.

"Am I going to die, ser?"

"Not if you don't get worse. Right now, it's not too bad. If it gets worse . . . that's the time to worry."

"You'll tell me true, ser, won't you?"

"I will." Alyiakal hopes he won't have to, but he's lost lancers with gut wounds before. "Right now's not the time to worry." He straightens up and heads for the larger tack room and almost a score of wounded Cerlynese.

He begins with the most severely injured man, with burns across more than half his body, and tiny bits of wound chaos already everywhere, with more around his broken arm, because the burns have already weakened the rest of his body. At the moment, his moans are almost inaudible, but that won't last, Alyiakal knows.

"Can't you do more for him?" asks the man on the nearest pallet, propped into a sitting position with a bulky splint on his leg.

"Even the greatest of the Magi'i healers couldn't do more," Alyiakal replies quietly, turning toward the questioner. "Any sharp pains?"

"No, ser. Same heavy dull ache . . . unless I twitch or move sudden-like."

Alyiakal infuses some order to deal with the wound chaos that might be fading. "How long have you been in Kraaslaen?"

"Since maybe the third eightday of Spring."

"You from Clynya?"

"Hardly. Cypraan, town near the mines. Didn't want to be a miner."

Alyiakal listens for a bit, then moves to check an armsman with a broken arm, and a burn on the other forearm. He adds a touch of order-infused water to the dressing. "It will feel better and heal sooner if the dressing is damp . . . but don't soak it."

"That helps," says the armsman.

"How did you become an armsman?"

The man offers a short bitter laugh. "Not much choice. Duke needed armsmen."

Alyiakal proceeds through the injured, not always asking questions, but he makes a deliberate decision to save the hard-faced man with the broken wrist and lightly burned arm for last. He dampens the light dressing with order-infused water, then checks the wrist splint and nods. Then he asks, "You're a squad leader, aren't you? Or if you're not, you should be."

"How would you know?"

"It's my business to know," replies Alyiakal, quietly adding order to the broken wrist bones.

"You're not just any officer." The man nods to the Mirror Lancers guarding the door. "They said you were their commander. Why do you bother with healing?"

"Someone has to. I have a talent for it. Why shouldn't my men have the best I can get for them?"

"Be nice if others thought that."

"You used to be a squad leader and got tired of bad orders and unnecessary cruelty." Alyiakal is guessing, but one way or the other, he'll learn something.

For several moments, the man says nothing.

Alyiakal just waits.

Finally, the man says, "Former squad leader. Busted and sent here."

Alyiakal nods.

"You talked to all the men here. Yesterday and today."

"Yes, they're injured."

"You say that after you ordered us to be burned to death?"

Alyiakal looks directly at the former squad leader. "I set all the flames myself, with my firelance. It was the only way to carry out my orders without risking too many of my men."

"Frig!"

"You asked," replies Alyiakal quietly.

"Your men follow you, I'd wager."

"That's their duty. Mine is to accomplish the orders in the most effective way with the least loss of lancers." *Which is critical because Cyador doesn't have that many lancers for the lands it rules.* Not that anyone has told Alyiakal that, but even in his comparatively short career it's become obvious.

"So why are you trying to heal us? Wouldn't it make it easier if we died?"

"No. If we let you die or killed you now, it would be murder, and sooner or later, everyone would know that we killed needlessly." Alyiakal pauses, then says, "That's what I don't understand about Cerlynese officers. From what I've seen they're cruel almost all the time, even when there's no reason."

"You're wrong," replies the former squad leader. "They're cruel *all* the time. That's what the Duke wants. He thinks other lands will fear Cerlyn."

"They will—until they destroy him," says Alyiakal.

The other laughs. "The Jeranyi won't. Neither will the Suthyans. They'd rather count their golds." Then he shrugs, unthinkingly, because he winces before he says, "He hasn't really tested Cyador. The border here is the only one touching Cyador."

"What do you think he'll do at the loss of . . . what . . . three companies?"

"I'm not the one you should ask. I'm just a wounded former squad leader."

Alyiakal steps away. "I'll be back this evening to check on your men. I assume you're the most senior . . . or at least the one that the others will accept as most senior?"

"That's fair. You and your lancers took out the undercaptains and the captain, and there aren't any squad leaders here."

Alyiakal nods. "Until this evening."

As he walks down the hill back to the supply wagon, Alyiakal considers what he's learned from the captives, especially the former squad leader.

So far, at least, it doesn't change his opinions of Cerlyn, and even if Duke Taartyn decides to back away from Kraaslaen for a bit, Cerlyn will present a problem for some time to come. All Alyiakal can do is to patrol and drive out any Cerlynese attempts to return to Kraaslaen—assuming Taartyn doesn't raise a massive army.

But the Duke will find it close to impossible to raise, equip, train, and dispatch such a force before Autumn, which means that such an attack is unlikely any time soon.

Unfortunately, unless you're relieved of duty, you'll be the one who has to deal with such an army for the next year and possibly two.

XCIII

Despite Alyiakal's best efforts, First Company does not ride out of Kraaslaen until threeday morning, but that delay allows Alyiakal to ensure that the thirteen surviving Cerlynese are well away from the town under the leadership of the hard-faced former squad leader, whose name he never learned. Alyiakal has also confirmed with him that there is a hamlet on the far side of the northern hills. He suspects, and hopes, that some of the wounded will "disappear" along the way. He wouldn't be surprised if none of them made it back to the nearest post for armsmen, which might also create nasty rumors about the Mirror Lancers, at least in Cerlyn. *That might not necessarily be bad, given Duke Taartyn's attitude.*

So far, the lancer wounded seem to be improving, except for Ashaar. Alyiakal has managed to keep the wound chaos from spreading, or increasing, and is hopeful that, if he can keep the wound chaos at bay, the young man will heal.

As before, Raayls and Maaetz ride ahead of First Company, with Alyiakal and Chaaltyn leading the main body. Although the calendar says it's now Harvest, the sun beats down through the heat-hazy green-blue sky as though it is still full Summer.

After a quint of relative silence, Chaaltyn says, "You haven't sent any messengers back to Lhaarat, ser."

"No, I haven't," says Alyiakal agreeably. "They'd only get there a day and a half before we will, and some events are best explained in detail."

"Ser?"

"Matters that seem straightforward in Lhaarat may not be viewed that way in Cyad. I'll leave it at that for now."

"When you say things like that, ser, it tells me I'm glad I'm not an officer."

"Every rank has its advantages and its disadvantages," replies Alyiakal. *The higher in rank, at least above captain, the less likely you are to be killed and the more likely you'll be blamed for matters you can't control. Occasionally, you might get fortunate, but that just means more is expected of you.*

"I like where I am, ser. Leastwise, right now."

"Then you're fortunate, Chaaltyn."

When the companies near Lastop, Alyiakal orders a brief break north of the hamlet where the force set up camp before. After the break, the Mirror Lancers start through the small hamlet. As Alyiakal nears the center of town, he sees the young chandler step out of the chandlery.

"Keep moving," Alyiakal says to Chaaltyn. "I'm going to tell the chandler what happened, but I don't want to halt again so soon." Then he urges the chestnut into a fast trot toward the chandlery.

The chandler looks worriedly at the approaching lancers and then up at Alyiakal as he reins up. "You don't look to have suffered much."

"We lost two men and have some wounded who look to survive. Most of the three companies from Cerlyn didn't. We destroyed the fort."

"They'll be back."

"If they're that foolish, they'll suffer a similar fate. The people in Kraaslaen don't want them back." Alyiakal smiles pleasantly. "I thought you'd like to know." He inclines his head politely, turning the chestnut and rejoining Chaaltyn. From what he senses, the chandler is stunned, and to Alyiakal, that suggests the man's family may well have ties to influential traders close to the Duke, unlike the headman of Kraaslaen, who definitely doesn't want any more Cerlynese armsmen around.

"From what I saw, ser," says Chaaltyn as Alyiakal settles the chestnut beside the senior squad leader and his mount, "he didn't look all too pleased."

"I have the feeling he and his family don't want competition, not that they'll have to worry for a while." *Most Cyadoran Merchanters aren't interested in out-of-the-way towns.* That's why Saelora's venture has been so successful, and why things will get more difficult as Loraan House expands.

Alyiakal returns his full attention to the road ahead, absently checking his chaos-collecting order funnel, knowing all too well that he'll never know for certain when he might need more chaos.

XCIV

After spending the night at the unnamed hamlet with the formerly Cerlynese waystation barracks, Alyiakal has his force set out at first light on fourday. Out of caution, he decides the three companies will take the high road all the way to the east road on the return to Lhaarat.

Even when Alyiakal and his force pass the cruder trader waystation on the high road, there are no tracks of Cerlynese riders. This suggests that, between the earlier first skirmish and the brief battle at Kraaslaen, the Mirror Lancers have cleared the high road of Cerlynese and the raiders they "encouraged" to attack the area around Lhaarat. The only tracks Alyiakal sees are of a few riders and carts and wagons, and no new hoofprints lead from the high road down to the old logging trail.

Once Alyiakal rides over the rough section of the road above where the River Lhaar tunnels its way under the long-collapsed hillside, he watches for tracks coming from the hidden northeast entrance to Lestroi. Neither he nor the scouts see any traces, although it's possible and probable that a rider or two may have used that way out of the hidden hamlet since the water flowing over the rock washes away any traces of entry. The tracks on the road intertwine enough that all Alyiakal can tell is that, if someone did, it wasn't within the last day or so.

Just past midafternoon, Alyiakal notes the various landmarks and the rocky ridge to his right that indicate they are approaching the log fort and the point where the high road joins the east road. As the scouts near the first of the log dwellings leading to the fort, a rider appears, heading south toward the fort. Unlike the last rider on Alyiakal's first approach, this rider shouts out, "Mirror Lancers coming! Mirror Lancers!"

"They didn't do that before, ser," says Chaaltyn.

"I suspect the announcement is to both parties' benefit. They want everyone to know we're coming so no one shoots and to let us know they're aware of us."

The companies continue riding toward the east road, and Alyiakal notices no one is close to the road. People in the fields and two youths herding mountain musk oxen in the alpine pasture east of the high road merely look for a few moments and return to their tasks. When First Company reaches the east road and turns west, past the fort that dominates the junction, Alyiakal sees that a section of the fort's log wall has been recently replaced, and he nods.

Then a semi-familiar figure—the gray-haired woman—appears behind the log rampart at the top of the wall.

Since she does not speak, he does, boosting his voice slightly with order. "We're returning from Kraaslaen. We removed the Cerlynese forces who were sending raiders. We did no harm to traders or factors."

The woman nods but does not speak. She continues to watch.

Once all three companies and the wagons with the wounded and some few remaining supplies are well past the fort and the hamlet, Alyiakal relaxes just a trace, but reminds himself that an evolution isn't complete until everyone's back in the post. *For an officer, not even then.*

The remaining long, hot descent to the post lasts until just past sunset, when Alyiakal leads the column through the gates and into the stable courtyard. While he knows that Majer Byelt will want an immediate verbal report, Alyiakal still dismounts and walks the chestnut to his stall, where he unsaddles, waters, and grooms him.

He hasn't quite finished when the duty messenger appears.

"Ser?"

"The majer requests my appearance?"

"At your earliest convenience, ser."

"I'll be there soon."

The ranker hurries off.

After finishing with the gelding, Alyiakal leaves the stable, brushing some of the road dust off his now-grimy uniform as he walks across the courtyard to headquarters and straight to the majer's study.

"How did matters go?" asks Byelt evenly.

"We did what we could," replies Alyiakal, seating himself in the chair directly facing the majer.

"That doesn't sound like what we need to report to headquarters. I just received a request from the Captain-Commander wanting to know how I'm dealing with the apparent Cerlynese 'incursions' into Cyador."

"We've removed almost all the Cerlynese armsmen and done what we could without getting into a possible war with Cerlyn, since starting wars is above my rank," says Alyiakal wearily, straightening slightly before he begins to relate the events of the last eightday. When he finishes, he just waits.

"So . . . if I have this straight, you've destroyed—not defeated, but destroyed—more than three companies of Cerlynese armsmen and gutted their only post on Cyadoran territory. You did this with only two deaths and eight wounded. Is that right?"

Alyiakal nods. "The problem is that it's really a two-and-a-half-day patrol out to Kraaslaen and another two and a half days back. We could cut that to two days if we could get the Mirror Engineers to rebuild the logging road all the way to the high road, but I doubt the Mirror Engineers are interested. We could hire locals, but we'd need golds to pay them. A better and shorter road north would make trading easier, but every patrol to the north would still take a minimum of four days, possibly five. Establishing a post in Kraaslaen might help, but supplying that post would be essentially impossible from late Autumn to mid-Spring, and while the post was isolated, it would be vulnerable to Cerlynese attack. Unless it were established with three companies, and they'd be of little use in supporting Lhaarat over the wintering period. I don't see Mirror Lancer headquarters wanting to put three companies in Kraaslaen." Alyiakal shrugs. "But those decisions would have to come from headquarters."

Byelt nods slowly. "Then it's fair to say that you've removed the immediate threat from Cerlyn."

"For now. Duke Taartyn's in Clynya, and he may not even learn of what happened for another few days. The survivors won't be in any hurry to inform him, if any of them even have any wish to do so. With the interior of the fort gutted, any small Cerlynese force would be vulnerable, and any larger force would require a great commitment of men and resources, which will be difficult to raise during Harvest. After that, he can only count on decent weather for four or five eightdays."

Byelt smiles. "So you've eliminated any immediate problem. Headquarters will appreciate that."

Headquarters might, but Alyiakal has doubts that the Merchanters trafficking in copper from Cerlyn will be pleased with anything that upsets the Duke.

"Write up your report," Byelt continues. "I'd like it sometime tomorrow so that we can go over it and what I send back to headquarters. Oh . . . I've ordered a hot dinner for all three companies and the officers shortly. I'll join you all in the mess."

"The men will appreciate it." Alyiakal stands. "I really need to see to the wounded now, ser. It's been an even longer day for them."

"Of course."

From the majer's study, Alyiakal makes his way to the infirmary, where the wounded are being settled. Some will be able to return to limited duty before long, after Alyiakal can replace temporary splints with more permanent casts.

His first concern is Ashaar, and he immediately checks the lancer's wound chaos, slightly higher than he'd hoped, but not out of control. While looking at the dressing, he infuses as much order as he dares.

"How is it, ser? You look a little worried."

"Any healer who isn't worried about a gut wound isn't a good healer," replies Alyiakal as lightly as he can. "You're about the same, and that's encouraging after two days' travel in a wagon. I'm thinking that now that you're here, things should heal faster."

"You're sure I'm healing?"

Alyiakal nods. "But with gut wounds, until you're fully healed, things can get worse, and I don't want that to happen."

"You're being very cautious, ser."

"Yes, but I will say you're doing better than I feared. I'm being cautious, but so long as you're improving, you don't need to worry."

Then Alyiakal turns to Aerek. "Let's see that shoulder."

"Doesn't hurt that much, ser. Even if I needed help getting into the saddle, riding's easier than getting jolted around in a wagon."

Alyiakal smiles wryly. "Meaning that it still hurts like you got it from the black angels."

"Not that bad."

The wound chaos is lower, but not much. "You're staying here for a while, Aerek."

"Is it that bad?"

Alyiakal shakes his head. "But if you're not thinking and you do something strenuous, you could tear some of the healing, and that wouldn't be good." Part of what Alyiakal says is close to nonsense, but without constant infusions of order Aerek's wound could get very bad, very quickly.

Then Alyiakal checks three other slash wounds, puts casts on two broken arms, and one broken leg, before leaving the infirmary and heading for the mess.

All the other officers are already there, including Staalt, when Alyiakal enters.

"I'm a bit late, but I had to deal with the wounded first."

"Quite understandable, and a higher priority," says Byelt.

"I imagine there are downsides to being both an overcaptain and a field healer," says Staalt.

Vaarkas tries to hide a wince.

"Not downsides," replies Alyiakal, "responsibilities." He looks at the hot lamb cubes over noodles, topped with brown gravy, and adds, "This looks wonderful."

"You can tell what we've been eating for an eightday," says Vaarkas dryly.

Paersol, his mouth full, nods.

For a time, Byelt just lets the three officers eat, but then asks, "Did you encounter any difficulties with the local people?" He looks to Vaarkas.

"No, ser. They didn't seem very happy with the Cerlynese. They were worried that more armsmen might come from Cerlyn, though."

"Traders were the only ones unhappy to see us," adds Alyiakal. "One other thing I didn't mention, the people in the log-fort hamlet made it easy for us to pass."

"Good," replies the majer. "Were the armsmen using those bronze shields that showed up in one of the hamlets here?"

"All the mounted armsmen carried them," replies Alyiakal. "They weren't that effective because we never mounted a direct frontal attack. We brought back all the captured weapons, including around thirty shields. The fire effectively destroyed the rest. I imagine some of the people in Kraaslaen have already scavenged the bronze." Alyiakal notices Staalt's momentarily puzzled expression and ignores it. "They also used mounted archers at the rear of their formations."

"You didn't have many casualties, so you must have found a way to deal with the archers," offers Byelt blandly.

"We set up a road ambush where the lancers were close enough to target the archers, and the attack on the fort was initially in darkness. We did take a few casualties there." Alyiakal stops talking and takes several more mouthfuls of the lamb and noodles. It's not that good, except in comparison to everything he's eaten in an eightday, but he definitely appreciates the hot meal.

"With what you three officers have done," says Byelt warmly, "I imagine that we'll have easier patrols in the next season."

Alyiakal certainly hopes so, but one thing he knows—for a Mirror Lancer officer, nothing is certain, at least, not for long.

XCV

Alyiakal begins fiveday by rising early and visiting the infirmary.

The wound chaos in Aerek's shoulder wound has increased, but he infuses the wound with more order, and senses immediate improvement. That suggests that he'll need to see the lancer three times a day. Ashaar's wound-chaos level has dropped, if slightly, and Alyiakal hopes that will continue. The other wounded are doing well, and Alyiakal suspects, over the next few days, he'll be releasing them to light duties.

His last healing stop is at the brig, to check Taaryan's arm.

The former raider looks at him. "I thought you forgot me."

Alyiakal shakes his head. "I took three companies to Kraaslaen. We largely wiped out three companies of Cerlynese and gutted the fort. How does your arm feel?"

In turn, Taaryan shakes his head, as if in disbelief.

"Most of the survivors were wounded. We sent them back to Cerlyn." While the young raider thinks over what he's just heard, Alyiakal trains his senses on the youth's arm, where he discerns only gray wound chaos, with the faintest hint of red. "Your arm's stopped hurting, hasn't it, unless you bump the cast against something?"

"How did you know that?"

"I'm a healer. I'm supposed know that."

"What are you going to do with me?"

"That's up to you. I'll see what the possibilities are, and we can talk about them in a day or two." That's ingenuous; Alyiakal knows exactly what those possibilities are, but with Taaryan's broken arm, there's no hurry, since he's not in shape for any of them yet. Alyiakal needs to deal with other, more pressing matters first. "I just wanted to make sure your arm was healing once I returned."

Alyiakal stands.

"You destroyed all those bastards, just like that?"

"Not just like that. We lost two lancers, and eight others are in the infirmary with their wounds."

"Only two? How many did you kill?"

"That's hard to say. They had three companies . . . sixty or seventy in a company, maybe a half score fled, and we sent thirteen wounded back to Cerlyn."

Taaryan swallows.

"I'll see you in a few days, and we can talk about what might be best for you. You *do* have some choices."

The former raider just stands there as Alyiakal leaves the cell, not exactly pleased with what he did, but Taaryan needs a jolt to understand his situation.

From the brig, Alyiakal makes his way to the mess, where Paersol and Staalt are quietly talking. Both stop.

"Good morning, ser," says Staalt quickly.

"Good morning to you both," replies Alyiakal, then looks to Staalt. "Did you encounter any raiders while we were gone?"

"No, ser. The majer ordered us to stay within ten kays of the post, but there weren't any reports of raids farther away, either."

"That's good to hear. Did you run across any traders?"

"A few, some from Cyador heading into the hills. Two from Kyphros. One of them claimed he was heading for Ilypsya."

"None claiming to be from Cerlyn?"

"No, ser."

Alyiakal senses someone else and turns as Vaarkas enters the mess. "Good morning."

"The same to you, ser. I have to say it felt good to sleep in quarters. Thank you for all you did for Gheryk and Maals."

"Now that they've got casts on those broken bones, they should be out of the infirmary in a day or so. They might be able to ride safely by the second eightday of Autumn, maybe a little sooner."

"Are there any other officers who are also healers?" asks Staalt.

"I'm only classed as a field healer," replies Alyiakal, "but when I was in officer training there were mentions that there had been a few. Just not many."

As the majer steps into the mess, Alyiakal and the others move to the table and seat themselves as the majer does.

"It's been a bit lonely in the mess," declares Byelt cheerfully. "Good to have you all back . . . and healthy."

"Any news from Cyad that we all should know?" asks Alyiakal.

"Except for a few directives and instructions, there's been nothing. Well, except an announcement that the Empress was delivered of a healthy daughter."

"Healthy daughter?" murmurs Paersol.

"What do you make of that, Captain?" Byelt asks Paersol.

"I don't believe that the Emperor has a son," replies Paersol.

So that the announcement of a healthy daughter and a healthy Empress suggests that the Imperial couple has time and the ability to provide a male heir. Alyiakal can't help but wonder if Imperial politics might well be improved if daughters could inherit. Certainly, Alyiakal's experiences with Healer Vayidra and Saelora have shown him that women often do better than men. *With less drama and violence.*

"They're young. They have time," replies Byelt not quite dismissively.

Alyiakal still wonders.

After breakfast, he goes to his study, hoping that there might be a letter from Saelora, though he knows that's unlikely. He'd sent his last letter just before he set out on the mission to Kraaslaen, little more than an eightday ago. There is no letter in his inbox, only a few directives and announcements from Mirror Lancer headquarters. Those can wait.

He has to thank the Rational Stars he only needs to write two letters informing the next of kin about the death of the two lancers, along with the death report to Mirror Lancer headquarters to initiate the payment of death golds. However, those will have to come after his patrol report for the majer. While the majer reviews Alyiakal's report, Alyiakal will have time to write the death reports and the letters to the next of kin.

Alyiakal first lists the history of events on a separate sheet of paper, then begins to write. After the first draft, he realizes he didn't mention certain related matters, including the polished bronze-surfaced wooden shields from Cerlyn used by some raiders, and identical to those used by Cerlynese armsmen. Four glasses later, he finishes the second draft and hands it to Byelt.

"Thank you," replies the majer. "I'll get back to you shortly."

While Byelt reads the report and, doubtless, makes notes, Alyiakal writes the next-of-kin letters for Vhaelyt and for Ketlas from Third Company, as well as the two death reports for Byelt to sign and forward to headquarters.

He's barely finished when Byelt appears in his doorway. "Good report, but we need to talk." He motions for Alyiakal to follow him, then turns and enters his study.

Alyiakal follows, bringing the two death reports with him. He closes the study door, walks to the desk to place the two sheets of paper in Byelt's box. "The death reports for Vhaelyt and Ketlas, ser," he informs the majer as he seats himself.

"Thank you. You do make matters easier, Alyiakal." He pauses. "You also make them more difficult."

"I wish that part were otherwise, ser, but I understand."

"Do you?"

"If I hadn't been so persistently curious about where raiders came from and where they obtained weapons, I wouldn't have discovered Lestroi, and you wouldn't have had a commander from headquarters here observing."

Byelt actually sighs, then offers a wry smile. "You're hard for an honest officer to hate or dislike. You're incredibly diligent and remarkably effective. You're also ruthless in pursuing an objective. Thankfully, you don't carry that ruthlessness beyond the objective. Remain careful that you don't. Unfortunately, your abilities make your immediate superiors look less effective."

"I've tried not to do that, ser."

"As I have seen, and I appreciate your attitude and effort. The plain fact is that both of us are in a difficult position. You're too competent and effective to be a deputy post commander here, and too junior to be one at a larger post or a commander at a smaller post. No majer or subcommander with any ambition, or brains, would want you as a deputy. The best we can hope for is that headquarters leaves us alone."

"Yes, ser. I see." Alyiakal pauses, then adds, "But if I hadn't done what I did, I suspect we'd both be in a much worse position a year from now."

Byelt snorts. "We both know that. So does headquarters, but I worry no one there wants to admit it. There's also the problem of Cerlyn: no one really wants to deal with it . . . and hasn't in years. So . . . as long as we're here, you'll be scheduling and making long patrols to the north."

"I hadn't thought otherwise. Putting a post in Kraaslaen is too costly and would be regarded as provocative—"

"We don't need to go over that." Byelt waves away Alyiakal's explanation. "Your report is strictly factual, as it should be. I'll forward it, with minimal comment, to headquarters, and we'll let headquarters tell us what we already know." Byelt raises his eyebrows. "Unless you have any additional thoughts."

"No, ser. Sometimes, less is better."

"Most times," replies the majer. "With a little good fortune, they just might let us be."

Alyiakal has doubts, but then, Commander Laartol would be consulted on any decision about Lhaarat Post, and in the past Laartol has generally been objective and practical.

"I share your sentiment, ser."

"We'll see. That's all I have . . . and thank you for doing those reports quickly. We can dispatch everything early tomorrow."

"Thank you, ser." Alyiakal stands, nods, and leaves.

Back in his study, Alyiakal begins to write a letter to Saelora. His comments on the recent directives and instructions can wait, and he wants to let her know, if in general terms, what has happened.

A glass later, he looks over what he has written.

> *My dearest lady—*
>
> *Since I last wrote, Lhaarat Post was required to take up arms to remove Cerlynese armsmen attempting to take control of the high road that provides traders access to Cerlyn, Cyador, and more distant places in Kyphros. Our efforts to remove them and return the survivors to Cerlyn were effective, and we managed the various evolutions in a fashion that minimized casualties, despite having to deal with them in the heat of Summer.*
>
> *I have just returned from those efforts, but I remain healthy and well, and fervently hope the same is true for you, and others dear to you. You will pardon me if I do not offer more specifics, but I know you understand that I cannot write about them.*
>
> *I have not yet received any letter from you in response to my previous correspondence. Given the distances which separate us, this is understandable. I hope that not only are you healthy and successful, but that we could have more time together—soon—unlikely as that is. I vividly remember every spare moment we have shared and how you brought warmth and love into my life. I could feel your joy and happiness for Catriana, and wish that I could provide the same for you . . . and for us, but I remain hopeful that special joy will not elude us.*
>
> *I could write pages, and I will, but not now, because I don't know when another dispatch rider will depart, and I want you to receive this as soon as possible.*

Alyiakal looks at the letter and the words, and hopes that Saelora can read between the lines, but at least she'll know he's safe. *For now, anyway.*

His eyes close for a moment, and he recalls Saelora's expressions, so many different expressions, all wondrous and beautiful in their own way, and he wonders if they're both too obsessed with proving to an indifferent world that they each matter and *will* make a difference—whether that indifferent world cares or not.

XCVI

For the next four days, Alyiakal returns to the patrols and other routine matters he established earlier, and on oneday, he and First Company patrol the road leading to the walled valley. As before, the gate to the valley is closed, and a single sentry stands within the wall watchtower. No hoofprints lead to the gate.

After a break, First Company returns to the wider road that climbs gradually for the next three kays to the flat, where Alyiakal had earlier ordered Paersol and Fourth Company to turn back. This time, Alyiakal has First Company ride another two kays to a point where the road heads south. He's about to call a halt when he sees a two-horse wagon approaching, flanked by four armed guards. He decides to investigate.

Two of the guards ride forward to meet the scouts, listen for a moment, and then ride back to the wagon.

Alyiakal orders, "Company! Halt!," then rides forward with the scouts reining up short of the wagon, where two men share the teamster's seat.

The older man, most likely the trader, looks at Alyiakal. His eyes narrow. "You're an overcaptain." The tone is almost accusatory.

"I am. I'm also the deputy post commander at Lhaarat. And you are?"

"Thaalmyn'mer, ser."

"Where are you coming from?"

"Quite a few hamlets, but the last town was Jakaafra."

"That's a long trip by wagon. Where are you headed?"

"Now, ser . . . isn't that my affair?"

"It is, but it's also that of the Mirror Lancers to make sure that you're not trading arms to raiders . . . or others. I'll ask again, politely. Where are you headed?"

"The place doesn't have a name."

"Might it stand at the crossroad on the high road to Cerlyn? Where there's a log fort?" Alyiakal concentrates on the trader, waiting for his reaction.

Thaalmyn laughs. "That'd be the place."

Alyiakal senses no deception, but replies, "And you don't want anyone to know what you bring back from there?"

The trader frowns. "I don't trade in arms, or anything like that."

Alyiakal smiles. "No. What they have is more valuable, and so far as I know, there's only one other source."

The frown becomes an expression of concern and puzzlement. "How . . . ?"

"Let's leave it at that. I would recommend that you don't travel as far as Kraaslaen."

"Kraaslaen? Where's that?"

The trader's ignorance feels genuine.

"The last town before you enter Cerlyn."

The trader shakes his head. "Nothing there for us. But why shouldn't we go there?"

"The Duke of Cerlyn decided to put a fort with three companies there. We removed them. He won't be pleased with anyone from Cyador."

"Good to know, but we've no intention of going that far."

"We're about to head back to Lhaarat," says Alyiakal.

"Be all right if we follow you until we turn off on the east road?"

"We don't have a problem with that," replies Alyiakal.

Less than a quint later, after re-forming, First Company heads back toward Lhaarat with the trader following a hundred yards behind, probably glad for what amounts to an armed guard.

"Ser," asks Chaaltyn, "you never said what he's trading for."

"He would have been upset if I named it." Alyiakal smiles. "He's trading salt and spices for mountain musk ox wool."

"What are those?"

"Do you recall those hairy-looking beasts near the log fort?"

"With the sharp horns?"

Alyiakal nods.

"How did you know?"

"I encountered them once before and asked."

"That wool must be something if he's traveling that far by wagon."

"I'm sure it is, just as I am certain he doesn't want anyone else to know." *It also explains how that hamlet could afford Cerlynese blades and shields.*

The return ride to the post is uneventful.

Once Alyiakal is back in the post headquarters, he doesn't even try to enter his study, instead stopping at the majer's door. "Is there anything you need from me?"

Byelt gestures for him to enter. "It's not urgent, but you'll need to handle this." He lifts a single sheet of paper. "It arrived just a quint or so ago. Sit down and read it. I'd like your thoughts."

Alyiakal takes the sheet and begins to read, scanning the necessary bureaucratic introduction until he gets to the core of the document.

> . . . *after careful consideration of the nature of the ruins and the isolated location of the hamlet known as Lestroi, as attested by Commander Laartol'alt, by a senior magus, and by senior officers of the Mirror Engineers, it has been determined that Lestroi and the surrounding area contain no devices or materiel of especial value, nor is the location of strategic importance. Therefore, it is decreed that Lestroi shall be considered as any other hamlet, provided that a visible entrance is provided and maintained. Said entrance may be gated, but access must always be available to Mirror Lancers . . .*

There is considerably more verbiage, but it does not change the basic conclusion. Alyiakal notes the signature and seal of the Captain-Commander of the Mirror Lancers. He hands it back. "That seems quite clear. It's in the middle of nowhere, and there's nothing there. They have no advantages except being a somewhat defensible retreat, not that the Captain-Commander said it quite that way."

"You don't sound that surprised. Did Commander Laartol intimate anything like that to you?"

"No, ser. He was exceptionally careful to tell me nothing past what he said at the last briefing before he left."

"You didn't speak with him after that?"

"No, ser. I didn't even see him except at breakfast the next morning. You were the last one to speak with him."

Byelt smiles wryly. "He didn't offer anything but courteous thanks. I got the impression that he's very cautious."

"He certainly was at Guarstyad." Alyiakal gestures toward the document. "We'll have to inform Kiefala that Lestroi will be left alone—provided they create a visible entrance."

"You should do that. She knows who you are." Byelt pauses. "On sevenday. You patrolled today."

"Yes, ser. It was a long patrol. There is one other matter, though."

"Oh?" Byelt's tone turns wary.

"We took the road leading to the walled valley and continued another six or seven kays." Alyiakal describes his encounter with the trader and his origin.

"So that road leads all the way to Jakaafra?"

"Through a number of hamlets, he said. But it's something that Mirror Lancer headquarters might like to know."

Byelt sighs. "Will you ever stop discovering things, Alyiakal?"

"Probably not, ser. So long as there remain things to discover."

The majer shakes his head. "Write it up so I can include it in my next report."

"Yes, ser."

Alyiakal heads to his study, hoping the dispatch riders have brought a letter from Saelora, but his box contains only a single sheet, a revision in supply procedures which effectively doesn't apply to Lhaarat Post.

He settles behind the desk to write what he can of his patrol report before evening mess.

XCVII

Sevenday morning dawns with a low haze across the valley, and slightly cooler than the previous few days. With the green-blue sky cloudless above the low haze, Alyiakal has no doubt the afternoon will be hotter—and damper. While Third Company heads up the old logging road to patrol the high road north of the River Lhaar, Alyiakal and First Company set out on the east road to Lestroi.

The ride to the River Lhaar overlook is without event, although the company has to wait for a logging wagon to turn off the road toward the logging area. Alyiakal wonders, as the company rides past the so-called mining road, why anyone would build a road, dig a tunnel, and then abandon it without a trace.

After a break at the overlook, the company continues on and reaches the hidden entrance to Lestroi several quints before midday. Maaetz and Raayls remove the dead evergreen, and the company rides down the short and narrow path and then along the ancient road.

A quint later, Alyiakal and First Company ride into the open area just short of the narrow gorge and its dwellings, where Alyiakal orders, "Company! Halt!"

Then he waits.

Before long, Kiefala appears on the balcony. She surveys the company, then asks, "Are you here to remove us?"

"No," replies Alyiakal, "I'm here for another reason, and I need to speak with you. I'll meet you at your door."

"You will disappoint me, Firstborn. That I know, but what can we do?" Then Kiefala leaves the balcony.

"Ser?" asks Chaaltyn.

"They won't do anything, but detail a pair of lancers to accompany me."

Chaaltyn gestures.

Haelsyn and Fuast ride forward and flank Alyiakal, and the three slowly ride into the narrow gorge, stopping before the first set of stone steps.

The silver-haired Kiefala emerges from the wooden door and descends two steps so that her head is only slightly lower than Alyiakal's. She looks at him, then at the two lancers, before leveling her gaze on Alyiakal. "You need no protection, Firstborn."

"Call it tradition, Headwoman Kiefala."

"What do you have to say to me that requires such force?" She gestures in the direction of First Company.

"The force is here to show you that what I tell you is backed by the Mirror Lancers. The highest of the Mirror Lancers have decreed that Lestroi will remain a hamlet for you and your people. No one will remove you—unless you raid others."

Alyiakal senses momentary stunned surprise before she asks warily, "What must we do for this great favor?"

Alyiakal doesn't miss the slight irony she places on the words "great favor." "There are two small conditions. You have already agreed to one, to allow Mirror Lancers to come to Lestroi, if necessary."

"What is the second?" Kiefala's voice remains wary.

"You must have a visible entrance to Lestroi. It can be walled and gated, but it must be visible from the east road."

"That is all?"

"That is all." Alyiakal smiles pleasantly. "I do have a personal favor to ask."

Kiefala's face freezes.

"Not that kind of favor. Almost half a season ago, we captured a young raider from the Grass Hills. He was injured, and his arm is healing. He's young and has no family. If he wishes to come to Lestroi, would you consider allowing him to come here?"

"Firstborn, you take, and then you give." She frowns. "Will you protect us as you do your valley?"

"Lestroi is not now a part of Cyador," says Alyiakal carefully. "We are too far from Lestroi to protect you at all times, but we will patrol the roads around Lestroi and do our best to keep raiders from you."

"You have kept your word, Firstborn. I will not ask more. I will meet the young man, and then I will decide."

Alyiakal inclines his head. "I can ask no more than that."

"We will make a gate and wall near the end of the old road that was blocked by the First, but that will take some time."

"But before the middle of Autumn?"

She nods.

"That is all I have to tell you or ask of you," says Alyiakal.

"Would that your forebears had been so honorable," she replies. "Bring the young man when you will, and we will decide."

"Thank you, Kiefala."

She nods, then withdraws to the top step.

Alyiakal nods in return, then eases the chestnut around. When he nears Chaaltyn, he orders, "To the rear! Ride!"

As the company withdraws from Lestroi, Alyiakal realizes that, in a vague way, with the silver hair, she reminds him of someone. Then he smiles wryly. *Healer Vayidra.*

XCVIII

An eightday passes, with days every bit as hot as Summer and no rain, during which Alyiakal takes First Company on two patrols. Among his other duties, he talks to Taaryan about either joining the Mirror Lancers or seeing if he will fit in at Lestroi, then tells him to think about the choices.

More traders than ever use the high and east roads, although few head north. Mirror Lancer headquarters has yet to reply to the high road mission report, which suggests other, more important, matters or a lack of consensus on how to instruct Lhaarat Post.

Alyiakal receives a letter from Saelora in reply to the letter he wrote prior to the high road mission. He appreciates her warm thoughts and support but decides not to reply immediately. He has nothing new to say, except for headquarters' decision on Lestroi.

On the second fourday of Harvest, since Alyiakal doesn't have a patrol, he sends word to Yosert to bring Taaryan to the infirmary. Once the two arrive, Alyiakal checks Taaryan's arm and removes the cast. "You'll still need to be careful with this arm for another season, but it's healed well."

"It's hard not to be careful when you're in a cell, ser."

"One way or another, you won't be here longer. Have you thought about your choices?"

The youth looks directly at Alyiakal. "You said I could join the Mirror Lancers or see if I fit in at Lestroi . . . or you'd just take me to a place and leave me."

"Somewhere outside of Cyador . . . most likely where the high and east roads meet. I wouldn't recommend that, but it is a choice."

"Why do you think I might fit in at Lestroi?"

"I don't know that, but I do know the headwoman at Lestroi would be able to tell. You'd have to meet her. You can choose Lestroi, but she'll decide. It will be better than the Grass Hills, but it won't be easy, and the Winters are much harder."

"How would she know if I'd fit?"

"Her hair is silver—and *not* because she's old. Most younger women with silver hair have a touch of the Magi'i about them." And Kiefala has more than a touch, from what Alyiakal has sensed.

"I'd like to try that . . . first. If she doesn't want me, I'll try the Mirror Lancers."

"Then you'll ride with us on the next patrol I lead to that area." Alyiakal nods to Yosert. "You can take him back to the brig now."

"Yes, ser."

After the two leave, Alyiakal smiles. He has a feeling that Yosert will be telling Taaryan just how fortunate he is.

Alyiakal heads back to headquarters. Seeing that Byelt's door is open, he steps inside. "I took the cast off Taaryan's arm. He wants to see if Kiefala will accept him. If she won't, he'll try recruit training at Terimot."

"You think she'll take him?"

"That's up to her, but it's likely."

"Why did you want to offer him that choice?" asks Byelt, a note of curiosity.

"It's closer to what he's used to, maybe a bit better, but I wanted to give her the chance to get a grateful young man. They don't have many young men left."

"Is that dangerous?"

"He was forced to raid by the Cerlynese, and Lestroi can't afford to raid, even with him. I also suspect that we removed Lestroi's hotheads."

"You have something more in mind."

Alyiakal grins. "Well . . . if the log-fort hamlet and Lestroi could become friendlier and accept having lancers around, we might not have near as many raiders to deal with."

"I have my doubts."

"I can always hope," replies Alyiakal, "but some of that will depend on what we hear from headquarters."

"You're taking First Company along the east road on sixday. Do you plan on taking Taaryan to Lestroi then?"

"I'd thought to. He's spent enough time here."

"He might miss a pallet bed and regular food," says Byelt.

"If he doesn't like it, so long as he's behaved himself, he can always come back and volunteer to be a lancer."

Byelt laughs.

XCIX

Because he's arranging for Taaryan to accompany First Company on patrol, Alyiakal is the last officer to arrive in the mess on sixday morning—except for the majer, who enters after Alyiakal.

Once everyone is seated and served, Vaarkas looks to Alyiakal. "I understand you're going to turn that young raider over to the headwoman of Lestroi."

"Not exactly," replies Alyiakal. "I'm going to allow him to present himself to her, and she'll decide whether he's acceptable. If not, he's going to lancer training in Terimot."

"I'd think he'd rather have it the other way around," says Staalt, "especially if he has any sense."

"He grew up in open spaces until the Cerlynese rounded him up," Alyiakal points out. "He never actually loosed a shaft against us, although he might have if a tree limb hadn't interfered."

"That's why he gets a choice," adds Byelt.

"More fortunate than most," says Vaarkas.

"Too bad he didn't shoot," says Paersol. "Then we'd be rid of him."

"Could be that he's not that inclined to fight," suggests Vaarkas, "for either raiders or us. Sounds like he didn't have much choice."

"You always have choices," declares Paersol.

"Until you don't," replies Byelt coolly.

Or until all your choices are equally bad, and circumstances demand you act. Alyiakal refrains from sharing that thought, happy to allow the majer the last word.

"Do you think the headwoman will accept him?" Vaarkas asks Alyiakal.

"That's her choice. We removed a number of her young men, because they were too rash. From what I've seen, however, she won't take him just to get another warm body."

"Just like the lancers," says Byelt dryly.

Vaarkas laughs softly.

"When do you think we'll hear from Mirror Lancer headquarters about the Cerlynese?" asks Staalt.

"It could be today, or it could be the middle of Autumn," replies Byelt. "For now, our only worry should concern raiders and unwanted intruders. We'll hear when they're ready, and not before." He turns to Vaarkas. "You may get your next posting before we hear. We're nearing that time of year."

"Where do you want to go?" Staalt asks Vaarkas.

"Wherever they send me." Vaarkas grins. "I'd like some places more than others."

The remainder of breakfast is cheerful.

After eating, Alyiakal walks swiftly to the stables, where he saddles the chestnut, spends more than a few moments under a concealment with the gelding before rewarding him with a carrot, then leads him out of the stable. He mounts and rides to where First Company is forming up, reining up and watching as Yosert walks Taaryan toward the company. In the rank behind Alyiakal and Chaaltyn, Haelsyn holds the reins to another mount.

Alyiakal gestures to the horse and says to Taaryan, "Mount up."

"Yes, ser."

After the youth mounts, Alyiakal says, "You'll ride beside Haelsyn and do exactly as he tells you."

"Yes, ser."

"Taaryan," says Alyiakal, "there's one other thing you need to understand. You're still a prisoner until you're either accepted by Lestroi or you enter recruit training at Terimot. If you try to escape, I will personally flame you."

Someone farther back in the ranks murmurs, "And the overcaptain never misses."

Alyiakal keeps a straight face as he recognizes Fuast's voice, who likely spoke to make Haelsyn's task easier.

Taaryan stiffens in the saddle. "Yes, ser. I understand."

"Good." Alyiakal turns the chestnut. "Company! Forward!"

As the company leaves the post gates and turns east, Alyiakal feels the morning's warmth, even though the white sun hasn't cleared the hills. While it will be a good day to be in the higher elevations, he knows Lhaarat will be hot and damp when they return.

He sees no signs of logging wagons or tracks on the side road to the logging area, nor does the company encounter any traders. Alyiakal notices only a single man with an empty cart, probably gathering firewood for the Winter, and the east road is clear to the River Lhaar overlook, and all the way to the hidden entrance to Lestroi.

Once the company halts, Maaetz removes the dead evergreen and sets it to one side.

Alyiakal senses order/chaos patterns near the end of the entry trail and quickly mentions, "They might be working on the entrance. Call out that Mirror Lancers are coming to see Headwoman Kiefala."

"Mirror Lancers to see the headwoman!" Raayls shouts.

Maaetz repeats the phrase before the two start down the trail.

A few moments later, Raayls calls back, "The workers are clear, ser!"

"You thought they might be working here, even if the entrance was still hidden?" Chaaltyn sounds astonished.

"I suspected they'd want something walled in place *before* they remove the tree," answers Alyiakal blandly.

Three older men and a woman around Alyiakal's age stand beside one end of a rough, waist-high stone wall running from the old road to a massive evergreen at the edge of the narrow trail to the east road. The three watch as the company rides by and re-forms on the old road and rides toward the gorge.

Kiefala stands at the top of the steps to her dwelling, waiting as Alyiakal halts the company and motions for Taaryan to ride with him. The two rein up at the bottom of the steps.

Alyiakal inclines his head and says, "Headwoman Kiefala, this is Taaryan. The Cerlynese forced him from his home in the Grass Hills. Taaryan, this is Kiefala, headwoman of Lestroi."

Kiefala looks directly at Taaryan and asks, "Why do you wish to join us?"

"I don't want to fight or raid. You're my only chance to avoid that."

"Life in Lestroi is not easy."

"Life in a mud-brick hut in the Grass Hills was not easy, Headwoman."

"What do you know about hunting and growing?"

"I have hunted grass antelopes, and helped my family grow potatoes and maize. I can learn."

"Your arm is healing. How did that happen?"

Alyiakal manages not to nod at Kiefala's order/chaos perception, something he has suspected all along.

"I tried to escape the armsmen and the Mirror Lancers. I didn't see a tree branch soon enough."

Alyiakal senses the truth of that statement and wonders why Taaryan never mentioned it before. *Because he didn't want to be thought a coward? And you never thought about asking? Would it have made a difference? You healed him, and he was fed better than he could have managed on his own.* But he'd assumed something that wasn't true, and that bothers him. *What else have you assumed?*

Kiefala continues to question Taaryan for a half a quint, listening to his responses, before saying, "You are welcome here, if you wish it."

"Truly?" asks Taaryan.

She nods.

Taaryan turns in the saddle, looking to Alyiakal.

"You can go," Alyiakal says. "You don't get to keep the mount, though."

Kiefala smiles. "We have horses enough."

Taaryan dismounts and hands the reins to Alyiakal. "Thank you, ser."

"You're welcome. Best of fortune."

Kiefala looks to Taaryan. "I need a few words with the Firstborn." She gestures for Taaryan to move away, which the youth does. Then she turns back to Alyiakal. "You are welcome here. You do not need to bring an entire company." She offers an amused smile. "But you must, I suppose, because they do not know what you are."

"It's better that way."

Her smile fades into sadness. "You're more a prisoner than Taaryan was." She pauses, then adds, "Before long Lestroi must become part of Cyador."

"Would you like me to mention that the hamlets east of Lhaarat should be considered for inclusion . . . if they wish?"

"It will happen anyway, but that would be helpful."

Alyiakal nods. "Then I will see what I can do . . . quietly."

"Thank you for Taaryan. He will be happier here."

Of that, Alyiakal has no doubt. "I will see you occasionally. Until then."

"Until then, Firstborn."

Alyiakal turns the chestnut and leads the riderless mount back to First Company, where he hands the reins to Haelsyn.

"She took him," says Chaaltyn.

"I thought she might. He'll be happier and more useful here." Alyiakal pauses. "And the living quarters are an improvement over the Grass Hills." He nods to Chaaltyn.

"Company! To the rear! Ride!" orders the senior squad leader.

Once the company leaves Lestroi and re-forms on the east road, heading back toward Lhaarat, Alyiakal thinks about Kiefala's assessment of him, then nods. *That's one way of looking at it, accurately, from her point of view.* Both he and Saelora know that they are prisoners of their ambitions and dreams.

On the return ride to Lhaarat, the company passes the man with the cart, now filled with deadwood gathered from the area around the abandoned mine tunnel, based on the wheel tracks Alyiakal observes.

After returning to the post, dismissing the company to duties, and settling the chestnut, Alyiakal walks to his study, noticing the closed door to Byelt's study, and finds two unopened envelopes from Mirror Lancer headquarters on his desk, as well as a note from Byelt.

We need to talk—after you open the envelopes from headquarters.

Alyiakal shivers, despite the warmth and moisture of the late afternoon. He seats himself behind the desk, picking up one of the large envelopes, then the other. Since one feels as though it contains more papers than the other, he decides to open it first.

He slits the end of the envelope carefully and eases out the single sheet, as well as a slightly smaller second envelope.

The single sheet is a letter under the printed letterhead of the Majer-Commander of the Mirror Lancers. Alyiakal frowns, wondering what he has done. The letter could be a reprimand or a commendation for his handling of the high road confrontations with the Cerlynese. He reads, his eyes widening as he takes in the critical paragraph.

> . . . *based on your accomplishments as Post Commander at Oldroad Post, as temporary Post Commander at Luuval, and as Deputy Post Commander at Lhaarat, ratified and confirmed by the Majer-Commander on Fiveday, Second Eightday of Harvest, 102 A.F., you, Alyiakal'alt, are hereby promoted to Sub-Majer, effective Oneday, First Eightday, Harvest, 102 A.F. . . .*

Alyiakal rereads the promotion letter again, word by word, to make certain that he correctly reads what the Majer-Commander wrote. The words don't change.

The smaller sealed envelope contains the insignia of a sub-majer.

Alyiakal's eyes narrow as he looks at the still-sealed lighter envelope. *What else could there be? A reposting?*

Carefully, he slits the remaining envelope and extracts the single sheet, carefully reading each word of the very short letter.

> *By the powers and responsibilities granted to me by the Emperor of Light, Protector of the Steps to Paradise, I hereby appoint you, Alyiakal'alt, Sub-Majer, as Commander, Lhaarat Post, with all duties and responsibilities required thereby, effective Oneday, Third Eightday, Harvest, 102 A.F. . . .*

Alyiakal shakes his head. *How did this happen?*

Somehow, it has to be the result of Commander Laartol's visit. There can't be any other explanation. *But why? The promotion alone would have been sufficient.*

Then he looks at the next lines.

> *A replacement company officer will be posted to Lhaarat shortly to fill your billet, and you will be notified when details are available. Since this is a continuation of duty and not a reposting, home leave is not authorized until the end of the present posting . . .*

Unfortunately, that makes sense in more ways than one. He slowly stands and walks from his study and knocks on the door to Byelt's study.

"You can come in, Alyiakal."

Alyiakal doesn't have to be told to close the door. He decides not to sit down, not wanting to impose on Byelt any longer than the majer wants.

"You look appropriately stunned," says Byelt wryly.

"That's a good word for it."

"You didn't have any idea, did you?"

"About the promotion? No. I'd hoped it might happen in another year or two . . . and I never even considered replacing you. But . . . what about . . ." Alyiakal doesn't know quite how to tactfully ask Byelt how it will affect him.

"Headquarters was kind. I've been promoted to subcommander."

"Congratulations!"

"*Mixed* congratulations," Byelt goes on. "I'm being detached, immediately, to full home leave, before reporting to Biehl, as both port and regional commander. That means I'll be in charge of the two companies at the port post, in addition to oversight of the District Guards."

Alyiakal senses no great enthusiasm and asks, quietly, "What am I missing?"

"It's essentially a pre-stipend posting. I'll have a few years there, at a higher pay grade, and then will be expected to fade into obscurity." Byelt straightens in his chair. "That may be kinder than what they did to you."

"Because I'll be a junior post commander with inadequate resources," *or resources they presume to be inadequate,* "but required to keep the Cerlynese and everyone else in line?"

"Exactly. If you succeed, your next promotion will get you a post command, likely either Isahl or Inividra, along with many more problems and only marginally greater resources . . . and without enough rank to object or request more resources."

Alyiakal has already suspected as much, but he only nods.

"I have something else for you to read. I think it was supposed to arrive before our 'promotions.' It's the reply to our reports on how you dealt with the Cerlynese. Since it's your problem now . . ." Byelt hands the response to Alyiakal.

He reads it quickly. Although the correspondence from the Captain-Commander begins with congratulations and vague platitudes of praise for removing "untoward armed intruders" from the high road, only one section really matters:

> *Given the existing priorities and requirements imposed upon the Mirror Lancers, it has been determined that establishing any additional post or facility north of Lhaarat Post in such an isolated area is not in the best interests of Cyador in the foreseeable future . . .*

Alyiakal hands the document back, but Byelt holds up a hand and says, wryly, "You might as well keep it. You earned it, along with the promotion." He pauses, then adds, "You're going to have some interesting years ahead."

"Thanks to you, ser."

"You earned them, but it won't get easier." He stands. "We might as well go to the mess and celebrate before dinner. There's at least one good bottle of Alafraan there."

ABOUT THE AUTHOR

L. E. MODESITT, JR. (he/him) is the author of more than eighty books—primarily science fiction and fantasy, including the long-running, bestselling Saga of Recluce and Imager Portfolio, including *Fairhaven Rising* and *From the Forest*. He is also the author of the new series the Grand Illusion (*Isolate, Councilor,* and *Contrarian*).

lemodesittjr.com